The Barnabas Chronicles

Volume 2

Brandon: Encouraged to Dream
Book 7
Brendon: Encouraged to Praise
Book 8
Brennen: Encouraged to Intercede
Book 9
Brody: Encouraged to Seek
Book 10
Buckley: Encouraged to Pray
Book 11
Burnie: Encouraged to Teach
Book 12

By

Ronna M. Bacon

Brandon: Encouraged to Dream Book 7

Asked to approach the beautiful Hagen Daltree with concerns about her 16-year-old twin sisters, Brandon Conaghan is not expecting to find a thriving educational toy and puzzle business. After Hagen and he are trapped in a collapsed building, Brandon is determined to protect the woman who intrigues him and who he has fallen in love with at first sight. Death threats, abductions, assaults - who is behind them and is it someone closer to them than they think? Brandon's friends from the Barnabas Foundation pitch in to solve the mystery but not before both Hagen and Brandon are left with what could be life-altering injuries. Their faith in God is tested, and Hagen wonders just how much she has to give up, including the dreams she and her father had worked on and that she kept up in his memory.

Brendon: Encouraged to Praise Book 8

When Brendon pulls Imly Dickerson out from where she had hidden herself in his workshop, little does he expect the danger that he would place himself in. Not a believer in love at first sight, he falls hard and fast for the beautiful red-haired lady, determined to protect her at all costs, even to the point of marrying her, from the man who had abducted her and threatened her very life.

Neither Brendon or Imly expected the danger that they would find themselves in. When Imly's parents are murdered and her beloved Brendon disappears and is presumed dead, Imly must deal with a critical injury of her own. Her faith and trust in God is tested severely.

With the help of Brendon's friends and the ladies of The Barnabas Foundation, Imly struggles to make sense of her life as she knew it and to find her husband, while bringing to justice a group that had entangled her in their deviousness, spanning two continents.

Imly and Brendon both find new meaning in praising God in all circumstances, even the most difficult ones, becoming a testimony to those around them of how God worked in their lives, even at their lowest point.

Brennen: Encouraged to Intercede Book 9

When Brennen Connolly is asked to fly to a town to meet with a J.J. Dering, he little expects a life-changing adventure is about to begin. The beautiful and petite Jaxcy Dering steps in to marry him to prevent his being imprisoned under a draconian town law. Even when the young couple return to his home, danger follows them every step of the way.

Jaxcy is shocked to discover that she is an heiress to a trust fund and property. Only, someone doesn't want her to collect either. When Brennen disappears, Jaxcy and his friends at the Barnabas Foundation struggle to decipher the clues and follow the trail to where he is. Added to the mystery is the death of her parents that sent her into poverty at age seventeen.

Who is behind it all? Will their fragile, developing love survive? And who was actually the recipient of the trust fund? Brennen and Jaxcy know that they must solve their adventure in order to survive. Learning to pray as intercessors is how God is leading and teaching them through it all.

Brody: Encouraged to Seek Book 10

When Brody Corcoran is abducted and then abandoned in the country with the beautiful Ker Deeks, he little expects the mystery surrounding her family to draw him in so deep. When Ker's father and brother disappear, she turns to Brody and his friends at the Barnabas Foundation for help in finding them.

Feeling that the only way to keep the woman he loves safe, Brody offers his hand in marriage to her. This only compounds the mystery surrounding them. Finding that Ker's mother is involved with the abductors of children and teens saddens them both but makes them more determined to solve the mystery and bring to justice those who are responsible.

Little do they expect to find themselves off on an adventure filled with abductions, attempted murder and death. Only God can protect them and led the couple and his friends at the Barnabas Foundation to the answer that they are seeking.

Buckley: Encouraged to Pray Book 11

When Buckley Cullen, beloved minister at the Barnabas Foundation, steps in to protect the beautiful Locklin Dinneen, neither one could ever imagine the journey that they are embarking on. When Locklin suffers amnesia after a motor vehicle accident, Buckley feels that the only way he can protect the lady he has fallen in love with is to offer her marriage.

Assaulted and then abducted, Buckley is found in a drug house. At the same time, Locklin has been injured in a hit and run that leaves her in critical condition. His friends at the Barnabas Foundation struggle to make sense of the mystery surrounding Locklin, with numerous curves and dead ends in their investigation. Locklin had lost her mother in childbirth and her father to an assassination, but did she really lose her father? That becomes one trail that the men must find the end to.

Through it all, Buckley and Locklin discover their love for one another growing, but more importantly, they discover the power of prayer and how God would want them to approach Him.

Burnie: Encouraged to Teach Book 12

After Burnie Cummings is injured in an explosion, he and his friends find the beautiful Muir Donachie on board their plane as a stowaway. Held captive by the storeowner, beaten, and forced to work for no pay, Muir is desperate to flee her home village and reunite with her beloved Granny.

Unaware that they have been followed, Muir is given a place to live in the Barnabas Foundation building and finds the friends that she had been seeking. Danger follows Burnie and Muir as the storeowner is out for revenge. Off on an adventure similar to that of his friends, Burnie is determined to protect the lady that he has fallen in love with.

Muir was left an orphan after her parents were killed in a plane crash. Or was she? The intrigue involving her spans two continents and draws in Burnie's friends from another town.

Who will succeed in surviving? What was really going on in Muir's village? And does she learn to trust God once more, leaning on Burnie to teach her how?

ISBN 978-1-989699-69-0

Table of Contents

2 Corinthians 1:3-4 (NKJV)

Blessed be the God and Father of our Lord Jesus Christ, the Father of mercies and God of all comfort, who comforts us in all our tribulation, that we may be able to comfort those who are in any trouble, with the comfort with which we ourselves are comforted by God.

Brandon: Encouraged to Dream

The Barnabas Chronicles
Book. 7

By

Ronna M. Bacon

Jeremiah 29:11

For I know the thoughts that I think toward you, says the Lord, thoughts of peace and not of evil, to give you a future and a hope.
NKJV

Table of Contents

Hands tucked in the pockets of his jean jacket, jacket collar turned up just because, a baseball cap tugged down over his mahogany-coloured hair, Brandon Conaghan sniffed the air appreciatively. The scent of hamburgers, hot dogs, peameal bacon, chips, cotton candy and caramel corn wafted through the late summer/early autumn air to tickle at his nose. He smiled. It was definitely the right day to be out and about and to wend his way through the arts and crafts fair. His blue eyes that reminded people of the deep blue of a summer's day assessed the area, his mind wandering to where he should go first.

Brandon sighed to himself as he tugged at the brim of his cap. He wasn't just here to amuse himself. He was also here for work. He was a social worker and a complaint had come in, one that his employer had handed him late the night before and asked that he look into for him. He didn't want any of the others in the office handling it, he felt it too sensitive. Ben had looked at him and told him that he trusted him to determine if there really was any truth to the matter.

Brandon walked past the booths holding the usual photos for sale, wood craft, hand crafts. He was on a mission. He wanted to find the woman he had been told to find and then enjoy his time. His friends from the Barnabas Foundation had asked him to go with them. He has hesitated and then said he would meet them somewhere at the fair.

Finally stopping near a booth, he frowned. This couldn't be it, he thought. He looked up at the sign: Honey's. It was the name of the company he had been given, but something just didn't seem to add up. Brandon approached, moving around the teenager who seemed to be working the booth, his eyes taking in the educational toys and puzzles. He reached for a wooden doll, feeling the fine workmanship that had gone into it, and then studied all the rest, moving around, a finger coming out now and then to touch a toy or a puzzle. There is no way, he thought, a woman did this. Then he sighed to himself again. No, that's not fair, is it, Lord? You have given them as much creativity and ability and talent to do these as you have a man.

"Can I help you?"

A soft voice with a lilt in it spoke from his left, startling him for a moment, his hand nudging against some of the toys. He reached desperately to keep them from falling over, horror on his face as he imagined the display totally toppling over, breathing a sigh of relief as he did just manage to prevent that very thing from happening.

A gurgle of laughter sounded as he turned. Brandon frowned. This could not be the woman, no, lady, he thought, that we received the complaint about. She was about his age, beautiful, with deep russet coloured hair and wide green eyes with hints of brown and gold and gray in them.

"I'm sorry. I almost destroyed your setup." He grinned, unable to help himself.

"You wouldn't be the first one. The girls and I have a time trying to get them set up sometimes. And there is always one clumsy customer that knocks over a whole display. I must say, you have quick reflexes."

He continued to grin, even as his mind was working through the possibilities. There is no way, he thought, that this lady would be guilty of abuse or neglect. That's what Ben was looking for. Proof that she wasn't.

Brandon pointed to a puzzle. "How do you make those?"

She laughed. "A picture is glued to a board, coats of Varethene applied and then a pattern is traced on top with a China marker. We use a scroll saw to cut the pieces. It sounds easy but it can be complicated. We aim for the younger children, up to about eight years of age, with these."

"I'm impressed. You do this on your own?"

Hagen Daltree. shook her head, turning for a moment to search under the canopy. "My twin sisters help. Holly and Haley. They're sixteen, and this is helping them to cope with our loss."

"I'm sorry. I don't understand." Brandon stepped backwards, to let customers flow by. He was impressed with the professionalism that the teens were showing and how rapidly the products were moving from the tables.

"We lost our parents about a year ago to a car accident. A drunk driver hit them and they didn't survive. Dad died at the scene. Mom died a day later in hospital without regaining consciousness."

"I'm sorry. I lost my parents to illnesses when I was younger than your sisters." Brandon looked around. "Listen. I need to talk with you. Ben asked me to."

"Ben? As in Ben Richards? Why?" A dark look covered her face. "They're at it again, aren't they? Trying to prove I abuse the girls by making them work for me. Or that I neglect them to work on this myself. They just don't get it. I have to do this. I am driven to do this." Tears glistened for a moment in her eyes. "And no, I don't abuse them or neglect. I work on this when they're at school."

Hearing a muffled sound, Brandon looked around, finding one of the teens standing near him, a black look on her face.

"You made her cry. Stop it!"

Brandon's hand went up as he steered Hagen away from the tent and outside. "I'm sorry. I didn't mean to."

"Fix it. And I'm Holly. You'll have to answer to Haley and I if you don't make it better." She glared at him as only a teenager could, then spun and flounced away, eager to find her sister and have her check Brandon out, she thought. He's just perfect for Hagen.

Hagen swiped at her eyes. "I'm sorry. It's just that today is a hard day. We're missing them so much, and then whoever this is keeps calling Ben. He's talked to me, but he was a friend of Dad's and has to step back."

Brandon nodded. "That's why he asked me to step in." He paused in his words, a frown on his face, as he looked around. He could hear the sound of a dirt bike. "I hear a dirt bike. There shouldn't be one here."

Hagen spun. "Not again. Run! He's heading right for us."

Brandon had already reached for her hand, tugging her with him as he ran towards the edge of the fair, thinking it was a blessing that's where she had her tent, heading for the buildings across the street, glad to see there was a break in traffic. He paused for a moment, to stare behind him, seeing the dirt bike waiting, as the rider gunned the throttle, before he began to inch forward. Hagen tugged at his hand this time, pulling him towards a one-story building that stood across from the fairgrounds.

"In here. He can't come in there. At least, I don't think he can."

"He could and likely would." Brandon slammed the door shut. "I need something to block it."

"Here."

Brandon stared in disbelief at the chair Hagen had handed him, before she took it back and jammed it under the door knob.

"That will hold for now. We need to find a way out." Hagen listened. "He's circling the building."

"Trying to spook us, hoping we'll run." Brandon paused, a sound echoing in his ears. "Hagen! We need to leave. Now!"

She spun from where she had been standing near a window, watching their assailant. "We can't. He's still out there."

"Hagen! Now!" Brandon reached for her, even as he felt the floor moving under his feet and ominous creaking sounding in his ears. He wrapped her tight in his arms, as the floor gave way, Hagen's scream echoing with the rending and crashing of the floor. Brandon hit hard, his arms still wrapped around Hagen, trying desperately to protect her and keep her from harm.

The dust swirled around them as debris floated down to settle on them. They didn't hear the screams and then the calls and shouts for help. They didn't hear the sirens as the emergency personnel sped their way. They lay, silent, blood trickling down Brandon's face, Hagen's face tucked against his chest.

—

Pausing by the paramedic rig that he had just jumped down from, Brady Coghlan stared at the building, not quite sure what he was seeing. The building looked intact, but word had come that the floor inside had partially collapsed. Someone had reported seeing a couple enter it, seemingly chased by someone on a dirt bike.

This isn't how I planned to end my shift, he thought. I was to meet Brandon here at four, just an hour from now. The call had come into their dispatch just before three, and Brady and his partner, Patrick had been assigned. Colin, their supervisor, had been apologetic, but with other teams out on the road, he had felt he had to.

Will Peters, chief of police for their town, walked towards him as they rolled their stretcher forward. His hand up to stop them, he hesitated before he spoke.

"Will? What do we have?" Brady's attention was on the building. "Dispatch said something about a couple inside?"

"Yes, they did." Will still hesitated to speak, catching Patrick's eyes, seeing the knowledge that one of Brady's friends were involved.

"Which one, Will?"

Patrick's words caught at Brady's hearing and he shifted to stare first at Patrick and then back at Will.

"Will?"

"Brady, it's Brandon. I have been told that he was here talking to Hagen Daltree, and then for some reason they ran for the building. Someone passing by heard the sounds of something structural collapsing inside."

Brady paled. "Brandon? I was to meet him here. At four. The rest of our guys and the ladies are here. We had planned to buy our supper and then picnic." He spun back to stare at the activity at the building. "Something doesn't add up."

"No, it doesn't. I wonder why they were in there." Will looked up as a voice spoke beside him. "Alice?"

Alice, one of the patrol officers who had responded, spoke quietly. "The fire chief asked me to come and talk to you. They've been able to see them, but he's not sure how structurally sound the building is. They're assessing that at the moment. He's not sure how long that will take."

"Brandon?"

"The firefighter who was able to lean over the hole said he's not moving. And neither is the lady with him." Alice frowned. "I wonder who she is?"

Will's phone chimed and he stepped away to take the call, his eyes resting on Brady. He sighed as he tucked the phone away. Another one, Lord? Can't these Foundation guys meet their ladies in a normal way?

Alice approached. "The fire chief needs to speak with you." She paused, her eyes on his face, catching the distress he was trying to hide. "Will?"

"Yes, Alice?" Will shook his head, his mind coming back to the present. "Roger needs to speak with me?" At her nod, he pointed to Brady. "Stay with him. I just had word that it's Hagen Daltree who is the lady."

"Hagen? Why?" Alice's face broke from its normal steady look. "It's him again, isn't it?"

"Him? Who? Alice, what are you talking about? Are you friends with Hagen?"

Alice nodded. "More than friends. She's my cousin. Most people don't know that. But, the point is, since their parents were killed and she became guardian to the twins, someone has repeatedly reported her to the social services office for neglect, abuse. Ben can't investigate as he was friends with her father. Unless?" Her voice died away. "Brandon. That's why he was here. I would hazard a guess that Ben asked him to talk to Hagen."

"And being the person he it, he stepped in to help when whatever happened. Do we have any sense of that?"

She nodded once more. "A dirt bike was seen hanging around the end of the grounds."

"And whoever it was chased them. Brandon would have thought they were safe in the house."

"Or Hagen would have. She's like that. Thinking of things I would never dream of."

"Like that, is she?"

Alice agreed. "You don't think God brought them together? All the others seem to have to be in danger to find their ladies."

"Not you, though, Alice. You found your life mate, Farr. But you wouldn't have if it hadn't been for Brady and Fynn going through what they did."

"No. I wouldn't have. Not that I would wish that on anyone." Her face litt up as she thought about her boyfriend before she sobered. "Do you want me with Brady or with you?"

"How be you go find the twins? They know you. Stay with them." Will paused. "They're what, sixteen? Who takes care of them if Hagen can't?"

Alice sighed. "That would be me. She didn't know who else to ask, not wanting to put a burden on them, not with what she has been going through. She has had a rough time, Will. She has refused to get us involved, but she has had threats against herself, against her home. Written threats. Emails to her business account. Phone calls. She even said someone has been following her."

"And she never said a word. That doesn't surprise me, but it stops now. When she's able, she will talk to me or to Dallas. Not you. You're involved as family."

"I know." Alice hesitated before she walked away, not sure if she should have said anything to Will. She looked up to see Fynn and Farr heading her way

"Alice? What's going on? We heard a building had collapsed." Fynn hugged her friend.

"It did. I have bad news. Brandon was in it when it went down. He and Hagen."

"Hagen?" Farr whistled in shock. "The girls?"

"I'm heading that way." Alice squinted at the sun. "Will asked me to. Thank goodness it's closing time."

"That it is." Fynn turned to walk with her, Farr standing staring across the street before he headed that way, to stand, his eyes shifting between Brady and the building, knowing how close friends all the men in the building were, all fourteen of them, he thought. Most orphans except for Barnabas Carey, the Barnabas Foundation CEO, and Breck. They were all paid through the Foundation, even though they were employed in the town, leaving their employers free to hire other workers without thinking of the cost.

Lord, their mandate is encouragement. How do we do this now? He paused as he felt someone beside him. Barnabas and Breck stood there.

"Brandon? Did we hear right?" Breck's voice held worry, his face concern.

"You did. I don't know why he's in there, but Alice said Hagen was there."

"Hagen?" Barnabas shot him a look. "She's still not safe."

"Safe?" Breck shared a look with him. "Farr, have Alice bring the girls to the building. We'll put them up there for the night. Doc and Anna would take them in."

Farr shook his head, as he watched Brady and Patrick finally moving towards the building, the fire chief and Will heading towards them. They stood before Brady nodded, his hand reaching for the doorframe of the building. He seemed to hesitate before he dropped out of sight, followed closely by Patrick.

His heart in his mouth for a moment, his professionalism shaken, Brady dropped down from the door to land on the clearest spot he could find. He looked up, seeing how much of the floor had come down. That should not have happened, he thought. It had to have been sabotaged. But why? And who?

Patrick dropped beside him and then reached up for the kits handed down to him.

"Let's assess them, Brady." He moved quickly towards the couple, pausing for a moment. "Brandon seems to have a tight hold on her."

"He does. Let's see what we can do."

Working quickly, the two partners assessed the pair, shaking their heads at one point.

"Backboards and collars, guys." Brady's voice echoed loudly in the building. He reached for the first one and then the second board. "How do we do this?"

"That's a good question." Patrick sat back on his heels before his hands reached for Hagen. "It looks as if they dropped straight now. Brandon took the brunt of it. Let's shift her to the board and then raise her to the guys up top."

Once they had been able to shift Hagen to the board and send her up as Patrick had stated, their attention turned to Brandon.

"Brandon? Can you hear me?" Brady was desperate to know his friend was all right.

Brandon stirred. "Brady? What are you doing here? And just where is here?"

"You've been in a building collapse, my friend. Lay still. Don't even think about moving an eyelash." Brady knew Brandon would try to move.

"I need to get up. Hagen needs me." Brandon lay still at Patrick planted a hand on his chest. "Please? Someone wants to hurt her. He chased us in here. Dirt bike." Brandon's voice faded away for a moment before his groans sounded. "I hurt."

"Where do you hurt?" Patrick shared a look with Brady.

"All over for starters. Can you sit me up?"

"Not a chance, my friend." Brady had been at work as he spoke, the neck collar in place.

"What is that thing? Get it off." Brandon, in his deep need to save Hagen, was starting to become combative, something Brady had not seen with him before. His hands reached for the collar, Patrick's hands there to pull Brandon's away.

"Brandon. Lay still." Brady's hand this time resting on his friend's chest. "We're going to roll you careful to slide the backboard under you. You are not standing up and certainly not climbing out." His hand leaned heavier as Brandon tried to move, to rise, to find Hagen. "Lay still. You're not helping us or yourself. You don't know what you have injured."

"I'm fine. Let me up." Pain shot through him as he moved, his eye closing against it as his consciousness faded.

"He's out again. Good." Patrick reached for the backboard as Brady held Brandon in the position that they had rolled him to. "What's with him and Hagen?"

"I have no idea. I'm not even sure I know who she is."

"She runs Honey's, the educational toy business. I think she's related to Alice."

"Alice?" Brady stood, reaching their kits up to willing hands before he stooped to help lift Brandon. "I've seen her then. Just didn't know who she was."

"That's her. She's had it rough. Brandon will be good for her." Patrick grinned at the look Brady shot him. "He's claimed her, just like the rest of you did."

Brady shook his head, reaching up with the backboard, and when it disappeared, reaching for the hands held down for him.

—

He was on his knees once more beside his friend, stethoscope in place, even as Patrick started the IV and placed the oxygen mask over Brandon's face.

Will stood, worry briefly crossing his face.

"Brady?"

"He's hurting, Will. I'm not sure where. When we asked him, he stated he hurt all over." Brady looked up, one hand up to shade the setting sun from his eyes. "He mentioned they were chased by a dirt bike."

"A dirt bike?" Will nodded before he walked away, leaving Brady staring after him before he was on his feet, lifting the backboard to the stretcher and then walking quickly towards their rig.

His eyes moving as he watched the activity around him, Brandon was forced to lie still, the blocks holding his head and the neck collar still in place. He could feel the straps across his body, unable to shift his position other than to move his arms, pain radiating from almost everywhere. His eyes raised as he saw movement near his head.

Doc Whitson, an Emergency Room physician as well as a close friend of the Foundation men, having his own apartment there, stood, watching the monitors on the wall behind Brandon's head before he reached for a wrist. He finally stood, hands on the bed rail, his eyes on his young friend.

"Brandon. What did you do?"

Brandon tried to shrug and then thought better of that idea. "I have no idea. I don't remember. Where was I again?"

"You were at the arts and crafts fair, but somehow ended up in a building that collapsed. Hagen Daltree was with you."

"Hagen Daltree? I don't think I know her." His voice died away. "I was trying to find her, to talk to her. Tell me. Did I?" His whisper held a desperation to it Doc did not understand.

"We suspect so, as she was found wrapped tight in your arms, in the basement of the building as well." Doc watched him closely, seeing the agitation in him that was not normal. Brandon was one of the most calm, level-headed men he knew.

"That can't be right. I wouldn't do that. Hold a lady like that." Brandon was becoming more agitated and Doc nodded at the nurse.

"It appears you found her. Now, how you ended up there in the basement, that's what we don't know." He looked around as he heard footsteps. "I'm sending you for a CT scan and some X-rays. I have to, Brandon. We need to determine if you have any broken bones or what's going on. You have feeling in your legs and arms, so I don't suspect any spinal damage."

"I need up, Doc." Brandon's voice had died to a whisper. "I need to find Hagen. She needs me. She's in danger." He slept, the pain medications taking over and sending him unconscious.

Doc shook his head. "Another one." He walked back out to the desk, seating himself, pulling up Brandon's chart to document his findings.

Will watched for a moment before he spoke, Doc shifting to stare at him over his half-glasses before he nodded.

"I'll be right there, Will. We do need to talk."

Will nodded, stepping back to lean against the wall behind him, his eyes watching the activity around him before he noticed Alice standing down the hall from him, her eyes on the room in front of her. He pushed away from the wall, striding towards her, ducking around the personnel mingling in the hallway as they went about their tasks.

"Alice?" Will waited, knowing she had heard him and knowing as well that she would speak.

"Will? Why? Who did this?" She looked up at him, for once not the professional police officer that she was but a hurt and confused family member.

"Alice? What did they say?" He handed her the handkerchief he pulled from his shirt pocket.

"She's hurting, Will. Brandon protected her as much as he could, holding her to him. But she's still hurt." Will's handkerchief twisted in her hands, her upset evident.

Will looked around, spying an empty room, and with a hand on her upper arm, drew Alice into it, almost shoving her down into a chair. He stepped from the room and with a quiet request, was handed a bottle of water. He returned, handing it in to Alice, who twisted it between her hand.

"Talk to me, Alice. What have they said? The younger girls?"

She sighed, looking up, tears sparkling in her eyes. "They're in the waiting room. Anna and Fynn are with them. They were back for a few minutes." She paused, having to swallow hard. "They think she has damage to a hand from a heavy piece of debris falling on it. If she does, she may need surgery. That means she can't work. And she needs to. Not just for the money, but it's her stress release, how she copes with what they've been through. Honey's is named for her mother, but it was a dream that she and her Dad shared, to make the toys and puzzles, to reach out in a way they didn't see others doing. Now what happens?"

Will crouched down in front of her, hearing steps stop at the door. "We'll talk to whoever it is we need to. The girls and you are welcome to go to the Foundation building. In fact, it might be best. Whoever it is may well go after you to get to Hagen. I need you to document everything you can, what she has told you, where she might have put any evidence. I know for a fact that she will have more offers of help than she will know what to do with. It's how our team works, Alice. She and the girls are part of our family. Her father worked with us on numerous cases as an attorney. Our people don't forget that."

"I know, Will. In my mind, I know that. I just don't see how we can go on." Alice blinked rapidly and was on her feet, almost running from the room, searching for Hagen.

Doc stood, Barnabas beside him, watching before Barnabas spoke.

"Cadee and Berneen are working on setting up one of the apartments for them. Burnie and Blair are working to clear out an area in the back of the gym, one of the extra rooms with an outside door, to set up Hagen's woodworking shop." Barnabas rubbed at his temples. Today had not been one of his better days. He had some personal stuff he was trying to deal with, but Brandon came first. "I just got word. There was a fire at Hagen's home. Her workshop is damaged. How bad, we don't know yet."

Will had stood as Alice ran, listening to Barnabas speaking. "Her shop? This makes it even worse. How much did she lose?"

Barnabas shrugged. "We're working on that. Brady headed there after his shift ended. Of all the guys, he would be the one best to assess her loss. Farr is with him. They've spent a lot of time over there with Alice and Fynn."

"Good. Find out what you can. I know you well, Barnabas. You've already spoken to your Board. Our association will help

<hr>

with whatever you need. I was telling Alice that officers have come forward to volunteer to help.”

Doc nodded. “I heard that. So have staff here. I don’t think Hagen or the twins are aware of how well thought of her father was. Her mother as well. She taught just about everyone your age and younger in town at some point, Barnabas.”

“She did. I remember having her for a teacher. I think she was one of my favourites.” Barnabas pulled out his phone as it chimed, a frown replacing the smile that had crossed his face at his memories. “I need to run, Will. Doc. Let me know what I can do.”

They wanted him stride rapidly away, not sure what was going on with him, but raising him up in prayer.

“Brandon? Doc, how is he?”

“I was waiting for some imaging to be done. Barnabas was gone before I could talk with him. He’s battered, bruised. No broken bones, but he does have a hairline fracture of his right femur. That will keep him down for a bit.”

“That’s not going to be easy, knowing Brandon. How do we do it?”

“We get Hagen on her feet and to him. They’ve connected, just like the others. She’ll work her magic. I would say she’s not able to go to her own home for now.”

“Not with what I’ve heard. I’ll head over there and then come back. Maybe at that point, one of them will be wake and can talk to me.”

—

Hagen shifted in her sleep, one hand coming up to cradle the other, the pain not dulled by the medications. She blinked, her vision blurry for a moment, before she held her eyes open, staring at the cream wall. The line running to the IV bag momentarily distracted her, and she reached for it, fingering it before she let it drop. She shifted once more, turning to her other side, pain filling her eyes with tears before she wiped at them.

Hagen, you do not cry, she told herself. You can't cry. You can't let the twins see you breaking down. You have to stay strong for them. She sighed to herself, knowing the usual pep talk was not working this time. Her head raised from the pillow as she saw a form sleeping in a chair near her.

The person stirred, and she realized it was Brady. Where is Fynn, she wondered?

"Brady?" Her voice was rough for a moment before she cleared her throat.

Brady roused, his eyes popping open as he heard Hagen speak.

"Hagen? You're awake. How are you feeling?"

"I have no idea. I think I was run over by something, only I have no idea what." She shifted again, this time to her back, reaching for the controls to raise the head of her bed.

Brady leaned forward, elbows on his knees, to watch her.

"You weren't run over. You ended up in a building where the floor collapsed. They've been around to get your statement, which you did give, but I'm not sure if you even remember that."

She nodded, weary to the bone as her mother would have said. "I do. They said Alice couldn't take it. How long?"

"How long? You mean, how long have you been here? It's about four in the morning, so about twelve hours."

She shifted slightly to her side, so she could study him without turning her head. "You were the one, weren't you?"

He nodded, knowing exactly what she meant. "I was. You weren't on your own."

"I wasn't?" Her eyes slid closed as she pictured the afternoon from the day before. "No, I wasn't. Brandon, was that his name?" At his nod, she sighed. "He tried to save me. I know he fell first. He just wrapped his arms around me. I could hear him praying as we fell. Does he really do that?"

"What? Pray like that? He does. He says his parents taught him that prayer is a day-long conversation with his beloved Father. So, he talks to God about anything and everything. He's got the rest of us started on that. It felt funny at first, none of us thinking of doing that or knowing that was how God wanted us to talk to Him. When he showed us the verse that talks about God being our Abba, our beloved Father, it made it easier." He paused, seeing that she was drinking in his words. "About your hand."

"My hand? How bad?"

"We think a piece of debris fell on it. Some broken bones. Some tendon damage. Doc seems to think you'll make a full recovery." At her cry of protest, his hand went up. "Your work. I know. Barnabas talked to the Board. They can set you up at the Foundation for now." He groaned. "About your shop."

"What about my shop?" She shoved at the bed, forgetting her injured hand until she put weight on it. She sank back, cradling her arm to her chest. "What about my shop?"

"There was a fire there yesterday after we brought you in. Some damage. Will says you can't work there for now."

"I need to, Brady. I have contracts I need to finish. And just how do I do that?"

"With our help, Hagen. The guys have all offered, as have the ladies. Will said he had officers coming forward to volunteer. You'll have so much stock, you'll have to have a sale to get rid of it." He grinned for a moment. "I don't think you know how beloved your parents were."

—

"I know." Her voice was barely a whisper. "I do know, Brady. That's why I want to do this. It was Dad's dream with me. Mom helped with the planning. I need to follow that dream, to make it a reality. Not just for me. For the twins. They need to see this dream of Dad's come true."

"It will happen. It already has. And the twins are aware of that. Alice took them home a while ago to an apartment in the building."

"I gather we can't stay at our place?" When Brady shook his head, she groaned, her own head dropping back on the pillow. "Then, where? I know Alice would take us in, but it's not fair to her, not when she and Farr are getting married in a couple of weeks."

"Barnabas has had Cadee fix up an apartment for you in the building. He was thinking ahead."

Hagen nodded, her mind already wandering to something else. "Brandon? How is he? He's not dead, is he?"

Brady began to laugh, drawing a frown from her. "No, he's not dead. He took the brunt of it, Hagen. We found you wrapped tight in his arms. Patrick said he claimed you." At her look of outrage, he began to laugh harder. "That's how it is with the Foundation guys. We stake our claim and hold tight." He sobered. "He's battered and bruised and has a hairline fracture in one femur. No concussion, either one of you, which we need to thank God for. Patrick and I could have been picking up you two hurt a lot worse. Or even dead. And that I think was the plan."

Hagen had been watching him, before her eyes slid closed and a single tear rolled down her cheek to drop onto the white pillowcase and soak into it. "That's the plan, I think, Brady. Someone wants me dead. And I don't know why."

Brady had finally made his way home, a yawn stretching across his face. He glanced at the clock and smiled to himself. He would hazard a guess that Hagen was already on her feet, searching for Brandon.

It was true, he would have discovered. Hagen had watched him leave through barely opened eyes, pretending to be asleep, hoping to convince Brady she was, but doubting that she had done that very deed. She slipped from her bed, searching the nearby closet for the bag of clothes Alice had brought her. Appreciation for her cousin's care wafted through her. Alice hadn't been able to retrieve any of Hagen's own clothes so had brought in some of her own. Hagen slipped into them, leaving the gown on the bed, and then shrugged into the zippered sweatshirt Alice had included.

Her sockless feet slipped into loafers, she paced the hallway, searching for Brandon's room. She need to see him for herself, to know that he was alive and not hurt too bad. She didn't doubt Brady's assessment but that was his. She needed to do her own.

Hagen's thoughts drifted to her sisters, and she almost wept in her fear for them. Whoever it was that was stalking her, threatening her, had moved on to threaten them. She needed to keep them safe but had no idea just how to do that. She sighed again, something she seemed to be doing a lot of lately, she thought, and that was not her. Hagen decided she needed to talk to someone, only she had no idea who. Alice, likely, but she was too close.

She finally found Brandon's room, watching as the nurse exited, making her rounds. The nurse paused for a moment beside Hagen.

"Hagen, can I get you anything?"

Hagen shook her head. "No, I don't think so." She peered past her at the open door. "Can I go in? I need to see Brandon. I need to know he's okay."

The nurse turned to study the room door before turning back to Hagen. "I shouldn't let you, but go ahead. I know what he did for you. If I were you, I'd want to do the very same." She moved past, pausing at the next door to watch Hagen.

Hagen hesitated before she moved forward, her uninjured hand rubbing against the jeans she wore. She paused in the doorway, looking up, asking permission to enter. Finally, her reluctant feet moved her into the room, where she paused once more before moving towards the bed, to stand at the end, her eyes on Brandon's face as his head moved restlessly.

Finally moving to stand near the head of the bed, Hagen's hand reached to grasp the one Brandon was using to pluck at the light blanket covering him. He stilled before his hand shifted from under hers to grasp hers in turn. His grip was tight enough she just could not pull her hand free. Now what, Lord? I can't get away. Is that Your plan? Make me stay? Her eyes slid closed as she prayed for healing for Brandon, not realizing that he had awakened and was watching her, drinking in her beauty, wishing she would open her eyes, eyes that for some reason drew him into their depths.

He was feverish, he knew, not quite making sense of what was going on around him. He shifted in the bed, bringing Hagen's eyes to his, before she gave a small, shy smile.

"Brandon?"

"Hagen, where am I? I thought we were talking at your tent at the fair. This doesn't look like that."

She stared at him, not quite sure how to explain to him what had actually happened to them.

"It's the hospital, Brandon. You were hurt." Her free hand, the one wrapped in a splint and bandages, came up to rest against his chest. "You need to lie still. Please?"

"I can't. I need to find Hagen. She's in danger. Someone is after her. Ben asked me to find her and talk to her." His eyes drifted closed as he licked at his dry lips.

Finally freeing her hand, Hagen reached for the glass of water near him and held it for him to drink from. He finally nodded, his head dropping back on the pillow, his eyes closing for a moment.

—

Hagen watched him, knowing she should leave, but reluctant to do that, not until she knew he was coherent, and that she had no doubt would take time. She was surprised when he reached for her hand again, his grasp warm on her hand. She felt the strength in his grip, and felt comforted and safe. Now, that doesn't make a whole lot of sense, she thought. I don't know him well enough to say that, but then again, I've heard Brady and Fynn talking about all the men from the Foundation. Guess I trust him without knowing a lot about him.

Brandon's eyes had opened, and his gaze had focused on her. He still wasn't quite sure where he was or even what day it was, but he knew without a shadow of a doubt that he did not want to lose the lady standing there. Only, he had no idea how he would go about keeping her in his life or if she would even want to stay.

He bit at his lip, before moistening them. His mouth felt suddenly dry. Lord, why this lady? Why now? I know she's in danger, but I have no why or who or how to keep her safe.

"Hagen?" Brandon's voice broke through the silence and he winced, thinking that he had spoken too loudly.

"Brandon? You need to be quiet. You have a fever." Hagen tried unsuccessfully to quiet him.

"You're in danger. I need to get up." He tried to raise himself and fell back, helpless for the moment, not seeing the concern and fear that flickered on her face. "I need to keep you safe but I don't know how." His eyes slid closed as the pain intensified. "Marry me, Hagen? Please, marry me. I can keep you safe that way." He slept, not seeing the shock on her face.

A quiet sound drew Hagen's attention to beside her, and she jumped, not having heard Buckley enter. He grinned at her before nodding at Brandon.

"How is he?"

"To tell you the truth, I'm not sure. I think that he's dreaming or something." She stared at Buckley for a moment, her eyes narrowing as she did so, knowing he was trying hard to hide a grin and not quite succeeding. "He didn't mean that. I know he didn't. He couldn't have."

Buckley sobered, the panic and hope mingling on her face driving away his mirth. "I think he did, Hagen. I truly think he did. He will remember it and will expect an answer from you." He grinned suddenly, looking like a small boy up to mischief. "I hear tell he claimed you."

Hagen groaned. "Not you too. What is it with you guys?" She flushed. "I'm sorry. I shouldn't have spoken to you like that."

"And why not? Right now, I'm here as Brandon's friend and yours. Not as your minister. So, it's okay to insult me. The other ladies do."

She stared at him, finally remembering to snap her mouth closed. "No, they wouldn't do that."

"On the contrary, they do. Fynn in particular delights in teasing me. But then, I was there when she proposed to Brady."

"She didn't! She wouldn't!" Hagen was shocked, for the moment her troubles driven from her mind.

"But she did. And then he proposed after I left. Ask them." He nodded towards Brandon, seeing his friend's eyes had opened and he was focused on Hagen. "He means it, Hagen. In fact, it might be the very best move you could make. You would have the safety and security of the building for you and your sisters, and the companionship of the ladies there. As well, us guys are around. We're a pretty tough lot, when you come down to it. We would be delighted to help solve whatever it is you are facing." A hand up stopped her words. "We know you're facing something. You wouldn't have been chased down by someone on a dirt bike if you hadn't."

"He's right, Hagen. I did mean it."

She spun, her eyes huge, as she became aware that Brandon was awake and had been listening to them.

—

Brandon sighed with relief as he settled down in his favourite chair in his living room, glad to set the crutches aside for a moment, his right foot resting on the ottoman. Being as tall as he was, it was no easy task to operate them, he thought. *I'm complaining, Lord. I feel entitled to but I know I shouldn't. But You let us do that, bringing whatever we need or are feeling to You.* He paused, his thoughts drifting for a moment, hearing quiet movement in his kitchen, soft voices talking quietly before he looked up to find Barnabas sitting near him, his head back on the chair, eyes closed, legs stretched out in front of him with his ankles crossed.

"You're wearing out, Barnabas. You need to take a break. What happened with the Langs really threw the Foundation into a turmoil for a while."

Barnabas nodded without raising his head. "It did. They almost succeeded in what they were trying to do. Guenivere and Branigan are fortunate they didn't succeed."

"That they are." Brandon paused, not quite sure what to say.

Barnabas raised his head, staring at his friend, before a grin crossed his face. "I hear you proposed to Hagen."

Brandon shot a glance towards the doorway before he nodded. "I did. I shouldn't have. She deserves to be treated in a special way." He groaned. "I'm not making sense, am I? Must be the pain medications. I don't handle them well."

"Really? I thought you were making perfect sense." Barnabas ducked the small pillow tossed his way, catching it and tossing it back, just as Hagen entered the room, a tray in her hands.

"Barnabas! Really?" She stared between the two men, catching both of them looking sheepish. "Okay. Which one of you started this?"

"He did!" Brandon and Barnabas both spoke at once, fingers pointing at each other, before they broke out into laughter, unable to contain it.

Hagen shook her head. "You're just like two toddlers, caught in mischief." She set the tray down on the coffee table, a little harder than she planned. "I'm sorry. I shouldn't have said that." Horror covered her face as she looked up, ready to turn and run.

Brandon reached for her hand, tugging her over towards him, shifting his foot so she could sit on the ottoman.

"Never apologize for something like that, Hagen. You're correct. We were like toddlers, but you have to understand. We've been through a lot with the guys here. Sometimes, we do goof around, but we would never do it to hurt each other or anyone else. We've been friends for so many years, it feels like we've known each other forever. I left New Brunswick to move here when Barnabas offered me employment." He stepped at the puzzled look on her face and then sighed. "Barnabas, explain it to her, please."

Hagen shifted to watch Barnabas, finding him intently watching the two of them.

"Barnabas? What does he mean? I don't understand."

"It's this way. The Barnabas Foundation pays the salary for the guys and when they marry, their ladies. That way, their employers can hire someone else and not worry about having to find the finances to do so. It is also a way to encourage others, which as I am sure you know, is the premise behind the Foundation."

"That I knew. I just didn't understand about the salaries. I can understand why you keep it as quiet as you do. You would be taken advantage of, I am sure."

"That is always a possibility." Barnabas reached for a plate and helped himself to the sandwiches she had brought in. "Thank you, Hagen. These look good." He looked around her at Brandon. "I think it's your turn to ask the blessing on the food, Brandon."

"You're right." He reached for Hagen's hand, holding it tightly when she tried to pull it away, a slight shake of his head stopping her. He knew her sisters had entered the room and found seats, and that she was likely ready to run.

Holly and Haley watched their sister closely, knowing that something had happened she hadn't told them. They exchanged glances and then a shrug, before they began to question Brandon about his work.

Hagen's eyes narrowed as she watched the pair, aware of what they were up to. And no, she was not prepared to tell them about the proposal. She thought he hadn't meant it, that it had been his fever, but deep inside, she really did wish he had. She was desperate for someone to share her life and worries. Hagen's life was not turning out how she had planned it, her dreams set aside for now, and perhaps forever. No man would want to marry me, she thought, not and take on the twins.

Brandon had leaned forward to reach for his mug of coffee, pausing as he watched her face.

"I meant it, Hagen. I really and truly did. Buckley will likely come up with a date for us, you know. He did for Fynn and Guenivere."

She turned, almost into his face, seeing his sincerity.

"We need to talk then, I guess, at some point."

"And we will. But for now, you and the girls need to head to your apartment. Just for now. We'll talk tomorrow, Hagen, my darlin'. That's a promise I have every intention on keeping."

—

Chapter 8

Standing at his office window late that night, Brandon stared out into the darkness, no lights on in the room and just faint light shining from his bedroom. His hand rested on the window frame, his thoughts troubled. He knew that he should have retired but his mind was too active for him to even think about sleeping. His right hand rubbed at his thigh, feeling the pain there, aware that he should be taking the pain medication Doc had insisted that he should do when he had popped in about an hour before.

His eyes drifting up, Brandon's thoughts drifted to Hagen. He smiled as he remembered her outrage at Barnabas over the pillow but then the sudden dampening of her spirit as she tried to back away and apologize for scolding them.

Hagen, he thought, what am I do to with you? Lord, I could use some direction about now. I'm not sure where I'm heading with this beautiful lady or how much danger we'll face. All I know is that I don't want to see her walk away from me. And the twins. Lord, they are such characters but I can see the sorrow in them. How do we reach through that to them?

He finally turned, letting the heavy blue drapes drop back into place, not seeing the man who stood in the shadows near his vehicle, eyes trained on Brandon as he had stood at the window, before he shoved a camera back into his pocket and walked away, heading towards the lake and the small boat he had anchored there. He knew where Hagen was, where her sisters were. Now, to find a way to separate the three ladies.

Rising early the next morning, Brandon perched on the side of the bed, his hand resting on his thigh, the pain level higher that morning than he had expected it to be. He heard quiet sounds from the kitchen and nodded. One of the thirteen other men in the building had found their way in and was working on breakfast for them. It was a common plan, breakfast and then prayer when they had an opportunity. He squinted at the clock and sighed. It couldn't be after nine. He never slept that late.

Struggling to shower and then shave, Brandon finally stood, balancing on his crutches, starting down at his feet. He had found a pair of sweatpants, not his usual style of dress, but today he really didn't care. He had struggled to pull on heavy socks, forgoing shoes for the moment. His mind was on Hagen and her problem and how he could best help her.

His crutches thumping along the hardwood floor, Brandon slowly made his way towards the kitchen, pausing for a moment, his head tilting before a smile lit up his face. It wasn't one of the guys, he thought, but Hagen. But who had opened the door for her?

Burnie peeked around the door frame before he appeared in the hall, a tea towel in his hand.

"Brandon, my friend. You are up and on your feet, or foot, rather." He grinned at the face Brandon made. "That good, huh?" He peered behind himself towards the kitchen before his voice dropped. "I was heading here this morning. Did you know that Hagen was standing outside your door, just waiting for you to open it? She said she had been there for a while."

Brandon paused, a frown on his face, before he nodded. "I can see that. She wants to mother, having had to do that with the girls." He suddenly gave a low laugh. "She told Barnabas and me off last night for tossing a pillow at each other before she apologized."

"She did? Hmm. I guess you deserved it?" Burnie grinned even wider as he pointed towards the kitchen. "Are you hungry? She had a basket of food for you, did you know that?"

"No, how could I? I haven't made it to the kitchen because someone is standing in my way and won't move." Hagen had appeared in the doorway, a question on her face.

Burnie continued to grin. "Then, I guess I must move and let you by so you can greet your lady. I'm off to my office, Hagen. Come see me when you can. I might be able to help with some of the research you need to do."

Hagen nodded. "I'll do that. I need to find some ideas for more toys and puzzles. Thank you, Burnie." She watched him walk away, not ready to face Brandon yet.

—

Brandon bit back his grin, knowing she was not going to turn around, not yet. He moved towards her, finally standing right behind her. His crutches went against the wall before he wrapped his arms around her, the toes of the one foot resting on the floor.

Hagen stiffened for a moment before she relaxed, feeling his chin resting on the top of her head. She waited, not sure what to say.

"Hagen? Are you okay this morning?" He felt her hesitation and then nod. "Okay. So. I hear you brought breakfast. Have you eaten?" Once more he felt her head move, this time in the negative. "Then, let's eat. We'll spend some time in prayer, too, if you wish."

She finally moved away, suddenly shy, reaching for the plates she had filled and setting them on the table, one across from the other. Brandon watched her carefully before he reached for her plate, moving it to the spot on the table next to his. She still avoided his eyes, and he bit back another grin, even as he pulled her chair out and seated her, before finding his own seat.

Late that morning, Hagen glanced at her watch, surprised to see how the time had flown. Breck and Brody had appeared a few hours before, simply stating that they were there to take her to her home. The insurance investigator needed to speak with her. Brandon had not given her any choice, simply reaching for his crutches and moving towards the door. She turned as she stood in the centre of her workshop, finding him slumped down on the stool near the workbench, pain evident on his whitened face.

"Brandon? This was too much for you. We should leave."

He looked up, a grin on his face. "No, it's okay. You need to do this. What have you left to do?"

She sighed, her eyes taking in the damage. "Everything here is pretty much ruined. I'll need to start all over, only I don't know how."

His hand reached for hers and stopped her movement away from him. "Barnabas talked to me after you and the girls left. He had spoken to the Foundation Board. They will set you up with everything you need to get back up and running." A finger came up to her lips, to stop her speech, even as he wrapped an arm around her and pulled her to him. Her arm went up instinctively around his neck. "It's what they do, darlin'. This is part of their mandate, how

—

to encourage someone. Bruce, Barnabas' father, was adamant we needed to do this. I think you've been told that there are many volunteers to help you. All we need from you is a detailed list, and I mean detailed, down to the last nail and paintbrush of what you had here and what you would like to have to continue."

"They can't do that." Hagen's voice was barely above a whisper, despair and disbelief in it, but deep in the secret part of her heart, the dream she and her father had shared raised its head once more. If they did that, she could continue and expand. Burnie had sent her text messages, with jokes but also bits and pieces of the research he had taken on. She had protested at that to Brandon, but he had simply shaken his head and say to let Burnie. It's what he did best.

Her arms wrapped tight around herself, the tears she refused to acknowledge trickling slowly down her cheeks, cutting through the devastation and bleakness of her face, Hagen stared around her home. She had finally be allowed in, Will Peters, the police chief, stopping by to assess how she was. She had not expected to find the rooms in shambles, broken ornaments and dishes on the floor, books torn and thrown around. Pictures had been pulled from the wall and the frames and glass on them broken. The food in the fridge and the freezer was tossed around.

Haley and Holly stood beside her, shock on their faces. Their arms reached for their sister and the three stood in a huddled heap, not moving, not wanting to see what the rest of the house was like.

Brandon balanced himself on his crutches, his heart breaking for the three ladies that he had begun to think of as his family. He could hear Will and Barnabas talking just outside the front door. Barnabas had appeared, eager to talk to Hagen to find out what it was she needed to get started. She had just stared at him, unable to answer for her emotions. That was when she had walked away towards the house, the twins appearing on the scene.

He moved forward, letting his crutches rest against the wall, his arms sweeping around the three sisters, his head bowing as he prayed for them. He found feel Hagen relaxing, her body leaning against him, as if in acceptance of what he was offering.

Hagen finally moved away from the security and comfort she found near Brandon, making her way through the house, the devastation and destruction in all the rooms destroying the hope she had begun to feel. She felt someone near her and turned.

Barnabas stood there and behind him stood Alice and Fynn. She simply shook her head, not sure what to say

"Hagen. Tell you what. We'll all pitch in and help you." Barnabas took a look around. "The guys will all be here shortly. The ladies as well. Alice tells me Farr is on his way as is Berneen's brother, Darby. We'll get your home cleaned up for you." He

———

waited for her to respond, a frown on his face as she stood, staring past him before she moved that way. He turned to watch, concerned, before he saw what she was moving towards. A quick movement on his part stopped her in her tracks.

Alice had been watching Barnabas and turned as he reached to stop Hagen. A gasp was drawn from her before her professionalism took over. Her phone was out to call for the crime scene techs before she went on a search for Will.

"Will? I need you to see something. Brandon, we need all of you out of the house for now."

Brandon nodded, his eyes moving towards the twins, a frown on his face as they approached him.

"Brandon? Who would do this?" Haley struggled to talk, her emotions overwhelming her, Holly's arm around her.

"I don't know but I can guarantee you this. We will find out who and bring them to justice." He looked past her to where Hagen stood, her eyes on him. "We'll let Alice and her friends look around. Then, my friends and the ladies will help you tidy up. Right now, we need to find a place to sit. Your sister has a list to make for Barnabas. Perhaps you could help her with that."

"A list? Of what?" Holly's voice had discouragement.

"A list of what she needs to replace from her shop. What her and your wishes are for equipment, material, designs. Mailing stuff. Whatever it takes to get her up and running again."

Holly's face lit up. "We can do that? Honestly?" She spun, her feet taking her rapidly towards Hagen, throwing herself into her sister's arms. "Is that for real, Hagen? We can start making plans to expand, just like you've been dreaming about?"

"That's right, Holly." Barnabas grinned as she peeked around Hagen at him, Haley at her side. "That's absolutely right. The Foundation is setting your sister up again and I have been told by the Board to provide everything that she needs, wants, wishes."

Haley's eyes grew huge. "Hagen! Oh, God has heard us, hasn't He?" She ran towards Barnabas, throwing herself at him to hug him before she danced away, reaching for Holly's hand and

———

pulling her towards the worn-out picnic table that sat midway between the house and the shop.

Hagen had watched them before she turned back to the house, moving closer so that she could watch the activity inside and outside. Brandon moved towards her, an arm around her.

"Why? Why do this? I don't know if the girls saw the message on the living room wall. It was brutal, Brandon. Who threatens to kill teenage girls?" She wept, fatigue and worry uppermost in her emotions.

Buckley spoke from beside her, meeting Brandon's gaze over her head. "God is in control, Hagen. I can't promise that you and heaven help us, the girls, won't go through any more difficulties. But trust me on this. All of us will try our utmost to keep you all safe."

"But that doesn't always work, does it?" Hagen's gaze had drifted towards the large maple tree in the front yard and she broke away from Brandon to approach it. She froze, seeing the enlarged picture of the twins leaving their high school. "That's from yesterday. Whoever it is is watching them." She reached to grasp it, to rip it from the tree, when a hand stopped her. She looked around.

Brendon stood beside her, his hand on her wrist, gently stopping her from the very deed she had contemplated.

"Leave it, Hagen. The police will need to see it. This has become more than just an arson case or your home being invaded. They are stalking your sisters and threatening them."

She gave an abrupt nod. "I know, Brendon. I know I shouldn't touch it. I don't want them to see it."

"But that's the thing, Hagen. We can't shelter them. They need to be aware of this, so that they can take precautions. If we don't and something happens, can you live with yourself?" Brendon watched her face and saw the moment she gave in.

Hagen looked up, trying to cover her feelings, trying to regain control of her emotions, turning as she heard Haley's voice, asking if she had any paper and a pen.

—

Late the next morning, Hagen rose from where she had been seated at the kitchen table, searching for her phone, and not finding it. She paused, hand to her cheek, trying to remember where she last had it and sighed. The three of them had been guests once more at Brandon's for supper the night before. That's the last she remembered having it.

Pausing at his door, Hagen finally raised her hand to knock before she turned, ready to walk away, freezing as she saw the man standing behind her. He wasn't one of the building men, that much she knew. She began to back away, before he reached for her, slamming her against the wall, his hands shoving hard against her shoulders. Desperate to escape, Hagen twisted and turned, unable to dislodge his hands, the force just becoming stronger.

His hot breath wafted across her face, the smell of alcohol and tobacco smoke causing her stomach to churn. He didn't say a word, just stared down at her before he gave a hard shove and then sauntered away, heading for the back stairs.

Hagen dropped to the floor, her head buried against her knees, shaking as she had never shaken in her life. She was terrified. Just who had that been? And why? Who was it that was after her, trying to destroy her dream, threatening her sisters?

She didn't look up as she heard footsteps, not seeing Brody stopping on the other side of Brandon's doorway before he knocked and then opened it, calling for Brandon. Brandon appeared, puzzled that Brody had not entered, before his eyes followed Brody's pointing finger.

He was beside Hagen, his crutches cast aside as he dropped to the floor, his arms cradling her, not understanding why she was fighting him, that was, until she heard his voice and then turned to him.

"Who was that man?" Her question stopped both men before they could ask anything, as they stared at her and then at one another.

—

"What man?" Brody stood, ready to search for whoever it was.

"That man! Where did he go? He shoved me against the wall. Hard. And wouldn't let me go. He threatened me. No, he didn't say anything, just his look and the force he held me with." She looked up at Brandon. "Please make him stop."

Brody turned and was gone on the run, flying down the stairs and then sliding to a halt at the security desk. The guard shook his head, before his fingers were moving quickly on the keyboard, pulling up the feed from the last little while. Brody stared in disbelief as they watched the man appear and then disappear through the back door.

"I thought we solved the problem of people accessing that." Brody was frustrated. It was not the first time someone had entered there, intent on nefarious purposes.

"We did." The guard was moving, heading for the door, Brody on his heels, his phone out to call Barnabas and then the police

Brandon finally managed to stand, taking the crutches Hagen handed him, his hand resting on her cheek.

"Are you hurt?"

Hagen shook her head. "I don't think so. Just shaken." Her anger was beginning to boil over once more, as her mother would have said. "I thought I was safe here."

"And you should be. Let security figure it out. Right now, in there." He pointed at his door. "I have your phone and was just about to head up with it when Brody knocked."

"That's why I'm here. I thought I had left it here." Hagen moved around the kitchen, finally reaching for the kettle, filling it and then lifting the coffee carafe before she dumped it out and made fresh. She could not settle to sit, her mind racing as to what the man had wanted.

Brandon watched her, seeing the conflicting emotions on her face, before he moved to stand in front of her, stopping her with a hug. She stiffened for a moment, before her arms hugged him back.

—

"What am I do to with you, darlin' Hagen?" Brandon's voice was soft in her ear. "Marry me? Let me protect you and the girls."

Hagen froze, her head on his chest, hearing his heartbeat in her ear. Lord? What do I do? Do I take his offer or refuse it? Is it fair to him, if I do? She waited, waited for God's leading, waited for the peace she should feel.

She finally nodded, her voice muffled somewhat as she spoke. "It's not fair to you, Brandon. What if we do marry and you find someone else?"

Brandon simply shook his head, reaching to tuck a russet curl behind her ear, one that had escaped her braid. "That won't happen, Hagen. I can promise you that. God has led so far. I have peace with asking you that. What about you?"

Hagen moved back enough to stare up at him, his arms loosening around her. "I do, I guess." She groaned. "That's not fair. God has not put a roadblock in place, I know that." She shifted from foot to foot, suddenly nervous, not quite sure what decision to make.

Brandon nodded, before his head bowed, his prayer raising for the lady he had grown to love with all his heart in such a short time, asking for wisdom in their decision, and that if it wasn't in God's will, that they would know.

Hagen turned when he finished, reaching for their mugs, hesitant as to where to sit.

"Hagen? How be we sit out on the balcony? I've been inside all day and could use some fresh air." Brandon grinned at her, and she froze, seeing in a moment, in the man standing in front of her the man who had haunted her dreams for years.

"Sure. Do you want anything to eat with your coffee?" Hagen was desperate to busy her hands, not sure if she should be even asking that.

"Not unless you do. I had a sandwich a while ago."

"No, I'm fine." She headed past him for the living room before his voice stopped her

———

"There's a balcony off the office. That's my favourite spot. I would like to share it with you."

She turned. "You have an office here?"

"A home office. I also have one on the main floor. Barnabas set us all up with one." He pointed down the hall. "Take a look in the rooms as we go by. Now, the girls? Do they share a bedroom or have their own?"

She blushed for a moment, the rosy colour on her cheeks fascinating Brandon who thought she looked even more beautiful. "They have their own but they could share."

"Not a problem. We can ask them."

Hagen nodded, even as she paused in each doorway, taking in the colour scheme, which was so much like hers. Creamy yellow walls in all the rooms gave a consistency that pleased the artist in her, contrasting with the dark wooden floors. Colourful drapes in all the room, each a different colour, set a tone that she liked. She paused in his office, staring around.

"This is nice, Brandon. I like it."

"Good. There's room in here to set up another desk for you. The girls will have a desk in each of their rooms." He waited for her to exit the office before he sank down in one of the brown wicker chairs, reaching to pull the ottoman over to raise his leg.

Hagen had been watching him closely. "Your leg?"

"It hurts but not like it did. Doc's been watching me."

"That's good. I just hate that you were hurt because of me."

"I'm not." Brandon raised his eyes to find her staring at him in shock. "Let me repeat myself, Hagen. I am glad I was there. Even getting hurt? I can live with that. What I can't live with would have been you being hurt or killed."

She nodded. "What happens with your investigation of me?"

"I talked to Ben last night. He's not going any further with it. In fact, he has go to the police services and put in a report of harassment on your behalf."

"He has? He didn't have to,"

"No, he did. It was a false report, many of which he has received. It needs to be documented with the authorities."

———

50

Staring at their sister before looking past her at Brandon, who stood, his hands on her shoulders, Holly and Haley were dumbfounded. They had talked about that very possibility, that Brandon would sweep in and save them, but never expected it to happen.

"You're engaged? Wow!" Holly finally reached to hug her sister, finding Brandon waiting to hug her as well.

Haley stood, not sure of what to say or do, before she stood in front of Hagen, searching her face.

"It's not because of us, is it, Hagen? I know you've had threats against us." She tried to control her emotions. "I didn't tell you. Someone has been following us. I don't know if Holly saw him."

Holly turned, Brandon's arm still around her shoulder. "No, I didn't. You didn't tell me."

"I wasn't sure at first. I saw him again today when we left school. He was walking towards us until he saw Breck waiting for us and then he left."

Brandon grew grim. "We'll need you to talk to the police. It's an active investigation."

Hagen nodded even as she reached for Haley. "I wonder if it's the same man."

"What man? Hagen, what aren't you telling us?"

"There was a man in the building today, who threatened me. Brody was looking into it." Hagen sighed. "This is not working."

Brandon's arm was around her as she spoke. "It will work, darlin'. It will work." He suddenly grinned, the twins staring at him, both with narrowed eyes. "This calls for a celebration. I would like to take all my ladies out for dinner."

"You would?" Holly's face lit up. "Oh, can we, Hagen?"

Her face tilted up to Brandon, she communicated with him in silence before she nodded. "I think we can do it. Is it safe enough, Brandon?"

"It should be. Brody and Burnie are heading in to town for a meal. We can all go together. I think they were heading for that little Italian place."

"Oh. Dress up?" This from Haley.

Brandon had not intended that, but at the excitement and eagerness on the twins' faces, he could not say no. "Sure. Why not?"

"Okay. Hagen, come on. You need to change. Dress up is not those jeans and T-shirt." The girls dragged her away, protesting, even as Brandon grinned in sympathy with her.

"They seem excited." Barnabas spoke from beside him. He had been watching the interaction between Brandon and the girls, a grin on his face at how they were reacting to him.

"They are." Brandon stared towards the spot they had disappeared in. "Just so you know, Hagen and I will be getting married, as soon as we can. Today really rattled her."

"I know. Are you sure, Brandon? I know you will have prayed about this."

"I'm sure. So is she." Brandon looked down at the floor, a bleak look on his face for a moment. "It's not how I imagined it would happen."

"None of the guys have, but they met the ones God meant for them." Barnabas nodded into the distance where Hagen had disappeared. "She's your lady, Brandon. We all can see it."

"She is, Barnabas. She is. I just don't know how to tell her that." Brandon turned, his crutches thumping on the floor, before he walked away from Barnabas, his apartment door shutting quietly behind him.

A couple of hours later, Brandon shifted in his seat at the table in the restaurant, uncomfortable for a moment, the feeling of being watched niggling at him. He couldn't see anyone that was overtly keeping an eye on their table, but the twins' excitement and chatter had drawn eyes and smiles their way throughout the meal. Hagen had tried to tamp down their chatter, but finally gave up, a shrug showing it was normal when they were excited.

Brandon reached for her hand, his clasp warm, before he leaned over.

"I take it they're not upset at our news."

Hagen shook her head, a smile on her face, before she spoke. "If they had been, you would have known. They can be vocal that way. They have always said what they feel." She shivered, her eyes searching the room or what she could see. "Someone's in here, Brandon. I can feel them watching us."

"I know. I have had the same feeling." He looked up as Brody stopped by their table, a grin on his face as the twins greeted him.

"Ready to head home, ladies? We can offer you a ride if you like. Brandon seems to have settled in here for the night."

Brandon simply shook his head. "No, we're good to go. Ladies, are you finished or do we need to wait longer for you?"

Haley stared at him, her eyes narrowing as she caught the grin he was trying to hide. "No, I think we're finished. Brody?"

"I would say you were. We'll be at the door." He shared a look with Brandon, who simply nodded.

Hagen had been watching the two and knew from the looks shared between then that her feeling had been accurate. They were being watched.

Brandon shifted on his truck seat, turning to talk with the twins in the back seat but obstensively to watch out the back window. Hagen kept glancing at him and he finally shook his head.

"Someone's back there?" Hagen kept her voice low

"I think so. With Brody behind us, they won't try anything. Not like what happened with Brady and Fynn."

"It was along here, wasn't it?" Hagen paled, remembering how Fynn had told her about the accident they had had.

—

53

"It was." Brandon breathed a sigh of relief as she turned in to the parking lot of the building. "We're home. Let's meet tomorrow, Hagen. We need to talk, but we also need to see if we can come up with some names."

She nodded. "I need to start working. My orders are backing up." She parked the truck, turning off the ignition and then handing him the keys. "Thank you, Brandon, for our meal. And thank you for being who you are."

The next morning, Hagen stared around her new shop, shock on her face, not quite sure what to say. She had not expected to see it up and running, not when she had just given Barnabas her list, what two days ago, she thought? This is amazing. Lord, it has to be You. That's the only explanation. She wandered around, touching the new equipment, the stain and paint cans set up at a nice large table that was covered with a laminate, easy to clean off, she thought. She looked at the wall beside it, seeing brushes in all shapes and sizes that would work for her crafts. She moved on to where the display shelves stood, a hand reaching out to touch them, before she once more walked further into the shop, seeing the stacks of wood on shelving, the papers and plastic laminates she would need.

Hagen stopped in front of another huge counter, this time, awe on her face. A shipping table, she thought. No more moving things around to pack her wares. No more packing them in the kitchen. A desk stood nearby, with a large printer and laminating machine beside it. Shelving behind the table held myriads of packing material and labels.

She stood, tears on her cheek. Dad, it's come true. Our dream has come true. We have a professional shop to work from. I just wish you were here. I need you to see this. Her tears continued unabated even as she felt gentle hands turning her into a body and arms hugging her tight. Brandon had found her. His chin rested on the russet head, even has his hand traced her braid.

"Hagen? What's the matter, darlin'? Did we miss anything? Haley and Holly gave a quite a list, but if there is something we need to add, we can." Brandon's voice whispered in her ear.

Hagen shook her head, unwilling to move away from him. "No, I don't think you did. It has everything I have dreamed about, in the way I wanted to set it up. The girls must have given you my plans."

"Fynn and Alice helped. In fact, all the guys and the ladies met with your sisters. They are quite opinionated, did you know that?" He gave a grin she couldn't see. "Haley and Holly laid it all out. What you wanted. What your father had wanted. What your mother had suggested. We just took it all and combined it. This is what came up. I just need to know. Is it what you want? What do you need changed?" Brandon shared a look with Breck who stood in the doorway, knowing that Hagen had headed that way.

Hagen raised her head to look up at him, wondering how she had managed to find a boyfriend so tall. That was not what she had planned.

"It's fine, Brandon. It's fine. I just didn't expect it, that's all." She turned, his arms loosening enough to let her. "It's Dad's dream. I just wish he was here. I need him to see this, and he's not."

Breck walked towards her. "Then, let's see what we can do to get you doing more. Blair wants to work on a website for you." He held up a hand. "I know, you have one. It's good, but Blair does that for a living for some people. He just wants to help. If you say no, that's fine."

Hagen stared at him. "I don't know what to say, honestly." She reached into a pocket of her jeans and pulled out a paper. "Maybe one of you can figure this out. I found it taped to the door this morning. Someone knows where I am and where my shop is. How do I keep all of you safe if that's the case?"

Breck's face hardened as he took the paper and read it. "I'll pass this one for you, Hagen. Dallas has been assigned to your case. He'll want to talk with you." He looked around. "Now, where do we begin?" He broke into a sudden grin. "I've always wanted to try my hand at woodworking."

She stared at him, before shaking her head. "Really? Just set that aside." She pointed at the paper. "I don't know that I can. Not that easily."

Breck studied her, realizing he had misread her and underestimated her feeling. "Hagen, I apologize. I did not mean to discredit your feelings or the danger you are in. Whoever this is means business. We have seen that. We need to sit down and go back over everyone you know, that may have a grudge against you or your family."

Hagen nodded, before moving away, heading for the filing cabinet and pulling open a drawer. She slapped a folder down on the table. "Here. This is what I have. Everyone and every business I can think of. There may be more and that we can figure out." She turned back to the cabinet, her back stiff, before she pulled out patterns and then moved away from the men, to reach for wood and her tracing pencils.

Breck and Brandon exchanged a glance before Brandon spoke in a low voice.

"She's hurting, Breck. Not just from that. With our plans she is missing her Mom. She hasn't told me that. Haley did."

"I am sure she is. The other ladies want to meet with her, to help with plans, but they're unsure if she wants them to. With Alice and Farr getting married this weekend and with what she's been facing on her own, her emotions are likely a mess."

Finally looking up, her right hand worrying the bandages and splints on her left hand, Hagen searched the room, seeing activity in just about every area. She had turned from her table hours earlier when Brandon had wrapped an arm around her and told her she had company. What did she want them to do, he asked?

Hagen had been surprised to see all the men there as well as the ladies. Doc and Anna had stood and watched as Buckley had prayed for her and for her work. She had not been able to say a word, her surprise that complete. Holly and Haley she could see near the mailing table, packing up what they had been able to salvage and repair, with Darby, she thought his name, Berneen's brother. She stretched as she rose, wandering the room, greeting each one, answering their questions, thanking them with tears in her eyes that she could barely contain. They had more than made up for the time she had lost and what had been lost in the fire.

Reaching the outside door, Hagen shoved it open, standing for a moment in the late day sunlight, feeling the fall chill coming. Early fall or autumn or whatever you wanted to call that season before winter, she thought, is one of my favourite times of the years. It gives me incentive to keep going, to be outside, to enjoy the wonderful works of God, to find ideas for her work. She was in the planning stages of a woodland set, trying to work through the intricacies of it.

Brandon stood for a moment, the door leaning against his arm, before he hobbled forward to where Hagen stood.

"You okay?" His voice was quiet, not sure how she had felt about them all descending on her. He had heard the comments over the hours, how they liked her work, that it was really great for the children she was trying to read to. Burnie, the author of the group, had turned at one point, a question on his lips, that died as he studied Hagen, before he shook his head. He wanted to use her handcrafts in a book idea that had come to him as he worked. He could talk to her later, he decided.

"I am, my love. That I am." Brandon's eyes shot to her at her words of endearment, not sure if she meant them or not. "I didn't expect them all to show up, though. They've caught me up to where I wanted to be weeks ago and couldn't get there." She looked up, a pensive look on her face. "How do I thank them?"

He reached to wrap her in his arms, content to stand near the garden entrance, not wanting to move away. "You did, just by how you reacted now. They don't want thanks, darlin'. They live to serve. I can guarantee you that they will be around when they can to help. You'll never be behind again."

She leaned her head back against him. "Then, that's that." She paused. "Brandon, are you sure?"

"Sure? About what? About us?" He felt her nod. "I am, darlin' Hagen. That I am. You are my heart, the one God planned from before time to be my helpmeet. I love you, Hagen. Never doubt that. I never believed in love at first sight, not until I met you." His head tilted as he looked at her face. "And you? You're sure?"

She hesitated for a fraction of an instant, causing him to despair, before she spoke. "I am, I think." She groaned. "That's not how I meant it. I am sure. I just need to be sure the girls are okay with it."

"And I can assure you that they are. Both came to me this afternoon, on their own, and thanked me for choosing you."

"They did? Wow! I guess that's that then." She looked away from him. "Brandon! Someone's here."

"There is. Run, Hagen. Head for your shop. I'm behind you."

Hagen began to run, hearing the thump of Brandon's crutches behind her until she heard a shout from him and slid to a stop, spinning to see him on the ground, not moving. Her eyes raised to the man standing over him and her heart sank. He was back. She retreated, not quick enough before arms wrapped around her from behind. She struggled to escape, unable to free herself and felt herself picked up and carried back towards where Brandon lay.

Set on her feet, an iron grip on her wrist that she could not escape, Hagen stared at the man, refusing to speak.

—

59

"So, you're back up and running? You don't listen very well. It would be a shame for something to happen to that building." The man standing over Brandon walked around him, to stand in front of her, close enough that she could once more smell the alcohol, tobacco and sweat coming from him. "Not talking? That's okay. You don't need to talk." He turned for a moment to stare down at Brandon and then turned back to stare past her at the building.

"Come on, man. Do what you have to and let's get out of here." The man holding her was getting edgy and nervous. He figured it would only be a matter of time before someone came out and saw them.

"Hold your horses. I'm getting there." The first man, his hair, face and clothing dirty and unkempt, stared at Hagen before a fist headed her way, driven into her ribs.

Hagen cried with the pain, feeling her ribs give way. Her wrist was released, and she fell to her knees, her arms wrapping around herself, tears of fright and pain on her cheeks. Her last coherent sight was seeing his foot raised and headed for her. She didn't feel the heavy steel-toed boot driven into her before she collapsed to the ground, to lie motionless just feet from Brandon.

The men stood over the couple before they shrugged. The older man pulled out a dirty once-white envelope from a pocket, studied it, and then dropped it onto Hagen's body before they moved away rapidly, suddenly aware that others would be coming out of her shop, and they needed to disappear before they were caught.

Laughing at something Brennen had said, Bradon and Brody headed out the door, the three men standing for a moment, sensing something off before they shrugged. Brennen was uncomfortable about walking away, his eyes searching through the dusk, before, with a cry for help, he was running away from the other two men. Bradon took off after him, Brody heading back in for Brady who was still around, knowing that if they needed help, their paramedic friend was the one to bring. His sudden reappearance startled the men and they rose, heading for the door, admonishing the ladies to stay inside. Haley and Holly reached for each other, just then realizing that Hagen wasn't in the shop. Fynn and Ennis moved towards them, asking questions to divert their attention.

Brennen dropped to his knees beside Brandon, a hand reaching for a pulse, his head dropping for a moment as he realized that Brandon was alive. It raised as he heard Bradon's cry of alarm, to find him on his knees beside Hagen, a hand reaching to push back her hair and then both hands in motion, trying to find out what was wrong.

Brady's steps slowed before he was on his own knees, assessing Brandon.

"It looks as if he was hit from behind. I can feel a knot on the back of his head. His leg?" Brady looked up at the question from Brendon. "I'm not sure. If he fell wrong, he could have injured it. We need the teams here."

Brady was on his feet, moving rapidly the few feet to where Hagen lay. He rolled her carefully to her back, hearing the moans that came from her as her arms wrapped around her abdomen. He didn't like the trickle of blood that came from her mouth.

"Brady?" Barnabas crouched down beside him, the other men standing with their back to the group, on guard, watching for anyone who was not to be there.

"She's hurt somewhere in the abdomen. The ribs, too, from what I am feeling." Brady sat back on his feet. "Who and how? I

—

would hazard a guess that she's got fractured ribs and from how she's trying to hold her abdomen? She's hurt there." He turned as he heard the sirens approaching. "Good. We'll get them in and get them assessed." He looked up at Barnabas. "Who tells the twins?"

Barnabas sighed. "That would be me, I guess. Hagen talked to me the other day, asked that if anything happened to her, before she and Brandon married, would I take on the care of the twins? They have no one else. We were in to the lawyers that day to sign the paperwork. Brandon as well."

"Good." He stood, giving his assessment to the paramedics who had approached before he stepped away, to stand beside Breck and Barnabas. "I'll ride with Hagen. Who's with Brandon?"

"Brendon is. He's not leaving his side, he said." Breck turned for a moment, seeing Dallas approaching. "Dallas is here. Head off, Brady. He'll catch up with you in town."

Dallas stood beside the two men, watching as the stretchers holding the couple were wheeled away, many hands ready to help as the men from the building walked beside them. He watched as well as Barnabas stood, arms around the twins, their hands clinging to each other before he moved them away towards his vehicle, Fynn and Ennis with them.

"What happened?" Dallas turned to Breck.

"We don't know. They walked out and then a while later some of the others came out and found them. Whoever it is, I must say, is really bold. This is the second time they've come after Hagen on our land."

"It is. How do we stop them? With the forest surrounding you and then the lake not too far away, you can't fence it."

"No, we can't. We've never had a need to, not until lately." Breck spun. "Someone is still out there, watching us. I can feel him."

"I know." Dallas looked around, motioning to some officers, sending them off on a search. "We'll not likely catch them. I just pray we're not too late."

Breck nodded. "Almost losing Bradon and Ennis was bad enough. I don't want to see it happen to anyone else." He watched

—

as Dallas headed away towards the shop, where Buckley stood waiting.

Watching carefully, Brady stood in a corner of the examination room, out of the way, as Hagen was assessed. He sighed. It was what he thought. A punctured lung. Abdominal injuries. There was talk that she would need to head for surgery. He left, intent on finding Barnabas, stopping as he saw Doc heading his way.

"Doc? I didn't know you were working tonight."

"I wasn't supposed to but Jeff called me, asking me to cover for him. His wife took sick and they had to head for Toronto to see her specialist there first thing in the morning."

"I see." Brady turned to walk back down the hallway with him. "I don't like what I'm seeing with Hagen."

"Me, either. I'm sending her for imaging. Just what happened?" Doc was angry, angry that friends had been ambushed once more on their home property.

"We don't know. Some of the guys had left her shop and found them." Brady paused outside another examination room. "How's Brandon? What damage was done to him?"

"So far, it seems as if he was just knocked unconscious. The leg is healing from what we can see on X-Ray. In fact, I think he can go to a cane when he leaves."

"That's good news. Now, about Hagen? What do we tell the twins?"

Doc shook his head. "I'll be out in a few minutes. Tell them I'll come talk to them." Doc peered over his half-glasses at Brady. "Who are they with?"

"Fynn. Ennis. And I think the other ladies. Someone had gone for Anna. I talked to Farr. Alice had to be out of town today to testify in another case. He's trying to reach her."

"Good. Go on, Brady. Find the twins. Stay with them for now." Doc shoved open the door and disappeared inside, the door swinging silently shut behind him.

—

Brandon stirred, a hand reaching for the back of his head, as his eyes flickered open and closed. He finally managed to crack them open partway, before blinking to clear his vision. A hospital room. Now what did I go and do? I don't remember. I don't remember things for a few weeks now. I have no idea what day it is. Hearing a sound beside him, he turned, frowning at the two young ladies who stood, worry on their faces.

"Brandon? You're awake? Are you okay?" The one who was slightly taller, her hair a beautiful red gold and having dark brown eyes, spoke.

"Yeah. I think so. Where am I?"

"You're in the hospital." This from the other girl, who had the same red gold hair but hazel eyes. "You scared us."

"I'm sorry. I didn't mean to. When can I leave?" He raised himself up, only to fall back down again.

"You can't leave yet, Brandon." Breck spoke from the other side of the bed. "Doc says you're staying overnight." He looked over at the twins. "Haley and Holly stayed just to see you were okay. Brady's heading home with them."

Brandon gave a small nod, a hand raising in a wave as the twins turned to walk away, their heads keeping turning to watch him

As the door closed, Brandon's head went back and his eyes closed for a moment. "Who were they?"

Breck stared at him. "What do you mean, who are they? They're Haley and Holly, Hagen's sisters."

"Hagen? Who's she?"

"Hagen? What do you mean? Who's she?" Breck stared at him.

"What I said. Who is she?" Brandon's eyes finally stayed open and he stared up at Breck.

"Hagen? Brandon! She's your lady. You're engaged to her. Those two are her sisters she's guardian to. What do you mean?"

Brandon sighed. "I don't remember her. Not at all. What day is it?" When Breck told him, Brandon stared at him. "That can't be right. Not at all. Didn't Branigan and Guenivere just get married?"

"Like about three months ago. Brandon? Are you saying you don't remember three months?"

Brandon sighed, his eyes closing. "I guess I am. What happened?"

"You and Hagen were attacked on our property. You two had left her shop. Some of the guys found you when they followed about thirty minutes or more after that." Breck ran his hands through his hair. "You really don't remember."

Brandon shook his head and then groaned. "You just had to have me do that. I don't know who she is. How did we meet?"

"You were at her booth at the arts and crafts sale for some reason. You two were talking and then were chased by someone on a dirt bike. You ducked into that old Farmer house and the floor collapsed, which it shouldn't have. The same day, she had a fire in her workshop at her home. Barnabas had her move into the building. You're in love with her, Brandon. How can you not remember?"

Brandon stared at the door, reaching for the bedside and raising himself up, waiting until his head cleared before he swung his feet over the side, balancing for a moment, a hand going to his thigh. "What did I do?"

"You had a hairline fracture there from the building collapse. Brandon? What are you doing?" Breck watched as Brandon hobbled to the closet, retrieved his clothes and then headed into the bathroom, before he reappeared, fully dressed, a hand resting on the wall.

"I want to see her. Now. If what you say is true, then take me to her."

Breck simply shook his head, reaching for the wheel chair. "You ride in this, or I won't take you."

Brandon nodded, at the end of his strength for the moment, before he pointed to the door. "Now, Breck. I want to see her for myself, to see if I do remember."

Barnabas and Brennen stood watching, seeing Breck's shrug at them, before they followed him down the hallway, stopping outside a room door. Breck's hand reached to push it open and then paused.

"Brandon, before you go in, pray, which I know you have been doing. If you don't remember her and tell her that, it will destroy her. She and the twins lost their parents a year ago to a drunk driver." His voice died away before he spoke again. "Now, I wonder." He spun to face Barnabas. "Has Dallas looked into that?"

"I'm sure he has. I'll mention it to him." Barnabas' eyes raised to stare down the hall, seeing both Will and Dallas walking towards them. "In with you two. I'll stall them."

Will stood, his eyes on the door, before he turned to Barnabas. "He's up and about?"

"He is, but somehow, I don't think it's good. Breck looked stressed when he wheeled him down this way."

Dallas shook his head. "Then I guess I'll need to talk to him." He looked around Will as Breck reappeared. "Breck?"

"We have a problem, guys. Brandon does not remember Hagen. Nor the twins. He thinks we're still living three months ago."

Pausing just near the bed, Brandon's eyes slid closed as he prayed. *Lord, I don't remember this lady, even though Breck says I do and that we're engaged. I just don't know, Lord. How do I get to remember? Please, Lord, I don't want to hurt her.*

Wheeling himself up the bed, Brandon's eyes first took in the monitors around Hagen, then the lines with the IV and plasma running to her arms. He shook his head. What had happened to her? He wished he could remember her.

His gaze dropped to her face, seeing the whiteness, no, gray look, he thought. What happened to her? He reached for her hand, the one with the splints and bandages, now replaced with clean ones. Brandon shook his head as he once more raised his face to watch her, seeing her eyes flickering open as she roused.

Hagen roused, not sure where she was, only knowing that she hurt, and hurt badly. She sighed to herself as she remembered the men, knowing one had already been stalking her. She needed to talk to Alice, no, not Alice. Was it Dallas who she needed to find? She felt her hand being held and nestled her fingers tighter to the man's hand, that she was sure of. It had to be Brandon.

Looking around, she finally spied him, his eyes glued to her, a puzzled look on his face. Licking at her lips, she was finally able to speak.

"Brandon? You're okay? I didn't know what they had done to you." She frowned as he didn't speak. "Brandon?"

He shook his head. "I'm okay. Just a bad headache. And whatever it was I did to my leg. And you?"

Hagen continued to frown, sensing something different. "Brandon?" She groaned as the pain hit and then she was away, unable to finish her conversation.

Brandon waited before he finally pushed away and wheeled to the door, struggling to open it and maneuver through. Brennen was heading his way and nodded at the door.

—

"How is she?" Brennen waited, puzzled at the look on Brandon's face and the length of time he took to answer.

"I'm sorry, Brennen. I just don't know." He wheeled past his friend, heading for the waiting room. He needed to go home, to be somewhere he knew where he was and to sort through his thoughts.

Brennen stared after him, not quite sure what to think. He looked back at Hagen's door before he walked after Brandon, hearing his request for someone to drive him home. Breck rose, shaking his head, before he pushed Brandon away, leaving the few who had gathered there to stand, staring after them, dumbfounded at Brandon's words.

Brennen stared behind him before he spoke. "What's that all about? Why is he leaving when Hagen's still here?" At the silence that greeted his words, he turned.

"He doesn't remember her, Brennen." Brady spoke, Fynn's arm around him. "He doesn't remember her, the twins, or even that he asked her to marry him. He thinks we still living just after Branigan and Guenivere were married."

Brennen stared at him before he shook his head, a groan coming from him. "Now, what? How do we get him to remember?"

"I talked to Doc about that possibility." Barnabas spoke up. "We talked about a number of issues he could face. It takes time, Doc said, or else it will take Hagen being in difficulty again for him to remember. And then again, he might never remember."

"And just how do we tell the twins? Haley and Holly adore him already. To have him walk away would be like losing their parents all over again." Brennen turned and stalked away, anger rising in him. Anger at Brandon. Anger at the world. Anger at the men who had done this. Anger at whoever it was behind them. He was determined to find them and headed for his truck and then the Foundation building, walking rapidly through it to the conference room, unlocking the door, flicking on lights in an angry manner before he slumped into the chair he preferred.

Lord, forgive me. I don't have the right to be angry. It's not my life. But it's a friend and his lady. Help me to help them. Let me find some clue, some word, some person, some business that will unlock this mystery. I don't want to see them hurt any worse. He

——

prayed for healing for Brandon. For Hagen, he hesitated, knowing that her condition was serious. A punctured lung, he thought, and internal bleeding. He shuddered at the words Doc had spoken to them all, that whoever had kicked Hagen had done so with work boots and with force. She was fortunate, he said, that she survived.

Two days later, staring in disbelief at Brennen, Hagen shook her head, slumping back on the couch in her living room. She had been stunned with his response to her question of where was Brandon and was he all right.

"That's not true, Brennen. It can't be true." The hurt she felt showed on her face, her mind unable to comprehend that the man she loved and who had said he loved her, didn't remember her any more, in fact, had not been around her.

"I'm sorry, Hagen." Brennen sat on the coffee table, facing her. "Doc said it was the blow he took, that caused him to forget."

"No, it can't be true. Haley and Holly are looking for him. Doesn't he realize how much he means to them, to me?" Hagen's eyes slid closed. "That's why he was like he was."

"When?"

"In the hospital. He just didn't seem himself, not the man I know." She looked up, shadows on her face and in her eyes. "What do we do? How do we get him to remember?"

Brennen shrugged, having asked Doc the very same questions. "I talked to Doc. He couldn't really tell me if Brandon would recover or when. He did say it might be you in danger that would trigger his memory."

Hagen snorted. "Like that will happen. If he's not around me, then how can he?" She rose, paced to the window and parted the sheers to stare out. "I'm moving back to my place, Brennen. I'll move my shop as well as soon as I can get my building redone."

"That's not necessary, Hagen. You're more than welcome to stay here and to keep your shop here."

She didn't respond. Brennen finally rose, his eyes on the fingers he has rubbing together, before he turned and walked away, anger rising in him. Anger directed at the men responsible. Anger directed at life in general. And anger directed at Brandon. He hoped he didn't meet him in the hallway. He just might help Brandon's memory along, and that wasn't what he needed to do. He prayed for the anger to disappear, prayed that Brandon would remember Hagen and the girls.

Hagen turned when Brennen had left, heading for her bedroom to pack her clothes and then to the office to pack what she had there. She hesitated in the twins' room but resolutely packed their belongings, carting everything down to her van, and realizing they really didn't have that much. Not any more. She stood for a moment, her eyes directed to where her shop was, and then slipped into the van, pulling away, not looking backwards. If she had, she would have seen Brandon standing there, staring after her, a puzzled look on his face. And she would have seen Brady watching both of them, before he shook his head and went to find Fynn, wrapping her in his arms, holding her as she wept for her friends.

Haley and Holly positioned themselves in the van, chattering away, telling Hagen about their day at school, before they realized they were heading to their own home.

"Hagen? Why are we going this way?" Holly turned to stare back at her sister.

"We're moving back to the house, girls. It's what we have to do."

"But Hagen? What about Brandon?" Haley waited for her sister to answer, not sure about what she was saying

Hagen didn't respond, simply drove to their home, and parked, before she opened the back of the van and began pulling out their luggage. Haley and Holly reached for theirs, once more exchanging glances.

Later that evening, the twins approached Hagen, finding her sitting on the couch in the office, where they used to gather with their father and mother, to hear him read their devotions and then pray for them. They looked over at each other, before they wrapped their arms around Hagen.

Hagen stirred, almost asleep when they came in, the pain in her ribs and abdomen less than the pain in her heart.

"Hagen? What happened?" Holly started the questions.

—

"What about Brandon? Does he know where we are?"

Hagen shrugged. "I'm sorry, girls. I'm just so sorry. Brandon doesn't remember us. To him, we're strangers. I can't stay there. I'm so sorry." The tears she had been resolutely holding back began to flow, the looks on the girls' faces opening the flood gates.

Arms around each other, the sisters grieved and then sat in silence.

"Why doesn't he remember?" Holly was trying to puzzle it out.

"I guess when he was knocked unconscious, he ended up with amnesia. He has forgotten the last three months. I just couldn't stay there. He doesn't know who you are."

Haley sat back, determination on her face. "We'll make him remember."

"No, Haley, we don't. We leave it alone. I guess it just wasn't meant to be." Hagen looked at the clock, fatigue weighing her down. "I think we all need an early night. Head off for bed, girls. We'll need to start sorting through the shop in the morning."

"The shop? Aren't you keeping the new one?"

Hagen shrugged. "Brennen said I likely could, but I just can't go there. I'll have to start over again, girls. All over." She rose abruptly, heading for her bedroom, the door closing quietly behind her.

Haley and Holly stared at one another, not sure what to say. They both quietly rose, tidied the kitchen from their simple meal, and then headed for bed, thoughts and plots and plans running through both their brains.

—

Three weeks had passed, with Hagen no closer to finding out what Brandon really thought. She avoided him whenever she thought they would be in contact. The twins were watching, ready to step in to help but whenever they approached Hagen about it, she had just walked away.

She didn't tell them of the increasing threats she was receiving, making her desperate to find somewhere to send them where they would be safe, but not knowing of anywhere. She had worked tirelessly on her shop, ignoring the fatigue and the pain she felt, the insurance adjuster lending advice but not questioning why she was determined to set up again in the old shop when he knew she had one all set up on the Foundation grounds. She had slipped in early one morning, early enough that no one in the building was around. The security guard on duty had been surprised when she asked for help, but shrugging, had done just that, her paperwork packed in boxes and loaded into her van. Once more, she drove away, this time for good, she thought, not seeing Brandon standing staring after her again, a puzzled look on his face.

Brandon was no closer to remembering Hagen or the girls. He would just look at anyone who commented to him about them, often turning his back and walking away. He avoided the conference room, where once he would have been in the thick of the research the others were doing. To him, she was a stranger, and at that, not one he would ever likely get to know. He ignored the niggling in his heart, that said she was his lady and he should be taking care of her.

Barnabas appeared in her shop doorway one day, startling Hagen. He didn't say anything, just walked around, studying her set up.

"Hagen? How are you feeling?" He finally perched on a stool, his eyes thoughtful as he watched her shuffle the papers on her desk.

"I don't know how I'm supposed to feel. Physically I am still healing. I shouldn't be working, I was told not to, but I don't have a choice, Barnabas. I am the sole provider for the twins. I have to start saving for their further education. This has set that plan back a long way." She raised a hand as his mouth opened. "No, don't say it. I will not accept any further assistance from the Foundation. You did too much."

Barnabas merely shrugged. "It was the Board, Hagen. They still want you to use the shop. That I have been told."

"I can't." Her voice was barely a whisper. "I can't, Barnabas. In fact, I am thinking of packing up and moving from here next year when the twins graduate. I can't stay in this town. The memories that were good are gone. All I have are bad memories."

Barnabas nodded. "I see. Talk to me again before you make a final decision. The men and the ladies tell me you and the twins are missed, but they understand. Alice said she's been in touch with you, but you're not saying much."

"Quit prying, Barnabas. I won't talk. Not to anyone." She looked down, her attention back on her work.

He watched for a moment before he rose, his heart breaking for her and also for Brandon. Now, Brandon, he thought, he's walking around lost, and I guess he's entitled, but he's hurting and he's hurting these three ladies. Lord, how do we do this?

That night, Brandon shot upright in bed, his heart pounding, fear coursing through him. He didn't know why. He sprang from his bed, rapidly dressing, glad he had been able to set the crutches and then the cane aside.

He ran for his vehicle, speeding away, leaving dust in his trail that drifted into the dark night. He had no idea where he was heading before he slowed to a stop in a subdivision in town, his eyes on the darkened house in front of him.

Brandon slipped from his truck, closing the door softly before he walked rapidly up the driveway and then around the house. Something was off, he thought, but just what. He didn't see the dark form that tackled him, taking him down, a hard fist to his jaw sending his head back to hit heavily on the lawn. His only thought was he was tired of this, but just why he thought that, he had no idea. His attacker stood over him for a moment before making his way to the back door. A few movements and the lock was jimmied, the door open. He paced through the house, his eyes studying the closed doors. He had been in there before, scoping out the rooms. He knew exactly what he had to do and who he had to get.

Quietly opening the door, he slipped inside, standing for a moment to accustom himself to the dim light before he approached the bed, a cloth soaked in chloroform in his hand. He slapped it over the young lady's face, combatting her struggles until they stopped. He scooped her up into his arms and paced back through the house and then outside, paced towards the back of the yard where his vehicle waited. He dumped her into the back seat, a blanket thrown over her, before he was behind the wheel and driving away. She would be his ace in the hole, he thought, one that would bring Hagen to her knees.

Hagen rose the next morning, knocking on the twins' doors as she walked down the hallway, before standing staring at the open back door. It had been locked when she went to bed. Now, how did it get open? She stepped through it onto the back patio, not seeing anything.

—

She sighed. Not again, Lord. Why do these things happen to me? I just want to live my life and get on with my business, get the girls through high school and then college. At that point, I can move somewhere out in the country, where I can live my life out in peace.

Pulling into the driveway, the responding officer studied Brandon's truck before he ran the plates, surprise on his face. Why would he be here, he wonder? He headed around to the back, meeting Hagen as she stood on the patio, worry on her face.

"Hagen? Talk to me. Tell me what you found."

"That." She responded, her finger pointing at the door. "That was open this morning. I distinctly remembering locking it last night."

"Okay. The twins? Would they have been up and about all ready?"

Hagen shook her head. "Their doors were closed when I came out." She frowned. "But they should be up. We had plans for today."

"Okay. How be you go get them up while I take a look around?" Donny Ellis paused. "Brandon's truck is on the street."

Hagen stared past him before she shrugged. "I have no idea why. He shouldn't be here." She spun on her heels, finding Haley standing in the kitchen, staring at the open door.

"Hagen, what is going on? Why is there a police officer here." She started to move past her sister until a hand on her arm stopped her.

"The door was open this morning and it seems we have had a break in." She looked around. "Where's Holly? Isn't she up?"

"No. That's unusual. She's always up before me." Haley spun on her heel, running for her sister's door, knocking and then opening it to look in. There was no sign of Holly. Haley quickly searched the room and then stood in the hallway, peering towards the single bathroom in the house. The door stood open, just as it had when she had left it moments earlier.

"Hagen!"

Hagen spun at the fear in her sister's voice, moving quickly to find her, an arm around her.

"Haley?"

"Holly! She's not here! Where is she?"

Hagen's face grew grim as she too searched her sister's room before, an arm around Haley, she rushed from the house, searching for Donnie, finding him helping Brandon to his feet.

"Brandon?" Haley's questioning voice drew his attention to her, and he shook off Donnie's hands, his own hand rubbing at his chin.

He walked slowly towards the two ladies, his eyes on Hagen's face before he looked at Haley.

"Haley? Are you okay?"

"But wait. You don't remember us."

"I guess I did forget you for a bit, but I do remember you now. Hagen?"

Hagen just shook her head, unable to speak, tears sparkling in her eyes before he swept her into his arms.

"Hagen? What's wrong?"

"It's Holly. She's missing."

Brandon stared down at her head before he swept her up into his arms, moving to seat in one of the white wicker chairs she had at the back of the house, shaking his head at Haley's comment that they would be wet. He watched Haley for a moment, standing forlorn, her face covered with tears, fear shaking her body before he reached out an arm and motioned her over, sweeping her into a hug as well. His arms encircled the two ladies, his eyes on Donnie, who had approached as he heard Hagen's voice.

"Donnie, can you check? They say Holly is missing."

Donnie nodded, his hand going to his service weapon, as he entered the house, to move through it quickly, to stop beside Holly's bed, his eyes on the discarded rag on the floor. Even now, the faint odour of chloroform hung in the air near it. He shook his head, walking rapidly outside, grabbing a blanket from the living room and

—

draping it around Hagen and Haley before he walked away, dismay on his face. He had been a schoolmate of Hagen's and considered her a good friend. His wife, Annie, had been one of her close friends for years.

Will stood, his head bowed as he listened to the report Donnie was giving, before he nodded.

"No signs of her around at all?"

"No, sir. We've searched the house and the shop. There's a crawl space, but it hasn't been disturbed. Hagen said she rarely goes down there, other than to check on the plumbing and the venting pipes. She opens the windows in the spring and in fact, just closed them up last night." Donnie looked around as he heard a vehicle pull to a stop. "There's Barnabas and Brendon. And Baird. And Buckley."

Will gave a quick grin. "I called Baird. Looks as if he brought reinforcements with him. I'm glad Buckley is here." Will peered towards the back of the house, watching Brandon and Hagen from where he stood. "We need to get them away from there."

Donnie nodded. "I know. Hagen has just refused to leave. I did get Haley to move to my car." He ducked to look through the window. "She's hurting, Will."

"I know. Those two girls are close, but what they went through losing their parents have made them even closer." Will walked towards Brandon. "Brandon? Can we talk?"

Brandon nodded, moving away from Hagen, feeling he was deserting her.

"Will? Any news?"

"Not that I am aware. Listen, we need to get Hagen and Haley out of here. The team is going to be here for a while. I can't let them back into the house." He squinted at the sky. "It's going to rain soon." He looked down to see Hagen standing in front of him, Haley with her arm around her sister.

"Will? Have you news?" Hagen was hopeful, but doubtful at the same time.

"No, I'm sorry, Hagen. I don't. Listen, I need to move you and Haley out of here. The team is going to be a while. Let Brandon take you back to the Foundation building."

Hagen sighed. "I just left there, you know."

Will gave a swift grin. "I know you did, but right now, that's where I need you to be. I know you were attacked there, and I know I am repeating my "I knows"." He grinned at Haley for a moment before sobering. "At least there, we have security that we can place with you."

Hagen turned to Haley, studying her sister, seeing the devastation in her face. "It's my fault, Will. If I hadn't come back, Holly wouldn't be missing."

"No, I don't think you're correct. We've heard rumours on the streets that someone has been following the twins. We just didn't have enough information to identify who it was. So, it wouldn't have mattered where you were. One of them would have still be taken. If they had been together, the other one may well have been injured."

Hagen had paled at his words, her arm tightening around Haley. "Then I guess we must." She turned to the house, intending on packing for them, when his hand stopped her.

"I'm sorry, Hagen. I can't let you go into the house. The ladies will make sure you have what you need." Will was apologetic but firm.

"Thank you. I wasn't thinking." She looked towards the shop. "If you can, there are some boxes with patterns and designs. Can you retrieve those for me? I take it we won't be back here for a while."

"No, I don't think you will. We'll look after getting those for you. Right now, we need you two to go with Brandon. Brandon, leave your keys. We'll get your truck to you. Barnabas is here. You can go with one of them."

Barnabas watched Brandon walk towards him, simply opening his vehicle door for Hagen and Haley to seat themselves before he threw a questioning look at Brandon.

"Brandon? What is going on? And where is Holly?"

"And why are you here?" This from Buckley.

"I was awakened in the night, feeling a fear for someone. I don't remember driving here but I didn't recognize the house. I walked around the house to check things out and got clobbered again. That removed the block to my memory." He looked down, momentarily overcome with his emotions. "It's Holly. She's missing. Their back door was broken in and she disappeared. Will said they found evidence that she was taken from her bed."

His words shocked the four men standing beside him, Buckley stepping back so he could watch Hagen and Haley.

"Let's get them home." Brendon spoke quietly. "I'll go find some of the ladies and take them shopping for the three of them."

"Do that, Brendon. Keep your bills and submit them." Barnabas turned back to watch the activity. "What about her shop?"

"She hadn't unpacked, I guess. Will said he'd get the boxes for her. And he'll make sure my truck gets to me." Brandon slipped into the seat beside Hagen, an arm around her shoulders, his hand resting on Haley, who leaned into it.

<hr>

Pacing the living room of the apartment she was once more back in, Hagen listened to the quiet conversation from the office and from the kitchen. Will had officers there, equipment in place to trace the call when it came. Hagen had snorted at that, drawing his eyes to her face.

"I doubt they'll call. They'll wait until I'm outside and just walk up to me. Can you prevent that?" She walked away from him before he could answer.

Haley watched her sister from where she had plopped herself down in a chair when they had entered the apartment, not moving, wishing it had been herself instead of Holly. Why, God? Why did you let it happen? Why Holly? Why here? She finally just wrapped her arms around her upraised knees and buried her face against them, not wanting anyone to see that she was weeping.

Brandon watched from the doorway before he moved towards Hagen. Sensing him near her, she turned and then walked into his embrace, his arms tight around her.

"Brandon, what am I to do? I need to find my sister."

"I know, darlin'. I know. Will's working on it. The guys are all in the conference room, working away. Fynn has called a friend who does searches on people. She's working on that."

Hagen nodded. "But who? My business isn't one that you can just take over. I don't ship on a regular basis, if that's what they're after. So why?"

"That's what we're trying to determine." He drew her down to the couch, his arm tight around her, a nod of thanks to Berneen, Baird's wife, who brought in a tray with hot drinks for them, and then stayed, her arm around Haley, as she perched on the chair arm.

"Who would do this?" Hagen looked up as she heard footsteps, and Burnie appeared, sinking down onto the coffee table in front of her. "Burnie?"

"Hagen, it's okay. I just have some questions, questions that arose as we were researching."

She nodded, watching as Haley's head raised, her heart breaking for her young sister.

"Okay. Your father, what did he do for a living?"

She told him, described what her mother had done, and then what had happened to them. She paused, a thought running through her mind, a thought that dismayed her but also scared her.

Brandon picked up on her emotions. "Hagen, what did you just think about?"

She turned to face him, her eyes haunted. "The man that hit them. He was drunk. The bar he had been at was charged for allowing him to drink over the limit. The bartender threatened us. I had forgotten that, tucked it away back in my mind. The bar owner didn't stop the threats, but I often wondered if he felt the same way. He lost his business because of that. The twins and I wouldn't sue. It wouldn't have brought Mom and Dad back. I have seen him around town, catching him watching me at times, and I have wondered what his mindset was."

Burnie nodded. "That's what we're looking for, Hagen. Thank you. Now, with your father's work, did he have any enemies that you know of?"

Hagen shrugged, her eyes on Haley. "There was one of the family that accused Dad of being biased and of doing shoddy, negligent work, but he hadn't. An investigation proved he had done everything as it should be done. You and Holly were about six or seven at the time, I think, Haley. Dad and Mom wouldn't talk much about it, but there is always the possibility that a grudge hung on." She reached for the pad of paper and pen that Burnie offered her, writing down that name and any other name she could think of. She looked up to see Dallas standing behind Burnie. "Burnie, Dallas is here. Can you give him a copy of that?"

"I can." Burnie stood, an apology on his lips that was never uttered as Dallas shook his head.

"It's okay, Burnie. You're asking the questions I would of Hagen and that I have of others." He stabbed a finger towards the paper. "Just give me a copy of that. On second thought, I'll just take a photo of it." His phone was out of his pocket as he spoke, the photo taken and his phone tucked away. He looked towards Hagen, his eyes catching Brandon watching her, his heart on his face. "Anything else, Hagen?"

She shook her head, her emotions in too much of a roil to clearly think or speak. "Just find my Holly." Her head went down on Brandon's shoulder and her eyes closed, even though she didn't sleep. Her mind drifted to years past and stayed there as her memories filled her with joy and sorrow.

I don't know who, Lord, but You do. Please, dear Lord, protect our Holly. Bring her back safe to us. Don't this haunt any of us for years to come. Hagen heard Brandon's prayer before her emotions took over and sent her into a sleep, a sleep she desperately needed but wanted to avoid.

Haley watched her sister, a woebegone look on her face. She huddled in her chair, tears on her face, as Brandon looked up. A movement of his arm had Haley flying to him, to be tucked up close to the man that she had begun to think of as her brother. She heard his prayer for her and for Holly before she too slept, her emotions overtaking her, just as they had with her sister.

Brandon looked up as he heard footsteps, and Will appeared followed by Barnabas. Both men sank wearily into chairs.

Brandon studied Will before he spoke.

"Any word?" He kept his voice low, not wanting to disturb the ladies he held tight to his heart.

Will nodded. "There is. We have sighting of the man who we think is involved. Plainclothes men are following him, ready to move in. We had word from the street about a possible hideaway for him." He sighed as he reached for his phone. Some days, he regretted being the chief of police. Today was one of them.

As he listened, his eyes shot towards Hagen and then Haley, before he was on his feet, almost running from the room, his voice calling for Dallas, who ran after him.

"Will?" Dallas paused at the foot of the stairs, waiting for Will to finish his conversation and pocket his phone.

—

"Thank the good Lord, they found her. She's still out, from what they said. Brady was the paramedic on call. Thank God for that. She knows him, if she awakes."

"We need to tell Hagen."

"And we will. Right now, they're working on removing her from the building she was in."

"Will? I don't like the sounds of that."

"No, I don't either. It's booby-trapped and they've made their way to her. It took time for them to clear a pathway. They'll bring her out and then bring her here. Doc has asked for that. I can't see the harm in it. If we take her to the hospital, they'll find her there."

"That they will." Dallas paced. "We need to awaken Hagen."

"We will, Dallas. We will. Once we have Holly here, we'll go get her."

Rousing, Holly looked around, a frown on her face, fear suddenly hitting her. This was not her bedroom, and it was late in the day, she could tell, just from the way the sun shone through the window. She raised herself up, staring at her nightclothes before she looked up, her face relaxing as she saw Doc.

"Doc? Where am I? I'm not at home."

"No, you're not, young Holly. How are you feeling? About like that. What I would expect. I just need to listen to your heart and lungs and then Will and Dallas want to talk to you."

"But where am I?"

"You're in the infirmary at the Foundation building. You went on an adventure and didn't ask any of us to come with you." He grinned as she frowned at him.

"I don't remember. Why not?"

"Because, young lady, you were chloroformed." Doc stepped back. "You're fine, just sleepy, I suspect. Now, here are Will and Dallas."

Dallas approached, a smile on his face that didn't quite reach his eyes. He was not used to talking to teenagers.

"Holly, Doc says you're fine. Do you remember anything at all about today?"

Holly shook her head. "No, I don't. I remember going to bed last night. We had planned to go for a hike this morning, I think it was. Just the three of us. Hagen said we needed some our time." She looked up at Dallas. "What happened? Why am I here?"

"You were chloroformed and taken from your bedroom sometime early this morning. We were searching for you, found out where you were and brought you here. You don't remember waking up at all?"

She shook her head, her eyes closing for a moment against the headache that had begun to pound at her temples and behind her eyes. "No, I don't. Can I see Hagen and Haley, please?"

Dallas shared a look with Doc, who nodded. "We can do that. Here, this is what we're going to do. I'm just going to pick you up and carry you to your apartment here. Hagen and Haley are waiting there for you."

"I'm glad we're back here. I like it here." Her head went down on his shoulder and she slept. Dallas tilted his head to look at her before sharing a look with Doc.

"It will take time to get out of her system. I don't know how much she was given, but she was either given a lot or else her system can't handle it. She shouldn't have still be sleeping when she was found. It was hours."

"I know, Doc. Let's move. I have two ladies who need to see this young lady." Dallas walked away, his concentration on getting Holly to her siblings, not seeing the men and ladies from the building who had gathered in the lobby at the news, relief and joy on their faces, prayers on their lips.

Doc opened the door for Dallas and then held it as Dallas entered, his eyes watchful that he didn't hit either Holly's feet or head. Brandon looked up at the sound of the footsteps, his eyes widening as he saw Holly. Doc pointed to the other couch in the living room.

"Right there." His voice was low and he reached for a blanket to cover her. "How long have they been sleeping, Brandon?"

He squinted at his watch. "About an hour." He felt Hagen stirring, her eyes opening before she looked up at him, a frown on her face.

"Brandon? Where are we?"

"In the apartment, Hagen. I have someone here who I think you want to see."

She frowned again, before she shook her heard. "I don't know who that would be."

"It's Holly, Hagen. She's here and she's safe."

Brandon watched as her beloved face continued to hold a frown before she sat upright, frantically looking around before she saw her sister. She was out of Brandon's arms and on her knees beside Holly, a shaking hand reaching out to touch her hair and then her face before her arm was around her sister and her face against her as almost silent sobs shook her body.

Haley roused next, blinking in the soft lamplight before she noticed Hagen was not there.

"Hagen?" She looked around, finding Dallas standing nearby, a smile on his face. "Dallas? Any word? I dreamt she was here."

"This time, your dream is true." He stepped back just enough so she could see Hagen on her knees. "Holly's home, Haley."

Haley sat, her mouth open, shock on her face before she scrambled to escape the blanket she had been covered with, tripping on it as her feet entangled in it with her rush to get to her sisters. She was beside Hagen, arms around both of her sisters as much as she could, sobs shaking her as well.

The men watched, compassion on their faces, before Brandon rose and pointed to the kitchen.

"Dallas. How?"

"I can't go into all the details, but we had been watching someone. Word from the street reached us as to a possible place where she was held. The ERT went in and brought her out." Dallas paused. "Brady is the one who took the call. Don't ask him. He can't and won't say much."

"I won't." Brandon took the mug of coffee that he had been handed, stepping back to stare into the living room. "I am thankful that she's here. Does she remember much that we'll have to work with?"

"No. She was never awake. It was a surprise to her to wake up downstairs." Dallas excused himself and walked away, rolling his head to try and relieve the tension in his shoulders. He still faced a long night, that much he knew.

Haley watched Holly closely over the next couple of days, not willing to be away from her, to the point, Holly turned on her one day, almost angry with her.

"Haley? Can you please leave me alone?"

Haley dug in her heels, not willing to admit her fear. Buckley had heard them as he approached where they were standing outside the building, facing one another.

"Ladies? Just who I was looking for. I'm hungry for some ice cream and am heading to town. Care to join me?" He watched, biting back as a smile as the twins continued to stare at one another before Haley agreed readily, Holly more grumpily.

Sitting in the ice cream parlour, Buckley teased them, bringing smiles finally to both their faces. Buckley was a well-loved pastor to his congregation, ready with a smile, a word of Scripture, or a helping hand or listening ear.

"Holly? If you need to talk, let me know. I listen really good, I'm told." Buckley grinned as she stared at him, her mouth open.

"It's really well. Don't you know your grammar?" She stared at him as he just continued to grin. "You did that on purpose."

He shrugged, watching Haley for a moment, before he sobered.

"Ladies, I know this has been tough on you both, in different ways. Don't let it come between you." He held up a hand at Haley's protest. "I know, Haley. You're afraid Holly will disappear again, this time for good. Holly doesn't understand how worried and scared you were. Just be patient with one another. Let each other have space like you used to." He grinned again as they stared at him, gathering up the debris from their treat. "How'd I do?"

"You nailed it perfectly." Holly bit at her lip. "I'm sorry, Haley. I didn't understand. And I should have. We're twins. We're supposed to know these things about one another."

"It's okay. I've been hovering, afraid you will disappear."

Buckley stood later and watched as Brandon walked towards him, a spring in his step for a change.

"Buckley? You waiting for me?" Brandon grinned, his whole face alight

"I am. Have you and Hagen set a date yet?"

Brandon shook his head. "Not yet, but we're talking about that. Why? You have a date available?"

Buckley just grinned. "I do. Let's see if you pick the same one." He looked around, then down at the envelope he held. "Listen. I found this envelope today outside Hagen's shop. She hadn't been around there, I don't think."

"No, she hadn't been. She had had some appointments to go to. What is it?"

"There was no name on it, so I opened it. It's a death threat, Brandon, directed at Hagen. How do we keep her safe? The guys are working as hard as they can to figure it out but are running into road blocks."

Brandon, who had been back to work, nodded. "That's what I have been hearing. Someone is deliberately blocking information. And I think I know who. I just don't have the proof I need." He said a name, Buckley staring at him in surprise, then consternation.

"Them? It makes sick sense, do you know that? Come on. Let's start our search. And I want to pass that on to Emma Finlay. We also need to pass this on to Dallas."

Brandon nodded. "We do. How do we stay safe, Buckley. They've proven that they can get into our building, into their home. Just how do we do that?"

"Prayer for one thing. Another thing is to get you two married. It may help but it may not. Whoever it is has proven they really don't care who gets hurt."

"And that is what bothers me. Someone innocent will be hurt."

"I know." Buckley held the entrance door open, waiting for Brandon to walk through, stopping short as he saw Hagen waiting for them.

Hagen walked towards them and in the arms that Brandon held open for her. He could feel her trembling.

"Hagen?"

"The twins have been threatened again. I can't do this, Brandon. I need to keep them safe, but how do I do just that when I have no idea who is after me. Or what they even want."

"They want revenge, Hagen. Come, over here to one of the sitting areas." Buckley pointed to one of the two areas on either side of the lobby that had been set up with couches, chairs, tables and a gas fireplace. "We need to talk. I found an envelope near your shop, with a death threat directed at you. Dallas is on his way out, when he can get here."

"The girls? They want to start riding the bus, but I'm afraid to let them."

"No, that's not a good idea. For now, let us take care of getting them back and forth. The guys have all volunteered to do just that."

"I can't thank them enough."

They talked for a while longer before Buckley excused himself and walked away, a meeting hanging over his head. Brandon watched him before he turned to Hagen.

"Hagen? We need to set a date."

"I know." She sounded grumpy and then sighed, apologizing to him. "I just wish Mom and Dad were here, but wishes doesn't make that happen." She turned her face up to him, surprised as he reached to kiss her and then kiss her again. "Brandon? We're supposed to be planning."

"I know. I'm planning on how I can sneak another kiss." With that said, he reached down and kissed her again. "Okay. So, planning it is. Any thoughts as to dates?'

She nodded. "I talked to the girls. None of us want me to have a big fancy wedding. That's just not me."

—

“No, but we need to have one we can look back on and cherish as the first step in our married life. Threats aside, we need to move forward.” He pulled out his phone and brought up his calendar. “I see I have this Saturday free.”

“Well, isn’t that a coincidence. I just happen to as well.” She leaned into his hug. “And Buckley was dropping hints. He said he was free Saturday as well. Would it do?”

Brandon shouted with laughter, startling Hagen for a moment, and drawing the twins towards them, just as they had entered the building.

“He did that with both Brady and Fynn and Branigan and Guenivere. One of these days, it will backfire and it will be his turn to be asked that.”

The twins shared a look before Holly hesitantly spoke.

“Hagen? What’s going on?”

“How about this Saturday for the wedding? Will it work for you?”

Brandon sat back as he listened to the excited chatter from the twins and the calm voice of his sweetheart. Yes, Lord, I hear. I am willing to go forward as is Hagen. Please, though, Lord, keep my lady and her sisters safe. Help Dallas to find out whoever this is and soon. None of the three can take much more.

Two weeks later, Hagen stood in her shop, staring down at the wedding band on her finger and the beautiful emerald stone in her engagement ring. She was happy, content, she thought, except for whoever it was after her. She had had more emails come to her business account, each more and more vicious. Dallas had sent them on to the lab, shaking his head, saying that they would try and track them but the lab was backlogged at the moment. He could not say when they would be looked at.

She looked around as the door opened and then began to back away. She knew this man. Her father had had dealings with him and had warned her about him.

"Well, Hagen. I see we are finally alone. Just how I planned it." He walked towards her, his overweight body heavy on his feet. "We need to have a chat."

"We have nothing to talk about. Now, please, leave." Hagen retreated behind the reception counter, her fingers feeling for the button she knew was there.

"Not until we come to an understanding, my dear. Your business is just what I need. Your dolls and wood crafts are perfect." He picked up one of her display dolls, turning the wooden toy over and over in his hands.

"No, I don't see how they would be perfect for you. You have no family."

"That's correct. However, these dolls can be hollowed out very easily. Drugs that I supply will go inside and you will ship them to where I tell you to. If you are reluctant to do that, I would hate to see something happen to one of your sisters."

"It was you, wasn't it? You're the one behind it. But now, you don't have the smarts for that." She was taunting him, desperate to delay him until help could arrive, if it ever did. "Dad always said someone smarter was behind you." She looked up at that point, her face blanching as she did so.

—

He reached for her, pulling her across the counter, sending anything on it flying, before he slammed her against it again and again. She collapsed when he let go, to huddle on the floor, the pain that was wracking her body taking every cohesive thought from her mind. She couldn't understand his words, only vaguely saw him walking away and then heard the door slamming behind him. She sank into a dark well of pain, not hearing the door fly open and the security guard dropping to his knees beside her, his phone out calling for help.

Brandon stood beside Barnabas and Brody, who had their hands on his shoulders, holding him in place, his eyes glued to the activity going on around his wife's shop. He had just arrived home from work when he saw the activity and feared the worse.

"I need to get there, Brody. I need to know Hagen is okay." Desperation laced his words.

"You can't, Brandon. You just can't. We'll get you to her, but they need to work on her." Brody shared a look with Barnabas who turned and walked away, searching for Dallas.

"Dallas? What's the word?"

"The security guard isn't sure what happened, but he said Hagen was attacked. The paramedics are working on her." Dallas was frustrated. "Can't I ever have a straightforward investigation with your guys?"

Barnabas cracked a grim smile. "I wish they didn't have to go through what they did but they have. God has allowed it. We just need to figure out who." He turned as he heard his name called. "What do you have, Joe?"

"This. We caught a picture of him as he was stalking around the buildings. I know him. He's high in the world of drugs."

Dallas and Barnabas shared a look. "This makes horrible sense, doesn't it, Dallas? Her handcrafts would be the perfect carrier for them. Who would think of toys?"

"True, but there is something else. What has happened doesn't just fit one person. Did she have to have two involved?" Dallas walked away, leaving Barnabas staring after him.

"Did he really say two parties?" Breck spoke from beside him

Barnabas turned, to find most of the men, except for Brody and Brandon, standing near him. "He did, and I think he's right. We've been focusing on one. But there are two. Let's see what we can come up with." He handed the photo to Blair. "Here, run with this. He's a nasty piece of work. He's the one who assaulted her today."

Seeing the stretcher moving towards him, Brandon broke from Brody's hand on his shoulder and almost ran towards it. He slid to a halt, his eyes on Hagen's white, pain-filled face.

"What happened to her?"

"Her back is injured, that's all we know for now." The paramedic shared a look with Brady, who had moved closer. "We need to get her to help, Brandon. Brady?"

"I'll get him there. Go on, fellows." Brady's hand kept Brandon beside him. "Come with me, Brandon. We'll head it. Brendon and Benen are heading for the twins."

Brandon nodded, almost too numb to comprehend what he has being told, heading for Brady's truck, Fynn holding the back door open for him. She watched him closely before exchanging a glance with Brady. Once they arrived at the hospital, he paced the waiting room, his eyes not leaving the doors to the examination rooms. He was anxious, distraught, he just didn't know what word to use for himself. He was sure Burnie could come up with a few, if he asked him.

Doc paused for a moment before he pushed open the doors, not wanting to talk with Brandon but knowing he had no choice. He knew the twins had arrived, word had got back to him. Why, Lord? Why? I know You're in control, but why Hagen? The twins need her. Brandon and she are just starting a life together. I shouldn't be having to go out and tell a young husband that I don't know how damaged his wife's back is, that I don't if she is permanently injured or not. Sometimes, Lord, life just is not fair.

He stood, his eyes on Brandon, before he looked around the waiting room, a small smile crossing his face. Yes, it was what he had expected. The Foundation building family, that was growing couple by couple, were all there, surrounding Brandon, comforting the twins, who saw him and were on their feet, running towards him.

Doc just opened his arms and swept them close. He and Anna had taken over as grandparents for them.

Brandon spun as he caught movement from the corner of his eye, seeing the twins moving towards Doc. His own feet took him that way, reluctant in part, but knowing he had to talk with his friend. He stopped short of Doc, a question on his face that he didn't want to ask, but knew he had to.

His hand raising to grip Brandon's shoulder, Doc then pointed to the outside doors, his arms still around the twins.

"Let's walk, Brandon, girls. I need some fresh air. And a break. It's been a bad day all around." Doc didn't tell them that he had lost a young mother and her infant to a motor vehicle accident, despite the best efforts of all involved. Then to have a friend appear as Hagen had, with questionable long-term injuries, he just didn't know how to cope for a moment.

"Doc?" Brandon paced beside him as they headed towards the picnic table under the trees.

Doc sank down, a sigh wrenched from him, a twin sticking close to either side of him. He watched as Brandon sat across from him, seeing some of the men from the building gathering close.

"Brandon. Haley. Holly. Hagen is alive, thank God for that. From what I understand and can see, it could easily have been a funeral home we were gathering in." He watched as the girls' faces whitened with fear. "That being said, we still have unknowns that we are investigating and then determining treatment. How much were you told, Brandon?"

"Not much, other than she was assaulted. Doc, I know you. What aren't you telling us?"

Doc nodded, moving his arms so he could clasp his hands together, raising his eyes to search for Buckley, who stood close by.

"Buckley? Will you pray for these three and for Hagen?"

Buckley nodded, slipping to the bench seat beside Brandon, an arm resting across his friend's shoulders as he prayed, asking for healing for Hagen, for wisdom of the medical staff, for release of fear from the three with him.

Doc raised his head when Buckley had finished, the verse coming to mind of the woman with the issue who had been healed simply by touching the Master's garment hem.

—

"Brandon. It seems that Hagen was repeated shoved against the counter in her shop. I can't tell you how many times. I doubt she even knows. At the moment, she's in imaging, for X-rays. And whatever else we may need to do. An MRI is likely as well. Her kidneys are badly bruised from this assault. How serious is it? We don't know. We do know there is a lot of swelling around the spine. That will go down. Until it does, we won't know if there is any permanent damage." He reached to hug Haley as he heard her start to sob. Fynn, he knew, had seated herself near Holly, an arm around her.

"Doc? Permanent? As she would be crippled?" At Doc's nod, Brandon's eyes slid shut, sorrow gripping him before anger took over. "How long before we know?"

"That I can't tell you. It will take time, days, weeks, I can't say for sure. The swelling needs to go down. As of tonight, she is still reacting to sensory touching on her feet and legs, but the swelling will get worse."

"Can we see her?" Holly's voice was barely above a whisper, choked with tears as it was.

"You can. Head back into the waiting room. I need to see whereabouts she is a present. I'm sending her up to a room as soon as I can."

Doc stood and walked away, Blair, Brendon and Breck meeting him.

"Doc?" Blair's voice held a question.

"It's not great, fellows. She may be crippled. Right now, we need to deal with those three. And find whoever the monster is who did this." Anger laced Doc's words, anger he knew he would have to ask forgiveness for.

"We're working on that, Doc. We have a picture of the man who did this. Dallas has sent it out to all the patrol vehicles. They want this over for Hagen and the twins." Breck's voice had a bite to it.

"Good. Now, I'm heading in there." Doc pointed at the door, before pointing back over his shoulder. "You stay with them. If whoever it is can't get to Hagen, he'll go after one of them. And I can almost guarantee you, this maniac was not working on his own."

Brandon stood, his arms around the twins, at Hagen's bedside an hour or so later. She had been moved to a private room, at Barnabas' insistence. He studied her, seeing her laying on her side, foam bolsters behind her back to keep her from rolling to that position. He traced her beloved face with his eyes, seeing the pain that it held, pain not relieved by the medications she had been given.

Holly hugged him, her head against him, her tears wetting his shirt. Haley hugged him as well, but she was not weeping. Not that showed, but he figured she was weeping inside. Each twin had their own way of dealing with this. All he could do, he thought, was be there for them, and pray for them.

Haley's hand reached to touch her sister's hair, just a light touch, not wanting to cause any more pain.

"Brandon? What if Doc is right? What if it is permanent?" Holly's question did not surprise him.

"Then, we deal with that at the time. Only God knows, love, and that's not a trite, off-the-cuff remark. He really is in control of this." He watched for a moment, before the twins walked away, leaving him on his own. He moved closer to his beloved bride, a hand on hers and the other hand on her face, wishing it was him and not her it had happened to.

Hagen's eyes flickered for a moment before she groaned.

"Brandon? Are you there? And just where is there?"

He gave a slight grin at the nonsensical way she was speaking, knowing it was the pain and the medications doing it.

"I'm right here, darlin'. And this is the hospital. You were hurt."

"I know. It was Barney Soles who did it. Dad had run-ins with him all the time. He warned me about him." She stopped speaking, the pain taking her voice for a moment. "What did he do?"

"He apparently slammed you into the reception counter. You have an injury to your back and kidneys."

"He was vicious, Brandon. He wanted to use my handcrafts to smuggle drugs. I can't let him do that. I'll close down before I do." Tears sparkled on her cheeks, tears of pain and fear and frustration, that Brandon reached to wipe away.

Brandon bent over the bed, his arm around his lady as he prayed, watching as she drifted off to sleep, a kiss dropped on her temple, before he stood upright, anger burning deeper inside him, before he prayed, asking for the anger to be removed and for the peace that only God could give. He didn't want to see Hagen give up her dream, but he knew she would if she had to.

He turned as he heard footsteps approaching. Breck and Bradon stood beside him.

"How is she?" Bradon's question brought through the silence in the room.

"She's hurting, Bradon, and ready to give up her dream to prevent him from using it. She named him."

"Barney Soles." Brandon stared at Bradon. "We have a picture. Weren't you told that?"

"I guess I was. There's just been too much thrown at me right now. Listen, the girls will want to stay, but I think they should head home."

"Fynn said she'd look after them. Alice is on duty, she said. If anything, Anna will step in. In fact, Anna's in the waiting room with them now."

Brandon nodded. "I'm not leaving, but I am really worried about them. I don't know how far these people will go. They have already tried by kidnapping to get Hagen to agree."

"I know." Breck looked towards the bed, his eyes doing his own assessment of both Hagen and Brandon. "We'll watch them. Fynn has suggested that you speak with their school, and have their work given to them that they can do at home or online. You know they will want to be where Hagen is."

"I know. Doc thinks she'll be here for a couple of days and then allowed home. He said he'd speak with the physician taking over her care, to see where she would stand with that."

Shifting in the recliner set near Hagen's hospital bed, Brandon pulled the blanket he had been given higher up on his neck, folding his arms across his chest when he was finished, just trying to find a comfortable position, an impossible task, he finally decided. He was exhausted, but didn't want to sleep, wanted to wait for Hagen to rouse and talk to him. The nurse had been in and out over the course of the evening and into the wee small hours of the night, speaking quietly to him, finding him a coffee and a muffin from their break-room.

He watched his bride, sorrowing because she was hurt, but with anger still burning within him. He didn't want to see her dream fail, he just didn't. But Brandon knew that was a real possibility. Hagen would just shut down her shop if she had to, putting aside what she really wanted for the sake of others.

His head turned as he heard footsteps approaching, and Barnabas appeared. Brandon glared at his watch, seeing how early it was.

"Barnabas? What are you doing here?"

"I had to come. I couldn't sleep, Brandon. Something is off about this whole thing with Hagen."

"I know. I just don't get it." Brandon looked behind him at the door and then at Hagen, as she moved restlessly, nearing time for more pain medications. "I worry about Hagen, and the twins. I talked to Dallas earlier tonight. He doesn't seem to be getting any sleep. Anyway, patrol officers found the man who assaulted her yesterday. He's in jail, but not talking. Dallas said he hasn't even asked for a lawyer yet. The charges are still being sorted out."

"It will take a while, I suspect." Barnabas reached for a chair, seating himself wearily. He was tired and worn out, needing a holiday, but refusing to go when his friends needed him. Lord, we need to get through this, and I just don't see how we will.

Hagen stirred, rousing more, the pain driving her to awake. She gave a small moan, her tongue moving over her lips, trying to moisten them. She sucked greedily at the ice chips Brandon placed in her mouth, his hand resting finally on her cheek before he bent and kissed her.

"Brandon? What time is it?"

"About three in the morning."

Hagen squinted at him. "You're still in the clothes you put on this morning. How come?"

Brandon gave a half-laugh. "I haven't had a chance to change. Somebody needed me more to stay with her."

"And who would that be?" Hagen sounded grumpy.

"You, my love. You're in the hospital again."

"I am? Why?" Her voice died away as she slipped once more into sleep, the nurse entering on almost silent shoes, ready to give the next dose of the pain medication.

"She's been awake?"

"Just briefly." Brandon waited for her to leave. "What else, Barnabas? I know you. You have something else on your mind."

Barnabas sighed. "You're right. I talked to both Will and Dallas. Even with this man arrested, Hagen is still in grave danger. Whoever it is behind it all? We think it was more than just the drugs. Somehow, someone else who her father had dealings with is involved."

"I would say they're right." Brandon bit at his lip, Hagen and he having discussed that very thing. "Hagen came up with some names, was it only a day or so ago? She couldn't sleep the night before last. I found her in the office, papers all over the place. She had been researching everyone she could remember having dealings with the family, or who she knew had threatened retaliation against her father. There is a list in the folder on the desk. Have one of the twins get it for you, or go on in and get it yourself. It's a green folder." He gave a low laugh. "Hagen wanted green. She said these men and women were envious of her father and her mother, and green was the colour of envy."

Barnabas gave a grin. "She thinks in colour, doesn't she? A true artist."

"That she is." Brandon struggled with a thought. "I think I know who we need to look into." His voice died away.

Barnabas shifted in his seat, his head turning as he watched Brandon.

"Brandon?"

"I think it's Ben or someone related to him. He knew Hagen's parents. There has been something off, with him saying he had had complaints about her. That doesn't make sense."

"No, it hasn't." Barnabas pulled out his phone, jotting some some thoughts. "We'll see where we go from there."

Brandon nodded, his chin dropping, and his eyes closing as he slept. The worry about Hagen had drained him to the point that he felt he could not go on. Hagen roused at one point, her eyes on him, before shifting to the door, a frown on her face as she saw someone hovering out there. She knew that person, just wasn't sure if she was really seeing him. Her gaze shifted to Barnabas, watching him for a moment before he looked up at her, a smile on his face, that didn't quite reach his eyes.

"Hagen?" His voice was low

"Barnabas, he's here. Why is Ben outside my door?"

Barnabas was on his feet, moving that way, stepping outside before he stepped back in

"He's gone, Hagen. You're sure?"

"I am. I have never trusted him. Dad seemed to but Mom always had a hesitation about him. I trusted her instincts."

"I have someone looking into him. Brandon mentioned him. Now, how are you feeling?"

"How am I supposed to feel?" Her grumpy response brought a glimmer of a smile to his face. "I'm sorry. I am not normally like this."

Barnabas leaned against the side of the bed, his eyes staring ahead of him, a thought crossing his mind before he spoke.

"It's understandable, Hagen. You have been through a lot, in what, the last fifteen or sixteen months. Losing your parents like you did? That would be enough, but to take on raising fifteen-year-old twins at the time, when you are all grieving? Yes, I would say that has been tough. And then through into the mix what has happened now. You're entitled."

"No, I'm not. I need to leave it with God, asking for His peace in this, and I struggle with that. I struggle with the fact that I will likely have to give up my dream." Her voice died away. When she spoke again, her voice was barely audible, and he could hear the devastation in it. "I won't let my business be used like he wanted."

Seated in a wheelchair, Hagen stared around the apartment, not sure what was off but she was sure something was. She pushed herself forward, pain moving through her back, but she persisted. It had been a week, she thought, since her attack. Insisting that she had to come home three days prior, she had just stared at Brandon when he protested before he held up his hands and nodded.

Brandon watched closely, knowing that she didn't want help, but his hands were still reaching for the chair, a slight smile on his face as he watched her emotions flickering across hers.

"Brandon? That folder? What happened to it?" Hagen stopped him at the desk.

"Barnabas has it. He said all the guys have a copy and once they have done all they can on their own, they'll compile it. He said it should be in the next day or so." He perched on the edge of the desk, hands resting on his thigh, staring past her.

"I see. Did I really do that?"

"You did." He brought his gaze back to her. "I gave him another name." He paused, not quite sure how to continue.

"Ben." At his surprised look and nod, she drew in a deep breath. "I never felt comfortable around him. To put it mildly, he was too inquisitive, wanting to know things that were none of his business. Mom always avoided him." She looked up, a mixture of emotions still running across her face. "How do you continue to work for him?"

"I talked to Barnabas and resigned from there. I think I have been remiss. We have not discussed how us guys are paid. The Foundation pays us directly, letting our employers hire more personnel as they need to without worrying about finances. And since we married, you have a salary settled on you."

"I do? Why? I don't need it. At least, I don't think I will." Hagen was surprised.

"It's how the Foundation set it up. When we marry, our wives automatically become part of the Foundation family and then receive a salary as well. They can do what they want, work, volunteer, stay at home, go to school. And as with Darby, Haley and Holly will receive funding, particularly for their schooling. It's part of the Foundation mandate for being encouragers." He watched the tears pooling in her eyes before he was on his knees, carefully wrapping her in his arms. "I'm sorry. I shouldn't have told you like that."

Hagen finally just laid her head on his shoulder, exhaustion over taking her, her eyes slipping closed against the pain as well. Brandon simply gathered her up and carried her to the bedroom, carefully letting her lie down before he pulled a cover over her. He left and returned with the wheelchair, glad the rooms were not small. He stood for a moment before he stretched out beside her, carefully cradling her to him, and then slept as well.

Haley and Holly went looking for them when they returned, Blair walking them to their door, before he headed for the conference room. Something was puzzling him and he needed to work on that. He knew Devaney would come and find him at some point. He could use her ideas, he thought.

Holly paused in the doorway, a faint blush on her cheeks, her eyes on her sister before she looked at Brandon who had roused and pushed himself upright.

"Holly? School all done?" He rose, heading to hug her and then searching for Haley to do the same.

"It is. And we don't have to go next week. It's a holiday." Haley looked past him. "We would usually do something fun, but I guess we can't."

"We still might be able to. Let's see how Hagen is at the beginning of the week. Now, what have you to tell me about your day?"

The twins chattered away, answering his questions, and just giving details of their day, responding with laughter at his teasing.

Holly finally shared a look with Haley. "Brandon, I have to tell you something, only I don't know how to."

"Just talk. That's all you need to do." Brandon leaned back against the kitchen counter, drying his hands and then throwing the towel over one shoulder. He had heard the faint squeak of the wheelchair, and know Hagen was heading their way.

"It's about Ben. I don't trust him. He's been hanging around the school, trying to talk to us. We've avoided him as much as we can. Why?" Holly looked frightened for a moment.

"That's what we're working on. Our guys are searching. Dallas is as well. I know what you mean. That's why I don't work for him anymore." He looked between the girls, seeing their startled glances at him and then each other. "It's okay. We'll be okay. I am going to use this time to help your sister heal, help you two through the rest of the school year and then decide what I want to do."

"But Brandon? You can't quit. How do you live then?" Haley reached to hug Hagen, who had wheeled into the kitchen at that point and sat listening to her sisters, and then stood, an arm around her.

"It's fine, Haley. I'm paid by the Foundation, as is Hagen now that we're married. And you two will receive funding from them, particularly for your schooling." He watched as the surprise and then excitement filled their faces.

"You mean, Hagen doesn't have to strive to save so much? She can do what she really dreams of doing with her work?" Haley danced around the room, reaching for Holly and pulling her with her. "God is good."

"He is that and all the time. Now, listen, what you said about Ben? Stay away from him as much as you can."

"It's hard." Holly flopped down into a chair. "He seems to be wherever we are."

"I understand that. The guys know that, too. They want to escort you two lovely ladies as much as they can."

A week later, Hagen approached her shop. She had not been able to bring herself to go there, but Brandon had been back and forth. He had grinned when she grumped at him for doing that.

"The guys and ladies are working in there. Darby is particularly interested, you know."

"He is? He's good with his hands. Maybe I need to hire him part-time, for now." She hesitated as Brandon pushed her chair through the door, her mind freezing as she remembered the assault. Looking around, her hands went out to stop the chair, a surprised and then delighted look on her face. "Brandon? What did they do?"

"Barnabas had it repainted and rearranged for you. The guys worked with him. I think I like this set up better."

Hagen nodded, seeing the wall that now stood between the work area and the lobby or reception area, noting as she wheeled through the door that there was a lock on it. Brandon caught her quick glimpse at it.

"Bradon insisted on that. Branigan has worked his magic with a security system for you. He had been planning on doing just that for you, but had wanted to talk to you first."

"I see." Hagen's thoughts were already on her workshop, wheeling her way around it, hands reaching out to touch and then withdraw. She sighed, still not quite comfortable. The attack had left her badly shaken and fearful.

"Hagen? What more can we do for you?" Brandon crouched down beside her, an arm around her.

"I don't know, Brandon. They have done so much." She looked up as the door opened and frowned. "Brandon, the door. Lock it please."

Brandon was on his feet, the door shut and quietly locked, watching the man who had entered. He had a bad feeling about him, his work in the social field giving him a sixth sense about people.

—

"Can we help you?" Brandon stood in front of the window, his eyes watchful, his hand reaching for the button just under the counter that Branigan had reinstalled when he was done his work.

"No, I am just looking around. I would like to come in there and see up close what there is."

Brandon shook his head. "Sorry. Not happening. It's all on a website that you can look at and order from. This is a private business."

"No need to be hostile. I'm interested in investing in this business. I hear the owner is looking for money to come in and help build it." The man, short, stocky, grizzled in appearance reached to try the door, surprised to find it locked.

Brandon heard Hagen's choked cry before he shook his head, his eyes going past the man to the security guards standing just inside the door.

"No, I don't think so. That's not why you're here. These gentlemen behind will escort you to the security office. We have a police officer on the way to speak with you." Brandon watched as the man jerked and then stepped backwards, surprise flittering across his face, an emotion that was quickly hidden.

"That's not necessary. Not at all. I'll come back." He made to move past the three guards, but was prevented by a hand on his arm. He was led away, protesting the whole time.

Hagen, who had stayed hidden, pushed herself forward, frustrated that she couldn't be on her feet. She was healing but the uncertainty as to if she would heal completely was still there. She paused beside Brandon, fear and anger on her face.

"Do you know who that was?"

Brandon shook his head. "No, I'm sorry. I don't." He was watching the door intently, not catching the look of frustration that showed momentarily on his bride's face.

"That was Ben's brother."

"Brother? I never knew he had a brother." Brandon finally looked down at her, puzzled.

"It's his half-brother. They always tried to pretend they didn't get along and didn't want anything to do with one another, but that's not the case." Hagen spun, reaching for the lock on the door, frustrated as she had trouble getting the door open, before she wheeled through, heading for the outside door, Brandon behind her, reaching to hold the door.

"Hagen?" He paused to set the alarm and then lock the door before he had to almost run after her. "Hagen?"

"I need to see your friends. To see which one is working on that name. Or are they?" She stopped suddenly, pain crossing her face for a moment. "I hate this, Brandon. I hate this chair. I hate that I'm restricted. How do I go on?" She shoved away from him, not waiting for an answer.

Brandon stood, shocked for a moment, his hands on the top of his head, not quite sure how to react. He knew Hagen was still hurting, and not just physically. He had tried to get her to talk to him, to talk to someone, but she had shut down and then wheeled away, heading for the balcony, struggling to open the door to get through, not willing to ask for help. Lord, how do I do this? How do I get her help? She has to be willing to seek it herself, but I am not sure she will, not unless something else happens. And, dear Lord, that scares me. I don't want to lose her, or one of the twins.

Brandon followed slowly, his hands jammed into his jeans pocket, feeling the coolness of the breeze blowing in from Lake Erie. He shivered, but not just from that. He stopped short, and then wandered around the building, intending to walk the paths before he sought Hagen once more. So engrossed was he in his thoughts that he didn't hear the running footsteps behind him, not until an arm snaked around his neck and a knife dug into his side. He was propelled forward before he could fight to free himself, a second man slapping a blindfold and gag roughly over his face before pulling his hands behind him and binding them with rough rope that scraped at his wrists. He was shoved into a waiting van which took off rapidly, the dust from its travel seeking the sky before it settled back down on the ground. He lay, his breath knocked from him with the force he had been slammed into the metal van floor, his head bouncing against the floor from the roughness of the ride as the van travelled rapidly over a gravel road, hitting ruts and potholes, finally with a hard enough force that he drifted off as he lost consciousness.

Lost in thought and in her research, Hagen didn't notice the passing time. She vaguely heard the comings and goings around her, raising her head once when Holly and Haley had approached her before they took off on their own tangent. She finally slumped back in the chair, her hands rubbing at her face, fatigue drawing deep lines in her face while adding a grayish shine to it. There had to be something here, she thought. There just has to be.

The noise of a chair sliding back beside her had her jumping, a hand to her throat, as she looked that way. Brennen grinned at her, Brody on his other side, both of them watching her.

"You have been deep in that, whatever it is." Brennen pointed to the papers she was tidying together.

"I have been and for too long." She looked around. "Where is everyone?"

"Gone for their meal or off to other activities. Where's Brandon?" Brody looked around, not having seen him since Hagen had entered the conference room.

Hagen shrugged. "I thought he was in here. Didn't I hear him?" When both men shook their heads, she sighed. "He was in the shop with me with Ben's brother, Billy, entered. We were heading this way. I haven't seen him since." She didn't tell the men how ashamed she felt for how she had reacted.

"No, he hasn't been. We haven't seen him. The twins were asking if we had. He had said something about a hike tonight with them." Brennen and Brody exchanged a glance, not liking the feeling they were getting.

"They haven't?" Hagen paused, ready to push herself away from the table, when she reached for the paperwork. "I need one of you to look over. I have determined that both Ben Richards and his brother, Billy, are involved. Billy was the one who was in the shop today."

"Wait a minute!" Brody's hand was up, stopping her words. "What man? In your shop?"

She nodded. "Earlier, just before I came in. The security came and took him. Brandon may be looking into that, mightn't he?"

"He might." Brody was on his feet, striding rapidly away from the room, searching for the security guard, not liking that they had not seen Brandon either since the incident. Brody headed outside, looking for Bradon and his dog, Kade, knowing that more than likely, Brandon had disappeared once more. Now, he thought, just how do I tell Hagen that, Lord? Thanks, You just had to hand it to me.

Brennen watched him walk away before he turned back to Hagen. His eyes narrowed as he caught how exhausted and in pain she was. Reaching for the papers she held, he took them gently from her, setting them on the table.

"Right now, Hagen, we need to get you home. You've done too much." He stood, his hands on her chair to pull it back and then head for the door.

Hagen gave a weary nod, wanting nothing more than to find her bed and sleep. Thanking Brennen as he opened and then closed the door to the apartment behind her, she slowly wheeled through the place, looking for the girls or Brandon, and not seeing any of them. She sat for a moment, contemplating the shower before she turned away, shifting instead to her bed and laying down, reaching for a light blanket. She was asleep almost instantaneously, not hearing the outside door fly open and the girls run through it, looking for either one of them.

The twins stood in her bedroom door, their eyes on her, before looking at each other. They had not found Brandon, no matter where they had looked. His truck was still there, so where was he?

"We can't wake her, Holly." Haley shifted from foot to foot. "We just can't. But, where is Brandon?"

"That we need to find out." Holly's phone was out, as she dialled his number once more, with it going straight to voice mail. "He's not answering. Where is he?"

"I know. Holly, I'm so worried. What if he's disappeared?"

Holly spun, anger briefly on her face. "He can't, Haley. He just can't. Hagen needs him too much." She ran as she heard a tap at the door, knowing it wouldn't be Brandon, but just praying it was someone who could tell them where he was.

Holly pulled the door open, Haley standing right behind her. a hand to her sister's back. They stared at Breck and Brennen, who stood there, trying to hide the grimness of their faces behind smiles but unable to do so.

"May we come in, ladies?" Breck pointed behind them. "We need to talk to Hagen."

"She's sleeping, Breck." Holly spoke as she backed away, not sure what to do or which room to go to.

"How about the kitchen, Holly?" Brennen headed that way, the ease of friendship with Brandon letting him do just that. "Have you eaten?"

The twins exchanged glances before Haley spoke. "No, we haven't."

"Sit. I'll make some sandwiches. Breck and I haven't eaten, and I'm starved." Brennen was desperate to lighten the mood, knowing that what they had to say would take the girls' appetites, unless they were fed first.

Rousing from her sleep, Hagen brushed at her long hair, finally braiding it and reaching for the tie around her wrist. She frowned, hearing men's voices from the other end of the apartment. Her head tilting, she listened before she shook it. No, that was not Brandon's voice. Who would be here?

Without thinking, she stood and walked towards the door, a muscle spasm in her back stopping her for a moment before she reached for the wall, her hand running along it as she walked towards the kitchen, pausing in the doorway, her eyes on the twins before they raised to the two men. Breck just shook his head at her, watching as she caught her breath in a half-sob and her face crumpling before she schooled her features and walked into the kitchen, Brennen pulling back a chair for her, his hand out to help her sit before it rested briefly on her shoulder.

<hr>

Haley and Holly stared at her, but before they could ask her where her chair was, Breck sat beside Hagen, handing her a cup of tea, knowing that her preference had changed.

"How are you, Hagen?" Breck's voice was low, almost as if he were afraid to ask.

Hagen shrugged. "To tell you the truth, I really don't know how I'm to feel. Exhausted. Overwhelmed. Burdened. Saddened. Lost." She kept her eyes on Breck. "And losing my dreams. How does that sound?"

"Sounds about right to me." Breck had heard a sound from Haley, he thought it was. "Have you eaten?"

Hagen shook her head. "No, I went right to sleep. A sandwich sounds good." She went to push away from the table, looking up with a word of thanks as Brennen served her.

Breck finally bowed his head, bringing the ladies to God, and then praying for Brandon, knowing he had news he did not want to share with Hagen.

Hagen studied him as he raised his head, his eyes steady on her. She nodded.

"You have word? He's gone, isn't he?"

Breck drew in his breath, still not used to the direct way that Hagen had of speaking.

"He is, Hagen. I'm sorry. We've searched. Bradon had Kade out and tracked him to the end of the forest." Breck's eyes met Brennen's. "I wish we could fence it off and stop this from ever happening again."

"It's happened before?" Holly's voice was barely audible as her hands reached for both Haley and Hagen.

"It has, Holly. In fact, Guenivere disappeared right out of her apartment. We have attempted to block any further attempt, but we can't lock up the outdoors, as much as we would like to."

Hagen's head dropped to her folded arms, a shudder running through her before her head raised again, determination on it.

"Do we know anything at all?"

Breck shook his head. "Dallas is out here now. They're searching. He'll want to talk to you about this afternoon."

"I thought he would. Will those two never leave us alone?" She grew pensive, not seeing the questions trembling on the twins' lips and faces. "Have they found Ben?"

"Not yet. And Billy wasn't arrested, for some reason, even though Barnabas pressed for just that."

"Who was the responding officer? Buddy Fuller?" At Breck's nod, she sighed once more, her eyes raised to the heavens as she prayed for peace, for strength, for courage, and for her anger to be removed. "That's Billy's son. He goes by his mother's name. I am sure that Barnabas would not have known that. If Will had, Buddy would not have been near here. We need to take out an order to keep him away from here and away from the twins and myself."

Breck was on his feet, excusing himself, angry that this had happened. His phone out, he spoke abruptly with Barnabas, who promised to talk to both Dallas and Will. He turned back, catching

———

Hagen for a moment as she sat, the sadness that he could sense almost overwhelming. Breck was back in his chair, listening as Brennen and Hagen spoke.

"Where would they take him?" Hagen looked around, Haley on her feet and running to the office, to return with paper and pens and Hagen's laptop.

"Where do we start, Hagen?" Holly leaned over Haley's chair, watching as Haley's finger flew over the keyboard.

"Breck? Brennen? What would you suggest?"

"We start with here. Then, we move outwards. Bradon said it looked as if the vehicle had taken off rapidly, heading down the gravel road that runs towards the highway."

"There are a lot of places that they could pull off and hide along there. A number of old abandoned buildings. Houses where the people are away or up north for vacations for the summer. The ones where people have already closed up and headed south for the winter." Hagen chewed at her lip, her hand idly twisting her cup, before Brennen stood, reached to refill it, and then sat back down.

"We can start a search but we can't go on private property. That we would have to leave for the police."

"Couldn't you drive in and then back out?" Haley was puzzled. "I mean, what if it is a place where you know the people? Couldn't you go see if they were home?"

"We could, Haley, but we have to be so careful. We can't compromise the investigation."

"And that might do it. I get it." Haley sat back, blowing out a breath that stirred her bangs. She began to pull at them before she reached for the laptop again, whispering to Holly, who nodded and watched as Haley pulled up a topographical map program.

Breck rose, to move his chair closer to the twins, watchful as he studied what they were doing.

"What are you planning to do with that? What's your purpose?"

Holly frowned at him. "You sound like one of our teachers." Her comment brought grins to the men's faces for a moment. "We want to see what the land looks like, if there are a lot of buildings, or if there is any provincially or federally owned land. We wouldn't need permission to walk on it, would we?"

"It depends, Holly, what the land is. Around here, I don't remember hearing of any that we couldn't do that with. I can check with a friend to make sure."

Hagen looked around. "I know who we can talk to. A friend of Dad's that used to work in the county. He can help." She stopped, biting at her lip. "No, I guess we can't. He's related to Ben and Billy."

"And he would be the perfect one to help them set up a hiding place, now wouldn't he?" Brennen bit out his words, anger lacing them. "Let me have his name, Hagen. He's just gone on our list."

Hagen supplied it, not seeing the surprise that flickered across the men's faces. They knew the name. He had been prominent in their church at one point until differences on the board had sent him away to another church, where they heard that he was causing similar problems.

Hagen turned as she heard her phone. "My phone? Where did I leave it now?"

Haley was on her feet, running for the bedroom and back, handing it to her sister. "I don't know that number, Hagen. Do you?"

Hagen nodded, swiping across her phone to answer it. "Elizabeth? Hi. How are you? Me? I'm hurting, but why are you calling?" Hagen gave a low laugh. "You heard what? Yes, I am. And yes, Abe and Emma have met him. So, he's approved." She listened for a few moments, her head nodding every once in a while, before she reached for a pen and paper. "What did Emma say? Is that right? Who? Yes, we have his name. I know. I wasn't to have an adventure like you and Nathaniel, now was I? You set an example for me, all of you." She laughed before she drew in a breath. "How much does she have? I see. And who is bringing it? Oh, wonderful. I would love to see you and Nathaniel. Who else? Good. The twins? They're good." Hagen paused, her eyes on her sisters. "Elizabeth? You've mentioned you heard I was having problems. It's Brandon. He went missing today." Hagen's finger

———

118

moved around the table, Hagen not really knowing what she was doing, the twins' gazes tight on her. "Thank you, my friend. I do appreciate that. Tomorrow? I think so. I mean, I'll be here. Since I was hurt, I haven't been travelling. Hurt? We'll talk. And thank you. And thank Emma. What was that? Do I need all of you? Like in how many?" Hagen laughed once more before she clicked off from her call and then set her phone carefully on the table, tears near the surface that she just could not hold back. The twins surrounded her, their tears mingling for a moment.

A week later, Hagen walked slowly towards her shop, her interest in it greatly diminished. *Where are you, Brandon? I miss you, my love. I want you with me. Lord, please? My heart can't take losing someone else I love.*

She stopped short as she stared at the door, before she walked forward to reach for the envelope that was tacked to it. Her hands shook as she opened in and dumped out photos and a piece of paper. They fluttered to the ground as she stood, her eyes on them, not comprehending for a moment what they were. Dropping to her knees, her fingers moved among them, looking with horror at the pictures of Brandon, each one with a consecutive date on them, up until that very morning. Hagen reached for the note, her hands shaking violently as she did so, unable to stop the paper from shaking so that she could read it.

Blair and Benen had been heading for the gym and stopped short as they caught sight of her before running towards her, dropping beside her, Benen's eyes on Hagen, Blair's on the photos. Blair reached to gather them, shock on his face, before he turned to Benen.

"Inside with her, Benen. To the building."

Benen's arm around her raised Hagen to her feet, her hand still clutching the paper. She was rushed inside and then set gently into a chair, the others in the room looking up in surprise and then with grim visages as they were told what had been found.

Dallas appeared an hour later, his eyes studying Hagen before he turned to Benen and Blair.

"What do you have?" He watched the anger simmering in them.

"This!" Benen shoved the photos and letter at Dallas, who barely caught them. "Hagen found these. On the door to her shop. All on her own. No one was with her. We found her on her knees, frozen and shaking so badly we couldn't get her to stand on her own."

Dallas shifted so he could watch Hagen, seeing her wrapped in a blanket, a cup of tea in front of her that he doubted she had touched. He looked down then at the photos, dropping them to the table to sort through them, a pen in his hand to do so.

"I know you've touched them, but who all?"

"Hagen. Blair. Myself. The others know what they contain but have not seen them or handled them."

"Good. We can eliminate your prints and Hagen's then." Dallas turned his attention then to the note. "Did she read this?"

"We think so, but we're not sure. She was shaking so badly when we found her that the paper was moving almost too fast to even catch a glimpse of what was on it. I am not even sure if she had read it. She hasn't responded to us at all."

Dallas nodded, having seen behaviour similar to this before. "Has Doc been around?"

"He was on duty but is heading here shortly. Brady took a look at her before he left. He said just to watch her and if she didn't respond, then to take her in. So far, we haven't felt we have had to." Blair was frustrated. "This is enough already."

"It is." Dallas' eyes dropped to the note. "Did you read this?"

"Blair and I did." Benen stared down at it as well. "It's brutal, Dallas. No young lady should be told that the only way she'll see her groom of a few weeks is in his casket. What do they want from her?"

"Her business. Word on the street that we have verified is that they want to use it for smuggled drugs and jewels. Something similar to what they wanted with Guenivere's father's business." Dallas looked up, a frown on his face. "Are these related?"

"No, they're not." The three men turned to find Hagen standing there, haggard as to appearance, still fairly shaky. "The Richards brothers have always been near the line. Billy has been over more times that you can count. Dad was getting ready to have him charged." Her voice died away. "That's why. It's revenge, blackmail, what have you. Who else are they after?" Tears clogged her throat for a moment. "Where is Brandon? Can anyone tell me that?"

Hagen stared at them for a moment before she turned and ran from the room, a hand to her lower back, and disappeared up the stairs, hitting the door of the apartment with her hands and twisting at the knob to open it, before she continued to run towards the bedroom, throwing herself facedown on the bed, to sob heartbrokenly, only too glad that the girls were away with some of the ladies in the building.

Haley and Holly approached her later that afternoon, finding her cuddled down in her favourite chair on the balcony, a blanket wrapped around her once more. She didn't look up as they approached, leaving them to stare at one another before they sank to the floor, their eyes on her once more.

"Hagen? What happened?" Haley was almost afraid to ask.

"I received photos of Brandon and a ransom note. No, I won't tell you what was in it. I can't. Dallas has everything."

"Is he okay?" Holly spoke up, her eyes on Haley, who shrugged.

"No, he's not, girls. He's not. And I don't know where he is. How do we find him?"

Losing track of the hours and days, Brandon paced his jail cell and that was exactly what it was. Whoever had abducted him had set up a mock cell, iron bars, rough bed, minimal facilities, just for him, he thought. He continued to pace, spending hours doing so, interspersed with standing at the small barred window, staring out into the day or night, whichever time of day found him there. He had become accustomed to the critters and insects that shared his cell, leaving crumbs for them.

Brandon despaired of getting loose. He had awakened finally two days after he had been abducted, his head pounding with pain. Being given nothing for the pain, he had suffered for days with a residual headache, just the last couple of days not being tormented by it. He was tormented with thoughts of Hagen and how she was and what this was doing to her. He knew they had taken pictures of him, they had forced him into a chair, to hold a paper he wasn't allowed to read, before he was shoved back into his cell.

Ben Richards stood and watched him through the bars, waiting for Brandon to turn. When he didn't, the anger began to burn within him.

"Brandon? Turn around." Ben's voice was harsh, not something Brandon had heard from him before.

Brandon refused to move, his eyes focused on the birds whirling in the sky, wishing he was as free as they were. He ignored his former employer, realizing for the first time that he had not really known him and wondered just how he had made it through the stiff interview and investigative process the Foundation put their prospective employers through. He was sure Barnabas would be looking into that with a fine tooth comb.

Ben began to yell at Brandon, his hands grasping at the bars, spittle flying from his mouth in his rage. It was a good thing, Brandon thought, that the door is locked and he doesn't have the key to it. He felt at his neck, feeling where Ben's hands would have been on them if they could have been.

Ben finally turned, a final taunt thrown over his shoulder, that Hagen would never find him and that Ben would claim her for his own. Brandon spun at that, horror on his face as he rushed towards the bars, reaching through in a desperate attempt to stop him. He sagged against the bars, unable to reach him to stop him, his mind racing as to how he could do that.

Brandon sank to the floor, his head bent to touch it, his arms wrapping around his head, sorrow and fear shaking him to the core. His heart cried out to God, but he just couldn't put into words his thoughts. Protect her, was all he could manage.

Two days later, he looked up, a frown on his face, from where he sat on the edge of his bed. Billy Richards stood there, an impassive look on his face, his eyes not moving from watching Brandon.

Brandon waited, not speaking, just waiting, he thought, for what, he had no idea. He refused to look away, refused to back away, refused to speak.

"Not talking?" Billy gave a sneer. "Ben said you would talk, that you couldn't help yourself."

Brandon didn't respond to the taunts hurled at him. He couldn't. He wouldn't do anything that would hurt the love of his life.

Billy finally stepped back from the bars, turning to speak to someone, a voice that had Brandon frowning before he covered it with an impassive face. He knew that voice and it was someone high up in the town council, someone he had had dealings with on multiple occasions. Why was she here?

Billy turned back to him, anger on his face. "Do you know my brother has been arrested? And that he has assaulted in jail? This is your fault. You will never leave here, not as long as you live, and I can guarantee you that won't be long." Billy spun on his heel and stormed away, his feet hitting hard on the stone floor.

Brandon sank back on the bunk, his head hitting the thin pillow, before his eyes closed. Lord, I can't do this. I can't live like this. It will kill me. That I know. I just want to be free, to be with Hagen, to help her reach her dreams, and just maybe have a few dreams of our own come true. He finally slept, exhaustion hitting him hard. He didn't see the man who appeared, looking over his shoulder, before he reached to unlock the cell and creep on silent fee towards Brandon.

A hand reached out to shake Brandon with no effect. The man shook his head at that, before he reached to draw Brandon to his feet and then over his shoulder, the cell door closed and locked behind him. The man, young but somewhat older than Brandon, a beard covering his lower face, a pulled down cap covering the rest, headed for the corn field behind the house, maneuvering his way through the cornstalks until he reached another road, where an old truck waited. He dropped Brandon to the passenger seat and buckled his seatbelt before carefully and quietly closing the door, his hand resting for a moment on the window as he looked around. He crept around to his own door, closing it quietly behind him as well, before he keyed the well-tuned motor to life, pulling away and heading towards the Foundation building and then past it, to arrive at a small working farm where he pulled through the open door in the drive shed, stopping the truck, pulling the key from the ignition and then running to close the doors after a careful look around.

Brandon stirred briefly as his door was opened and his eyes flickered open before he slept again, the nights of little or broken sleep and the strain and stress that he had been under with Hagen's injury combined to drive him back down in the depths of sleep and unconsciousness. The man shook his head before pulling Brandon from the truck, driving a shoulder into his abdomen and carefully situating him over his shoulder. He turned, heading for the loft in the drive shed where a soft clean bed waited for Brandon.

Brandon sighed as he sank down, murmuring a quiet thank you, not feeling his boots being pulled from his feet and then the socks that he had worn for so long. The man stood over him before he headed for the small bathroom attached, wringing out a cloth in warm water and soap and returned to wash Brandon's face and hands and then his feet.

He stood back, eyes on the far wall before he turned and headed back out the door, closing it quietly before he walked down the steps, his boot heels sounding hollow on them. He. stood, his eyes on the loft before he shook his head and walked away, closing the side door to the building after himself. Brandon would sleep, he thought, for a while, at least until he was able to find some food for him.

Chapter 33

Her head hurting from lack of sleep, Hagen paced her workshop. She was alone, the door to the reception area locked. She should be working, but she had no interest in it. Her heart cried hourly to God, asking for Brandon to come home, so that they could go on with the dreams that they had been starting to talk about.

She turned to her work, picking up a puzzle and staring at it, her mind working overtime for a moment in what she wanted to do. She dropped the puzzle, reaching instead for a pad of paper and a pen, ideas flowing from her with detailed description as to colour, size, material, age group. Hagen finally sat back, drained, not sure why she felt she had to put down all her ideas. She was on her feet, finding samples for each plan, each plan going into its own folder, her ideas transferred to her design program and copies printed.

Hagen finally sat back, drained, unsure why still but knowing that was what God had wanted. She reached for her water bottle, taking a deep swig, as she heard the outside door open. She stepped to where she could see who had come in, a surprised look on her face.

"Daniel? What are you doing here? I thought you were deep in farm work at this time of day." She reached to unlock the door, heading through it to stand in front of an old friend, Daniel Fields.

"I should be, Hagen, but I had to see you. Can we talk in here without being overheard?"

She nodded. "We can. Everyone is away or busy. The twins are at school."

Daniel rubbed his hands down his jeans, not sure how to start. He stared at the young lady in front of him, knowing that what he had to tell her would rock her world and set her on a mission, but he had to be sure first that she would be safe

"Daniel?" Hagen stared at him. "You usually don't have any trouble talking to me."

He gave a small grin, before sobering. "I know, Hagen. I know. But this time, it's hard. It involves more than just you and me." He spun to pace, his hand running through the blond hair he kept cropped short. He spun back, to come to stand in front of her. "Hagen, is it true? You're married?"

Hagen nodded, her smile sad. "I am, Daniel. Only he was kidnapped by someone trying to take over my business."

"It's growing? I have heard good things about it. He's from here, isn't he?"

"He is. I think you've met him at church. Brandon."

"I have." Daniel looked down for a moment at the fingers he was rubbing together. "Hagen. I need you to do something for me. I need you to pack a bag for yourself and for Brandon."

Hagen stared at him. "A bag? For both of us?" At his nod, she frowned before her face lit up. "You know where he is? Where?"

Daniel shook his head. "Not yet. Go, do what I asked. I'll meet you at the rose garden. Try and keep it less than obvious what you're doing."

"I can try." She turned before she spoke. "The twins?"

"Ask Anna and Doc to look after them for you. Tell Doc I need to talk with him too."

Hagen turned back to stare at him before she turned and almost ran for the building, slipping up the back stairs to the apartment. She quickly grabbed clothes for both of them, hesitating for a moment before she called Anna.

"Anna? Can the twins stay with you and Doc? I have been called away to help a friend. That's great. Also, can you have Doc call Daniel Fields? That's right. Daniel. I ran into him today and he asked for Doc to call, that he had to talk to him. Okay. No, I'm not sure when I'll be home. I'll leave a paper authorizing you and Doc to look after them for now."

Hagen raced for the office, moving as quickly as she could, scribbling out a note for Doc and Anna and sealing it into an envelope before she left one for the twins.

"Haley and Holly: I've been called away for a few days. I'm okay. I am with a friend to help another friend. Doc and Anna will look after you. I'll try and call in a day or so, but I can't make any promises. Pray, dears, please pray. Help where you can in the research.

"I have left a whole whack of plans and whatnot in the shop. If you and Darby want, you can work on them, or whoever else wants to. I think we're caught up, just needing to do some new stuff. Love you.

"Hagen."

Hagen dropped the note on the kitchen table, beside the envelope for Anna, where she knew the twins would find it. She grabbed the charger cords for the phones, dropping them into a pocket, and then ran for the door, ignoring the twinges of pain that coursed through her at times.

Daniel was waiting for her near the perennial garden, motioning for her to be quiet and then heading away from the building, taking a path that Hagen didn't recognize, that came out near a paved lane. Daniel held the truck door for Hagen and then ran for his own seat, heading away as quickly as he could.

"Daniel?" Hagen waited until he glanced at her. "Brandon?"

"I have Brandon, Hagen. He's in my drive shed, in the loft you helped me design for whoever needed it. I never expected it would be you."

"Your drive shed? But how?"

"I'll explain. Just let me get you to him. I think he's beginning to give up, Hagen. I found him locked in a cell, one I think that was designed just for him."

"Ben and Billy Richards."

Daniel shot her a startled glance, his face not able to hide his surprise. "I think so, but there's someone else involved."

"I know. A woman. Only a woman would or could be this vindictive. And I think I know who."

"If you do, have you told anyone?"

Hagen shook her head. "No. I need to but I don't know which of the guys to tell."

"Who do you know the best?"

"Brady." She sighed. "He's married to Fynn, right, and Alice is married to Fynn's brother, Farr."

"Then, that's who you'll tell. Wait for a bit, just until you find Brandon."

Reaching for her duffle bag, Daniel merely pointed to the stairs to the loft, before he headed to roll down the door, and then followed Hagen as she slowly made her way to the landing. He reached past her to open the door, setting the bag inside, and then reached to hug her, a prayer whispered in her ear. He watched as she hesitated, a hand to her mouth, tears sparkling in her eyes before she stepped through into the living room, not even acknowledging the door closing being her.

Daniel stood, his head back against the door, his eyes closing for a moment as emotions roiled within him. Hagen had been his best friend growing up, a sister to him. He hated to see what was happening to her. He finally moved away, heading for his fields, to see what he could accomplish, but his mind puzzled through what Hagen and Brandon were facing.

Moving quietly towards the bedroom, Hagen hesitated for a moment before she touched the door with her fingertips, her other hand across her mouth to still her sobs. She stood for a moment in the half-light, searching for Brandon, finally seeing him on his side on the bed, an arm wrapped around his chest, the other wrapped around his head. She gave a half-cry before she fled towards him, dropping to her knees, arms trying to surround him, unable to lift his weight to do just that. Her head was buried against him as sobs shook her body.

Thank you, Lord. He's out. He's safe. Now, please, Lord, help us to solve this, to find out who it is. I can't live like I did. It's not fair to the twins, either.

Brandon stirred, his arm coming from around his head, a hand dropping on her head before he slept once more, relief that he didn't realize he was feeling coursing through him. Hagen finally raised her head, her eyes on his face, a hand reaching to touch him, unable to fully comprehend that he was here and that she was with him. She finally rose, reaching for the blanket draped across the footboard, shaking it out to cover him, and then heading to find a hot damp washcloth to wash her face. Her tears had been cathartic, much needed. Hagen stood at the window in the living room, seeing the darkening of the evening, and knowing she would need to find Daniel.

Daniel turned as he heard her footsteps approaching him where he stood contemplating his house garden. He needed to get into it, he had been thinking, and pick what was ripe, and that was a lot.

"Hagen?"

"Thank you, Daniel. I don't know how you knew where he was or that he was even missing. Or that he belonged to me or me to him. He's sleeping more soundly now, not as restlessly." Hagen wrapped her arms around herself against the chill of the evening. "What can you tell me?"

"The old Richards place? He was there but hidden." Daniel felt his anger growing. "They had built a jail cell for him, and that's where he was. I happened to overhear Billy talking on the phone this morning. You know how loud he can talk and how most times he really doesn't care if he's overheard. I had to search for the room. It was in the old barn, at the back of it. If you hadn't been looking for it, you would never have found it. Why go to all that work?"

"Simple. They want my business. Billy had someone assault me. I hadn't connected them until Billy showed up in the shop one day. I was told they were taking over my business and would use it for transporting drugs and stolen jewels."

"That's what we always expected from them, but no one has ever been able to prove it. How did Brandon end up working for them?"

"Ben hid his true character. Brandon was hired to work as a social worker for him, being paid by the Foundation. Greed took over, I think. Dad suspected something and I think was getting ready to go to the authorities." Hagen paled. "There's a safe in the office at the house. I haven't had the heart to open it." She looked at Daniel, horrified. "What if there's proof there, that I could have brought out? And prevented this from happening?"

"I don't know that it would have made a difference. Can I get it for you?"

Hagen nodded. "I'll get the keys and the combination in the morning." She turned slightly, looking back towards the drive shed. "We need to let the Foundation guys know." She signed as her phone rang and she pulled it out, reaching to mute it. "It's Brady. Now, what?"

"Answer it. You have to talk to one of them. Brady knows you. Or else talk to Barnabas. He'll need to know where Brandon is, but I'm not sure that is such a good idea."

She shrugged. "I have no idea." She finally swiped to answer the phone, Brady just kept calling her.

"Hagen? Where are you?" Brady's voice held a quality that she didn't think she had heard before.

"With friends. Why? I talked to Anna."

"We know you did. Elizabeth was here, looking for you. Emma sent more material. We need to discuss it."

"I can't, Brady. I'm in the midst of something right now." She was desperate not to give away anything but she couldn't be sure that she wouldn't.

"At least, Hagen, let me call you in the morning and do a conference call with some of the guys. They're worried, Hagen. I don't think you understand that you're part of our family now."

"I know I am, Brady. It's just so hard." She blinked rapidly, and then was running across the lawn, her phone tossed towards Daniel, who caught it and then swiped it to end her call, Brandon's name on her lips.

Brandon slowed to a stop, unable to believe what he saw. He just opened his arms and caught his bride, wrapping her tight to him, their tears mingling.

Daniel stood, watching for a moment, before he turned and walked towards his house, setting Hagen's phone on the table on the porch.

———

Staring at his phone, Brady shook his head. Hagen was hiding something, that much he knew. He looked up, to see the other twelve men staring at him. He shrugged.

"She won't say where she is." He was apologetic.

"That doesn't surprise me. She doesn't know us well enough, I think." Brendon paused, a frown on his face. "You don't suppose...?" His voice died away, as he stared at Brady.

Brady nodded. "I think your supposition is likely correct. She's somehow found Brandon and doesn't want to give away where they are."

"Would she do that?" Blair lifted his mug to sip from it, grimacing at the cold taste, before he rose, dumped it out and fixed himself a fresh mug, sitting back where he had been.

"I can see that." Barnabas spoke. "We have to let her do what she feels is best. If we push, she may grow stubborn on us." He looked around as the door opened, and Doc walked through, a tired look on his face. "Doc?"

Doc sat, scrubbing at his face with both hands, before rubbing at the back of his neck.

"Barnabas, what I am about to say, goes not further. It is third-hand knowledge." He looked around at the men, knowing that they would not break confidence with him. "I talked to Daniel Fields a bit ago."

"Daniel? What has he to do with this?" Buckley spoke for the group before he nodded. "The loft."

Doc nodded. "Daniel wouldn't say, but that's what I suspect. He said in a roundabout way that he had a friend who had been hurt in some manner, and that he had connected that friend with another friend."

Burnie snorted, causing the other men to smile. "He couldn't come right out and say, now could he? He has Hagen and Brandon with him, they're safe in his loft, and what do we want to do about it? That sound about right?"

Breck began to laugh. "Burnie, I think you need to go write something. You're beginning to talk in riddles."

Burnie grinned. "But I'm right, am I not?"

Brady nodded. "I think so. Doc, did Daniel say anything else?"

"He did. In a rambling manner, totally unlike him, he mentioned Ben and Billy Richards but also a woman. Carol Richards Balsam."

"Their sister?" Blair sat back. "Of course. She works for customs. That's the inside person we were trying to find." He sat forward, reaching for a pen and paper. "Now, we'll get somewhere, won't we?"

"Where's that stuff Elizabeth dropped off?" Bradon was on his feet, reaching for it and then sorting it out, handing some off to Brennen and Benen. "Here. It's going to be a long night, I suspect."

"I suspect you're right. Carol Richards has at least two other names. She's been married, what two or three times?" Baird spoke up.

"Try four. We know her by her last marriage. Unless you know her history, you wouldn't know that and therefore, wouldn't connect her to her brothers. They avoid each other." Breck turned to his laptop, beginning to search, not liking what he was finding in just a cursory one. "She's a nasty bit of work."

"What about properties? Do we have a list of those?" Baird reached for some of the paperwork.

"No, I don't think we do." Buckley paused, a thought crossing his mind. "Now, if memory serves me correctly, there is an old abandoned farm of theirs, not too far from here."

"Perfect. We'll look into that. Do you have the address?" Brody's hand was out, waiting for Buckley to drop the slip of paper into it. "Has anyone heard from Emma?"

"I did." Branigan spoke up. "She said she has material she will either courier to us in the morning or send with someone. I suspect that someone to be Elizabeth and Nathaniel."

"Or Emma herself with Abe." Baird's voice held a note of amusement before his face sobered. "I don't like this, fellows. There are more than just the three siblings. Did anyone know that?"

Doc nodded, from where he had sat himself into a corner, watching the men at work. "There are five that are living. A brother and a sister were killed in a house fire when they were young. It was always thought to be arson."

His legs stretched out in front of him, Brandon lounged in one of the green wicker chairs on Daniel's back porch in the early morning of the next day, a Bible open on his knee, a mug of coffee, his third already that day, on the small glass table beside him. He tilted his head to listen to the calls of the awakening birds and insects and other creatures, and the softening sounds of the night creatures seeking their rest. He tilted his head even further to watch a cricket meandering across the floor, stopping every few feet to sing. He was content, he thought, for the moment, here with Hagen. Brandon was worried about the twins, knowing that he had disappointed them that night, even though he could not prevent it.

Hagen watched from the large kitchen window over the farmhouse sink she was working at, helping Daniel prepare their breakfast, quiet conversation of long-time friends between them.

"Daniel? Are you in the fields today?"

"Today? It's Saturday, right? I have to check them out but I don't think there's much to do. It's getting late in the year and I only have the soybeans and corn to harvest. The corn will be done next week. Why?" He turned from the stove, spatula in hand from turning the frying ham and French toast. "Was there something you needed?"

"There is." Hagen pointed with a soapy finger. "I left my keys and the safe combination there. If you could retrieve whatever is in it." Her brow wrinkled as she tried to think of what all would be in there. "Just dump it into a bag and bring it here. But, please be careful. The back door would work best."

"The twins won't be around?"

Hagen shrugged. "I highly doubt it. They haven't been there much since we moved to the Foundation building. I think they've cleared out everything." She sighed, her eyes resting back on Brandon, watching as his head bent once more over the Book he held. "I need to talk to Brandon. I'm not sure the twins will want to keep the house, but I think we should likely sell it. There are too many memories there for me. Besides, we're content where we are."

"No rush for that." Daniel reached for some plates, dishing up their meal, and then pointing to the door. "If you would, I think everything is out there."

"Just the coffee and my tea. Here, let me." She reached to open the door, the sound startling Brandon and causing him to jump, a white look crossing his face.

"Brandon?"

"I'm okay." He stood, reaching for a plate and then a new mug of coffee she handed him.

Hagen finally stood, clearing away their meal, before she sat back down, a pad of paper in front of her, twisting a pen in her fingers.

"Brandon, we need to talk to Dallas today, but how do we do that? We have to have him take your statement."

"I know." Brandon sighed. "I just wish that we didn't have to." He rubbed at a wrist, unaware of what he was doing. "I don't want to go around them. I saw what has happened before. They get attacked and hurt. And with their ladies involved now, I don't what anything to harm them."

"We get that, Brandon." Daniel sat back, before he rose. "I'm heading in to get what you asked for, Hagen. Anything else?"

Hagen shook her head. "I don't think so. I want this to end, Daniel, and maybe what you retrieve from the safe will do that." Her eyes rested on Brandon, seeing he was not listening to their conversation. "You're friends with Dallas. Can you ask him to come out this morning, if possible? Find some ruse to do that?"

"I can." Daniel suddenly grinned. "I've been promising him produce. There's a lot that needs picked. He can come help himself today." He turned and walked away, his face sobering, his eye thoughtful. Lord, I have no idea how we do this. Someone is going to get hurt. I pray it isn't Hagen again, but I know it will be. Protect her and Brandon right now, Lord. I want to see her live to fulfill the dreams she has had and that she and Brandon have now.

———

Brandon watched Hagen turning her phone over and over. "It won't bite."

"I know." She sighed, her eyes on her rings before she spoke. "I was talking with Brady last night. He wants a conference call this morning. How do we do this, Brandon? It's not safe for you to reappear, at least not yet. You have to give your statement to Dallas." She jerked as she heard a car, ready to run for shelter, before she sat back. "And there's Dallas."

Dallas stood at the bottom of the few steps, his eyes on Brandon, before he spoke. "Hagen?"

Hagen sank back down, her hand reaching for Brandon's. "Dallas? You're here? Did Daniel call you?"

"No, actually, he didn't. I heard that Daniel had been in touch with Doc, and surmised I might find you there. You're not hiding very well from your family, you know." He walked up the steps, past them into the kitchen, and returned a few minutes later, a plate with a warmed up breakfast on it and a mug of coffee. He sat, his head bowed for a moment, before he began to eat, ignoring the couple, but with a sparkle of mischief in his eyes.

Finally, Dallas sat back, pushing away his plate and rested his elbows on the table, his eyes on Brandon. He knew Hagen was watching him closely, and he bit back his smile. It's okay, Hagen. I won't tell where you are. I come out to see Daniel every two to three weeks. People know that, so they won't think this strange. And where you are sitting, you're sheltered by the blinds that Daniel or you drew down this morning. And they know you and Daniel are friends, so they wouldn't think anything of you being here. Except if they thought you knew where Brandon was, and then they would be looking for you.

"Brandon? Can you talk to me? Tell me what transpired?" Dallas drew out his notepad and pen, his eyes searching Brandon's face.

"I don't know how much I can tell you. I remember being taken from the building, blindfolded, gagged, bound, and then thrown into a van. A very bumpy ride, I must say. One of the deep ruts caused me to bang my head extremely hard and I don't remember anything until I woke up in a jail cell. There was a row of bars and then a barred window. Very primitive. Billy Richards would show up every little while asking, making demands that made no sense. The last day, I remember hearing a woman's voice, but I don't know who that was. They were arguing, I think, their voices raised but I couldn't hear well through the solid wood wall that stood about five feet away from the bars. The last thing I remember was laying down and falling asleep. That is until last night when I walked out from that building over there and saw Hagen running towards me. I can't tell you much more. I was on my own. Billy would bring in my food once a day and then leave."

Dallas nodded. "It is about what I expected. Here, let me have a moment to transcribe into my program and then I'll print it for you to sign. Once I've done that, we'll talk about other things."

Hagen looked down at her phone she had her hand on. "It's Brady, Brandon. He wants to do a conference call. What do we do?"

Brandon reached to kiss her, before laying an arm around her shoulders. "Now that Dallas has my statement, we need to talk to him and the others. They're too good of friends to me for me to hide more than I am."

Hagen searched his face before she nodded, reaching for her phone, putting it on speaker after she had dialed Brady's number.

"Brady? Good morning."

"Hagen? You're okay? Can you talk to the twins for a moment?"

"Hagen? Where are you?" Haley's worried voice sounded across the air waves.

"I'm at a friend's, and no, I won't tell you. It's not safe. I'm in hiding. How are you two?"

"We're okay. Just miss you." Holly's voice sounded choked with tears. "Hagen, when are you coming home?"

"Soon, I hope and pray, Holly. Now, what are you two up to?" Hagen spoke to her sisters for a few moments, her eyes never leaving Brandon's face. "Okay, is Brady still there?"

"He is. Love you, Hagen."

"Hagen? Are you really okay?" Brady sounded worried.

"Are the twins gone? If they are, who all is with you?"

"All the guys are, Hagen, as well as Will. The twins are gone." Brady waited for a moment. "Hagen? What are you up to?"

"It's not Hagen that's up to something, Brady. It's me. Someone freed me, but I don't want to come home, not just yet. We need to go over some things and find out some more information." Brandon's voice left silence on the other side of the call.

Shock on his face, Brady stared at his phone before looking around, seeing similar looks on everyone else's face but Buckley, and that was no surprise, he thought.

"Brandon. You're free. What can you tell us?" Barnabas spoke up.

"Not a lot. I was told I was held in the Richards old barn. They had done up a real-life cell for me. I was released by a friend, brought to his place, and that's where Hagen and I are right now. We don't want to come around until we can talk about how we do it. It was Billy Richards. He kept coming in, ordering me to tell Hagen she had to let him in as a silent partner, that they were taking over her business."

"We figured that one out." Bradon spoke up. "Who else?"

"I heard a woman's voice that last day."

"His sister. She's involved all the way. We're finding out stuff that we'll pass on to Dallas." Burnie heard a snicker from Brandon. "Brandon? Did I say something funny?"

"Considering that Dallas is sitting here with us, not really." Dallas snickered, bringing a grin to Brandon's face for a moment. "Now, what?"

"Now, what?" Barnabas spoke again. "What else can you tell me?"

"Not a lot. I only saw Billy and that briefly. He never stayed more than five or ten minutes. I saw no one else. I can't even tell you who abducted me, he nabbed me from behind."

"Your height?"

Brandon paused, not having thought of that. "I would say so, or close. I can't describe either one."

"Okay." Breck took up the conversation. "We've been at work, as has Emma. Dallas, she is still shooting us information, where she's finding it I have no idea."

"Have a patrol pick it up. I'll look at it later. Right now, we need to come up with a way to get these two home safely and without being seen." Dallas rubbed a finger along his forehead. "I'm at a loss."

"We could do what we did before, vehicle into the loading dock, and then up to the apartment. But with the twins here, that would be more difficult." Blair was thinking aloud.

"It would be. They wouldn't mean to say something, but they're teenagers. Something would slip it." Hagen knew her sisters and would defend them with her life, but she was also a realist, knowing that teenagers didn't always think before they spoke.

"We'll see what we can do, Brandon, Hagen. It's likely better if you are here and stay inside and stay put. Where you are now puts your friend in danger." Breck spoke, his voice slow as he pondered different scenarios.

"I know, Breck. I know that." Hagen was almost in tears, leading Brandon to slid his chair closer and wrap her in his arm, Dallas watching with a look of sympathy on his face. "Knowing Dallas, he probably wants to lock us up somewhere, and Brandon can't do that again."

"No, he can't." Dallas finally spoked. "Give me the highlights of what you have."

He wrote his notes rapidly, sometimes interrupting to clarify a fact, before he stared down at his pile of notes, and there was a pile. His pen tapped gently against his hand as he sank into deep thought.

"Benen? That comment you made about Carol. What was that again?"

"My comment? That I wondered if it was her or if it was her other sister. They are very similar in appearance and their voices are quite a bit alike. Carol has always seemed on the up and up. That Caren, that's a different story. From what I understand, she has always been one to take advantage of others, considering it due her. Would she be the one who was there?"

"I think it was, Benen. I know Carol's voice and it didn't quite sound like her. I thought it was the deflection through the door and my not being quite alert."

"I'll look at bringing her in for questioning. We seem to be tripping over her every time we turn around." Dallas shook his head at Hagen. "Hagen?"

Hagen sighed, her hands gripping together until her fingers turned white. "It has to be her. She and Dad locked horns many times, he had her in court over numerous issues. I could see this being revenge driven for her." She looked away. "And their other brother, Byron. He hasn't been around a lot lately, but I did see him in town a few weeks ago. In the rundown part of the Main Street."

"It was reported to the homeless shelter, Hagen. They've been watching for him for something else." Buckley's drifted through the phone to her. "I'm sure, if he's still there, he'll be turned in. He's done too many dirty tricks for them to let it go."

"I know he has. Their kids are the same." Hagen's voice stopped. "Have you looked into their families?"

"We're working on it. Dallas, Emma has been back in touch just now. She said Abe and the guys were heading this way for work and he would drop off a bundle of documents for you at the precinct. I just love the way she uses words." Burnie's happy beam could be heard loud and clear.

That broke the heaviness of the conversation as they all laughed, leaving a huge smirk on his face.

"Dallas, where do we stand with the investigation?" Brennen voiced the thought they had all been trying to avoid.

"Right now? Not where I want to be or would like to be. With these new names and with what I am sure Emma has sent on, I'll be working long hours on this and my other cases." He rose to his feet. "Listen, guys, I have to run. Keep in touch. Stay safe all of you. I have no doubt they would use any one of you to get to Hagen."

With that sobering comment, Dallas walked away, leaving Brandon and Hagen staring at one another, as they were sure the others were.

———

"Listen, I have Daniel going in to my home to retrieve some stuff from a safe. I'm not sure what I'll find, but I know there might be something." Hagen bit at her lip, knowing she had placed her friend in danger. "I shouldn't have done that. I placed him in danger, didn't I?"

"Not necessarily. He's been in and out of your house for years, Hagen." Barnabas hastened to reassure her. "They would not like think anything of it, other than he had gone in for something he needed."

"I hope so." Hagen stared at Brandon, seeing the fatigue beginning to show. "Barnabas, how do we do this? How do we come home? I can't hide from the girls, they need me too much."

Brandon's hand rested on her arm, as he leaned over, a kiss on her cheek. "Bring us home, Barnabas. Send someone out to Daniel's and bring us home. Reroute him to the building."

Standing in the kitchen of their apartment, Hagen shuddered, her mind thinking how close it had been for Brandon. Thank you, Lord. You protected him and brought him back to me. Now, what, though, Lord? Where do we go from here? How do we find the ones responsible? We can't begin to go on with our dreams unless and until the Richards are caught. Will it take me going out there, putting myself on the line to bring them to justice?

She felt arms around her and she leaned back against Brandon, her own hands wrapping around his. Her head tilted to rest on his arm, she felt safe, loved, and secure, but not necessarily in that order.

"What are you thinking about so hard?" Brandon waited for her to respond, content just to hold her.

"I was wondering how we catch them. What if it means that I have to put myself out there?"

"If you do, we'll do everything to keep you safe. I can guarantee you that. The guys won't want anything to happen to you."

"I know that, Brandon, but there is always a danger. Did Breck say where they were in their investigation? I know they are looking, feeding stuff on to Dallas and Will."

"He didn't say." Brandon moved past her to fridge, an eye on the clock. "How be I grill something for supper?"

"Sound good." She heard the sound of the door opening and her eyes slid closed. "Are you ready for this?"

"No, but I don't think we have much choice." He grinned at her even as he sat the meat and vegetables he had pulled from the fridge on the counter. He turned, his grin becoming larger as he heard the bickering between the twins before they appeared in the kitchen doorway, their eyes on him before finding Hagen.

"Hagen!" Holly's squeal of joy reverberated in his eardrums and he watched as she launched herself at her sister.

Haley stood, mouth open, shock on her face before she too was throwing herself at Hagen, before turning to him, standing for a moment, uncertainty on her face before he simply held out an arm and she threw herself at him, her arms tight around him, tears wetting his shirt.

"Brandon! You're home! I didn't think you would ever come home!" Holly stood watching, before she too moved into his hug.

"I am, girls, but we need to talk, and I mean really talk. But first, go get cleaned up and changed. I was about to grill but I'm not sure if I should. Maybe no supper tonight?"

The twins joint squeal of "Brandon" echoed through the kitchen before they took off on a run, their happy voices drifting back to the couple in the kitchen.

Hagen leaned against him, reaching up for his kiss.

"You made them happy. They always wanted a brother."

"I never had any brothers or sisters. They're great. For what it matters, I worry too much about something happening to them."

"Me, too." Hagen moved away from him, her hands reaching for the meat to hand to him and then reaching for the vegetables. "Brandon?"

Brandon paused from walking through the doorway, to turn back, a puzzled look on his face.

"What if we don't catch them in time, and we lose one of the girls or each other? How do we go on?" Hagen refused to look around, not wanting to see shock and condemnation on his face.

Brandon was back across the room, the meat dropped on the table as he gathered Hagen close to his heart.

"I pray that doesn't happen. We don't know what God has planned, but we will go on, serving Him, following the dreams He has given us. My dream is a long life with my lady." He kissed her thoroughly, leaned back to study the face of the woman he adored, and then turned back to pick up the meat and head for the balcony and the grill, a whistle trailing behind him, warming her heart.

Hearing a tap at the door, Hagen headed that way, giving Haley the plate of vegetables to take out to Brandon and asking

Holly to dig out the plates and flatware. She stood on tiptop to peek out, her one hand flat on the door, the other hand on the lock. She twisted the lock and stepped backwards as she opened the door.

"Daniel?" She peeked out, not seeing anyone. "How did you get here?"

"Let's see. Baird, Brady, Brennen and Burnie paid me a visit and made me an offer I couldn't refuse." He handed her a box, a grin on his face. "This is what I found. The fellows were really interested in it. Burnie kept asking if he could look, it might be a bestselling novel in the box."

Hagen began to laugh, picturing Burnie doing just that. "He would, wouldn't he? Maybe, just maybe, I'll let him take a peek." She set the box down in the kitchen and then pointed through the living room. "Brandon and the girls are out there. Head on out. I just have to grab some rolls and the condiments." She reached for an extra plate and flatware and stepped back as Daniel grabbed up the tray.

"Lead the way, milady. Let's find that fellow of yours."

Hagen finally stood, flushed with laughter, to gather the remnants of their meal, the twins reaching for what she had in her hands, pointing back to her seat. Shaking her head, Hagen headed into the apartment, her hands resting for a moment on the box, before the twins approached, a tray of fresh coffee and juice and a plate of cookies in Haley's hands.

"What's that, Hagen?" Holly touched the box.

"It's from Dad's safe. Daniel emptied it for me. I need, rather, we need to go through it. I think there might be something in there but I can't be sure."

"Did Dad have a safety deposit box?" Holly looked uncertain as she asked.

"He did. I cleaned it out when I was settling the estate. There was only some old mortgage information on the house. I handed it over to the lawyer, who has it in his safe."

Hagen seated herself, her hands resting on her lap, her eyes on Brandon, who nodded.

"Daniel, we need to bathe this with prayer. Will you lead?"

149

Her hands shaking, a prayer on her lips, Hagen reached into the box, pulling out the papers and then setting the box aside, Brandon reaching for it and setting it on the table behind him. He watched her carefully, ready to step in if he had to.

"Hagen? What is there?" Holly and Haley had moved from their seats to stand beside her, the two men moving so the twins could sit beside her.

"I don't know." Hagen paused for a moment. "I don't know what we'll find, Haley, Holly. I really don't. Dad never said much, only told me if something happened to him, I would have to deal with it."

She sighed, reaching for the first piece of paper and unfolding it. "This is just tax information that I have dealt with." She looked around, finding Brandon heading back outside with a pile of blank folders, labels, and pens in his hands.

"Here, girls. You can label the folders as Hagen decides what each piece of paper is. If you can, sort it by date or by alphabet, depending on what there is."

Hagen moved rapidly after that, sorting through the material with the girls' help until she reached the very last piece of paper, a sealed envelope with her name on it, written in her father's handwriting. She paused, her finger tracing the writing, blinking back tears before she loosened the flap and opened the large brown envelope.

"What is that?" Holly's finger touched the documents.

"I'm not sure, Holly. Let's see what Dad left. A passport, but it's not his photo or name. A list of phone numbers with only initials. Photos of? That's Billy and Ben, isn't it, Daniel?"

Daniel reached for it, Brandon leaning over to look. "It is, I would say about 10 years ago. Around the time, I think that you landed here, Brandon, or just before."

"About that time. I transferred in to finish my degree, I had about 18 months left." He reached for the photo. "Is this the old farm?"

"Not that one. This is another one." Daniel sat back before he looked at him. "I wonder if there's another jail cell."

Brandon sat back, shocked. "I wonder. We'll let Dallas worry about that, shall we? Hagen? What else do you have there?"

Hagen looked up, her face drawn and white. "This. A letter written by Dad, or almost a journal, detailing the crime the Richards had been up to. He states he was afraid for his life and for Mom and us." She heard the intake of breath from the twins. "Brandon, what if their accident wasn't an accident? What if it was deliberate?"

"How? Wasn't it a drunk driver?" Brandon was puzzled, his eyes on her face, trying to understand where she was heading with her questions.

"That driver was notorious for being able to drink a lot and not seem drunk. He was often stopped and blew well over the limit. In fact, at the time, he didn't have a driver's license." Daniel shared a look with Hagen. "Unfortunately, I can see the Richards setting him up and having him play chicken with your parents, Hagen. Only he was too drunk to have the proper reflexes."

"And then his family found out, began to blackmail the Richards, and they decided to set me up for revenge." Hagen was on her feet, anger driving her to pace, before she swept the material back into the envelope. "Are the guys in the conference room, Brandon?"

"I think they planned to be." He squinted at his watch in the dimming light. "They should still be. Girls, how be you and Daniel clean up and then head on down there? We could use your insights."

"You can? I mean, you want us to help?" Haley was incredulous.

"We didn't think you did. So we never offered." Holly was on her feet, almost running for the kitchen.

"We have been remiss, I think, my love." Brandon's hand reached for Hagen's. "They may have the insight we've been lacking."

<hr>

"They have good imaginations. Will that help?" Daniel grinned at the couple, before he headed in to help the girls, finding them almost finished. "What? You didn't wait for me?"

They turned before they began laughing, teasing him with the ease of old friends.

Brandon stood for a moment outside the conference room door, his hand on Hagen's cheek.

"When we go through here, and give them this, and ask for help, there will be no going back."

Hagen nodded, her hand coming up to grip his. "I know, my love. But we need to do this. We need this over. We can't go on with our dream of making my work your work in a more educational, teaching way."

Standing just inside the door, Hagen and Brandon watched the beehive of activity, as he termed it later on, going on in the room, all thirteen men there, the wives, Farr and Alice, Eric, Fynn's cousin and his wife, Sandra, and Will. That shouldn't have surprised them, but it did.

"I thought Will was on holidays." Hagen's whisper to Brandon, though quiet, seemed to echo through the room, raising heads and then with glad cries, raising the occupants to their feet, to come and greet Brandon and herself.

Daniel, Haley and Holly slipped quietly inside, heading for seats near Will, dropping into quiet conversation with him.

"Brandon? You're okay?" Barnabas stood beside him, his hand on his friend's shoulder.

"I am, Barnabas. I wasn't harmed, which is the strange part of it all. Just held in a jail cell, set up just for me."

"A jail cell?" Burnie exchanged a glance with the others. "Arranged just for you? That's bizarre."

"Not if you know the people involved." Hagen spoke quickly. She held up the envelope. "I have information here that I didn't know Dad had. I hadn't looked in the safe since they were killed. I'm sorry." She blinked back tears before heading towards her sisters.

"Sorry? For what?" Benen watched her walk away with the ladies in the room heading after her.

"Her father named the Richards. He had dates, a list of initials, a passport that we don't know who it belongs to, an almost diary of facts and details about them. She feels guilty, that if she had found it, perhaps none of this would have happened."

"God's timing, Brandon." Buckley spoke quietly before he headed towards Hagen, a hand on her arm drawing her to one side.

They could see him speaking with her before their heads bowed and the men know Buckley was praying with and for her.

"It's all in here." Brandon handed it off to Brody. "Make us copies and then hand the originals to Will. He needs to have this. I think that it will likely aid in other investigations they have on the go."

The men scattered, back to what they had been on, quiet conversation mingling with the click of keys and the rustle of paper. Haley and Holly had finally given in, and headed for bed, Daniel walking them up before he returned, a thought crossing his mind.

He approached Breck, who was free for a moment, standing staring down at the coffee pot.

"It won't pour itself into your cup, Breck." Daniel grinned as Breck looked up, shaking his head to clear it.

"I know. I'm just puzzled."

"About what?"

"The Richards. There just seems to be something or someone missing."

"I know. I think the same thing, but I can't imagine who it is." Daniel turned as he heard a throat clear near him.

Brady stood there. "Fynn and I have been talking. I think I have a name to suggest. Emma's running it for me." They stared at him when he gave the name before Daniel nodded.

"Perfect sense. That's who is behind them. Now, how do we prove it?"

"With a lot of hard work and searching. Daniel, I'm going to pass that name on to Dallas." Breck walked away, the two men watching him before Brady's eyes strayed to Brandon, seeing the fatigue weighing his friend down. "We need to solve this, Daniel. We can try all we want to encourage him, to keep him motivated and moving forward. That's the mission of the Foundation, to provide encouragement. But if it doesn't resolve soon, he'll lose hope."

"I know and so will Hagen. I can tell you this, after being friends with her all our lives. If she starts to lose hope, she will hide it and hide it well. I'm not sure either myself or the twins would be able to read her well enough to discern that."

"That would be true. What do you think about the person Brady named?"

"High in the government, in exports and imports, customs? Absolutely. There have been rumours around about him and his daughter for years. She runs a customs business, helping businesses and individuals make their way through the customs process. It would be a perfect cover."

"I agree." Brady turned for a moment, finding Hagen standing beside him. "Hagen?"

"Daniel, what name did Brady give you?" She kept her eyes on Brady. When he stated it, she nodded, then help up some papers. "These were in with Dad's stuff. Will needs to have it, but take a look at it first, please."

Hagen watched Brady walk away before she turned to make herself another tea, hesitation in her manner, so unlike her that Daniel frowned.

"Hagen?"

"What if we're wrong, Daniel? What if we accuse the wrong person?"

Brandon's arms surrounded her. "It will go no further than our friends, Will and Dallas. They will verify it either as true or not. Trust them, Hagen. I know that is something that is difficult for you at present."

"It is, Brandon, and it shouldn't be." She leaned her head against his arm, her arms wrapped around his. "I hate this, Brandon. And you're about out on your feet."

"I am, but I want to stay." He frowned as she giggled. "What did I say?" He looked up at the snicker from Brady.

"You sounded like a little kid who was told to go to bed and was refusing." Brady grinned as he walked away. "Listen to your wife, Brandon."

Hagen bit back her own snicker before she pulled Brandon from the room and walked towards the stairs. "He's right. You do need to sleep. Your body needs to recover."

Hours later, Hagen curled up in a corner of the couch, a blanket over her, her cup of tea beside her. She studied the cup, a china cup, she thought, with a picture of her favourite bird, a Baltimore oriole on it. Brandon had sought it out for her, she thought. Thank you, Lord, for him. He has brought so much to my life. I don't feel alone and frightened any more. And he's helping with the girls, stepping in as a brother and also a father figure for them that they need. She turned her head as she heard footsteps and Brandon appeared, reaching to shift her over so he could sit with her and then drew her tight to him.

"Can't sleep?"

She shook her head. "Too much on my mind, I guess." Her head went to his shoulder, even as her hand reached for his. "I didn't mean to wake you."

"You didn't, not really. I hadn't got into a deep sleep. Too much to think about." He tilted his head to study her face. "About that name?"

"Yeah, that name. What if we're wrong?"

"At this point, I don't think we are. Dallas will work his magic, or let God work through him, I should say, to prove or disprove it."

"I know." She reached forward to retrieve her phone from the coffee table. "Nathaniel sent me this. Apparently that group has been working on it as well, along with Emma and her employees. He said that given the name Daniel had mentioned, it is more than likely to be the right one. He had found information on that person, but couldn't connect to us. He thought it was old information. Emma apparently has been tracking this person for years."

"She has? You mean, we're the means to bring this person to justice?"

"It would appear so." Hagen tossed her phone to the table and yawned, turning her face into Brandon's shoulder and sleeping.

———

Brandon watched her sleep, a cry rising from his heart that God would solve this soon, that she would be safe. He wanted so much to be an encourager for her, but he felt he had failed in that.

Looking up from his desk as his secretary, Amy, appeared in his office doorway, Barnabas beckoned her in.

"Amy?"

"Amos Thomas is out there, Barnabas. He is insistent that he has to speak with you, and right now." Amy was disturbed, that was easy to see.

"Amos? No, I can't. Not right now. I have that conference call with Dad and the rest of the Board in five minutes."

"I told him that. He is refusing to leave. He scares me today, Barnabas, and that is not easy to do."

"I see." Barnabas pushed back his desk chair, preparatory to rising, when Amy shook her head.

"I called security, and I can hear them now. You stay put. They'll handle him." She walked away, but Barnabas still rose, to stand just inside his office doorway, listening to the loud voice echoing down the corridor before the shutting of the outside office door cut it off.

"Amy?"

"Barnabas, he's gone, but he's vicious today. I have never seen or heard him sound like that. Ever." Amy appeared in the hallway, her eyes still on the outside door.

"No, it's not like him. Can you let Breck know and ask him to follow up on it? If he's refused to leave the office, have Breck ask that he be held for questioning and possible trespass charges." Barnabas disappeared back into his office, his mind already on the conference call he needed to be part of.

Amy threw up her hands. "I'll do that, Barnabas. I'll just do that." She jumped as she heard Breck's voice behind her

"You'll just do what?"

"Talk to you. Amos Thomas was just escorted from here. Barnabas wants you to follow up and ask that he be held for possible trespassing charges. The fellows had a hard time getting him to leave."

"I can do that. Listen, is he the one that you mentioned when this all started with Brandon and Hagen?"

"He is. And now look where we are."

"We'll sort it out, Amy. Is Barnabas free?"

Amy shook her head. "No, he has that conference call." She turned to look towards his office. "What's going on with him? There is something more than the guys."

"I know, but he's not talking." Breck hesitated before he shook his head and walked away. There is no way that would be true, he thought.

Opening the conference room door, Dallas looked around, not seeing Brandon or Hagen, but he entered anyway, knowing he had to speak with each of the men and that would take time, time he needed to be spending on other investigations as well. Will had met with him that morning, asked him to concentrate on this case and a couple of others, and let some of the other team members pick up for him in the meanwhile.

Two hours later, Dallas rose, heading for the outdoors, needing to walk for a bit, to digest what he had been told, and to determine how he could fit it in with his own investigation. These guys are great, he thought, and with Emma shooting him so much on the ones that he was investigating, he didn't think it would be long before he could make arrests. But how to keep Brandon and Hagen and the twins safe? That was a question that he didn't know if he had an answer to. He knew Hagen. He knew that she was at her limit and would soon step out of her safe zone and go after the Richards and whoever else it was that she had determined to be involved. She's like her father in that, he thought. When Gallagher and Emily were killed, we lost a power couple in the community. They were both quiet, worked in the background, but they made things happen.

Hagen watched him pacing from the balcony above, before she headed back inside. The twins were home from school already, excited about another few days off, the reason why she just couldn't think of for the moment. Brandon, she knew, was meeting with Breck, looking into a new line of work, but she knew his heart was not in the social work field as it had been, and she blamed the Richards for that. His volunteer work as a mentor to young college students had had to be put on hold for now, he didn't want to risk any harm coming to them, and he missed it, he told her.

She sighed, pacing around the kitchen, her arms folded around herself. Now, what was that thought? Something is niggling at the back of my mind, Lord? Can you help me to remember?

"Hagen?" She spun as she heard Brandon's voice, a frown on her face as she headed for the hallway, to meet him heading into the kitchen.

"Brandon? You're in a rush."

"I just needed to see you." He wrapped her in his arms, kissing her soundly, before hugging her tight, his head on hers.

"What is going on?" Hagen felt that she could barely breathe, Brandon had her in such a tight hold.

The twins slid to a stop, having heard the excited sounding voices, and frowned at first one another and then at their sister.

"Hagen?"

"I have no idea, Holly. Ask this big oaf, if you must know."

"A big oaf, am I?" Brandon winked at the twins, who had to smother their grins. "Barnabas found Breck and I. He had a meeting this morning with the Board. There is a whole new avenue of work that they want me to look into."

"There is?" At his silence, Hagen pushed back, her eyes narrowed. "And that would be?"

"To work with teens in the courts. There is a need that no one else has tried to meet. Someone from the courts approached the Foundation, and the Board thought of me. It's definitely something that we will need to pray about."

The twins hugged the couple, their hands meeting around them.

———

"This is so cool, Brandon. You would suit that to a T." Haley watched her sister's face. "Hagen?"

"Sorry, I was wool gathering, I think. This is great news but we need to pray that it is God's will."

"And I talked to Dallas. They are getting ready to arrest the Richards, all five of them, on other charges, but they won't forget about us. Dallas thinks that this will be critical to solving our mystery, or adventure, or whatever you want to call it."

"This is dangerous, right?" Holly stepped back, fear on her face. "It won't end it, will it? When do the people stop following us everywhere we go? We have guys at school trying to trap us into meeting them, into going out with them, into going for pizza with a group."

"Holly? Is that what has been happening?" At her nod, Hagen's eyes slid closed. "How be, for now, I talk to your teachers and see if we can let you work online or at home? Would that help?"

"It would. You worry about us when we're away from you and we worry about you." Haley reached for Hagen, hugging her tighter than she had in years, her fear palpable.

Benen froze as he read the article on his monitor, sitting back before he printed numerous copies of it. He rose, heading for the printer, grabbing the sheets of paper and tidying them into a neat pile before he sorted them and then stapled each set. He looked around. Not all the guys are here, he thought, noting Brady, Bradon and Buckley were missing. Benen stood for a moment, staring down at what he held, before he walked over to the centre table and cleared his throat, bring all eyes to him, with frowns at the interruption on some faces, frowns that smoothed out as they glimpsed his face.

"Guys, I have an article here that I think we all need to look at. It's not pretty. I don't know how I found it, other than it was God and He knew that we were at a point we needed to see it." He handed around the papers, watching as he saw the moment each man caught the meaning of it.

"Who wrote this?" Burnie was the first to speak.

"I looked into that. She's a lawyer from a town about thirty miles or whatever kilometres away from here. She's been known to walk the line. The law society has been after her, but they had not enough proof."

"Is she the one behind it all?" This from Brody, who had been highlighting sections of the article.

"I would like to think so. She really had it in for Hagen's father, that much is clear from that article. We need to research to see how she would be related to the driver that hit her parents." Benen looked around as he heard footsteps. "Hagen? Brandon?"

"Who were you just speaking about?" Hagen stopped beside Benen, tilting his hand to read the name. "Her? Yes, the driver was her son. Is that the connection? I knew she despised Dad, that he had called her on things on different occasions and had shown her up in court on some cases. She is vindictive, always has been."

"You know her?" Baird moved closer, his eyes on Brandon as he spoke.

"Not personally. Dad made sure that he kept his ladies, as he called us, away from the people he had difficulties with. He didn't like to mix his family life and work life if he could help it. But I remember him talking about her." Hagen had paled. "Did she put her own son up to that, to killing Mom and Dad?" Her hand clamped across her mouth as her stomach roiled. "Who would do that?" Her voice was barely audible.

"Someone who is very sick mentally and emotionally." Brandon wrapped an arm around her. "Have you talked to Dallas?"

"Not yet. He said he would be interviewing the Richards regarding this case today, so he didn't think he'd have time to talk with us." Breck pulled out his phone, his face turning white as he listened, his eyes on Hagen.

"Breck?" Hagen was almost afraid to hear what he would have to say.

"Two things, Hagen. Ben Richards died today from a ruptured brain aneurysm that no one knew he had, not even likely himself. Given that, Dallas said Billy has begun to talk, and give names and details that they didn't have yet."

Breck paused, a compassionate look coming over his face. "Your home, Hagen?"

"My home? What about it?" She paled. "They got to it, didn't they?"

"They did. What you didn't know was that Dallas had asked that we clear it out for you, to put everything in storage here. Brandon didn't even know that." He watched as her face moved and then crumpled, tears on her cheeks.

"Thank you. I needed to do that, just wasn't ready to do it myself." She frowned once more. "But that's not all."

"No, it's not. We were finished just after 10. Barnabas had a professional mover go in yesterday and pack everything up, ready for us to go in today." He held up a hand as she went to protest. "We had to move fast, Hagen, in case someone tried when one of you ladies was there. It is a good thing we did. The house exploded about thirty minutes ago."

"Exploded? How? A gas leak?" Hagen searched her mind, trying to comprehend what would have caused the explosion.

"No, not a gas leak, Hagen."

Brandon finally spoke, his shock wearing off. "I think what Breck is trying to say, Hagen, is that someone planted a bomb and blew the house up."

"A bomb?" Her voice rose to a squeak, as she stared around at the men who had gathered closer. "A bomb? Were they trying to kill us?"

"More than likely send a message." Blair spoke up, his hand rubbing at his cheek. "They want you to stay silent and not say anything. Somehow, I don't think that will work."

"No, it won't." They could hear the anger in her voice. "That was our home. I was holding on to it until the girls reached majority. Then, we would have made a decision as to what we all wanted to do with it. They have taken that decision away from us, and they had no right to do that."

"No, they didn't." Breck spoke. "And we will catch them." He tapped the paper he held. "Would she do something like that?"

"Absolutely. We had suspicions that she had done this in the past. People would have their cars explode or burn, or there would be a fire in the home. Arson, but without any proof as to who did it. Not just in this town, either." She looked up at Brandon. "How do I tell the twins?"

"We'll do it together. Buckley will be there, if you like."

She shrugged, before snatching the papers from Breck's hands and stalking away, to slam herself down into a chair, the papers slapped down on the table in front of her, as with pen in hand, she stabbed at the sheets.

"I gather she's a little upset?" Breck stared after her in awe, not quite sure he had really seen what he had just witnessed.

Brandon grinned. "That she would be. Touch her family and she becomes a mother bear. She has had to do that over the last year, to protect the girls but more importantly to protect her heart. She's learning to share that with me."

"Does that mean what we just saw, you'll do?" Burnie spoke up, a smirk on his face.

"You just might. So don't be surprised." Brandon turned back to his friends. "So, how do we go about getting the goods on this woman and giving them to Dallas?"

"For starters, we have a surveillance video from a neighbour's outdoor camera. They had trouble with trespassers and set one up. They called Barnabas and offered it to him, as well as giving a copy to the investigating officer today." Breck paused, not quite sure how to go on.

"Who was it, Breck?" Blair's heart sank, not really wanting to know.

"It was someone who had dressed up as Daniel, but it wasn't him. Burnie and Brody were within him at the time. He was being set up, to cause even more anguish to Hagen."

"I hope they have him hidden away." Brandon could feel the anger beginning to burn in him.

"He is. Dallas won't say where, and frankly, if we don't know, we can't compromise his safety." Breck reached for another copy of the article. "So, who gets to go see Dallas?"

A hand to her throat, Hagen stared at the woman standing in front of her, an arm out to shove her sisters behind her. Why was this woman here, in the middle of Hagen's town, in broad daylight, tracking her down and standing in her way?

"Girls, when I give the word, turn and run like you have never run before. We're not that far from the police department. Head there." Hagen continued to back up, shoving her sisters behind her. "Now, run. Send help."

The twins took one last look and then did exactly as she asked, running for the police department, shoving open the door to the shock of the officer on duty, who came out as they called for help. A quick question and he was calling for help, sending the responding officers on their way, his arms encircling the twins and drawing them away from the door, into a sheltered area of the lobby.

Hagen heard the girls' feet pounding on the pavement as they ran, and she thanked God that their parents had drilled into them that they responded instantly when asked to do something in an emergency, not stopping to ask questions or find out the reason why.

"So, you think that will save you and the brats?" Leanne Fuller stared at Hagen, before she shook her head, a taunt on her face. "That won't work. I'll track them down and hold them hostage, to make you do what I want."

Hagen was puzzled. She knew what Leanne wanted, or at least she thought she did.

"What on earth do you mean? I thought you wanted my business to transport illegal goods."

Leanne snorted. "That was the Richards' idea. Not mine. No, I have another plan." Her words were drawn out, as if she were just coming up with her nefarious plot. "No. Your parents weren't to have died that night. It was to have been a warning. Only my stupid son had to be drunk."

"He was drunk all the time, Leanne. Didn't you know that?" Hagen was still puzzled, trying to read the other woman and unable to.

Leanne's hand shook as she pulled it from her pocket, a weapon in it. "No, he was not. He was never drunk. Those were all lies about him." She waved her hand. "Lies your father told and had everybody believing."

Hagen continued to frown, even as she began to inch backwards, knowing there was a doorway she could slip into if she could only reach it. Just a few more feet. She just had to keep Leanne talking and distracted.

"No? Sorry, Leanne. He did it to himself. Everyone knew how much he liked his alcohol, and his drugs. Did you supply him with those?"

"Of course not. We're not talking about him. We're talking about you. I need to kill you, my dear, to exact revenge. Your father thwarted me too many times. I could have been rich and retired except for him."

"I doubt that, Leanne. Someone would have stepped into your path and stopped you. How close are they to doing just that? Oh, and my house? That was you, wasn't it. Trying to pass yourself off as Daniel."

"No, that was Daniel. He's lied to you all your life." Leanne had stopped walking, distracted by a sound behind her.

"No, it was you." Hagen made a lunge for the door, pulling it open and letting it slam behind her, running through the stock room, desperately seeking for a place to hide. She scrambled into a narrow opening, pulling piles of rolled plastic in front of her, and crouching down, her head buried in her arm, one hand across her mouth to silence her gasps for breath. She listened intently, hearing the door slam open against an outside wall and then the clatter of high heels on the concrete floor as Leann entered, searching for her.

"Where are you, you little...!" Leanne's anger was such that she could not even finish a sentence, her free hand hitting at the boxes and packages on the shelves, not finding Hagen.

Leanne finally stood, close to where Hagen had hidden, before she spun in a circle, off balance, the alcohol she had consumed for courage beginning to work against her. She didn't realize just how much she had imbibed.

Hearing a sound, she walked as quietly as she could on her high heels towards it, her weapon up. She saw the shadow moving quickly towards her and her weapon discharged. She heard the sound of a surprised cry, frowning as it sounded more male than female, and that couldn't be right, she thought. Leanne stumbled forward, to stand, tottering on her heels, staring down at the crumpled form in front of her, not hearing the running steps heading her way or the jerk as her arms were pulled behind her or feel the cuffs as they closed with a metal snap around her wrists. Her weapon was taken and bagged before she was led away.

Will dropped to his knees, hands outstretched to turn the officer over, his heart clenching as he saw it was Dallas. He looked up to nod at the comment that help was on the way.

Alice stood beside him for a moment, before she looked around.

"Who was she after? It had to be someone."

Will rose, stepping back as other officers moved in to help Dallas, the paramedics almost running their way with the stretcher loaded down with their kits.

"It was Hagen. The twins appeared in the lobby of the building, asking for help. Dallas responded and this is what happened." Will spun. "Hagen had to have come in here. This is close to where the twins said they were."

"Then, she's hidden herself away." Alice gave a grim smile. "We used to do that to one another when we were small, hide and not say a word when the others were looking for us. It was good practice. Only I never expected to have to have Hagen do that as an adult."

"None of us did." Will beckoned to some officers. "Hagen is here. Hiding from what we suspect. Start a search, making sure that she knows we're the good guys."

A soft sound had Will spinning once more, to find Hagen standing behind him, her eyes on him, staring from a white, white face, with fear etching lines on it.

"Will? Alice? Where is she?" Hagen tried to see around him, spotting the body on the floor. "Oh, no! Who is that?"

Alice was beside her, an arm around her. "Leann has been arrested. She will not trouble you any longer. She's facing some stiff charges."

"But who is that?" Hagen's finger shook as she pointed.

"It's Dallas. He was shot by Leanne as he approached this area. It's in his shoulder, so we'll see how severe it is." Will's hand reached to steady her.

"Is it over?" Hagen's voice was barely audible.

"We think so, Hagen." Will gave a gentle smile as he pointed behind her for Alice to walk her out that way, his steps matching theirs, a hand out to steady her if needed. "We'll sort it all out, find out who all she has had dealings with, and then lay the charges."

"She's the one who planted the bomb." Hagen stopped suddenly, swaying as the adrenaline released itself. "I'm tired."

Will gave a quiet laugh. "I have no doubt that you are. Let's get you to the department, get your statement, and then get you and the twins home. Brandon will be waiting for you, no doubt. His friends have been busy, Dallas tells me, his hands apart to show how much material they brought him."

"They're good. They've had practice." Hagen yawned, the only thing holding her upright Alice's arm around her.

———

Late that night, Hagen wrapped herself in a blanket and sank gratefully down into her favourite wicker chair on the deck, the china cup of tea beside her. The twins had taken time to settle down, overwrought as they were, but they had finally succumbed to sleep, Hagen watching closely before dropping a kiss on their heads, pulling the covers up tight as she had when they were tiny and she was tasked with putting them to bed, whispered a prayer over each one, and then closing their doors, walked away to find Brandon standing, waiting for her with open arms, to gather her close. His tears wet her hair as her tears wet his sweatshirt, before he prayed for her, whispered some verses in her ear, handed her the blanket and her cup of tea, and told her to go and spend some time with God.

Hagen was grateful for the man she had married, who she loved so deeply, and had so quickly. God had provided just who she needed, she thought. Brandon was the one who had walked through her dreams as a teen, refined as a young adult, but who she had never expected to find. She shifted in her chair to be able to rest her head against the chair back, her eyes on the dark sky, watching the stars in their twinkling and the moon as it sent its rays earthward. It was a favourite time of day for her, a time that she could relax and reflect, to gather her thoughts and her ideas from that day, and to look forward to the next.

She lifted her head as she heard the door open and close and then felt herself lifted up as Brandon scooped her to his heart and then sat back down, cradling her close to him.

"Okay, my love?" His breath whispered across her ear.

"Getting there. It will take time. The twins will need help, I think."

"Buckley thought of that. He has a list of people they can talk to, including a friend of Emma's."

"Darcy, Doug's wife. They had an adventure that almost killed her and almost destroyed the town of Riverville. Revenge from a rogue police chief. Yes, she would be good. A retired forensics psychologist."

"You know interesting people." His chin rested against her head and he was content to hold the lady he loved more than his own life.

"We'll get there. Did you talk to Will? I haven't heard about Dallas. Alice has been tied up with the investigation."

"I did. Dallas is fine, just staying overnight in the hospital for observation. She winged him and when he went down, he hit his head hard. He's fighting mad, Will tells me."

Hagen laughed. "He would be. He always did hate for injustice to win." She snuggled closer. "I never expected this, you know."

"Expected what?" Brandon had no idea of where she was heading with her words.

"You. Me. My shop. Your friends who are now my friends. The ladies. It's so overwhelming what God has provided for us. Darby and the twins are becoming close friends, and I'm glad. He'll look out for them. They need that at times."

"And they're good for him. They put him in his place, Berneen tells me."

Hagen laughed. "That they do." She was silent for a while, her thoughts chaotic until she just gave up trying to sort them out. "Brandon, if we had to choose a verse for us, given what we've gone through, what would you choose? I know we'll be asked, but I just can't seem to settle on one. My mind is too full of puzzles and hurt and sadness, that it seems that I have lost sight of my dreams."

"Never that, darlin'. Never that. Your dreams are there, just waiting to surface. Your Dad and Mom's dreams are there as well, those they chose to share with you. And the twins? They will have their own dreams, some to share, some to keep private even from one another. As to a verse? That's a good question. I might not be able to come up with one tonight."

"That's okay. I just thought we should be looking at something. Dad and Mom chose a verse when they married for them as a couple, even though they each had a life verse."

———

"I like that idea. I know you have a life verse. So do I." Brandon's voice paused. "I know what we can do. A dream that was my mother's. I had forgotten it. How be we take part of your business, and dedicate it to making plaques or signs with people's life verses? Have them choose a favourite picture or scene and incorporate it into the project?"

"I like how you think. Mom wanted that, but she never pushed, wanting the educational portion to be first. We need to update our website and include that." Hagen shifted again, this time her mind racing with possibilities.

"Turn off the thoughts, my love. Just rest. You've been through a lot. The next few days and weeks will be exhausting for you as you release the stress and strain that you and the twins have been under."

When Hagen didn't answer, Brandon shifted her enough to see her face. He smiled, and then sat back, his own eyes closing as he too slept. It had been an emotional day for them both, and God had granted them what they needed most, sleep.

Three months later, Brandon stood for a moment in the shop door, watching as Hagen concentrated on a project. He walked towards her, a hand resting on her shoulder as she looked up, a smile lighting up her face

"You're home and early!" She was on her feet and in his arms, her face raised for his kiss.

"I am and free until the middle of next week. Barnabas sent me home, told me to go find the lady I loved and spend the days with her. Know who that would be?" He laughed as she playfully swatted his arm. "What are you working on?"

"A new idea. God has been giving me too many dreams and ideas. I start on one and then another and another comes from that." She was glowing and he loved that.

"God is using you in a way I don't think even your father would have imagined. Go with the creative juices. We have been able to hire, through Buckley's contacts, and those men and ladies are happy for the work. You are providing encouragement to them and through them to others. It's snowballing. You are doing exactly what the Foundation envisioned."

"As are you. I talk to the youth that you work with. They hunt me down in town or at church, singing your praises, telling me how much better they feel about themselves because of you." She moved away from him. "I did this today."

"Did what?" He approached her as she stood, staring down at a framed picture, his arm coming around her. "Our verse. As for me and my house, we will serve the Lord. Joshua 24:15. New King James Version. And you chose a picture of your home. That's is nice. I like it." He kissed her again, before staring down at it, frowning as she moved it to one side. "What's this? Hagen?" He stared down at the picture that lay on the table.

"Brandon?"

"Hagen? Is this what I think it is?" He turned her to face him, surprise and awe on his face. "What are you telling me?"

"That I think you'll make a great father. I have seen how you react and teach the twins, not belittling them but building them up even when you have to reproof or correct them."

"When?" He just hugged her tighter and tighter.

"Brandon! I need to breathe!" Hagen's happy laughter spilled out and around the shop. "In about six months more or less. And we need to set up for two. That means the twins have to share."

Brandon stepped back, his hands on her shoulders. "Two? As in twins?" At her nod, he had to reach for a stool and sit. "Twins! Wow!"

Hagen laughed even as she reached for her phone, a frown in place as she saw it was Dallas.

"Dallas? We haven't talked in a week or two. I thought we weren't talking." Hagen could feel Brandon staring at her in shock.

Dallas' laugh carried across through the phone. "I know. I thought that too. I need to meet with you two. Is now a good time?"

"As good as any, I guess. Where?"

"Seeing as I'm standing right outside your shop door, will that work?" She spun as she saw him heading in, tucking his phone away in a pocket, a grin on his face, and then looked past him to see thirteen men and six ladies following in his footsteps.

"What is this? A party I didn't know I was hostess to?" Hagen was grinning as she greeted each one.

"No, we're giving the party and it's for later." Barnabas gave her a hard hug and then shook Brandon's hand. "Dallas asked to meet with us all. He wouldn't tell me why." He grinned at the face Dallas shot him and smirked in response.

Dallas studied each of the ones sitting or standing around, his gaze resting last on Hagen and Brandon, a frown on his face for a moment before he nodded.

"I just needed to update all of you on the investigation. Leanne Fuller has turned around and pled guilty to the charges facing her, including assault on and attempted murder of a police office, namely me. She has faced a slew of charges from this town and numerous towns around. The forces are glad to have her off the street.

"It is as you suspected, Hagen. Revenge. She was plotting revenge on your father, not realizing that the Richards were plotting the same, and using her son in their devious plans. He wasn't to have died, as we thought. He was to have just run them off the road and then disappeared. The Richards had it all worked out to move him from town, change his identity and then forget about him. We suspect they had hired a hit man to get rid of him, but Billy Richards has refused to confirm that.

"It all comes back to what you had found. Your father had information on Leanne that he was ready to turn in. She found out about it and then tried to find it. She is also the one who set the bomb in your home, pretending to be Daniel.

"The Richards had wanted your business to use for smuggling contraband, namely jewels and drugs. They had planned to frame you if anything was found. They were the ones who set your original shop on fire, as a warning, only it took a much bigger hold than they planned. Not the brightest ones, those five. Yes, all five were involved.

"Ben is the one on the dirt bike. He had it planned, where you had your tent, that Brandon would meet you, that you would step away and talk. He knew you would do just that. He had arranged for the floor joist to be almost cut all the way through in strategic spots, likely doing it himself. He's the one who had your sister kidnapped.

"Now, let's see. I think that covers it all. Any questions?"

Hagen's voice could be heard softly in the quiet that followed Dallas question. "I do not need to avenge. God will avenge. In so much better a way for us." She looked up at Brandon, who nodded, before she rose and went to each individual with a hug and a thank you.

Brandon stood for a moment, his eyes on his friends, knowing that he and Hagen had not faced what the six of them had.

———

175

"I can't find the words, guys, ladies, to thank you. You have been what true friends are. Thank you, each one of you." His hands rested on Hagen's shoulders. "Hagen has been busy. I know she has found out what verse is important to you and what kind of scenery you like the best. In those boxes sitting by Buckley's left arm, you will find a framed photo, with your verse on it, as a small thank you from Hagen, Haley, Holly and myself."

There was silence before laughter and talk broke out, the boxes distributed and each one standing in amazement at the artwork that Hagen had prepared, awed at her ability to choose a photo that so encompassed their dreams

Dear Readers

Thank you once more for picking up one of my books, this time the story of Brandon and his lady, Hagen. Once more these two characters have taken me on a windy, twisty road of adventure, not letting me see the road map in advance. Hagen's name was not originally Hagen. She chose this one. The twins, Haley and Holly? Not planned at all. In fact, I had no idea she has not an only child until they just showed up, and in my thoughts, enhanced the story and added a bit of fun to it.

My dream since a child was only known to my Mom, and that only a couple of years before she graduated to heaven in 2010. The dream? To write a novel. That novel, *The Sparrow*, started off a three year so far adventure of meeting characters and telling their stories, usually with the author not having a clue what was to happen, and with their unruliness, a chance to explore occupations and what not that I normally would not have done.

God knew my dream. He let it sit for probably fifty years before I set hands to the keyboard and wrote that novel. He knows your dreams. He knows when the timing is right. He knows who you need to reach and why. Trust Him with those dreams. Wait on His leading and timing. He'll guide you through the process.

The verse from Joshua? My father chose that when he and my mother married, for it to be the verse for their home. It has special meaning to me because of that. Isn't that what we, as believers, are to do? Serve the Lord and with gladness.

God bless each one of you. May He grant you the fulfillment of your dreams.

Ronna

Brendon: Encouraged to Praise

The Barnabas Chronicles
Book 8

By

Ronna M. Bacon

Nahum 1:7
The Lord is good,
A stronghold in the day of trouble;
And He knows those who trust in Him.
NKJV

Psalm 34
1. I will bless the Lord at all times;
His praise shall continually be in my mouth.
2. My soul shall make its boast in the Lord;
The humble shall hear of it and be glad.
3. Oh, magnify the Lord with me,
And let us exalt His name together.
4. I sought the Lord, and He heard me,
And delivered me from all my fears.
NKJV

Table of Contents

Hearing the bell signaling someone had entered the front of the cabinetry shop where he worked, Brendon Conroy sighed, staring down at the dark-stained latex gloves he was wearing and then at the end table he had almost finished staining. A quick decision had him returning to the staining. It just can't wait, he thought. If I leave it, then I have to start all over with a new table, and that I just can't do. Lord, why now? I'm on my own, Lawrence is away doing deliveries. He finally stripped off the gloves, tossing them into a waste receptacle on his way to the front, his mind still on the work he needed to accomplish that day. Not a lot, he thought, given that it was a long holiday weekend coming up and he was looking forward to that. The cabinetry shop had become quite busy, and Lawrence was happy, but Brendon just wanted a break. He hadn't had time off in a close to a year, he thought, other than when he had taken time to work on finding the culprits in the adventures his friends at the Barnabas Foundation seemed determined to have.

Running a hand through his jet-black hair, Brendon paused just inside the workroom, peering through the doorway, not seeing anyone in the showroom, but he knew he had heard the doorbell. He shook his head before he walked out onto the floor, searching about the model furniture that Lawrence had set up in it. He frowned as he studied the short, heavyset man who was standing at the window, staring out, appearing to be just a customer, but something about him rang alarms bells in Brendon's mind. He had seen too many of his friends go through danger not to be concerned. Lord, I have no idea what I am about to face, but You do. Please, protect me.

"Can I help you?" Brendon paused in the middle of the room, his eyes scanning quickly for anything that was out of the ordinary. He faintly heard the buzzer as the back door opened and frowned some more. That couldn't be Lawrence, he thought. He had indicated that he would not be back today, at least not until dark.

The man turned slowly, a sneer covering his face, as he looked Brendon up and down. "I'm looking for a young lady. She was seen entering these premises." The man's hand flicked in disdain at the furniture. "Though why she would do that is beyond me."

Brendon shrugged, his dark gray eyes watchful. "haven't seen or heard anyone today. I've been too busy. If that's all you want, there's the door." His head nodded that way as he squinted at his watch. "I need to lock up. It's closing time."

"No, it's not." The man pranced forward, his shiny dress shoes seeming too small for his feet. "It's not four o'clock yet."

"But you see, I can close up early. I'm in charge this afternoon, and I say the business is closed." Brendon paced over to the door, anger briefly flaring in him, as he yanked open the door and held out a hand for the man to leave. "I have no idea who you are, or who you are looking for, but I do know that you're not looking for any furniture. So I would suggest you leave and leave now."

"I'll have your job, young man." The man's anger became palpable.

Brendon suddenly grinned. "Go for it. I doubt that will work." He barely let the man get through the door before he had slammed the door, shoved home the locks, turned the open sign to closed, and then pulled down the blind on the door. He moved to one side where he could see the man, who stood in the parking lot, staring around before he walked around the building. He stood once more in the parking lot before he approached the door, shaking it and then hammering at it, demanding that it be opened for him. Brendon grinned to himself. This time, it wouldn't work. He had a good idea of who this was, a new import to an accounting firm in town, and one who had alienated everyone that he had been in contact with.

Brendon moved back through the showroom, flicking off the lights before he paused at the doorway to the workroom, feeling someone was there, but not seeing anyone. He shrugged, putting it off to being tired and needing to get away. His thoughts turned to his plans for the next week, a week that he had booked off, desperately needing a break. He had no real plans, he decided, but just knew he wanted to get away.

Cleaning up from his staining and setting everything back into its place, Brendon walked back through the showroom, ensuring all the windows were closed and locked, and everything there was ready for the weekend. He ducked his head to stare out the window, a smile creeping across his face as he watched his unruly guest pacing the parking lot, every so often glaring at the building. He turned, heading for the office, and setting it to rights for the weekend, before he paused, a frown crossing his face. No, he thought, there can't be anyone here but I did hear the back door buzzer. He began a systemic search, finally stopping near a large table and waiting before he ducked, a hand coming out to grasp the arm of the person hiding under it, pulling them out and to their feet.

Shock covered his face as he realized that the young man that he thought he was pulling out was really a young lady, around his age. His hand dropped from her wrist before he reached for her arm, leading her to a chair and then shoving her down, crouching down near her.

He watched carefully as she refused to look up before he sighed, rising to his feet and heading for the kitchen, to return with a bottle of water, finding the young woman heading for the back door. His long legs covered the distance quickly and a hand on her arm had her stopping, a whimper coming from her. He frowned once more at that and then spun her to face him, a gasp that he couldn't control wrenched from him at the bruising he could see on her face.

"Who did this to you?" His demands were met with silence. "I asked you, who did this to you?"

She shook in fear before she glanced up at him. "He did." Her voice was barely audible.

"Who did?" Brendon was at a loss to know who she meant.

"He did. The man that you were talking to." She wrapped her arms around herself, her face white with fatigue and pain and fear, the dark bruising, some of it turning yellow and green, showing ghastly against it.

"He did? When?" Brendon shook his head. "What am I do to with you? I can't let you out there. He's still waiting." He watched her shivering and sighed once more, pacing to the office and returning with his jean jacket, wrapping it around her, feeling her flinch at his light touch.

She pulled away from him, intent on finding the door and disappearing. Only, Brendon wouldn't let her. He reached past her, a hand flat on the door, holding it closed even as she tugged at the handle.

"Please? Let me go! I need to disappear. If you help me, he'll hurt you." Tears of fear and fatigue trickled down her cheeks and she swiped at them angrily.

Brendon's heart broke for her. Lord? Is this why I didn't take today off as I had planned? I needed to be here for this lady, whoever she is. And I feel myself being drawn into an adventure, just like my seven friends have already had. I hadn't planned on that, but You did. You planned this, didn't you, Lord? And now that I've met this lady, even without knowing her name, I just cannot walk away from her.

His hand slipped to her wrist and grasped it lightly, not letting her pull it away from him. He reached into his pocket for his keys, quickly opening the door and pulling her through before the door closed behind him, the security system set. He pointed to his truck parked nearby.

"That's my vehicle. In you go. Here, crouch down for a moment until we're out of here and then you can sit upright." He watched as she did that very thing before he closed the door and headed around the truck to climb up and behind the wheel, pulling away and out of the back of the lot, noting that the man had appeared, hands waving at him to stop. He grinned. Not this time, buddy. Not with this lady on board. I'm taking her to Anna and Doc. They'll help with her. He had referred to an older couple in the Barnabas Foundation building, Doc an emergency room physician, and his wife, Anna, who mothered all fourteen of the men and now the wives of some of the men.

Brendon pulled to the side of the road, shoving the transmission into park before he turned to the young lady with him. By this time, she had sat up on the seat, the seatbelt tight around her, and her hands clutching at his jacket, trying to get warm. She had no idea who he was or where he was taking her, but she felt safe for the first time in months. He will want an explanation, and I don't know that I can give him one, at least one that will make sense.

Brendon studied her in the fading daylight before he grinned.

"I'm Brendon Conroy. I am happy to meet you. And you would be?"

She shook for a moment, terror getting the better of her before his even baritone voice soothed her. She fingered her shoulder-length deep red hair before her dark brown eyes looked at him.

"Imly. Imly Dickerson."

"Emily? I am pleased to meet you." He watched as she shook her head. "What did I say?"

"It's not Emily. It's Imly - spelled i-m-l-y. A hangover from my mother's Irish heritage." Her head went back and her eyes closed for a moment, despair briefly flickering across her face. "I need to leave, Brendon. Being here with you puts you in danger. He won't stop until he finds me."

"And just what is it that he wants from you?" Brendon could feel the anger burning in him again, and had to pray hard to have it tamped down.

Imly stared at him. "You don't know him?"

"I know of him. I've seen him around town. No one likes him or wants anything to do with him." He stared at her, determined to get to the root of the issue. "But why is he after you?"

"He wants something from me. Something that isn't mine to give." Imly blinked rapidly. "My parents are not rich, not in money, but in heritage and ancestry, they are. He's not. He wants from my parents documents that would allow him to claim a heritage to a clan that isn't his to have. It can only go to the oldest in the family. And that is me when I turn 28, which will be shortly." She turned to face Brendon. "He is determined to get it one way or another, even if he has to marry me. That's why he beat me. I refused. I can't stand him. He is evil personified."

"Then, we will defeat him. That I can promise you. What else does he want?" Brendon waited before he spoke again. "There has to be something more."

188

"There is. There are rumours that the clan here in Ontario that Mom and Dad are part of has a hidden trove of jewels, gold, and documents that would indict leadership in this town in crimes. He's part of it, I think." Imly looked up, a scream rising from her throat, as a heavy object slammed against the window beside her, fracturing the glass into tiny pieces, but that didn't totally shatter the window.

Brendon took one look at the window and at Imly and then, transmission in drive, floored his accelerator and took off, leaving the man standing behind him, shaking a fist and waving the tire iron he held in the other hand.

"Is he for real?" He sped away from town, driving as fast as he felt he should, heading for the Barnabas Foundation building and safety. "I'm taking you to the building that I live in. There's an older couple there who will take care of you. Doc can assess your bruises, and don't refuse. We need to document these for the police. We also have a friend, a detective, who would come and talk to you."

Imly merely nodded, not sure of anything anymore. It was the first time in five or six months, she thought, that she felt safe and protected. Lord, are You still there? It seems You haven't been, but You must be, to lead me to this man, who is so willing to help where others wouldn't.

Finishing his examination or as much of it as he could, Doc Andrews finally moved from their spare room, leaving Anna with Imly, who was trying hard to convince the older woman that she just could not stay. She had brought danger with her, she insisted, staring in disbelief at Anna as the older woman just laughed. Anna explained that they had had danger come to their building with seven other couples, so what was one more? Anna laughed even harder when Imly stated that she was not part of a couple. Anna had reached to hug her, telling her to just wait, that the men in the building staked their claim on their ladies at their first meeting. Imly finally remembered to snap her mouth closed.

Doc headed for the kitchen, yawning, a hand rubbing at the back of his head. It had been a long day for him, the emergency department where he worked seemingly overrun with patients. He paused at the doorway, his eyes on Brendon, watching as the younger man just sat, his hands folded on the table in front of him, a puzzled look on his face. Brendon had slipped away long enough to his apartment to shower and change, returning as quickly as he could. He was deeply worried about Imly. Doc shook his head. Another one, Lord. Why is it that these young fellows have to meet their ladies when the ladies are in danger? He reached to pour himself a mug of coffee and then filled Brendon's mug again before he started searching through the cupboards.

Anna stood and watched him, a smile on her face, knowing exactly what he has looking for.

"You won't find them, Doc." Her smile widened as he glared at her.

"And why not? You know that I need my sweets."

"I know you do. Sit. I'll get them." Anna reached into the one cupboard that he had not searched and pulled out the container of squares. "Here you go."

"Thanks, love." He looked towards the door. "Imly?"

"I finally convinced her to have a shower. She didn't want to put us to any work, she said. She is adamant that she is leaving tonight. She didn't want to take the clothes that I handed her to wear until I sort of promised that she could pay for them. You know we won't let her do that very thing." Anna poured her own cup of tea and sat beside Doc, her eyes on Brendon, looking around as the door opened and then closed and footsteps headed their way.

Barnabas Carey, chairman of the Barnabas Foundation board, greeted them before his eyes lighted on Brendon.

"Doc?"

"He found a lady in distress, Barnabas, and brought her to us. I don't think he's planning on leaving until he sees her again. Besides, he tells us that his front passenger window needs to be replaced before he goes anywhere."

"And he's to be away on vacation next week." Barnabas moved around the kitchen with the ease of familiarity, finding a mug to fill with coffee, sitting at the table, and reaching into the container of squares that Doc shoved towards him.

Barnabas watched Brendon closely, concerned. He was like that with the other men in the building. What most people didn't know was that the Barnabas Foundation paid the men's wages, freeing up their employers to hire other staff without having to search for funds. It was part of the Foundation mandate, to do this in a way to encourage others. The foundation had been named in part for Barnabas by his father, Bruce, but it was also based on the Barnabas of the Bible, who had been an encourager to Paul.

Brendon finally looked up, surprised to see he was no longer alone. He opened his mouth to speak just as he heard a whisper of sound from the hallway and was then on his feet, moving towards the door. He found Imly standing just outside the kitchen door, her arms wrapped around herself, her hair still wet from her shower. She had a woebegone, lost little kitten look to her that instantly endeared her to Brendon, even more than she already was.

He moved to stand in front of her, waiting for her to look up, his heart breaking for her.

"Imly? Are you okay?" His voice was low, low enough that only she could hear him.

"I don't know, Brendon. I just don't know. I shouldn't be here." She looked up at him, fighting to regain control of her emotions, but losing the battle.

Brendon simply reached to enfold her in his arms, tightening them as she fought at first to free herself before she relaxed against him. He took the blanket that Anna handed him and wrapped Imly in it, surprising her when he simply lifted her into his arms, before he headed back to sit in the kitchen, not letting her go. He cradled her to him, looking up with a word of thanks as Doc set a cup of peppermint tea in front of him.

"Imly tells me that she likes her peppermint tea." Doc grinned at her as she peeked out from under the mess of wet hair. "You'll find that we keep a cupboard with just what our friends like to drink." He seated himself again, pushing over the container of squares. "Here. Help yourself. Anna won't let me eat them all."

She stared at him before turning her head to Brendon, discomfort showing briefly on her face at his close proximity before he nodded.

"Help yourself. They are good. But wait? Have you eaten at all today?"

She dropped her head before she shook it. "Not today. Nor yesterday. I think, I don't know. I think it's been four or five days."

Anna made a sound and was on her feet, heading for her pantry, returning with a container of soup from the freezer.

"Imly, here. I'll heat this. In the meantime, Doc, make the girl a sandwich. She can start with that."

Imly opened her mouth to protest just as Brendon's arms tightened slightly around her, stilling her words.

"It's okay, Imly. Let them. It's part of who they are, caregivers to us." He tilted his head to watch her, seeing the moment she acquiesced.

"Thank you. But it's a lot of work." She glanced around, startled to see Barnabas sitting near her, his eyes on his mug. "I'm sorry."

Barnabas looked up. "What are you sorry for?"

"For all this. I'm sorry. I don't know you." Her voice was soft, a natural softness, that brought a sense of peace to those who heard her.

"I'm Barnabas Carey."

Her eyes grew round. "You're him!"

"I am?" He grinned at her, receiving a wavering smile in return. "But, who is that? I mean. I know that I'm Barnabas, but that doesn't explain what you meant."

"Barnabas, you'll confuse the poor girl." Anna patted him on the top of his head as she moved to set the bowl of soup in front of Imly.

"I did, didn't it?" His grin widened. "I'm the Barnabas, or one of them, of the Foundation. Dad named it after me, in part."

Feeling uncomfortable at being the only one eating, Imly finally reached for the spoon and dipped it into her bowl of soup, Brendon moving them closer to the table, but definitely not letting go of her. She wondered at that, then shrugged inwardly. He made her feel safe and secure, and she wondered at that, too. No one, not even her father, had that effect on her.

Brendon didn't speak, content that Imly was eating, his heart raised in prayer for this lady. He just knew that he couldn't walk away from her, not yet, perhaps not ever. He sighed to himself. I did it, didn't I, Lord? I found my lady, one in distress, just like the others. I was praying that it wouldn't happen, but I just can't walk away from her. Lead in this, Lord. She's scared, worried, beaten in spirit and body.

Imly finally pushed the bowl and plate away, not able to quite finish either the soup or the sandwich, fatigue weighing down on her. Doc had made her another cup of her peppermint tea, just grinning at her protest that the cold cup would be just fine.

She looked around, finding Anna had moved away, intent on something, just what she wasn't sure. She didn't know that Anna had headed for the spare room, finding brand new sleepwear for her, laying out fresh towels, and then kneeling by the bed, to pray for her new friend. She didn't know the circumstances, but that was okay, she knew. God knew them. All Anna had to do was to pray.

Brendon reached for his mug of coffee, groaning slightly as his phone rang. At some point, Imly had simply stood up and moved to the chair beside him, keeping as close to him as she could. He scanned his messages, a grin on his face at one of them, Doc watching him keenly.

"Brendon?" When Brendon looked up, Barnabas drew in a breath, seeing the determination in his friend's eyes to keep the lady beside him safe. "Are you still planning on leaving in the morning?"

Brendon shook his head. "No, I don't think so. I had no real plans, after all. I was just going to drive around, find a likely spot to camp, and then move on. I have to have the window replaced and John said he'll have to order one in, that it likely wouldn't be in before Tuesday." He shrugged. "I'm fine with that." He glanced at Imly, finding her watching him.

"You were going to go away?" Imly fought the fear that she felt rising in her.

"I was, but I'm not. You need me here." Brendon raised a finger as she went to protest. "You do. Besides, God hasn't said that I can leave, and unless He does, I stay."

"You believe that?" She knew that was how her father thought and how she had, until the last two weeks. She despaired of ever having that certainty again.

"I do. With every fibre of my being." He shared a glance with Barnabas. "You mentioned your parents. Do they know where you are?"

Imly shook her head. "No, I don't think so. And they will be so worried." She rubbed at her face, and the two men with her could see the worry and stress that Brendon's question had raised. "I need to talk to them, but he took my phone. He smashed it in front of me."

Brendon pulled out his phone again, looking over at her. "What is their number?"

"I'm sorry?" Imly didn't understand exactly what he was asking.

"Your parents' phone number. Do you remember it?" He grinned at her as she stared at him before she remembered to snap her mouth closed, a frown coming on her face.

"I do. But why?"

"Because you are going to call them now, put their minds at rest. Where are you from?"

"From up north, near Sudbury. We live out in the woods, which is how he managed to kidnap me. Do you suppose that they put out a missing person's report on me? Or did he do something to make them think I had gone willingly with him?" She glanced up as Barnabas rose and moved to the hallway.

———

Barnabas turned slightly so he could watch her, his voice quiet as he spoke with their detective friend, Dallas.

"Dallas? Are you still on duty? Good. Brendon has a situation that we need you to look into. What's that? A lady?" Barnabas began to laugh. "It is. Her name is Imly Dickerson, from Sudbury way. It seems that she was kidnapped and brought her by Lewis Wills. That's right. Kidnapping. Assault. He's beaten her. Doc would be the one to tell you how bad if we can get Imly to agree. That's right. That's how you spell it. Thanks. No, we're at Doc's. Okay. Let me know."

Barnabas stood for a moment, his eyes thoughtful as they rested on Brendon, before he moved away, sending a group text message to the other twelve men in the building, asking for a meeting in the morning. Brendon needed their help this time. His phone chimed with prompt responses in the affirmative. He knew a couple of the men had planned to leave early in the morning, but this is what their friendship was like. Unless it was life and death that they leave, they simply postponed what they needed to do.

Buckley, the minister in the group, sent a separate message, asking for more information. Barnabas sent a quick reply before he pocketed his phone, walking back towards the kitchen, pausing as he heard Brendon and Imly speaking.

He drew in a deep breath as he realized just how close it had been for the two when Brendon's truck window had been shattered by Wills. Brendon had not mentioned that in front of Doc and Anna, and Barnabas was determined to find out why.

Hearing a tap at the door, he moved towards it, comfortable in letting in whoever it might be. Doc and Anna were around, Doc peeking around the doorframe of his office.

Dallas, the detective that Barnabas had contacted, stepped inside, a question on his face.

"What happened?"

Barnabas shrugged. "I haven't got the whole picture, but Imly has a lot of bruising on her face. She was abducted, brought here, and then somehow escaped, finding her way into the cabinetry shop. Brendon hasn't said much."

Dallas nodded, his eyes finding Doc, who had approached them. "Doc?"

"I need Imly's permission to tell you what all I found, but Barnabas is correct. She has been beaten, not given food, and then running for her life. I have no doubt of that fact."

Dallas nodded, moving slightly so he could watch the couple in the kitchen, seeing Brendon on his phone, his voice quiet, his eyes on Imly as he spoke.

His eyes on Imly, Brendon hesitated before he glanced at the kitchen clock, noting it was still early evening. He was exhausted, but he knew his emotions were all over the place, given what he had been through and from what Imly had detailed to him. He would need to talk with Barnabas and his friends, surmising that Barnabas had already put out a group text to set up a meeting. That is what he did, take care of them.

Dialing the phone with the number Imly had given him, he listened to it ringing on the other end, ready to leave a voice mail, when a male answered, his greeting abrupt.

"Mr. Dickerson? My name is Brendon Conroy. You don't know me, but I am a new friend of your daughter's, Imly." He stopped speaking as he heard a sound on the other end and then silence. He waited before he spoke again, his eyes on Imly, a hand reaching to cover hers that she was rubbing together. Imly's eyes never left his face.

"Imly? Do you know where Imly is? Do you know where my daughter is?" The voice was broken and full of emotion, her father close to tears.

"I do, Mr. Dickerson. I met her today and she is safe here with friends of mine. I work for the Barnabas Foundation, and she is safe in the building here with a physician and his wife who are some of its residents." Brendon's eyes slid closed as he heard Imly's father trying to control his sobs. He heard a feminine voice in the background. "Mr. Dickerson? I will let Imly have the phone but before I do, I should state that she is in grave danger. My friends and I will do what we can to protect her."

Brendon handed the phone to Imly and started to rise, remaining seated as she shook her head, her own hand reaching for his, her fingers cold as she grasped it as tight as she could. She stared down at the phone before she raised it to speak into it.

"Dad?" Her voice was barely audible and clouded with tears.

"Imly? Oh, thank God. You're safe. We have been so worried. You just disappeared and we didn't know what happened. No note. Nothing. Are you okay, lass?"

Imly could hear her mother as well, and for a moment, could not speak, tears clogging her throat before she could gain control.

"I will be, Dad. Mom. I'm sorry. I'm so sorry. I couldn't stop him. I couldn't get away." She could not continue, the phone falling from her hand as she bent over the table, her head buried in her arms.

Brendon's arm was around her even as he reached for the phone, hearing her father's pleas for her to answer him.

"Mr. Dickerson? We do need to speak about what happened. But first, Imly will need to give a statement to the detective who is waiting." Dallas had moved into the kitchen, quietly fixing himself a mug of much-needed coffee before sitting down across from them. "But what I can tell you is that a man by the name of Lewis Wills kidnapped her, brought her to my town where he is part of an accounting firm, has beaten her, threatened her life, tried to marry her, and mistreated her."

"What? Wills? Of course. The scoundrel. I wondered why he had been hanging around town and then coming out to our place, even with a restraining order against him." Imly's father, Ian by name, was growing angry. "We'll leave in the morning to come but it's a long drive."

Brendon spoke quickly. "No, that's not a good idea. Let me talk to Barnabas here. I'm sure he'll send his pilot, Andy, and the Foundation plane up there to get you." He looked up to see Barnabas nodding, his phone already out to call Andy. "In fact, he's right here and making arrangements. We'll make sure Andy has your contact information.

"I have to ask. Did you put in a missing person's report on your daughter?"

"We did, and it was to go province-wide but somehow I don't think it did. The officer we spoke to seemed to shrug it off, that Imly being an adult meant she had simply walked away without telling us. That is not our daughter."

———

"No, sir, I don't think it is. I'll have the detective ask around, but he's sitting here, shaking his head that he never received any word on that report."

Ian Dickerson sighed. "Somehow, we knew that. The officer is one that has been accused of shoddy work before but always manages to escape without any disciplinary action. This time, that won't happen."

Brendon spoke for a few more moments before handing the phone back to Imly, rising and walking away, needing to control the emotions and in particular, the anger, building in himself.

Setting Brendon's phone down finally, Imly swiped at her face, wincing at the pain from the bruising as she hit it. She jumped as a warm wet washcloth appeared in her line of sight before she took it was a murmured word of thanks and sweeping it at her face, relishing the warmth and how it made her face feel better. She looked up, startled to see she was alone with the detective, she thought he was, and looked around, panic beginning to build when she didn't see Brendon.

Dallas spoke. "Brendon is just outside the door. I need to get your statement and then he can come back." He grinned at her. "Now, if we're quick, you won't be long without him near you."

Imly frowned before she nodded, suddenly fatigued. "What do you want to know?"

"Take me back to what happened at your home."

Imly nodded, her eyes raising to catch a glimpse of Brendon, praying for courage to do what she had to, to bring Wills to justice.

"It started about five months or so ago, I think." Her brow wrinkled as her mind returned to the past. "Wills started hanging around town, sitting out in front of the office where I worked, coming in and asking me to go with him for meals, for coffee. It came to the point that my employer didn't let me go anywhere for work on my own. He went with me or he had one of his sons or nephews escort me.

"Dad knew and went and talked to him, with Wills promising to stay away from me, but he never did. We would find cards, flowers, and gifts from him on the front steps or the back porch or on my car. It came to the point that I took a leave of absence from my work, hiding at home. We talked to the police up there and took out a restraining order, but it never worked. He would come and go and not be seen. Even with the security cameras that Dad put it, it wasn't clear if it was him. He disguised himself that much.

"Anyway, about two weeks ago, I think, I had had to go into town for an appointment. When I came out, it was pouring rain and really dark. I hesitated for a moment, and that was all it took. A hand came around my mouth and an arm around me, trapping my own arms to my sides. I fought to get away but couldn't loosen the arm from holding me. I was picked up, carried to a vehicle, dumped inside, my hands bound and a gag over my mouth before I was shoved to the floor of the car and a blanket thrown over me. It wasn't Wills that did this. The man was too strong, too tall, and too young. But I heard his voice from the front seat. I don't know how long I was left like this before the blanket was removed and I was pulled up on the seat.

"Wills wasn't there but there were three other men, one driving, and one on either side of me. We would stop on occasions, I would be let out, but a hand was on my arm at all times. If I had to use the facilities, one of them stood outside the door. I couldn't escape. I tried. I fought them. After a day or so, we arrived here and I was taken to a building outside of town and locked into a room. It was bare, with just a mattress on the floor with some blankets. The attached bathroom only had the bare minimum of supplies. The windows were sealed. I had nothing to break them other than my hands and I tried that. They wouldn't break." She paused at that moment, reaching for the glass of water that Dallas had set in front of her, taking a drink. She tried to compose herself, barely able to.

Imly looked up at Dallas, knowing she needed to finish her statement, but ashamed of what had happened to her.

"Wills appeared the next day, unlocking the door, and standing there, not saying anything. He did this for a few days, many times a day, before he finally spoke, telling me that he wanted the heritage that would be mine. I was shocked, I think, unable to respond at first. When I finally did a few times later of his saying this, I just told him that he couldn't have it. It was a trust that came down to the oldest in the family and could not be passed on. He just laughed, an evil maniacal laugh.

"It was after that he started to hit me." Imly felt her face, feeling once more the blows that she had received. "I tried to avoid them, backing away from him, but he just followed me. Finally, I think it was about four days or so ago, he simply said that we would marry, and when I received my heritage documents, I would sign everything over to him. I knew then I had to escape or I would die. He had no plans to let me live, that much he had made obvious.

"Somehow that night, I shoved at him as he was hitting me, sending him off balance and to the floor. I stood, horrified for a moment, before I turned and fled, finding the stairs, running down them, reaching for the back door, and finding it opening under my hand. I hid for a while, watching as he searched for me before I ran for the road and followed it back the way I had been taken, reaching town the next day.

"I hid in the downtown area, seeing his men searching for me. I must have been spotted at one point as I hid near the cabinetry shop. Wills was there. I wanted to go in the front, as I had seen Brendon and thought maybe he would help me. I had heard comments on the street about how the Barnabas Foundation men would help and that Brendon was one of them. I couldn't go in the front door, but the back door opened. I didn't think it should have. I ran in and hid, not knowing if Wills would see me. Brendon found me and was bringing me here. He had stopped for a moment and that's when Wills appeared again. He must have followed us. That's how the window was damaged. He hit it with something. Brendon drove away after that and brought me here."

Imly stopped speaking, her emotions overcoming her for a moment, feeling drained in every way. Her spirit had been beaten down over the past two weeks, and she wondered if she would ever be free of the monster. The memories would linger, driving her awake in the night, to pace, looking over her shoulder for Wills to appear.

Dallas studied her for a moment before his eyes dropped back to his laptop, to scan through her statement, clarifying items as he needed to before he printed it and slid it across the table to her, a pen placed on top of it. He didn't wish to approach her any closer, seeing how close she was to running.

"If you would read through it, note anything we need to adjust, initial each page and then sign the last one and date it, I think that will do it for now." He smiled at her. "It's okay. This is how we'll do it. If I have to have you come into the department, then Brendon will bring you."

Imly stared at him for a long time before she dropped her eyes to the papers, not reaching for them again for long moments, leaving Dallas to wonder if she ever would. She finally began reading, her eyes heavy as fatigue weighed them down. Lord, will this end it? I can't do this anymore. He has taken too much from me, from Mom and Dad. From how many others? She finished signing her name and looked up, finding Dallas reaching for the papers, his eyes on her.

"How many?" Her voice was a bare whisper.

"I'm sorry." Dallas was puzzled.

"How many? How many others? How many others has he done this to?" Imly was on her feet, running from the room, searching for Brendon, finding him standing in the hall, just outside the kitchen door, his arms open to scoop her to him, his head bending over hers as she sobbed heartbrokenly.

——

Late that night, Brendon slumped in the corner of the couch in Doc's living room, his mouth against his hand as he braced his elbow on the arm. His thoughts were muddled, some dark, some questioning, some hopeful. He had tried to pray but felt his prayers went nowhere. Doc paused beside him, to set down a fresh mug of coffee, and then tucked a blanket around the younger man, before standing beside him, laying a hand on his head as he prayed for him.

Doc sank gratefully down into his recliner, popping the footrest up, a sigh coming from him. It had been a long day, he decided, and far from over. He was thankful that he did not have to work on the next day. He watched Brendon closely before his eyes moved to where Imly lay on the couch, her head resting on a thin pillow laying on Brendon's lap. Anna had covered her with a soft yellow blanket before she had headed to bed. Doc knew that she was not likely sleeping but instead holding vigil for her young friends. It was what she did. He sighed to himself again. Lord, this is what, the eighth one? Are we going to go through all fourteen of the young men? I mean, I know that You are there, that You have protected them, brought the ladies into their lives that are their soul mates, helpmeets, the ladies that they were looking for and praying for, but to have almost lost some to death? I don't know that we can continue like that. But You are almighty and in control.

Brendon's arm rested around Imly, protecting her from what, he wasn't even sure, but he only knew he had to. That danger was imminent to approach her, but he didn't know if she would let him be her protector. Her actions that night had given him hope. He only knew that she had captured his heart, already. He had laughed when the others had said that was how it was, but he couldn't laugh. Not now. Not when it had happened to him.

Doc finally spoke, breaking into his thoughts.

"Brendon? What are your plans?"

Brendon's eyes turned to him before he shrugged and then gestured with his hand. "To tell you the truth, Doc? I have no idea. All I knew today was that Imly needed someone to protect her, to get her away from Wills. This was the safest place I could think of to bring her."

"She's what, almost 28, she said?"

"She is. Why?" Brendon rubbed at his temple, a headache starting. "Her heritage. That comes to her when she's 28. How do we protect her? She said her birthday is in two weeks. Even with her parents here, that won't protect her from Wills."

"No, it won't." Doc remained quiet for a while, his thoughts muddled, an event totally unlike him. "Listen, Brendon. Don't say anything until I am finished. And when I am, I want you to earnestly pray over what I have to say.

"The only way to protect her is for you to marry her." Doc's hand went up as Brendon opened his mouth. "No, listen, please. As her husband, you would be able to guard her heritage, I suspect. She had indicated by her actions that she needs to be with you, that she thinks you will protect her. She is hesitant with the rest of us, but not with you. You rescued her from danger, and part of her reaction is that she is grateful, but it goes deeper. She sees you as part of her life. I am not saying that you should but it is something to consider."

Brendon's eyes had not moved away from Doc's face as he spoke, the words clarifying his thoughts.

"Doc, those are my thoughts. I have been trying to come up with something, short of that, to protect her, and I just can't. I am not sure if she would ever agree, but we need to do something until we can prove Wills' actions and have him arrested. Dallas is working on that, but he didn't hold out hope that it would be quick. Somehow, I don't think that Wills is working on his own. He didn't strike me as being that smart." He looked down as he felt Imly stirring and then sitting up.

Imly pushed the hair from her face, her eyes on his face, a wonder crossing hers, and then hope.

"You would do that, Brendon?" Her voice was soft, soft enough that he had to lean down to hear her. Doc watched them closely, confirmation in his mind that these two were meant to be together.

"Do what?" He had an idea of what she was asking.

"Marry me? We don't know each other. I didn't think that couples did that." She looked askance at him as both he and Doc laughed.

"It's okay, Imly. A friend of ours, Baird, married like this. His wife, Berneen, married him to save his life. They are very much in love." Brendon just shook his head at the memory.

"She did? Wow!" Imly looked over at Doc to see him nodding.

"That's true, Imly. And our friend, Buckley, who is also our pastor, was taken with them and forced to perform the marriage."

Imly looked back at Brendon, then down at the hand he was holding out. She prayed, desperate to have an answer, before she reached to lay her hand in his, finding his closing over hers.

"I will do my best, Imly, with all my being and with God's help to keep you safe." Brendon made his pledge to her, knowing that his life may well be on the line and that he might not survive, but that was his character and his heritage. His parents had been survivors, living in the Yellowknife Territories, as missionaries there, both meeting their death from illness, leaving him an orphan at age 19. He had been in trade school at that point when Barnabas had approached him about moving to Southern Ontario. He had questioned Barnabas, who merely shrugged, said God told him to find orphans who shared his initials and offer them employment.

Imly finally nodded, surprised when he reached to hug her and drop a kiss on her forehead. She felt safe with him, something that she had not even with her father. Why that was, she wasn't sure.

Brendon stood, a hand reaching for her, pulling her to her feet, before he was still and unmoving, his eyes on the far wall, biting at his lip. He looked down at her, not remembering that Doc was in the room, but that would not have mattered if he had remembered.

"Again, Imly. I will do everything with my being to protect you. Only God knows how difficult that will be." He smiled at her uncertainty. "Now, how be you head off to bed? We'll talk in the morning. Doc or Anna will come to get me if you need me. They have also left a phone beside your bed, unlocked, and it has my name and number programmed into it. Call me, no matter what time, if you need me. Do you understand?"

She gave a hesitant smile. "I do. Thank you." She surprised both of them by reaching to hug him before she reached to fold the blanket, whisper a goodnight to Doc, and head down the hall, Brendon moving so that he could follow her progress.

His head turned as he felt Doc's hand on his shoulder and heard then Doc's prayer for him and him alone. He knew Doc prayed for each of them daily, but this was different. Tonight had changed the course of his life and he would not step back from Imly, not when she needed him.

"God bless you, Brendon. Head off for your own bed. I suspect you'll be here early in the morning." Doc paused, a yawn cutting into his words. "Barnabas said Andy was heading up to Sudbury tonight and would connect with her parents early in the morning. He has taken three security guards from the team with him. Barnabas is taking no chances. Two of them will stay at their place for now, until we can sort out what they want to do. He doesn't think that her parents will be safe nor their property."

"I doubt it will be. Thanks, Doc." Brendon hesitated and then turned and walked away, the door closing quietly behind him, heading for his own apartment and his bed. Only he never made it to his bed. He dropped to his knees instead and spent hours in prayer, before he rose, showered and dressed for the day, and then wandered his apartment, imagining Imly moving around it, assessing what he needed to change. He finally sighed. He would wait until he found out what her likes and dislikes were. He searched for his wallet as the dawn broke, heading for his truck, broken window and all, intent on rousing a friend who had a jewelry store. He had some rings to buy and he wanted to find the right one. His friend was an early riser, Brendon knew, and would not hesitate to open up his store for him.

Later that morning, Brendon stopped just inside the door of the conference room, his gaze roaming the room, seeing all of the men except for Barnabas, gathered there, quiet conversation, teasing, and laughter filling the air. He smiled. Each one was from a different province or territory, but all had become close friends, dividing without intention into two teams of six, with Breck and Barnabas as their leaders.

He jumped as he felt a hand come down on his shoulder. Buckley stood there, a grin on his face, but concern in his eyes. He had been through similar situations with seven of the men and had prayed that the other seven, including himself, would not face adventures as they termed it.

"Brendon?"

"Buckley?" Brendon mimicked his tone of voice, a grin covering his face.

"Brendon? You too?" Buckley shook his head. "I thought that we told you, seven was enough. The rest of us aren't to undergo adventures."

Brendon began to laugh, bringing the attention of the others to him. "Sorry, Buckley. Somehow, the memo regarding that missed me." He sobered. "I am sure before you ask." He grinned suddenly. "Do you have a date free for us?"

Buckley laughed as well, his own words coming back to haunt him. He had offered dates to two of the couples, only to have his words come back at him from them.

"I do. Today, in fact." He grinned again as he moved away, Breck moving into his space.

"Brendon?" Breck's voice held the concern he felt, his eyes studying his friend closely.

"Breck? She's in trouble, just like the others. I can't walk away from her. She needs me."

"I know you and your heart. You have prayed over this?" Breck watched him carefully. Serving as Barnabas second-in-command, Breck assessed the men on a weekly basis, meeting for prayer with each one.

"I have, most of the night, in fact." Brendon rubbed at his tired eyes. "I have not had God say no. If anything, it's as if He's given His permission and His blessing. Her parents are being flown in today from Sudbury. Andy went to get them."

Breck nodded. "That's what Barnabas said." He looked behind Brendon. "Here's Barnabas now. Let's find our seats, Brendon."

Breck moved away. As Brendon took a step after him, Barnabas' hand rested on his shoulder.

"Brendon? Doc said I should talk to you." Barnabas' voice held concern.

Brendon hesitated and then nodded, a bleak look crossing his face for a moment. "Doc said that, did he? He suggested something last night. Imly had awakened as we were talking. We are going to marry, Barnabas, as soon as we can. I, no, we, need to talk to Buckley about that."

"You're sure?" Like Breck, Barnabas had no doubt that Brendon had prayed it through.

"I am. So is Imly. Doc pointed out that I seem to be the only one that makes her feel safe. I know that's no reason to marry, but I can't do anything less."

Barnabas studied him before he nodded. "Another one. Brendon, she has your heart. That I can tell. I watched her last night. It went beyond just feeling safe with you. You make her feel cherished and wanted and loved. She needs that after what she went through. I can't guarantee, none of us can, that it will turn to love, but it's a basis that God can and will work on. We've seen it with Baird and Berneen, for example. Come. Find your seat. We need to spend some time in prayer for all of us but particularly you two. You're setting off on an adventure, and I fear for you both."

The men had broken off into groups of two to pray, a common practice for them. Brendon finally shifted around his chair, his eyes on Barnabas as he sat, his head down, his hands laying on the folder on the table in front of him. No one spoke, knowing that Barnabas would open the discussion when he was ready.

Barnabas finally raised his head, his searching for the seven friends who were married: Baird and Berneen, Benen and Cadee, Blair and Devaney, Bradon and Ennis, Brady and Fynn, Branigan and Guenivere, and Brandon and Hagen. Now, Brendon and Imly. He thought it was heading that way last night, but he didn't expect it to happen so soon.

He had heard from Andy. When they had arrived at her parents' home, the house was empty. The doors were broken in and there were signs that her parents had fled quickly, leaving everything but it seemed their identification behind them. Andy and the security guards were searching, but they needed to speak with Imly to see if she had any idea where her parents would flee to. Andy said there seemed to be a vehicle missing. He had been in touch with Dallas, given that he was involved in the case.

Buckley watched Brendon closely, knowing he would have to have a talk with him. He prayed for him, and was it Imly? He wasn't quite sure on the name, his attention going back to Barnabas as he cleared his throat.

"Fellows, Brendon here has become involved in a situation, similar to what seven of you have gone through. He has rescued a lovely lady by the name of Imly Dickerson, who actually hid in his workroom yesterday to escape the man who had her kidnapped and brought here. There are details that are still being investigated. Dallas is involved and has been in contact with the police in the Sudbury area. Imly was kidnapped by Lewis Wills, who we are all familiar with. I can safely say, I think, that each one of us has had a run-in with him at some point.

"Imly has indicated that Wills is determined to obtain a heritage that she has coming to her when she turns 28, in what I believe is two weeks. He has beaten her and also told her that she would marry him. We have no doubt that she would not survive any length of time.

"Imly has been frank with us, I believe, in stating that the heritage only goes to the oldest in the family. There are other issues that we are investigating that may be related to this." Here, he paused, his eyes on the men, hearing the quiet comments and the subdued anger in the voices.

"Andy has flown up to bring her parents back, but they seem to have disappeared. He thinks that they have gone on the run and into hiding, but he's not certain on that. Two of the security guards will stay there and search. One will drive back and search on the way down. Andy is flying back today, but will head back up, if he needs to."

Barnabas waited for questions, but none came. He nodded. He knew the hearts of the men and knew that they would be in prayer for the situation and in particular for Brendon. His attention turned then to Brendon, finding him looking down, his hands rubbing together. He is nervous and uncertain, Lord. Only You can bring him the peace He needs. We need to praise You all the time, but it is so difficult in these situations.

"Fellows, Brendon has shared something with me. I know that he has prayed it through and feels it is the only answer for this situation. He tells me Doc suggested that he and Imly marry. We know Doc. He does not suggest something unless he is positive that God has laid it on his heart to do so. Brendon says that Imly overheard the conversation. Their agreement is that they will marry, and as soon as possible. We need to bathe them in prayer as they undertake what will be a dangerous step, for Imly, but in particular, for Brendon. Wills, from what I know of him, will not take this without a fight. We need to stand together. And, yes, we will be working this, just as we did for each one of you seven. Any questions?" He looked towards the door as a tap came to it, and it cracked open.

Anna appeared, distress on her face, searching for Brendon, who had risen and walked towards her.

"Brendon? Can you come? Imly needs you. She tried to call her parents and can't reach them."

"Certainly." He glanced back at Barnabas, who waved him away, concern on his face.

The men all stood, watching intently as Brendon walked away. They turned in unison to Barnabas, finding him staring at the closing door, a shuttered look on his face, that smoothed away quickly.

Branigan spoke. "Where do we start, Barnabas? We can do some today, but Guenivere and I do need to leave by noon." He paused. "Can the ladies meet with her?"

"I agree. I think they should." Baird spoke up. "Not all of them at once, of course. But who would be best? Berneen, I think, given how we married."

"Berneen, for sure. Cadee? Fynn?" Buckley named two other of the ladies.

"Let Anna decide." Breck spoke up. "I agree with Berneen. But Anna will have a sense of who Imly needs to speak with. And just make sure you spell her name correctly. It's i-m-l-y, Brendon tells me."

Brendon's footsteps slowed as he approached the lobby of the building, Anna's hand on his arm before she pointed to one side. Both sides of the lobby had a sitting area, with a gas fireplace facing each other. Imly paced near the one area, her arms wrapped around herself, panic in her movements. Brendon's steps picked up speed as he walked towards her.

Imly spun as she heard footsteps, her panic increasing until she recognized Brendon. She flew towards him, her arms around him as his surrounded her, hugging her tight. Anna stood to one side, distress on her face for the younger woman.

"Hey, sweetheart. What happened?" Brendon waited patiently, knowing Imly would speak when she was ready. He was not about to push it.

"I tried to call Dad and Mom. They didn't answer their cell phones. I tried to call the landline. He answered, Brendon. He was in their house and answered their phone. He laughed when he recognized my voice. He told me that he was coming for me, that I would marry him and sign over everything to him."

Brendon felt her tears wetting his flannel shirt as he hugged her tighter before he simply swept her into his arms and headed over to one of the chairs, sitting down, hugging her tight to him again. He looked up at Anna and then at Berneen and Hagen as they appeared, concern on their faces.

"It's okay, sweetheart. Andy and the men are searching for your parents. He said that he thinks they're fine. But we need to talk."

Imly leaned back so that she could look up at him, studying his face, seeing the strength in it that she thought she had imagined last night. He had a look in his eyes that said she was important to him, the most important thing besides God, and that he cherished her. She sighed. He fit the picture of the knight that her mother had woven into her bedtime stories. Imly had convinced herself that he didn't exist, but he did and he was holding her.

"We do?" Her voice was soft, with traces of tears lacing it.

"We do. I talked to Buckley just a bit ago. He's our minister. We could be married this afternoon if we had a license. And that we could likely get. I know the clerk at the city hall. He would help us."

"He would?" She just shook her head. "I don't know, Brendon. I just don't know."

"I know, sweetheart. It's a big step." He looked up at Berneen sat down near them. "Here's Berneen. She's the one that we told you about last night, who married Baird to save his life. If you want to talk to her, she's willing to do just that."

"She would? She doesn't know me." Imly jumped as Berneen spoke.

"No, I don't know you, but I want to. Brendon has chosen you to be his family. That makes you part of the Foundation family. We help each other out." Berneen grinned. "I was the first one, so I guess you can blame me for starting it all."

Imly stared at Berneen, a frown on her face. "I saw you."

"You did? When?"

"Two days ago. You were downtown, helping someone. I almost approached you but I saw Wills looking for me."

"Oh, I wish you had. I would have gladly helped you to hide from him." Berneen grinned at her, seeing Imly beginning to relax. "So, do we talk? If Brendon is planning on marrying you today, we need to do some fast work." Berneen stood, waiting for Imly to stand as well, in no hurry.

Imly stared at her before she turned her attention back to Brendon. "Brendon?"

"It's up to you. It is your decision. If you want to just sit here and let me hold you, I will gladly do that. If you want to go with Berneen, and maybe meet some of the other ladies, then I'm fine with that." He looked up to see Buckley standing beside Anna. "And here is Buckley. He would like to meet you as well." Brendon's tone was gentle, not as one talks to a child, but it held understanding that he knew it was difficult for her. He would let her make her decision and then back her, his voice said.

Imly finally nodded, standing and moving towards Buckley.

"You're the minister?"

"I am. I am pleased to meet you, Imly. We've been waiting for years to do just that." Buckley grinned at her frown. "You see, each of the fellows has not dated or shown interest in anyone until they met their lady. That made each of us anxious to meet the ones who would be chosen. You are a beautiful lady, and Brendon will take care of you and cherish you." Buckley nodded towards Brendon. "Now, we have to set a date. I understand if you want to wait until your parents can be here, or we can track down our friend, the town clerk, obtain the license, and then you can marry this afternoon. Berneen and Anna will take care of fixing you up, I would suspect."

"That's exactly right, Buckley." Anna's arm came around Imly and Imly leaned against her. "But it is your decision, Imly, just as Brendon has said. Unless you agree, we go no further until you do."

"I think." She turned in a panic, searching for Brendon, finding him right behind her, reaching for her, to gather her close. She finally nodded. "Today, Brendon. I feel doom hanging over us, and I want this over. He will try his best to do something before my birthday, and I can't let that happen. Once I have my heritage, no one can touch it. That much Dad has said. This is the dangerous part."

"Then, sweetheart, go with the ladies. I am sure the other ladies are around and I know Hagen's twin sisters will want to be in on it." He bent, kissed her forehead, and then stepped back, letting Anna and Berneen move in and sweep her away.

"She's anxious, Brendon." Buckley came to stand beside him. "She was in panic mode, Anna said."

"She was. He has her scared. And I can't say that I blame her. We need to pray and pray hard for her and her parents. Wills will try anything, and when he's thwarted, her life will be meaningless to him. I can't let him hurt her."

"No, you can't. Listen, I talked to Eddie. He can access what he needs for us, just needs your identification. Do you have Imly's?"

"I do. She gave it to me last night for some reason." Brendon turned. "I gather you're driving."

"That I am. Let's go get what we need. You need flowers for your sweetheart. Anna called the florist. She's expecting you to stop by. Rings?"

"I have those. Frank opened up for me early this morning."

"Of course, he would." Buckley headed into town, his eyes watching the vehicle behind him. "We have company."

Brendon twisted to look behind him. "And we do. I don't think it's Wills. Imly said he answered the phone at her parents when she called. I need to pass that on to Dallas."

"One of his henchmen then. Now, do you want the ceremony in the church or in the chapel in the building? I would suggest the chapel."

"I agree but I want Imly's opinion on that. I won't make any decisions for her."

Imly turned to stare at herself in the full-length mirror in Anna's bedroom, not recognizing herself in the long lace-covered white dress, her hair covered by a lacy veil. Sadness wafted through her. Her mother should be here to share this moment. Her father should be the one to walk her down to Brendon. And neither were here. Brendon had sent in her flowers, with a note she had read in private, simply stating that he was glad that she had agreed to be his sweetheart and signed with all his love. Her fingers had covered her mouth when she read that, not sure if he really meant it. She was scared for him, not wanting him harmed but knowing that it was a real possibility. Wills would not take her escaping from him lightly. She prayed, prayed hard, and then her prayers turned to praise, as she had been taught, praise that God had protected her and provided for her.

Doc watched as she walked towards her, her bouquet in her hands, a sad look flittering across her face. He sighed. He had walked his own daughter down the aisle to her groom, and Imly's father should be the one walking his own daughter to her groom.

Doc smiled as she looked up at him, surprise on her face to find him in a suit and tie, a simple flower on his lapel, confused for a moment.

"Imly. Your father's not here. Will you let me meddle in your special day? May I have the privilege of standing in for him, not taking his place, of course? Will you do me the honour of letting me walk you to Brendon?"

She stared up at him, silent for a moment, tears blinding her before she blinked them away.

"Doc, I don't know how you knew, but yes, I would like that. You have become special to me. Thank you." Imly reached to hug him. "Now, where do we need to be? I'm not familiar with the building."

"Then, my lady, I will show you." Doc crooked his elbow, a grin on his face, as he waited for her to tuck her hand into it and let him lead her away, down to the main floor and then down a corridor to a chapel.

They could hear the sound of music before Doc opened the door, allowing her to glance in before they entered. She was surprised, shocked in fact, at the number who had gathered. She glanced up at Doc.

"They're all friends, Imly. The men from the building. The ladies. Some of our security team. Brendon's employer and his family. You have become part of a large family now. No, we are not a cult but a group of believers who care deeply for one another."

An hour later, Imly stood in the rose garden on the Foundation grounds, the late roses scenting the air heavily as Brendon kept an arm around her, laughing at the comments directed his way, making sure that Imly knew she was part of them now. None of them heard the rustling of approaching bodies. The two men stopped, shock briefly on their face as they saw Imly in her wedding dress, tucked close to Brendon. A few minutes of angry conversation occurred before one raised a weapon, pointing it at Brendon.

Brendon looked around suddenly, feeling someone watching them, but not seeing anyone. A sudden jolt to his body had him flying backward to lie still, Imly falling with him, a scream breaking from her.

The men spun, the husbands shoving their wives to the ground and covering them with their bodies. The security men searched and then headed towards the woods, directly towards the two men who fled.

Brady, a paramedic, crawled rapidly towards Brendon, trusting that he would be kept safe, Doc heading that way as well. They paused, their eyes on Imly, who lay still, shock keeping her that way.

"Imly?" The sharpness of Doc's voice cut through her shock. "Are you hurt?"

"No, I'm not." She twisted in Brendon's limp arm. "Brendon! Oh, dear Lord, please, don't let him die because of me."

"Imly. We're going to take a look at him. Brady here is a paramedic. But we will need you to move." Doc waited patiently as Imly shook her head.

"No, I'm not moving. It's his shoulder, Doc. What happened?"

Brady crawled closer, his hands already assessed the wound. "He was shot, Imly. We don't know by who." He looked up at a sound from her, almost the sound a wounded animal would make. "We'll look after him. He would want you safe. What we need you to do is to crawl towards Breck over there. He's right behind you. He'll look after you. We'll be right behind you, but Brendon would want you to do what we ask you to do."

Imly stared at him before she nodded. "Yes, he would. Please? Don't let him die because of me." She turned, her eyes on Breck as she crawled towards him, fear lending speed to her pace.

Breck wrapped an arm around her and then lifting her to her feet, swept her rapidly towards the building and inside, heading for the infirmary, knowing that was where Doc and Brady would bring Brendon.

Imly paced, fear in her heart that Brendon was indeed dead. She looked up as she heard shuffling in the hallway and then Brendon appeared, a hand clamped to his shoulder, pain on his face, supported by Doc and Brady.

Brendon groaned as he sank down on the bed, his eyes closing from pain before they opened and he squinted, looking for Imly. He beckoned to her, reaching out a hand to her. Imly took it, disregarding the blood that covered it, fear on her face.

"Brendon?"

"I'm okay, sweetheart. Doc and Brady will patch me up. They want to take me into Emergency. Will you go with me? You need to change." His eyes closed against the pain as he bit his lip to keep from groaning.

Imly stood, horrified that he had been shot. She jumped as a hand touched her arm and Anna spoke to her, gently drawing her away and to another room, helping her from her wedding finery and into jeans and a sweater, a wet cloth in her hand to wash the blood from Imly's hand.

———

Imly stood once more beside Brendon, watching as Doc and Brady worked on Brendon, before he was helped to his feet and walked out to Doc's vehicle, to slide onto the back seat, his head going back on the seat for a moment from the pain, before he looked for Imly, reaching a hand for her, and then tucking her close to him.

221

Imly perched on the edge of a seat in the waiting room, her eyes on the door to where she knew Brendon was being assessed. She didn't see the men gathering close around her, to hide her and protect her. Berneen sat beside her, an arm around her, knowing only that Imly needed a friend with her. And Berneen considered Imly a friend, even if she was just a new friend.

Anna sat on her other side, her heart hurting for Imly, her thoughts changing to prayer, watching as Dallas spoke with the men and then the ladies before he approached Imly, pausing to study her before he crouched down in front of her, into her line of sight.

Imly jumped as Dallas suddenly appeared before her, not having seen him approaching her.

"I'm sorry."

"What are you sorry for?" Dallas was puzzled.

"I'm sorry Brendon got hurt. It shouldn't have happened. I brought this to him. It's my fault." Imly refused to look at Dallas, her eyes locked on the door, wishing someone would just come and get her. Doc stood for a moment, watching her, before he walked towards her, standing out of her line of sight.

"It's not your fault, Imly. Brendon knew what he was doing. He would have assessed the risks and made his decision. You were his main concern, not himself. We'll talk more. But right now, Doc is here to take you to Brendon." Dallas rose, letting Doc move towards Imly.

Imly was on her feet, almost running towards the doors, Doc reaching to stop her.

"Just a moment, Imly. I will take you in, but we will be taking Brendon to surgery. The bullet didn't hit anything vital, but it did tear through some muscle. That will heal."

"It will?" Imly shifted impatiently, just wanting to be with Brendon. "But then he can't work."

"That's not important right now. He's worried about you, Imly. He's afraid Wills will have you taken from here. It's a perfect opportunity." Doc paused outside a room, a hand on her arm. "Dallas is taking precautions. Barnabas has brought in some of the off-duty security people to help guard you two, who, by the way, came in willingly. We'll do everything we can to protect you, but you need to stay with one of us or the police, and if we say run, you run."

Imly nodded, her attention not really on Doc and what he was saying. Realizing that, he sighed. *Another lady, Lord, who is so focused on her man that she is putting herself at risk. Protect her Lord. I don't know if we can go through what we did with Bradon and Ennis, almost losing them.*

With Doc's hand on her arm, Imly stood for a moment, her eyes on the nurses as they moved around a stretcher before Doc nudged her forward. She stopped at Brendon's bedside, her eyes only on his face, not lifting to any of the equipment. *He's too white, Lord. What did I do? I brought him to this. I hurt him. I can't do this.* She moved backward, intent on running and hiding, leaving Brendon to his friends. She just knew that she was responsible and hated that.

Brendon shifted uncomfortably on the bed, his eyes opening before he groaned, a hand reaching for his shoulder. He searched, looking for Imly, finding her standing near him, but not close enough. He frowned at the fear on her face as well as an emotion showing that he just could not read. His hand out, he beckoned her closer, reaching to grasp hers as she came closer.

"Imly? You're okay? You didn't get hurt?" His eyes narrowed against the pain, but he kept focused on her, ignoring the activity around him.

Imly shook her head. "No, I didn't, but you did. It shouldn't have happened, Brendon. I'm sorry. Maybe we shouldn't have married."

Brendon struggled to sit up, against the protests of the medical staff, his only focus Imly. He wrapped her in his good arm, feeling her struggle when he did so until she relaxed, her arms coming around him.

"It's okay, sweetheart. I knew the risks. God didn't stop us from marrying. He will protect us. We may not like what we have to go through, but He is there. What's the saying? Praise Him in the storms? That's what we will do." His head dropped against the softness of her hair. His voice whispered softly in her ear as he continued. "We met under difficult circumstances, but I would be lost without you." He glanced up and past her as he heard the clatter of wheels and the team from the operating room appeared. "They've come for me, sweetheart. Stick with the men from the building. They'll protect you. They'll also work on solving this. It's what we do."

Imly nodded, unable to trust her voice to speak. Her arms tightened around him, reluctant to let go.

Brendon's voice softened even more as he prayed for his lady, not himself, his prayer turning to praise for God's protection. When he was finished, he paused before he kissed her forehead. His eyes on her face, he nodded. "I love you, Imly. Remember that." With that, his arms loosened and he dropped back on the stretcher, his eyes closing against the pain, giving up the fight to stay alert.

Imly stood, Doc's arm around her, watching as Brendon was transferred to the other stretcher and then wheeled from her sight. She followed as close as she could, Doc walking with her. She didn't see Brady and Barnabas approaching and then walking with her. Doc shook his head at the two men before he directed her steps to an elevator, to walk her into the surgical waiting room and make her sit. Anna was waiting and just swept her into her arms, holding her as she shuddered, unwilling to let any tears fall.

Barnabas watched closely before he turned to Doc, finding Dallas standing nearby.

"Doc?"

"The bullet tore through muscle. They'll repair it. He'll not be working for a few weeks. Once it has healed, we'll get him into physiotherapy. It's Imly I'm worried about. She's about ready to run." Doc tilted his head to watch her. "She blames herself."

"I know she does. They all have." Barnabas spoke quietly. "I heard from Andy. They still have not located her parents, but someone that they talked to mentioned another home halfway between here and their home. Imly didn't mention that."

"They have?" Dallas spun. "I'll be back. I still need to talk to Imly." He was away before Barnabas could continue.

Barnabas shook his head even as Brady grinned at him.

"Didn't expect that?" Brady sobered. "Listen. Those of us who had planned to be away aren't leaving. We'll be heading back to the building and the conference room, setting up to research as we have. Does she know Emma, by chance?"

Barnabas gave a bark of laughter. Emma Finlay was well known for tracking down people and addresses and whatnot that no one else could find.

"It would be nice, but I have no idea. See what you can find." Barnabas turned as he heard his name called. Hagen's sisters stood there, Berneen with them. "Girls?"

"Barnabas, does she have any clothes? I mean, of her own?" Holly was upset, not quite framing her words as she should.

"I don't think so, Holly. Why? You want to go shopping for her?" Barnabas grinned before he reached to hug each of the twins. "How be you head off then? Berneen, you're with them?"

"I am. I have a good idea of what she wants and likes." Berneen's head turned as her brother, Darbi, spoke from beside her.

"I'm in, too. Breck was looking for you two, Haley. He said something about needing to take you to some stores?"

Haley grinned. "He did? Good." She turned as Breck appeared. "Breck?"

"Here you two are. Come on. I want to go shopping." He winked at them, causing them to grin, before they reached to tuck their hands into his arms that he was holding out for them. Breck was a favourite of theirs and they knew that he was ready to have fun with them shopping.

Berneen shook her head before she grabbed at Darbi's arm.

"Let's go. They'll leave without us."

Doc just shook his head, knowing that Breck would pay for everything for Imly, without saying anything.

"Doc? How is Imly?" Barnabas had turned to watch her.

"That is a good question. The last two weeks have beaten her down, I think. She's subdued, terrified, looking over her shoulder. Now, this with Brendon. He's been the only one to reach through to her and he's not available to her right now. That concerns me. That and the fact that her parents aren't here. What's the story on that? Are they on the up and up or are they involved deeper than we know?" He walked away, leaving Barnabas staring after him.

Late that night, Brendon raised the head of his bed, wincing as a shaft of pain shot through his shoulder. Thanking God that it was not his dominant hand, he searched the room, not finding Imly there. He found the release to the bed rail, lowered it, and then shifted himself to sit on the side of the bed. He glanced around before he stood, waiting until his head cleared before he moved towards the cupboard, finding a pile of clothes that someone had brought in for him. He dressed quickly, leaving the room, searching for Imly, finding her curled up in a chair in the waiting room.

Brendon paused, a smile on his face. She hadn't left him. He had been afraid that she would run, and then he would have just followed her. He looked up to find Benen and Burnie standing nearby.

"You two are here?" Brendon looked around. "Who else is here?"

"Brady. He's getting your discharge paperwork. Doc has taken responsibility for you. Your surgeon said you can leave, unless you would rather stick around here." Burnie grinned before he nodded towards Imly. "Go and find your lady. She refused to leave." He sobered at the thought of the fight that they had had.

"He's right. We tried to get her to come back to the building, promised to bring her back first thing in the morning. She just refused. Branigan was afraid that she would run, hide, and then come back without anyone around here for her. We have word that Wills has men watching here." Benen watched Imly closely before he looked at Brendon.

"So, we sneak out in the middle of the night? Is that the plan? Thinking they won't be watching?" Brendon shook his head before he headed to where Imly was curled up. He sat beside her, his eyes on her before he reached to drop a kiss on her head.

Imly roused, instantly awake, fear running through her before she realized that she was still in the hospital waiting room. She straightened, her eyes finding the two men near the doorway, watching her before they looked away. She sensed someone beside her and jumped, her eyes huge as she stared at Brendon.

"Brendon? You're here? You shouldn't be." Imly tried to stand, to grab for his arm, to try and make him rise and go back to his hospital room. "You're dressed. Brendon!"

"It's okay, Imly." Brendon could not get her to calm down, so he simply swept her into a hug, waiting until she had stilled. "I'm going home. Doc has made arrangements for that. We're making an escape during the night. Wills has men watching us."

"He would." Imly sounded disgruntled. "When will I be free of him?"

"Soon, I pray, sweetheart." He looked up as Burnie approached. "All set?"

"We are and we need to leave now. Brady spotted one of the men heading this way. We're heading for the service elevator."

A while later, Brendon stood in his kitchen, resting his hand on the countertop, hearing soft rustling as Imly wandered through the rooms. Then, he heard silence and turned his head, wondering where she had gotten to. He sighed. He was almost asleep on his feet, the pain medications given him kicking in. He headed for the bedroom, stopping for a moment as he found the bedside light on.

Brendon frowned, stepping back to look into the spare rooms. He didn't see Imly, but he could hear her, muttering softly to herself. He simply shook his head, and instead of heading for bed, he walked to his office, dropping down into his desk chair, reaching to click on the desk lamp, a gift from his own father when he graduated high school.

Dad, you would love my bride, Imly. She's soft spoken, like Mom, but I think I will see a fiery side to her. It has to be, given her deep red hair. Hair like Grandma's. She's the lady that Mom wove into my bedside stories. I love her deeply already, Lord, how I don't know. Help me to protect her, to bring her to safety, to do what I can to reach down and bring her back to who she was. That, dear Lord, has been driven down inside her. Help me to teach her to praise You in all circumstances, no matter what.

———

Imly stood just outside the doorway, watching him, wanting him to rest but not comfortable enough to approach him. She sighed, sorrow filling her for a moment as she watched him, and she just didn't know why. She turned, heading for one of the spare rooms, to creep into bed, but not to sleep, at least not at first. She listened for Brendon to move around but she dozed off without hearing that.

Hours later, Brendon stood, disoriented for a moment, before he headed for the door, cracking it open to find Breck standing there, Brandon and Bradon with him. He stood back, balancing himself for a moment with a hand against the wall.

"You're here early." He complained as he walked towards the kitchen, squinting at the clock. It couldn't be ten already, could it? "You're supposed to be at church. I'm not going to make it today."

"We know that, Brendon." Bradon simply moved him to one side and reached for the coffee carafe to start a pot of coffee. "We need to talk to you and to Imly as well. Is she up?"

"I have no idea. I just woke when you hammered at the door." Brendon was grumpy, an unusual circumstance for him.

'Sit, Brendon." Breck's voice was stern, not a usual tone for him. "You'll fall over if you don't. And I for one do not want to explain to your bride why that happened." He had noticed Imly hovering in the doorway, not sure if she should come in or not. "Imly? Will you talk sense into Brendon?"

"I'm sorry. I can't do that." Imly turned and walked away, the men hearing a door close softly in the distance.

Brendon stared at the doorway, not sure what had just happened. He was torn, wanting to go to Imly, but also needing to hear what his friends had to say. Brandon finally turned him to the doorway.

"Go, find Imly. She needs you."

Imly had merely nodded when Brendon had approached her, not turning around, not wanting him to see the tears on her cheeks, the cheeks with the darkening and yellowing bruises. She was ashamed of her looks, ashamed that she had been treated like she had by Wills.

Brendon had given a small sound and then just swept her into his arm, holding her, not finding her struggling to escape. That concerned him. He tilted his head finally to look at her.

"Imly? Please? Don't shut me out." He waited until she nodded. "I will not leave you until I know you are okay. Breck has some information and questions that he needs to talk to us about. Please?"

Imly had had a suspicion that was why the men were there. "But they're supposed to be in church. It's Sunday. It's not right that they are here and not there."

"That doesn't matter. They are where God wants them. Now, let's go see what they are wanting. If I know Bradon, he has probably started his French toast for us."

"He cooks?" Imly was surprised.

"We all do. In fact, we have a potluck supper once a month, just to get together for some fun times, without worrying about anything else."

Breck looked up from the papers that he had spread out in front of him, opened his mouth to speak, and then snapped it closed. His own face grew dark with anger as he studied the bruising on Imly's face before he caught the anger quickly flashing across the faces of the other two.

Imly sat, not speaking, her demeanour withdrawn. Brendon sighed, his hand going to feel his arm. It was beginning to be painful but he refused to take anything. Not yet, at any rate, he thought. Pushing away his plate, not able to finish the meal set before him, he watched Imly closely, before he spoke.

"Breck? I know you. I know Bradon and Brandon. As much as I enjoy your company for breakfast, and it is something new for Imly to discover, that we do like to gather and eat, you are here for more than that."

Breck nodded. "I am. First, Imly. Your parents? Did they have another home or some place that they might have fled to?"

Imly looked up, startled, before she shook her head. "Not that I am aware of. I was raised in that house, Dad saying it was one that had been in the family for a long time. I don't remember his parents or Mom's. They said that they had died before I could remember." She searched Breck's face. "Why? What aren't you saying?"

"That we have not found your parents. Not yet. The men up there have searched. The police have been involved. And no, that officer has not been in the loop at all. We have traced him back to Wills and he is now off duty and will be until he is cleared. He has admitted not passing on your parents' report on you."

"I knew that. What else?" Imly's hand rubbed against the wood of the table until Brendon's hand covered hers, his grasp light but tight enough that she stopped her movements.

"We have evidence that there is another house that they own, between here and Sudbury. There is also a house here in town that is in their name. This is concerning, Imly, that they have these and you don't know about it." Breck's voice, while stern, held compassion for the young woman in front of him.

"I didn't know. I'm sorry. I'm so sorry."

"Don't apologize, Imly." Bradon spoke up. "We have found information on your father. What does he do for a living?"

"Dad? He has a woodworking business. Why?"

"Because the evidence that we have found shows that is not where his income comes from. The heritage you said you had coming? There is nothing like that. There is no clan that they belong to. Not how you would think, that is."

Imly sat back, devastated at the words that she had heard. "If not, then who are they? Who am I? Am I really who I think I am?" She looked up at Brendon. "I'm sorry. I shouldn't have come into that shop. I'm so sorry."

"There is nothing to apologize for. You didn't know. You were raised thinking one thing." His arm went around her in a hug. She didn't see the look of pain that briefly crossed his face. "What else?"

"Jim is heading this way. Dallas is feeding him some addresses. He's searching as he comes." Breck paused, not quite sure how to phrase what he needed to say. "Imly, it is my turn to say I'm sorry. The evidence that Dallas has been able to find is that your father was involved in white-collar crime in Ireland and fled to here. There is a warrant out for his arrest over there."

Imly stared at him. "Then, who is Wills and what does he really want? If there is nothing that comes to me, why do what he did?"

Barnabas looked around the conference room that afternoon. Sunday afternoon and a long weekend, and the men were here. He could see a few of the ladies as well, Berneen, Cadee, Hagen, and he smiled, Haley and Holly were there. So were Alice and Farr, Fynn's brother and his wife, Alice being a police officer. He knew that she would have asked for permission to be there from her supervisor.

He turned as he heard footsteps stop beside him. Benen stood there.

"How is she?" He was concerned, knowing that it would have been devastating for her to learn what Breck had told her.

"Breck said that she didn't really react, just asked who Wills was and why he was after her. His gut feeling is what we thought. She had no idea that her father had been involved in crime."

Barnabas nodded. "Listen, how free are you in the next week or so? Can you fly over there? I can give you some names to approach. Something just doesn't ring true with this."

"I can make the time. Cadee will go with me. That would work. Anyone else?"

Barnabas studied the men. "Branigan. Take them with you. Amy will be in tomorrow morning, she tells me. She'll give you what you need. Andy will fly you over and stay there until you're ready to come back. He's fighting mad, he tells me. He saw Imly's face last night."

"Wills was brutal, but so were some of the others." Benen walked away, heading for Cadee, to draw her away from the others, his thoughts dark as he remembered how he had almost lost her to a poisoning.

Breck paused before he entered, his thoughts muddled and troubled. He had spoken with Brendon again, to try and make sense of what was going on. Neither one of them could understand it.

Brendon turned as Imly approached, a woebegone look on her face. He simply enveloped her into a hug, waiting for her to speak, his hand entangling in her hair as it rested on her shoulder.

"Brendon? Why? I'm sorry. That seems to be all that I can ask."

"It's okay, sweetheart. We understand. You don't want to know what the other seven have faced. Bradon was in fact drowned and revived. Ennis was stabbed, and Doc wouldn't remove the knife, which was a good thing. Cadee almost died from a poisoning."

Imly simply nodded. "I see. Wills? He seemed convinced I had something coming to me. How do we find out? Do we need to go back up there?"

"No. Dallas is heading that way, he says. He needs to, as part of his investigation. He stated he would simply pack up everything he thought he would need and bring it back. He has the warrants he needs for that. He's been working with the force up that way. He asked if there was anything you wanted to be brought back."

Imly stared up at him. "He'd do that? Then, my Bible and my laptop. They're on the desk in my bedroom. Tell him if he needs permission, he can bring anything he thinks he needs. Dad has a safe. I'll give him permission to search that. Just let him have the code, that all he needs." Imly thought through what she needed to do. "I guess that I'll need to head that way at some point. Pack my stuff. I won't be going back there, now will I?" She turned to walk away, stopping as Brendon spoke.

"How be we have the men up there pack everything up for you? They can rent a truck and bring it back down with them. Would that work?"

She turned slowly, her eyes on him. "They would do that?"

"They have already offered. In fact, Levi has already begun to gather boxes, just in case. As to cost, the Foundation covers that."

"They can't!" Imly was horrified at the thought. "That's too expensive."

"Imly, I haven't had a chance to speak with you about something. You know of Barnabas?"

She nodded. "I do and I don't know why. I heard Dad talking about him one day, and the name stuck as well as the Foundation name. Why?"

"Because part of what the Foundation does, is just this. They help, without asking. It's part of the mandate to be encouragers. What did you do for work?"

"Me? I was a secretary. Not that I'm going back there."

"No, but Lawrence asked. He's been looking for someone to take over in the office. He's busy doing deliveries, I'm busy in the shop. He's looking at hiring to help with sales and in the workshop. If you want, you can have the work in the office." Brendon paused, biting at his lip. "The thing of it is as well, once we married, you automatically became an employee of the Foundation. It's how they have it set up. The men's wages are paid. When we marry, that extends to the wives. That's part of being encouragers to the couples."

"They do that?" Imly was shocked. "I see. I guess I didn't expect this. Now, what, Brendon? Wills is out there. How do you go back to work, and how do I go about a normal life?"

Hearing footsteps rapidly approaching from behind him, sounding heavy, Brendon began to turn and step to the side. Before he could, he was slammed into the building wall, deliberately on the side with his wound. His senses swirled as the world around him darkened. He dropped to the ground, his hand on his shoulder, breathing heavily from the pain. The footsteps faded even as other steps were heard running towards him.

Blair and Burnie reached to help Brendon to his feet, letting him lean against the wall behind him. His eyes were closed against the pain. It had been a week since he had been shot, and he had ventured into town, just to see Lawrence and find out where work stood. He had certainly not expected to be ambushed and end up almost flat on his face on the sidewalk.

"Did you get the number of that truck?" Brendon's eyes cracked open slightly.

"No, but we have a description of him." Burnie's hand under his elbow helped Brendon maintain his footing. "Blair headed that way and said he'd make the call. What are you doing here? And is Imly with you?"

"I came in to see Lawrence. I had not planned this, you know. Imly is with some of the ladies, having lunch they said. They are trying to include her, but she's withdrawn, Burnie. I can't even reach through some of the barriers that she has up."

"It will take time. It's been a shock. Being kidnapped, assaulted, escaping, marrying, having her groom shot on their wedding day, having her parents disappear and then finding out she had not been told the truth about them. How does that sound?" Burnie was angry, not at Brendon or Imly, but at whoever it was behind it all. "I don't think that Wills is the brains behind it. He doesn't strike me as having the ability to plan all this."

"Sounds about right." Brendon's hand found his shoulder. "Is it bleeding?"

Burnie shoved aside the collar of Brendon's sweatshirt. "No, and it wasn't for trying. He really hit you hard. On purpose." Burnie's eyes dropped to the ground and he stooped to pick up an envelope. "He dropped this."

Brendon, by this time, had managed to open his eyes all the way. "An envelope?" He reached for it. "And addressed to me." He stiffened his knees. "Can we sit somewhere?"

"Let me have your keys. Blair drove us in. I'm driving you home and this time, you're staying there." Burnie eyed his friend. "That man meant business, Brendon."

Hearing the door close and then silence, Imly carefully peeked out from the kitchen, finding Brendon standing in the hall, a hand braced against the wall. His face was white and pain-filled, and that scared her.

"Brendon?" When he didn't reply, she approached him. "Brendon?"

He looked up, bleary-eyed, before he reached an arm to tuck her against him. "Sweetheart? I didn't expect you to be home yet."

"Yeah, well. I am. What happened to you?" She tried to support him as he walked, directing him into the living room. "Here. Sit on the couch." She watched as he dropped heavily down before she was away, fixing his coffee and her tea and then reaching for the pain medication.

Half an hour later, Brendon looked up, feeling slightly better, before he reached for the envelope Burnie had stuffed into his pocket.

"I was knocked down outside of my work, and someone left this for me." He looked over at Imly before he reached to pull her to him. Tucking her close, he fingered the envelope. "He left this for me."

"Wills?"

"That's what we think, but we are not sure. None of us got a good look at him." Brendon sighed. "But, first, how was your lunch?"

"Okay, I guess. I just wasn't in the mood for it. I'm sorry. I still think that I don't belong here."

Brendon sighed. He suspected that was how it had gone. "Sweetheart, you do belong here. All of the ladies have expressed the same sentiment in different ways. I know it's tough." He waited for her to speak. When she didn't, he tilted his head to look at her, seeing once more the woebegone look on her face. "How can I help you? How can I make it better for you? I am praying for you, for your parents. For resolution of this."

Imly shrugged. "I don't know, Brendon." She looked up, her eyes troubled. "I wish I could talk to them, find out what is going on." She poked at the envelope. "You need to open that."

"No, first, my bride needs me to help her. What can I say, sweetheart?" Brendon watched her before he sighed to himself. This is working well, Lord. Now, what? Before he could stop himself, he reached to kiss her, startling both of them. He drew back, mouth open to apologize before he reached to kiss her again.

Imly had been startled with the first kiss, but she welcomed the second one, reading in it Brendon's growing feelings for her, and knowing that she was attracted to him as well. How that was possible in such short a time, she didn't understand.

Brendon finally drew back, leaving Imly with rosy cheeks, and looked down at her.

"I will not apologize, sweetheart."

Imly shook her head. "No, don't." She poked at the envelope again. "Now, will you open that?"

Brendon opened the unsealed flap and pulled out a single sheet, unfolding it. His eyes dropped to the bottom.

"It says your Dad's name."

"That can't be right." Imly leaned over. "That's his name, but not his writing. What is going on? What does it say?"

Brendon began to read. "*If you continue to investigate, you will lead to our deaths and Imly's death. Stop now. Ian Dickerson.*"

"Dad wouldn't word anything like that. Who is this?" Imly stared at the paper before looking up at him. "Brendon, didn't Barnabas say some of the men went to Ireland?"

"He did. They're due back tonight. Barnabas wants a meeting tomorrow." Brendon groaned. "It's Sunday tomorrow. That means on Monday."

"How? They all work."

"We all work, but when we need to, Barnabas pulls us out and in to investigate or travel or whatever it is that he needs us to do. Our employers are all aware this can happen and are in agreement with it."

"That's a strange way to run businesses." Imly sat back once more, surprising herself by feeling content in Brendon's arm.

Monday morning found all the men gathered in the conference room, wanting to know exactly what Benen and Branigan had discovered. They could read them to a certain extent, and somehow, they didn't think it would be what they had expected.

"Benen?" Barnabas looked over at him. "What do you have to report?"

Benen and Branigan shared a look. "It's not what we were told or what Dallas was told. I don't know who he talked to, but there is no warrant out for Ian Dickerson. In fact, we were able to determine that the Ian Dickerson we were sent to investigate has never stepped foot in Ireland. The description of the man that we were given does not match Imly's father in any way. That man is the one who was involved in white-collar crime. The investigator we spoke to was surprised to see us. However, he was able to shed some light on what she was told.

"In the older days, there was an inheritance that passed to the oldest male in the family. That included lands, jewels, and a certain standing in society. But we were told that is no longer in effect. We were not able to determine, no matter how we tried or asked, when or why, just that it was at least two hundred years since this had been done. Even if it were in effect, it would not go to the eldest daughter. If there were no male heirs, it simply died away. Whatever monies or jewels or land reverted to the town they were resident of at that time."

"So, Wills is after something that he has heard or read about but isn't in effect?" Breck paused, a thought running through his mind. "What if it is a crime family that had set this up? Kept it as a secret society? Kept it running without anyone in authority knowing? Is that possible?"

Branigan nodded. "We asked that. The investigator wouldn't confirm that, but he did say that there were rumours of that happening. We found someone who will look into that for us over there. He was able to give us names here in Ontario to talk to. That would be our next step. He did say that Benen and I should not be the ones to contact them, that we should find someone outside of our group to do that."

"Emma and Abe." Brady grinned. "They would, or one of their men or friends would do that. In fact, I was speaking with Abe the other night, just to get his feelings on this, and I will come to that. He suggested either his Uncle Eddie, a retired officer, or a good friend, another retired officer, Ben, to look into that."

"That would work." Barnabas paused. "Where do we stand right now?"

"Right now?" Brody spoke up. "We have bits and pieces of information. Not enough to even put together a picture of what is going on with Imly. We have heard from the streets that Wills is still looking for her." His attention centred on Brendon. "He knows about you two. I can say that he was not the one who shot you, but someone involved with him did. I spoke with the owner of the accounting firm that he said he worked for. He was never employed there. And would never be, I'm told."

"Strange." Breck looked up from his notes. "Brendon? Has Imly said anything at all?"

Brendon shook his head. "She is at a loss to explain this. She is also at a loss about her parents. That has caused so much anxiety for her. I wish I could find her father and talk to him. The note that we got? It was signed by him, but it wasn't his handwriting. Nor was it her mother's."

"So, they are either being held captive somewhere or have gone into hiding and someone is using that fact to torment your wife." Blair shook his head. "How has Jim made out on his search?"

"He has found out nothing and that surprises him. There have been no sightings at all." Barnabas looked up, studying each of the men. "I would suggest a couple of you head that way, starting from here. He's searching the main roads. Take the back roads and side roads. It's a long shot, but it may pay off."

Bradon shared a look with Burnie. "We'll go, Barnabas. In fact, I can start first thing in the morning."

"Okay. Talk to Amy for what you need." Barnabas paused. "Anything else?"

"Yes. Fynn mentioned that we might want to talk to Emma and see if she can help. She has resources that we don't and she's good at finding the people who want to hide." Brady spoke of a friend's wife.

"Do that, Brady. Now, let's break off and spend some time in prayer." Barnabas closed the folder in front of him, set his pen down, and rose, heading for Brendon, to partner in prayer with him.

Staring at the late-season, dark yellow roses on the bushes in front of her, Imly stood, deep in thought, not really aware of where she was. She certainly was not thinking of her safety, that was a definite fact. If anyone had asked her what her thoughts were, she could not tell. She started as she heard a sound and spun, a hand to her throat.

Brody simply shook his head. Lord, she's out here on her own, not even watching or aware of what is around her. That's not good.

"Imly?" Brody walked towards her, a hand up to shade his eyes against the late day sun. It was days since Brendon had been shot and came home.

"Brody? I'm sorry. I didn't hear you." She paused, seeing the look on his face. "What did I do now? I don't understand."

"Just being out here. On your own. Without anyone knowing where you are. Brendon was looking for you, he said." Brody's hand on her arm stopped her forward rush. "He said it's not urgent. I happened to find him in the lobby and said I'd take a look for you." He grinned at her even as his eyes raised to study the area. "This is a nice seating area. The fellows and their ladies use it a lot. We have quite a range of gardens here." He reached for her hand, to tuck it into the crook of his elbow, before he turned them to walk back towards the building.

"I know. I shouldn't have come out here." She sighed. "There are just so many rules right now. And I know I will break every one at some point."

Brody laughed. "We all do, but just keep in mind, let someone know where you are, even if it is just the security guard at the desk. He'll come with you. That's not a problem. The fellows that are married? Their ladies have done that. In fact, a couple were taken right out of the building."

Imly looked at him, shocked. "There is no way that would happen. It couldn't." She continued to stare at him, disbelief growing on her face. "It can't, not with the security you have in place."

"It did happen, Imly. That's why the security is stronger. Barnabas and the Foundation Board have insisted on it. Even still, out here?" Brody waved a hand before he reached to open the door for her. "They can come in and get you and then disappear with you without anyone knowing. That has happened as well. We can't fence off the property. It's too big." He suddenly grinned. "When Brendon's better, have him take you for a walk that way." He pointed over his shoulder. "That will take you to Lake Erie. It's quite a view, to look over at the United States, or even when it's stormy, to see the waves breaking against the rocks. And then the sunsets or the sunrises. You haven't lived until you've seen them."

Imly simply shook her head. "I'm sure that they are spectacular, but right now? I don't think so."

Brendon caught her last sentence and frown. "You don't think what, sweetheart?" He looked over at Brody as he laughed.

"I was telling her about the lake and the views." Brody waved as he walked away.

"He was, was he? They are wonderful. We'll pack a supper or lunch one day or even a breakfast and go down there. I've done that many times." Brendon wrapped an arm around her and turned her to one of the seating areas, waiting for her to sit before he dropped down beside her.

"We will, will we? Not yet, that's understood?" She leaned back on him. "Brendon?"

"Hmm?" He shook his head, coming back from his dreams of sitting with Imly on his favourite rock at the lake, watching the sunset, and maybe, if God willed, watching their little ones frolic at their feet.

"Have you heard anything about Mom and Dad?" She sounded desperate, wanting to know where they were.

"No, I haven't. Barnabas or Breck would have made sure that we did if they had any word." His arm tightened on her. "We'll find them, or they'll find us. The fellows are still working their way up north. They've been in contact with Breck."

Imly sighed, her head going down on Brendon's shoulder. "You shouldn't have been hurt, Brendon. That's not right."

"Yes, it is. If I have to give my life to protect you, I will." He paused, biting at his lips. "I love you, Imly. It's that easy. You are my life, right below God. I will do what I need to in order to protect you."

Imly nodded, sadness filling her heart. "I know that, but I don't want you to be hurt again. I don't know that my heart can handle losing you or seeing you hurt once more." She stopped, unsure of how to express her thoughts and her wishes. Her voice was barely audible. "It appears that I love you too, Brendon. But, where do we go from here? We can't live a normal life until this is behind us."

"Not true. We go on with our lives, living them each day to honour God. That's how we do it." Brendon settled back on the couch, his shoulder aching but not like it had been.

Imly had been listening to him, but her attention had been drawn to the outside, a frown coming on her face as she watched a vehicle pull in, before she was on her feet, pulling Brendon up and away from the lobby, stopping in a hallway to watch the front doors, even as they opened and Wills appeared.

"It's Wills! How dare he!" Imly hissed the words, keeping her voice low, the anger and fear evident in it.

Brendon drew her back further, his phone out, a call placed to the security desk and then to the police department. He looked around, desperate to find somewhere to hide with her, to keep her safe. An arm around her, he swept her into the chapel, snapping the deadbolt on the door to lock it.

They stood, leaning against the door, hearing the heavy tread of Wills as he wandered the building. Brendon frowned. That shouldn't be happening. Where were the security guards? Brendon frowned as he heard the heavy steps hastening away, towards the back of the building.

Imly leaned against him, her eyes on the door, a frown on her own face, before she looked up at him, the frown changing to a question. Brendon shrugged. She reached up to whisper in his ear.

"Did he leave?"

"I think so." Brendon listened to the noise outside. "We'll wait here until they come and get us." He turned, the fading adrenaline causing him to stagger, Imly's arms out to catch him and help him to a pew. He sank down gratefully, pulling her down with him, to tuck her against him.

"Brendon?"

"Imly?" He gave a quick grin, causing her to frown at him again. He sobered. "I know. He came right into our home building. He shouldn't have made it down these hallways. Security should have stopped him."

Brennen and Breck stopped at the chapel door, frowning that it was closed. They knew Dallas was around, coming out when the call about Wills being on the premises went in. Will Peters, the police chief of the town, and also a good friend, had appeared along with him, walking through the building. They had not found any sign of Wills, but they had found his vehicle in the parking lot.

Breck turned the knob on the door, surprised to find it locked, an unusual circumstance during the day. He dug out his keys, the frown deepening on his face. They had searched the building for Brendon and Imly, even as far as Breck entering their apartment, but not finding them. This was the last room in the building that they could search. He shoved the door open and stepped in, surprised to find no one in there.

Brennen stepped in as well, searching, before he stooped, to pick up a phone.

"This is Brendon. He wouldn't have gone anywhere without it."

"Not on his own, that's for sure." Breck walked through the chapel, opening the doors to the cupboards before he paused at the outside door. "They must have gone out this way. And it's hidden to the security cameras." He shoved open the door, stepping outside, then stopping and turning back to the door. "It was not locked, and it always is."

"I don't like it that we found Peter unconscious behind the security desk. He took quite a heavy blow." Brennen stepped out after Breck. "Someone took him down from behind, while he was on the phone. I don't know that he was able to put through a call to the head office."

"No, he wasn't. He hadn't had a chance to even call." Breck walked around the building, searching for just what, he wasn't sure.

Brennen kept pace with him. "I don't understand it. They should have been in the chapel. Unless someone took them from there."

"And that is exactly what I think happened. But who?" Breck stopped in from of the chapel door, his finger touching the lock. "This isn't marked. They had to open it for whoever it was."

"Brendon wouldn't do that for just everyone. He would have had to be certain of whoever it was." Brennen was frustrated and suddenly afraid for the couple.

"I know. Unless it was Imly's parents, and she let them in."

"But that doesn't explain why Brendon's phone was there. Did you see Imly's?" Brennen used his shirttail to pull open the door. "I didn't see another phone."

"I think that it was likely hers on their kitchen table. Brendon had commented that she was refusing to carry one, afraid that Wills would find out the number and keep calling her."

"That's not helpful." Brennen bent to look under the pews on both sides of the aisle, before he stood, a hand rubbing at his cheek. "I don't see anything. Can you access Brendon's phone?"

Breck shook his head. "Not likely. He told me that he had it secured so that no one could access it."

"That's no help." Brennen turned as the door to the hallway opened and Will, Dallas, and Barnabas appeared.

"No sign of them?" Will's keen eyes scanned the room.

"No, but we found Brendon's phone. And the outside door was unlocked." Breck held up the phone. "I can't access it."

Will and Dallas shared a look before they headed for the door and then disappeared through it. Barnabas watched them before turning to the other two, hearing the door click shut.

"We need to meet. The others are gathering in the conference room. The ladies are arranging to bring in food for us all. It will be a long night." Barnabas ran his hand through his hair. "I don't like this. I heard from Brody. They talked to a police detachment halfway there. Imly's parents' car was found in the ditch near that town. No sign of them. The officer couldn't tell if there were any signs of violence. There wasn't anything in the car, but that was the feeling the guys had when they searched Imly's home. There didn't seem to be anything missing."

Breck shook his head. "First, her. Then, her parents. Now, Brendon and Imly. How do we even know that the incidents are related?"

"We're assuming that they are but you are correct, Breck." Will spoke from behind him, causing him to jump. "Sorry. I didn't mean to startle you. Dallas is heading up that way now. He's gotten the statements that he needs." Will looked around, puzzled. "I don't see Brendon just leaving with whoever it was."

"No, he wouldn't. Not unless Imly was threatened. And that is likely what happened." Brennen's words had a bite of anger to them, unusual for him. "And just how do we find them?"

"That I can't answer, fellows, but we need to clear this room. The crime scene techs are heading this way."

Barnabas nodded. "Let's meet in fifteen in the conference room. We need to start making some plans. Those of us who are here."

"The fellows are already there. Brady was reaching out to Abe and Emma, but he said he was having trouble reaching them. He wasn't sure, but he thought this was the week that they usually took off and found Emma's mountaintop and her eagles."

"Is that right?" Barnabas shook his head. "Well, I guess that's that."

"Not quite. Brady did speak with Jace at her business. He's starting a search, but he said Emma was much better at it than him."

"We'll take what we can get." Barnabas held the door to the conference room open before he stopped. "I just had a thought. Would her parents have landed here already?"

Breck and Brennen shared a look before Breck spoke.

"That's a possibility. How be Brennen and I head into town, see what we can find out?" Breck was already moving away from the door, Brennen keeping pace with him.

———

Two days later, Buckley raised his head from his sermon notes, listened, and then shook his head. He was alone in the church, or so he thought he was. Hearing a sound again, he once more raised his head. Staring down at his notes, he sighed. He was struggling with this sermon, trying to write the words God was giving him on how to praise in the storms, but it just wasn't happening. He sighed once more, threw down his pen, and rose, a prayer on his lips that he really was alone and he could return to his study of the passages that he felt he was to use.

Buckley stood for a moment outside his door, looking down the sanctuary towards the main entrance but not seeing anyone. He frowned. He knew the sound of the front door as it had a very distinct noise when it opened. It hadn't been fixed, at his request, as it alerted him to an intruder if someone did enter the building.

He walked towards the front of the building, searching each row of pews before he stopped, shock on his face, a shout dying on his lips. He sprang forward, dropping to his knees beside the huddled form, reaching to turn the face up.

"Imly? Dear Lord, thank You for bringing her home. Imly? Can you hear me?" Buckley tried to elicit a response from her but to no avail. He reached for his phone and then muttered to himself. He had forgotten it at home that morning, shrugging it off at the time, knowing that he had the church phone he could use.

Buckley rose to his full height, staring down at Imly, torn between running to call for help and not leaving her. Not leaving her won. He reached to gather her into his arms, finding no resistance from her, and elbowed his way through the door, shoving it closed. He shifted Imly around enough in his arms that he could reach into a pocket for his keys and lock the door before he was almost running down the few steps to his car. Wrenching open the door, he carefully set her down, fastened her in, and then slamming the door, he ran for the driver's side. His own door slammed behind him as he headed away rapidly towards town, his glance shifting between the road and Imly.

Parking in the designated clergy spot at the hospital, Buckley twisted in his seat, praying that Imly had responded. She had not, he sighed, and that concerned him. He was out of his seat, around to wrench open the door once more, and gather her close, almost running for the entrance. Surprised looks shot his way before the charge nurse was on her feet, heading for an empty room, Buckley following close behind her.

Doc watched from where he was reading a chart, a frown appearing on his face, before he turned his attention back to his patient. Whoever it was that Buckley had brought in would have to wait. There was nothing he could do about that.

Doc finally moved to that room, his hand reaching for the chart, his eyes on Buckley. Buckley had refused to leave, and the nurse had simply nodded at his explanation. It was not the first time that Buckley had stayed with a patient.

Frowning, Doc looked down at the chart, his steps halting as he read the name before his eyes shot to the bed, and then he was moving rapidly towards it.

"Buckley? What on earth?" Doc was already reaching for his stethoscope from around his neck.

"She just appeared in the church, Doc. I couldn't get her to respond. So I have no idea what is going on."

"I see." Doc looked towards the door. "Brendon?"

"She was by herself." Buckley was torn. He felt that he needed to stay with Imly, but he also knew that he had to report it.

"Go, make your calls."

"Yeah, that. I'll have to see if I have change. I forgot my phone this morning." Buckley was frustrated as he dug into his pocket, finding no change.

"Here. Use mine. I'll come and find you when I'm done here." Doc handed over his phone and then motioned him away.

Buckley hesitated, one last glance at Imly, before he turned and walked away, already dialing Barnabas' number.

"Doc?" Barnabas answered in a distracted manner.

"It's Buckley. I had to borrow Doc's phone. Imly showed up at the church just a few moments ago. She's here in Emergency." Buckley held the phone away from his ear at the exclamation from Barnabas.

"Imly? She's there? Brendon?" Barnabas was on his feet, waving at Amy as he passed her desk, heading for the conference room. Bradon and Burnie whom he had sent north were on their way back, just hadn't reached home yet. He shoved the door open hard enough that it startled the men gathered inside, causing them to rise to their feet.

"No, no Brendon. And she's not responding. Doc's with her. I am thanking God that he was here today." Buckley paced, unable to sit.

"Okay. We'll head in. Brady said Abe or Emma were heading this way, or else he was sending someone with material for both us and Dallas." Barnabas stopped his words. "Dallas! Have you called him?"

"Not yet. You were the first. She'll need some of the ladies. Anna for sure."

"They will all want to come, they have been that worried. Call Dallas and then call me back if there is word before we arrive."

Buckley finally ended his call with Dallas, unable to supply much more information than what he had given to Barnabas. Dallas promised to head over as soon as he could, but at the moment, he was on the scene of another crime and he couldn't promise when he would be free. Buckley had simply told him to come when he could, that he doubted Imly would be leaving any time soon.

He looked up as he heard Doc's voice, rising from where he had been sitting, before Doc approached him, pointing to the chairs.

"Sit back down, Buckley. I need to. At least for a few moments." Doc sank down with a sigh of relief, his eyes closing for a moment, before he spoke. "Any word on Brendon?"

"Not a one. He wasn't with her. Dallas was having officers head over to the church." Buckley groaned. "And I locked the door. They'll need to get inside."

"Not right away. One of them can come to get you when they need to." Doc's eyes slowly opened and he rubbed at them. It had been a long day, he thought, busier than normal. He would not leave the hospital until he knew what was going on with Imly.

———

Doc paused in the doorway to Imly's room, his thoughts on Brendon, before he began to pray. Imly was in critical condition, that much he knew, and he just didn't know who to turn to if she needed more treatment than what they had planned. He turned as he felt a hand on his shoulder.

Barnabas and Breck stood on either side of him, sober looks on their faces.

"Doc? What can you tell us?" Breck knew how careful Doc was about saying much about patients.

"It's difficult, Breck. Her parents aren't here, nor is Brendon. They would be her next of kin, I suspect. If she needs further treatment, who authorizes it?" Doc walked forward, to stop by the bedside, his hand automatically reaching for his stethoscope. He finally wrapped in around his neck again, his hands reaching to feel at the side of her head, a frown on his face.

"She's had X-rays, fellows. There is a hairline fracture on this side of her head. How serious? That we can't tell until she awakens."

"And we don't know when, is what you're saying." Barnabas blew out a breath. "So, where does that leave us?"

"Nowhere." Doc's words were abrupt, from his frustration and fear. "All we can do right now is pray for her. And even at that, I can't guarantee what the outcome will be. God alone knows."

Breck had turned slightly as he heard a sound at the door and then beckoned Berneen in.

"Doc. Berneen's here."

Doc shot her a glance. "Berneen. Has she said who her power of attorneys is?"

"No. We never talked about that." Berneen stood at the foot of the bed, her eyes on her friend. "Doc? How bad? Or can't you say?"

"She's critical, Berneen. I can't go into the details. I have to talk to Barnabas and Breck, but she is under the Foundation care, so that is necessary." Doc watched Berneen closely. "Berneen, will you stay for a while?"

"I can, Doc. That's what I'm here. Baird is waiting outside. I think that he wanted to talk to either Barnabas or Breck."

Breck nodded and walked away, searching for Baird, finding him standing in the waiting room, staring out the window into the darkening sky.

"Baird? You were looking for us?"

Baird nodded. "I was." He drew a deep breath. "I heard from Dallas. It's not good news. He was trying to reach one of you two." He turned, a devastated look on his face, before he swallowed hard.

"Brendon?" Breck's voice was barely audible.

Baird shook his head. "No. Her parents. The authorities up north found them." Baird's words cut off, his emotions getting the better of him. "I should say, they found their bodies. They had never left their property. They were hidden in a shed, and the authorities just found them, doing a more thorough search."

"What!" Breck was shocked, to say the least. "Dear Lord, You will need to comfort Imly. This is not what we had expected."

"No, it isn't. They are looking for Wills now. Dallas said that there was evidence he was involved in it. That day that he answered her call? He was there, but they were already dead. They think that their car was driven this way and then dumped to make us think they were heading this way. It just gets more strange." Baird turned, looking towards the hallway. "How is Imly?"

"Doc's not saying much, but he did say that she is critical. We need to pray, Baird. We also need to find Brendon. I fear for his life."

"You and me both." Baird sighed. "I prayed none of the rest would go through what some of us did. I'm not the same person that I was. It's not possible to go back to that." He nodded towards Imly's room. "She not likely is. And I know Brendon won't be." Baird was frustrated. "How did she end up at the church, anyway?"

"That we don't know." Breck looked around as he heard footsteps. "The rest of the fellows are here. All of us." He frowned as he studied Bradon and Burnie. "How do we tell them that they were on a wild goose chase?"

Bradon stopped near Breck. "Breck? You've heard?" Sorrow flickered across his face. "Dallas called when we were halfway home."

"We have. I'm sorry, fellows."

"Not your fault. You didn't know. None of us did." Burnie looked around. "Brendon?"

"No sign of him. And it's not looking good for Imly." Breck opened his mouth to speak, snapped it closed, and walked away, leaving the men staring after him before they exchanged glances.

Hearing new footsteps, Baird looked once more towards the doorway, a frown on his face before he moved through the men, bypassing the ladies who had gathered, and stopped in front of the couple who stood there. He has to be an officer, Baird thought.

"Can I help you?"

The man nodded. "I am looking for either Barnabas or Baird."

"I'm Baird."

"I'm Lieutenant Doug Foster. And this is my wife, Darcie. Emma sent me this way." He reached to shake his hand.

Baird's eyes narrowed. "Emma sent you? Is that correct?"

Doug grinned. "She did. She said you would question whether I was legit or not." He continued to grin even as Darcie shook her head.

"Don't pay him any mind, Baird? May I call you that?" At his nod, she looked around him at the waiting room. "This is all of you? We were told at your building that you were here but not why."

Baird's face grew grave. "We are. Imly, Brendon's wife, is here. She showed up today, critically injured. There is no sign of Brendon."

Doug frowned. "I'm sorry. I'm not following what you mean."

Baird sighed. "Let's have a seat. Barnabas will be around shortly, I suspect." He waited until they were seated before he continued. "Brendon and Imly disappeared two days ago from the chapel in our building. Imly showed up today in our church. Buckley found her when he heard a noise in the building. There was no sign of Brendon." He paused, sorrow crossing his face.

"Baird?" Darcie reached to lay her hand on his wrist, her eyes raising to Berneen as she sat down beside her husband, an arm around him.

"We received confirmation today that her parents are dead." Berneen leaned her head against Baird's shoulder. "They were missing."

"Oh, no!" Darcie stared at Berneen before she looked down at the notepad and pen that Doug was waving at her. "Thank you, my love. Okay. Talk to me. Tell me everything that you can. Each one of you. And I want to talk to Doc, is it?"

"That is correct." Baird was puzzled, before he looked up at Doug, finding a smile on his face.

"It's okay, Baird. Darcie owns an arts and craft store and has one online, but she was trained as a forensics psychologist. She can do a profile for your detective, without having much information. And I can guarantee you that it will be spot on. She did it for us."

"She did?" Barnabas had slipped into a seat beside Berneen. "Darcie? I've heard of you. Your material is still used for teaching."

"It is? I didn't expect that." Darcie was lost to them after that comment.

Doug simply shook his head and then nodded at Barnabas.

"Where can we talk?"

Barnabas looked around. "Follow me. There's a conference room just down the hall. Baird, make sure Breck knows where we are. I assume the ladies are waiting here."

"We are. We'll keep Darcie company." Berneen smirked at him. "Go. Figure this out. We need to find Brendon for Imly, and it's not happening with us just standing around here in this waiting room."

Her head moving restlessly, Imly grimaced with pain, but also with the memories that were flooding her mind, destroying the peace that she needed to have in order to heal. She licked at her lips before she turned abruptly to the side of her head that was injured. Pain flashed through her, drawing a moan from her, and then her movements stopped.

Cadee was watching her closely, reaching to press the call button for the nurse, her hand then resting on Imly's. Distress coloured her face. Lord, we need her awake, but it doesn't look as if it's going to happen. How do we praise in times like this? How do we? We can't on our own. That's not how we are. But You can do that in us. You can bring us to praise you in whatever situation we find ourselves.

The nurse entered on almost silent shoes, pausing for a moment to study the monitors, before she reached to take Imly's vitals.

"She was moving. I thought that she was waking up. Then, she turned wrong and stopped moving." Cadee's voice was barely above a whisper.

"She hit the wrong spot, is that what you're saying?" At Cadee's nod, the nurse reached for Imly's chart, to make her notes. "She will be restless. Doc expected that. Doctor Watts is on duty today. I'll let him know. Doc said Dr. Watts would be taking over her care, now that she's on a floor."

Cadee nodded, not taking her eyes from her friend. "Who is in the waiting room?"

The nurse laughed softly. "A better question would be who isn't. All of you ladies, the twins, Darbi, and some of the men from there. There is also a police lieutenant and his wife from outside the area. They were around yesterday but haven't left yet."

"Doug and Darcie. Good. They can help." Cadee's heart was sore for her friend. "Is Benen out there?"

"He is. I'll send him in, if you like."

"Please." Cadee just needed her husband, to have his arms around her, and to hear his prayers. She knew that others were praying for their friends, but sometimes, she thought, it didn't seem that their prayers went very far.

Benen hesitated for a moment, his eyes on his wife, before he was beside her, his arms around her. His eyes then sought out Imly, a frown coming across his face as he studied the fading bruises on her face but the new enlarging purple colouring on the side of her head.

"What happened to her, Benen?"

"That we don't know, Cadee. We haven't been able to even figure out how she made her way to the church or from where."

Imly stirred once more, hearing voices near her. She squinted as her eyes opened before she sighed and drifted off again, the pain in her head driving her down into darkness. Her lips murmured Brendon's name even as a tear crept down her cheek.

Cadee leaned closer, horror crossing her face as she heard Imly's whispered words. She spun, her arms around Benen as she clung to him.

Benen's arms tightened around her. "Cadee? What did she say?"

"Oh, Benen." Cadee's voice was thick with tears. "She thinks Brendon is dead. That he was killed because of her."

"Oh, no!" Benen looked around as the physician entered. "We'll need to leave, Cadee." He turned her towards the door before he stopped to speak with the physician. "Cadee heard something Imly said. She was alert for a moment and muttered that she thinks her husband is dead, killed because of her."

The physician nodded, a sober look on his face. "That's what we've wondered. Until it's confirmed, we must keep up our hope and hers."

His arm around Cadee, Benen walked back towards the waiting room, knowing their friends would ask how Imly was. And that he couldn't say. Not yet. Cadee stopped, bringing him to a stop as well.

"What do we tell them, Benen?"

"The truth, I guess. We can do no less." Benen hugged her tighter, his eyes on Barnabas as he walked towards him, Doug beside him.

"Benen?" Barnabas' voice held the question that he would not ask.

Benen shook his head, sorrow wafting across his face. "Imly had roused but not enough to know that we were there." He paused, his eyes on Cadee, who still hid her face against him. "Cadee heard her say something that is upsetting."

"And that would be?" Barnabas waited for Benen to speak, finally opening his mouth to question him further when Benen spoke.

"Cadee heard Imly muttering that Brendon was dead, killed because of her." Benen paused, a bleak look around his eyes. "How do we prove that he isn't? It's going to be hard enough for her to find out her parents are dead, let alone having to deal with this."

Doug had been listening closely. "How sure is she?"

Benen shrugged, his eyes on the others who had gathered close. "I don't know for sure. We won't know until she wakes up completely and the Lord alone knows when that will be."

Benen looked past Doug as Darcie as she paced. "What's with your wife?"

Doug shrugged. "She's thinking. She does it best lately by pacing. Just so you know, she was treated very badly years ago and that affected her wish to continue in her chosen line of work. She rarely goes back to it, only two or three times. Once was when we reconnected and went through a horrible situation that almost took out our town." Doug looked past Benen. "Is that the detective that's investigating this?"

Barnabas nodded. "Dallas. He refuses to let us use his last name. Doesn't explain that."

Darcie spoke from beside Doug. "No, he doesn't have to. Is there somewhere we can meet? I think we need to get out of the way here and do some brainstorming."

Doug sighed, even as he reached to shake Dallas' hand, realizing they had met a number of years ago. "Dallas. Good to see you again."

<hr>

“Doug? I didn’t realize you knew these fellows.”

“I didn’t, not until yesterday. Abe and Emma sent Darcie and me over. You’re the one I have a stack of material for.”

A week later, Imly lay back on her hospital bed, her arms crossed across her chest, not willing to look at anyone. She had done this, she thought. She had brought devastation to this group of friends. The ladies of the building had been in and out for the last few days, each one taking the time to spend with her, praying with her as she would let them.

Her eyes closed as her head dropped to the pillow, the nagging headache not letting go of its grip on her. She was frustrated, to say the least, unable to state where she had been, who had taken her, or even how she had managed to escape. Or even, she thought, that she had been released for some reason. Her heart hurt as she thought about Brendon, convinced that she was a widow. She could hear the words drilled into her brain that last night, that he was dead and it was all her fault. Flashes of a picture showing him on the ground, his eyes closed, a large red stain on his chest, haunted her. Imly frowned as she pondered it. There was something off about the picture, but she just could not think of what it was.

Barnabas turned from the window that he had been standing in front of, watching Imly's reflection in the glass, not seeing the coloured leaves on the trees outside or the clouds scudding across the blue of the sky. He was concerned, to put it mildly. Doc had not been able to tell him much, but he had indicated that Imly would need at least six weeks to recover. And that was being generous. They needed to do something to find Brendon and bring him home, Doc declared, not convinced that he was dead.

"Imly? What can we do for you?" Barnabas leaned back against the window, his hands resting against the window sill.

"I don't know, Barnabas. Everyone asks me that, and I don't know." Her head raised as she squinted towards him, the light hurting her eyes. "What can I say? If I had not hidden in the workshop, Brendon would not have found me and he would still be alive."

"Not necessarily, Imly." Barnabas shoved away from where he had been standing, to pace over to take a seat in the chair beside her bed. Buckley, you need to the one giving this talk, not me. "God has control of this, Imly. Not us. Not whoever it is."

"I know that in my head, but it's my heart that's having the trouble." She sighed. "I just wish it was different." Imly looked down at her fingers plucking at the blanket. "Is it really true about Mom and Dad?" Her voice was barely audible.

"It is. I'm sorry, Imly. We couldn't have prevented that." Barnabas leaned forward, his elbows resting on his thighs. "The coroner says that they were likely killed not long after you spoke with them. There is not a lot of evidence that the police are releasing out to anyone, other than Dallas and the team here."

"I know." She bit at her lip even as she blinked rapidly, the headache intensifying. "I just wish it was different. Have we learned anything else that you can share?"

Barnabas shrugged. "Not a whole lot. We know it wasn't your parents that were involved in the insurance fraud and black market sale of those items. Dallas says that he is investigating someone but won't say who. Our fellows are working round the clock right now. And Fynn's friend, Emma, is throwing information at us almost too fast for us to read. Doug's Darcie left a profile for us and passed that on to Dallas."

Imly's eyes narrowed, not altogether from the headache. "Can I see it?"

"You can, once you're released. The physicians won't let you leave right now." He grinned. "Feeling caged?"

Imly stared at him, her face whitening to the point that it startled Barnabas and had him on his feet, reaching for the call button. Imly's hand stopped him.

"No, don't call. It's what you said."

"What did I say?" Barnabas thought back over his words and really wasn't sure which one she meant.

"Cage. I was in a cage of some kind. Not in a house. An outbuilding. A shed. A barn. A cabin. I couldn't quite see what it was, it was dark. And they didn't let us have any lights. Brendon was taken away before I was locked up. I don't know where they put him, but I know that he was fighting them, to try and get back to me." Imly blinked rapidly. "It was early the next morning, I think, that they told me that he was dead and that it was all my fault. They left the cage door unlocked. I think that was done on purpose. I tried to get away, but someone shoved me and I fell, hitting my head, I think, against a rock." She looked up. "Is that when I did that?" Her voice, naturally soft, was barely audible.

"More than likely. It is a miracle that you were able to make your way to the church. We still haven't figured out which way you came from." Barnabas studied her, hoping that she would or could remember.

"Barnabas, when can I leave?" Imly eyed the door, ready to jump from the bed and run from the room. "I need out of here. How many?"

Barnabas frowned as he rose to stand beside her, his hand resting lightly on her wrist. "How many? How many what, Imly? I don't understand."

"How many days? How long have I been here?" She was getting more and more agitated.

"Seven days. Why? Is that important?"

"It is." She shifted away from him, off the bed and heading for the door, a hand held to her head in an attempt to control the pain. "I need to leave. Something is to happen today. And I just can't remember what."

Barnabas stood, dumbfounded that she was walking away, no almost running, he thought, before he was after her, a hand out to her arm to stop her.

"Imly, you just can't leave. Not with the head injury that you suffered."

"I have to, Barnabas. I have to go home. Something is going to happen and I don't know what or how to prevent." Imly was almost in tears, not seeing the physician and Doc heading her way.

———

"Imly?" Doc's voice barely broke through her agitation, and he turned to Barnabas for an explanation.

Barnabas shrugged. "She's convinced that she has to leave, that something is to happen today. Only she can't remember what."

Pacing the apartment, unable to settle down into a chair or even to lay on her bed, Imly searched for any sense or hint of Brendon. She swiped at the tears trickling down her cheeks. She did not cry. Ever. Never ever. She seemed to be doing that lately, she thought. Imly was grieving, for her parents, for Brendon, for his friends.

Pausing at the French door to the balcony, Imly rested her hand against a windowpane, feeling the coolness of the glass. My life is like that, was her thought. My life and my heart. Lord, how do I go on? How do I live, knowing that I brought this to Brendon, to his friends, to my parents? I just can't go on, not with that burden. Brendon would tell me I need to praise You, but I can't. Not yet, anyway. Lord, is he really dead? Something isn't right about that picture.

Hearing a tap at the door, Imly sighed. It had to be one of the guys, she thought, or one of the ladies, or Doc, or Anna. She didn't feel hospitable right now, not wanting to be around anyone. The tap sounded again, and she finally moved to walk through the living room, pausing for a moment to stare around, before her steps turned to the door, a hand holding the side of her head.

Hand on the door, Imly stared at the lady who stood there, a frown etching across her face.

"I'm sorry. I think you have the wrong apartment." Imly started to close the door but paused as the lady shook her head.

"No, I'm in the right place. You're Imly Conroy. Darcie described you."

"I'm sorry. Darcie?"

The lady laughed. "Darcie Foster. A retired forensics psychologist and a good friend. She and her husband, Doug, a police lieutenant, were here this past week at the request of other friends. Let me introduce myself. I'm Rylee Allison, a friend of Emma and Abe, who I don't think you have met yet." With a grin on her face, she held up the box in her hands. "Darcie asked me to bring you some sweets."

Imly finally stood back, motioning for Rylee to enter. "I guess, the kitchen. I'm sorry, this is all so new. Brendon and I had not been married long when we were kidnapped." She reached for the kettle, but paused, fighting the tears she could not stop.

Rylee gave an inaudible sound and simply swept Imly into a hug. "It's hard. It's so hard. I know that." She finally maneuvered Imly to a seat, before she reached to wring out a cloth in warm water to hand to her. Then, with the kettle on, she searched for tea and the teapot, and then the sugar and cream.

Imly looked up, her eyes red from her tears. "I should be doing that."

"No, you're to rest. I met your Doc downstairs. He was adamant that I look after you." Rylee searched for cups and small plates, opening the box to display a selection of baked goods. "You wouldn't know, but I have a bakeshop. Darcie told me that you needed some sweets." Rylee sat, her eyes on Imly, before she reached for one of Imly's hand, her head bowing as she prayed.

"Dear Father, my new friend is hurting, in so many ways. I know some of the pain she feels, dear Lord. But it's not the same. Our pain is so individual, just like us. It's hard to see the good stuff in all this, Lord. That's when You need to shake us and remind us that You are the One we look to and offer our praise to. It is You, dear Lord, who cradles us in Your hands and shelters us. We can only praise You for that. We can't totally understand it, now can we, Lord?"

Imly stared at Rylee as she prayed, never having heard someone talk to God in such an open and honest way. Rylee, looking up, caught the surprised look on Imly's face and laughed.

"I'm sorry. It's how I talk to God. I was taught that prayer is not just for certain times. It should be a day-long conversation with my Abba Father."

Imly finally nodded, the surprise wearing off. "That is so true." She sighed. "I wish it was that easy. Brendon told me that when he would brew coffee, he would pray for someone."

"That's it. Exactly." Rylee watched as Imly nibbled at a cookie. "I'm so sorry about your parents, Imly. I think that is why Darcie wanted me to come and see you. My parents were murdered when I was young, leaving my paternal grandmother to raise me and my two brothers."

"Wow! Your brothers must have been young."

"They were, but we made it. Dave, my husband, is the love of my life. If we had not moved here from Ireland, I would not have met him."

"Ireland? Strange that you came from there. Barnabas sent two of the men over there to investigate. I can't remember if he told me what they found. It was told around that my father was involved in crime, but it wasn't him at all." Imly's finger moved crumbs around on the table.

"They said the same about my father, but he wasn't involved, not at all. In fact, he was one of the ones who was trying to bring men to justice. They killed him because of that. But when Dave and I went through what we did, we were able to solve that with the help of detective friends and bring them to justice." Rylee paused speaking, staring across the kitchen. "I almost died, Imly. And if Darcie were to tell you Doug and her story, you would not believe it. It sounds like something from a novel. Doug is the ETF lieutenant. A rogue police chief wanted revenge on all the emergency services. He almost took out a large number of people in our town. He also shot Darcie. If another friend who is a paramedic had not been there, she would have died. And my Dave is a paramedic as well. He's been involved in so much that we can't even talk about."

"I get that, Rylee." Imly sat back, a hand rubbing at the side of her head. "I hate this, you know. I really do. I don't see what purpose God has in me ending up with a skull fracture and Brendon dead. Or my parents dead."

"Do you know for sure that Brendon is dead?" Rylee looked past Imly towards the hallway, hearing the door open quietly and then close, the sounds of shoes being removed and then equally quiet footsteps heading their way.

Breck, Brody, and Dave, Rylee's husband, appeared in the kitchen, moving quietly around the two ladies, to make coffee for themselves, before they were seated at the table, reaching into the box for some of the goodies.

Startled at the feeling of more people in her kitchen, Imly looked up, her face whitening for a moment. Dave watched her closely before he shared a look with Breck.

"Imly?" Breck's voice drew her eyes to him. "How are you? And don't say that you're fine, because we know you're not."

Imly stared at him, not used to being spoken to in such a blunt manner, before she shrugged.

"I really don't know, Breck. I have a horrible headache, I look like something that the cat dragged in, my parents are dead, Brendon is gone, likely dead." Her words paused as she frowned. "They showed me a picture, Breck. But there was something off about it. I can't put my finger on it."

Chapter 23

Breck nodded, his eyes on Brody for a moment, before he spoke.

"Talk to us, Imly. Tell us what you can remember. It doesn't have to make sense, if that's what is holding you back. Experience has taught me that sometimes it's what seems the least in an investigation or an event that could make or break the outcome."

Imly sighed, her head really beginning to hurt. "I can try, Breck, but I'm not thinking too clearly right now."

"We understand that, Imly." Brody spoke up. "Just start talking. If we need to clarify something with you, we can."

Imly finally nodded, pain showing in her eyes. "I think. I'm not sure of anything, Breck. Does that make sense?"

"It does. With your head injury, you may not remember exactly what happened. That we understand. Dallas is trying hard to track your steps but he can't seem to find anyone who saw you. Or at least, anyone who will acknowledge that."

"Wills has them scared. That much I know. He terrifies me, Breck. But I don't think that he was the one this time. I don't recall hearing his voice. It was someone different, someone I know but I can't remember who at the present." She reached for her cup, her hand shaking as she raised it to her mouth to sip from it, her other hand coming up to help steady it.

"Just take your time, Imly." Breck had reached for the pad of paper that he had set to one side, his pen in his hand. "I'll take notes and then we can go back over them."

"Old school, Breck? I didn't think anyone used pen and paper anymore."

Breck grinned as Brody laughed. "I do, Imly. I find I think better if I write it out this way. Okay. So, where do we start?"

"At the beginning, I guess." Imly frowned. "I know that person who was there. Quite well, I think, but I just don't know. I can't remember who it is." She sighed. "I have to go back, I think, to when it all started. We talked about it, right?"

"We did, Imly. You were upfront and honest with us. Wills had you kidnapped and brought down here. He had been stalking you, trying to date you. A man his age? He'd be in his fifties at least."

"He is. Fifty-five in fact. He made sure that I knew that. I hated him being around him. He made me feel dirty and unclean. I can't quite explain what I mean. I think I told you that my employer protected me as much as he could until I had to quit. This took a lot of my freedom away from me.

"When we arrived here, he was waiting in a house outside town. I had no freedom until one day I was able to escape, shoving him from me. He told me that we would be married that day. I couldn't stay here. I know he looked for me here in town. I made a few friends over the three or four days I was on the streets. They protected me. Not one of them liked Wills. He is linked to more crime that what you have discovered. One of them told me that he tried to recruit some of them to break into homes and businesses and steal artwork and jewelry, that he would then sell on the black market or ship overseas.

"Now, to come to the present. I think Wills was behind our abduction, but I can't say for sure. I always felt that there was someone else involved, someone who had power over him. He's a coward and a bully. I just don't know who." She paused, reaching for her tea, sipping it even though it had grown cold.

"To go back to when you had told us about a heritage you had coming to you. The fellows have confirmation that there is none. And that there has not been in years. The official they spoke with would not confirm if there was a criminal element still promoting that idea." Brody looked at Breck, finding him watching Imly closely.

Imly nodded, fatigue weighing her down. "I understand that. I just don't know why Dad would have told me that." She paused before she shook her head. "As to this kidnapping, I can't tell you much. I don't remember, excepts for bits and pieces that aren't clear. Except for that photo."

"What is striking you wrong about the photo?" Rylee spoke, her eyes on Dave as he nodded. They had faced something similar.

"I'm not sure." Imly turned to her. "It just didn't seem to be Brendon. The man's build was off. He was laying in such a way that I couldn't see his face." A cry came from her. "There was no wedding band. I could see his left hand. There was no wedding band. And Brendon had one." She held up her hand. "He bought me one to give him that matched mine. A rose gold one and engraved, which is unusual. Does that mean it wasn't him?"

"Quite possibly. They would have been playing mind games with you, Imly." Breck looked down at his notes. "You said there was blood on the chest?"

"There was, but there was no hole in his shirt." She paused once more. "And it wasn't the shirt Brendon had on. I doubt they would have made him change it. It was somewhat similar in colour, but it didn't match."

"Then, I think we can safely say, it was not likely Brendon who you saw. Whether that man is alive or dead, that we will have to leave to the police." Breck looked up, a thoughtful look on his face. "What else, Imly?"

"I don't know." She buried her face in her hands, her headache increasing. "I don't know. I seem to remember walking to the church. From the lake or thereabouts. Does that make sense?"

"It does. There is a direct road or several paths that come up to the church from there. We can start looking that way." Brody rose at a nod from Breck. "I'll go find some of the guys. We have time yet today that we can search."

Breck watched him walk away, the door closing quietly behind him, before he looked back to Imly, seeing how white and drained she had become.

"Imly, we'll leave it at this today. You do need to be resting."

"I know, Breck, but resting does not bring Brendon back." Her face whitened even more as a look of absolute horror crossed her face and a cry was wrenched from deep within her. "I know who it was." Her eyes rolled back as she collapsed, sliding from her chair.

Dave had been on the move before she had spoken, catching her in his arms and then looking around.

"Down the hall, Dave. The last room on your left is the bedroom. I'll find Doc." Breck was out of his chair, heading for the main floor, knowing Doc would be there somewhere.

Rylee reached to pull the blankets back before Dave gently laid Imly in her bed, pulling them back up before she stood to one side, watching as Dave worked over Imly.

Doc walked back through the apartment, a grave look on his face. He simply shook his head at Breck before he walked to the apartment door and through it, looking for Barnabas among their friends gathered there.

"Doc?" Brady approached, Barnabas beside him. "How is she?"

"We need to admit her, Brady. I am not convinced that there is not something going on. We need to do imaging and I may need to call in another specialist." He paused, not quite sure how to express what he needed to. He wasn't all that familiar with Imly, not enough to know how she would react if he said much about her condition.

"Doc? Are you thinking bleeding?" Barnabas shared a look with Brady, who nodded. That had been his thought.

"I am. It may be nothing, but I would rather err on the side of caution. Brady? Who's working today?"

"Tammy and Luke."

"Good. They'll take care of her. Request them when you call it in."

"Already done." He walked away, heading for the main entrance, to wait for his colleagues.

Barnabas watched him walk away before he spoke.

"How serious, Doc?"

"Now, that I can't tell you. Breck seemed to think that she had remembered something. He was grateful that God had placed Dave there today."

"It is how He works, isn't it?" Barnabas rubbed at his face. "Mom and Dad are heading this way, he said. They are concerned. He is not sure if he knows her parents."

"Then from who? Do either one of them have siblings?"

"Her father. And no one knows exactly where he is right now, not that I know of."

"I can tell you exactly where he is." Burnie spoke from beside him. "He's here in town. Dallas is back in town and has confirmed sightings of him."

"He does?" Doc shook his head. "Is he the one behind all this?"

"I would suspect so." Burnie shook the sheaf of papers in his head. "This is only part of what we have found. He was estranged from her father, had been for a number of years, but confirmation is coming that he was seen frequently in her home town and around their home."

"This has to hurt. Finding out this will set her back in her healing." Barnabas turned for a moment, his eyes on the door to the apartment. "Buckley called a bit ago. He's got the prayer chain working and has set up the room in the church and in the chapel here. He said there have been many calls, asking how the people can help."

"That's good." Doc paced away before he spun and returned. "Has she said anything at all?"

Breck spoke from behind him. "She's adamant now that the man in the photo was not Brendon, but just who it was, we don't know. Imly has been able to remember enough of what bothered her that convinced her that they were lying to her about the photo. But she is not convinced that Brendon is still alive. She thinks she walked to the church from the lake area. Some of the men have taken a look this afternoon but came back as soon as word reached them about her."

"She won't like that." Doc shook his head before his hand reached for the doorknob to the apartment door. "I'll be with her. We need to solve this, men, and soon."

They watched as Doc disappeared before turning to the others gathered around them, the men and their ladies, the single men, the teens. Barnabas drew a deep breath. Every time one of his friends went through something, it seemed to be worse. He had a dread of what the others would face, but he also acknowledged that God was in control.

—

Rylee met Doc as he paused in the kitchen, concern on her face.

"Doc? Imly is awake and is adamant that she will not go back to the hospital. Dave has checked her vitals, her vision, and said they are within normal limits."

Doc sighed. "We can't force her, but she'll be here on her own." Doc made a move to head for the bedroom when Rylee's hand stopped him.

"She knows that, Doc. She told us that she was fine with that, that if she needed someone she would call. She has expressed her desire to be on her own." Rylee was concerned, that was evident. "I can understand that, Doc. You don't know my history or Dave's. My parents were murdered when I was sixteen, leaving my younger brothers and me on our own except for Dad's mother. I know that feeling of wanting to be on my own, to grieve, to come to terms with what she has to face."

"But you weren't injured." Doc pointed past her. "She has a head injury. This episode today? It could be a bleed on the brain."

"It could, but we can't force her to treatment." Rylee watched with compassion as Doc's mouth worked as he tried to control his emotions. Imly had a way, with her soft voice and her demeanour of not wanting to make trouble for anyone, of wrapping herself into their heartstrings on first meeting.

"No, we can't." Doc sighed, turning as Brady tapped at the door and entered. "Brady, sent the crew away. Imly won't go."

Brady nodded. "Already did. We talked, the three of us. We figured this would be the situation." He shook his head in turn. "We'll watch for her."

"But not overnight. She is adamant that she won't have anyone around her. She doesn't want to put anyone out, as she stated it."

Brady stared at Rylee. "She said that? She doesn't know us. We won't let that happen."

"Unfortunately, Brady, we have to respect her wishes. I made sure all our numbers are on her phone." Doc walked away from them, heading towards Imly.

———

Dave had a few quiet words with Doc before he moved away, finding Rylee waiting for him.

"Dave?" Rylee walked into his hug.

"Imly won't budge." Dave sighed, knowing he would have done the same. "It's her choice."

"It is. A voice inside me says something is going to break loose soon. And she will be hurt once more."

Dave nodded, his hug tightening. "I know, love. I know. All we can do is pray for her."

A week passed and then a second one. Imly wandered the apartment and then the building and then the outdoors, trailed when she did that by one of the security guards. She was now on a first-name basis with them all, she thought.

She had lain awake each night, finally rising around four to pace the apartment before she would find her Bible and spend the next hours in prayer and Bible study. She was growing in that way, coming more aware of God working in her life. She was trying hard to learn to praise in this situation, but it was tough, she acknowledged to the ladies, who would spend time with her each day, taking turns. They had agreed with her but told her that all she had to do was be willing. God knew her heart and how hard it was for her.

Imly also spent time in the conference room, as much as they would let her, reading through the material that she would find on the table in front of the chair she favoured. The men would study her and then look at one another, shaking their heads. They had each returned to their normal occupation, knowing that at some point, they would be called away again.

Brody had taken to spending his time seated next to Imly. He was concerned, monitoring the whiteness or grayness of her face, as the case may be. When he questioned how she was feeling, she would simply shrug and respond that she had no idea how she was to feel, that she had never been in such a situation before.

Imly frowned as she stared at the pages in front of her four weeks after she had returned home. Her strength was gradually returning, not because she has keeping up the diet Doc had given her. She was grateful for his loving care but it didn't make it any easier. She rubbed at her forehead, the headache still there but only a dull roar, was how she now termed it.

Looking up, she searched for someone who could help her understand what she was reading. It didn't make sense, but then in a bizarre way, it did. She had not told anyone who it was that she suspected of being behind Wills. She still had not come to terms with that.

"Imly? You look puzzled?" Brennen sat on one side of her, Branigan on the other.

"I am. This? These dates? Who came up with them?" Imly's finger tapped at the paper.

Branigan leaned over to read what had caused her concern. "Jace or Emma, I think. We didn't. I don't think that we've seen those. I don't remember them at all. Brennen?"

Brennen had reached for the paper, leafing through them. "No, this is new stuff. Emma has sent it. We haven't had it given to us yet. How?"

Imly shrugged. "It was sitting here, where I usually sit. I thought one of you had put it there."

"No, I don't think that we did." Branigan was on his feet, his phone out, questioning each man before he returned. "Burnie did. He has copies for each of us, which we haven't got yet. He said they're in a pile on the table." He looked around. "I don't see them."

"They're not here. That is strange. Who would have taken them?" Brennen was on his feet in turn, heading for the security guard.

"Does it matter?" Imly was puzzled at their reaction.

"It does, Imly. If someone has taken them, then either it was one of the security personnel or someone was in here, getting in through a locked door, and removing all the copies but that one." He reached for her copy. "May I borrow this for a few minutes? I want to make copies."

Imly shrugged. "Sure. Whatever."

Branigan was back in his chair, a stern look on his face. "That's not right, Imly. It is not "whatever". You matter to us. Whether you have accepted it or not, you are part of the Foundation family."

She sighed. "I know that. I just have trouble remembering that. For so many years, it was just my parents and me." She looked up at him. "What do we know about that?"

"The police are not saying. Nor is Dallas. He wants to meet with you sometime this week, I think."

"He said that. I'm not sure I'm ready to. Not without Brendon." Her voice was quiet enough that Branigan could barely hear her.

"We know, Imly. We know. Now, about this?" He was on his feet, heading for the photocopier, making his copies, and then back in his chair beside her, her copy in front of her. "Talk to me. Tell me what you see."

"What I see? I see dates that don't make sense. These dates for my parents' birthdays? That's not what we always celebrated. Mine is correct. Their anniversary is wrong." A thought crossed her mind. "Branigan, do you have photos that would go with these dates?"

His hand stilled from where he had been running his finger down the page, the other hand with his pen jotting notes. "I'm not sure. What are you thinking?"

"That may be the people who I believed were my parents, weren't. Is that a possibility?"

"That is what I need to talk to you about, Imly." Dallas' voice from beside her had her jumping in her chair even as she turned, a white look on her face.

"They weren't my parents, were they?"

"No, they weren't. I'm sorry, Imly. I truly am. They were the ones who were connected to Wills at some point. We also have evidence that they were connected to the criminal group in Ireland who noised around about that heritage you were to receive."

"Then, who am I?" Imly could barely whisper the words, tears near the surface.

"You are Imly MacDermott. That we have proven. We are working on finding your real parents, but have hit a roadblock there."

"How old would I have been when this happened?"

"We're not sure, but likely a baby or young toddler. You don't have any memories, do you?"

"Not of anyone but them. They loved me, Dallas. How could that be?" Imly rose, running from the room, unable to stem the tears, brushing past Ennis and Hagen as they called to her.

<hr>

The two women stared after her and then at one another, before looking at Branigan, who had followed Imly from the room.

"Branigan?" Hagen turned to watch where Imly had fled to. "What just happened?"

"She just found out her parents were not her parents."

"What? Oh, my!" Ennis turned as well. "Someone needs to be with her."

"Let her be for now, Ennis. Check on her later." Branigan turned away from them, returning to the conference room, determination of his face to find out just who that couple was.

That night, the moon and stars were hidden behind the heavy dark clouds that dripped a cold misty rain on the ground. The wind was strong, blowing in from the lake, a bitter chill to it, sending the late autumn leaves scurrying to the ground in front of it. The man paused for a moment outside the Foundation building, searching for anyone that might see him, before he adjusted his hold on the second man, leading him to the back door. He reached for the keys in the man's jacket pocket and unlocked the door, letting him in and then handing him his keys. He waited as the man hesitated and then walked forward, his steps slow and weighted, his hand running along the wall to help balance himself.

Brendon slowing climbed the stairs to the third floor, each stair seeing higher than the one before it, needing to stop every few steps to catch his breath. He didn't know where the man was, who told him to call him John, that he would get him to safety. He needed his help to continue, only he was on his own.

Finally reaching his own door, he leaned against the wall, his face gray and drawn in the overhead lighting. He fumbled with his keys to unlock the door, stepping into the apartment, the door closing behind him, and reaching down to remove his shoes, out of habit setting them into the closet. He drew a deep breath as he straightened back up.

John had found him the day before, he thought, freeing him from his prison and taking him to safety. After four weeks, Brendon was grubby and unkempt, his hair long, his face covered in whiskers that he hated but hadn't been able to do anything about.

John had let him sleep, rousing him only to get broth and water down his throat. He had watched Brendon carefully, his skills as an armed forces medic coming into play. Brendon had roused about three hours previously, a question on his lips that never was asked. John had helped him into the shower, Brendon shaky on his feet, leaving clean clothes for him, before he had seated him at a table, and without waiting for Brendon to refuse, played barber for the younger man.

Brendon, once more clean-shaven and with his hair trimmed neatly, had gratefully eaten the soup placed before him, too tired to even ask who John was and how he had found him. He had paid little attention as John had walked him from the lake area to the Foundation building, not even questioning how John knew where he belonged.

He walked slowly through his apartment, a frown puckering his forehead, as he saw the dim light from his bedroom. That is strange, he thought. I don't remember leaving a light on. He stared down at the wedding band on his finger, his thoughts on his bride. Lord, they told me she was gone, but they wouldn't tell me if she had left me or if she was dead. That played on my mind. It was so hard to try and praise You in those circumstances. I tried, Lord, I really did.

Making his way through his apartment to the bedroom, Brendon rifled in his dresser for his nightclothes, heading for the ensuite bathroom to change, before he headed towards the bed. His steps slowed and then stopped. Wonder lit his face as he saw Imly, asleep, her hand on his pillow, traces of the tears that she had wept in her sleep on her face.

She is here, Lord. I didn't know that. I wonder if John did. Thank you, Lord, that she is here and alive. He slipped in beside her, his arms coming out to wrap around her and cradle her to him. His own tears wet the red hair that he loved, even as he slipped away to sleep, his body unable to keep him alert or awake.

Awakening in the early morning hours, as had become her custom, Imly lay, her eyes closed, sensing something different around her. She slowly opened her eyes, a frown on her face as she realized she was held firmly in someone's arms. Momentary fear drove through her until she raised her head and saw Brendon. Her own wonder grew before she raised herself even more, to drop a kiss on his cheek, before she slipped away, to dress and then head for the kitchen.

I will let him sleep, won't I, Lord? I have no idea where he came from or when, but I am thankful that he is here with me. Time enough to talk later today. She hummed a praise chorus without realizing that she was, as she fixed her tea and then set the coffeemaker, ready to turn it on when Brendon awoke. She paused, her hand resting on the fridge door, her eyes turning towards the hallway, listening for Brendon's movements.

———

284

Imly reached for her phone, to check her messages as had become her habit on a daily basis. She smiled. Breck had sent his usual good morning message. He had taken on the role of a big brother to her, one that she desperately had needed. She scrolled through the messages, tears briefly blinding her as she read them. Each one of the fellows, including Barnabas, had sent messages of encouragement for her. The ladies had each sent a thought or a prayer or a Bible verse for her. She hadn't realized just how they had taken her into their growing family, but today, she finally understood.

Lost in thought, she had not heard Brendon moving around in the bedroom or the soft sounds of his footsteps as he padded towards the kitchen. Brendon paused in the doorway, his eyes on her, thankful once more that she was alive and that he was home with her. Now, he thought, we need to find out who is responsible for the destruction and devastation that they had both undergone.

He walked towards her, his arms coming around her, causing a small squeak to come from her, before she wrapped her arms around him.

"When did you get home, Brendon?" Her voice was muffled against him.

He shrugged. "I'm not sure. I wasn't too awake last night or rather early this morning. Somewhere around one, I think. John didn't tell me."

"John? Who's that?" Imly was puzzled. She didn't know a John, or at least, she didn't think she did.

"He's the one who found me, fed me, cleaned me up, and brought me back to you." Brendon's arms tightened around her. "They told me that you were gone. I just didn't know if you had left me or were dead."

Imly shuddered at her own memories. "They told me that you were dead. They even showed me a picture, but we've figured out that it wasn't you. We just don't know who it was."

"No? Maybe I can help." He swayed slightly, fatigue hitting him unawares. He reached for a chair to sit, Imly's hand resting on his shoulder. "Imly? Are you okay?" He searched her face, seeing that she had been through a trial without him.

———

"I'm getting there, my love. I was hurt. I escaped from Wills but fell somehow. I'm not even sure how now. Anyway, I hit my head hard enough to fracture the skull." She watched as his eyes slid closed before she wrapped her arms around him once more. "I made it to the church and Buckley got me to help. I'm better every day."

"Oh, sweetheart, I wish I had been there. They have taken so much time from us."

"That they have." Imly moved away, to switch on the coffeemaker before she turned back to him. "We are researching and investigating. Someone named Emma is sending information to us and to Dallas."

"Emma? That's good. She finds things no one else can, but can't explain how she does it."

Imly looked towards the outside door as a tap came to it. "That will be one of the fellows or one of the ladies. They have made it a habit of appearing each morning, just to make sure I'm okay."

"They're a great bunch." Brendon took the mug of coffee she handed him before he reached to kiss her, not wanting her to move from his sight, his arm around her waist to keep her near him.

"Brendon. I need to answer the door." Imly shook her head at him even as she smiled, content for the moment.

"I know." He sighed. "I guess that means it will get out that I'm home."

"It will. You don't know how worried all of them have been." Imly moved away from him, to open the door.

Doc stood there, as well as Dave and Rylee, his mouth open to speak before he snapped it closed.

"When did he get home?" Rylee's soft question came even as she hugged Imly.

"Sometime last night. I didn't hear him at all." Imly looked up at Doc. "He's not in great shape, Doc. He said someone named John found him and brought him home."

Shaking his head, Doc stepped away from Brendon, who was seated in his office chair. He was not sure what all Brendon had been through, but he seemed to be in good health, and that Doc could not understand. The wound from the bullet had healed well, Doc was glad to see.

"Brendon? What can you tell us?" Dallas spoke from where he was perched on the corner of the desk. He had appeared just after Doc had entered their apartment.

"I'm not sure what all I can tell you. I never saw the faces on the men, and there were only two that came around me. I was locked into some sort of hole in the ground, with a door to go in and out. I could see the sky above and yes, it did rain down on me. It was not a pleasant place to be." He shook his head. "I didn't really see them much. I slept a lot, I think, and when I would be asleep, that seems to be when the food and water that they provided appeared in my cage. They would come around, ask me questions that didn't make sense and then disappear."

Dallas looked up from his notes. "What sort of questions?"

Brendon shrugged. "Just about who I was, where I was from, who my parents were. I didn't answer, and they didn't like that. About two weeks ago, they told me that Imly was gone, but refused to clarify that. I didn't know if she had left me or was dead."

"And that played with your mind." Dallas stared at him for a moment, before his eyes dropped to his notes. "Now, you mentioned a John. Who is he?"

Brendon shook his head. "I have no idea who he is. He just appeared, not yesterday, the day before, opened the door, dragged me to my feet, and led me from there. I couldn't tell you where we ended up. I just couldn't concentrate. He fed me, let me sleep, helped me to clean up, and then brought me here. He didn't say a word the whole time. And I can't remember what he looked like."

Dallas nodded. Brendon's comment was about what he expected him to say. "How about the men that held you captive?"

Brendon shrugged, not willing to say. "Average height. Average weight. Neatly kept. One had blond hair, one brown. Clean-shaven. I really wasn't paying that much attention." He sighed. "And no, I won't work with a police artist. I don't remember enough to describe them. Besides, it was dim, with only the light coming from the hole above me."

"Okay." Dallas shared a look with Doc and then Dave, who was closely watching Brendon.

Dave mentally shook his head. *He knows more, doesn't he, Lord? He's just not saying. They must have threatened Imly, that would be the only reason that he won't say.*

Doc and Dallas finally walked away, Dave's head turning to watch them, before he looked over at Brody and Brennen, who were seated nearby, their eyes on Brendon.

"What didn't you tell him, Brendon?" Dave's voice was quiet.

"What do you mean?" Brendon wasn't sure about Dave, only having met him that morning, although Imly seemed to trust him.

"You know more than you said. Or you suspect more than what you told him." Dave leaned forward, reaching for the pad of paper and pen laying on the desktop.

Brendon sighed. "You're right. What I couldn't say are impressions that I had." He looked over at Brody. "You two know me. I don't make accusations."

"No, you don't, but you have an impression that you can't shake." Brennen looked towards the doorway. "Right now, Brendon, I would say that you need to rest. Doc's heading back this way, and I think you'll find Imly with him."

Imly appeared in the doorway, a frown on her face at Brennen's words. "Brennen?"

"It's okay. We're just trying to get Brendon to take it easy."

"I know. Brendon, Lawrence is here. He's asking about you."

Brendon gave a slow nod and started to stand. Lawrence had appeared behind Imly, and then moved past her, motioning Brendon to stay seated before he seated himself in front of the desk, nodding at the other three men and motioning Imly to stay.

"Brendon? What did Doc have to say?" Lawrence was concerned, more about Brendon's health than that he was behind in his orders in the shop.

"That I need to rest. I want to come back, Lawrence, even part-time. Is that possible?" Brendon knew that he was pushing it.

"You can. Edward has stepped in for now, but he's not interested in full-time work. His work with the teens is where his heart is."

"I know. This is Thursday. How be I start part-time again on Monday?" He looked up at Imly, who was standing beside him, her hand on his shoulder, his arm around her waist. "And Imly will come with me. She's eager to take over in the office."

Lawrence's face lit up. "You are?" At Imly's nod, his smile grew bigger. "That is an answer to prayer. With you in the office, I can go back into the workshop."

"But, Lawrence, what if I bring danger or trouble to your business?" Imly had considered that many times while Brendon was missing.

"I thought of that. Barnabas has been in touch. He sent a security guard over to assess what I need and I have made the changes he suggested. No one gets into the workshop or office area. We have a locked steel door. The showroom has been redesigned to some degree, with more of the items showcasing on the website. We'll make it work, Imly."

Lawrence finally left, Brendon secretly glad that he had. He was exhausted but he just couldn't rest, not until he talked to his friends. It looked as if Dave was now a friend as well.

"Dave? What do you do?" Brendon was searching for answers to questions he didn't know how to ask.

"I'm a paramedic. I'm friends with Doug and Darcie. And Abe and his men. Abe, Doug, and I grew up together. And if you need more information from a security standpoint, talk to Abe. I'm sure Barnabas already has."

———
289

"He has." Brody spoke up. "But for now, we're not doing anything more. Brendon, your volunteer work with the badminton club has been taken care of. Burnie was glad to step in. He states that he needs some new ideas for his novels and this is a perfect opportunity to try and find some."

Brendon grinned, his mind eased on that front. "He does, does he? I'm sure the teens will give him plenty of that."

Dave was finally the only one left in the room with Brendon, the two friends leaving to head to their employment, and Imly had left with Rylee to find some of the ladies in the building. Dave studied Brendon closer, seeing the fatigue, but also something else.

"What else is bothering you, Brendon?"

Brendon looked up, surprised at the question. "I'm not sure what you mean."

"I mean, there is something else, something that you haven't told anyone else. And before you deny it, I've been there. Rylee and I went through some pretty intense stuff around the time we got married. I almost lost her. So, I do have a sense of what you are feeling."

"You did?" Brendon drew in a breath. "Yes, there is something. Imly said her parents are dead, that they have been identified, but that it has been proven that they were not her biological parents. I don't see that. How do we prove or disprove that?"

Nodding, Dave leaned back in his chair, a thoughtful look on his face. He finally looked up at Brendon, finding the other man watching him closely.

"You have doubts? How were they identified?"

"Imly said it was the police in her hometown. I don't trust some of them. One of them had connections to the man, Wills, who had her kidnapped and brought down here. And then, there's John. How does he fit in? He never said anything. I have no idea who he is or where he is even from, or how he even found me."

"I can have Emma or Jace look into him. If you can describe him, that is."

"I can only in a vague sort of way. My mind was so fogged with a lack of sleep and nutrition. I am not sure that I wasn't drugged at some point."

"You more than likely were. You have no idea where you were?"

Brendon shook his head. "I don't. So, how do we prove that it was them? And how do we prove that they were or were not her parents?"

"Let Emma work on that. And a friend's wife can as well. She has a family tree program that she will gladly use. Just let me have all the information you can on Imly's family."

Later that afternoon, Imly found Brendon still seated at his desk, his computer up, his cold mug of coffee on the desk beside him. She simply shook her head, removed the mug, and headed for the kitchen to make him fresh. She paused as she did so, a thought niggling at her mind, before she shook her head. No, she didn't think that she knew the man Brendon called John, but when he had described what he could remember, he seemed familiar.

Having spent a number of hours in the conference room with the men and the ladies, Imly was exhausted, her headache returning. She had overdone it, she knew, but she was pushing herself to solve this mystery surrounding herself. It was only when it was solved and the culprits in custody that she felt Brendon and she could go on with their lives.

Brendon finally looked up, rubbing at his eyes, squinting towards the window. He was shocked to see that dusk had fallen. His eyes dropped to his work. He had made progress, he thought, but just what that was, he wasn't quite sure. Brendon knew he would need to talk with his friends, to get their perspective on what he had found and to see how it all correlated with what they were working on.

He rose, searching the apartment for Imly, standing beside the bed where he found her curled up, her arms wrapped around her, a gray look on her face. His finger reached to gently trace the track of her tears. Brendon sighed. He wanted to make it all better for her, but just couldn't. Lord, why? Why Imly? How do we praise You in these circumstances? This is taking a toll on her, on her body, on her mind, on her spirit.

Brendon reached for the blanket that Imly had folded neatly at the end of the bed and tucked it around her, a hand resting gently on her head as he prayed for his bride. He turned finally, heading for the kitchen, a glance at the clock showing it was past their supper time. He wasn't hungry but knew he needed to eat.

An hour later, Brendon stood in the conference room, facing Baird, Benen, and Blair, who were grouped in a half-circle in front of him. He could see the other men watching closely, all but Barnabas, and he knew that Barnabas had a meeting that he had to be out of town.

"What are you saying, Baird?" Brendon shook his head, not quite comprehending what he had been told.

"That Imly's parents are not dead. The couple that they found? They looked similar to them, but Barnabas asked that DNA testing be done. Dallas called, looking for either one of you. He asked that I tell you or Imly that her parents are still alive. We just don't know where they are."

Brendon's eyes slid shut, his emotions getting the best of him for a moment. "So, they are alive? How do we find them?"

Baird shook his head. "That we don't know. No one has seen them since that day Imly spoke with them. Emma's working on that, but she had a rush investigation that she had to take on. She apologized but said she'd be working on it again as soon as she could."

Brendon felt a hand on his back and reached to wrap an arm around Imly. "Imly? I thought you were sleeping."

"I was." Imly still had the gray, drawn look on her face, and the pain from her headache showed in her eyes. "My parents are still alive? Is that what you just said?"

"They are." Baird shared a look with Benen and Blair. "We just don't know where they are at present."

Imly nodded, a hand resting on the side of her head. "I have no idea where they would be. Unless Wills has them in his control and has hidden them somewhere." She paused. "Brendon, this John? Can you describe him again?"

Brendon proceeded to do so, his eyes on Imly as she frowned and then turned, breaking away from him to head for a computer, seating herself. He watched as her head bowed for a moment before he was in the chair beside her, an arm around her, Breck moving in on her other side, the other men gathering around.

"Imly? Sweetheart?"

Imly looked up, a clear look in her eyes again. "I think I might know him. You said he seemed to know how to treat you medically?"

"That was my impression. His care went beyond just an ordinary person."

Brady spoke up. "In other words, he assessed you and went from there in how he treated you?" At Brendon's nod, Brady continued. "Then, he's either in the medical field, has had training, or is retired from some sort of service or healthcare company."

"Then, I think that I do know him." Imly's fingers flew across the keyboard as she searched for a name, finally pulling up a news story. "Is this him, Brendon?"

Brendon stared at the photo on the screen, before he swallowed hard and then nodded. "It is. How?"

"I haven't seen him in years. He's Dad's brother, but we haven't seen in him something like five years. No, more like ten. He was in the armed forces, serving as a medic. He retired, suffering from post-traumatic stress disorder. He hadn't really remained in one place for too long." She looked up. "But, how did he end up here? And to find you?"

"That's something we will ask him when we find him. And find him we will." Brendon's arm tightened on her. "I guarantee you, we will find him."

Lawrence turned from where he had been sanding a table and watching Brendon closely. Brendon had been back to work for almost two weeks, not saying a lot about what had happened to him, but that was alright with Lawrence. He knew Brendon kept a lot inside but would talk to him if he felt he needed to. His eyes turned to where the office was, and a smile crossed his face. He could hear Imly singing to herself, and he nodded. She had made a difference in his workload, taking on the office work.

Brendon paused his staining, staring at the dresser he had just finished, before he tapped the lid back on the can of stain and walked over to the large stainless steel sink that they used for cleaning their equipment, setting the brush into the container of paint thinner to clean. He shook his head. They were no further ahead, he thought, than they had been.

Imly thoughtfully replaced the phone receiver. Whoever it had been really didn't want to order furniture, now did they, she thought. A fishing expedition was more like it. She had not taken the bait, simply keeping her comments on the products that Lawrence carried or could manufacture. She rose from her desk, stretching, her eyes on the monitor for the security camera at the front of the store. He's back, isn't he? She almost ran from the office, searching for Brendon, throwing herself at him as she shook with terror.

Lawrence took one look at her and ran for the office, his eyes on the monitor as well even as he reached for the phone to call for help.

Brendon hugged her tight, his chin resting on the top of her head, feeling her shaking in her fear.

"Is he out there, love?"

"He is, pacing around the front of the building. What did I do, Brendon? I've brought trouble to Lawrence."

"No, you haven't, Imly." Lawrence spoke from behind her. "I know that man, but not by the name you call him. He's tried to weasel his way into part ownership of the shop. I won't have him on the premises. Stay back here, you two. I called for the police to come, and I was assured there was a patrol car in the area. Hopefully, they will be able to arrest him and keep him in jail for a while."

"Not long enough, Lawrence." Imly shifted in Brendon's arms, turning to face him. "He'll make bail and be out in no time."

"I don't think so, love. When I spoke with Dallas last, they were looking for him. Apparently, he has been involved in incidents in other jurisdictions as Dallas put it. The charges against him include murder and extortion."

Imly relaxed back against him. "Does that mean he won't be around?" Her voice was barely audible.

"He won't, but someone else will be. That is guaranteed." Dallas spoke from where he had come to a halt beside Lawrence. "We know he's not working on his own. We also know there is someone over him. That person is staying well hidden."

Imly nodded, not liking what Dallas had to say. It had just confirmed what she thought.

"So, now what? I'm not staying hidden away for weeks or months. I can't live like that. Nor can Brendon."

"We realize that, Imly, and are trying to investigate, but we keep hitting a blank wall. And that we can't understand."

"That's because you're not looking in the right places. I told you about that officer in my hometown. I am sure, if you look hard enough, you'll find someone on your own force, near to the investigation that is stonewalling you." Imly broke away from Brendon and headed back to the office, her hand reaching for the phone receiver to answer an incoming call.

Brendon watched her walk away before he spoke.

"Dallas? Had you thought of that?"

Dallas sighed. "We have. We are investigating a few of our officers. We're not liking what we're finding. Will is speaking with their supervisors today. Unfortunately, we're not confident that we have found the one or ones that we need to."

"Find them and find them soon. If you don't, I'll do the looking. I don't want this to drag on. She's stressed and that's stressing me. It's not helping her heal. And she's missing her parents. Do you know where they are?" Brendon walked away, heading towards Imly, to find her with her head pillowed on the arms she had folded on the desk, her body shaking with her subdued sobs. He dropped to his knees beside her, gathering her close, his lips moving in prayer for her.

"Dallas?" Lawrence didn't ask anything more.

"I know, Lawrence. I know. It's been the same for all of them, hasn't it?"

"It has, but something about Imly makes me want to help her. And it's not just because she's part of the family. It's her."

"I know what you mean. She's the little sister everyone wants to have and doesn't have. That makes us protective of her." Dallas blew out a breath before he shook his head and then walked away,

Early that same evening, Brendon stood in the conference room, staring at the whiteboards on the walls, noting the new information written on them. He walked towards one, a finger tracing the name.

"Who is this?"

Branigan looked over his shoulder. "Dwayne Easton? He is a son of Wills. No one seemed to know that here in town. He's involved in the shady side of life in town."

"How deep?"

"About as deep as you can get." Brandon shoved a photo at him. "This is him."

Brendon stared down at it. "He's one of them."

"One of who?"

"The two men that held me." Brendon's finger tapped the photo. "He's the blond. Now, who's the one with the brown hair?"

Bradon's hand reached into his line of sight, to drop a photo on top of the one Brendon was still holding. "Here. This is a cousin of his. They're always seen together."

"And this is the other one. Do we know where they are?"

"We do. They're up in Imly's hometown, sitting in jail at present. They were arrested for break and enter at her home up there."

———

Berneen and Cadee watched Imly walk towards them a few days later. They had agreed to meet for lunch, Imly not sure if she should put the ladies at risk. They had laughed at her, telling her that all the younger ladies in the building family had faced things and came through victorious. She would be no different.

Imly hesitated as she approached them, her eyes tracing past them, a frown on her face as she saw the man watching her before he turned and walked away. That was John, she thought. But why was he here? He obviously didn't want her to acknowledge him.

Berneen had watched Imly closely before she turned, her own eyes following the man walking away, making a mental note to talk to Baird that night.

"Imly? Ready for some lunch?" Cadee grinned at her, pointing towards the restaurant near Lawrence's building.

"I am. This is a restaurant?" Imly looked up in awe at the round building. "I thought it was a tower of some kind."

"Not at all. The owners wanted to build a castle but weren't allowed by the town council. They compromised on just a tower. They call it The Turret."

"Interesting name. British food?"

Berneen laughed as she waved at one of the owners and then pointed to a table near the back of the restaurant. "Not at all. Canadian is the predominant choice. But they do have a wonderful fish and chips or fries or whatever you want to call them."

An hour later, Imly waved goodbye to the two and walked back towards the shop, her thoughts not on the lunch, but on the man that she had seen. Was that really John? She would likely never know for sure. Her steps slowed as she neared the back door, her hand reaching to key in the code before she slipped through the open door, closing it tightly behind her.

Frowning, Imly looked around. Brendon and Lawrence should be here at work but she could not hear anything. She searched, not finding either one, before she hurried to the office, her eyes on the monitor to the shop. She drew in her breath sharply before reaching for the phone.

Brendon and Lawrence stood side by side, just inside the showroom, in front of the shop door, their hands raised, their eyes on the man in front of them. No, Brendon thought, it isn't Wills, but he has to be connected to him in some way.

Lawrence shifted his weight slightly, his eyes on the windows behind the man, seeing the police officers approaching quietly. He nodded to himself. Imly must have returned and found us.

"What is it exactly that you want?" Brendon's voice held a touch of anger and also fear. He didn't want the man to know where Imly was.

"Your woman. That's who. She needs to come with me." The man pointed to the door. "She's back there. How be we go on back there and you find her for me?"

"Not happening." Brendon shook his head. "I just can't do that." His head turned for a moment as he heard a sound, leaving the other man an opportunity to raise the piece of wood he held and bring it down heavily on Brendon's head. Brendon collapsed, not a sound coming from him, as Lawrence watched in horror.

Imly's hands covered her mouth, containing the scream that she had almost released. Please, Lord, don't let him be hurt. I can't stand it if he is. She reached for her phone as it danced on the desk from the vibrations shaking it.

"Hello?" Her voice was hesitant, relief coming to her as she recognized Dallas' voice.

"Imly? Where are you?"

"In the office. Please? He just struck Brendon. Please?"

"We're outside, Imly. Officers will be going in the front. I need you to come to the back door. I'm right out there."

Imly ran for the door, hesitating for a moment, before she cracked it open, to find Dallas and officers waiting for her. He swept her from the building even as the officers entered, rushing her to his vehicle and shoving her inside it, to stand with his back to it, his eyes searching the surrounding area.

Imly watched as the man was finally led from the building and then paramedics moved in, Brady one of them. How does that happen, Lord? He's there whenever we need him, isn't he? That has to be Your hand.

Dallas moved away from the door, opening it before he crouched down, his eyes on her.

"Dallas?"

"Brendon's on his feet. He's refusing to go to the hospital. He's desperate to find you. They were told that you had been kidnapped and that he had to go with them."

Imly stared at him. "I saw that man, the one who I think helped Brendon. He was watching out for me when I met Berneen and Cadee. I think he is my dad's brother. We haven't seen him in years."

Dallas nodded, his eyes following the man walking towards them. "Here's Brendon. Brady's with him."

Imly almost shoved Dallas out of the way. She ran towards Brendon but never made it. She stumbled and fell, to lay still. Brendon stopped his forward walk, stunned, even as Brady pushed past him, to drop to his knees, a hand on Imly's back, shocked to see the blood spreading across her mid-back, before his hand was on his radio, calling for his partner to hurry.

Brendon's knees hit the pavement hard, sending a shock wave through his body, even as horror grew on his face.

"Brady?"

"She's been shot, Brendon." Brady glanced up quickly and then past him to where his partner, Patrick, was running towards him, the other team of paramedics on his heels.

"Shot?" Brendon's hand reached to touch her red hair, tears suddenly blinding him. "How?"

Dallas stood behind him, a hand on his shoulder, even as he spat out orders to the officers, who scattered.

Hours later, Brendon raised his eyes, a haggard look on his face, expecting to see the surgeon in front of him. They had rushed Imly into the Emergency Department and then to surgery. He frowned, staring at the man who had stopped in front of him.

"Brendon? Imly?"

Brendon shook his head. "I'm sorry. It's John?"

"I am. I just heard. Imly?"

Brendon pointed to the chair beside him. "Sit. I have no idea how much longer it will be." He scrubbed at his face with the heels of his hand, suddenly overly tired. "She's in surgery."

"Surgery? I heard on the street that she was hurt. I didn't know it was that bad." John's eyes were raised as he saw the men from the building gathering around them, the ladies keeping back, Anna among them.

"Yeah, well, it is. They've had her in surgery for over two hours. They were sure what all they would find when they went in, the surgeon said." Brendon slumped back, a devastated look crossing his face. "Why?"

"Why?"

"Yea, why?" Brendon looked up as Buckley sat beside him. "Buckley?"

"I don't have that answer for you, Brendon. I wish that I did." His heart hurt for his friends.

John shared a look with Buckley before he looked up at Barnabas, who waited beside him. He stood, a hand out to shake the other man's hand. "Barnabas Carey. I'm Imly's uncle. John Dickerson."

"That's who we thought you were. First, thank you for rescuing Brendon. Now, talk to us. And make sure it's the truth you tell us." Barnabas nodded his head towards the men surrounding them. "They won't take it lightly if you don't."

———

Brendon was on his feet, shoving his way past them, leaving them to stare after him, before Buckley was moving after him, to stand beside him as the surgeon met him.

"Doctor?" Brendon was almost afraid to ask.

"Brendon? It went better than I hoped." The surgeon's hand reached to catch his arm, to steady him on his feet. "I stayed with her through the recovery process. That's why it's been so long. The nurse said she had been out to see you."

Brendon nodded. "She has been. How is my wife?"

"She's in ICU for now but if it goes as I suspect, she'll be moved to the surgical floor tomorrow. Come, walk with me." He nodded as Buckley walked with them. "God was with her, Brendon. I hope you know that."

"I do, Doctor. I do. But what aren't you saying?"

"That it could have been much worse. The bullet missed the organs. It did nick an artery, but the quick work on the part of the paramedics helped her to survive."

"It did?" Brendon's steps slowed before he walked forward again. "Can I see her?"

"You can. For a while. And then we'll ask you to leave. There is an officer outside her door. Dallas placed him there." The physician stopped Brendon. "She will need time to recover. With the head injury she had a while ago, we need to watch her closely."

"The head injury? Does that factor in?" Buckley was watching Brendon, knowing that he really wasn't listening anymore.

"It could. We had to be careful what we gave her in the operating room and what we can give her for pain medications. I understand she's still be having headaches?"

"She has. She doesn't say much, but she does." Brendon walked away from the two men, heading for Imly, to stand beside her bed, a hand on her cheek, the other hand on hers. He finally lifted his eyes to study the monitors, before he looked back down at her.

Buckley watched him walk away. "He's hurting, James."

"He is. We've been praying for them, but it just doesn't seem to end, now does it?"

John had watched Brendon and Buckley walk away before he spoke.

"Any word on her parents?"

"Why would you ask that?" Breck had moved to stand beside John, not sure about him.

"I know they're missing." He shot Breck a look before he pulled out his wallet. "This needs to be kept quiet. I work for an organization that tracks people like Wills. That's how we knew about Brendon. It just took me some time to find him. Did you know he was only about a mile from the building?"

"A mile?" Breck shook his head. "Now, why would you say that?"

"Because it's the truth. Wills has control of a property that borders the Foundation land. It's buried deep in numbered companies and phony names." He looked up as Bradon moved closer. "I have all the information that your detective will need." John handed over a thick envelope to Barnabas. "There are copies in there for you as well and my contact information. I need to leave." He was gone before any of the men could stop him

Breck stared after him. "Did that just happen?"

"It did." Bradon was frustrated. "Now, how do we find him?"

"He'll find us, I suspect." Burnie poked at the envelope. "We need to take that back to the conference room."

"And we will, once we know how Imly is." Barnabas handed Breck the envelope and walked away, his phone out as he took a call.

Four days later, as Breck parked in front of the Foundation building, he smiled grimly to himself. He had watched in the rearview mirror as the car following him had been pulled over by a patrol car. Dallas was taking no chances, that he knew. He shifted in his seat to peer back at Brendon.

Brendon roused from his thoughts, his arm tight around Imly.

"We're home?" He was surprised. He didn't realize that they had arrived there.

"We are. Let's get Imly inside." Breck slipped around to the back door to open it for Brendon, watching as Brendon stepped down from the truck, then reached to gather a sleeping Imly tight into his arms, a soft sigh coming from her as he did so.

Hagen waited to hold the building door open for them before she headed for the elevator, intent on helping. Breck had waved as he returned to his truck, to head back into town to a meeting.

Brendon gently laid Imly down on the bed, a murmur of thanks to Hagen before she moved away. He knelt beside it, his hand on his bride, his heart lifting in prayer. It could have been so much worse, he thought. He could have lost her and he didn't know how he would have ever lived on if he had.

He finally rose, tucked the blanket around her, and then headed for the kitchen, the aroma of freshly-brewed coffee heading down the hall to meet him. He reached for a mug, poured his cup, and then stood, staring at the fridge.

Hagen watched from where she stood near the sink, a slight smile on her face.

"Brendon?" When he looked around, she continued. "How is she? Really?"

"Lucky to be alive. James told me today that they almost lost her a couple of times during the operation. That's why he stayed in the recovery room with her, not just leaving the surgical assistant to do that." He sighed, reaching to pull a chair out from the table so he could sit, weary beyond what he had been. "God was good, Hagen. He was good. It is hard to praise Him at times, but I have no choice."

Hagen nodded as she took her own glass of water and sat with him, a hand rubbing at her abdomen. Brendon frowned at her as she laughed.

"It's okay, Brendon. I'm fine. The twins are kicking up a storm today. That's all." Hagen and Brandon were expecting twins, the first little ones in the building, and everyone was eagerly anticipating meeting them.

Brendon smiled. "They will be spoiled, you do know that? With all us in the building, how could it be anything else?"

Hagen laughed. "Haley and Holly say the same thing. They drive me to distraction at times. They want to know if the babies are boys or girls. We chose not to find out." She looked closer at him. "You need to rest, Brendon. Working the hours you have as well as being at the hospital as much as you have been is wearing you down."

Brendon sighed. "I know. I just couldn't do anything else."

"We get that, Brendon. For now, one of the guys will drive you back and forth to work. Dallas and Barnabas have worked out a schedule. There will also be an officer in plain clothes in the building with you. From what I understand, the one who will be there is eager to learn the furniture trade. He's wanting to move on to something different, he tells Barnabas. He retires in four months and says he too young to sit around."

"Lawrence said that he had someone in mind. With the way the business is growing, even given the times we're living in, he wants to hire someone. He's spending more time designing than he really can afford to right now." He sighed once more. "But I don't want to leave Imly on her own."

"We understand that." Hagen picked up the sheet of paper that she had laid on the table and waved it at him. "The ladies have gotten together and drawn up a schedule, including Anna and Amy and the two teens. Darbi wants to help out with you. We are splitting the hours that you will be away among us, making sure for the first few days that she is not on her own. She'll grow tired of us."

Brendon paused as he raised his mug to his mouth and then shook his head. "No, I don't think so. She told me this morning that she finally had realized just how much she was a part of this family, that she felt wanted for the first time in years."

"She did? She is a part of us. But for years? What did she mean?"

"That I am not sure. She was asleep again before I could ask. Her uncle has been around when I've been there on my own. He's done some talking. I need to let the others know what he has been saying." He yawned and then apologized.

Hagen merely shook her head at him. "They're in the conference room. Head on down there, if you like. I can stay. Brandon expects you to come there."

Brendon finally stood, reached to hug his friend's wife, and then headed to check on Imly, finding her still sleeping, not having moved from the position he had left her in, before he headed down to the main floor. He paused outside the conference room door, hearing laughter coming through it as someone was being teased. His heart eased some in its sorrow, knowing that his friends were there for him, just as he was for them.

Staring at the chart on the wall, Brendon was puzzled. He moved to stare at the map next to it, a finger coming up to trace the highway from Imly's hometown to where he lived. Somewhere along there, he felt her parents were. Whether they were free and on their own, or held captive to get to Imly, that he wasn't sure of.

Brody moved in beside him, Bradon on his other side, exchanging a glance behind his back.

"What are your thoughts, Brendon?"

Brendon's finger stabbed at a name. "John mentioned this village. He seemed to think that Ian had contacts there. How he knows that, I am not sure."

Bradon tilted his head. "That name did come up, but I can't remember why. Do you, Brody?"

"It was one of the ones the guys stopped at. They mentioned that the people were hesitant to talk to them, almost as if they were afraid." Brody shook his head. "One of us needs to head back there. It's only about forty-five minutes from here."

"That close and yet so far." Brendon paused. "If it wasn't that Imly was just home from the hospital, I would head there. Tomorrow's Saturday."

"Devaney's scheduled to be with her tomorrow, Brendon, even though you're home. The ladies want to take some of the burdens from you. This is how they feel they can serve you two. They don't want to step on your toes and will back away if either of you wants them to."

Brendon shook his head. "No, it's fine. I know that they care deeply for Imly. She told me she's realized how much she is part of this family now." He turned to stare at the room. "You two want to make a road trip in the morning?" He sighed as his phone chimed. "Now what? It's John. How did he know?"

"Know what?" Breck had approached.

"We're heading to Littleton in the morning. John wants to go. We just made that decision." Brendon's eyes lifted, concern on them. He looked down at his phone and then handed it to Breck. "Have someone check this out, please? Someone is spying on us and it may be through that. I have felt that way for weeks."

"And I'll have the room here swept again. Security does it every day but we'll pick up the number of times. This is just too coincidental." Breck's eyes never left Brendon's face. "How far do you trust John?"

Brendon shrugged. "Not very, I would say. I mean, he seems to have been the one who brought me home, but how did he know where I was? And if he knew, why did it take so long? Do we have any proof that he's who he says he is?"

"We have proof that he isn't. The man that's been around? That's not John Dickerson." Burnie held up a sheaf of papers from where he was seated near them. "Imly's uncle is, I am sorry to say, deceased. He was run down a year or so ago, in that very village you are heading for, Brandon. His identification has been used over the last year, but what we can determine is that the man using it looks like him but it is an imposter."

"What about that material he gave us?" This from Benen.

"Emma took a look at it as has Dallas. It is all nonsense, they tell me." Branigan had risen, heading for the coffee pot, needing another cup of coffee.

"So, where do we stand, then?" Brendon rubbed at his forehead, a headache starting.

"Not where we were. We are making progress, Brendon, in spite of all the setbacks. Andy is flying Buckley and I back up to her hometown on Monday. There are some names we need to track down and people we need to talk to." Blair spoke from the end of the table, his head still bent over his papers. His voice died away before he was on his feet, the sheaf of papers in his hand. "Fellows, I think I know who is behind Wills." He looked up, seeing the expectant looks on his friends' faces before he looked at Barnabas. "Barnabas, how well does your father know Philip Baker?"

"Not that well. He's never felt comfortable around him, I know that. Mom avoids him. Is he the one?" Barnabas reached for the paper he was handed. "Is it him?"

———

310

"He's part of it. My research shows that he and Wills go back to school together, a boarding school, from the looks of it." Blair pointed to the paper. "There are notes there from what I could find. I have photos of them together that I saved to a file. I will pass it on to Dallas at some point, but for now, I'm holding on to it. Until or unless they escalate their attacks on you."

"That will happen." Brendon felt exhausted, his body sagging until his arms were braced for friends on either side of him. "Sorry, guys. I don't know what's wrong with me."

"You need to relax and get some sleep, Brendon. You haven't this week." Breck reached for his arm, tugging him from the room. "If you're planning a trip tomorrow, how be we take you home and let you get some sleep? Imly may be awake by now and looking for you."

Imly watched Devaney closely the next morning, a frown on her face, not quite sure why she was in her apartment. She sighed. I guess I have a babysitter, don't I, Lord? And then she sighed again. Forgive me, Lord. That's the wrong attitude. I know. I need to be thankful for friends who care. It's hard to praise in all this, but I'm trying.

Devaney watched Imly closely before she handed her the cup of tea she had ready for her.

"Here, Imly. Have a seat at your own table. And here's your peppermint tea I understand that you like. Forgive us if we have stepped in where we shouldn't have. I'll leave, and let you be."

Imly shook her head. "No, it's okay. I'm just not good company right now. Brendon explained it to me last night, what you ladies have planned, but I think I was too much out of it to really understand."

"It's okay. We tend to step in and out of one another's lives. We have all told each other off at times, asked for forgiveness, and moved on. I can't say that we have held grudges, not with what we have been through. Then, too, our fellows are close friends, and it would make it difficult if we were enemies."

Imly watched her closely. "I get that. I've never had a friend like that, you know? I mean, I have had friends, but none as close as you ladies are already."

"Oh, Imly. We didn't know that. I'm sorry."

"What's to be sorry for? You didn't know. I've been so used to it, that I didn't realize it could be different." Imly shifted uncomfortably. "Do you mind if we head for the living room? I think I'll be more comfortable there."

"Sure. What would you like to eat? Just some toast?"

"That would be great. And thank you."

Imly was asleep later that afternoon when Brendon returned, tired and spent, but with a sense of having accomplished something that day and he really needed to talk to his bride. He gave Devaney a quick hug as she was leaving with a thank you for staying and then headed to shower and change. He felt grubby, he thought.

Heading back for the kitchen, he could hear quiet sounds and stopped in the doorway, to watch Imly as she moved around, slowly to be sure, but on her feet. He approached her, talking to her as he did so.

Imly turned slowly, her hand resting on the counter, as she looked up at him, a smile breaking through the pain on her face.

"Did you have a good day, love?" He gently hugged her, holding on just a little bit longer, before he reached down to kiss her.

"I have no idea. Poor Devaney. I think I slept a lot of the day."

"She understands. She's been there, hurt and needing care." He pointed with his chin. "It seems that she has left a meal for us in the crockpot. How be I dish it up and set us up in the living room? You'll be more comfortable there."

"That would be great." Imly watched as he moved around his kitchen, content just to be near him. "How was your day?"

"Good. We managed to get the people in the village to talk to us. I need to go over what we found, but we need to eat first. Head on in, love. I'm right behind you."

Brendon finally wiped his mouth on the napkin he had been holding, before he rose to clean away their dishes, returning with her tea and his coffee. He sat beside her, an arm around her, as he bowed his head and prayed for the love of his life, knowing that when he spoke to her, it would change how she saw herself and her parents.

"Who's here tomorrow?" Brendon was delaying the talk, trying to frame his mind to put out the words in the way he needed to.

"I'm not sure. Hagen left a schedule on the fridge, I'm told." Imly's head went down on his shoulder, even as she yawned. "I hate pain medications. It makes me so sleepy. But, you found out something."

"I did. I didn't get a chance to talk to you last night. John, the man who claimed to be your uncle, is not him. We have confirmation that your uncle died a year or so again in an accident."

"He did? I wonder if Dad knew that. He hadn't seen or heard from him in years."

"I'm not sure. We can clarify that when we find your father." His voice dropped off, as he thought through the day. "What we found out is still to be verified, but we have confirmation of some of it. The fellows want to meet tomorrow, Sunday and all, just to work on it. It's okay, Imly. We've done it before. We'll do it again if we have to."

"And we will. Do you really think this stops with us?" Imly grew silent. "Somehow, sweetheart, hearing the stories of the adventures the other seven went through? It won't stop with us. It won't stop until it reaches Barnabas. Devaney mentioned that everyone felt something was missing in each of their investigations. I think that you'll find it ends up with Barnabas, that someone is after him, and is going after each one of you. It's as if someone targets us, someone hears about it and then starts working on that."

"I suspect you're right." Brendon was content for the moment just to sit quietly with Imly secure in his arms. "But we have to talk, Imly. I'm just not sure how to tell you what we found out."

Finally speaking, Brendon tried to organize his thoughts in a way that made sense. Only, he thought, *nothing makes sense about this.*

"What did you find, sweetheart? It can't be any worse than what we already know." Imly's quiet confidence in him helped him to find the words.

"We went there, not really expecting to find out much. It was a long shot, as they say. The people had not been forthcoming when the other fellows stopped there. But it changed. When Bradon introduced me to the waitress in the family-style restaurant as your husband, that changed. She began to talk to us and drew others over to be introduced.

"It seems your father has an interest in that town. He spent time there as a child. That's why your uncle was there. He had gone home. I'll come back to him." Brendon paused, a prayer raising in his heart for what he had to say. "Anyway, we finally met the oldest person in town. A tiny little lady. She's a relative of yours, I think. She definitely wants to meet you. She gave us information on your family that I don't think you even know. She may be in her eighties but her mind is still razor-sharp."

"So, what did she have to say?" Imly waited, her head turned up to watch Brendon. "Brendon?"

Brendon shook his head to come back to the present. He had been lost in thought for a moment, wondering just where Imly's parents had gotten to.

"Your parents are not in that village, nor in the ones nearby. That much we determined. Your dad has been back there over the years, but he didn't have any contact with John. Apparently, John did not want to see him. I couldn't find out why. I was told I had to talk to your father about that. The impression left with us was that they had had a falling out of some sort and your uncle just refused to see your father."

"I can see that. Dad could be dogmatic about things. About the time Uncle John left, Dad had been in a bitter mood, unlike him. Mom wouldn't say what about. At the time, I was graduating high school, planning on college, and then a career."

"That's what Abigail told us. Your uncle had been specific with words about you. I am not sure if she would have opened up to you if you had been there."

Imly shrugged. "I don't know. I don't think it really matters now. What else?" She glanced towards the hallway as a tap came to the door. "Were we expecting anyone tonight?"

"Not that I know of." Brendon sighed, reached to kiss her, and then rose, heading for the door. He stared at Bradon and Brody and then past them at Breck. "Guys? Didn't you just go home?"

"We did, Brendon. But we have come across something that we need to talk to you two about." Bradon motioned towards the hall. "Can we come in?"

"Oh! Yeah, sure. We're in the living room. Coffee is on." Brendon turned and walked away, heading back for Imly, finding her almost asleep. "Imly? Some of the fellows are here. They need to talk to us."

"What? Can we do that tomorrow?"

"No, I think we should tonight. Can you stay awake for a while?" Brendon's arms were around her again, a quiet thank you to Breck for the refreshed mugs of coffee and tea that he placed on the table beside him.

"What do they need to know?" Imly squinted at them. "What do I have to tell you now?"

Bradon grinned. "This time, it's our turn to tell you something. We're hoping it's good news, but we're not even sure about that."

Imly shrugged, her head back on Brendon's shoulder, a sigh rising up from deep within her.

"If we must, we must." She yawned. "Sorry. The pain medication is working." She frowned. "Brendon, what did they give me this time? I thought it was a mild one. I can't handle heavy-duty ones."

Breck was on his feet heading for the kitchen, returning with the bottle in his hand. "It was a mild one." He popped the top from the bottle and shook one into his hand. "Imly, this is not what you were prescribed. I recognize this. This is too strong." He headed away, his phone out to call Dallas, leaving a voice mail for him, before he returned, setting the bottle beside him on the small table. "I'm taking these to give to Dallas. Brendon likely has something you can take."

"Thanks, Breck. Now, what did you find?" Brendon searched the faces of his friends, seeing a look on them that gave him hope they have found a clue that would lead to the end of this for them.

"We need to go back, Imly, Brendon. Back to when your father was young, Imly, around his mid-teens from what we can determine." Bradon looked down at his notes. "Your father was raised in that village that we visited today. We have confirmed that. But Wills was also from around that area. They knew each other from high school. Wills was always a bully, even to this day."

Brody spoke up, picking up from Bradon's words. "Abigail called me a while ago, Brendon. She tried to call you, but couldn't get through. She wants to send us some more information, but I told her I'd go and get it. It's critical that we have what she has." He paused to sip at his coffee, trying to gather his thoughts. "She said that she had been mailed documents in the last few months from someone, no name on the envelopes, but it contained tax documents, shipping credentials, and other forms that she thought we should have. They have your father's name on them, but she seemed to think his signature was forged."

"Did she say where they were going to or coming from?" Imly sighed. "Those aren't the right words. Forgive me. I'm sorry. My brain is not functioning well tonight."

Brody grinned. "Understandable. We know what it's like, unfortunately. Now, about your father? Any other family members that we should know about?"

"I'm sure that you have discovered all of them. He had some cousins, but I have no idea where they are. If he has seen them in the last few years, I would not know that. As for Mom? She was the only child of an only child. That doesn't help, now does it?"

Brendon finally locked the door after his three friends, his hand resting flat against it as he drew in a deep breath. They were still so far away, he thought, from finding out what was going on. He hadn't told Imly about the letter he had found taped to his vehicle that morning, a threat against her. Wills was still around, he was sure, or else he was paying someone.

"Brendon?" Imly's voice came from behind him and he spun around to face her, watching her closely.

"Yes, love?"

"Who did this? Who gave me the wrong medication? You had it filled at the pharmacy. Are they involved?" Imly walked into his arms, holding tightly to him.

"That's what we think. Breck is looking into that. He knows the owner of the pharmacy, but not all the pharmacists he has working for him. He spoke with Dallas just as they were leaving. Dallas is taking over that investigation as it is part of the bigger picture." He turned them to walk back towards the living room. "It doesn't end. We'll figure it out."

Imly sank back down on the couch, her arms wrapping around herself. "My mind is starting to clear a bit. It's been hours since I took one of those pills." She looked up as he sat beside her. "I guess church is out tomorrow."

"I think so. You're not able to sit for any length of time, that's a given." He reached for his Bible. "We can do our own church. But for now, let's just spend some time reading our favourite verses and praying."

"I would like that. I miss that." She leaned against him. "Thank you, Brendon, for being who you are. That is one thing I can praise God for in all of this."

Waking early the next morning, Brendon rose and moved around the apartment quietly, finally dropping down into his desk chair, reaching for the computer mouse to wake up his computer. He read through his emails, responding to Lawrence's questions, and then pulled up the file he had been working on.

He added the notes that he made from the day before and then sat back, studying what he had written. Brendon was frustrated. There had to be a better way to sort this. He looked up as he felt a hand on his shoulder and then wrapped an arm around Imly to pull her down onto his lap, kissing her before she could react.

"Brendon? You're up early." She looked at his computer monitor. "What are you making?"

"A mess, I think. I don't know what to do with this."

"Let me look at it. Can you print it? It's sometimes easier to look at something in black and white. And then we can scribble all over the pages."

"Scribble, is it? Do you have crayons?" He grinned as she gave him a playful swat.

"No, I don't but different colours would be a good idea. How many colours of pens and highlighters do you have?"

"Not enough. I know there are plenty in the conference room." He reached for a thumb drive, to transfer the file to it. "We can move down there after breakfast." He sat back, his eyes on her face. "You look much brighter and in less pain this morning."

"I think I am. My mind is not foggy like it was. What was I given?"

"Dallas hasn't responded to that question just yet. Whatever it is, when we find out, you'll never be given it again."

Hours later, Imly stood and stretched, a hand resting over her incision. Doc had been by, to ensure that she was not overdoing it, and she knew Brady was keeping a close eye on her. Brody had returned with the documentation from Abigail and had made copies of it all for each one, putting the originals back into the envelope to hand over to Dallas.

Ennis and Fynn approached Imly, drawing her away and to Fynn's apartment. Brendon watched her leave before he turned back to Burnie, frowning at the paper that the other man kept shoving at him.

"What is this, Burnie?"

"This? This is a crucial part of the evidence, I think, Brendon. I checked the signatures with what Imly provided. This is her father's. It is on a customs form shipping jewels to Ireland. Did he know what he was doing?"

"What's the date?" Brendon drew in a deep breath. "This is three days after Imly disappeared. Did they do this to try and get her back?"

"That is something that we'll need to ask them, if we ever find them." Burnie sat back, his eyes thoughtful. "I just don't get it, Brendon. Where are they? Are they involved after all and in hiding? Or are they being held hostage or captive or what?"

"That I don't know." Brendon looked up as Branigan sat down beside him. "Branigan? I don't like the look on your face."

"I don't like to be the bearer of bad news. Remember how we had DNA testing done? Barnabas was able to get a rush on it." Branigan looked down at the papers he held. "We got the results back. Imly and her parents? Their DNA does not match. I'm sorry, Brendon. It's not what we had hoped."

"No, but it is what we expected." Brendon reached for the paperwork. "I'll talk to her tonight. Right now, she's with the ladies. She needs that. Devaney was almost in tears today when she spoke with me. She said Imly had admitted that she never really had a close friend, not like the ladies are here."

"That makes sense, in a sick way." Brennen had sat down at the table. "They would want to keep her away from too many people, just in case someone found out that she wasn't theirs. How do we find out who she really is?"

———

"We discussed this, Imly and I. She is adamant that Imly is her correct name. Her birthdate seems to be correct, from what she can figure out." Brendon sat back, before he was on his feet, heading for a box that had been packed up from Imly's home and brought back. "Imly had the fellows pack everything up, paperwork and all. I don't think we've gone through it." He was pulling off the tape and opening the box flaps as he spoke.

"Here. Let us all take some. There's a lot there. Hopefully, we can sort this out."

Late that evening, Brendon ventured back into his office, a frown on his face as he thought of the conversation that he and Imly had had over their dinner. Imly was not surprised at the DNA results, disappointed, she admitted, but questioning who and why. And how was Wills involved in it all, she had asked, and who was behind him and that.

Brendon reached to flick on the desk lamp, pausing for a moment at the gift-wrapped package on his desk. Shooting a glance towards the door, he carefully unwrapped it, opening the flaps on the box, a delighted grin on his face as he stared down into it before he began to laugh. He carefully lifted out the large box of crayons, then the large box of colouring pencils, the huge number of coloured pens and markers. Imly had been busy, he thought. Who would have done this? Then, his grin widened. Darbi, he thought, Darbi, Haley, and Holly. He had thought they had been up to something. Now he knew what.

He sank into his chair, bracing his elbows on the desktop, his chin resting on his clasped hands. Where do we go from here, Lord? I feel like we have hit a dead end. Do we turn around and head back the way we came or do we find a tangent to follow?

Looking up at the clock, Brendon was shocked to see it was after three in the morning. He stared down at the papers he had been working out, colour coding them as Imly had requested. It was beginning to make sense, he thought. He had traced back the couple who had raised her, finding discrepancies in their information that he needed to talk to the fellows and Dallas or even Will about. He also had a fair idea of where she was from. And that concerned him. A small village should have been aware that a child disappeared and sounded the alarm, but it would appear that none had gone out. Who had prevented that?

Rising from his chair, he padded through to the kitchen, where he had left on a low light and reached for the coffee pot, to rinse it out and make fresh. He didn't think he would be sleeping that night. He yawned widely, rubbing at the back of his neck, before he wandered through the apartment, trying to see it from Imly's point of view and just not doing that. Brendon wanted her to make changes, had asked her to, but she had just looked at him. For now, she was content, she said, to live in it as he had decorated it. It would come, she promised, once she was feeling better and could see what they needed.

He stood for a moment, watching her sleep before he stooped to drop a kiss on her cheek. He was so thankful she was in his life. Turning away, he headed for the kitchen and his mug of coffee and then back to the office.

Finally, throwing down his pen and rubbing at his tired, bloodshot eyes, Brendon felt confident that he knew who was behind it all. And that person lived here in his town. And had been in his hometown. So, he thought, who was this person really after? Was it him or Imly? It really didn't make sense, he thought, that this person had tracked him down. He hadn't known Imly until the day she appeared in the shop. Of that, he was certain.

Imly stood for a moment in the shadows of the dimly-lit hallway, watching Brendon as he worked away. He's discovered something, hasn't he, Lord? Is this where we praise You, for letting him find something? I guess it is. She moved quietly away, heading for the living room, searching for her phone. Scrolling through the messages, she stopped at one. Her father, or who she thought had been her father, had sent a text message. One that really didn't make a lot of sense.

Jumping as she felt someone near her, she spun, directly into Brendon's arms, her phone trapped between them.

"Good morning, love. Sleep well?"

"I think so. You didn't, did you?"

"No, I worked all night." He looked down at her. "Let me shower and change, and then I'll let you know what I have been up to." He grinned suddenly as he swooped down to kiss her. "Thank you for the gift."

"Gift? What gift?" Imly was puzzled.

"The one on my desk. You know, the one with the crayons, pencil crayons, pens, markers?" He frowned at her puzzled look. "You didn't know?"

Imly began to smile. "No, I didn't. But Holly was around when I was telling the ladies about how I had threatened to get you them. She must have."

"Holly, and Haley, and Darbi. They can get up to mischief when they're together, but never anything bad." He kissed her again before walking away, leaving her staring after him, her face rosy with a blush.

Hearing a tap at the door, she frowned, thinking that she was frowning a lot. Standing on tiptoes, she peeked through the peephole, seeing Breck standing there, his attention on someone beside him.

"Breck?" Imly peeked around the door she had opened. "It's early. Didn't you sleep either?"

Breck grinned. "And who didn't sleep here?"

"I did. It was Brendon. He's been colouring in his office all night." She grinned, knowing that Brendon was standing right behind her.

"He has been, has he?" Breck held up the papers he had in his hand. "Then, maybe he needs these. And this is Gus Wilson. He's an investigator who Barnabas contacted. He has some interesting information for you."

"Come in then, Breck." Brendon reached to draw Imly back from the door. "What do you have?" He led the way to his office, an arm around Imly to draw her with him.

"As I said, interesting material."

Pacing the conference room, Brendon watched his friends closely as they intently worked away, quiet conversation sparse at best. He was frustrated, he had to admit, but at least they were making progress. He stopped beside Brody, who had risen and headed for the map on the wall, placing another blue dot on it.

"A blue dot, Brody? What are all the dots for?" Brendon's index finger touched them.

Brody grinned. "Darbi suggested that, muttering something about you colour coding things. The blue dots are where Ian Dickerson has been over the years. Does Imly know he is that well-traveled?"

"Imly didn't know that. He would be way for a day, a couple of days, sometimes a week, but he always said it was to do with his woodworking." Imly spoke up from behind the men. "Why?" Her eyes widened as she saw the number of blue dots. "Those are all from his trips?"

"Just the ones that Emma has been able to verify. She says there are many more they are working on. Did you know he traveled like that?"

"No, I didn't. I guess I never thought much about it." Imly chewed at her finger. "When I was little, I never really paid that much attention, I don't think. As a teenager, I really didn't care. When I started working, I had no interest in his travels. I was concerned about making good and then finding my own place." She paced behind the men. "What else is there to learn?"

"We're working on it, Imly." Brody looked down for a moment. "I have to say this. I am sorry this happened to you. It shouldn't have."

"Thank you, Brody. But I know that God allowed it. For whatever reason, He placed me there." She looked up at the ceiling, blinking rapidly. "Do we know anything more about my past?" At their silence, she looked back at them and then turned to look at the other men, surprised to find them all standing around her and Brendon, the ladies there as well. "What?"

———

"Brendon found some information that he wanted us to verify. He was not going behind your back, Imly." Brennen spoke for the group. "He wanted to be sure of his facts before he approached you. Brendon?"

Brendon nodded, his hands reaching to pull Imly close to him, to wrap her in a hug. "Buckley?"

Buckley nodded, knowing exactly what Brendon was asking. As the heads were bowed, he prayed, for Imly, for Brendon, for her real parents, for themselves and also Dallas. He prayed for resolution of the mystery surrounding her, and that God would be praised in all things.

Imly's head raised, a determined look on her face. "Brendon?"

"I have managed to trace you back to where you came from. It's a small village not far from here. Not the one that John and the man calling himself your father came from. That was a red herring, we think." He paused, wrapping his arms tighter around her. "I asked Emma to do some research. And her friend, Kataleen, helped with her family tree program. We have found the lost child posters, the reports of you being missing and likely abducted. Why you were never found, we don't know. They were sent out province-wide."

"I don't understand, Brendon. Who am I?" Imly turned slowly in a circle, her eyes searching each face around her. "Brendon?"

"You really are Imly Anna Dickerson. Your birthdate is the one you have always celebrated. Why they did this, we may never know. Dallas is working hard on the trail of them in his investigation. He called when you were out with the ladies a bit ago. He has information that he wants to verify. Then, he will be by." Brendon hugged her tight to him. "I'm so sorry, Imly. I wish it had been different for you. So much was stolen from you."

Imly drew a deep breath. "Thank you, sweetheart. Now what?" The friends around them could hear the devastation in her voice and see it on her face, noting that she was blinking rapidly to contain the tears she refused to shed.

"Now, we finalize everything we can, turn it over to Dallas, and protect you at the same time. He said that he had been warned someone other than Wills was looking for you." Breck spoke up. He turned to the others. "Let's go, fellows. Let's solve this today, if we can. Imly deserves to be free of what has been hanging over her for years.'"

The men scattered, the ladies as well, to find seats, the rustle of papers sounding loud in the room. Imly watched from where she still stood in the shelter of Brendon's arms before she turned back to the map.

"What were you planning on finding, Brendon?"

He shrugged. "I wasn't sure, love. I was just finding all these places. Why?"

"Has anybody researched thefts, or drug busts, insurance claims in these places?" Imly moved away from him, a finger tracing the dots. "It's like we're trying to connect the dots, as they say, whoever they are. Will it lead to the one behind it all? Someone other than Wills? Someone in the insurance game?" She spun, determination on her face, a sparkle back in her eyes. "I remembered something. I wasn't supposed to be home but I heard them talking. Something about insurance fraud and theft. I had forgotten, I guess thinking it didn't really matter. But it does, doesn't it?"

"It does, love. Come. Sit with me. We'll start looking at that angle. I'm sure one of the fellows is working on it as well."

Barnabas had been nearby as they spoke, his hand reaching for the coffee pot, before he paused, setting his mug down. He turned so he could watch Imly, the overhead light catching her profile. He drew in a deep breath. He knew who she reminded him of. But, how did he prove it?

The conference room door closing quietly behind him, Barnabas walked rapidly towards his office, nodding at Amy as he entered.

"What paperwork do I need to look after for you?"

"You're all caught up for now. You must have been in here early this morning." Amy smiled and shook her head at him.

"I was. For some reason, I felt compelled to be here. I also spent a good portion of time in prayer." He looked down for a moment, his fingers rubbing together. "You've talked to Dad and Mom. Do you know if they're planning on stopping by soon? I've only gotten voice mail when I try."

"I have. They have no plans, not before the board meeting in a couple of weeks. And then it would just be your Dad. You're missing them."

"I am, Amy. This bit with Imly? It has really driven in how fortunate I am to have my parents. The fellows don't and that saddens me."

"I know it does. Go. Phone your parents. I'm done for now. Do you need anything?"

"No, thanks, Amy. Take off and enjoy your evening."

Barnabas sank into his chair, his phone turning over and over in his hands, before he dialed the familiar number.

"Hi, Dad."

"Barnabas!" Bruce Carey's voice echoed over the phone to his son. "You've been calling and haven't been able to reach us. We were away to the island." Bruce referred to the island in the lake near where they lived, which had a cottage they occasionally ventured to.

"Were you, Dad? I wish I could join you."

"You should, son. You need some time away." Bruce asked about the men and the ladies before his voice died away. "You called about something in particular, didn't you, son?"

"I did, Dad. Ian and Emily Dickerson. Do you still see them?"

"We do. In fact, they are here now. Why?"

"What do you remember about their daughter? I seem to recall them mentioning they had a daughter, but she is not around." Barnabas almost held his breath.

"Their daughter? That's interesting that you would ask. They were speaking of her today, missing her greatly. They never really knew what happened. For all their searching, they never found her."

"Dad, I am going to send you a photo. Will you take a look at it for me?" Barnabas sent the text with the photo off to his father and then waited, a prayer in his heart that he was right.

"Barnabas? Where did you get the picture of Emily?" Bruce was puzzled.

"It's not Emily, Dad. It's a lady, Brendon's wife, in fact, who has become involved in one of those adventures. We haven't had a chance to speak, other than sending our emails. Does she look like Emily?"

"She does. It is incredible. This is what Emily looked like when she was around thirty. Who is she?"

Barnabas could hear his mother's voice speaking with his father. "Dad, are you two by yourselves? If so, put your phone on speaker, please. Mom?"

"Barnabas? I don't understand. Your Dad says this is Brendon's wife. She looks like Emily."

"I think she is their missing daughter. What was her name?"

"Imly." Bruce spelt it for him. "It's unusual, but they wanted something close to her mother's without it being identical."

"Then, she is here. Brendon's Imly, we have discovered, was kidnapped as a young child. I don't know all the details that the men and in particular, Brendon, have discovered, but they have proof that Imly was that child. Brendon has even been able to track back to the village she was from. He can't explain how it happened. He said a name or an idea would cross his mind and he would follow that tangent. It has to be God, Dad, Mom." Barnabas grew silent.

"And we need to tell them, and then get them there. Son, I will leave it to you to discuss with Brendon and then tell Imly. We'll work on our part up here. Knowing Ian and Emily, they'll want to head there tomorrow."

"They will, I guess. Dad, one other thing? The couple who raised Imly? They were murdered. Imly was kidnapped and brought down to our town, finally escaping and then hiding in Lawrence's shop, where Brendon discovered her. We'll let you know the rest when you get in."

"We'll be praying, son. Have no doubt about that." Bruce clicked off his phone, a thoughtful look on his face, before he looked up at Elizabeth. "Lizzie, we need to talk to them."

"We do, but first we pray."

They moved at last towards their back yard, finding Ian and Emily walking towards them. Bruce hesitated before he spoke.

"Ian? Emily? How be we have a seat in the house? Barnabas has called."

"Barnabas? How is he? And the men? How many are married now?" Ian's smile lit his face as he thought of Barnabas. "It's been a long while since we saw him."

"It has been, Ian. Here, Lizzie, let me take the tray for you." Bruce headed for the sunroom, a room they used a lot.

Ian finally set his mug down, his eyes on his long-time friend. "Bruce? Something is troubling you."

Bruce drew a deep breath, a prayer raising in his heart. "There is. Barnabas called for a reason." He reached into his pocket for his phone, drawing up the photo that Barnabas had sent him. "He called asking about you two. He also sent a photo on to me, one that I would like you to take a look at." He looked up at Lizzie. "First, let's pray. If it is what I think it is, it will rock your world."

Finally handing his phone to Ian, Bruce sat back, his hands lightly clasped, his eyes on his friends. Elizabeth linked her arm with his as she too watched them.

Ian shot Bruce a look, one of puzzlement, before he looked at his wife. She shrugged and then tilted his hand to look at the photo, a shocked sound coming from her.

"Bruce? This is me, I think. How did he get this photo?" Emily studied it closer. "No, it's not me. It's too modern. Who is she?"

Ian's mouth worked as he tried to control his emotions, tears momentarily blinding him before he spoke, his voice barely audible.

"Imly!"

"What?" Emily stared at him.

"It's Imly, darling. All grown up. She always did look like you." He drew a deep breath, his arm around her. "Bruce? What is the meaning of this?"

"It's a long story, Ian. But apparently, she showed up, Brendon rescued her, fell in love and married her. Barnabas didn't go into all the details, but for now, she is safe. Brendon has traced her back to your village."

"I don't understand. Where has she been?" Emily stared at the phone, her finger coming out to trace Imly's face. "I want to see her."

"We'll take you there. I told Barnabas that you would want to go tomorrow?"

"Tomorrow? Tonight!" Ian's voice was forceful.

"Tomorrow. We need to let Brendon have time to talk to Imly and warn her that you are coming. She has just found out that she is a missing child, the couple who raised her are dead. By the way, the man used your name, Ian."

That same evening, Brendon had gone looking for Imly, finding her curled up on the love seat in his office, a forlorn look on her face. She didn't move when he sat beside her, reaching to pull her over to him and just hold her.

"Brendon? Why?" He could hear the suppressed tears in her voice. This has rocked her world, as they say, he thought.

"I don't know, love. That's what we're working on. Dallas called earlier when you were cleaning up the kitchen. He's not going to make it today after all. He's tied up on another case for the night. He sends his apologies."

Imly shrugged. "I didn't expect that he would come." Her head dropped onto his shoulder. "Where do we go from here? How do we find my parents? Are they even alive? And would they even want anything to do with me after all these years? I am sure they have moved on."

"That's something we need to talk about. First, though, we need to pray. I miss my parents are times like this. It's hard being an orphan." He prayed for them, knowing that when he talked to her, it would change what she thought of things and people.

Imly finally spoke. "You wanted to talk to me, Brendon?"

"I do." He paused, not quite sure how to proceed. "The fellows took what I had done, followed more of a trail, confirming names and dates. I wanted to be sure before we talked." He paused, biting at his lip, trying to sort out his thoughts. "I found your parents, Imly."

She was quiet, not sure that she had heard him right. Her face raised to his. "Did you say that you found them?"

"I did. They still live in that village. From what we can determine, they have never lost hope of finding you. The detectives have been working on your case on and off over the years, not willing to let it go to a cold, unsolved case." He paused again, a slight smile on his face that Imly frowned at. "But there is more. Barnabas took a photo of you this morning and sent it on to his father, whom you have not met yet. Bruce confirmed that friends of theirs are your parents. In fact, Barnabas said they were staying with them today."

"They are? He did? How?"

"His Dad and Mom took one look at you and asked where he got the photo of Emily. That's your Mom's name. They showed the photo to their friends, and they were shocked. Your father confirmed it was you. If we need to, we have the DNA testing that we did. And I guess they had submitted DNA testing to some missing children's site."

"Oh, Brendon? Really? You found them. Thank you." She reached to kiss him before snuggling back down. "I guess we need to meet then. When do we leave?"

"We don't." His finger came across her lips as she went to protest. "Bruce said your father wanted to head down here today. He convinced them to wait until tomorrow, to let us talk to you and prepare you."

"Thank you." Imly grew silent, sorrow in her heart over the years that had been missed with her real parents. She finally spoke, talking at length about her childhood, how sheltered she had been kept, how she had few friends, that the couple who had raised her had frowned on her leaving home at all. Her words spent at long last, she turned her face against him and slept, shedding tears that soaked his shirt, breaking his heart for his beloved Imly.

Early the next morning, Barnabas stood in his open apartment door, watching his parents and the Dickersons walking towards him. Doc stood just outside his door. Barnabas had asked him to be handy, if he could, and he readily agreed.

Hugged by his parents, Barnabas reached to shake Ian's hand, only to find himself swept into a tight hug by the other man and then hugged even tighter by Emily, a whispered, tear-filled thank you in his ear.

"Dad? You made good time."

"We did. Andy flew up early this morning. He called for something else and then when I said we were heading down, he volunteered to come. He's been that concerned about Imly."

"He has been. He was one of the ones who went north." Barnabas beckoned them in. "I have breakfast just about ready. We'll eat, spend some time in prayer and then go find Imly and Brendon."

"Brendon?" His mother shook her head, a smile on her face. "I never thought he would marry. He's been so much of a big brother to the girls here."

"He has been, Mom, but he has found the one lady who completes him." Barnabas waited until they had finished eating and the table and kitchen cleaned up before he spoke again. He detailed how Imly and Brendon had met, what had transpired just prior to that, and what the couple had faced.

Ian and Emily's faces grew grave and tense, hearing what had happened to their daughter.

"She's okay now, Barnabas?" Ian's voice was barely audible, his emotions that much in play.

"She's getting there. She tells me that she still tires easily and the headaches can come and go, but overall, Doc here says she's better."

"Ian, Emily, I can't tell you from a medical standpoint what happened with Imly. I have treated her and can't break that confidence. But I can say she has healed remarkably well. Even when Brendon was missing, she had to be told to rest, to heal, and fought us on that at times."

The five finally rose, heading for the conference room, standing just outside the door Barnabas opened. They watched the activity in there, heard the quiet comments, and then gentle teasing and laughter. Ian and Emily exchanged glances, not having been aware this was what the men had done.

"This is normal now for the fellows. Dad and Mom, we'll go in first, I think. We need to let Brendon know Ian and Emily are here."

Brendon looked up as a hand touched his shoulder and he rose, a hand out to shake Bruce's before Elizabeth hugged him.

"Brendon? I hear you have been having one of those adventures that you fellows seem to think you need to have."

Brendon grinned. "I have been. We told the others that it stopped with Brandon, but it didn't. Good to see you two again. Imly's upstairs with the ladies. She's extremely nervous." He rubbed his hands together. "And so am I. There is a lot riding on this."

"There is, but God has gone before us. Listen, Ian and Emily are waiting outside the room with Doc. Come, meet them." Bruce turned Brendon, towards the door, nodding to the other men who had risen and then followed them.

Ian stood, an arm around Emily, watching the door closely, a sigh drawn from him when only Brendon approached him, Bruce and Barnabas on either side of the younger man.

"Brendon, is it?" Ian spoke first.

"It is, sir. I am so sorry for what you two went through. You have missed a lot. Your daughter is a wonderful, compassionate, caring lady who I love deeply." Brendon didn't know that his words had helped to ease the worry and burden the Dickersons had carried for close to twenty-five years.

"Thank you." Emily reached to hug him. "God bless you, son."

Brendon looked past her, gave a small sound and excused himself, long strides taking him to Imly. She stood, her eyes on Ian and Emily as they watched the younger couple before she looked up at Brendon, a woebegone look on her face, a lostness to her that broke his heart. He swept her to him and then turned her away, taking her outside to a bench in a nearby garden, nodding to the security guards who had followed.

"Talk to me, Imly." He waited for her to speak, letting her have the time she needed.

"Was that them, Brendon?"

He nodded. "It was. They really want to meet you, but I only allow it if you are agreeable. If you can't today, we don't. It is entirely up to you." He raised his eyes to see Imly's parents waiting nearby, Barnabas and his parents beside them, and behind them, his friends standing in solidarity with Brendon and Imly, the ladies standing in front of their men.

"I know we need to, Brendon, but I'm scared. I am so scared. What if whoever it is that is after me goes after them? How do I live with myself if they are hurt?"

"They have been hurt, and have been for years. You three need to heal. But I won't push you. Let God lead you in what you do. I will stand beside you and behind you, whatever your decision is. If you need me to speak for you, I will. If you want to walk away and move somewhere else, that's what we'll do."

Imly looked at him in horror. "You can't do that, Brendon. This is your home. Your work is here. So are your friends."

"You are the most important one right now. They understand that. The ones who are married? They have all felt the same." He looked up, staring into the distance. "I want to do what is best for you. You are the most important person in my life, next to God."

Imly leaned against him, a deep sigh that was almost a sob rising from her. "I guess that I can meet them. I'm just so nervous."

"And they are." He looked down at her, his heart breaking, wanting to prevent any more hurt for her, but knowing that he could not. "When you are ready, we'll go meet them."

"Are they out here?"

Brendon laughed. "They are, and so is everyone else. They are that concerned for you, but also pulling for you to find your family and become whole again."

"Is that what this will do? Will it fill that spot deep inside me that I couldn't ever fill or get rid of?" She finally stood, her eyes on him. "Let's go, Brendon. At least, let me meet them. Whatever happens, God is in control. I can only praise Him that He is."

Brendon stood, hugging her, and then dropping a kiss on her forehead, a prayer whispered in her ear. "If you are sure, then I will walk beside you, every step of the way. You will not go forward into anything without me."

"Thank you, Brendon. I love you." Her whispered words warmed his heart, even as he echoed them back to her, before he turned her to face the ones who were waiting for her, desperate to reach out and touch her, to love her once more.

Her eyes on the couple as she walked forward towards them, her hand tight in Brendon's, Imly drew a deep breath. She was shocked to see how much like the woman she looked.

"Brendon? I look like her."

"You do. It's uncanny how much you do." He stopped their forward walk, staying a few feet apart from the couple. "Imly, this is Ian and Emily. Ian and Emily, Imly."

Emily's hand covered her mouth as she sobbed, Ian's arms around her, tears on his face. The shock of finally seeing their daughter after so many years shook them both to their core, leaving them unable to speak.

Imly was puzzled for a moment before she spoke.

"Hi! I feel like I should know you, but I don't."

"That's understandable." Ian had to clear his throat before he continued. "It's been too many years, Imly. Too much has happened. But, this? You are here. Back in front of us. A lady grown, a beautiful one at that."

Imly nodded, her eyes on her mother as she listened. "Thank you. I'm sorry. I'm so sorry. I'm sorry they put you through all this." She looked up with a frown as a sudden buzzing sounded, a scream breaking from her as Brendon swept her away from the couple and to the ground, his body covering hers. They could hear the commotion and shouts of the others, even as an explosion sounded close to them, shaking their bodies violently.

Shouts rang through the area, even as the men scrambled back to their feet, the ladies running for the building, Ian and Emily with them, Elizabeth holding the door for everyone. She stood, heart in her mouth, as she watched Bruce and Barnabas outside. They could hear the sounds of the sirens as the emergency vehicles approached.

Doc was on his knees beside the young couple, Brady beside him, hands reaching to move Brendon away from Imly, to assess them. Barnabas squatted beside them.

———

"Doc?"

"They're okay, Barnabas. Just had the breath knocked out of them. Brendon?"

Brendon nodded, a hand on his chest, the other on his head. "Doc? What happened?"

"An explosive device of some kind." Breck crouched down near them. "You're okay?"

"I think so. Imly?" Brendon shook away the hands reaching to help him sit up, instead rolling to his side and reaching for Imly.

"Brendon? Where are we?" Imly's eyes were not focused, concerning him.

"We're at home, love. Someone just dropped a bomb near us."

"They did? Why? Who would do that?" She sat up carefully, frowning for a moment. "I'm having trouble seeing."

"Imly?" Doc's voice was stern as he spoke. "Can you look at me?"

"I would if you would stop moving and there weren't so many of you."

"Sounds like a concussion. We'll need to take you in." Brady stood, ready to help her to the stretcher wheeled nearby, when she shook her head, a grimace covering her face.

"Why did you make me do that?" She grumbled, even as the men around her grinned at her comment. "No, I need to go lie down, I think. Brendon, please?"

"That we will do. We'll take you to the infirmary here. Doc and Brady will watch out for you, but you will go in and be assessed if you don't come around soon." He stood, on shaky legs before he stopped and swept her into his arms, heading for the building, a wall of men around him.

Dallas stood watching. He had been on his way out there when word reached him that an attempt was planned on Imly's life that day at the building. He had requested backup and it was those sirens that Elizabeth had heard.

Emily and Ian followed closely behind him, concern and fear on their faces, watching as Brendon laid Imly down on the bed before he tried to step back, Imly's hand grabbing for his arm, preventing him from doing just that.

"Brendon? Don't leave me !" She blinked. "Who else is here?"

"Doc. Brady. Anna. And Ian and Emily."

"They're here? I thought they had left, that they didn't want me." Sobs shook her body, increasing her headache, even as Brendon swept her close to him, his cheek resting against her.

"No, love. They didn't leave. They are wanting to spend time with you." He finally set her back, stepping away, motioning for Ian and Emily to approach.

Emily stopped beside the bed, a hand out that she kept drawing back before she dared lay it against the red hair so close in colour to her own.

"Imly?"

Imly started, her face turning towards Emily. "Mom? Where have you been? I looked for you, but I couldn't find you. I was so scared. They wouldn't let me go." Imly began to sob, deep heart-wrenching sobs that shook her body, bringing tears to Emily's eyes as she gathered her daughter to her arms, glad to have her there, but missing all the years they had been apart. Ian's arms surrounded his ladies, his own face wet with tears.

Brendon stepped back and then from the room, to stand with an arm folded against the wall, his face buried against it, as sobs shook his own body. His friends shared looks of compassion for him, even as Bruce approached, an arm going around Brendon just as he would his own son. Bruce considered all the men his family and would treat them no less than that.

Brendon finally roused enough to hear Bruce's prayer for him, knowing that his lady was back with her family. But just where that left them, he wasn't sure.

Looking around later that afternoon, Brendon frowned at the footsteps he could hear. They didn't sound familiar. He was on his feet, heading for the door to the infirmary room where Imly still slept, when he slid to a sudden halt, his hands rising in the air. He backed away until the hospital bed stopped him.

"What do you want? I think you have the wrong building." He frowned at the men standing in front of him.

"No, we don't. We're in the right place." The speaker, a heavyset man that reminded Brendon of Wills, spoke before he pointed towards Imly. "She's the one we want. She's going with us."

"I don't think so." Brendon's hands clenched, ready to protect his lady.

"Oh, I think so. Move." The man beckoned to one of the men with him when Brendon made no movement away from the bed.

A sudden blow across his face had Brendon stumbling sideways, a hand out to catch himself from tumbling to the floor, the other hand reaching to wipe the blood from his mouth.

"I'm not leaving her. And you're not leaving with her." Brendon straightened back up, his hands raised and clenched, ready to fight for his lady, despite being outnumbered.

A few minutes later, the man stepped away from Brendon, leaving him crumpled and unconscious on the floor, the beating brutal at times. The leader nodded and then approached the bed, staring at Imly dispassionately before he spoke.

"Take her." When his men didn't respond, he repeated himself. Uncertain as to why there was no movement around him, he began to turn and halted quickly, feeling the small round end of a gun barrel against his back.

"I don't think so. She's not going anywhere. You are." Dallas reached for his cuffs and snapped them around the man's wrists. "For starters, Tyron Wills, you are under arrest for conspiracy to commit assault, threatening, attempted kidnapping. There is a slew of other charges just waiting to be laid. You won't be taking anyone anywhere." He nodded to the officers, who filed out with their prisoners.

Doc was on his knees beside Brendon, finding him moving, pain on his face as he did so.

"Brendon, here let's get you on your feet. I need to look you over." Doc helped him to stand, an arm around him to steady him.

"Imly?" Brendon tried to move away from Doc, to approach Imly.

"She's still sleeping, Brendon. Here, down in this chair." Doc worked quickly, quiet words to Brady who helped. "God was looking over you today, Brendon. You're bruised and battered, but considering everything, fortunate you didn't have any worse damage done to you."

"Imly?" Brendon finally shoved away their hands, stood, and approached Imly, finding her just rousing. "Imly, love."

"Brendon?" She squinted at him. "What did you do? You look like you've been in a fight and lost."

"That's about what happened. You're safe, love. Dallas is here."

"Imly?" Dallas spoke from beside her. "We have them all now. Brendon is correct. You are safe. At last, you are safe."

"I am? I'm so sorry, Dallas, to have made all this work for you." Imly drifted off, leaving Brendon shaking his head, and grinning at Dallas.

"Did she really just apologize?"

"She did, Dallas. She does that. For some reason, she feels that she has to. She can't explain it."

Dallas just shook his head, commented that she was certainly unique, and walked away, stating he would be around the next day. He definitely had to talk to them.

——

Brendon looked up as he felt an arm around him. Emily stood there, hugging him, Ian on his other side, an arm around his shoulder.

"Welcome to the family, Brendon." Ian had trouble getting his words out. To have found his daughter and then almost had her disappear again had shaken him badly.

Searching the faces gathered around them in the conference room the next day, Imly snuggled closer to Brendon, his arm around her, her hand in her mother's. The couple had spent the morning with her parents, getting to know one another, to talk over what had happened, to weep with one another but more importantly, to spend time in prayer and praise.

Dallas looked up from his papers, nodding to Barnabas, who looked at his father. Bruce rose to his feet, his voice raised in prayer and also praise as well, bringing them into God's presence with his words, asking for understanding and a blessing on all that had gathered.

Dallas finally began to speak. "Imly? I know this has been so difficult for you. To find out that you were kidnapped as a child, not aware of that, losing the couple that had raised you, to be kidnapped and then suffer as you have with physical assaults and having Brendon disappear as he did? I cannot fathom how you have kept your spirit in an attitude of praise. That was certainly God at work.

"Now, to go to Wills, the younger brother, the one who had you kidnapped and brought down here. He had threatened the couple who had raised you. Tyron Wills had you kidnapped at age three, placed you with them, telling them that you were an orphan. He saw you outside your home and took the opportunity to have his men take you. He apparently searched for a couple who bore the same name as one of your parents and found one who was named Ian. They were a Christian couple, but Tyron Wills had information on a crime that the man had committed and gotten away with before his conversion. He used this as blackmail, forcing him to use his woodworking skills to prepare furniture and boxes and whatever else you remember to be used in smuggling jewels, artwork, documents, and even drugs out of the country. All of these were stolen. When you asked about insurance fraud and theft, this was part of it. We are working with the federal officials here and with officials overseas to try and recover what we can. It will be a long process.

"Brendon, when you rescued Imly and then married her, you became a target. Wills for some reason decided that Imly had an inheritance coming to her. He was led to believe this by his brother. He never worked in this town, not in a legitimate business at any rate. We have arrested all the men that were involved in everything you two went through."

"This John? Who was he?" Brendon was puzzled.

"John? That's a mystery, Brendon. We can't find anyone who knows him or has seen him. It is as if he is a ghost."

"Or an angel." Imly's head went against Brendon's arm. "It is possible, but God placed him where He needed him, to rescue Brendon and bring him home."

Dallas clarified what little he could, stating simply that it was still an ongoing investigation and that he would be around, just to keep them all updated on what he was finding. And yes, he stated, they would be required to appear in court, to testify at some point.

Mingling with his friends, Brendon felt fatigued, his body sore and bruised from the beating he had taken the day before. He stopped beside Breck, not saying anything.

"Brendon? Any regrets?" Breck's voice was quiet.

Brendon shrugged. "I guess I do. But I'm not sure how to exactly express them."

"That's fair." Breck nodded towards where Imly stood with Emily and Elizabeth. "This is what we do. And we praise God when we do. Listen, Barnabas is going to talk to you, but he asked if I would give you a head's up. He wants to send you to school, to learn investigations. He would like to set up a section of the Foundation to find missing children. The board is agreeable, quite eager in fact. Your name has been raised by all of them as the one to head it. Only if you're interested and willing."

Brendon nodded, then turned to Breck. "Going through this? I found the love of my life, Breck, in Imly. Finding out what happened to her? That changed my focus. I love my woodworking, love working with my hands, but this? This has my heart. So tell Barnabas, it's a yes. Just let me know where and when I'm heading off to school."

Breck laughed before he moved away. "I will do that, Brendon. God bless you, my friend."

Six months later, Brendon searched through the apartment for the lady he still called his bride, not finding her. He paused in the hallway, a hand on his head, frowning before he nodded, heading for the balcony off his office. He stood for a moment, watching the love of his life as she sat, curled up on the love seat, a blanket wrapped around her against the cool spring breeze.

Imly looked up, a smile on her face, reaching for his kiss and then snuggling into his arms as he sat beside her, content with her life. She had found the missing part of her heart, when she found him, or rather God had led her to him. She had her parents back in her life. She was saddened that the people who had raised her had been killed by Tyron Wills as a threat against her that she never understood.

"Have a good day, love?" Brendon was content as well. He was deep into his studies at a local university, eager to learn, and more than ready to set up the department the Board was looking at.

"I did. Hagen was around with the twins. They are so cute. Tiny, but cute. She says Brandon spoils them, but she's content with that. She says that they have what they both wanted. She wanted a boy, he wanted a girl."

Brendon grinned. "He's been walking around six feet off the ground since they came. I am happy for them." He grew silent.

"Mom and Dad were by today. They finalized the sale of their home and found one here in town. I think Bruce helped out that way."

"I'm sure he did. He has a wealth of contacts that are always willing to help him out. He doesn't abuse the contacts that he has."

"No, he wouldn't." Imly bit at her lip. "Brendon, where do we go from here? You're deep in your studies. I'm at loose ends."

"I know you are. You need this time, love, just to be you, to learn how to live once more."

"I know I do, but I'm used to being busy. Bruce suggested that I volunteer at the shelter, but I don't want to. It brings back too many memories."

"It would. You're still working for Lawrence, and he is so thankful for you to be there."

"I know, but I'm not sure I want to continue working in an office. What I really want to do? Learn to paint and stain the furniture as you did. I talked to him today. He wasn't surprised and has promised to teach me, but he made me promise that if we have children, I will step back so the babies aren't harmed."

"I agree with him there. When and if that happens, we'll talk about it."

The young couple grew silent, content to be with one another, sure of the other's love for each other, ready to move on to where God was leading. Just where that was, they weren't sure.

Brendon sighed as his phone chimed. He pulled it out, pulling up a text, and then began to laugh.

"What's so funny?" Imly reached for his phone, beginning to laugh. "Buckley! He just doesn't stop. No, I don't want to help him in the church office. But what else is he asking?"

"He has asked if you would be willing to give some talks on what you went through, to show how God protected you and led you to be so thankful and praise Him through it all. We'll pray about it. He'll pester you, no doubt, but he will accept it if you say no."

"I should say yes." Imly laughed. "It would serve him right."

Brendon laughed, then reached down to kiss her before snuggling her back against him. They had no plans that evening, content just to sit and watch the setting sun as it sank over the lake.

Thank you for choosing to read the story of Brendon and the love of his life, Imly. What a ride they took us on. I joke that the characters only allow me to be the driver, that they don't share the map or GPS coordinates with me to tell me where the story is going. Each character has their own unique story and character. That's what I love about discovering each one.

Characters have a habit of showing up in the stories. Dave and his Rylee are from a town I named Riverville. Their story is *A Touch of His* Garment. Doug and Darcie's is *The Heart of a* Lion. But I love it as well when beloved characters walk in and out of other stories. The Emma mentioned? She is from Riverville as well, her story and that of her husband, Abe, being *His Protection* from the *His Guardians* series.

When do we praise God? When skies are blue, everything is rosy, and nothing bad is happening? Or do we praise Him in all things? We need to practice the power of praising Him in all situations. As I write this story, the province and country I live in, Ontario, Canada, is in the second wave of the COVID-19 pandemic. It is difficult to praise in this, but I must. He is in control, even though in our humanness we doubt that.

God bless you, my friends.

Ronna

Brennen: Encouraged to Intercede

The Barnabas Chronicles
Book 9

By

Ronna M. Bacon

Ephesians 6

18 And pray in the Spirit on all occasions with all kinds of prayers and requests. With this in mind, be alert and always keep on praying for all the Lord's people.

Ezekiel 22
30 I looked for someone among them who would build up the wall and stand before me in the gap on behalf of the land so I would not have to destroy it, but I found no one.

Table of Contents

Standing in front of the window in the living room of the small, rough-framed cabin that she called home, Jaxcy Dering wrapped her hands around the brown stoneware mug of tea she held, trying to control the shivers running through her. It was late spring and damp in the province she lived in, that of Newfoundland and Labrador. A late spring snowstorm was blanketing the ground in white, making it difficult for her to see the towering pine trees that surrounded her home. She finally turned to set her mug down on a pine table near her favourite chair, to reach for a log to drop into the fireplace, and then moved to the kitchen to replenish the wood in that stove. Living out in the country as she did, she didn't have electricity. It was too expensive to bring in.

A sound from the bedroom had her heading that way, a puzzled look crossing her face that settled into the deep gray eyes that almost seemed too large for her face. She pulled at the black hair she had in a braid, uncertainty in her very movements. She sighed once more. This is it, isn't it, Lord? I have to face the music as Mom would have said. How do I do just that?

Jaxcy paused in the bedroom doorway, a smile crossing her face as she watched her blue merle Shetland Sheepdog curled up tight to the form lying there. He had refused to leave the man, claiming him as his own.

"Kerry, you do need to move, you know? You can't stay there all day." Jaxcy moved quietly around the room, tidying an already tidy room, delaying the inevitable, she thought. She finally turned to the bed, to slip to a seating position on it, a hand reaching out to lay on the man's forehead, finding it cool once more.

His head tossing restlessly, the man's eyes flickered open and closed, finally remaining open. He licked at his dry lips, sipping gratefully at the mug of water that Jaxcy held up to his mouth. He swallowed hard, before he focused on her, a frown momentarily crossing his face.

"Where am I?"

"You're in my home." Jaxcy watched him closely. "How are you feeling?"

"Sore. What did I do?"

"What did you do? Let's see. You apparently arrived here on the Rock a week ago, got yourself in trouble somehow, were beaten up, and taken in by me." She stared across the room. "What do you remember?" When he didn't reply, she looked back at him, finding his hazel eyes focused on her. "I asked, what do you remember?"

"Not a lot. I remember you. You helped me." His hand laid gently on her arm. "Thank you."

Jaxcy shrugged. "I had to. They wouldn't have stopped, you know. They are the troublemakers in town, but they shouldn't have targeted you. You're a stranger in town. That much we determined."

"Why am I here?" His head moved restlessly. "This isn't a hospital room."

"No, it's not. You were there for a day or so before I brought you home." She looked down at her hands, studying them. "You had nowhere else to go."

The man shifted his position, his eyes on her, before he scrubbed a hand at his face, frowning. "I have no whiskers."

"No, you don't. You insisted on being shaved every day. You didn't ask for much more than that. I couldn't trim your hair." She lightly touched the dark auburn waves. "I tried, but you refused."

"I did? That's not like me." He sighed. "I need to introduce myself. I'm Brennen Connolly." Brennen watched as her face tightened momentarily before his hand rested on the dog laying with his head on his chest. "Who is this?"

"That's Kerry. He has claimed you. I have had trouble getting him to leave you. You need to rest, Brennen. The town doctor was to be out today, but it's snowing too hard."

"Snowing? It's spring!"

"I know it is. This is what happens here. It snows in the spring." She rose, walking away from him, not answering his call for her to come back, that he needed to know her name.

Brennen sighed, his eyes drifting closed as he slept. Jaxcy returned to watch him, to reach and tuck his hands back under the covers, her finger lightly resting on the wedding band he wore before she turned and almost ran from the room, tears blinding her briefly.

Lord, what did I do? What did I do? Mom and Dad would be shocked, horrified, I think. I know, Lord. You didn't say no, did You? I had to, Lord. I just had to. He had no one.

Jaxcy huddled down on the rickety couch in her living room, reaching for the threadbare blanket to wrap herself in, her eyes on her hands, studying the matching wedding band on her finger. She had had no choice, she thought. She sat for hours like that, before she heard a shuffling sound and jumped as Brennen sank down beside her, dressed in the clothes that she had washed and left on a chair, not knowing when or if he would ever use them again.

"You shouldn't be up." She shoved back the blanket wrapped around her, ready to rise before his hand rested on her arm.

"Please? Talk to me? I don't understand." He stared at his hand. "I'm not married. I don't understand why I'm wearing a wedding ring."

Jaxcy sighed and then swallowed hard. I guess the time of reckoning is here, isn't it, Lord? How do I explain to this man, this stranger, that we are truly married?

"You are. We had no choice. There is a law in this village or town or whatever you want to call it. Unless strangers have a reason to be here, they have to leave. If they don't, then they are jailed. The only way around it is if they marry someone local. It doesn't matter if they are only in town for a day or longer. The authorities here are a law to themselves. They have driven so many young people away. I would have left if I could have." She blinked rapidly.

"But I don't understand. Why am I here? If I'm married, where is my wife?" He frowned as he saw the devastation crossing her face. "Can you tell me what is the matter?"

Jaxcy sighed. "I guess I have to tell you who I am. You were alert enough that we could question you, to find out a personal history on you, enough that we could save you. The minister in town, an old man by the name of Brown, helped us." She blinked rapidly against the tears that she was refusing to shed. "I am Jaxcy Joelyn Dering Connolly. I am your wife." She was on her feet, running across the room, reaching for her jacket, shoving her feet into her boots before she wrenched open the door and was through it, the door swinging shut behind her.

Brennen stood, a hand on the top of his head, as he stared after her, shock on his face. What did I do, Lord? What did I do? I was asked to come to this village. I know I talked to Barnabas and Breck about it and they agreed I needed to. There was someone here who had requested that I come. But, who was that? It doesn't sound as if I made that contact.

He sank back on the couch, Kerry jumping up beside him, a paw on his leg, before Brennen's hand rubbed at the dog's head.

"Well, boy, what do we do now? I'm a husband and have no idea of how to be just that. I don't remember the ceremony and that's not fair to her. Lord? Where do I go from here? Please, Lord? I need help. I am definitely in over my head." He finally rose, heading for the kitchen, stopping to replenish the logs in the fireplace, finding the room chilling.

Brennen searched the kitchen, finding only tea and no coffee. He wasn't a tea drinker, he thought, but it looked as if he had no choice. He searched for food, finding a loaf of homemade bread and butter, and then searching for meat or something he could use for sandwiches. He was hard at work making a meal when the door opened and a flurry of snowflakes blew in with the cold wind. He shivered before he turned, finding Jaxcy not looking at him.

"Jaxcy? Thank you. We will talk, but first, have you eaten?"

"No, I haven't. I haven't had much of an appetite. Are you sure you want that sandwich? I have broth as well." She moved past him to reach into the fridge or icebox, he thought, to retrieve the container of broth and then dump it into a pot to heat, sliding it onto the stove, rattling around it as she did so.

"Let's have that, shall we, or do you want the tea that you have in the cupboard?" Brennen's words were careful as he worked away, watching Jaxcy as he did so. "Where do you normally eat?" He eyed the small table, seeing the makeshift repairs to it. How has she ever lived, Lord? This place is not where she should be. That much I can see. She's a princess, a princess in denim and flannel, and she's my princess. I need to change all this. He didn't stop to think why he muttered that to himself. He didn't realize that Jaxcy had already claimed his heart.

"I usually eat in front of the fireplace. Especially in the cold weather." She took her plate and mug of broth with a quiet word of thanks before leading the way back across the long room that held both the kitchen and living room.

"We'll talk, Jaxcy. First, we eat. Then, we pray. Then, we'll talk."

Jaxcy looked at him in surprise and then relief. A believer, she thought. Thank you, Lord. It could have been so much worse.

Brennen finally rose, gathering their dishes, carrying them through to stack them tidily in the sink, a frown on his face as he realized she didn't have running water. He turned, reaching for the tray he had readied, setting the teapot on it, and then returning to the living room, to set the tray on the table in front of them. He reached out his hand, palm up, waiting for her to respond, feeling her tentative touch as she finally took his hand.

He prayed, not sure afterward what it was that he had prayed, but knowing that something he had said reached to her. He felt her fingers relaxing from their tenseness, tightening slightly on his. He waited after he had finished, his eyes on the floor, before he looked up, to find her studying him.

"Just who are you, Brennen?" Jaxcy was curious, to know about the man that she had married.

"I work as an illustrator for children's books. But there is more to that than what it implies. I am employed by The Barnabas Foundation, who pays my wages, allowing me to work for my employer. This allows the employer to hire on others as he needs to without worrying about cash. I am an orphan, raised in foster care in Labrador. Barnabas Carey, the chairman of the Barnabas Foundation, found me and offered me work. I accepted. There is something interesting about all this. He has hired twelve of us, plus one other man. The twelve of us are orphans, coming from a different province or territory, but we all share the same initial. He said God told him to do that. Part of the creed of the Foundation is to be encouragers, based on Barnabas of the Bible."

"So it is named for him as well as your friend?" Jaxcy watched as he nodded. "I see. That's interesting. But it doesn't explain why you are here."

"That is the strange part. I was contacted and asked to come here. I talked it over with both Barnabas and Breck, prayed about it, and then flew here. I was to contact a J.J. Dering." He paused, his eyes suddenly on her. "That's you!"

"Those are my initials, but I didn't contact you." Her eyes slid closed. "It had to be Johnny. He's the minister. He's old enough to be my grandfather. He knew what I was facing."

"And that would be?" Brennen reached for her hands, rubbing his fingers along hers, trying to warm hers.

"I have been threatened. We don't know why. We can't find the ones behind it. But the toughs who beat you up are employed by someone. It really seemed as if they were watching for you."

"And why would they be doing that?"

Jaxcy shrugged. "We don't know. I don't have money." Her hand waved in the air around her. "I'm not rich." She paled. "I forgot. How could I forget?"

"What did you forget? Jaxcy? What did you forget?"

She scrambled from the couch, running towards a desk in the corner of the room, yanking open the drawers and rifling through the papers inside, finally pulling out a long envelope. She walked back slowly towards him, her face pale, before she sank back beside him, handing it to him.

"What is this?" At her nod, he slid out the paperwork inside and read it. "Jaxcy? Do you know what this is?" She shook her head, her eyes not leaving his face. "Jaxcy. This is a deed to the property and for stocks and bonds that come to you when you turn twenty-eight." He looked up at a sound from her. "Jaxcy? When are you twenty-eight?"

"Yesterday. It was yesterday. But, what does this mean?"

"It means that you have come into a certain amount of wealth. How much, I can't tell from this. We need to talk to someone." He studied the deed, and his face paled. "Jaxcy, have you ever traveled to Ontario?"

"No, I have never been outside of this village. Why?"

"Because this is property near where I live. It borders the Foundation property. We need to head back there."

"We do? But how? And who?"

Brennen's face grew grim as he read through an attached letter. "It names the person here. I know him. He is brutal. He would kill you to get his hands on this. And it says that if you are not married by the time you reach that age, the property will revert to a trust, which then turns over to this man. Oh, Jaxcy. Thank God I was here."

Brennen paced the cabin the next morning, waiting for Jaxcy to return from outdoors. He smiled at how she had had to persuade Kerry that he really needed to go outside, finally just picking up the dog and walking away, muttering to herself as she did so. He wasn't quite sure if he had heard her right, but she seems to be muttering about men and their stubbornness.

Jaxcy circled her cabin, seeing the fresh footprints that led from the forest to the cabin and then back to the forest. More than one, she thought. What would have happened if Brennen had not been here? There is nothing here now, she thought. Nothing to hold me here. I know Brennen needs to return to his home, but I am not sure if I am to go with him. He hasn't said. She sighed, her eyes on Kerry as he growled at something he was picking up on. She trusted him in a way that she didn't trust humans.

Hanging her jacket up on the hook near the back door and sliding out of her boots, Jaxcy slowed turned, to find Brennen standing near her, a mug of tea held out for her. He's made himself to home, hasn't he, Lord? But what do I do when he leaves? Even in such a short time, I've gotten used to him being around. I will miss him. With a quiet thank you, she took the mug and then headed for her usual spot on the couch, stopping as his hand rested on her arm.

Brennen looked past her, biting at his lip. He had tried to bring up his phone, but it needed recharging. He knew his friends would be concerned, having been unable to reach him.

"Jaxcy? We need to talk."

She nodded, not looking at him. "I'll make sure you get into town. My truck will run that far, I think. It's really not that far. You can catch the ferry to Labrador and then a plane from there. Your friends must be concerned." She waited for him to remove his hand, frowning when he didn't. She looked up at him, wondering at how tall he was. Jaxcy had always been teased about how short she was, and that had affected how she saw herself. She didn't understand or know that Brennen saw not a short woman, but a beautiful petite lady who could take care of herself. "Brennen?"

"We do need to talk, Jaxcy." He sighed before he swung an arm around her and walked her over to the couch, waiting until she was seated before he dropped down beside her, a prayer raising from his heart for wisdom.

"Brennen? What is it?" Jaxcy's eyes closed. "I know what it is. You are planning on leaving. I'll take you into town. There is a ferry that leaves tonight that you can catch." When he didn't respond, she looked up at him, to find him studying her.

"I'm not leaving, Jaxcy, not without you. I repeat, I will not leave you here. With us marrying before you turned twenty-eight, that has changed everything for you. Now that you have thwarted his plans, he will be after you for revenge."

"But, what about you? Aren't you in danger?" Her voice was barely audible.

"He will be after me, I suppose. That's why we'll head back to Ontario as soon as we can." He saw the moment she caught his words and stared at him, her mouth open. "I am not leaving you here. For one thing, I need to protect you. You need someone to do that for you. Most important? You are my wife, my bride. It doesn't matter how it happened. You are my family. I protect my family and take care of them." He suddenly grinned. "I need to introduce you to eight other ladies."

"Eight ladies? Why? I don't understand."

Brennen began to laugh. "Eight of my friends have gone through what we term as adventures. They have each married a wonderful lady. Some to save each other's life. I'll let them tell you their stories, but one thing is clear. God protected them and brought them through what they faced."

"They did? Eight of them? How many of you are there?"

He laughed harder. "There are twelve of us, all orphans. Then, there is Breck, and then Barnabas."

Jaxcy continued to stare at him. "You're serious!"

"I am." He reached for her hands, bowing his head to pray, asking for guidance for them and protection for Jaxcy. She wondered that he didn't ask that for himself.

Brennen reached for his mug of tea, sipping slowly, giving himself time to compose himself and to find the words he needed to say.

"Brennen?" Jaxcy's hand rested lightly on his until he flipped his over and clasped hers.

"Jaxcy? I need to head for home. I can't leave you here on your own. Please? Come with me? I pledge to do my best to protect you, to give you all the honour that you deserve." He waited, his eyes on hers, as she searched him and then her own heart. He saw the moment that she made her decision, and he drew a deep breath, ready to contact Barnabas and tell him he wasn't coming back.

"I will, Brennen. God help me, I will. I have nothing here. I can barely put food on my table. I scrape and scratch for what I have." She waved her hand to indicate the cabin. "This is all I have. I lost everything in town when Mom and Dad were killed in a landslide. This is all I could find. It has been so hard." She didn't cry, she had done enough of that.

"Thank you, Jaxcy. Now, what do you need to pack to take with you? Did you say there was a ferry tonight?"

"There should be, provided they can run it. We need to leave soon, though." She was on her feet, heading for the bedroom.

"Jaxcy, wait. What do you need to pack out here?"

She spun. "Just the stuff in the desk. The rest doesn't matter. I need Kerry's crate, his food, or enough to get by with, his harness, leash, and his grooming tools. Oh, and his toys." She spun back and almost ran for the bedroom. She felt relieved, able to escape the life she had been living, just existing, she thought.

Finally, standing on the ferry deck, watching the land fade into the distance, she drew a deep breath. This is is, Lord, isn't it? My past is there. My present is here, with a man I don't know, that I am married to. My future? That's in Your hands. You know the path I will walk. My hand is in Yours. Lead, please, Lord.

Jaxcy's hand tucked tightly in his, Brennen watched her face closely, not surprised that there was no emotion on it. She seemed to hide her emotions. I need to talk to her about that, Lord, don't I? I need her to talk to me. He pulled her backward with him, to the sheltered alcove that they had claimed as their own, Kerry in his crate, the bag with his belongings resting on top of his crate, the one bag that Jaxcy had packed sitting beside it. That saddened him, and he became determined to change that.

———

It was late when they disembarked the ferry, Brennen carrying Kerry's crate and one of the bags, Jaxcy carrying the other one, her free hand tight in his. She was shaking slightly, her emotions suddenly mixed and overwhelming her. She refused to say anything, not realizing that Brennen had picked up on what she was feeling.

Brennen searched for a free area and spying one, headed over there, setting down the crate and bag and just sweeping her into a tight hug. Jaxcy was surprised, her body stiffening before she relaxed against him, hearing his quiet prayer in her ears.

He leaned back finally, his eyes on her face. "Okay?"

"I think so. Just overwhelmed. I have never been on the mainland, in all my life. Is that strange?"

Brennen shrugged. "Not necessarily. If you had no reason to come here, then I guess you wouldn't have." He looked around. "We need to find a ride to the airport. I'm not sure what time the planes leave."

"Brennen!"

Hearing his name called, Brennen jumped and spun, shoving Jaxcy behind him, a frown on his face that smoothed out.

"Andy? Brody? You two are here?" He reached to shake the pilot's hand and then reached to shake Brody's.

"Barnabas sent us. He hadn't heard from you as you had arranged. When he couldn't raise you, he sent us. We just flew in today and were heading for the ferry to go over but found out we had missed it. We were putting in time when we saw you." Brody's face turned to a frown as he heard a dog woofing. "Brennen? Where's the dog?"

"Right here. He's named Kerry, and he's coming with me." Brennen turned slightly, watching Jaxcy as she hid behind him, slight fear showing on her face. "It's okay, Jaxcy. These are friends. And our transportation home."

Brody tilted his head, watching the black-haired beauty trying her best to hide behind Brennen. He frowned. "Brennen? Care to introduce us?"

"Brody, Andy. This is Jaxcy. She's been a friend in need. But I need to give her full name." Brennen watched as she shook her head. "We have to, Jaxcy. We have to. These are friends. They will help us. Andy is the Foundation pilot. We don't have to search for a flight and then wait for it to leave."

"Brennen?" Jaxcy's voice was quiet.

"It is okay." Without taking his eyes from her, or dropping her hand, he spoke. "Brody. Andy. This is Jaxcy Joelyn Dering Connolly. She is my bride, my princess. We are off on an adventure, just like the others."

Andy stared at him. "Who beat you up, Brennen? The bruises haven't faded yet."

"No, they haven't. It's kind of a long story, but I was beaten when I arrived in Jaxcy's town. She stepped in, married me, and then took care of me."

"Welcome to the family, Jaxcy." Brody stepped to the side where he could see her better, seeing the fear in her face. "How be we move off then? Andy has a car here that we rented. Let's head for it."

Brennen nodded, watching as Andy and Brody gathered up their bags, and moved away before he followed, Jaxcy's hand in his.

"Brennen?"

"It's okay, Princess. It's okay. Andy will fly us back to Ontario, to our home. You will be welcomed and loved, just for you. And you will be welcomed and loved because you are my family."

"But they don't know me! How could he say that?"

"Brody? He said it because he means it. He's not one of the ones who have married. But I can tell you that Baird and Berneen married something similar to us. She married him to save his life. One of our friends is our pastor. He was there and forced to marry them. Blair married Cadee to bring her to safety from a war-torn country." He opened the car door, waiting for her to slide in before he shared a long look with Brody, who nodded.

Brody slide into the front passenger's seat, his eyes on the mirror on the door as he closed it, a frown on his face. Brennen was being followed. Who knows what would have happened if he and Andy had not shown up? He was interested to hear Brennen's story but knew Brennen would wait until they could all meet. He shifted slightly to watch the couple in the back seat.

Brennen kept Jaxcy's hand tight in his, shifting his gaze to where the dog crate sat on the seat beside her. He could hear low whines coming from Kerry and knew that Andy would insist on the dog being let out of the crate once they were in the air. Bradon had often traveled with Andy, taking his Australian Shepherd, Kade, with him. Kade was always allowed to roam the cabin unless there was bad weather or turbulence or when they were taking off or landing.

"You'll be able to rest once we're in the air, Princess." Brennen's hand tightened on hers. "I know Andy will have stocked the plane with food." He looked towards Andy. "Do you have coffee, Andy?"

"Gee, that's the one thing I forgot to pack, Brennen." Andy grinned as Brennen shook a finger at him. "Devaney made sure that I had a large supply. For some reason, she thought you would need it."

"Bless her. I do. Nothing against the broth or tea that you supplied, Jaxcy, but I miss my coffee."

"Why? It's so bitter." Jaxcy made a face, causing the men to grin.

Seated in one of the seats in the plane, knowing Andy was flying them home through the night, Brennen felt fatigue settling in on him. Jaxcy had dozed off, Kerry tight in her arms, a blanket covering them. He had tucked a pillow under her head, a sleepy thank you his reward. He frowned down at his cup of coffee, suddenly not wanting it. He wanted a mug of tea shared with Jaxcy in her cabin.

"Brennen? Are you okay?" Brody's quiet voice broke the silence in the cabin.

Brennen shrugged. "I don't know. Physically, I know I am healing. Emotions are all over the place, as you can imagine. She's had a rough life, and it's about to get a lot rougher. Jaxcy said her parents were killed in a landslide when she was seventeen and she's been on her own since then. Her home was taken from her, and I am not too sure how legal that was. She was living out in the boonies, no electricity, only wood for heating. She carried in her water to use, heating it if she needed hot water." He glanced at her. "It was a rough place, Brody. One of the worst places I have ever seen."

"I'm glad you're bringing her home, but I don't understand how you ended up married."

"There's a lot to it. One is a law about strangers in their town, either having to marry or end up in jail. Jaxcy pulled out paperwork last night. She had to marry by the time she was twenty-eight to inherit wealth or it went into a trust and the trust turned over to someone we know. Dylan Smithers."

"Smithers? I knew he was slimy but how does he figure into this?"

"That I'm not sure of. More research for us, I guess. She turned twenty-eight a couple of days ago." Brennen sobered even more. "Do you know, she told me that she has never ever celebrated a birthday since her parents died. No one helped her to do that."

"Oh, Brennen. That's sad. We'll make up for that, if she'll let us." He paused, a thought crossing his mind. "Smithers? Isn't he living on that property bordering us?"

"He is. And it happens to belong to Jaxcy. I can see a fight on our hands to get him out of there."

"Dallas will help. Or Will." Brody mentioned a detective friend of theirs and the police chief of the town they lived near.

Brennen yawned, setting down his mug and reaching for a blanket. "Sorry, Brody. I'm still rocky to some extent. The men who met me in her town beat me badly. Jaxcy and her minister stepped in." Brennen's voice died away as he slept.

Brody watched him for a while before his attention turned to Jaxcy, and then to Kerry, finding the dog watching him with bright eyes.

Rousing as the plane landed on the Foundation airstrip, Brennen rubbed at his eyes before he shook out his blanket and folded it. He rose, stretched, and then helped Brody tidy up the cabin. He stood, his eyes on Jaxcy, who still slept, Kerry in her arms. Reaching for the dog and tucking him into his crate, Brennen undid Jaxcy's seatbelt and then gathered her close, surprised at how little she weighed before he nodded to Brody and followed the other man down the steps. Brody tucked the dog's crate onto a seat and then walked back towards Andy, who was approaching him.

"Did he say much, Brody?" Andy was concerned.

"Not a whole lot. We need to watch for Smithers. He's involved." Brody shook his head.

"I just don't get it. How did Brennen get involved?"

"That I don't know. He hasn't said. Nor has Barnabas. We didn't have a lot of time to get any information, other than we needed to leave right away, that he hadn't heard from Brennen." Brody stood for a moment, his eyes on Brennen, who had wrapped an arm around Jaxcy and laid his head down on hers. "He's in love."

Andy ducked his head to study the couple. "He is. He's like the others. Love at first sight. I would not have thought that nine of our friends would have fallen in love so quickly. Let's get them home."

Jaxcy roused as Brennen shut the apartment door behind them, a quiet word of thanks to Brody and Andy. She stared around and then pushed at him, dropping to her feet, a hand rubbing at her eyes.

"Where are we?" She was confused.

"In my, sorry, our apartment in the Foundation building. That's something that we didn't talk about. Each of us has our own apartment here. And an office on the main floor." He watched her closely before he reached to switch on more lights. "Head off to bed, Princess. There are three bedrooms. Take your pick."

Jaxcy nodded, not quite awake enough to understand totally what he was saying. With a soft thank you, she reached for her bag, noting that someone had let Kerry out of his crate. Brennen watched her walk down the hall, pausing at each doorway to study the room, before he turned to reach for Kerry's leash, closing the door softly behind him as he walked the dog outside.

Brennen yawned as he hung up his jacket and then the leash, fatigue hitting him. He squinted at his watch. Three in the morning, he thought. Not a lot of time to sleep, but he would catch what he could. He strode towards his bedroom, changed, and then slid under the covers, startled for a moment before he smiled. He simply reached to cradle Jaxcy near to him. He felt Kerry jump on the bed and then curl up tight to his legs. This is what I have been missing, isn't it, Lord? A family. He slept even as his prayer of thanks rose.

Early the next morning, Jaxcy rose, staring back at Brennen before she moved to claim her clothes and then search the apartment. She stood in awe of the bathrooms in each bedroom before choosing one, her hands on the soft, thick, aqua-coloured towels that filled the towel racks. Tears blinded her for a moment. She had never had or seen such luxury in her life.

Heading for the kitchen finally, she stopped to study each room, thinking that her cabin would have fit at least three times in the apartment. She paled at the thought of having to clean it but then stiffened her spine and decided that as Brennen's wife, that was exactly what she would do. She didn't have training in anything else.

Surprise halted her forward walk as she stood in the kitchen doorway. Jaxcy walked around, her hand touching the appliances and then the smaller appliances on the counter. Opening a door, she stood once more, her mouth open as she stared at the well-stocked pantry. She shook her head, finally reaching for a loaf of bread.

Brennen stood, in turn, watching her, Kerry tight to his leg. Sadness filled his heart for a moment, knowing what she had come from. He could not imagine living as she had.

"Jaxcy?" Brennen's voice startled her. "I see you have the loaf of bread. You don't have to have toast, you know?"

"I don't? It's what I usually have." She hesitated, then set the loaf of bread back down, unsure of herself.

"You can if you wish. I didn't mean you couldn't." Brennen stepped towards her, an arm around her shoulders. "We have cereal if you like cereal. Hot or cold. There are waffles in the freezer. There is probably fresh fruit in the fridge as well as eggs."

"All that? I don't know, Brennen. This is so hard." Tears sparkled in her eyes, turning them almost black.

Brennen sighed, reaching to hug her. "It's okay, Jaxcy. I'm sorry. I didn't mean to lay it out so roughly for you. I'm not sure how to treat a lady in my life."

"I'm no lady." Jaxcy pushed at him.

Brennen refused to let her go. "You are, Jaxcy. You are a very beautiful lady. One that I am so glad to have in my life. You are a princess, and don't let anyone tell you any different." He felt her finally relax.

"So, what do we have to eat?" She refused to answer the unspoken question in his voice.

"What would you like? Tell me and I'll cook for you." When she refused to tell him, he simply moved her to the kitchen, seated her, and then prepared their breakfast.

Jaxcy rose to clear away the dishes, awe on her face when he pulled open the dishwasher.

"A dishwasher? I've never seen one." She watched as he stacked their dishes and then turned to her.

"Jaxcy, we need to talk, but I'm not sure if this is the right time or not. Come. Let's head for the office. I have some paperwork in there that I need to do, but I want to start us off with prayer."

She nodded, reaching down to scoop Kerry into her arms. "Kerry? Has he been out?"

"He has. He's already made some friends."

Jaxcy frowned. "That is unusual. Where do I walk him?"

"I'll show you." Brennen reached to retrieve a set of keys from his desk. "Here. These are yours. I'll show you which keys work which doors."

Brennen finally sat back, his hand still holding hers, a frown on his face. "We'll need to meet with Barnabas. But I really don't know what to do."

"I'm not sure what you mean." Jaxcy watched him closely.

"I mean. We need to start investigating Smithers and your property. We need to get some advice on what your trust is." He sighed. "They told me not to have an adventure. We told Brendon it ended with him. It doesn't look as if it did."

"Brennen? What are you talking about? Who is Brendon? What adventures?" Jaxcy was confused.

<hr>

Brennen began to laugh. "Eight of my friends here at the Foundation had what we call adventures, some life-threatening. But through it all, they met the loves of their lives. In fact, Brandon and Hagen are new parents to a set of twins. There are eight ladies who will welcome you. If you feel overwhelmed, tell them or tell me. They don't mean to do that, but they can."

"I see. It's been so many years since I've had a friend. Even then, they were not close friends." She sighed, her head going down against his arm.

"Speak up for yourself." He sighed as he heard a knock at the door. "We're not finished our talk yet, Princess. Let me see who is there. Look around here. I want your input on what we should change. This is your home. We need to make it that for you." Having said that, he rose and walked away, leaving her staring after him, her arms tightening around Kerry.

"Did he mean that, Kerry? Did he really mean that? I feel as if I died and went to heaven. That God heard my grumbling and shoved me into something so wonderful, just to shut me up." Tears sparkled on her cheeks before she swiped angrily at them.

Barnabas Carey stood beside Brennen, his eyes on Jaxcy, hearing her words, and hearing Brennen's faint muttering. He had stopped by, Brody letting them know that they were home and that he really needed to talk to Brennen. Brody had not told him what was up, but his very silence had alerted Barnabas.

Brennen simply sat beside her, swept her into a hug, and prayed for her. She was startled at his quick movements but then listened to his interceding on her behalf. She wondered at that, not used to it.

Jaxcy realized suddenly that they were not alone, as her startled eyes saw Barnabas sitting quietly near them, his head bowed as Brennen prayed before he took up the petition.

Smiling at Jaxcy, Barnabas waited for Brennen to speak, knowing his friend was having difficulty forming his words. He finally shook his head.

"I'm Barnabas Carey." He frowned for a moment as Kerry alerted and then jumped from Jaxcy's lap to head towards him, standing up to sniff at his face. "Does your dog always do that?" He was grinning as he held out a hand for Kerry to sniff at.

"He does. He has never bitten anyone yet. That's Kerry. He's protective of me."

"I would imagine he would be. Now, tell me about yourself. Brennen seems tongue-tied at the moment."

Brennen began to laugh. "And that is unusual for me, is what you're not saying. This is Jaxcy Joelyn Derring Connolly." At Barnabas' quick look at him, he nodded. "We are married. There is a story there. You can see by the bruising that I was attacked when I arrived. Jaxcy stepped in. There is a law in her town that if a stranger stops in and doesn't marry someone from the town, then they are jailed. I don't remember it at all, but Jaxcy tells me she felt she had to." He tilted his head to watch her face. "This is the J.J. Dering I was to meet."

"She is? We didn't know, did we? Thank you, Jaxcy. Welcome to the family."

Jaxcy finally remembered to snap her mouth closed. "Thank you. That wasn't what I expected."

"It wasn't?" Barnabas nodded. "I know what you expected. You expected blame and recriminations, to be made to feel like an outsider, not wanted?" At her nod and sad look, he shared a look with Brennen. "That doesn't happen here, Jaxcy. All of the eight men who are married faced danger, but we all stood by one another. It made us closer. The eight ladies of the Foundation building are close. I am sure they will welcome you into their midst. Anna, Doc's wife, will be around, I suspect, once she hears about you. Now, talk to me." He glanced at his watch. "We are in no rush. Take your time. We will meet later with the men, Brennen. This afternoon, late afternoon, after they're all home."

Jaxcy sighed. "I don't know where to begin. My parents were killed in a landslide when I was sixteen or seventeen. It was right around my birthday. I lost the house. The bank just took it. They shouldn't have. Dad had insurance that would have paid it off and let me live in it. The only place I could find was a little cabin in the woods and I found a truck to use." She looked up at Brennen, resignation in her glance. "I didn't have a lot, scratching and scraping to survive."

"Her house was a little cabin, Barnabas. She had only a fireplace and wood stove for heating and cooking. No electricity. No running water." He hugged her to him, even as he looked up at Barnabas. "This is such a contrast for her."

"I am sure it is. You mentioned Smithers?"

"I did. The land and house he is using? It belongs to Jaxcy. We need to talk to someone about evicting him. She also had stocks and bonds that we will need the accountant to look at and explain to her. I took a quick glance, but I'm not into numbers."

"We can do that. Now, Jaxcy? May I call you that?" At her nod, Barnabas paused for a moment, his eyes on the floor before he looked up at her. "What can we do for you? I can only imagine that Brennen wants to do what he can for you. So do we."

Jaxcy shrugged, unable to say what she needed to. She didn't want to be obliged to the Foundation, not fully realizing that she was now part of a family.

"I need to take her shopping, Barnabas." Brennen simply shared a look with Barnabas, who nodded. "Today, I think."

Jaxcy looked at him, horrified, before he simply shook his head.

"We will, Jaxcy. Trust me. Please?" He waited until she nodded. "Anything else, Barnabas?"

The other man shrugged. "I'm not sure, Brennen. Let me have what you can of the documents. I'll talk to Dallas and Will and see what we can do about the property. I would suggest that Jaxcy not go near there until I have."

"No, it's not likely a good idea." Brennen was silent, just nodding when Barnabas stood and said his good-byes.

Jaxcy finally shifted away from Brennen, her arms wrapping around herself.

"Jaxcy? If you don't want to go shopping, I'm fine with that."

"No, it's not that." She blinked rapidly, finding tears almost overcoming her once more. "It's that I don't have any money, Brennen."

"Jaxcy? Please look at me." Brennen waited until she did. "You are my bride. It is part of my duty and honour to provide for you." He sighed. "There is something else. When we marry, the Foundation provides for our wives. They are paid wages, just like we are. It's part of the Foundation premise of encouraging."

"They can't. Not for me. They don't know me." Jaxcy would have continued to protest but Brennen's finger was laid on her lips.

"No, they don't. It doesn't matter. This is what they do."

"I've never heard of that before." She watched as Brennen rose to his feet, heading for his desk, to pull open a drawer and remove something.

Brennen stared down at the small ring box that he held in his hands. It was the only thing that he had left of his parents, his mother's engagement ring. He couldn't remember them, but he felt certain that they would approve of his bride. He simply returned to sit beside her, reached for her hand, and slipped on the ruby ring, her mouth opening and closing before she looked up at him. He nodded and then reached to hug her.

———

Feeling eyes on him, Brennen shifted his stance as he waited in the clothing store for Jaxcy. She was feeling overwhelmed, he knew, but when one of the ladies from the building had approached him, he had quickly introduced her to Fynn, his friend, Brady's wife, who simply took Jaxcy under her wing and led her away. He could hear Fynn's quick laughter and comments, but not a lot of talking from Jaxcy. That concerned him.

His eyes searched the store before he moved to look out the window, his eyes finding the short thin man standing across the road, his focus on the building. Smithers! How did he know? Brennen reached for his phone, sending off a quick text to Barnabas.

Jaxcy approached him, Fynn beside her, bags in their hands.

"I spent too much, Brennen. I just know I did." Jaxcy had a tight, worried look on her face. It was obvious she was not used to spending money without counting every penny.

Fynn hugged her, surprising her. "No, you didn't. Brennen would say that. Besides, I had fun helping you. If you want to shop at any time, come find me. I'll gladly come with you. So would any of the others. See you two later." She was away before Jaxcy could respond.

"She's like that, Jaxcy."

"She is? She's so down to earth. I like her." She took the hand that Brennen was holding out.

"She is. Would you believe she is a doctor?" He laughed at the look Jaxcy gave him. "She is. Fynn is an entomologist. I'll take you out to her building one day." He stuffed the packages into his truck and then pointed across the road. "Come, let's go out for lunch. We need to celebrate."

"Brennen! I have cost you so much already."

"No, you haven't. I want to." He held the door for her, his eyes on Smithers, seeing the instance the man recognized Jaxcy. He sighed to himself. Now what, Lord? How do I protect her?

Their lunch finished, Brennen reached for Jaxcy's hand as they exited the small, family-style restaurant. He had had to persuade her to have what she wanted, not just what was the simplest or the cheapest. She had frowned at him, and he had thought she looked just adorable when she did so.

"Now what, Brennen? I should get back to Kerry. He's not used to me being away from him for long." Jaxcy was worried about her companion.

"We'll go get him and take him for a long walk. How's that? I can show you some of the gardens, even though they are not in bloom yet."

"Okay. Do you have time?"

"For you, I will always have time. You will come first with me, right after God. I want you to understand that." Brennen waited until she looked back up at him and then nodded.

Jaxcy opened her mouth to respond when a look of horror crossed her face. Before she could even scream, Brennen's hand was torn away from her as he was tackled and taken down to the pavement. She stood for a moment, watching as Brennen was struck repeatedly before she ran forward, throwing herself at the man's back, her hands scrabbling and scratching at his face.

The man simply shook Jaxcy off, swinging her around to face him by the arm that he held in a tight grip, before his fist struck her violently in the face, not once but twice, sending her to the pavement, to tumble over and over and then to lay sprawled facedown, not moving. The man stood for a moment watching her, hearing the sounds of shouts and running feet coming his way. He turned back to Brennen, a booted foot coming back before he kicked the younger man in the ribs with the steel toe of that boot. He shot a look over his shoulder and then scuttled away down the nearby alley, like the cowardly bully he was.

———

Smithers knew how to hit and run. He had been doing that all his life. He ran for the car that was waiting, scrambling in before it tore away. The two men who had chased him were too late. They could only stand and stare at the dust raised, obscuring the car, before they shook their heads and ran back towards the street.

Brody and Branigan ran forward, ready to help. They could hear the rise and fall of sirens in the distance, drawing near.

"It's Brennen!" Branigan was on his knees, his hands trying to keep Brennen from moving.

"Let me up! I need to find Jaxcy!" Brennen fell back, his head spinning, a hand cradling his ribs. He shook off the hands, trying to rise.

Brady, another friend, and a paramedic, slowed his steps. "Brennen?" He shared a look with his partner, Patrick, even as they stopped their forward movement with the stretchers.

"Yeah." Branigan looked around, not seeing Brody for the people crowded around them. "Where's Brody?"

"He's here?" Brady looked at the officers who had responded. "We need these people moved back. We can't work like this."

The officers nodded, before with arms outstretched, they moved the men and women back and began to take statements.

"Brody?" Brady shot him a glance even as he tried to restrain Brennen.

Brennen kept shoving at the hands preventing him from reaching Jaxcy. He needed to know she was alive and okay. It didn't matter about him, he thought.

"Jaxcy?" He slumped back to the pavement, his hand coming up to wipe at the blood that had started to trickle from his mouth. "Where is she?"

"Jackie? Who's that?" Brady reached to try and take Brennen's vitals, his partner with Jaxcy.

"Jaxcy." Brennen shoved harder against Brady. "Brady, move. I need to get up."

"No, you need to stay still. You're hurt, Brennen. I need to find out where."

Brennen rose to his hands and knees and crawled away from Brady, despite Brady's best efforts and protests to keep him where he was. He collapsed beside Jaxcy, a hand out to touch the back of her head, a groan coming from him as he lost his fight to stay alert.

Brody's hands were there to help as Patrick worked on Jaxcy, his eyes shifting to watch Brady as best he can.

"Who is she, Brody?" Branigan stood behind him, worry on his face.

"Jaxcy? She's Brennen's wife." His concentration on Jaxcy, he didn't see the looks the other three men exchanged.

"His wife? What are you talking about?" Brady turned as an officer approached to help shift Brennen to a stretcher.

"A long story, Brady. One that we were to hear this afternoon at our meeting." Brody stood, his eyes on Jaxcy.

"How is Jackie, Patrick?" Brady shot a glance at her as she was transferred carefully to another stretcher.

"It's not Jackie, Brady. It's Jaxcy." Brody spelled it out for him. "What now, fellows?"

"Off to Emerge. One of too many trips we've made today." Patrick rose, his hand on Jaxcy's wrist as the stretcher she had been placed on was raised.

"Brody, you're riding with them?" Branigan had his phone out, ready to make the call that they always dreaded making.

"I am. Jaxcy knows me, to some degree. I met her last night when Andy and I tracked them down in Labrador."

Branigan nodded, his attention on the call he had placed.

"Barnabas? Brennen and Jaxcy have been assaulted. How bad? I'm not sure, but it looks bad. No one can tell us who or why. What's that? Smithers? Him? Who knows. Brody is riding with Brady and Patrick. What's that?" Branigan covered one ear to hear Barnabas better over the chatter around him, moving away from the scene and towards his truck. "No. Brennen was conscious, sort of, when we arrived. Jaxcy, is it? It is? She was unconscious. Sure. I'll keep you updated as I can. You're heading in? Oh, after that conference call? Okay. If anything changes, I'll call." Branigan's phone was tossed on the passenger's seat as he pulled away, knowing that it could well mean life and death for his friend. He shook his head. He had not expected to hear that Brennen had married. That was a story that he really wanted to hear.

Doc looked around as Brady and Patrick wheeled the stretchers in, the nurses helping.

"Brady? Who do you have?"

"Brennen. He's not great, Doc. It looks as if he took a bad blow to his ribs. He's bleeding from the lung, I am assuming." He nodded to the other stretcher. "That's Jaxcy. She's taken a bad blow or two to her face."

Patrick spoke up. "When I touched it, she whimpered and moved away from my hand. I couldn't get a good feel of how bad it is."

Doc nodded, before pointing towards the rooms. "In there. Brennen? Can you hear me?"

Brennen's eyes flickered before his lips formed Jaxcy's name. "Jaxcy? Where is she?"

"Jaxcy's here, Brennen. I need to examine you." Doc's hand on Brennen's chest kept him still. "Brennen, you need to stay still."

Brennen moved to roll to his side, let out a groan, and then laid still, his face whitening from the pain.

Later, Doc stood beside Jaxcy's bedside, his eyes on the computer monitor showing the X-Rays she had had taken. He shook his head. Not a total fracture, he thought. Hairline at best. She would be sore.

He turned as he heard footsteps, and Barnabas walked towards him.

"Barnabas? You're here?"

"I am. First, Brennen?"

"Pneumothorax. A punctured lung from a rib. He took a heavy blow. There is also a lot of old bruising." Doc sent him a questioning look.

"Yeah, about that. He was beaten badly about a week ago. He told me this morning he had been in the hospital there for a day or so, and then moved to a home. He thought he was recovering."

"He had been, but this beating sets him back. He'll be in for a few days. The surgeon on call is heading in. We'll need to place a chest tube."

"Ouch." Barnabas studied his friend's wife. "I'll sign off on his paperwork. Jaxcy is not able to."

"What on earth are you talking about?" Doc spun, a questioning look on his face.

"Jaxcy? She and Brennen are married. A long story, Doc, but apparently she saved him from going to jail in her hometown. How is she?"

Doc shook his head, and Barnabas grinned at his muttering about the younger generation and how they met their ladies. He nodded at Jaxcy.

"There is a hairline fracture of her jaw. The surgeon will take a look at her as well. Likely she'll need it wired for a few weeks to heal. Find who did this."

"We're working on it, Doc." Barnabas watched Jaxcy for a few minutes, his heart rising in prayer for the young woman before he turned, walking across the hall to stand beside Brennen before he moved to the waiting room, his eyes searching the faces gathered there, a faint smile on his face. It was as he had expected. The Foundation building fellows were there as were the ladies. He could see Anna, Doc's wife, as well.

Brody approached him, his eyes looking past him.

"How are they?"

Barnabas shook his head. "Both are heading for surgery. Brennen has a punctured lung and needs a chest tube. Jaxcy has a hairline fracture of her jaw." Barnabas frowned. "She is so tiny."

"I know. Brennen didn't say too much, but I got the impression that she didn't have a lot. He said she lived in a really ramshackle cabin, no electricity, no running water, with little income."

Buckley, the minister in the group, spoke from beside him. "Who is Jaxcy, is it?"

Barnabas sighed, his eyes sliding closed even as he prayed for his friend and his bride. "Buckley, we need to meet as a group. See if we can use a room here. That will free up the waiting room for others."

"We can. I already asked." Buckley moved away, a puzzled look turned back towards his friends, before he started moving among their group, to shuffle them from the waiting room to a conference room nearby.

Looking around the room from where he stood speaking with Will Peters, the police chief of the town, and Dallas, a detective who was also a good friend, Barnabas studied each one who was present. He didn't have a lot of information to give them and that concerned him. Brennen had handed him the package of documents on his way out of the building with Jaxcy but he had not had a chance to more than glance through them.

"You suspect Smithers?" Dallas had had his own problems with Smithers in the past.

"We do. Brennen didn't get a chance to go into too many details but Jaxcy owns the property he has been using. She had forgotten, I guess. There is also a trust fund that came to her when she married Brennen and then had her birthday. Brennen suspects Smithers was after that."

"I'm sure he was." Will gave a sound of frustration as his phone vibrated. He squinted at the number. "I need to take this. I'll be back."

"Barnabas, what do you really know about her?" Dallas asked.

"Not a lot. Brennen had a letter before he went east, asking that he contact a J.J. Dering. Breck, he and I talked about it, prayed it over, and he decided to go. We didn't know that Jaxcy was that person."

Dallas shook his head. "And he ended up married to her? There's a story there."

"There is. I need to tell the others. I have some documents that we'll need to take a look at. Brennen handed them over to me." Barnabas moved away, heading for Buckley who nodded.

Barnabas stood for a moment, studying each one who was in the room before he nodded. He knew the hearts of the men and the ladies and that they would do their utmost to help Brennen. He had always been there for them.

"Okay, fellows, ladies. This is what is up. As you know, just over a week ago, Brennen headed for the east coast, to meet someone named J.J. Dering. When he arrived in that town, he was badly beaten. A young woman stepped in to help him, along with the minister of her church. There is a law in that town that states that any stranger who arrives must marry someone from that town or go to jail." He paused, hearing the low murmurs and then the nods. "Brennen was married that same day. Unknown to him at the time, the J. J. Dering he was to meet was a young woman. Her full name is Jaxcy Joelyn Dering. She is the one who stepped in and married our friend, to save him from jail. From what research I have been able to do, it is a long sentence that they are given."

Benen spoke up. "Is that the lady who was with him today?"

"It is, Benen. Andy and Brody flew down yesterday at my request, as Brennen did not check in with me as we had arranged. They found Brennen and Jaxcy heading for an airport, returning this way." He looked around. "Bradon? She has a dog that I would ask you to take care of for now."

"How are they, Barnabas?" Burnie spoke up, worry on his face, and in his voice.

"Brennen has a punctured lung from the beating today. Doc says it looks as if he was brutally kicked. Jaxcy was also assaulted and has a fractured jaw." He tamped down the anger rising in him. "This is not how we welcome people to our town."

"Do we know who?" This from Brandon, Hagen's arm around her husband.

"We do. Dylan Smithers." Dallas looked up from his notes. "From what Barnabas has learned from Brennen, Jaxcy is the owner of the property he has been living on. She was unaware of that until a few days ago. Barnabas, you have paperwork to turn over to me?"

"I do." He handed over the envelope he had been worrying with his hands. "I took a quick look. Deeds and other papers."

Dallas nodded. "Good. We need to stop Smithers. He's been the bane of everyone's existence for years. We just had not been able to prove anything."

"We can from today. There are numerous witnesses to the assault." Will Peters spoke from where he was leaning against the wall.

"That's good." Barnabas stared down at the floor, letting his friends talk among themselves. He looked around as the door opened and Doc looked in, beckoning at him to come out.

"Doc?" Barnabas spoke as soon as the door closed behind him.

"Brennen is headed for surgery now. I just wanted you to know. The surgeon felt he couldn't wait any longer."

Barnabas drew a deep breath. "We've been through so much with all of the fellows. God has provided and healed."

"He has." Doc was silent, his thoughts on his young friends. "Now, Jaxcy? What has that girl been doing to herself? She is underweight."

"I know. She's been on her own since she was seventeen. Brennen said she lived out in the woods in a ramshackle cabin, with no electricity. She scraped for everything she could get."

"We need to fix that, Barnabas. See to it." Doc paced away and then back. "She'll have her jaw wired for a few weeks. This is not going to help her get to where she needs to be."

"I know that, Doc. I know that. I stopped by this morning to talk with Brennen. She will not ask for anything. He mentioned that when he told her there was a lot of food, she put the loaf of bread back, thinking he didn't want her to have toast."

Doc blinked rapidly, his emotions getting the better of him for a moment. "We need to change that. I don't think we've faced that with the others, now have we?" With that, he walked away, leaving Barnabas to stare at the wall in front of him, his thoughts muddled, unlike him.

———

Fynn slowly approached Jaxcy's bedside, not quite sure of how she would be received. She studied her new friend, wincing at the bruising that was starting to colour her face. Lord, why? This shouldn't have happened. Please, Lord? Heal my friend. Heal Brennen.

Walking away after a time, Fynn sought for Brady, finding him standing right outside the door waiting for her. He simply enveloped her into a hug and stood, his head on hers, his eyes on Jaxcy.

"Was she awake?"

"No, she wasn't. Brady? This had to hurt. Why?"

"Likely to keep her from coming here to get her property. Smithers was to get it if she hadn't married by the time that she was twenty-eight."

"And is she?" Fynn leaned back to look up at him.

"She is. Barnabas said about three days ago." Brady sighed. "We need to do something to help her celebrate. She hasn't celebrated a birthday since her parents died, from what Brennen told Barnabas."

"That's so sad. Was it only this morning that I took her through May's clothing store? She didn't want to spend any money. I had to convince her that was what Brennen wanted."

"It's understandable." Brady looked around. "I have to head back out. You're staying?"

"I am. I have the time. Ennis and Cadee are here as well."

It was after midnight when Jaxcy finally aroused and stayed awake, her eyes opening as she stared around, fear in her heart. She had no idea what had happened until she moved and pain shot through her face. Tears blinded her as she reached to touch the jaw, finding the sore spot. She remembered, then, a man tackling Brennen before she had run at him. Brennen? She sat up abruptly, waiting until her head cleared.

She slipped from the bed, searching for clothes, finding some of the ones that Fynn had convinced her to buy, was it only yesterday? She dressed rapidly and then headed for the open door, stopping for a moment to catch her breath and her balance. Where is Brennen? Lord? Where is he?

Jaxcy looked around for a nurse and didn't see one before she walked quietly down the hallway, searching through the open doors, finally spotting Brennen. Looking over her shoulder, she hesitated before she headed towards him, her hands coming out to grip the bed rail, her eyes on him.

"Brennen, what did I do?" Her voice was barely audible, pain evident on her face. "Why? Why didn't you just stay away?"

Jaxcy stood for hours that way, refusing to move when the nurses suggested that she would be more comfortable in a chair. She simply shook her head. She felt responsible for his being there and just wanted it to be different. Her heart was raised constantly in prayer.

Barnabas stood for a moment in the doorway, watching her, before he moved towards her. He frowned. She had not even noticed that someone else was in the room, her focus solely on Brennen.

"Jaxcy?" His hand went out to help her keep her balance as she jumped. "Should you be here?"

"I have to." He had to strain to hear her words. "I have to. It's my fault."

"No, it's not. It's Smithers' fault." He sighed, knowing that she didn't believe him. "Here, you need to sit. The nurse said you've been standing here for hours."

"I can't. I'm sorry. I need to stay here." Jaxcy looked at him, a tortured look in her eyes. "I have to be here."

"We get that, Jaxcy. All we want is for you to sit. You're hurt as well." Barnabas was growing frustrated.

Brennen had roused as he heard the voices, a frown on his face for a moment, before pain shot through his chest as he moved. His hand reached up to touch hers, causing her to jump.

"Jaxcy? You can sit, Princess. I know you're here." Brennen watched through pain-narrowed eyes.

Jaxcy turned her focus to him. "Brennen? You're awake!"

"I am, Princess. How be you sit?"

Jaxcy just shook her head. "I can't, Brennen. I just can't." She turned and ran from the room, leaving Brennen trying to rise and go after her.

"Stay put, Brennen. I'll find her." Barnabas was out of the room, searching for her, finding her standing in the waiting room, staring out of the window into the growing daylight, Fynn's arm around her.

"Barnabas? Is Brennen worse?" Fynn was confused.

"No. He tried to get Jaxcy to sit. She's been standing by his bed for hours, the nurses have said."

"Jaxcy? Why?" Fynn waited, knowing Jaxcy would talk when she was ready.

"I had to, Fynn. I had to." Jaxcy stopped speaking, her body shutting down, her eyes closing as she collapsed. Barnabas was there to catch her, turning with her in his arms and striding back towards Brennen's room, Fynn beside him.

"Barnabas? Aren't you taking her to her own room?"

Barnabas simply shook his head. "They need to be together. If I don't take her back to Brennen, he'll be up and looking for her. And he can't just now."

Brennen had managed to sit, his legs over the edge of the bed, but the pain had stopped him. He sat, his hand wrapped around his ribs, watching the door.

"Barnabas?"

"She collapsed, Brennen. She has a fractured jaw, which none of us have been able to tell you about yet."

Grimacing in pain as he did so, Brennen slid over on the bed, the arm on his uninjured or less injured side out to cradle Jaxcy as Barnabas laid her beside him. He could hear the soft footsteps as the nurse approached. Worried, he looked up at her.

"Katie?" He was thankful it was one of the nurses that they knew from church.

"She stood here for hours, Brennen. She had been here for a while when we found her. I would say likely five or more hours. We just could not get her to leave." Katie reached to check Jaxcy, a frown on her face. "She just wouldn't leave you, Brennen. Her fingers would be white at times, she was holding on that tight. I don't know that she took her eyes off of you the whole time."

Barnabas shook his head. "Even when I approached her, she didn't look around." He shared a look with Brennen.

"She doesn't have anyone, other than me, Barnabas. She hasn't totally learned to trust me. It will come." He looked up, a tortured look in his eyes. "I pray it is soon. I pray also that she learns to trust the rest of us."

Jaxcy gave a soft moan as she turned her face against Brennen, a flicker of pain crossing her face. Katie was away and back, ready to give a pain injection when Brennen held up his hand.

"Do we know if she has any allergies?"

Katie paused. "Now, that's a good question. I am not sure that we do." She looked down at the syringe and sighed. "I gather that you're refusing to have her given a shot."

"For now. Until Jaxcy can tell us or we can reach out to the minister in her hometown and see if there are any health concerns. He seems to be the only one she had contact with."

Barnabas shook his head as Katie walked away. He frowned, a thought running through his mind.

"You two didn't talk much?"

"Not about medical stuff." Brennen sighed, pain shooting through him as he moved, and he struggled to breathe. "What did he do to me?"

"Kicked you with his steel-toed boot. Your rib punctured your lung. You have a chest tube for now."

Brennen paled. "How do I take care of Jaxcy?"

"That's where we come in. It's your turn to receive, Brennen. You are always giving to us." Barnabas waited for a while, watching as Brennen dozed off, the pain medications taking hold before he walked away.

Breck walked towards him as he headed for his truck, and he paused, waiting for him to catch up with him.

"How are they?"

"Jaxcy was up. They found her standing by Brennen's bed. She refused to leave. He's been awake. Right now, they're together." He stopped, a thought running through his mind. "Where do we stand with Smithers?"

"He's gone underground by the sounds of it." Breck was frustrated. "I still don't get it."

"Get what?"

"How is Smithers involved? Did Jaxcy know him?"

Barnabas stared down at the keys he was rubbing his fingers on. "I don't know. I got the impression that she didn't."

"Then, I don't get it. How does he fit in?" Breck rubbed at his face, a puzzled look on it.

"That's what we're going to have to determine. You're heading in?" At Breck's nod, Barnabas paused, thinking through his day. "Send out a text message. Whoever is around and free, we'll meet later this afternoon."

"How long is Brennen in for?"

Barnabas shrugged. "Depends on how the lung comes along."

Breck looked up a couple of hours later from the book that he was reading, his attention down the hall. He rose, heading that way, finding Dallas heading his way. He shook his head as he noted the teenager Dallas had a grip on.

"Dallas?" Breck paused, waiting for Dallas to speak.

"I found him outside Brennen's room." Dallas held up an evidence bag, with a switchblade knife in it. "He shouldn't be here. It's not visiting hours. Besides, he's not family or friend to either one of them. Not that I know of."

Breck watched the younger man, seeing the fear flickering in his eyes. "He's been with Smithers, Dallas. I've seen them together."

"He has, hasn't he? I was here to talk to Brennen." Dallas sighed. "Now, I'm off downtown. I'll be back. How are they?"

Breck shrugged, not willing to say much in front of the teenager. "About what you would expect."

Dallas shared a look with him and then, nodding, walked away. Breck stared at the door to Brennen's room before walking towards it, to stand in the doorway. The surgeon was there and he could hear quiet conversation between the two men. He turned away to find Bradon and Burnie walking towards him.

"How is he?" Burnie's question was quiet, but Breck could hear the worry in his voice.

"I haven't talked to him yet. He was sleeping when I got here." Breck pointed towards the waiting room. "Any word from the investigation you fellows are running?"

"Not yet. We're having trouble accessing any records from that town. It's locked down tight." Bradon was frustrated.

"We should be able to access something. Do we even know their marriage is legal?" Burnie was puzzled.

"It is. Barnabas has verified that, he said. The Foundation lawyer is working on that. Apparently, this town has been on the radar of various authorities for years. They just could not prove anything. People were too afraid to talk."

"And it will fall to Brennen to do just that." Bradon paced. "How do we know that the trust fund and the documentation giving it to Smithers is legit?"

"The lawyer is working on that. He's pulled in someone else skilled and accomplished in estate and trust laws."

"That's good." Burnie watched the surgeon walk away from Brennen's room. "Can we see him?"

"Likely. Jaxcy is with him. Barnabas said she found him last night and refused to move from his room."

"Guilt?" Bradon took a guess.

"Likely. Say, did you retrieve Kerry?"

"I did. He and Kade are best friends now." Bradon sobered. "Ennis was in tears last night, Breck. She can't imagine how it came to this point for Jaxcy. Or how she had even lived. Fynn was by our place. The ladies are planning on meeting for prayer, and then to see what they can do for Jaxcy."

———

Walking slowly through the apartment, her hand rubbing at her temple trying to ease her headache, Jaxcy searched for something to do that wouldn't disturb Brennen, who was sleeping. She had stood and watched him, knowing that the effort of coming home had drained his stamina. She sighed. What did I do, Lord? I didn't know we were getting into this. I never meant for him to be hurt.

Finally searching for cleaning supplies, Jaxcy was surprised to find them well stocked, but not well used. She frowned. The apartment was clean, sparkling clean in fact. This did not make sense. She turned to her laundry but was unsure how to even work the washer. She had washed her clothes by hand for years, hanging them to dry in front of the stove in the winter, outside in the better weather.

Heading for the door as she heard a knock, she opened it, frowning at the three women standing there.

"I'm sorry?"

"Hi, Jaxcy. I'm Berneen, Baird's wife. This is Cadee, Benen's wife, and Imly, Brendon's wife. We won't stay for long, but we want to pray with you. Will you let us?"

Jaxcy shrugged, stepping back so they could enter. She pointed down the hall.

"Which room? Kitchen or living room?"

"Kitchen." Cadee held up a tray she had been holding. "I have muffins for us, but some delicious purée for you. If you want, that is." She was suddenly hesitant, not sure if she had overstepped her bounds.

"That's fine." Jaxcy was getting more and more frustrated. "I wish..."

"What do you wish?" Berneen moved around the kitchen, fixing coffee for those who wanted it and then tea for Imly and Jaxcy. She had heard Jaxcy liked her tea, not realizing that it had been all Jaxcy could afford.

Jaxcy shook her head, pointing to her jaw. "This. Why?"

"Because you are standing in his way. Brennen as well. He's known to be a mean, vindictive man." Cadee looked up from where she had been fixing the purée for her. "Benen said he's been like for as long as he has known him. The victims are too terrified to speak up."

"So, that leaves me?" The three ladies had to strain to hear Jaxcy's voice.

"I guess. We have all had that, Jaxcy. Had to stand up for ourselves and our fellows. To bring evil to justice." Imly's hand was laid on the one Jaxcy had on the table. "It's not easy. Some of us have almost died. Ennis did. She was stabbed. Bradon was actually drowned and revived. My Brendon was shot trying to protect me and then disappeared for four weeks."

Jaxcy's eyes were on her, wonder in her eyes. "There is no way that happens."

Cadee laughed. "It does. Berneen here? Forced to marry Baird to save his life. Me? Benen married me, as my father's request, to protect me and bring me home from a foreign country. I almost died from a poisoning."

Jaxcy studied each woman. "Where was God?"

"Right there. Even at the darkest point, He was there. He did not walk away from any one of us." Berneen sat beside Jaxcy, an arm around her. "He is here with you, Jaxcy, with Brennen. If Brennen had not married you, you would not have survived. Smithers would have seen to that."

Cadee began to pray, with the other two ladies following suit. Jaxcy was quiet, not saying much because of her injury, but she also was not sure how to talk with other ladies. She had never been comfortable doing that.

<hr>

Jaxcy jumped as she felt an arm come around her and a kiss was dropped on her temple. Brennen slipped into the seat beside her, a word of thanks for the cup of coffee Cadee slid in front of him.

"Brennen?" Jaxcy watched him closely, seeing he seemed more rested.

"I'm fine, Jaxcy. And you?" He studied her before nodding. They would need to talk, he decided, but just how to approach her, that was the question. She was feeling guilty, of that, he had no doubt.

Later that afternoon, her hand tight in Brennen's, Kerry on his leash beside her, Jaxcy wandered some of the grounds and gardens with Brennen, awe on her face.

"This is huge!" Awe was on Jaxcy's face.

Brennen laughed. "It is. We are not far from Lake Erie. We'll walk there once we're better. I think Kerry might like to see the waves."

She glared at him for a moment. "Sure. Teach him to herd waves. We'll never keep him at home."

"No, we will. We'll make sure he's on a leash." Brennen's arm around her drew her close to him. "Now, Princess. I need to head for my office to see what I have waiting."

"I've taken you away from your work, haven't I?"

Brennen simply shook his head, walking her back to the building and in the back doors, to stop at an office door, unlocking it, and then reaching in to flick on the overhead lights.

Jaxcy stood in awe once more, spinning in a circle to study the rooms. Brennen reached to let Kerry off his leash, and the dog headed around the rooms, sniffing and familiarizing himself with them.

"Take all the time you need, Princess. I'll be in that room over there, checking my emails and whatnot." Brennen waited for a moment, not sure if she had heard him before he headed for his desk and was soon immersed in his work.

Looking up later, he found Jaxcy standing in front of him, uncertainty on her face. Not sure what was going on, he rose and headed around to her, drawing her into a hug, a grimace of pain crossing his face for a moment.

"What's wrong, Princess?"

Jaxcy finally answered. "I can't find the cleaning supplies. How do I clean your office if I can't?"

Brennen realized then that he had made a grievous error on not talking with Jaxcy, but then again, they had not had a lot of time to do so.

Chapter 13

Brennen turned later that night, a mug of coffee in his hand, and leaned against the kitchen counter. He was exhausted, ready to sleep, but he needed time with God. He had no idea how to be a husband, how to protect Jaxcy. It didn't seem as if he had done that great already. Dallas had been by, just to update them and take what information they could give him, just to complete more of what he needed in the investigations. He had their statements, but he told them, things were remembered afterward.

Jaxcy had finally admitted that she thought that she had to clean the office and the apartment and do the laundry and cook. He had simply wrapped her into a hug and prayed for his princess. She kept looking at him as he called her that, but he had just shaken his head. She was not ready, not yet, to hear that she was the princess of his dreams, that he had fallen hard and fast for her.

She had shaken her own head when he told her that she didn't need to clean, that the Foundation had paid for years for housekeeping for the men, just as part of their mandate to be encouragers. When she had mentioned that she thought she had to, he had smiled and hugged her tighter. He told her that he had been looking after himself for years and that he didn't expect her to wait on him. They were partners, he stated, and would work together. She had protested that she had no training in anything else. Brennen had simply smiled, said that was okay, and that they would figure it out together, what she wanted to do. Right now, they both needed to heal.

Walking through the apartment, the lights low, he sighed to himself. He wanted this over, he thought. He knew it would only get worse and that scared him. He didn't want his Princess to be hurt her any more than she had been. He was in full realization that if he was hurt again, it would hurt her. He had seen something in her eyes that night as she had whispered a good night to him, something that gave him hope that just maybe she might, at some point, return his feelings.

He sat at his desk in his home office, pulling up his emails. He had not gotten too far that morning, and he knew the publisher he worked for had books waiting for him. He would need to work hard and long to catch up. He sent off the emails he needed to, took a quick look at the books waiting for him, his mind racing with the possibilities of what he could do, and then he turned to a search engine, searching for just what, he wasn't quite sure. He brought up news article after news article about Smithers, his face growing grimmer with each one.

Brennen finally sat back, exhaustion draining him, before he reached for his keyboard, sending off an email to a friend, asking her to search. A quick response startled him and then caused him to smile. Yes, he responded. He was having an adventure. No, he stated, he was not enjoying it, other than he had found his princess.

Startled, he looked up as he heard a noise, and then heard Kerry's low whine. He was on his feet, moving towards the bedroom, not finding Jaxcy. He began to panic, tracking Kerry's whine, finding the dog huddled down in the living room, protecting the door to the balcony.

"Kerry, what is it, boy? Where's our Princess?" Brennen dropped a hand on the dog's soft head as he stood, before he turned to search the living room, hearing soft sobs that he had not when he had entered. He approached Jaxcy, watching her closely, before he was on the floor beside her, gathering her to him,

Jaxcy pushed at him, bring a groan from him before his arms tightened. She pushed until she could push no longer, then collapsed against him, feeling his strength in how he held her, reading in it as well his feelings for her, and knowing that she was starting to love him, but she had decided it was too soon. She also quieted as she heard his prayer, before her eyes slid closed and she slept, her emotions and her physical injury stressing her body past its limits.

Brennen slept as well, unmindful of how hard the floor was. Kerry dropped his head on Brennen's leg and kept watch, growling as he heard a noise on the balcony, rising to stand at the door, his growl growing louder.

Jaxcy stirred late the next morning, feeling cold, a frown on her face as she realized that she was in Brennen's arms but that they were seated on the floor in the living room. She sighed. Another nightmare, she thought. She had not had one for weeks, but they were back. Kerry nudged at her, and she rose, heading to dress and then to take him outside. She didn't see Branigan and Buckley watching her or Brandon following her.

Brennen was at his desk when she returned, rising to greet her as she approached him.

"I'm sorry, Brennen. I had a nightmare."

"Did you? Do you have them often?" His arm around her, he walked them towards the living room.

"I haven't lately, but I used to have them every night." She sighed. "Kerry is upset about something."

"Is he?" Brennen had watched as Kerry had headed for the balcony door. "That's strange. Why is he at the door?"

"He kept wanting to go out there this morning. And just why did we sleep in the living room?"

"Because that is where I found you. You went to sleep and I couldn't lift you."

Jaxcy stared through the open door, seeing the package sitting there. "Brennen? What is that? It wasn't there last night."

"No, it wasn't." Brennen back away, shutting the door. "I need to call Dallas. He'll send someone out, I know. Meanwhile, let's get your tea and my coffee and head for my office."

Brennen looked up a couple of hours later as Dallas opened the door to his office and then entered, a shuttered look on his face as he stared at Jaxcy, who was ignoring him, engrossed as she was in a book. Rising, Brennen approached him.

"Dallas? I know that look."

Dallas nodded. "I know you do. Listen? Can we talk without Jaxcy being present?"

"Why?" Brennen felt Jaxcy's hand on his side.

"What is wrong? Why would you ask that?" Jaxcy's voice held a tinge of anger.

"Because of what was in that box. Did you place it there?" Dallas' voice was tight.

"What? How dare you accuse me of something like that?" Jaxcy's voice was barely audible as she spat her words out through her wired jaw before she ran, Kerry at her side, the door slamming behind her as much as any door in the building could slam.

Brennen glared at Dallas. "You had better have a good reason for this. I'm going after my wife. If I can convince her to return, we'll meet you in the conference room. If I can't, then we don't meet. I will not tolerate anyone treating or talking to her like this."

Dallas' hand went up as he opened his mouth to speak, but Brennen was gone before he could say a word. Dallas ran a hand through his hair. That went well, Lord. I let my anger and worry get the better of me. I know I shouldn't but these fellows have been through enough. He turned from the room, heading for the door, knowing he had other cases to work on but he really did need to talk to Brennen. He would return, hopefully before nightfall.

Brennen searched for Jaxcy, not finding her, not even finding Kerry, though he tried hard. Branigan and Brendon approached him, a frown on their faces, not quite sure what he was doing. Brennen turned as he heard his name, an arm wrapping around himself.

"Brennen? You look horrible!" Brendon's hand came out to steady his friend. "You should be inside, not out here. Not when it's about to rain."

"I can't find her."

"Who? Jaxcy? Is she out here with Kerry?" Branigan turned in a circle. "Where would they be?"

"That I don't know. She ran from my office, Kerry with her. Dallas was around. She didn't like that he accused her of placing a box on my balcony."

"A box? Wait! Brennen, what are you talking about?" Branigan looked up as others approached.

"There was a box placed on the balcony sometime overnight. Dallas retrieved it. We didn't get into what was in it. We didn't have a chance. He wanted to talk without Jaxcy present, she heard him, asked why and then ran." Brennen sighed. "I guess I wasn't too polite to him."

"It's understandable. Now, where would she have run to?" This from Benen.

"That I don't know. She's not familiar with the area. We walked through some of the gardens earlier but neither one of us was up to much. I'm afraid, fellows. Afraid that Smithers has her in his control."

"I just heard that Smithers has been found." Breck spoke from behind Brennen. "It's not good, fellows. He was found dead, shot."

"What?" Brennen spun, then struggled to keep his balance. "How?"

"That's what they're working on. Dallas called, looking for you. He's sending out a patrol car to provide some security for here until he can get more understanding of the situation. He has asked that we watch out for you two. Now, what is happening here?"

Buckley spoke up. "Jaxcy's missing. So is Kerry." He turned as he heard a sound and found Hagen and Devaney walking towards them.

"Hagen?" Brandon went towards his wife even as Blair headed towards Devaney.

"Where is Jaxcy? We found Kerry but we can't get him to rouse." Hagen pointed to the dog Devaney carried.

"Where?" Brennen was beside them, ready to head off to wherever it was he needed to be.

"By the roses. He was just laying there, Brennen. We didn't see Jaxcy and couldn't think of where she would be."

Brennen was away towards the garden before she had finished, not caring that his hurried movements caused his pain to increase. He ignored it even as he searched for Jaxcy.

"She's not here, Brennen." Branigan's hand stopped his movements. "Come on. Back into the building. Breck called it in. Dallas is heading this way. It's getting dark."

"I know, but I need to find her. Where is she?" Brennen was beginning to panic.

The men shared looks and then spread out, Hagen and Devaney forcing Brennen to go with him, using the fact that Kerry was hurt and that Jaxcy would want him to look after the dog.

An hour later, Brennen still sat in the lobby area of the building, the heat from one gas fireplace not warming him. He cradled Kerry in his arms, the dog awake and alert, but not willing to leave Brennen. There had been no reports yet that Jaxcy had been found. It was dark now, with a misty rain falling, chilling the searchers.

Barnabas halted beside Brody. "No sign?"

"Not yet. I don't like this, Barnabas. Too many of us have disappeared from here."

"I know, Brody, but we can't fence it off. Dallas said he was heading for Jaxcy's property in the event she might be there."

"As if she'd be in the open. I'm not sure that she evens knows which area is hers."

"No, I don't think she does. Brennen said he hadn't talked to her about that yet." Barnabas frowned as he heard a soft sound. "Did you hear that?"

"I did." Brody spun, before pointing. "That way, I think." He was off on a run, following the faint sounds that came his way. He slid to a halt, a hand out to stop Barnabas. "In here, somewhere, Barnabas. If it's Jaxcy, she can't yell."

Barnabas hesitated, his head tilted to listen, before he was reaching for the bushes, parting them, an exclamation drawn from him. "Jaxcy!"

Brody pushed past him, dropping to his knees, his hand reaching for his pocket knife, to slash the bonds that had held her prisoner. "Jaxcy?" When she barely nodded, he was pulling off his jacket, to wrap it around her before he rose, Jaxcy in his arms. "We need to get her to Doc."

"We do. You're okay?" Barnabas held the bushes back once more before he headed almost on a run for the building, Brody following at a rapid pace.

"I am. She's freezing, though."

The men headed directly to the infirmary, finding Doc walking towards them.

"Brody? You found her?" Doc had the door open and the lights on in the room, heading for where he had left his stethoscope.

Brody was away, looking for Cadee, who was training as a nurse, knowing Doc would want her help. Anna was already heading his way.

"Brody? I just heard. Have you found her?"

"We have, Anna. In the infirmary. I was looking for Cadee." He paused, not sure which way to go.

Anna simply reached to hug him, turning him to walk back with her. "Benen will find her. The ladies were heading for the chapel, to spend time in prayer." Anna watched her young friend, a frown puckering her forehead for a moment. Something is going on with Brody, Lord, and I am not sure what. The fellows are feeling the stress of the last months and into years, not sure who would be next. Please, dear Lord, walk with each one. Guide their steps. Help us to intercede on their behalf. Before we even speak, You have heard and answered.

Cadee approached Jaxcy's bedside during the night, her hand reaching for her stethoscope. Doc, Anna, and she had worked frantically to warm Jaxcy, Doc sending Cadee to find Brennen and then sending her to find warm dry clothes for the younger woman. Jaxcy had not roused at all, the chill coming from her worrying Doc. He had not said much, simply shook his head, started an IV, and then asked for hot water bottles and heavy blankets, to try and warm her. It had finally succeeded, the blue of her lips fading to normal pink.

Cadee's gaze shifted to Brennen, who slept on the stretcher that Blair and Burnie had wheeled in, refusing to leave Jaxcy, simply shaking his head. Brennen had refused to state what he thought, that somehow Smithers was still alive, that Dallas had been wrong, and that Smithers would somehow make his way to find her and take her somewhere Brennen could not find her.

Brennen had roused as he heard Cadee moving around, opening his eyes to a small crack, watching Jaxcy. His thoughts drifted to the night before, when Breck had found him in the lobby. Breck had dropped to a seat beside him, after he had taken off his jacket, frowning at the ice crystals that had formed.

"We found her, Brennen." Breck's hand kept Brennen in his seat. "Wait. We need to talk before you go to her. Barnabas and Brody found her. She was found, lying in some bushes. With the rain now turning to sleet, she would not have survived overnight. Doc, Anna, and Cadee are with her. Brady here will stay with you for now." Breck had shaken his head at Brennen's protest. "He stays. Dallas caught up with me. With the sleet moving in and changing to heavier ice, he won't be out tonight. He's not sure when he will be able to get out. He did ask that I talk to you. He sends his apologies."

"Yeah, well, about that. He needs to apologize to Jaxcy. I won't have her accused of a crime." Brennen's look was mutinous.

"He knows that and he feels bad. That's no excuse that he doesn't know her. She's the innocent party in all this."

"He left a voice mail for me, telling me that there was a direct threat against me in that box. It held pictures of me over the last week and from when I was at Jaxcy's. Someone is following me." Brennen rose, staring down at Breck. "Again, she is not the culprit here. I don't know who is." He turned and walked rapidly away, not looking back.

Brandon shared a look with Blair before he spoke. "He's right. She is the innocent party in this. So is he. If it's not Smithers, then who is it?"

"He had to be working for someone. He never had a traceable source of income, not that we can determine." Barnabas spoke from behind them. "How be we spend some time in prayer for our friends and then try to get some work done?" He squinted at his watch. "It's early yet. Unless you have plans?"

"No, none of us. The ladies are in the chapel, praying. We can work." Buckley strode away, heading for the conference room, following by the others.

Watching Cadee leave, Brennen hesitated before he rose, a prayer rising within him, a prayer for healing, for peace, for wisdom, for resolution of this that they found themselves in. He cried out for protection for his princess, knowing that the day before could have turned out so differently.

He stood, his hand on her cheek, wincing at the fading bruising, anger burning within him. He wanted revenge on whoever had done this, whoever had been behind Smithers. Then, he grew repentant. Vengeance was God's, not his. He breathed a sigh, his eyes closing as he surrendered his will, once more, and surrendered his Princess to God.

Jaxcy stirred, her eyes opening as she awakened, searching the dimly-lit room. The hospital again? She closed her eyes, a deep breath trying to calm her agitation. She felt the hand on her cheek and turned into it, recognizing Brennen's touch, even though their touches had been minimal to that point. She searched his face, seeing the peace that he was obtaining starting to flood it. She raised a hand to touch his, bringing a smile to his face as he opened his eyes.

"Princess? How are you?" He leaned closer to her.

"Sore. Where am I? The hospital?"

"No, in the infirmary in our building. You had an adventure and didn't take me with you."

"I did? I'm sorry. Dallas, was it?" At his nod, she sighed once more. "I need to apologize. I let my fear and anger speak and then drive me away."

"He wants to apologize to you as well. He realized that he didn't approach it correctly."

"I'm not used to interacting with people. I only saw a few on Sundays when I could get out to church, or if I had to shop, which was only every four to six weeks."

"No excuse for his anger. He told me that he was afraid for us." Brennen dropped the bed rail, and then sitting beside her, cradled her to him. "I can see his point."

"True, but what was in that box?"

"Pictures of me. Threats." He looked down. "I have some news. Smithers was murdered."

"He was?" Jaxcy twisted to look at him. "But that doesn't mean it's over, does it?"

"No, it doesn't. Barnabas was around late last night, just to see how we were doing. The fellows have started their investigation. They've become pros at this, seeing as I am the ninth to have an adventure."

"Nine? That's a lot. And it won't end until we get to Barnabas, now will it?" Jaxcy shifted once more. "Kerry?"

"He's at home. He was hurt, but Brady took a look at him. He doesn't think he was hurt too bad."

"I tried to stop the man from hitting him. He just shoved me away and when Kerry was down, he came after me. I tried to fight him off but he was too strong. He tied me up and dumped me in some bushes." Jaxcy stared down at her clasped hands. "I'm sorry, Brennen. I'm so sorry."

"It's okay, Princess. It's okay. You're here and safe." Brennen's arm tightened on her.

"Take me home, Brennen. I need to go home."

———

The tears and pleas in her voice broke his heart. Without saying a word, he simply gathered her into his arms, heading for their apartment, and then wrapping her in a blanket, dropped into his favourite armchair and sat, his head on hers as they both slept.

Standing at his kitchen counter, his focus on the scenery he could see outside of the window above the sink, Brennen listened as Branigan, Brendon, and Breck discussed what they had discovered. He shuddered at what they were saying, how Smithers had been behind so much destruction and devastation in the area. He knew only too well how he had worked. Both Brennen and Jaxcy had been his victims, Jaxcy more so than he had been.

He turned, his mug of tea in his hand. Staring down at it, he wondered when tea had become his beverage of choice and not the coffee he loved. He sighed, setting down his mug, and walking away from the men, leaving Breck staring after him for a moment.

Brennen stopped in the hallway, his eyes on Jaxcy as she stood, arms wrapped around herself, unwilling to enter the kitchen. She looked up at him, her eyes huge in her pale face, the effects of the chill from the day before still there. He simply reached to wrap her in his arms, his embrace tightening as he felt the sobs starting, sorrow in his heart for her. He stood, hearing footsteps behind him that paused.

"Princess? What's wrong?" He finally spoke, not sure if she would even respond.

"Take me home, Brennen. Please?"

"You are home, Princess. This is our home." Brennen was puzzled.

"No, take me home. To my cabin. I want to go back there. I felt safe there. Here I don't." Her sobs deepened.

"Princess? Do you want to go back there? It's not safe for you there. Breck is here. He has information about the law and the townspeople that he needs to talk to you about." Brennen was unable to reach through her distress, finally just scooping her into his arms and heading for his chair in the kitchen, a quiet thank you to Breck who pulled it back.

The three men watched as Jaxcy's tears were finally spent, and she just laid back against Brennen, not saying anything.

"Brennen?" Branigan finally spoke, breaking the silence.

"She wants to go back to her cabin. And we know that's not safe. And it doesn't seem to be any safer here. So what do we do?" Brennen felt awkward, even asking that.

"We keep you both here. Your work is here. You are both exhausted in more ways than one. Jaxcy has been thrust into a building and among people she doesn't know. She has not had a chance to relax or recover. That's something that preys on her feelings. You two were married without being able to discuss it or even truly agree to it. She stepped in to save you, Brennen. She will have questions as to whether she did what was right."

Jaxcy had looked up at Branigan was speaking, finally nodding. "All that and more." She was frustrated that her wired-together jaw kept her from talking a lot. Brendon finally shoved a pad of paper and his pen towards her, finding himself the object of her intense regard before she nodded and took the pen, her fingers forcing it to fly across the paper as she filled and then turned page after page. The four men watched her closely, not sure of what she was thinking.

Finally pushing the papers towards Breck, Jaxcy sank back against Brennen, exhausted, and suddenly realizing he still held her. Her head tilted back to study him, finding his eyes on her, a compassionate look on his face before he nodded.

"So, what do we have here, Jaxcy?" Breck spoke as he gathered the papers and looked them over, a shocked look on his face as he looked back up at her. "Jaxcy? You're sure about this?"

She nodded. "I am. I want this wire out now." She was frustrated at not being able to speak correctly.

"Not for a week or so, Princess. That's what the surgeon said. If we take it out too soon, you won't heal properly."

Branigan had been reading her notes and looked up, surprise on his face. "Jaxcy, this bit about Smithers' family. Do you know them?"

———

"I guess. I never connected them with him. I know the name is the same. Why?"

"Because we came across those very names last night when we were researching. They seem to have traveled back and forth between here and your town." Branigan handed the pages over to Brendon.

"When was that law set up?" Brendon's mind had taken off on a tangent.

"Twelve years ago, I think. I'm not sure." Jaxcy paled. "It was around the time that my parents died." She twisted to stare at Brennen. "Brennen? I never got an accident report. I was just told it was a landslide."

"And you think now that maybe it wasn't just an accident?" Brennen nodded. "I have been wondering that. We can't get those reports. Dallas has tried and been denied."

"The next step would be Emma, wouldn't it?" Breck pulled out his phone. "I'll call her. I have the information here." He was on his feet, walking away, leaving Jaxcy staring after him.

"What did he say?"

"We have a friend who is very good at finding information that no one else can. He's calling her to get her started on the search." Brennen sighed as his phone rang and he pulled it out. "Emma? She's sent an email."

———

Late that night, Brennen sat back from his computer. He was feeling physically better, he thought, but he was worried about Jaxcy. She had been quiet, quieter than she was normally. When he had approached her, she had just shaken her head, said she was tired and walked away, Kerry standing watching her before he turned to Brennen.

He had a handle on what work he needed to do, and the ideas were flowing. He sighed. As much as he wanted to work on the investigation, at present he had obligations to his publisher. He hadn't realized that he had so much work outstanding.

Walking through the low-lit apartment, Brennen studied it, trying to see it from Jaxcy's point of view once more. He just couldn't. He couldn't get past the huge contrast and that worried him. He was afraid she would just pack up and leave him, overwhelmed with her new life. His prayer was that he could reach her and help her. At the present time, he was just not sure how he could.

Standing in the living room doorway, Jaxcy watched Brennen, realizing that she had come to love him, but too unsure of herself to approach him. She finally walked towards him, sitting beside him, her hands clasped on her lap. She didn't speak, not wanting to disturb him, just in case he was praying.

Brennen tilted his head to study Jaxcy, not saying anything, his hand resting on Kerry's head. He finally spoke, talking about his life in foster care, how he had never known his parents and had always wondered what they would have been like. Jaxcy's eyes were on his face, sympathy on hers.

"You never knew them?"

Brennen shook his head. "I don't, I don't think. I was only two or three when I was taken into custody and placed in foster care. I have tried to find out why, but the records have been sealed by the courts. I have put in a petition through the lawyers here to have them unsealed, but we are still waiting."

"That's so sad." She looped an arm around his, laying her head on his shoulder. "I had mine. We had our disagreements as all families did, but I knew they loved me." She paused, a thread of thought catching at the edge of her mind. "Do you think this Emma will find out something?"

"I am sure that she will. She's good. The best in the business is what I have heard."

"Then, that's how we pray. I am tired of living like I am. I want stability."

"You have that with me, Princess. No matter what we go through, I am not walking away from you." He turned to face her. "I heard from Dallas earlier."

"And?" She looked up at him. "What did he want?"

"Just to let me know that they have the man in custody who shot Smithers. It was unrelated to our adventure, he said, but that we needed to be extremely careful. They are sorting through all the paperwork they found in his office. He has contacts that are still dangerous to us. In fact, Dallas said he had put out a contract on us. He was wanting revenge."

"Did we ever find out what happens to the property if I die after I was married?"

Brennen nodded. "It still goes to a trust, but this time it goes to a trust that can't be transferred or broken. It is to fund high school scholarships."

"Wow! Who set that up?"

"Burnie was working on that, along with Blair. They're searching through all sorts of dummy companies and whatnot."

"So that may not even be true. Who owned the property, to begin with?"

"That's what we can't determine." Brennen sighed. "I'm sorry. There doesn't seem to be many answers for you."

"It is just so strange. Why me? What did my parents ever do to have this come down on me?"

<hr>

Brennen raised a finger to halt her words, a thought running through his mind. "What did your parents do?"

"What do you mean, what did they do?"

"For a living, occupation, whatever you want to call it."

"Dad? He was a police officer. Mom stayed home. She was a proofreader for technical manuals. Do you think that this is it?"

Brennen nodded. "We have not looked closely at your parents, at least, I don't think so. Maybe it was revenge for your parents or something." He groaned as his phone chimed and he twirled it on the coffee table to look at it. "Emma. She's sent an email that she needs us to look at right away."

"She does that?"

"She does." Brennen stood, reaching for Jaxcy's hand, pulling her to the office with him, before he shoved her into his desk chair, pulling up another beside her. "Let's see what she has to say."

Jaxcy was confused. She knew about emails and stuff like that, she thought, but she had never used them herself. Brennen failed to see the look on her face at first until he turned to speak.

"I'm sorry, Princess. I'm just so used to this. Here. Let me explain. You have heard about emails and email addresses?" At her nod, he continued. "Emma has sent an email and has attached documents that she wants us to look at. I'll put them up, print them and then we can look them over."

"That's a lot of work." Jaxcy tried to protest at him doing that.

"Not at all. I'll need to print them anyway, I suspect, for the fellows." He was on his feet, retrieving the papers before he was back to his desk, in his chair, finding Jaxcy reaching for the stack. "Jaxcy?"

"I can at least sort it for you. How many copies?"

"I did six. One for each of us. One for Dallas. And then three for the fellows. They'll copy them as they need to." He reached for the copies, stacking them neatly before he turned to her. "Now, we take our highlighters, pens, and whatever, head to the living room or kitchen, wherever you wish, and work away."

"It's late, Brennen."

"I know, but neither one of us will rest easy until this is over. I want it over yesterday. You need it over."

"I do." She sighed. "I just don't get why God has allowed this. I'm not someone who would have chosen this."

"I know, Princess. I know. Let's pray first and then we'll find a late-night snack to tide us over."

Chapter 18

Late the next morning, Brennen looked up at a tap at his office door and watched as Dallas entered. Dallas was on a search for the couple, needing to speak with them.

"Jaxcy?"

"She's with the ladies, at Anna's. Do you need to speak with her?" Brennen dropped the pencil he had been holding. "I can get her."

"Not right away. I do want to speak with her, apologize, and then update her. But, you. What did you go and do, Brennen?" Dallas spoke half in jest.

"I don't understand." Brennen was puzzled, pointing to a chair for Dallas to sit.

"I received a raft of material from Emma and then from the Foundation lawyer. They have been researching you. The lawyer has finally been able to unseal the court records concerning you. He said he had tried to call you this morning."

Brennen groaned. "I always mute my phone when I am working." He reached for it, accessing his voice mail, wonder growing on his face as he listened to the lawyer's message. He set his phone down carefully before he looked at Dallas.

"Did you know?"

"Know what? That you were an orphan, that your mother gave you up because she was dying from cancer. That your father had been killed in a road rage incident before you were born?"

"That. I never knew." Brennen sat back, his hands rubbing at his face, blowing out a deep breath. "I never imagined that, you know. He said he has pictures and other things for me, including a letter from my mother."

"That's interesting. I would like to know why it was never given to you before."

———

"He's looking into that. He has approached the powers that be down there and is raising a ruckus, as he put it." Brennen looked down, overcome for a moment. "Now, about Jaxcy?"

"About Jaxcy. Can we go find her? That way, I only have to talk once." Dallas grinned at Brennen.

"Sure. I'm not sure exactly where she is." Brennen held up a hand. "And no, she has refused a phone. She admitted that she is somewhat scared of the phones nowadays."

"That's interesting. I wouldn't have thought that." Dallas followed Brennen down the hallway.

"She is quiet, not saying a lot of what bothers her. She has been beaten down by life and just trying to survive. I have to pull things from her, although she is getting better at talking with me."

Jaxcy looked up from where she has seated on Anna's couch, Fynn and Ennis on either side of her. She went to rise but Brennen motioned for her to stay put. He headed for the kitchen, Dallas in tow, and she heard his laughter as Anna teased him.

Fynn rose as Brennen approached, moving to let him sit beside Jaxcy, a word to Anna as she left, an eye on her watch. The other ladies gradually found their way out, calling back to Jaxcy that they had enjoyed themselves and they wanted to meet every week, if she would let them.

Brennen wrapped an arm around her, feeling the fatigue as she leaned against him. Knowing that she would not say a word, he smiled.

"Overdid it, did they?" He grinned at her frown. "They don't understand, Princess, how it is with you. You aren't used to being around people. I can talk to them or you can."

"You can't!" Jaxcy was horrified at the thought of him doing just that. Then she looked over at Dallas. "I need to apologize, Dallas. I let my temper get the best of me and I should have stayed and listened to what you had to say. It has been a while since you have been here."

Dallas grinned. "It has been. Apology accepted. I need to apologize as well. I shouldn't have approached our last meeting as I did. That being said, I do need to talk with you both."

———

Brennen spoke up, his eyes on Jaxcy. "It's okay, Jaxcy. I have some stuff to talk to you about, but we'll do that later. Right now, Dallas has some information that he needs to tell us."

"I do." Dallas opened the folder he had been carrying with him. He handed over some photos, watching Jaxcy closely as she took them. "Do you know these men?"

She stared at him for a full moment before her eyes dropped. She nodded. "This one? The gray-haired man? He's the mayor of my town. He has been for twenty years or so. No one has ever run against him. This second photo? That's his brother. He's the town accountant. The next one? He's the chief of police. The next one? That's the town's attorney. The minister and I suspected that they were all involved in drafting and ramming through the law. Does that make sense?"

"It does. Considering the law came on the books just before your parents died? We think it was directly to target you." Dallas looked down, discomfort and sorrow on his face, before he looked back at Jaxcy. "I'm sorry, Jaxcy. Your parents did not die in a landslide. It was made to look like that. We brought in the provincial police force, who have now taken over the enforcement in your town. The four men? They are under arrest. Thanks to the Foundation lawyer and friends he has in high places down there, we have been able to pull some records. With your permission, we would like to exhume your parents' bodies and have a medical examiner from outside the area do a new autopsy. In fact, there was never one done. It was blocked by the police chief."

"That's what I could never understand. They just told me that they were dead. They wouldn't even allow me to see their bodies. They sealed the caskets at the funeral. I protested, the minister and his wife protested, but they didn't allow it. They gave some flimsy reason." She blinked rapidly to dispel the tears. "How do I even know it was them? I never saw them. I only had their word it was my parents. How do I know for sure that it was? Will this examination prove that?"

———

Two weeks later, Brennen stepped back from the apartment door, his eyes on Dallas and then Barnabas as they entered. Something was up, of that he was sure. He had been out and about, feeling that he was being followed, but not seeing anyone that he could pinpoint.

"Dallas?" Brennen pointed to the living room. "I'll get Jaxcy."

"Just a moment, Brennen, before you do. We need to talk to both of you, but it is mostly what we have found about her parents." Dallas shook his head at Brennen's questioning look.

Jaxcy hesitated as she approached before Brennen reached to sweep her close to him. She was puzzled at the comment that she had overheard.

"Dallas?"

"Jaxcy? How are you?" Dallas grinned for a moment before he sobered. "I have news, Jaxcy. Can we sit?"

She shrugged. "I guess. I don't know why everyone wants to sit when it's bad news."

"Perhaps so that their legs don't give out and they end up in a heap on the floor." Barnabas grinned at her in turn. He waited until they were seated before he prayed, knowing that what Dallas had to say would be disturbing, to say the least.

"Dallas? What news do you have?" Brennen waited, his hand clasped tightly by both of Jaxcy's.

"Jaxcy, we have a report back on the landslide and then from the medical examiner. It has been determined that the landslide was deliberate but that the people in the car were not killed by it. They were dead already when the landslide hit the car."

Jaxcy paled. "Dead? Before? But how?"

"They were shot, according to the report. The bullets were still in the coffins. No one did an examination on them at all." Dallas paused, his eyes on Brennen before he looked at Jaxcy. "Now, according to the report, the people would have been in their mid-thirties."

"That can't be right. Mom and Dad would have been in their forties. I don't understand." She looked between Brennen and Dallas, a bewildered look on her face, not seeing how Barnabas was watching her.

"I think that it means that they weren't your parents. Is that correct, Dallas?" Brennen spoke up, wanting to change it for his princess but unable to.

"That is correct. They were both males. The force is looking into that, and say charges are pending."

"The mayor?"

"That is who they suspect. Now, as to your parents? We can find no evidence that they are dead. Where they are? That is the question. We have expanded our search to outside of Newfoundland, to across the country, and even into the States."

"What? You mean they may still be alive? But how?" Jaxcy was even more confused.

"That is what we don't know. We're still digging into records and conducting interviews. We're still a long way from where we need to be."

Jaxcy nodded, a saddened look on her face. "They are dead, Dallas. I don't doubt that. I would suggest you search his property outside of town. It's a large forested area. There have always been rumours about bodies that he had buried there."

Dallas nodded. "We have heard those too. There will be cadaver dogs going in to search. I'm sorry, Jaxcy. I was hoping to put this to rest for you."

"It is what it is." Jaxcy hesitated and then rose, walking away, only Brennen seeing the tears on her face.

"Excuse me." Brennen was on his feet, following her, reaching to wrap her into his arms, holding her as she sobbed. He knew that the investigation had opened wounds that hadn't healed. He had no idea what to say or even if he should say anything. He just prayed for his princess, asking for healing for her. "You okay, sweetheart?" He finally broke into the storm of tears.

"I don't know. I just don't know." She frowned at him. "Brennen? Why that word?"

"What word?"

"Sweetheart. You always call me Princess and that I don't even understand."

Brennen hugged her tighter. "You are the princess of my dreams, the one I was waiting for all my life. And you are my sweetheart. I never knew when the time would be right. This is not likely it, but I just wanted you to know that I love you, more each day."

Jaxcy stared at him, finally remembering to snap her mouth closed. "You do?" Her voice was barely audible. "Oh, Brennen. I was so afraid. Afraid that you would never care for me. I thought you were only doing what you were because you thought you had to as a husband. Taking care of me, making sure I was okay."

"That's part of it." Brennen looked towards the doorway of the office. "I need to go back and talk to those two. But understand this. Our conversation is not over. Not by a long shot. Stay here. I'll talk to them, see what else they can tell me."

The three men talked for a while longer before they rose. Brennen shut the door behind them, standing with a hand braced against it, suddenly unsure of himself. And that was not like him, he knew. He felt Jaxcy's hand on his back and turned suddenly, just sweeping her to his heart and kissing her. They had to talk, they both knew, but their mutually discovered love was too new and fresh to disturb it with words.

A week later, Jaxcy curled up in the large easy chair that Brennen had found and moved into his office. He wanted her near him, he said. She had laughed, shaken her head, and then circled it. She needed to find something constructive to do, she knew, but just what that was, she wasn't sure. Brennen had gladly let her have a sketch pad, bought her the pencils she refused to ask for, and left her to sketch.

Brennen looked up after a time, finding Jaxcy intent on her work, a pencil between her lips, another stuck behind her ear, her face a study in concentration. Who knew, he thought, that he would find a bride who liked to draw as well? God was in that, he knew. He had to be.

He looked towards the door as a tap came to it and then Brady peeked around it, beckoning Brennen to come outside. Brennen rose, a glance thrown towards Jaxcy before he closed the door behind him.

"Brady?"

"Brennen, we have found something in our research. We need to talk to you about it. It concerns your parents."

"And? I have a deadline I'm working on. I have to have the sketches in today." He frowned. "Can I have a couple of hours?"

"Sure. Come and find us when you're done."

Brennen watched Brady walk away before he shook his head and then returned to his work, the illustrations coming to life under his fingers. He felt Jaxcy's hand on his shoulder as he finished and sat back, an arm out to sweep her to his lap, his kiss on her lips stilling her protest.

"Brennen? What did Brady want? You were so deep in your concentration when you came back that I didn't want to disturb you."

"Thank you, Princess. He needs to talk to me. Something about my parents. And no, I will not let you stay away. You're going with me." He reached around her to the keyboard. "I just need to save these and then send them on. There. Another book done."

"Just like that? They're gone?" Jaxcy was always surprised at the speed at which the emails traveled back and forth.

"They are." Brennen reached to kiss her again, hearing Kerry whining at his feet. "It's okay, Kerry. We are not ignoring you, now are we?" He laughed as Jaxcy playfully swatted at him.

Jaxcy watched him, waiting for him to move, but he seemed to be content just to sit and hold her. And she was content to be held. "Brennen? Don't we need to go find Brady?"

"We do. I guess that means we have to get up?"

"It does." Jaxcy slipped from his knee, her hand held out for him. She was becoming more accustomed to showing her emotions with him, although she struggled at times. "Dallas was around when you were deep in concentration."

"He was? I didn't know that. How did I miss him?"

"It was when I had Kerry outside. And no, I was not on my own. Eric followed me." She sighed. "Dallas needs to talk to us too at some point over the next couple of days. He warned me to be extra cautious right now. Whoever it is that they are looking at, he said, is in the area and word on the street, as he put it, is that they are looking for us."

"That's what they always do. Put out a contract on the couple. It's what happened with the others." Brennen locked the office door and reached for her hand, heading for the other hallway and the conference room. "Listen. We need to go out for a dinner. Dress up, if you wish."

"Dress up? I don't know, Brennen. It's been so long."

"I know it has, Princess, but we'll work on it. We'll just take what time you need."

"Thank you, love. Now, are we going in or are we just going to stand out here?" She was becoming freer in how she teased him, his love and confidence in her bringing more confidence to her.

———

"Going in, I guess." He opened the door and waited until she entered, his eyes searching the faces that turned their way. All of them were there, including Barnabas. And Dallas, as well. This can't be good, he thought.

"Brady? You wanted to talk to us?"

"We did. Here." Brady was on his feet, heading for the coffee that was on and then heading for Brennen and Jaxcy, their coffee and tea mugs in his hands. "Sit. This is going to take a while."

"That doesn't sound good." Brennen sighed. "How long has it been, fellows? And how soon can we have it over?"

Rising from where she had been sitting, Jaxcy moved around the room, her mind whirling at the information being thrown at them. She turned to face the room, leaning back into a corner, a hand rubbing at her temple. She still suffered from headaches on occasions, and this was one of those, she thought.

Fynn approached her, a mug of tea extended. "How are you, Jaxcy?"

"To tell you the truth, I really don't know. I don't know how I am to be. There is just so much." She nodded towards the men. "How do they do this? They just absorb it and continue, new questions, ideas, and thoughts flying at each other."

"That's how they work. They have been friends for so long, they really do understand to a degree how each one thinks. What one doesn't think of, the other does." Fynn grinned. "Anna maintains that it is a good thing they are not small boys. They would be in constant trouble."

Jaxcy smiled at that. "I can see that. They like to tease and torment each other, as my mother would have said." She paused, a sad look crossing her face. "I talked to Dallas a while ago, when he came back. He didn't have good news for me."

"Oh, no! Your parents?"

Jaxcy nodded. "They still have not found any sign of them. He said he talked to my minister and his wife, but they were not much help. Whatever happened to them, it has been well hidden." She sighed a deeper sigh. "This has been so hard, you know? Marrying as we did. Moving here. It is such a contrast."

"Talk to me, Jaxcy. Here. Let's go sit in the lobby. Some of the other ladies are around. Do you mind if they join us?"

Jaxcy stared at her for a moment, shocked. "You really mean that?"

"I do. Oh, Jaxcy! Did you think we didn't want to know you, knowing that you had little in your life, that you had had to scrimp and scrape to get by? That's not it. We just weren't sure if you were ready to be inundated with our friendship."

"I would like that friendship. It's just been hard. I wasn't around people a lot in the last few years. I just couldn't."

Fynn reached to hug Jaxcy, before she pointed to the door. "Let's head out there." She waved at Brennen as he stood watching them. "Brennen knows you are with me."

"He does? Okay."

An hour later, Brennen stood where he could watch the ladies, without being seen. He frowned as he watched Jaxcy, seeing that she was trying hard to join in but showed to him that she was overwhelmed.

Brady nodded towards the ladies. "Your lady? You need to rescue her from my lady. Fynn sometimes doesn't get the personal touch that she needs to have, particularly if someone doesn't stand up to her. She's trying, but she's used to dealing with creepy-crawlies."

Brennen grinned. "That she is. I know I need to go rescue her, but I don't want to interfere if that is how she would see it."

Brady simply shook his head, walked across the lobby to the ladies, and scooped Fynn into his arms, sitting back where she had been. Fynn let out a squeal, bringing laughter from most of the ladies, but a shocked look from Jaxcy that she quickly covered.

Brennen crouched down beside her chair, an arm around her.

"Having fun, Princess?"

Jaxcy turned to him, seeing his concern for her in his eyes. "I am, but I need to leave, Brennen. How do I do that? I know Dallas needs to talk to us."

He dropped a kiss on her temple. "It's very easy. You stand up, excuse yourself, and walk away hand in hand with me."

She stared at him, shocked, then rose as he tugged at her hand as he stood.

"If you will excuse us, ladies, Brady, Jaxcy and I need to go find Dallas before he thinks we have run away." He waved at their laughter, not seeing their concern as they watched Jaxcy.

"She's really hurting." Ennis commented.

"She is. I notice that she had become quieter as time went on." Hagen sighed. "I think it was too much."

"Not too much, Hagen." Brady spoke up. "It's that she has never really had a close friend, from what Brennen said when he asked for prayer for her. And I am not betraying a confidence when I say that. He has given permission for us to talk to our ladies. And going through what she has now? The uncertainty about her parents? That is hard on her."

"And she has only finished high school. The rest of us have some college education or university education. She likely feels inadequate based on that." Cadee blinked to clear away the tears she refused to shed, thinking of what it must be like for Jaxcy. "She reminds me of the ladies and girls I worked with in the mission."

"Then, how do we reach her, Cadee?" Berneen leaned forward. "We need to do that. It breaks my heart to think of this."

Brady had been listening. "My advice? Just be yourselves. Be her friend. Include her when she is willing. Let her have her space. Cadee, didn't your parents say they wanted to start a garden at the shelter? Then include her with that. That was how she had her food. She grew it."

Chapter 22

Dallas watched Brennen closely as he seated Jaxcy at the table that he had taken over, spreading out his documents and notes. Jaxcy rubbed her hands along her legs, nervous for a moment, her eyes on the paperwork.

"Dallas? Where do we start?" Brennen sat, knowing that the room had quieted for them.

"Let's spend some time in prayer first, if you don't mind. I need it, and I know you two do as well."

Finally looking up, Brennen kept his eyes on Jaxcy.

"What do you have, Dallas?"

"For starters, your minister friend, Jaxcy, is a wealth of information, information that he really didn't know he had. The skilled investigators have pulled it from him. And the police force in your town has been disbanded for now as has the town council. The mayor and the police chief are under arrest. The plan is to set up a new council and a new police force, using some of the same men and women who were on the force."

"That's good. They weren't all bad." Jaxcy leaned against Brennen. "But, where does that leave us?"

"Sitting at a table, trying to make sense of everything?" Dallas grinned at her. "Seriously, it does move the investigation along. There are some things that I can't discuss with you.

"First, your parents. The land belonging to the mayor has been searched. The cadaver dogs made no hits, which was good in a sense. They are moving on to other properties."

Jaxcy nodded, a thought crossing her mind. "Could my parents still be alive? I know it has been a lot of years. Could they?"

"That is a possibility we are strongly looking at. I can't go into those details at the moment. Have you thought of anyone, anything else that you can tell me?"

Jaxcy shook her head. "I have had 11 years or so to do just that. Think. Not to think. To avoid people because of the looks of pity sent my way. To avoid people because of the anger directed at me, the hate, the physical abuse. Why, Dallas? Why did they do this?"

"That is what I needed to talk to you about. The trust fund? It comes from your parents. Even if they had been alive, it still would have come to you. It is money that they received as inheritances that they pooled into a trust fund for you. They tried to keep it a secret, but the banker talked and that's how this all started.

"The law in town? That was set up specifically directed at you. They wanted you to avoid marriage, to stay out of touch with people, to keep to yourself. Every young man in town, who had remained, was warned to stay away from you, or they would be jailed for some reason."

Jaxcy looked at Dallas in horror, Brennen's arm around her to comfort her.

"They did that? All to get my money? I don't want it. What can I do with it?" She swiped at the tears on her cheeks, not willing to acknowledge them, but knowing she had to wipe them away.

"We can discuss that later, Princess." Brennen pointed to the paper that Dallas was holding out for her. "Dallas needs you to take that."

Jaxcy reached a tentative hand to take it, turning it to read it, shock on her face. "There is that much?"

"There is. You are a wealthy young lady. It may not seem like much, but it would be enough to keep you for life, if you use it frugally. If you had still been at your own home, you would not have had to scrimp and save and scrape to get by."

Brennen tilted Jaxcy's hand to read the financial paper, then bent his head to study her.

"Jaxcy? We don't have to decide anything today."

"I know. I just don't get it. We never had a lot when I was small. We had enough to get by with, with some left over." She looked up at him. "They did this for me?"

"They did." Dallas handed over other papers. "These go with that. Now, as to Smithers? He was not the main person, the main one responsible. He had heard of the trust fund, how we are still tracking through the web of deceit that he wove. But he did have contacts there, shall we say of the unsavoury kind? How he found out about this? Likely by someone talking that shouldn't have. The investigators are appalled at how the information has been noised around town."

"And if Mom and Dad were gone, and I didn't marry, or marry too late, it went to Smithers?"

"That's what they have tried to say, what paperwork you were given at some point said. Where did it come from?"

Jaxcy stared at him and then felt anger growing in her. "The banker. How is he related to Smithers?"

"I like how you think. Brennen, she went right to the heart of the matter, something that took us a while to figure out. He is a cousin of Smithers."

"But who killed him?" Jaxcy turned to study Brennen. "Someone did. And why?"

"That we are working on." Dallas sighed. "I know that I keep saying that, Jaxcy, but that is how investigations work. We nibble away at information, trying to connect it, praying that it will be over soon. Sometimes it is. Sometimes it isn't." He groaned as his phone rang and he pulled it out. "Excuse me. I have to take this call. I will be back."

Brennen watched him walk away before he spoke, his eyes connecting with Branigan.

"Jaxcy? Are you okay with all this?"

She shrugged. "I have no idea. It's just so much information." She frowned as she read a portion of one of the papers. "This is not right, Brennen. This lists Dad's family. He was not an only child. He had two siblings, a brother and a sister. His sister? I knew her. She moved out to British Columbia when I was about ten or so. They kept in touch but then when all this happened, I lost contact with her."

———

"We can work on that." Brennen reached for a paper. "Let me have the names."

"Sure. His sister was Jacqueline. My name is Irish, but they wanted something close to hers. His brother? He was Joseph, but I didn't know him well. I don't remember seeing him since before Aunt Jackie moved west. Mom said that Dad and he had words and he refused to apologize for what he said. They would never tell me what it was. He disappeared a couple of years before this happened."

"Okay. Do you know birthdates?" Brennen scribbled down the information and then was on his feet, heading for Branigan, who rose and took the paper from him, a few quiet words between them.

———

Jaxcy wandered the apartment the next morning, Kerry keeping pace with her. Brennen was in his office downstairs, she knew, but she refused to disturb him. She had checked the phone that he had insisted she carry. She was receiving calls from an unknown number. When she checked the voice mail, the viciousness of the messages had her dropping the phone and cowering away from it.

Heading for the door, she hesitated, jumping as a knock came to it. She peeked out, then pulled the door open.

"Branigan? Aren't you supposed to be at work?"

He simply grinned. "Not today. Today, I am working to solve your and Brennen's adventure. Would you come downstairs with me? We have some things we need to ask you about."

"And who would we be?" She slipped Kerry's leash on and then closed and locked the door. "I forgot. I should leave a note for Brennen."

"No problem. Simply send him a text."

"A text? And how would I do that?" Jaxcy was puzzled.

"On your phone." Branigan frowned as she paled. "Jaxcy? Where's your phone?"

"I left it in the apartment. I didn't tell Brennen. I have been getting calls and messages from someone. I don't know who it is. They are horrible."

Branigan reached for her keys. "Where is it?"

"On the kitchen table." She stood, arms wrapped around herself until he returned, locking the door behind him.

"We'll look into that. Dallas will need to know. Did you recognize the voice?"

Jaxcy shook her head. "No, I didn't. But then, I'm not used to talking to people over the phone. Doesn't that change the sound of the voice?"

"It can. Dallas will have the lab techs take a look at it for you. They'll retrieve the messages, analyze what they can, and then hand it off to him."

"It sounds complicated." She paused just inside the conference room door. "Branigan, what would you do, if you were me?"

"Hunt like crazy to find out if my parents were alive. Find my aunt and talk to her. See where my uncle was. Think about the trust fund and what I really wanted to do with it." He seated her, then drew up a chair beside her, his eyes on the door as Brennen entered, heading to sit beside Jaxcy.

"Jaxcy? Are you okay, Princess?" Brennen's voice soothed her fears.

"I am not sure." She pointed to the phone Branigan had laid on the table. "He's taking that. I have had calls and messages that Dallas needs to know about."

"Have you? I thought you might have. It's what they do. Threatened both of us, am I correct?"

She nodded, unwilling to put that into words. "Branigan said he needed to talk to me, but he's just sitting there, not saying anything. So, does he really need to or not?"

Branigan grinned at her, even as Brennen laughed softly. "She's got me there. Now, we have tracked down who we think is your aunt, but we need you to tell us if she is." He handed over some photos.

Jaxcy reached for them, laying them down on the table, a hand covering her mouth. "Aunt Jackie? Oh, you look so much like pictures Dad had of his mother. Where are you?"

"She's living in BC, just like you thought. Barnabas has Brody and Buckley flying out there tonight, to speak with her, not letting her know about you until we can determine why she left."

"He is? Oh, he can't do that!"

"He can and he will. He has before, Jaxcy. And he will again if he has to. The Board is in full agreement with this."

———

They spoke for a while longer, Jaxcy confirming more details for them as they went along. When she was not sure, she adamantly told them that. Brennen nodded. This was the Jaxcy he was falling deeper in love with. He could see her blossoming. His only fear was that she would blossom and then move on.

Late that night, Jaxcy found him as he stood on the balcony, watching the clouds playing hide and seek with the moon and stars. She slipped under the arm he held out for her, her own around him.

"Brennen? What now?"

"Now, we wait for the fellows to come back from the west. We continue to live our lives." He hugged her tighter. "I still want to take you out for a meal. We need to do that on a regular basis. Go on dates."

"Dates? Married couples do that?"

"They do. It's part of keeping fun in our lives. So, will you go out with me tomorrow night for dinner? Your choice."

She shrugged. "I guess it's safe enough. I feel afraid, Brennen, more afraid than I have ever felt. Someone is out there, watching us, just waiting for the right time to take us. I fear that we will not survive if they do."

"We are in God's hands, Jaxcy. Never forget that. He is in control. I trust Him to protect me. If He calls me home, then I am ready to go."

"I know, Brennen, but I am still afraid." She stood for a moment. "Do you think we'll ever find out what happened to my parents?"

Early the next morning, Brennen roused, his head coming up from his pillow as he squinted around the still dark room. He could hear Kerry giving soft growls from where he was positioned on the end of the bed, facing towards the door. Rising, Brennen reached for his jeans and sweatshirt that he had discarded the night before, a quick glance at the bed showing him that Jaxcy was already up. He shook his head. She rose so early, he told that if she got up any earlier, she would meet herself going to bed. She had just shaken a finger at him as she laughed.

He pulled on his socks and then motioned for Kerry to come with him. He paced through the house, Kerry's hackles rising higher and higher as they both did so. Brennen paused at his office, a frown on his face, seeing a low light, and hearing voices. Kerry was away before he could stop him, a bark sounding loudly through the room, even as Jaxcy's scream pierced the air.

Brennen was through the door, heading towards the man who stood over Kerry, who lay at his feet, blood coming from a slash on his side. Jaxcy was restrained from heading for Kerry by a second man, who had his arms tight around her, trapping hers to her side. He didn't see the third man standing just out of sight inside the room. He heard Jaxcy's scream once more before a violent blow sent him to the floor, where he lay still, sprawled facedown. He could vaguely hear Jaxcy's fear-filled voice begging them not to hurt him.

Yanked to his feet and shoved towards the balcony door, Brennen's hand rested on the back of his head, his senses still spinning. He couldn't tell if Jaxcy was with him or not, but he thought he could hear her protests that he couldn't climb down from the balcony. Shoved outside, he stood for a moment, a hand resting on the railing, before a gun poked him relentlessly in the back, and he was forced to climb over the railing to the rope ladder and then down it, one of the men heading down it before him.

Jaxcy scrambled down the ladder, fear on her face as she landed on her feet and then ran to wrap her arms around Brennen, her support helping him to stand. His arm was around her as he squinted at the men around them before they were pointed towards the woods and then through them, towards a delivery van that stood waiting, a fourth man watching closely.

Brennen stumbled inside, dropping to his knees from the hard, sudden push that sent him into the van. Jaxcy landed beside him, falling to her side, a cry of outrage and pain coming from her. The door was slammed shut and Jaxcy heard the lock clicking into place. She was on her knees, reaching for Brennen, moving them to lean again a van side, trying desperately to brace them, unable to do so as the van sped through the forest, the ruts and bumps shaking her hold on Brennen, and banging them against the metal.

"Jaxcy?" Brennen finally found his voice. "Did they hurt you?"

"No! But they did you! Brennen, your head."

Brennen shook off her hands, instead wrapping her tight to him even as he shifted them towards a corner of the van, bracing them better against the movement.

"It's okay. What happened? Where did they come from?"

"I don't know. I was up and in the kitchen, making my tea, when I heard a sound behind me. One of them slapped a hand across my mouth and then pulled me into the office. That's when I heard Kerry growling and then you coming towards me." She tucked herself tighter to him. "They came up that ladder and broke into the office through the door. They were waiting for you. If you hadn't come, they were ready to go find you." She sniffled, trying to control her tears. "Kerry!"

"I know, Princess. I know. Bradon was to head our way this morning. If we don't answer, he'll come in and look for us. He knows I would have sent a text to him if we weren't planning on meeting him. He'll look after Kerry for you."

"I know. I just don't like him laying there, hurt."

"Did they say anything?"

"No, not a word, other than they wanted you." She thought for a moment. "No, nothing more than that. Why? What would they want?"

"That's what we need to figure out." Brennen squinted towards the back of the van, feeling the vehicle slowing down and stopping. "We've stopped. If you get a chance, run. Don't worry about me. I'll follow as best I can."

"We can't, Brennen. I won't leave you."

Brennen shook his head, his hand resting on her cheek. "Please, Princess? For me? I need you to run as fast and as far as you can, finding somewhere to hide if the opportunity presents itself." He dropped a kiss on her lips. "Please, Princess?"

Jaxcy finally nodded. "Only if you do too. I can't go on without you, Brennen."

Prevented from responding as the van door abruptly opened, Brennen raised an arm to block the strong light that blinded him. At the command to come out, he rose, Jaxcy's hand in his, and walked towards the light, a hand running along the side of the van to help him keep his balance. He was hauled from the van, landing on his knees, hearing Jaxcy's protests as pain shot through him, and his head spun from the earlier blow. How long they had been in the van, he had no idea, but he could see the faint pink on the eastern horizon.

Jaxcy twisted her body and broke free from the hold the man had on her, running to Brennen and dropping to her knees, her arms around him as his body bent forward, a hand flat on the ground bracing him to stay upright. His face contorted with pain, even as the other hand rested on the back of his head.

"Leave him alone! You've hurt him enough!" Jaxcy's cries broke through the quiet of the early morning, startling the birds and insects into flight and into quiet. Tears sparkled on her cheeks, tears that she didn't know she was shedding.

Pulled upright and away from Brennen, she watched as he was roughly hauled to his feet and pushed down a path. She continued to struggle to get away, to get to him, afraid that they would be separated. Her desperate prayer for help and safety rose, even as a damp cloth was slapped around her face. Her struggles became weaker and weaker until they ceased as her body went limp. The man holding her shook his head before he slung her over his shoulder, gruff words shared with the man who had stayed with him. They headed off towards the path, to follow the steps that Brennen and his captor had taken. The van drove slowly away, the man heading out for his normal day of deliveries.

Stillness reigned in the early morning air until the critters, birds, and insects cautiously peeked out and then began their normal daily routine. It was as if there had been no disturbance.

A frown on his face, Bradon knocked again at Brennen's door before he glanced at his watch. It was thirty minutes later than he had planned to be there, but a call from Barnabas had delayed him. He pulled out his phone, sending off a text message to Brennen and then waiting, scrolling through his own messages to see if Brennen had sent him one. None.

This is strange, he thought, before his face tightened. This was not Brennen, not to respond to a message or not to send one of his own. Lord, he prayed, I have no idea what is going on, but You do. I fear for them. Protect them. He hadn't seen them around the building, he thought, running for the stairs and then outside, searching for them.

"Bradon? You're on a hunt, I can tell. Who are you looking for?" Breck stood in the building doorway.

"Brennen and Jaxcy. I don't see them anywhere. Nor Kerry. We were to meet over thirty minutes ago. I got delayed but when I knock at their door, there is no answer. And I don't hear Kerry barking."

Breck stared at him for a moment before he had turned, running for the stairs, a dark look on his face.

"And no word from him?"

"Not a one. And that's not him. He's one of the better ones of us to respond promptly to a text message."

"He is." Breck pounded at Brennen's door, causing Burnie to pop his head out of his own door before he approached them. "I'm going in, fellows. I don't like this."

Breck had keys to each of the apartments but never used them unless it was an absolute emergency or he had been asked to enter by one of the fellows. He had a bad feeling, he thought, his heart raised as well in prayer for his friend and his wife.

Searching the apartment, Breck finally approached the office, a cry drawn from him as he rushed towards Kerry. Bradon and Burnie were on his heels, Bradon dropping down beside Kerry.

"He's been slashed, not too deep, thanks to his heavy thick coat. But where are Brennen and Jaxcy?"

Burnie searched back through the apartment, finally approaching the office door to the balcony. He reached for the handle and then stopped.

"This door is open, fellows. He always locks it." He looked back over his shoulder. "I think we need to leave."

"We do." Bradon was on his feet, Kerry in his arms. "I'm heading in to the vet's with Kerry. Call me when you hear something."

"Take off, Bradon. Let us know how he is." Breck's hand rested on Kerry's head and he received a quick lick on his arm from the dog's tongue. "You're okay, Kerry. I just wish that you could talk and tell us what happened."

Two hours later, Barnabas, back from a meeting in town, approached the men, a frown on his face, as they gathered in the parking lot of the building.

"Breck? What is going on?" He searched the faces of the men, seeing the ladies waiting in the lobby.

"It's Brennen and Jaxcy. They are missing. Someone got to them." Breck kicked at a stray rock, an unusual sign of worry and frustration.

"How? The doors are locked at night." Barnabas was puzzled.

"That's not how." Burnie spoke up. "They used the office door from the balcony. The police officer we talked to thinks they had a ladder, like rope."

"They did? And they're gone?" Barnabas looked past the men as Dallas and Will walked towards them. "What about Kerry?"

"He was hurt. Bradon had him in to the vet's and now has him settled down in his crate in their apartment." Buckley shook his head. "Who would have thought?"

———

"I know, Buckley." Dallas spoke from beside him. "Who would have thought?" He searched the faces of the men. "When is the last time any of you saw them or heard from them?"

The men exchanged glances and shrugged.

"I guess it was likely around supper time?" Baird had a question in his voice. "Berneen had been up to see Jaxcy about going out to lunch next week. She said they seemed fine, no problems that she was aware of."

"I had a text from Brennen about seven." Bradon spoke up. "We were to meet around nine this morning. I was running late and headed there about thirty minutes later than planned."

"So, it has been what twelve to fourteen hours?" Dallas jotted notes into his ever-present notepad. "No one heard or saw anything?"

"Not a thing. Brennen's office balcony is hidden to a certain degree from the security cameras." Breck shook his head. "We thought we had it all covered."

"These people are desperate, Breck. They would have found a way." Dallas turned to study the building. "Can we go inside? It's going to take a while for you all to be spoken with. The ladies as well." Dallas watched as Doc headed their way. "Doc?"

"Any word?"

"Not a one. Did you see them this morning?" Dallas spoke up, his eyes on Will as Will studied the other man.

"No, and that's not like Brennen. He was to call early this morning. Anna said he wanted to talk to me about something to do with an illustration for a book he was working on."

Barnabas paced his office later that afternoon, his hands clasped behind his back, praying for his friends. *This is what, the ninth one, Lord? Do we have to go through all of us? How do we keep going on? This is draining all of us. It has gone on for so long. Please, Lord, bring Brennen and Jaxcy back home. And soon. And well.* Then, he sighed. *It's Your will, Lord, not ours.*

He turned as Amy, his secretary, knocked at his door.

"Yes, Amy?"

"Barnabas, I have a call from someone. He says he works for Abe and Emma. His name is Nathaniel?"

"Nathaniel? That's strange. It's usually Abe or Emma that call. Thank you, Amy." Barnabas dropped into his chair, his head bowing for a moment. He knew Abe and Emma had been searching for Jaxcy's parents, hoping to have good news. *Lord, we could use some good news.*

"Nathaniel? How are you? And Elizabeth? That's good. Yes, we do need to get our people together. Soon, I hope. But you had called?"

"I did. Abe asked me to. He's in a meeting right now with the rest of our team and Emma and Jace. We found them, Barnabas."

Barnabas stared at the wall in front of him, not seeing the enlarged photograph of an angry Lake Erie. He wasn't quite sure he had heard Nathaniel correctly.

"Barnabas? Are you there?"

"I am, Nathaniel. I'm sorry. I wasn't quite sure that I had heard you correctly." Barnabas breathed a sigh of relief.

"You did, Barnabas. We had someone in that country track them down. He's been able to move them into hiding. We're heading there shortly." Nathaniel paused, before he continued. "I tried to contact Brennen. I couldn't get any response."

Barnabas shook his head and then spoke. "No, they've disappeared. Sometime overnight, we think. We're not sure. They were taken from the apartment."

"Oh, no! This is not good. Listen, I have to run." Nathaniel could hear his name being called by Abe. "We're off, Barnabas. We'll be in prayer for those two. Abe will be in touch once we're back."

"Keep me updated as you can. We will pray here. I just hope Jaxcy and Brennen are home soon."

Barnabas set the receiver back down, before he buried his face into his hands, shudders running through him at his deep emotions. This was almost too much, Lord. To hear that her parents have been found, in another country. He raised his head, his fist resting against his chin, as he stared once more at the photo, unsure of how to approach the men, or even if he should. He looked up at the tap on his door and beckoned Breck in, asking him to close the door as he entered.

Breck sank into the chair in front of the desk, weary beyond what he had thought possible. They had searched. The police had searched. There were no signs of them. Bradon had taken Kade, his dog, out and Kade had alerted to a trail, that ended at a road. The crime scene techs were working that scene as well as the apartment and below the balcony. Dallas had privately told him that there was not a lot of evidence. It was like the couple had vanished into thin air.

"Breck? Any word?"

"Not a one. There is little evidence from what Dallas has said. We didn't think there would be. Kerry is on his feet, stressed beyond what Bradon has seen in a dog."

"I can imagine. He was there when Jaxcy disappeared. Those two share a bond that I have not seen before."

"They do. All we can do is pray. The fellows and the ladies are in the conference room. Haley and Holly have the twins. They said that was their job right now. Darbie is around somewhere. I'm just not sure what he is up to." Breck studied his lifelong friend. "Something has happened."

"There has been a development. I need to let you in on it, but we need to keep it between us for now. If Jaxcy was here, I would go to her and talk to her. Nathaniel called."

"Nathaniel? As in Abe's Nathaniel?"

"That one. He said the team is heading out. They found Jaxcy's parents."

Breck stilled as he stared at Barnabas. "What did you say?"

"I said, they found her parents. They're heading out to bring them home." Barnabas slumped back in his chair. "To tell you the truth? I thought that they were dead and buried somewhere or dumped into the ocean."

"That's what I thought. Brennen told me that he and Jaxcy had come to the conclusion that her parents were dead and had been for years. Now, what do we do?" Breck leaned forward, reaching for the pad of paper and pen on the corner of the desk.

"The apartment next to Brennen? Have the cleaners go through it. Make sure it's ready for us. Once we know more and when Abe will bring them here, I'll have you stock it with supplies. Talk to Anna and Doc. Prepare them. Nathaniel didn't say where Jaxcy's parents were, what country, so I have no idea what to expect."

"None of us do." Breck sighed as his phone rang. "Dallas? Any word?" He shook his head at the question on Barnabas' face. "Nothing? That's what we had thought. No, I don't know what to think. They wouldn't leave like that. Jaxcy would not leave Kerry hurt unless she was forced away. I agree. We'll spread out later and look. That property? I see. Sure, we'll keep in touch."

Barnabas had been listening closely. "No word?" His question was out almost before Breck had finished his call.

"Not a word. Not a sign. There is just nothing there."

A day later, Barnabas reached for his phone, setting down the towel that he had dried his hands on. It was late evening and he had just managed to prepare his dinner. He sighed as he stared down at his plate, thinking it would be another night that he didn't eat.

"Carey." He struggled for a moment to hear before the sound clarified. "Abe? That's you?"

"It is, Barnabas. This is a quick call. We're on our way to the plane and heading home. We have the packages that Nathaniel talked about. Give us about twenty-four hours and we'll be setting down near you." The call dropped before Barnabas could ask anything more.

His head dropping, he breathed a sigh of relief, before he reached for his plate and headed for his office. He didn't often eat in there, but this was one time he would. Barnabas sat, his head bowing as he prayed, thanking God for the fact that Jaxcy's parents were finally on their way home. He had gotten the sense that it was still dangerous for Abe and his men and would be until they were in the air and then home. He didn't think he could do what they did.

His prayer finished, Barnabas reached for his fork, eating quickly and absentmindedly as he jotted notes. He wiped his mouth on his napkin and then reached for his phone, pausing to pray once more, to plead for Brennen and Jaxcy to come home and soon.

"Breck? Are you at home?"

"I am. Do you need me?"

"I do. We need to meet. I have news." Barnabas heard the silence of the phone before Breck blew out a breath.

"Brennen?"

"No. Jaxcy's parents. Abe got a message to me. We need to make some plans." Barnabas could hear Breck's apartment door slam and then shortly his own apartment door opening and closing.

"In the office, Breck. The coffee's fresh."

"Thanks. Do you need a refill?"

"No, I'm fine for now." Barnabas was on his feet, heading for a filing cabinet, pulling out paperwork. "We'll need to talk to Doc and Anna. The cleaners have been through?"

"Just today. They said everything was good. No issues with anything." Breck sank into a chair, his mug of coffee landing on a coaster on the desk. "Where do we start?"

"We have. With the apartment. As to food? That is a big question. I would start simple, with the basics. Fresh fruit, vegetables, fish, chicken."

"Right. We have no idea where they have been?" Breck sighed as Barnabas shook his head. "Maybe Abe will call again and that will let us know what to do."

"He might. Doc will need to see them. Who do we have that we can bring in on the quiet to assess them psychologically?"

"I would say go out of town. Maybe Doug's Darcie?"

"Good idea. I know she would help. Call them in the morning. Now, we need to talk to the fellows. Set up a conference in the morning. Ladies included." Barnabas watched as Breck sent out a text, setting up the urgent conference, and smiled at how quickly the phone chimed in text messages.

"They never let us down." Breck smiled at Buckley's comment. "Buckley wants to know if we need to up the urgency on the prayer chain.'

"That won't hurt. Just put it out as an added unspoken request for Brennen and Jaxcy." Barnabas rose, then stood, staring down at the paperwork he had pulled. "We have no idea where or why."

"I suspect it was one of his siblings, Barnabas."

"I agree. Emma has been working that for us?"

"She has. Burnie said he had found some interesting information that he needed to share with us concerning them. I will ask him about it tomorrow."

The following morning, Barnabas stared around the chapel, seeing each one of the men and the ladies there. Doc and Anna and Amy were there. He had asked Andy to be present, thinking that if Abe landed in his own town, he would send Andy that way.

"Fellows. Ladies. We have news." Barnabas' voice broke through the chatter and created silence. "No, we have not found Brennen or Jaxcy. Abe has called. He is on his way home from somewhere with Jaxcy's parents."

Stunned silence followed as they all stared at him and then one another.

Early the next evening, Barnabas walked towards the Foundation plane, watching as Doc, Brady, and Breck emerged, an older couple with them. Abe had been in touch early that morning, requesting that Barnabas send his plane to meet them. He felt that they had been followed and he didn't feel comfortable heading to them. Barnabas had agreed, set up a meeting at a remote airport. All the men and the ladies had volunteered to go. He had thanked them, picked the three men, and sent them on their way.

Breck moved quickly towards him, pointing to the vehicles. "We just made it off the runway when vehicles appeared. Someone has been watching us too closely, Barnabas. Let's get them out of sight in the Building."

"Agreed. Have they said much?" Barnabas watched as Brady and Doc headed the couple for the van.

"No, not a lot. Other than a thank you, and how did we know?" Breck shook his head. "They're not in great shape at the moment. He did mention that things had gotten rougher the last couple of months."

"About the time this started with Brennen and Jaxcy. Did you tell them about Jaxcy?"

"No, I thought that it would be best coming from you. They have not asked how or why we found them. Abe didn't give much information, we were that concerned about getting them transferred and then getting back in the air."

"I understand. Head off home, Breck. I'll follow when Andy is ready."

Andy approached him shortly. "Barnabas? Did Breck tell you?"

"He did." Barnabas reached for the thumb drive Andy was holding out. "Captured some pictures, did you?"

"I did. I can't guarantee how clear, but we did our best." He shook his head. "To think they have been alive and Jaxcy thought they were dead."

"I know. It's going to be tough for each of them, isn't it? I just wish we had Jaxcy here."

"I know. It's going to go hard. Any idea on who is behind it?"

Barnabas shook his own head. "Just speculation at the present."

"I would say her aunt."

"Why?" Barnabas parked in his assigned slot and then shifted to stare at Andy.

"I don't know. It would just make awful sense, now wouldn't it? But then again, it could be her uncle. Did her mother have any family?"

"That we can't determine. For some reason, it's too hidden. Emma and Jace are working their magic as is Kataleen with her family tree program. She was finding some interesting items, she tells me."

Andy grinned as he shut the SUV door. "She will do her best. She finds things I couldn't imagine finding. By the way, Abe said Darcie is willing to come to talk with Jaxcy's parents."

"That's good to know. Thanks, Andy. Have a good night."

Andy waved as he walked away, Barnabas standing for a moment in the quiet of the twilight, his face tilted to the sky, his eyes closed as he breathed a prayer of thankfulness but also of intercession, begging for his friend and his wife to come home and soon.

Breck watched him from nearby, waiting until Barnabas turned towards him.

"Did you get them settled?"

"As well as we could. Her father said it is such a contrast. They basically lived in a rundown shack that had no amenities and had holes in the roof and walls. I would like to get my hands on whoever it was."

"You and me both." Barnabas held the lobby door. "I'm heading up to meet them. Do I need to know anything in particular?"

Breck gave a shake of his head. "Not really. They're quiet, as could be expected. They are in shock at being free after all these years. I would say to give them a few days to get accustomed to that, then have Dallas meet with them. Buckley has already been around and introduced himself, planning on meeting with them in the morning. Doc has assessed them quickly, he said, but he would like to do more, run bloodwork, and whatnot, as he puts it." Breck suddenly grinned. "Jaxcy is almost the image of her mother. Both are petite ladies."

"That's good to know. Have a good night, Breck. Thanks again." Barnabas headed for the stairs to climb to the second floor, Breck watching as he walked away.

———

The next morning, Barnabas watched as Jaxcy's parents walked towards him across the lobby, fear and apprehension on their faces. He sighed. This is not how it was to be, he thought. Lord, this time, You need to work through this. It will take years for them to become accustomed to being free once more. What was it, eleven years or so?

"Mr. Carey?" Jaxcy's father, Jeremiah, held out his hand. "Once more, thank you. Jemma and I can't begin to tell you how grateful we are."

"It's Barnabas, please. I just wish we had known before. We would have brought you home sooner if we had known."

Jaxcy's mother simply reached up to hug him. He grinned to himself. Breck was right. Jaxcy was a lot like her petite mother.

"I just wish Jaxcy was here. Let's have a seat here in the lobby." Barnabas looked up as Fynn approached, a tray in her hand. "Here, thank you, Fynn. This is Fynn, Brady's wife."

"Brady's wife? The one he says likes to play with creepy-crawlies?" Jeremiah gave a small grin. "He talked of you last night, in part I think to help ease us into here. Between the three men, we have a good idea of who is who here."

"That's great. We just keep expanding our family. I won't stay." Fynn turned to leave, when Jemma grasped her hand.

"Please? Brady said you had connected with Jaxcy. Please? I need to know about her. We both do. It's been too long. We were told she had overdosed and died, that we had to leave the country because the police had determined we had provided the drugs to her." Jemma shared a look with Jeremiah. "We couldn't defend ourselves. We were never given a chance."

Fynn sat beside Jemma, her hand tight in the older lady's grip. "That is so wrong. And Jaxcy was told you two were dead. Did you know that?"

"Breck told us that last night. Who would be so cruel?" Jemma wiped at her eyes.

Barnabas had been watching Jeremiah and then spoke quietly to the older man. "You have an idea?"

"I do. I would like to talk to you and that Breck, today, if possible. I don't like to accuse anyone but someone is responsible for breaking up our family. Jemma and I have talked it over until there was nothing left to talk over. We could barely scrape by to make a living. It was hard, Barnabas. Almost like being in a prison. And in fact, that is what we were told we were in. I can't thank you or that Abe and his men enough."

"That's what Abe does, goes in and rescues people. We'll talk. The men are working away today, hoping to bring a swift resolution to this." Barnabas spoke quietly with Jeremiah, listening to Fynn draw out Jemma. Brady, you sell your wife short. She is doing just what needs to be done, asking the questions that need to be asked.

Jemma finally looked at him. "Do you know where our daughter is? I want to see her so much."

"I am so sorry. I don't. I wish I did." Barnabas looked at Fynn, who was watching Jemma with a compassionate look on her face. "Jemma, would you feel comfortable meeting some of the other ladies?"

"I guess." Jemma shared a look with Jeremiah before she nodded. "If that is what you wish, I can."

"No, it's not what I wish. It is what you wish and want to do. You are free here. You decide how you live your life." Barnabas watched with compassion her struggle before she nodded.

"It's hard, Barnabas. We have not had freedom in so long."

"We understand. Now, let's go find the ladies. I'm sure you'll enjoy Hagen's twins." Fynn rose, drawing Jemma to her feet, and linking an arm with Jemma.

"Twins? Oh, my!" Jemma walked away with Fynn, Fynn chattering away.

"That's not Fynn, to chatter like that."

"I didn't think it was. Now, Barnabas, tell me what you couldn't or wouldn't in front of Jemma."

Barnabas rose and pointed to a hallway. "Let's go meet with the men. Dallas, the police detective, will be out shortly. And Will Peters, our police chief, is heading our way. He stated that he wants to meet Jaxcy's parents and thank them."

"Thank us? For what? Bringing trouble to Brennen?" Jeremiah was puzzled.

"No, he wanted to thank them for raising a resourceful daughter who brings sunlight to everyone who meets her."

Brady moved across the room to where Breck stood, staring at the map they had placed there.

"Any thoughts?"

"I wonder how close they are to here. I can't see them being too far away." Breck traced a finger along the road that tracked along a portion of the Foundation grounds. "Dallas said they have gone into the house that Smithers was using. No sign of anyone there in a while, he said."

"No, that would be too obvious. But then, obvious is how things usually work out." Benen spoke from behind them. "We have had them close to us or farther away. Blair and I have been monitoring the lake. No signs of any boats out there that don't belong."

"Good thought." Burnie reached for a tack and a string, tying the string to the tack, which he then placed in the centre of the Foundation building. "If we start with a small circle, can we trace who has the land or buildings? Most of them we know and would not be involved in anything against us. At least, not willingly."

"No, they wouldn't." Breck stepped back to let Burnie work, hearing the steps behind him as the other men approached. "So, where does this leave us?"

"We tackle what's in this circle and then keep expanding." Burnie looked over his shoulder as Dallas made a sound. "Dallas?"

"You've thought of something that I'm not sure we have. We have been struggling with trying to determine properties and owners, given the workload that we're under right now." He suddenly grinned at Burnie. "Want to come join us? We have an opening in the detective pool."

Burnie gave him a horrified look. "No, thank you very much. I'll stick to writing the mysteries. I couldn't solve them in real life."

"But, Burnie, that is exactly what we are doing." Brandon grinned at him. "Or did you think this didn't count that way?"

Burnie glared at him for a moment before he grinned. "I know. That's not how I meant to say it."

"We know, Burnie. You're better at writing than at speaking at times." Brendon ducked the pretend blow that Burnie sent his way.

Jeremiah stood beside Barnabas, a frown on his face as he listened to the men joking, not quite sure how life worked anymore.

"It's okay, Jeremiah. They're just letting off their worry and frustration. They are all good friends. They come from every province and territory, are all orphans for some reason or another. They care deeply about one another. I am sure that you are aware we've been solving the mysteries and adventures that the others have been involved in."

"The men mentioned it last night." Jeremiah gazed around the room, seeing the piles of paper, the computers, printers, faxes, and other equipment that he just could not name. "I really didn't understand."

"No? It's strange when we are all involved in different lines of employment and volunteer work. Brennen is a child's book illustrator and he volunteers with a baseball team for small children. They love him."

"Breck, I think it was, mentioned that last night. Jaxcy? What does she do?"

"That's the thing, Jeremiah. Here, have a seat." Barnabas waited until the older man had sat, a mug of coffee set in front of him, before he too sat and then began to talk. "Jaxcy doesn't talk a lot about what she wants to do. The house you had was taken from her. We're working on that. She had to scrimp and scrape just to get by. Coming here was a sharp contrast for her, she has said. She didn't have an opportunity to go away and go to college. She is really not sure what she wants to do. Brennen is content just to let her heal and then make her choices. She will not want for money. As a member of the Foundation family, she is provided with an income."

"She is? Thank you, son." Jeremiah's face worked as he tried to control his emotions. A second broken thank you came from him even as he reached a handkerchief to his face to wipe away his tears. He jumped as he felt a dog stand up at his knee and lick at his face.

"This is Kerry." Barnabas' hand rested on Kerry's head. "He belongs to Jaxcy. He was hurt the night that they disappeared."

"Kerry, is it? She has always liked that name." The older man's hand rested on the dog's neck even as he studied him. "Thank you, then, Kerry, for trying to protect our girl."

The men had found their seats as Barnabas and Jeremiah were speaking, breaking into groups of twos to pray before they straightened their chairs around, their gaze on Barnabas.

The men had tossed ideas around, listened closely as one another spoke, before Dallas rose, heading to renew his mug of coffee, a frown on his face. His mug hit the table with a bang, before he was back at a computer, working through his various passwords to access a secure site. He typed rapidly, watching the monitor as screens flicked over one by one. Will sat beside him, quiet conversation between them before Dallas sat back, pointing to a name.

"That one. That's the one that I think we missed. How did we do that?"

Will nodded. "I agree." He sighed. "Who was working on that portion?"

Dallas shot him a look and then sighed. "Are you thinking they overlooked this on purpose?"

"I do." Will rose. "I know who it is. You don't need to say anything. I'm heading in to talk to Ralph. He'll pull the detective in."

Dallas watched him walk away, seeing Brendon slip into the chair that Will had just vacated. His fingers moved to close the program.

"Dallas?"

"Yeah, Brendon. We have someone who wasn't doing what they were supposed to be doing. Will's heading in to talk to Ralph."

"That doesn't sound good." Brendon studied Jeremiah, seeing the fatigue that was starting to him down. "We need to get Jeremiah out of here. He's weary."

Dallas turned to watch him. "He is. And I need to be on my way. Thanks for the input. You fellows always have insight into a situation that is different from ours."

"That's because we aren't police officers. And coming from our varied backgrounds, it is a given that we see things differently." Brendon rose as Dallas did. "I just wish I knew where they were. We need to get them home."

"That we do. We're working on it, Brendon. Keep on doing what you fellows are. Send me any information that you can. Emma and Jace are doing that. I just don't get where she finds what she does." Dallas shook his head at that even as he turned to walk away.

Two hours later, Brandon rose abruptly and headed for the map, his finger tracing outside the circle that Burnie had drawn before he nodded. His gaze dropped to the paper that he held. A small cry rose from him, causing the others in the room to turn and stare at him.

"Brandon? Care to share with us?" Brody rose, to stand beside him, staring at the area that Brandon still had his finger planted on. "There? Why?"

Brandon shook the papers in the air. "Because of this. Emma sent over some addresses. This is one that we would never have looked at. It's buried in numbered companies." Brandon turned to the room, searching for Jeremiah, and breathing a sigh of relief that he wasn't there. "It's connected to Jaxcy's aunt and uncle."

"The two of them? I thought there was a split in the family." Benen moved towards the map. "There? Of course. So close, but so far. When do we head over there?"

Barnabas had entered as they were speaking. "First, let's get organized. Brandon, talk to us. Then, we pray. Then, we make plans."

Late that night, the black SUV crept slowly down a side road before it pulled into a laneway and stopped, the lights going off. Three men emerged and headed quickly and silently down the laneway, pausing frequently to listen. The agreement had been to head into the building and search it, being back out before daylight fell.

Their steps paused as they heard hesitant, staggering footsteps heading their way, looks exchanged between them before they faded into the overhanging limbs. A slight cry came from one before the three were running towards the man heading their way, a burden in his arms. They moved the man quickly towards the SUV, one of them taking his burden from him, the other two swinging his arms over their shoulders to support him. They shoved him onto a seat, placing his burden near him, and climbed in, the SUV disappearing quickly from sight down the road.

The driver gave a quick glance behind him, a questioning look on his face, before he nodded at the explanation given him. He drove towards the back building entrance of the Foundation building, the large overhead door to the loading dock raising to allow him entry, closing silently behind him.

Doc and Brady stood beside the two stretchers pulled up near the vehicle, watching closely as the doors swung open and the men emerged, pulling Brennen out and leading him to a stretcher, countering his attempts to get back to the vehicle. Doc's hands were there as Jaxcy was pulled from the vehicle, her body limp and unresponsive as she was carried carefully to the other stretcher and laid there, a blanket pulled up over her to try and counter the shivers that shuddered through her body.

Barnabas stood watching, thankful that his friends were back, before he looked up at Breck.

"Breck?"

"We found them walking towards us, Barnabas. I don't know how. It was as if Brennen was determined to walk all the way back here."

"And he would have. Go with them. We'll meet shortly." Barnabas rubbed at his face. "It's late. The five of us will meet, the rest of us in the morning." He walked towards the building infirmary. "I'll speak with her parents in the morning, once we know more. I don't like her looks."

"No, she's struggling to breathe. Brennen is worn out. He looks as if he's been beaten again. She's been beaten too. Who does this?" Breck was worried and frustrated.

——

"We'll find then, Breck. We'll find them. We need to keep these two safe, and just how we do that, I'm not sure anymore."

Standing back from the door, Jeremiah pointed to the kitchen of the apartment that they were using. Barnabas rested a hand on his shoulder for a moment before he headed to the kitchen, a greeting for Jemma sounding from him. Buckley followed, a prayer raising in his heart, knowing that what they had to say would bring happiness but also worry.

Jemma turned from the counter, reaching to return Barnabas' hug. She had never liked to hug in the past, at least hug those who were not her family. She had discovered that she now liked that contact with people, finding it was helping her to heal. The ladies of the building had started that with her, hugging her every time that they met her. They were a blessing, she thought.

Buckley hugged her as well before reaching for the coffee pot and pouring coffee for them all, just grinning at her protest.

"It's okay, Jemma. It's what we do, serve one another. We don't even think about it anymore."

Jeremiah finally spoke, his eyes on Jemma as he did so. "You two boys are here early this morning. As much as we have come to enjoy your company, you must have a reason."

Buckley spoke up. "We do, Jeremiah. First, may I pray with you two?"

Jemma nodded, having become accustomed to Buckley's way of dealing with life and stress. "Prayer would be good. I have been awake all night, burdened for our girl and her man."

Barnabas sipped at his mug of coffee when Buckley finished, trying to organize his thoughts, something unusual for him.

"Barnabas? You have word?" Jeremiah's words were hesitant once more, fear evident in them.

"We do, Jeremiah. Jemma. Last night, Breck took Benen, Burnie, and Branigan. They headed out just about dark, to a place that Brandon had discovered. The rest of us waited in the chapel, bathing their trek in prayer. I won't go into the details of how or where. That has been given to Dallas, and he is dealing with it. Breck, Benen, and Branigan headed down an overgrown laneway. Partway down it, they heard a noise and drew off to the side. They recognized the man heading their way, met him, and brought him home."

"Brennen!" Jemma's quiet voice held confidence that she was right. "He's home. Jaxcy?"

Barnabas shared a look with Buckley, seeing the worry in his friend's eyes. "We have her. She's home, Jemma. Jeremiah." He struggled to control his own emotions as the older couple simply held each other and wept, the emotions overcoming them.

When he could finally speak, Jeremiah had to clear his throat frequently. "Take us to her. I assume that she is in a hospital."

"No, she's here. We have an infirmary set up on the first floor. Doc is with her. So is Anna. Cadee is training as a nurse and is there." Barnabas' hand on his arm kept Jeremiah in his chair. "She is sick, Jeremiah. Pneumonia, Doc tells me. She has also been beaten as has Brennen. That worries Doc. We don't know if there are any residual effects from that."

"Please, Barnabas? Take us to her?" Jemma was on her feet, her hands reaching for the mugs, to rinse them out, rinsing out the coffee pot, and emptying the grounds into the garbage before any of the men could stop her.

Barnabas hesitated at the infirmary door, his eyes on the couple. "Doc is here. He'll let you stay for a while, but only for a while. He's trying to find a treatment for her. He'll need to get a medical history from you. When she had her broken jaw, Brennen refused some treatment for her, just because he didn't know her history."

"I see." Jeremiah's arm tightened around Jemma. "Unless she has developed something since we last saw her, then the answer would be that she has no history."

Jeremiah and Jemma entered the room hesitantly, their eyes on Doc before they moved forward, to stand at their daughter's bedside. Jemma's hand shook as she reached to touch her daughter's face and hair in ever so many years.

Doc and Cadee stood back, watching, Doc's eyes concerned that this might be too much for them. He had assessed the couple completely the day before, concerned that Jeremiah had developed what he was sure was heart disease. This was not good, he thought, the stress that having Jaxcy back but sick would bring.

Jeremiah kept an arm around his wife, his heart breaking for her and for their daughter, and the young man who was now part of their family, one that they still needed to meet. His hand rested on his daughter's, feeling the fever wracking her body. His eyes lifted to the monitors and then to the IV line running to her other hand. He traced her face, seeing it in the young girl he had lifted to his shoulders so many times as she had asked him to, seeing the young teen he had helped with her homework.

As he stood there, Jeremiah grew angry as he saw the young lady that he needed to learn to know once more, anger burning in his heart at the years taken from him, before he repented and asked for forgiveness. Forgiveness for his anger but forgiveness for whoever it was. He had a suspicion as to who it was. It had become clearer overnight as he too had spent the night in intercessory prayer for his daughter and all those involved. He had stood on the balcony overlooking the parking lot, watching the men run for the vehicle and then drive away. He had still been standing there, the lights off in the apartment behind him, as it had returned and then driven out of sight around the building. He had prayed then, that his daughter had come home, as well as her groom.

It had shaken both of them, he knew, to find out that Jaxcy had lived as she had, had married in such a manner, but they knew her character of the past. They knew that she would have stepped in as she had, without a thought for her own safety. So much had been taken from them, so many years that they would never get back. His eyes were raised as he heard footsteps, footsteps that sounded unsteady, before a young man stopped on the other side of the bed, his hand reaching to cup Jaxcy's face before he bent to kiss her, his cheek resting against hers.

Jemma stood for a moment before she was around the bed, a mother's arms encircling a hurting young man, a young man who could not even remember his own mother's arms. Her soft prayer reached to him, and he began to weep, sobs rising within as her arms tightened, and then Jeremiah was there, beside them. His arms encircled his wife and son-in-law even as his prayer was raised. Doc and Cadee stepped from the room, Cadee opening weeping as Benen found her. Doc wiped at his eyes, before he raised them, shaking his head.

"It's just so much, boys." He looked around at the group gathered, each man in the building present, as were the ladies, the twins, and Darbie. Amy was there as well. He saw Bruce and Elizabeth Carey headed their way and nodded. Barnabas needed his parents, given the high emotions that all of them were dealing with.

Jeremiah finally stood back, his arm around his wife, as he studied the tall young man who stood in front of them. A hurting young man, he decided, and hurting in more ways than just physical. How he reached him in the hurt, he had no idea, but God did. He prayed for him, and then for Jemma and himself, and then for his daughter.

"You must be Brennen." Jemma reached to hug him again, feeling him clinging just a moment longer than she had expected.

"I am." Brennen was confused for a moment before his brow cleared. "Jaxcy's parents? But how?"

"We are. I'm Jemma and that's Jeremiah. A young man named Abe swept in and rescued us from where we had been taken all those years ago. We had no way of getting away or coming home. We were on an island miles from here."

"Abe did? That's wonderful. Emma must have found out where you were." Brennen's body sagged for a moment and he was grateful to sink down in the chair that Jeremiah pushed forward. "I'm sorry."

"Sorry for what?" Jeremiah rested his hand on Brennen's shoulder.

"I'm sorry that you lost all those years with Jaxcy. I'm sorry that you were treated like you were. I'm sorry that Jaxcy can't meet you again. I'm sorry that she's sick and been hurt. I'm sorry that I couldn't protect her any better than I did." He looked up at them, a lost little boy look on his face that endeared him deeply to Jemma. They had learned his story from Barnabas the day before. "But I am not sorry that Jaxcy is my love. I love her deeply, more than I ever thought I could love someone. She is a wonderful, compassionate lady. Jaxcy has had it rough but she has not let it destroy her."

"Thank you, Brennen." Jemma's voice died away as she dropped a kiss on the top of his head. "Welcome to the family. But I understand that all your friends are working hard to solve your adventure as they call it. The ladies have taken me to their hearts, and I love that. I have craved for female companionship that I would just relax and enjoy."

Brennen's gaze went back to his bride, his heart hurting that she was suffering to breathe. He wanted a piece of each of the men who had held them captive, making her slave for them, holding him away from her and against a wall as he watched her struggle to cope the last couple of days, the fever slowing her steps and fogging her mind. He knew that she had wanted to quit, but kept on going, just because of the threats levelled towards him. He had tried to intervene, told them that he would do the cooking and cleaning that they insisted she do, but blows to his face and body had stopped him.

He rose, a hand on her face, a kiss on her lips, as Doc approached, a hand out to help him from the room. Jemma and Jeremiah followed, a long last look at their daughter, before confusion in the hallway took their attention. They watched, horrified, as Brennen's legs gave way and he collapsed, only the hands of his friends keeping him from landing hard on the hardwood floor.

Doc pointed to the second infirmary room.

"In there. I thought that this would happen." He looked around, spying Dallas. "Find them, Dallas. Find the monsters who hurt these two. This building family? It's had enough. Stop this insanity." He was behind the closed door, Anna and Cadee with him, Brady on his heels.

Late the next afternoon, Brennen stood once more beside Jaxcy's bed, his eyes worried, as he listened to Doc. Jaxcy was not responding how he wanted her to. It might mean that she needed to be in the hospital and that Brennen was reluctant to do. But, he thought, if she had to be, he would do that.

"What can we do for her here, Doc? That we haven't already done?"

"Not much else, but if she needs more aggressive treatment, then that's where we'll need to move her. I would rather do it sooner than later."

Brennen nodded, knowing that Doc was being brutally honest with him. "I know, Doc. I know. It's just such a risk, taking her there. She can be reached there."

"And she can here. Not as easily." Doc sighed. "I'll wait until later tonight and see where she stands."

"Thank you, Doc." Brennen didn't move as Doc walked away. He couldn't. He prayed harder, he thought, than he had prayed in his life. Please, Lord, don't let my lady die. Please? I need her. Her parents need her. The ones in the building need her. Someone is out there that she needs to reach.

Late that night, Brennen looked up from where he sat, his head bowed, the bruising on his face looking garish in the soft light. He was on his feet, his hand reaching for Jaxcy as she moved, a moan coming from her even as she coughed. Her hand reached for the oxygen mask that covered her face. Brennen's other hand stopped hers from moving it.

Jaxcy's eyes flickered open and closed even as she licked at her lips. She frowned at him.

"Brennen? What time is it?"

"Almost midnight."

"What day?"

"It's Saturday. Why?"

"Then, we have to move. They're going to take us away from here. That's what they said. The leader didn't care if I heard them. They're taking us out of the country." She was becoming agitated.

"We're safe, Princess. We're safe. We're home."

"Home? We can't be. They won't let us go."

"No, they didn't. I managed to get us away. Breck and some of the fellows met us and brought us home."

She nodded, her eyes fever bright. "Take me home, Brennen. I can't do this anymore. Take me home, please." She slept, her sleep natural for the first time in days.

Brennen stood, his eyes on her, a thought crossing his mind that he shrugged off. Did he really just walk out of there, or had they let him go for a reason? What did Jaxcy mean when she said they were to be taken out of the country?

He watched her closely, her words asking him to take her home resounding in his mind. If that was what she wanted, then he would. He would take her back to the Rock, fix up her cabin, and live there with her. He would bring in electricity, figure out the internet somehow. He could work from anywhere. He would miss his friends and the community that the building people were, but Jaxcy came first.

Jemma had entered quietly as Jaxcy was speaking. She had hesitated about moving forward, not wanting to disturb the younger couple. Her hand on Brennen's back startled him.

"She was awake?"

"She was, Jemma. She was. She's confused." Brennen's brow wrinkled for a moment.

"She never does illness well. And for her to be this sick, makes it worse." Jemma's arm was around him. "Don't rush into any decisions. She asks things in her sickness that she would never ask otherwise. She never means them."

"I think she does this time. She wants to go home."

"And this is your home. She will make it hers. You two have not had what you would even consider a regular marriage, now have you?"

Brennen shook his head, a smile crossing his face. "None of us have. You have heard the adventures that my friends have had. How do we continue?"

"By trusting God. Trusting your friends. Trusting that police detective who comes around every once in a while." Jemma paused. "He is a troubled young man, seeking for something that he hasn't found yet. He will not stay in that department much longer."

"You don't think so? Strange. That's how I feel."

Jemma nodded towards her daughter. "Don't make a decision based on her illness. If you want to keep her home down there, fix it up. Use it as a retreat. Or let someone else use it, who really needs it."

Brennen stared down at the lady that he was beginning to think of as his mother. He dropped a kiss on her cheek. "Thank you. You are a wise lady."

"I have had a lot of years just to think and pray. A forced retreat, if you will." She studied him for a moment. "Jaxcy loves you. I heard her responding to you. She doesn't do that with people who are not important to her."

Brennen nodded, his eyes on his princess. "I always dreamed of a princess, of being a prince or a knight riding in on a white horse to save her. She is my princess, Jemma."

"She is, Brennen. And you rode in to save her. Not on a white horse, but nonetheless, you saved her from a fate that her father and I can only imagine awaited her." Jemma reached to kiss her daughter, reached to hug Brennen, and walked away, leaving Brennen with his thoughts, some of which were black.

A day or so later, wrapped in a heavy blanket, her feet tucked up on the couch, Jaxcy rested tightly against Brennen, unwilling to move too far from him. Kerry was draped across her lap, he too unwilling to leave either one of them. He had licked and washed at Jaxcy's face when he saw her, not ready to leave her alone. Her arms had tightened around him, unable to let him go.

She nodded as she listened to the quiet conversation around her. Barnabas and his father, Bruce, were there. Her mother and father moved quietly around, handing out the mugs of coffee and tea that had been requested. Breck had come in, checked on her, and then quietly sat where he could watch them both.

Buckley had been around earlier, as had Fynn. Praying for them both, Buckley had asked no questions, not needing to. Fynn had been there, helped Jaxcy to shower and then change into clean clothes. Her kindness and willingness to serve had brought tears to Jaxcy's eyes and earned her a long hard hug. She had not stayed, waving at Jeremiah and Jemma as she left.

Jaxcy was not quite sure how to handle having her parents back in her life. To find out that they were still alive had been traumatic, but to actually have them in her home? That would take some getting used to. She thought of all the tears, sorrow, rage, fear, and whatever other emotion she had been through in the past years. Lord, You need to help me. I can't do this. Not anymore. I just want to go home, but this is my home. I know Brennen would move back east, but that's not his home. I just am so confused.

Brennen's arm tightened around his princess. He knew she was at her limit but she had refused to leave him. He could understand that. Looking up as Bruce started to pray, his eyes slid closed and he felt the presence of God in the room. He always did when Bruce prayed.

No one wanted to break the silence when the prayer time had ended. Jeremiah finally spoke, his eyes on Jemma as he did so.

"Have you talked to that police detective, Brennen?"

"We have. I can share some of our story, but some of it has to be kept silent."

"That we can understand. Just tell us what you can." Barnabas sat forward, his eyes on his friend. "How did they manage to surprise you, with Kerry here?"

"That's what we're not sure of. We talked about it. Kerry was still on the bed when I woke to his growling. Jaxcy hadn't been up for long, just long enough to make her tea. She said that as she finished, she sensed someone in the room with her. A hand was over her mouth and her arms were trapped to her sides before she was carried to the office.

"I think it was at that point I woke to Kerry's growling. I don't understand why he didn't leave me. I got up dressed and starting searching for Jaxcy, hearing men's voices that I didn't recognize. I found her in the office, saw her being restrained, and then I was down. I didn't see the third man standing beside the door, waiting for me. Jaxcy managed to get to me, but I couldn't help her escape. We were forced out on the balcony and then down a rope ladder."

"We wondered at that." Barnabas spoke up. "Dallas said there wasn't much evidence."

"No, I don't think there would have been. They had us down the ladder, the ladder retrieved Jaxcy said, and then we were forced to walk to the side road near us. They had a delivery van of some kind. We were forced into it. They drove around for a while, always on rough roads, but it felt like they had been driving in circles.

"When they stopped, we were forced out. I was led away before Jaxcy was. I am not sure what happened next. Jaxcy was chloroformed, that we figured out."

"Chloroform? That's an old trick." Bruce looked up from his notes. "Did you get a good look at the van or any of the men?"

"Not really. I know the van was high enough that I could stand almost upright. That's not much help."

"A delivery van, then." Bruce nodded. "We'll see what we can do. Now, what else?" His gaze shifted to Jaxcy, a small smile creeping to his face as he noticed her nodding off. "Jaxcy, what can you tell us?"

Jaxcy blinked, bringing her attention to Bruce. "I'm not sure. I was too worried about Brennen to see much. I know there were four, but only three went with us. The three that were in the apartment. One of them headed away with Brennen first. I don't remember what happened after that until I awoke." She shivered for a moment, her fever starting to spike again. She blinked again, her eyes sore.

"Just tell us the basics, then. We can always get more information later." Bruce smiled at her.

Jaxcy had awoken during the late morning, disoriented for a moment, shivering at the chill in the room. She had reached for the blanket crumpled beside her, wrapping herself in it, before looking around through blurry eyes. Frowning, she stared at the body lying near her before she scrambled to her knees, to crawl towards it.

She pulled at the man, turning him towards her, shocked to find Brennen there. She shook him, calling his name, unable to rouse him. Sitting, a hand on his chest, she stared around, trying to make sense of what was going on. Unable to, she had reached for the blanket on the floor beside him, spreading it out to cover him, laying down beside him, her own blanket covering her. She pulled his arm around her, a hand on his wrist to keep it there, her other arm across his chest. Head on his shoulder, Jaxcy slept, unable to stay awake.

Neither one heard the door open or the heavy footsteps that approached them. The man stood, staring down at them, hatred on his face. It was their fault, he decided. Their fault that he didn't get the money coming to him that should have come. They would pay. He turned and walked away, the door clicking shut behind him and the lock snapping closed.

Brennen had awakened in the early morning, a toe shoving at his ribs doing that. He had sat up, rubbing at his head, his eyes on the man. He rose when he was told to, finding Jaxcy on her feet, her wrist tight in the grasp of another man. Jaxcy had shaken her head at him, her eyes trying to communicate with him, but his head was pounding too much to understand what she was attempting to tell him.

Jaxcy had been pulled to the kitchen, finding it in shambles, uncertain as to what was expected of her. She heard Brennen's stumbling footsteps and tried to look around the man holding her. The leader of the three stood in front of her, a black look on his face.

"You will clean this kitchen. You will cook for us. Then, you will clean the house." His words were abrupt, guttural, almost, she thought, as if he was trying to disguise his voice.

"No. I won't. I'm not your servant." A sudden blow across her face had her on the floor, tears blinding her. She could vaguely hear Brennen's shout of outrage and the struggle he put up to get to her. Hauled to her feet, shaken by the hands that held her, Jaxcy was again ordered to clean and cook. She started to refuse until her eyes found Brennen and drew in her breath.

Brennen was held to the wall in front of her, his arms twisted near his side, pain evident on his face. He could barely stand, she thought, seeing the red marks the blows to his face had left. Her own hand touched her face, finding the cut on her lip and the blood trickling from it. She shook, more from fear than anything. Lord, what have we gotten into? Protect Brennen. Set him free. She finally nodded, not looking at the man.

Working quickly, Jaxcy had cleared enough of the debris and dirty dishes to be able to prepare the men's breakfast, wanting to slap it on the table, but knowing that if she did, Brennen might pay. The men sat to eat, ordering Brennen to stay where he was and Jaxcy to move to the other side of the room. They were warned to stay exactly where they were or the other one would be hurt.

Jaxcy grew fatigued, the effects of the chloroform still evident in her body, as she finished scrubbing the kitchen and then moved to clean the rest of the house. She sighed. How could men live like this? Her mother would have had a few choice words about the state of the house. Jaxcy was blinded by tears as she worked, just missing her mother and wanting to see her. Anger at herself drove her forward until the house was clean, but not sparkling. That, Jaxcy decided, would never happen. It needed paint and new flooring for that, and she doubted that the men would be bothered doing that.

Brennen turned as the door opened to the room they had been shoved into. He waited, his eyes on Jaxcy as she stumbled through the door, the leader of the men standing staring at him, a warning on his lips to not try anything. No sooner had the door closed and the lock clicked then Brennen was across the room, catching Jaxcy as she collapsed, her head hitting his shoulders. He looked around, finding no chair, only the rough mattress shoved into a corner. He hurried that way, sitting down and just cradling her to him, a blanket wrapped around her.

Jaxcy was too tired, she thought, too tired to do anything. Too tired to talk to Brennen. Too tired to sleep. She just stayed in his arms, feeling the strength and caring and love in them.

"Jaxcy? Are you okay?" Brennen kept his voice low.

"I think so. Just overly tired." She tilted her head back. "And you? Did they hurt you this morning?"

"Not really. They did you." His finger gently touched her face and lip. "I wanted to hurt them, Jaxcy, for hurting you."

"I know, love. I know. We have to stay strong. We have to find a way out, only I'm not so sure that we can." She grew quiet, finally sleeping.

Brennen didn't stir that night, his head going down on hers as he too slept. He had tried to stay awake, tried to plan what to do, but the effects of the blow to his head and the beating he had taken that morning were too much. His body needed to recover, and sleep was part of how it would.

The same pattern happened day after day. Jaxcy still refused the initial request to clean and cook, until she saw the abuse that Brennen took. They both realized that it was happening to force her to work for the men. She stared at them in distaste, wishing she could somehow escape but knowing that was not a possibility. She grew desperate as the days went by.

Brennen searched the room they were in, trying to find a way out, but unable to. It was an older home, with older wooden windows. He had inspected them closely, only to find the window frames had swollen over time with the weather and neglect. He could not open them. He could only hope to break the glass, and that was not a possibility when at least two of the men were always present.

Jaxcy grew tired. She was beginning to have trouble breathing, her chest hurting with each breath. She couldn't think, not with the pain she was in, and her high fever. Brennen had tried to lower it with cold cloths at night, but it didn't work for long. He had begged for medication to give her, but the men had just looked at him, sneered, and locked the door in front of him.

That last day, Jaxcy stumbled through her chores, not even aware of what she was doing, long moments spent trying to catch her breath and think of what she had to do next. She knew the men were beginning to be freer in their conversation around her, and she wondered at that.

Catching their names, she listened closely even as she worked on the meal. She drew in her breath as best she could. They were planning on taking them away on the Sunday. That was only a couple of days away, she knew. Out of the country, they said. Where? She drew in her breath again, pretending to be busy. She knew of that island. People went there and never returned. She had heard talk of it.

Shoved back into the room, she fell into Brennen's waiting arms, not seeing how he was feeling, that he was trying hard to stay strong for her and failing. He swept her close, dropping to the floor, to just hold her, feeling the heat from her fever through his shirt. Desperate to escape, Brennen finally laid her down and rose, pacing the room once more, the light growing dim as dusk approached. He headed for the door, his hand twisting the knob, not expecting it to turn under his hand and the door open. He paused, listening.

Turning at last, Brennen gathered Jaxcy close to his heart and crept out, down the hallway, to the door that led to the outside, listening for footsteps coming after him. He frowned. He didn't hear the men and he usually could, their voices were that loud.

Creeping slowly across the yard, Brennen headed for a path, or laneway, he wasn't quite sure what to call it. He listened carefully, not hearing anything, his eyes on his beloved princess. He moved forward, step after step, each step a momentous task. He finally was stopped by men, and he grew afraid, ready to turn and run.

"Brennen? Are you okay? Talk to me." Breck's voice was kept low.

"Breck? You're here? Did they kidnap you too?" Brennen was confused.

Breck gave a low laugh. "No, we're not captive. And it doesn't look as if you are anymore. Here, let me have Jaxcy." Breck waited for a moment for Brennen to respond before he simply gathered Jaxcy into his arms, the other two men stepping up to help Brennen.

They moved quickly back the way that they had just emerged along the trail, heading for the SUV. Breck tucked Jaxcy inside and turned, a frown on his face.

Brennen was protesting, trying to turn back the way that they had just come, insistent that Jaxcy was back there, that he had lost her. He pleaded with them to let him go. Breck shook his head and watched as Brennen was shoved onto a seat beside Jaxcy.

The men watched as Brennen realized Jaxcy was there and gathered her to him, tears on his face as he murmured quietly before he too was lost to them. Their emotions hard to control, they had seated themselves and watched the area as Burnie drove away, heading for the paved road and home.

———

"I didn't expect you back so soon." Burnie glanced at the seat behind him.

"We met them heading our way. I have no idea how or where they came from."

"The old Smothers' place. It's that way. It's the one Brandon had pinpointed."

"I know. I wonder if Dallas has checked it out." Breck shifted so he could watch the two in the low light inside the vehicle. "They have had it rough, by the looks of it. Jaxcy is sick."

"She's got a high fever." Benen's voice held the concern he didn't want to admit to.

"I know. I could feel it. Pray that Doc and Brady can treat her. I don't want to think of what could happen if we have to take her to the hospital."

Burnie was soon pulling into the loading dock at the building, the SUV in park and the motor shut off. He was out of the vehicle, as were the other men, watching as Doc and Brady approached with the stretchers. They all helped to move the couple to them and then followed as they were moved quickly to the infirmary.

Breck stood beside Barnabas, shaking his head at a question.

"Breck?"

"We found them walking towards us, Barnabas. I don't know how. It was as if Brennen was determined to walk all the way back here."

"And he would have. Go with them. We'll meet shortly." Barnabas rubbed at his face. "It's late. The five of us will meet, the rest of us in the morning." He walked towards the building infirmary. "I'll speak with her parents in the morning, once we know more. I don't like her looks."

"No, she's struggling to breathe. Brennen is worn out. He looks as if he's been beaten again. She's been beaten too. Who does this?" Breck was worried and frustrated.

"We'll find then, Breck. We'll find them. We need to keep these two safe, and just how we do that, I'm not sure anymore."

Brennen finally stopped speaking, his eyes on Jaxcy, wishing it had been different. She had not needed to be taken captive, to be forced to perform what amounted to slave labour. He had not shared with the group what Jaxcy had told him in the infirmary. Her parents didn't need to hear that. He had spoken to Dallas about it, who had frowned at him and then nodded.

"Brennen?" He looked up at Bruce. "What else?"

The younger man shrugged. "Not a whole lot. I was basically locked up in the room, except when Jaxcy was in the kitchen. They wanted me there at that point for some reason."

"Intimidation towards her. If they threatened you, she would do what they wanted." Barnabas shared a look with Breck. They knew Brennen. They knew that he was holding something back. "Look, you need to get your wife to bed. She's still sick. And you need your rest." Barnabas stood, the others rising as well. "Don't get up, Brennen. I'll be back in the morning. Call me or Breck, if you need to."

Brennen nodded, weary to his bones, he thought. He just sat, his eyes on Jaxcy before he moved, rising with difficulty, to carry her through to her bed, covering her tightly with the blankets, watching as Kerry jumped up and cuddled close to her.

"It's okay, Kerry. I feel the same way. I don't want her out of my sight." He paused for a moment before he headed for the office, pulling up his email, and scanning it. He sent a quick email off to the publisher, begging his forgiveness for not responding, but giving a shortened version of what had happened. He smiled at the quick email back. The Christian publisher that he worked for knew the men of the Foundation building, had been a frequent guest of Barnabas and the board.

Brennen finally pulled his phone towards him. He could not sleep without talking to either Barnabas or Breck. Breck won on the call.

"Brennen? I thought you would be calling." Breck shifted back in his easy chair, a hand automatically reaching for the pad of paper and pen he kept on the table beside it.

"Thanks, once more, Breck, for what you fellows did. I know. You don't want thanks, but you have it anyway." Brennen paused, not quite sure how to continue.

"What didn't you say, Brennen? What was it that you felt you could not be open with in front of her parents?"

"What? You're reading my mind?" Brennen grinned for a moment at Breck's laughter before he sobered. "There is something. You told me that her parents had been sent overseas. Did they know they were being sent?"

"That's an interesting question. Burnie asked them that. They said no. They had been given something, didn't know they had left Canada until they woke up on the island. There was no way off for them. Very few inhabitants, mostly prisoners, from what we can determine. Abe has not said how difficult it was to get in and out, but I am sure it was. Jeremiah mentioned armed guards."

"Ouch. No, Abe won't say. Nathaniel said they never do. It's not important in their mind. It's the people that are important."

"That is so true. It's been the same with all of you fellows, when Barnabas had had the opportunity to do just that with you twelve. You are there for each other as well." Breck paused to sip at his cold cup of coffee, grimacing at the taste. "But there is more. I know you."

"There is. I didn't want to frighten Jeremiah or Jemma, now that Jaxcy and they are together. Jaxcy mentioned something the other night. She didn't say anything when we were still captive. And I can't figure out why the door was left open, in order for us to escape."

"It had to be done on purpose, Brennen. There is no other explanation. Which one of the men didn't fit in?"

"I would say the driver. He would be around once in a while." Brennen groaned. "And he was there that day. The men had to leave to meet with someone. He always appeared when they needed a ride. He could have had the opportunity to unlock the door on the way out. We were not that far from the outside door."

"Okay, so, someone there is playing both sides. How do we find him?"

"I don't think we will. I would imagine that he is either dead or has disappeared on his own. They were too vicious for it to be anything else." Brennen grew silent, a prayer raised for that man. "But, that's not what I needed to say. When Jaxcy awakened in the infirmary, she thought we were still captive. She asked what the day was. She had overheard plans to send us overseas on Sunday. They were planning on sending us out of the country."

"I see." Breck paused, his thoughts running ahead of his ability to form words. "Do you think they were planning on the same island, now that you know?"

"I doubt it. They would not want Jaxcy to know her parents were alive. I would suspect an island close to there." Brennen caught himself yawning. "I need to go, Breck, but I needed you or Barnabas to know this tonight."

"I'll make sure I tell him. Have a good night's sleep, Brennen. You two are in our prayers." Breck had risen, hearing the apartment door open, and seeing Barnabas in his kitchen. He set his phone down on the kitchen table, taking the mug of coffee offered to him with thanks.

"Brennen?" Barnabas nodded towards the phone.

"It was. He called with some additional information. Jaxcy overheard a plot to send them overseas last Sunday."

"Overseas? Not to the same island, I doubt. They wouldn't know yet, I don't think, that Jaxcy's parents are here."

"I think they do. Eric has mentioned seeing evidence that the building has been watched. It's happening all over again. I thought we told Brendon it stopped with him?"

"We did, but it doesn't seem to work. We need to make some plans, and then meet with the men in the morning."

———

"They're all pulling back from their work until we can get this solved. Brennen has gone above and beyond for each of them. They want to repay in some small way that favour."

"He has. It's his character. Now, where do we stand, and what do we do? Dad's hanging around for a couple of days. He'll want to be in on the planning." Barnabas reached for a pad of paper and pen, laughing at Breck's apology for having one waiting for him.

The next afternoon, Jaxcy stood where Brennen could not see her as he worked away at the kitchen table, his ever-present mug of coffee beside him. She had just awakened and rising, had wandered through the apartment looking for him. She watched as Kerry stood up at him, sniffing at his face, receiving a hug and a good rubbing on his head from Brennen.

Brennen raised his head, to stare across the room. Blair had been around, dropping off material for him to look through. He was impressed at the amount of work that had accumulated the pile of papers in front of him. But, then again, it was how they worked. Brennen had nodded at Blair's request to call when he spotted anything unusual. The thing was, he thought, that he wouldn't know what was unusual or different.

A hand held out behind him, he spoke softly to Jaxcy.

"Hi, Princess. Have a good sleep?"

"I guess. You should have awakened me." She clasped his hand, feeling him pull her towards him and down on his knee.

"You needed to sleep. Feeling any better?"

"I guess." She sighed. "That seems to be the extent of my vocabulary." She poked at the papers. "What is this?"

"Research from the fellows. I am not sure where they were headed with what they have here."

Jaxcy leafed through it. "They have really dug deep. This is Aunt Jackie. This is Uncle Joseph." She sorted through the material, setting it into different piles. "But what is this?"

"That? I wondered at that. The names? Do you recognize them?"

"No, I don't. I have not seen names like that in any of our family histories. Mom and Dad might recognize them."

"Someone will ask them, I am sure." Brennen's head tilted to watch her. "How do we solve this, Jaxcy? And how do we keep you safe?"

"You too." Her voice was barely a whisper. "We need to keep you safe too, Brennen. I can't lose you."

His arms tightened around her. "Nor I, you. So, what do we do?"

"I can't stay inside all the time, Brennen. It will kill me. I need to be outside, working in the earth. Do you understand?"

"I do. It's part of who you are. All we can do is be as cautious as we can, and pray lots."

"Yeah, well, that. It doesn't seem to be working too well."

"We are alive, Princess. God has kept us alive. Sure, we have been through stuff, been hurt. You're sick. But God has been there."

"I know." She sighed. "It's just so hard." Her voice died away as she stared at the papers. "Brennen, what if Dad and Mom didn't set up the trust fund? That has puzzled me all along. They never had extra money. Their parents were not rich. There were no rich relatives, not that I am aware of."

Brennen's hand froze for a moment before he reached for his pen and then he flipped over one of the pieces of paper. "Okay. We've assumed all along that it was them. If you're right, and I suspect that you are, who would have done this?"

"That's what I have been trying to think about. Someone known to Aunt Jackie? Uncle Joseph? He disappeared so many years ago. What if it wasn't someone from the town, but someone who wanted to set Mom and Dad up for something, and to do that they had to be removed. That way, they could go after me. Get rid of me and then let Mom and Dad come home?" Jaxcy shuddered at the thought. "I don't like the way I'm thinking, Brennen."

"Nor do I, but I think you are on to something." He sorted through the pages. "Here. Brandon mentioned something or someone. He wasn't real clear on it. We need to talk to him."

"Where is he now?"

———

Brennen glared at the clock. "If he's not working, then he would be in the conference room." He reached for his phone, sending off a quick text to Brandon. "He'll come up here, Princess. That way, you can still rest."

"I feel like an invalid." Jaxcy was grumpy and knew she was showing it.

"That you are still, Princess. I know that it's tough. You didn't ask to get sick." He studied her. "I just thank God that we got away and got you to help."

"That's what I don't understand, Brennen. How did we get away?"

"The door was unlocked. We suspect that it was the driver who unlocked the door for us."

"I think that you are correct. He just didn't seem to fit. I thought that he was watching the men too closely, and not us at all."

"You did? You never mentioned that."

"I thought that I had." Jaxcy sighed. "Brennen, have you been receiving messages that don't make sense, that threaten us?"

"I have been. I need to talk to you about them as well. Dallas has them."

"He does? And what does he say?"

"That it's typical to receive them. I know the other fellows did." Brennen hesitated before he spoke. "Princess, I need to ask you something. Are you happy living here?"

She turned to him, surprised at his question. "I am. You're here. I am making the friends that I could never make in my hometown. Why do you ask?"

"Because when you were in the infirmary, you asked me to take you home. I thought it meant back east."

Jaxcy gave a sad smile. "Did I? And you've been trying to figure out how to do just that? Oh, Brennen, no. This is our home. I don't think I ever want to go back there."

———

Brennen breathed a sigh of relief. "Well, I guess that's that, then. We stay here. I'll talk to Barnabas, if you like, about your place. He'll look after it for you." He frowned as his phone chimed. "It's Brandon. He's on his way up here."

Jaxcy was off Brennen's knee and heading for the bedroom. "I need to get dressed then."

Brennen stared after her, realizing that she really had been in her dressing gown. He shook his head even as he headed for the door to answer the knock. He was losing it, wasn't he, Lord?

Brandon stared at Jaxcy for a moment, realizing that she had pinpointed something that he knew the men had overlooked. He sighed, before he looked at Brennen, finding his attention on Jaxcy.

"Jaxcy? Did you have to complicate our search?" Brandon shook his finger at her.

Jaxcy starteed at him, her eyes narrowing as she caught the grin that he was trying hard to hide. "You fellows needed my help, obviously. It's only logical that it had to be someone outside the family. How do we find them, and then how do we prove it? I can tell you how to use natural stuff for fertilizers and how to grow plants. This I can't do." Her finger flicked at the papers in front of her.

"But you see, you have. You sorted through this, didn't you?" Brandon looked at the piles. "Your aunt, your uncle, others. But what is this pile?"

"That? Those people? I have no idea who they are or how they fit in. They are not from my town. I can tell you that much." Jaxcy looked up as Brennen gave a small sound. "Brennen?"

"Jaxcy, the man from the bank? The one we connected to Smithers? What was his name?"

"Wayne Johnston. Why?" She leaned against him as she looked at the list he had compiled. "He's there and you have his brother, son, nephew, daughter, sister, cousin. Who don't you have?"

"That's what I am wondering." Brennen stared at her as she sat back, her gaze intense as she stared at Brandon.

"Jaxcy?" Brandon's voice stirred her to shake her head.

"Brandon? Did you come across anything that showed their relatives from another province? I think they had family out west."

"As in British Columbia? Where your aunt is?" Brennen watched as her face paled. "I am not saying that she is involved. Did your aunt marry?"

"She had been. That I remember. But I don't remember her husband. I can't remember if he died, they divorced, or if one of them just walked out on the other. Mom or Dad would know."

Brandon had been sorting through the pile of papers on her aunt. He read the bottom paper and looked up. "He died, under suspicious circumstances out west. The police felt that he was killed, but they could not prove it. It says here that your aunt remarried within a month of his death."

"That quick? Wow!" Jaxcy reached for the paper and then paled as she read the name. "This is a cousin to Johnston. How?"

"That we will ask." Brandon pulled out his phone, a finger in the air to pause her questions, as he read his text. A stern look crossed his face, one that Brennen recognized.

"Brandon? Where is she?"

Jaxcy stared between the two men, not quite sure what was being asked.

Brennen's hand reached for hers. "Your aunt isn't out west anymore, Jaxcy. I would hazard a guess that she is in our vicinity."

"She is. Emma just sent word to Brady. Your aunt and her husband have been seen in the area. Together with the Smothers' family. That is where you were held, at one of their properties. They are not even trying to hide it anymore, Brennen."

"I know. That scares me, Brandon." Brennen leaned forward, a frown on his face. "So, if they are not hiding it, what is their plan? And how do we combat it?"

The men spent some time discussing their thoughts, Jaxcy noting down the highlights before a train of thought sidetracked her. She rose, heading for the office, searching for a map, returning to the table to unfurl it.

Brennen watched her closely, not quite sure what she was up to.

"Jaxcy?"

"Okay. I'm not sure how to really say what I need to, so I just have to talk." She paused, gathering her breath, knowing it was taking a lot from her just to speak. "This is a map of Canada. You are all from different provinces and territories? Am I correct?" At their nod, she pointed. "This is where I am from. Aunt Jackie moved across the country years ago, before Mom and Dad disappeared. They were taken to an island in the Southern Hemisphere, at least, I think that is where. Suppose someone on the west coast needed to set up on the east coast? How would they do that?"

Brennen and Brandon exchanged glances.

"I think you are onto something, Jaxcy. And using the property next to us? Saying it was yours? That would implicate you in whatever it was they are planning. We are readily available to Lake Erie and then through the canal system, to Lake Ontario and then the Atlantic Ocean." Brandon was on his feet, gathering their papers. "Are you well enough to come downstairs, Jaxcy?"

She shrugged, knowing that she wasn't, but she was determined to end this. "I will be. I want this over, for Brennen's sake. And for my parents. Enough time has been stolen from our family."

Approaching Brennen, Bradon and Burnie sat on either side of him. Jaxcy had gone to stand in front of the map, her finger tracing the area that Brendon was pointing out to her.

"Brennen? What's up?"

"Jaxcy has come up with an interesting idea. She asked Brandon and me if someone wanted to expand their criminal activities to the east coast, how would they do that?"

His two friends exchanged glances.

"She's right, you know. That trust fund? Laundered money? It was never meant to go to her." Burnie paled. "Does she still have it?"

Brennen shook his head. "No. We turned all the information over to Dallas, and he has had the Foundation attorney look into it. It never really existed."

"It didn't? You two went through all this for nothing?" Bradon shook his head.

"No, it's not for nothing." Brennen was trying to understand what was going on and then explain it. "It was a setup. What we haven't had a chance to tell you fellows is that our captors planned to ship us out of the country, just like her parents."

"And no one would have ever found you?" Bradon paused. "Who?"

"That's what we need to determine. In the paperwork that Brandon gave me, it showed that her aunt had remarried and that they are in the area. We are not sure why."

"When did they arrive?" Burnie was on his feet, heading for his own chair, returning with a sheaf of papers. "Is it in these?"

Brennen took them, quickly finding what he wanted. "Here. This is what we found. We need to talk to the officers out west."

"Dallas can do that." Bradon was on his feet, moving away, his phone out to call Dallas. He turned to watch Jaxcy, seeing the fatigue that she was trying hard to hide, the whiteness of her face a sharp contrast to the dark shadows under her eyes. We need to solve this, Lord, and soon, he thought.

Breck stood in the doorway, eyeing each one of the men, before his focus stayed on Jaxcy. He moved towards her, watching her closely, seeing just how close to collapse that she was. His hand drew her to a chair near Brennen, before he was away and then back with a cup of tea for her.

"Here, Jaxcy. Drink this. And then, Brennen needs to take you home."

Jaxcy shook her head. "No, I need to stay. Please, Breck? I need to be part of this."

Breck stood for a moment, considering her words before he was out of the room, beckoning for Brady to come with him.

"Brady, she won't leave, and she's almost ready to collapse."

"I know. I was watching her. Even Brennen isn't going to be able to make her leave." Brady headed down the other hallway. "Let's take that cot over for her. At least, that way, she can rest."

"I agree. I was heading for it. What else?"

"Her medications? I think she needs some oxygen as well. Maybe an IV?"

The two men worked quickly, gathering what they needed, meeting Doc as they headed back.

"Brady?"

"Jaxcy is refusing to go back to the apartment. She's in the conference room. We're hoping to get her to rest."

Doc nodded, reaching for some of Brady's burden, before he followed them. He approached Jaxcy, finding her sitting with her eyes closed, her arms wrapped around her. A gentle touch had her jumping and then nodding at Doc's quiet words. He settled her on the cot, oxygen in place, and an IV started. He was worried, he thought. Lord, heal this girl. That young man over there is head over heels in love with her and needs her. Resolve whatever it is that they are going through and soon.

Brennen had lifted his head and watched as Jaxcy settled down on the cot, a relieved sigh rising from him. He had tried to get her to leave, to let him take her home, but she had refused and moved away from him. He turned as Buckley sat beside him.

"Brennen? What's this I hear that they wanted to ship you two out of the country?"

"Jaxcy overheard them. I don't get why, though."

A sound from Branigan had them all turning his way, watching the grimness that began to cover his face. Branigan shot a look at Jaxcy, noting how still she had become.

"Fellows, I think I know why. And I think I know why Jaxcy is so sick. Doc, how sure are you that it's pneumonia?"

"As sure as I can be without X-Rays. Why?"

"If she was exposed to a chemical, would she have symptoms like this?"

Doc paused, his eyes on Branigan, before he nodded. "Maybe not the high fever, but the breathing issues? Yes. Why?"

Branigan was on his feet, heading for Doc, a paper held out. "Check out this. I think she had chemical exposure. Dallas sent over some information, off the record, that puzzled him. He wanted me to talk to Brennen or Jaxcy."

"Is that ethical that he did that?" This from Breck.

Branigan shrugged. "I have no idea. He's bouncing around ideas, he said. And one of them is a chemical that he has heard about on the street. That it would be released into the air and affect many people, allowing the perpetrators to take over a government. He wonders if Jaxcy was a test case."

Brennen's face grew dark with anger. "They did that? Is that why they had her cleaning all the time. She said that they made her clean the whole house every, single day. She didn't think it needed that much cleaning."

"And somehow, somewhere, they exposed her to this." Doc's face grew grave. He spun, searching. "Breck, we need to get some supplies and quickly. I can't tell how serious it is. Is there someone with a portable X-Ray machine?"

Brady lifted his phone. "Already done, Doc. They'll be here in fifteen."

"Good. Now, Breck, come with me. Brady, you stay here. Call me if she worsens or call 911 and take her in."

Watching as Jaxcy's condition worsened, Brady finally rose, gathering her into his arms, and running for the door, Branigan at his heels, holding the doors for him, and pointing to his truck. Brennen had looked up, thrown down his pen, and ran after them.

"Brady?"

"She's worse, Brennen. I need to take her in. I can't wait for the crew to arrive."

Brennen slid into Branigan's truck, reaching for his bride, cradling her to him, watching as she struggled to breathe.

"Brady?"

"We don't think it's pneumonia, Brennen. Dallas questioned if she had been exposed to any chemicals. I guess they found traces of something."

Brennen paled, even as he kept a watch on her. "And if it is? Can we treat her?"

"That's our plan, Brennen." Brady was monitored Jaxcy as closely as he could. "Unfortunately, I think we'll have to intubate her and place her on a ventilator until we can get the treatment started."

Brennen paled even more before his anger rose. "Find this person or persons. I want to face them, to ask them if a young lady's life was worth it."

"They'll tell you that it was. We'll do our best, Brennen. Buckley will have the church and everyone that he can reach praying for you two."

Three hours later, Brennen looked up as a hand rested on his shoulder. His face was pale and drawn, fear and grief showing on it and in his eyes.

"Doc?"

Doc sat wearily into a chair. He had not been on call but had come in when Brady had alerted him to bringing Jaxcy in. He had fought with the physicians and nurses to save her. So far, they had been successful. Dallas had been around, bringing in what information that the techs had provided him.

"Brennen, we have had a fight. She is not out of the woods yet. Not by a long shot. Dallas has given us what he can. We've found a treatment and have started it. She'll be going up to ICU shortly."

Brennen nodded, already convinced in his mind that he was losing her. Her parents sat beside him, Jemma's arm around him.

"Can I see her?"

"Give us time to get her settled. Head on up, Brennen. I'll meet you there." Doc stood, hesitated for a moment, and then moved away.

Jeremiah watched him walk away. "Brennen? What can we do for you?"

Brennen's head shot around to stare at the older man, surprise on his face. "I'm not sure. I should be asking you that."

Jemma spoke up. "Jaxcy has made it obvious that you are the love of her life, the one that she was waiting for. We need to keep you healthy, Brennen. She will survive this. She will need you when she awakes."

Brennen rose, staring down at the fingers that he was rubbing together. "I guess. I wish I had your optimism and faith." He pointed to the elevator. "Let's head up there. Doc will find us."

Jeremiah's arm was around his wife, knowing that she was grieving already, thinking that they had found their daughter once more, only to lose her.

Brennen paced the waiting room late that night. He had sent Jeremiah and Jemma home finally, stating that he would call. He had no idea who still remained of his friends, but he knew some had. He turned to face the doors to the ICU rooms before he shook his head. It wasn't time yet that he could go back in. Brennen knew that the staff was working their magic or whatever you wanted to call it to keep his princess alive. He was losing hope that they would.

Doc stood and watched his young friend. He shook his head. Why, Lord? Why have all these young men and ladies gone through life and death struggles? I just don't get it. But You are in control. That much I know. Please, Lord, give us the wisdom that we need to treat this young lady. She is responding, I know, dear Lord, but not quite how we would expect her. He paused, feeling his phone vibrating. He pulled it out. Bruce Carey was on the phone, stating that he had found someone to come in and consult. Did they want him? He had courtesy privileges at the hospital and was an expert in chemical contamination.

Doc breathed a sigh of relief. He had not even asked for that, and the Lord had provided.

"Yes, Bruce. We could use his expertise with Jaxcy. We're treating her but we need more information."

"That's what I thought you would say. He should be there in ten minutes. I told him to ask for you or Terry."

"Thank you. We need to find the treatment we need for Jaxcy." He turned to watch Brennen. "I could use someone to talk with Brennen. Do we know anyone?"

"I'll see who I can track down." Bruce was gone before Doc could even say anything. He turned to speak with Brennen, instead seeing a tall, distinguished man walking his way.

"I'm looking for Doctor Whitson."

"That would be me. And you would be?" Doc reached to shake his hand.

"I'm Jake Webster. Bruce Carey sent me your way. Said you needed some assistance with diagnosing and treating a young lady." Jake turned slightly as he heard footsteps behind him.

"That we do." Doc's hand reached to draw Brennen close. "This is Brennen, Jaxcy's husband. They were kidnapped a few days ago. Jaxcy has been running a high fever but developed breathing difficulties. We assumed it was pneumonia, but she became much worse today. We brought her in. Right now, she's on a ventilator."

Brennen studied the physician standing in front of him, a frown on his face. He looked familiar, but he could not place him.

"Dr. Webster? What can you do for my princess?" Brennen's desperation came through in his voice.

"I'll what I can do, young man. What can you tell me?" His keen eyes studied Brennen closely.

"Not a lot. She was made to clean the house where we were kept every day, even though it didn't need it. We think she might have been exposed to something. The last day, she could barely function."

"I see. Dr. Andrews? Where is this young lady? And what else can you tell me?" His hand stopped Brennen from moving away, drawing him with them towards Jaxcy's room. "I want this young man with us. He may have information that we need, without being aware of it."

An hour later, Doc stood back, watching Jaxcy closely, breathing a sigh of relief. Jake had thrown off his jacket, rolled up his sleeves, and plunged right into determining what Jaxcy was exposed to, based on the information provided by Dallas earlier. He had questioned Brennen extensively as well, drawing from him details that had not been provided earlier, simply because no one had known the questions to ask.

Brennen stood beside the bed, his hand on Jaxcy's face, his own face white and drawn. He was beginning to weave from the fatigue that was crippling him. Doc caught him as he collapsed, Jake reaching to help, drawing up the chair that had been provided for them.

Doc crouched down beside Brennen, assessing him before he looked up at Jake.

"Has he been exposed to the chemical?"

"More than likely, I would say. Can you run blood work and ask for them to check for that particular chemical, just as we did for Jaxcy?"

"I can. Terry will be around shortly as well, he said." Doc stood. "I just don't get it."

"Get what? Their exposure? This particular chemical is manufactured in an illegal lab, used for criminal activities. I have no idea why they were exposed, though. It is usually part of criminal activities overseas."

Doc paled. "And there's your answer. Jaxcy mentioned that the plan was to take them out of the country. But if they were testing it on them, that doesn't make a lot of sense."

"No, it doesn't. Now, let's have a look at this young man."

Looking up the next morning, from where he was seated in the waiting room, Brennen stared at the man standing in the doorway, watching him. He frowned, started to rise, and then stopped as the man turned and walked away. That was strange, he thought. Who was that?

Branigan stared after the man, thinking he looked familiar but not sure why. He headed towards Brennen, handing him a takeout cup of coffee and a bag containing a muffin.

"Doc said you hadn't eaten." Branigan dropped down beside him.

"No, I haven't. Thanks, Branigan." He sipped at the coffee, before setting it aside to open the bag and pull out the muffin. "Where is everyone else?"

"Hard at work, trying to figure out who is responsible for all this." Branigan nodded towards the door to the unit. "How is Jaxcy?"

"Better, much better. Bruce found someone who could come in and treat her. Whatever he found to treat her has worked. Doc and Terry think they'll be able to pull the ventilator later today. Doc isn't supposed to be up here, not being an Emergency physician, but they have allowed him to do just that."

"I wondered. I know Terry has been glad of his assistance." Branigan's eyes closed for a moment. He had been up all night, working away on trying to track down Jaxcy's uncle. "I have a line on her uncle."

"You do? And?" Brennen waited for Branigan to speak.

"He's not in Canada. As far as we can determine, he moved to the United Kingdom years ago and has not been back since."

"I see. Does Jeremiah know that?"

"Not yet." Branigan peered around Branigan, seeing Breck and Brody heading their way. "Barnabas said he'd talk to him."

Breck and Brody waited for Brennen to speak, sharing a glance when he didn't. Neither were sure just why he didn't.

"Brennen?"

Brennen's head shot up, surprise on his face. "I didn't see you two. I'm sorry." His eyes slid closed for a moment, fatigue weighing them down.

"How is Jaxcy?" Breck was almost afraid to ask.

"Better. Thank you for the prayers. She is better." Brennen's eyes caught the nurse approaching, and he was on his feet, a muttered excuse me thrown at the men, before he was striding rapidly towards her. "Nurse?"

She smiled. "It's okay, Brennen. Terry asked me to come and find you. He needs to update you." Her hand on his arm stopped his forward movement. "They pulled the ventilator already. She is breathing on her own, with just oxygen by nasal prongs."

"She is? Oh, thank God." Brennen almost hugged her before he was away, striding down the hall, a lighter movement to his steps.

Breck had risen and watched him move away from them. "That must have been good news."

Two days later, Jaxcy sat cross-legged on the bed, dressed in leggings and a heavy sweater. She had been allowed to be up and moving around, no longer needing the oxygen. Fynn and Imly watched her closely, trying to read how she was. Imly finally just approached her, sat on the bed, and reached for her hands, her head bowing as she prayed for her friend.

Jaxcy wiped the tears that had fallen on her cheeks. "Thank you, Imly." Her voice was still a hoarse whisper. "You have no idea what this means for me."

"I think I do. We have all had to go through things that we could never have imagined. We have formed a close group. We want you to be part of that. That being said, when are they springing you?"

Fynn laughed at the expression. "Imly? Really?"

Imly just grinned. "I know. Darbie and the twins are corrupting my language, aren't they?"

Jaxcy smiled, content suddenly with the knowledge that she was a welcome part of a group, no longer an outcast, to wait on the sidelines. She no longer had to long to belong. She did.

"Terry said tomorrow. I'm just afraid, ladies. I am afraid that whoever it is will come after Brennen."

"I know what you mean." Fynn dropped into a chair. "Now, the other ladies are planning on preparing meals for now for you two. Brennen said that he needs to work, he has a couple of books waiting for him."

"I know he does. I told him to stay away today and work on them. He hasn't listened to me." Jaxcy caught sight of Brennen in the doorway.

Brennen laughed as he approached, bending to hug and kiss her.

"You did, and I did, but I needed to be here. Terry called. He wanted to talk to us." He looked up as Fynn and Imly started to rise. "It's okay, ladies. You can stay, if you wish. Jaxcy and I talked it over. We can't hide what happened, and if you being here will help us solve this, then we welcome you here."

Fynn and Imly exchanged a glance before they looked at Jaxcy, seeing her smile of agreement.

"You know, you fellows have not asked us for any input." Imly grinned at the look on Brennen's face as he realized how true that was.

"You are so right." Brennen looked at Fynn. "Fynn, what would you suggest?"

"I suggest that we blow this joint, taking Jaxcy with us." She pointed to the door, where Terry stood, waving papers at them. "Here are her discharge papers. At least, I think that's what Terry is waving at us."

Staring down at the papers that he was holding, Brandon could not believe what he was reading. He turned, searching the room, not seeing Brennen around.

"Where's Brennen?" His call raised the heads of the men who had gathered in the room.

"Brennen? He said that he had some work to do. Why?" Benen was on his feet, heading for Brandon.

"Because I think I just figured out who is involved." Brandon shoved the paper at Benen. "Are you seeing what I'm seeing?"

Benen stared at his friend for a moment, before he took the paper that Brandon kept shoving at him.

"What are you talking about?"

"Read it. Tell me if you see what I see." Brandon pointed at the paper, turning his head as he heard the door open and close. "Brennen? Take a look at this."

"At what?" Brennen walked wearily across the room. He had moved Jaxcy home the day before, settled her that morning in their living room with some of the ladies, and then headed to work. He had needed a break, he thought, and had headed to the conference room. "What are you talking about?"

"Here." Benen handed him the papers, his face grim as he nodded at Brandon. "I see it, Brandon. I think that you are correct. In fact, that correlates with what I just found." He turned, hurrying back to where he had been seated, and printing off the work he had just done. "Here. This goes with that."

The other men had gathered around them, exchanging glances, not quite sure what was going on, but knowing Brandon and Benen had made a discovery.

Brennen rubbed at his eyes and then his forehead, a headache growing that he refused to take anything for.

"What?" He stared at the paper, and then looked up at Benen. "Him? She trusted him. He's the only one that she really trusted in her town."

"I know. But he had the perfect cover, now didn't he? Who would suspect a minister?" Brandon looked around as snickers from the men filled the room. "Sorry, Buckley. We know you're honest."

"Well, I guess I have to say thanks then, I think." Buckley reached for the paper, a frown. "Her minister? Wait a moment. That's not the name she gave."

"No, he has been using a different name. He played her, Brennen, and well. And I doubt that he is as old as she thinks he is."

"No, I don't think so. He had to have known who I was. He's the one who sent me the letter, that much Jaxcy and I figured out." Brennen sank down into a chair, his elbow bracing his head. "Where do we go with this?"

"Here. Emma just sent some information that goes with that." Brady handed a sheaf of papers to each man. "She said that she suspected him, but had to do some digging. He's been involved in a lot of criminal activities on the sly, she says."

"And her parents would have trusted him enough to take what he offered in food or drink. That's how they did it." Brendon spun, heading for the map. "Let's see. Emma says that he was from this area, just north of us a way. There." His finger found the spot of a small town. "And guess what? That's where we tracked both Smithers and the Smothers families to."

Brennen stared at the paper, not really reading it, a frown in place. "Are you saying that they are all from the same town? How did we miss that?"

"I don't think that we did." Blair spoke up. "It wasn't until you two were kidnapped and then we found you on the Smothers' property that it all began to gel. Now, what do we do about it?"

"Set a trap." The men turned to stare at Devaney as she moved into their midst. "Trap them. I have no idea. You fellows always have such great ideas. But draw them out. Bring them together."

"She's right. That may be what we have to do." Blair wrapped an arm around his wife. "Is the minister around here?"

―――

"He is. Emma says that they have tracked him to our town. He arrived, when?" Brody looked at his paperwork. "The day before you two were kidnapped, Brennen."

"So, he has to be involved. But who is behind it all? Someone has to be, to have access to the chemicals needed to manufacture what they tested on Jaxcy." Brennen rose and began pacing. "Where do we go from here?"

Jaxcy stared at Brennen and then Burnie, listening carefully to their explanation of who was involved and how. She shook her head and then waved her hand at them to stop their talking.

"Johnny? I don't see that. He's old."

"Actually, Jaxcy, he's not. He played old, but he's around your father's age." Brennen sank beside her, an arm around her.

"He is? I wouldn't have guessed that. So, if he is, he knew all along that you would show up. Why you?"

"That is something that we will ask him." Burnie held up a finger as he pulled out his phone, frowning at the text message. "I guess that we won't after all. Breck just sent out a text. They pulled the minister's body from the lake this afternoon."

"Getting rid of the ones who could bring their organization down?" Brennen sighed. "So, we're back to square one, I gather."

"Not necessarily." Burnie held up the folder that he had dropped onto the coffee table. "This is some of the research that we have done. Some that Emma has sent us. In it, I think we will find the answers. Or at least, I pray we do." He handed it over to Jaxcy. "Jaxcy. You know your town. Read through it. Tell us what you think." He grinned as he handed over pens and highlighters. "Mark that copy up all you want."

"I can. Okay." Jaxcy began to read, a frown of concentration on her face.

Brennen pointed to the kitchen, motioning Burnie to come with him. He reached into the fridge, a glance at the clock showing it was lunchtime. Burnie worked with him, preparing a simple meal.

"Will she find something, Brennen?" Burnie glanced towards the living room.

Brennen stepped to where he could watch her, finding her staring into space, her hand upraised with a pen in it.

"I think that she has. Give her some time. She needs to think through it all. Then, she'll tell us what she thinks." Brennen shook his head. "I hate this, Burnie. Whoever this is, it has been her family through a horrible experience."

"And it's hard not to hate them, isn't it?" Burnie studied his friend. "All the other fellows have struggled with that as well."

"I guess." Brennen stood for a moment, staring out the kitchen window. "It's just so hard not to."

"Hard not to do what?" Jaxcy's arm came around him, her question turning his face towards her.

"Not to hate whoever is responsible."

Jaxcy nodded. "I know, Brennen. It is hard. You have no idea of the number of hours that I have spent asking for the hate to be taken away. I have had to do that for so many years." She looked up at Burnie. "Burnie, I think that I have an answer for you. But we need to talk to everyone else." She swayed for a moment, fatigue hitting her.

"You, Princess, need to rest for a bit. Here, let's eat in the living room. Then, you can stretch out on the couch and tell us exactly what you have found."

Brennen and Burnie stared dumbfounded at Jaxcy an hour later as she finished her summation of the findings that she had discovered. Brennen reached for the papers that she had dropped to the floor, sorting through them, reading her notes. He sighed.

"You have complicated it, Princess."

"No, I have not. I have clarified it." She shot him a mutinous look, then glared at Burnie as he choked back a laugh. "Laugh all you want, Burnie. But this is what I think. You asked me that." A hurt tone sounded in her voice.

Brennen sighed, moving to sit beside her and gather her close. "It's okay, Princess. We believe you. I just don't see how we missed this or missed naming that person."

"Because you don't know the town. I don't know it as well as I should. And if you ask Mom or Dad, they won't know what has happened or the dynamics of the town in the last eleven years. It has changed that much." She pointed at the papers. "And that person and their family are responsible for that. They have relatives all over Canada, their family is that large."

"I see." Burnie reached for the papers, reading her notes. "I see some names that we had looked at, but we didn't have that connection." He looked up, a grin on his face. "I nominate you as lead detective."

"Save that for a book, Burnie. By the time we'll all done, you'll have more fodder than you know what to do with in a novel." Brennen shook his head, feeling Jaxcy's body relaxing, and looking down at her. "She's asleep, Burnie. This has taken too much from her." He studied the thinness and paleness of her face, the black shadows under her eyes.

"It has. She's so petite to begin with, Brennen." Burnie watched her closely. "Is she recovering okay?"

"Terry seemed to think she would. She still needs oxygen every once in a while. We have to monitor her oxygen stats all the time. We won't know for a while if there has been any permanent damage."

"We are all praying that there isn't." Burnie's eyes closed for a moment before they popped open again. "So, what do we do with this?"

"Take it to the fellows. Let them start what they need to. I want to confront these people, and I know that I'll be fought on that."

"Not necessarily, Brennen." Burnie nodded towards Jaxcy. "We'll all be there. I'm off then. One of us will be by later to update you." With that, Burnie was gone, the apartment door closing quietly behind him.

Two days later, Brennen approached Breck, a quiet question asked, and then he walked away. Breck stared after him, not quite sure what Brennen was up to, before he was running after him, a hand out to stop him.

"Brennen? What did you just ask me?"

"I asked you how well does Bruce know that specialist that he sent in?" Brennen was puzzled.

"I can ask. Bruce knows so many people."

"I know, but it's just strange how all of a sudden he appeared. I know Bruce does this, but I have to question that physician."

Breck nodded. "I know. I would do the same. Let me talk to Bruce, find out what I can. You'll be around?"

"I have to head to town for a bit. I need to do some research in the library." Brennen paused at the look on Breck's face. "What? You don't think I should?"

"It would likely be best if someone went with you. They'll try and take you again, just to get to Jaxcy. She has to know something or someone."

"I think that she has given everything that she can. She's still not healing well, Breck. I want to find someone else for her to see."

"Leave it with me. I'll find you someone." Breck watched as Brennen walked away, a stoop to his shoulders that was unusual. *He's wearing out, Lord, and we need to help him. Only, I don't see how.*

Bruce Carey stared at Breck thirty minutes later as the younger man stood in front of him. Bruce had still been around the building, and Breck had tracked him down.

"He asked what exactly?" Bruce knew Brennen well enough to know that it was not an idle question.

"He just asked how well you know the physician that stepped in." Breck was hesitant to speak, not wanting to shed any wrong on the physician.

"I see. Not that well. We've met at meetings and he is on the board of a local hospice. I can see why Brennen would ask." Bruce paced away and then back. "You know, it is strange. He approached me, asking how the men were." He stared hard at Breck, an inscrutable look on his face. "He specifically asked about Brennen."

Breck nodded. "There's our connection then. Bruce, we need to research this. Come with me."

Bruce's hand was out to stop him. "Your office, Breck. We keep this between us until we find out for sure."

"Of course. That's where I was heading." Breck sighed as his phone chimed and he pulled it out. "That's strange. It's an email from Emma." His face paled. "Bruce, it's about that physician."

"That's not good. What does she say?"

"That he is up on disciplinary measures, has been relieved of his duties and privileges at all the hospitals, including ours." Breck looked up, shock on his face. "He should never have been in there, treating her. She goes on to say that the authorities from out west, Alberta, are looking for him in connection with criminal activities that he has been connected to." He groaned.

"And it has to do with chemical warfare?" Bruce took a guess.

"It does. I just wish this was over. Brennen stated that he wants to find another physician to assess Jaxcy."

"And that I will do, personally." Bruce sat in front of Breck's desk. "Okay, Breck. Let's start our research. We need to prove this, and then get that proof to that young Dallas."

Two hours later, Breck tidied the papers that he had printed into a neat pile and looked up at Bruce.

"I think that we have what we need."

"I do as well. You head off to find Dallas. I'll find the men. I would assume that they are in the conference room?" Bruce grinned, knowing the men too well.

"The ones that can be are. The ladies were taking turns with Jaxcy, as much as she will let them."

"Her parents?"

"They have been in and out. They don't want to settle in the building. And I can't say as I blame them."

"No, I don't. If they are looking for a place in town, send them to Sally. She'll find them one of our houses." Bruce was away before Breck could respond.

Breck waited for Dallas to approach him, a frown on his face as he studied the top paper. Bruce and he had determined so much, but would it be enough? He knew Dallas would have to confirm everything.

"Breck? The duty officer said you needed to speak with me?" Dallas waited for Breck to speak.

"I do. Bruce and I took a question that Brennen asked and did a lot of research." He handed over the folder. "Here. This is on the physician that came in and treated Jaxcy. He's involved."

"He is? Sandy was getting red flags on him, but had to set it aside." Dallas glanced quickly through the material. "I don't know how you all do this. You find information that we don't."

"Like it's been said before. You think like a police officer. We don't. Just a different perspective."

"And that is true. Thanks, Breck. Watch Brennen and Jaxcy." Dallas looked up when Breck didn't respond and then groaned. "No, they're not, are they?"

"Brennen wants to confront them. He's working on a plan, I just know. I only hope that he informs us of what he is planning."

"I do too. Let me know what it is and I'll make sure that he's protected."

The next day, Jaxcy wandered the rose garden, unable to stay inside. Cadee, Ennis, and Guenivere were with her. She was tired, she thought. Tired of what they were going through, tired of scrimping and saving, a habit that Brennen was trying his best to get her to break, but it is so hard, she thought. Lord, when will this be over? I need it over today. Please, Lord? Let it end. We both need to move on and can't. Her hand rested on her cheek as she turned at Cadee's question.

"I'm sorry, Cadee. What did you ask?"

"Mom and Dad have asked if you might be interested in helping them to set up a community garden at the shelter."

Jaxcy's eyes grew thoughtful. "I would like that. Barnabas has also said that there would be a large garden area here as well. What did he do?"

Guenivere laughed. "It's just Barnabas being Barnabas. He thinks so far ahead of all of us, we can't keep up with him. He has suggested it and has asked, no doubt, if you would like to be in charge?" She continued to laugh at the look on Jaxcy's face. "It won't be all on you, Jaxcy. I can guarantee you that. We will all pitch in. Just think, ladies. We can grow our own veggies."

"And there are to be some fruit trees." Jaxcy sighed, sitting on one of the nearby benches. "That I don't have experience with."

Ennis shook her head as she sat beside her. "Never worry. He'll have found someone to look after that and train us." She studied Jaxcy. "Jaxcy, just how are you feeling?"

"Not great. The medication I was put on doesn't seem to be working. Bruce has found someone else to see me, and that appointment is for early next week. I just wish this was all over with."

"We have been there, Jaxcy. We know what you mean." Guenivere spoke up. "What are your thoughts on who did this?"

"That, I'm not too sure of. There are just so many names."

"Then, let's talk them all over, list the whys and why nots, and see who we can narrow it down to." The ladies laughed as Cadee pulled out a pad of paper and pen from her jacket pocket. "Sorry, this is a habit."

Thirty minutes later, Jaxcy stared at them. "It was him? All along?"

"And her. I don't get it, Jaxcy. Why?" Ennis was upset about her friend.

"I don't know. I want to face them and ask them just that." Jaxcy jumped as she felt a heavy hand on her shoulder and saw the fright on her friends' faces.

"And that you can do, Jaxcy. We have been waiting out here for too long. You will come with us." Brian Ellsmere stood behind her, his wife, Carol, at his side.

"Brian? You were my friend. Or at least, I thought you were."

He sneered even as his wife gave a cruel laugh. "Never, Jaxcy. Never. We just pretended to be. We had this plan for years."

"Plan? What plan?" Jaxcy was desperate to keep them talking, hoping that some of the fellows would appear. She gave a subtle nod at the look on Ennis' face and knew Ennis was somehow sending out a text.

"A plan to take over a country. Not this one. Who would want that? But there is a nice little island country in the warm ocean. Your parents were on one of the islands in the chain. You and Brennen are headed to one of them. This time, you will not escape us." Carol sneered at the look of fear on Jaxcy's face.

Jaxcy's heart dropped. They had been the ones all along. She had been right. Now, how did she manage to escape and get her friends away as well? It wasn't right, Lord, she thought, that they are here in danger because of me.

"Who wrote the letter to Brennen? We know that Johnny was part of it?"

"Johnny? Oh, yeah, him. He was part of it and then decided that he wanted out." Brian's hand tightened on her shoulder, and she bit back a cry of pain. "We dealt with him."

"What did you do, Brian?" Jaxcy could feel the anger rising in her, anger that was totally unlike her. She was afraid as well, afraid of what the couple would do to her friends. "Who else is here?"

"No one. Just us." Carol sneered at her.

"No, there has to be someone else. You two would never work on your own." Jaxcy bit back the tears that threatened to fall after the back of Brian's hand slammed across her face. She could hear the distressed sounds from her friends.

"Leave her alone." Ennis spoke up. "How do you expect her to answer you if you beat her." She had caught sight of movement behind the couple and prayed that it was their fellows.

"If you want the same, keep flapping the mouth." Brian's growing rage was showing. His hand gripped Jaxcy's wrist in a cruel grasp and he hauled her to her feet, ignoring her cries of pain and the cries of the other ladies to leave her alone. "You're coming with us, Jaxcy. We really don't care if your man does. He's not the one that we want. You are."

Jaxcy's legs gave way at that point and she collapsed, held upright only by the tight hold that he had on her. Brian began to drag her with him, Carol facing the ladies, a gun pointed at them. She backed up into Brian and then began to curse and shout at him, not seeing the men who had surrounded the area.

Brian's head turned as he desperately sought a way out, and not finding one. He hauled Jaxcy once more to her feet, an arm around her, using her for a shield, even as his own curses were directed at everyone present, including Carol.

Brennen stepped to the forefront, his eyes hard, as he stared at Brian, seeing Jaxcy drooping against the other man, her eyes closed. She was having trouble breathing, that much was obvious.

"Let her go."

"Not a chance. She's coming with us." Brian trained the gun that he had pulled from a holster on his belt and directed it at Brennen. "Get out of our way, all of you."

"I don't think so. This is what you call a stand-off, Ellsmere. You're not getting by anyone of us." Brennen caught a slight movement of Jaxcy's part, as she sagged even harder, pulling the man's arm down and sending him off balance.

"Out of our way." Carol peered around Brian, her own gaze as hard as her husband's, keeping her gun trained on the women.

No one saw exactly what happened or even knew how Kerry managed to be there. He took a leap towards Brian, his fur glistening in the sun, his hackles raised all the way down his back. The growls that he emitted were loud in the sudden silence. Brian screamed with shock as Kerry latched onto the wrist of his gun hand, dragging it down, forcing him to drop it.

Brennen's toes dug into the gravel as he launched himself forward, a fist coming down on the other man's arm. He scooped Jaxcy into his arms and ran, hearing the ladies coming after him. He shot into the lobby of the building, heading for the infirmary, hearing Brady's voice behind him. Running footsteps sounded loud behind him even as he slid to a halt, waiting as Brady shoved open the door and flicked on the lights.

Trying to set Jaxcy down, he found he couldn't. Her arms were tight around his neck, even as she buried her face against his neck, refusing to look up. Brady finally just pointed to the bed and told him to sit and hold his princess.

Barnabas and Dallas found them an hour later, standing in the doorway watching the young couple. Jaxcy had finally moved to sit beside Brennen but refused to let him move away from her. Dallas just shook his head as he approached them.

"Jaxcy? Are you okay?"

She peered at him from under her brows, a dark look on her face. He could see the fear still showing in her eyes.

"About like that, huh?" Dallas sat in the chair that had been moved closer to the bed and watched Brennen, finally nodding. "We have all of the players now, Brennen. Jaxcy. I am sorry that you had to be assaulted and almost kidnapped again."

"The other ladies?" Jaxcy's voice was hoarse with her emotions and barely audible.

"They are shaken, have given their statements, and at the moment, are standing right outside the door behind me, waiting to see you."

"They are? They need to go home."

Dallas simply grinned. "They won't." He shared a look with Brennen and then nodded.

"Who all, Dallas?"

"Who all? That's a good question." Dallas pulled out his notebook, Barnabas coming to lean against the foot of the bed. "We have finally solved this, rounded up everyone, and are sorting out the charges. I must say, I have never had a group of criminals trying to put the blame on each other like these ones are."

"The physician? Was he involved?" Jaxcy felt sorry for the man.

"No, actually, he wasn't. He was legit. But what you were given has proven difficult to actually determine what the chemicals were. We have finally done that. He is aware of that and that you had reservations about him. Barnabas has spoken to him and agreed to speak with you, to see if you will allow him to continue to treat you, given what I am about to tell you."

"Mom and Dad?"

"I have a team with them. They are being briefed on the same information that I will share with you. First, your minister? He was part of it, as you have been told. He left a detailed letter in his home down east. He was being blackmailed, forced to pretend to be older than he was. The lady who posed as his wife was not his wife. She was placed in his home to monitor his activities.

"The Ellsmeres were part of it, but not of the upper echelon. They were used to threaten people. He was involved in drug trafficking among other crimes. She was as deeply involved as he was. They saw this as a way to get rich, but they didn't realize that they were considered expendable and would have been killed once they had no value to the group.

"The group? It consisted of members from across Canada. I can't go into details, as it is part of the investigation and charges yet to be laid, but Ellsmere was correct when he said the plan was to take over another country and run it for their own profit. A small island chain was just perfect, or so they thought. There were members who talked too freely and to the wrong, or should we say, the right people and that was how it all began.

"Your parents? They were removed, all within the express purpose of driving you to ask for help from the group. They didn't expect you to survive on your own. They had been monitoring the Foundation fellows. For some reason, Brennen, you were chosen. The minister was forced to write the letter to you. As we suspected, the law was drawn up just to get to you, Jaxcy. They thought that they had succeeded in bringing you under their control when you and Brennen married, planning to blackmail both of you. Why and how? They have never said, and we can't determine. When you left the province, they had to make other plans."

"Is that why they followed us? How does Smithers fit in?"

"Smithers was a low-level criminal, related as we had already learned, to the banker in your home town. The banker is the one who set up the trust fund, forging your parents' signatures to make it look legit."

"Who all from this area was involved?" Brennen shared a look with Barnabas, seeing regret on his friend's face.

"Smithers, the Smothers family, Dale Lewis, the librarian. And then there were a couple of patrol officers, some probation workers, two lawyers, a general practitioner. A pharmacist. A chemist." Dallas paused. "I will let you have names later, but for now, we are still sorting through their charges. Our public relations team is preparing a statement and will be speaking with the press sometime tomorrow or the next day."

"The chemical? How did they do that?" Jaxcy was puzzled.

"The chloroform they used on you, Jaxcy. It was combined with the chemical and there were lesser doses in the cleaner that you were forced to use." Dallas paused, regret on his face. "I am sorry, Jaxcy. I wish that we could have solved this before all that happened."

Jaxcy shrugged, leaning harder against Brennen. "You did your best, Dallas. That's what I prayed, that everyone would do their best. God answered that prayer." She yawned, her ebbing adrenaline playing with her body.

Brennen gave a sound and then slid from the bed, gathering her close.

"If there is anything else, can we talk later? She needs to be resting." He walked away, speaking briefly with his friends and the ladies before he headed for their apartment, finding Jeremiah and Jemma hesitating in the hallway.

Brennen stared at them, realizing that they were all a family now and sighed. He finally had a mother and father that he could get to know. He would always regret that he never knew his own parents, but Jaxcy's parents had taken him into their hearts.

"Mom? Dad? Come on in. I'll get Jaxcy settled and then we can talk." He didn't see the look the couple shared or the tears that sparkled on Jemma's face.

Three months later, Jaxcy straightened up from the garden that she had been working in, rubbing at her lower back. She eyed the long, straight rows of tomato plants, satisfied that they were growing just the way that she wanted them to. She stood and watched some of the ladies who had become friends with her work away, the men from the building around at times. Barnabas had just smiled when she thanked him, for giving her something to do in the outdoors that she loved.

Kerry gave a happy yip and was running from her as she spun, a hand coming up to shade her eyes. A huge smile lit her face and she had dropped her hoe and was running after Kerry, to be swept into Brennen's arms, hugged tightly, and kissed thoroughly.

"You're home, love. I didn't expect you until tomorrow."

"I am home, Princess. And I don't have to travel for months. I spoke with the publisher. He has agreed that I don't have to travel, not unless I choose to and not unless you go with me. It's been a long three days."

"Three days? That was all? It felt like three months." She squirmed in his arms until he set her back down, his arms still loose surrounding her.

"It has. What have you been up to?" He looked past her. "The garden is looking good."

She turned as well, waving at Imly as she walked past her. "It is. The ladies are enjoying it so much. And so are your friends. They are hilarious with their comments, you know."

"I know. And I can only guess that Buckley's are the worst."

Jaxcy began to giggle. "His are. He has already given the garden a date by which he wants to be eating produce. It's far too early. He's doing that on purpose."

"He is. Did they tell you that he gave dates for the weddings for two of our couple friends?"

"They did. They could hardly speak for laughing so hard on how it went back on him."

Brennen shouted with laugher at that. "It was priceless, I must say. I can't wait to meet his lady."

"Me, either." Jaxcy hesitated. "Mom and Dad were around earlier today. They want to head back to our hometown for a bit, just to clear up things, and then resolve whatever it is that they need to."

"It will bring closure for them. Do you want to go along?" He held his breath, waiting for her answer.

"No, I don't need to. I have everything that I want and need right here." She twisted to look up at him. "Now that my lungs are better, and I can do things, I want to explore the area. Will you come with me?"

"I would be delighted to do just that. I know some great hiking trails, places we can camp out overnight. I'll even take you out in a kayak on a beautiful lake up north."

"That sounds delightful." Jaxcy grew quiet, the setting sun reflecting off her face. "Brennen, what would have happened if you had not come to town, if you had ignored the letter?"

"I don't even want to think about that. I'm sure that they would have forced you to marry someone and then you would have disappeared."

"Just like Mom and Dad. They don't talk much about their time."

"No, they won't. They just want to forget it. Listen, how be we head into town? I would like to take my Princess out for a meal."

"I would like that, love. Sorry, Kerry, you can't come. Not this time." She waited for him to move. When he didn't, Jaxcy looked up at him, finding him watching her closely.

"Do you know how much I love you? Do you know how I grieved when you were so close to death? I prayed so hard, Jaxcy. So hard. I really thought God would refuse my request."

—

"I know, love. You've talked in your sleep." She reached up to kiss him. "We'll set that aside, Brennen. We're not ready to talk that all over. Maybe we will never be." She leaned into him. "One thing that I did learn? We need to be more assertive in our prayers, to be the intercessors that God wants us to be."

"That we do, Princess. When did you get so smart?"

She shrugged, her hand reaching for his to draw him towards the building. "It's just how God teaches me. I study, think, and then learn."

"Never stop learning. You teach me so much as well."

Thank you for choosing the story of Brennen and his Princess, his Jaxcy. Once more, the characters have decided on their own what their adventure would be and how they would learn to trust God through it all. Jaxcy was not the name I had chosen for her. It had been Jemma, which became her mother's name.

How do we pray? Do we pray for our own wants and needs? Or do we spend time in intercessory prayer for our friends, families, and those in need? That is how we need to pray. It is something that I have been relearning as I have written the story of Brennen and his Jaxcy.

Evil is rampant, no matter where you live. Things and events that at one time we would only see in a novel? They have become commonplace. All we can do is trust in God and pray for His protection and strength for our daily walk.

Abe and his team just had to show up again. Their stories are in the *His Guardians* series. Those men and ladies I missed when the series finished. That's why, no doubt, that they show up every once in a while.

And of course, a Shetland Sheepdog, or Sheltie as they are referred to, had to show up. I owned a beautiful blue merle named Noah, his black, gray, white, and tan coat just beautiful. I have two tri-coloured Shelties at present, Liam and Natalie. They add adventure to my life.

God bless each one of you.

Ronna

Brody: Encouraged to Seek

The Barnabas Chronicles
Book 10

By

Ronna M. Bacon

1 Chronicles 16:11

Seek the Lord and His strength; Seek His face continually.

Psalm 9:9-10

The LORD also will be a refuge for the oppressed, a refuge in times of trouble. And they that know your name will put their trust in you: for you, LORD, have not forsaken them that seek you.

NKJV

Table of Contents

Tucking his pen back into his portfolio, Brody Corcoran glanced around the tastefully furnished reception area of the business office that he found himself in. He was to meet with a Ker Deeks. I wonder what he is like, he wondered, trying not to listen to the voice of the lady who had answered the phone. He could not see her, but her low voice was melodious and drew him to want to meet her. He sighed. No, he decided, he would not have an adventure as nine of his friends from the Barnabas Foundation building had had. They had almost lost some of his friends and their ladies to death. It had been too close.

Shifting in his chair, Brody glanced at his watch. He had been early for his appointment, something that he was trying to change, but couldn't. He stood for a moment, moving to stare out of the window, watching the parking lot of the building. Located at the edge of a town near where he lived, Brody studied the area, a prickling sensation tingling at his neck. He didn't like that feeling. Not one bit, he decided.

He turned as he heard his name called and studied the young lady, around his age, he thought, as she approached him. Red gold hair. Dark gray eyes. Freckles sprinkled across her nose. He mentally shook his head. There was no way that she was real. This was the image of the lady that he had always thought he would find.

"Mr. Corcoran? I'm sorry. I was on a call that I just couldn't end. Please? This way?" She pointed to a conference room. "Have a seat. Can I offer you a coffee or tea?"

"No, thank you. I'm okay, but don't let me stop you from having something." He grinned at her, laughter for a moment sparkling in his deep blue eyes.

Ker Deeks studied the man in front of her. Tall, she thought, too tall. Dark brown hair. Blue eyes. Dad, what did you do? You asked me to meet with him, and then you ducked out. I hope my suspicions are not correct, that you are trying to set me up.

"No, that's okay. I'm Ker Deeks." She looked up at the silence and then smiled. "Expecting a male person? That would have been my father that you spoke with. He's out of the office, but you can speak to me. Or we can reschedule for when Dad is around."

Brody shook his head, desperate to collect his thoughts. "No, it's fine. I just wasn't expecting a lady."

Ker gave an unladylike snort, which caused Brody to grin in return. "Blame my brother. He wanted a younger brother and got me. He had already picked out the name. Mom and Dad just feminized it."

"Feminized it? Is there such a word?" Brody shook his head, dropping his face to hide his grin. This was going to be an interesting meeting, wasn't it, Lord? And I can see Your hand in it already. "Now, your father asked me to stop by. He said he had some documents that he needed to have drawn up?"

"He does." Ker reached for the folder she had placed on the table. "These are the ones that he is thinking of. Just for an explanation, Dad's business is highly confidential. He does searches for missing children and teens. He tries hard to keep out of the news. So far, we have managed to do that."

"I see. I wasn't aware of that. And you are in the office, then?"

Ker nodded. "Most of the time. Sometimes, if there is an emergency, and we can't get our teams to go in and bring out the children or teens from another area, I go in. We work closely with all law enforcement authorities and courts. We never go in without clearing it first. That's how Dad has always worked."

"Then, what forms are you needing to draw up? I am sure that you have had them already in place."

"We have." Ker sighed. "But for some reason, the law office that we usually work with has become difficult to do just that. There have been some changes in personnel. A new lawyer has been taken into the partnership there. Neither Dad, Keefe, or I trust him. There has been something off about him, and we just don't know what. I'm sorry. I shouldn't have said anything." She looked troubled.

"No, it's okay. It goes no further than our conversation here in this room. It just helps me to understand why you are looking for someone new. May I?" Brody reached for the papers, glancing through them, a frown on his face. "Have you used these yet?"

"No, not yet. Dad looked at them, and then he refused to. That's when he talked to Bruce Carey, asking if he knew someone who could look them over and then help us."

"Bruce? Your father knows him?"

"He does. They have been friends for years." Ker studied him, suddenly not sure of him. "You seem surprised."

"I shouldn't be. Bruce's son, Barnabas, asked me to come. I work for the Foundation, even though my employer is a firm of paralegals."

"You do? Then, that's why." Ker paused, her head turning as she heard a soft click of a door. "Excuse me for a moment? That's the back door. No one should be coming in there. Dad is away. Keefe is on vacation this week."

Brody was on his feet, a hand stopping her from moving forward. "Wait. Let me go, please?"

"It's not your office." Ker tried to disguise her discomfort at his stepping in.

"Doesn't matter. I won't let a lady go out into danger." Brody strode out of the room, heading for the back door, searching the offices as he passed them, not seeing anyone. He stood for a moment just inside the door of a large, multifunctional room, seeking to find the person or persons who had entered. He had no doubt that they were no longer alone in the office.

A scuffling sound behind him had him turning. Only he never made it all the way around. A blow to his head dropped him to his knees, his hands going out to stop himself from landing facedown on the tiled floor. He vaguely heard Ker scream and then the sounds of a struggle. He was hauled to his feet, swaying as his vision darkened before he felt himself shoved forward and through a door, the cool breeze hitting him in the face.

Ker struggled to escape from her captors, anger rising within her, her eyes on Brody as he has hauled across the parking lot and then pushed into the back seat of a large SUV. She froze, her feet not working for a moment, as the man holding her yanked at her arm to drag her towards the same vehicle.

Pushed down beside Brody, she glared at the three men, one sitting beside her, a cruel grin on his face as he watched her. She didn't know them, that much she knew, but she would remember them. Her memory for faces had always been excellent. She shifted closer to Brody, feeling his hand reaching for hers and tightening on it. Ker turned her head, her focus on Brody, seeing the pain that he was trying hard to hide, even as he watched the three men closely.

Ker had no idea who they were. She had not seen them before, but her father had warned her to be careful after Keefe had spoken out of turn. There had been threats coming into the office, by fax, by email, by phone, that she had just found out about. Her father hadn't told her of the packages that he and Keefe had found and turned over to the authorities.

Brody shifted his gaze from man to man, watching Ker as well, as best as he could. He didn't like that they were being driven from the town. Not one bit, he decided. Then, he began to pray, begging God to protect the lady with him, and give him the ability to save her.

The SUV was finally stopped in a density of a forested and marshy area. The door beside him was pulled open, and both he and Ker were shoved out, landing hard and awkwardly on the ground, to lie still for a moment. Brody rolled to his back, staring in disbelief as the vehicle drove away at a rapid pace, before he was on his feet, running towards the road. He slid to a stop, unbelief still on his face. He heard muttering from beside him and turned, watching Ker as she stood there, anger on her face.

"Just who were those men?" Brody's question drew her attention to him.

"I have no idea. All I know is that I am out in the boonies somewhere, it's late afternoon, and I have no idea how we are going to get home."

Brody's phone was in his hand. "I have limited service. Let me send off a text. Do you know where we are?"

Ker shrugged. "About 10 miles from town. On Old Whyte Road. Do you know the area?"

"No, I don't." He pocketed his phone, his hand reaching for hers. "Let me help you."

She shrugged away from him, heading back down the road. "I can do it myself, thank you very much."

Brody stared after her before he ran to catch up. This will be interesting, he thought. I am not sure what they wanted, but my head is aching like crazy, Lord. I have a miles-long walk and a lady with me who doesn't want any help.

Brody finally reached out to stop Ker's forward progress, needing to rest for a moment, and thinking that she did as well.

"Again, Ker? Do you know those men?"

"No. I don't." She bit at her lip for a moment. "Dad didn't want to tell me, but Keefe let something slip. There have been threats against our company."

"And you are just telling me now? Ker!"

"What? What can you do? You're not involved." She refused to look at him.

"Not involved?" Brody stared at her, shock on his face. "Not involved? Just what do you call the lump on the back of my head and the headache that I have? Isn't that being involved?"

She glared at him, anger burning through her. "I don't want you here. Go away." She's turned and stomped away from him. Her white long-sleeved blouse was no longer the pristine colour that it had been that morning, with a rip across one sleeve where she had caught it on a wayward branch. Her black pencil skirt was dirty and stained. She limped, not willing to take off her shoes, and not willing to admit that her feet were hurting and hurting badly.

Brody stared after her, a hand on his head, before he called after her. "Ker. You're limping. What did you do to your shoes?"

Ker spun, stomping back towards him. "You have dragged me all over this forsaken area. Through bush and shrub and I don't know what all to call it. A short cut, you said. I didn't see any short cut. And during that time, a heel came off my shoe. What do you expect me to do? Walk around on who knows what in bare feet?"

"Ker! Stop! I didn't know that. You should have told me."

"Told you?" Her voice rose in anger. "And just what would you have done? Left me there?" Her hands reached to yank off her shoes, and she pitched them at him. "Here. You take them. You walk in them." She turned and almost ran from him.

Brody caught the shoes that she threw at him, staring at them before he stared after her. Running after her, his hand on her arm stopped her.

"Ker? Please? Don't walk that way. You're going the wrong way."

"And just how would you know that? You told me that you didn't know the area." Her words were bit out, almost needlelike in their delivery.

Neither one of them heard the truck slowly approaching them, nor heard it pull to a stop not far from them. Brandon and Benen, friends of Brody's, exchanged a glance, grins on their faces, as they watched their friend from the safety of Brandon's truck.

"I think that Brody has a live one there." Brandon continued to grin.

"I think he does. Ouch!" Benen winced. "Did she just throw her shoes at him?"

Brandon laughed. "I think that she did. Should we rescue him?"

Benen shrugged. "I suppose that we must. After all, he did send us a text message, didn't he? I wonder why he's out here, though."

Brody finally turned, hearing the truck approaching him once more. "Ker. There are friends. We can leave."

"You can leave. I'm not going anywhere." Ker was being stubborn, but the fear and panic that was rising within her drove her anger.

"Yes, you are. We are not leaving you out here." Brody waited. "Ker? Let's move." When she still stood, a mutinous look on her face, refusing to move, he simply reached for her arm and pulled her to the truck.

Standing with the door to the back seat open, Brody waited for Ker to jump up on the seat.

"Ker? Let's go."

"No. Absolutely not! I am not getting into another vehicle with you. I don't know these people."

"Ker. In the truck, now!" Brody waited, finally tossing her shoes on the floor, picking her up and seating her, pulling the seatbelt around her.

"How dare you!" Ker spat her words at him.

"I dare because you need to be in here! I dare because I am tired, my head is hurting, and I need to get it looked at! I dare because someone is out there watching us, waiting for night to fall so that he can kidnap you again! Is that enough?" Brody's anger had flared, and his words were like barbs directed at her.

Brandon and Benen exchanged a glance, their amusement barely contained.

"Ready to go home, Brody? And maybe you would like to introduce us to your lady?" Brandon's voice rippled with his laughter.

"Shut up, Brandon. And you too, Benen. This has not been a good day!"

"We can see that." Benen shifted to watch them, noting that the lady had refused to look at any of them. "Hello. I'm Benen, and this is Brandon. We're friends of the man back there who seems to have mishandled you."

Ker stared at him, unable to believe that she had heard what he had said.

"Benen, shut up. It's been bad enough already today without you starting. How does Cadee put up with you?" Brody sighed, suddenly weary, his head beginning to pound heavily. "I'm sorry. I didn't mean that."

"I know. You're just frustrated and in pain. And we can see why." Benen turned back around, his laughter filling the cab, Brandon barely containing his. "And Cadee puts up with me because we love each other."

Brody just shook his head, hearing the snicker that came from Brandon.

"Did you say these were friends of yours?" Ker's finger stabbed towards each one. "What friend says that?"

"Draw in the claws, kitten. We've been friends for many years. We've also been through too much together to bear any grudges." Brody twisted to watch behind him. "Did you see any vehicles waiting?"

"No, we didn't. And we would like to hear what happened to you." Brandon glanced in the rearview mirror to find Ker staring at Brody and nodded. She's the one, isn't she, Lord? She's his lady. Another adventure. "And by the way, didn't we tell Brennen that nine was enough?"

"Shut up, Brandon. Just get us home."

Brandon's comment and Brody's response had Ker staring at Brody once more, a puzzled look in her eyes. She really was not sure what she had landed into. She never talked to friends that way, nor did her brother. Her mother would not have allowed it.

Benen had looked down at his phone as it chimed and then spun around. "You're Ker Deeks?"

"I am. What do you want to do about that?" Ker was scared, and for Ker to be scared, her anger flared.

"Because Barnabas just sent word that your home has burnt, there has been a bomb threat at your office, and Brody's truck is still there at your father's business. They're looking for you two."

"Tell Barnabas that so far, we're okay. We'll talk when we get back." Brody stared out the side window, not seeing the looks that Ker kept throwing his way.

———

"Barnabas said to bring Ker with you. He'll settle her into one of the suites for the night. Her father and mother are heading our way."

"That's good."

Ker stared at the three men. "Don't I get a say in where I go?"

"No!" The three men spoke as one.

Pulling to a stop in front of the Barnabas Foundation building that they all called home, Brandon shifted to study Brody. He frowned. Brody is hurting, Lord, and I don't know why. All we got was that cryptic text, asking someone to come and pick him up and then where he was. He shared a look with Benen, who shook his head.

Ker stared up at the building as best she could from inside the truck, finally remembering to snap her mouth closed. She had heard of the Foundation, knew her father was friends with the founder but had never been here. The three-story building was a mixture of dark brown brick and dark brown board and batten siding, with balconies for each suite.

Brody roused, his eyes narrowed from pain, before he reached for the door handle, to shove the door open and then slid down, the slight jar of landing on the pavement causing his head to pound even more. Benen was out of the truck and around to stand beside him, waiting for him to ask for help.

"Brody?"

"It's okay, Benen. Doc's around, isn't he?"

"He should be. Brady's not. He's on shift tonight."

"That's what I thought." Brody turned to Ker, finding her watching him closely. "Come on, kitten. Let's get you inside. My friends will help you out."

She shook her head. "No way, buster. I am not going into that building. I have had enough for the day."

"Ker, you don't have a choice. The police have asked that you be kept safe here. If necessary, they will arrest you." Brody hated to be stern with her, but she was not leaving him much of a choice. When she still refused to move, he simply reached into the truck, undid her seatbelt, slid her towards him, and gathered her into his arms.

Ker was shocked, to say the least, that Brody simply picked her up and walked towards the building. She began to struggle.

"Let me down. I can walk,"

"On those feet? I don't think so." Brody nodded at Benen as he held the door open for him, not paying attention to some of his friends and their ladies, gathered in the lobby seating area, who stared at him, some open-mouthed.

"Put me down, buster." Ker's fear was driving her anger.

"Ker, enough. I'll let you down once we get to Doc's apartment. He's an Emergency room physician. He'll need to assess both of us."

"You, maybe. I'm okay."

"Really?" Brody stared down at her, seeing how the day had fatigued her, leaving dark shadows under her beautiful eyes, and loosening the curls from the ponytail that she had put her hair in that morning. "I would say otherwise."

Abruptly dropped to her feet, Ker bit her lip, realizing that Brody had been right, after all. And she hated that. Keefe was always trying to get the best of her, and she refused to let him or any male do that to her. She stared down at her hand, caught tight in Brody's strong grasp, and for once didn't try to move away from him. She refused to let anyone touch her or hold her hand, she thought, and here this man had carried her and was now holding her hand. She paled as she realized that she had let him do that very deed earlier in the day.

Benen waved as he walked away, amusement still in his eyes, looking for Cadee. Her parents ran the local homeless shelter, and Cadee was always gathering new clothes to take in. He figured that Ker would need some, even if she really didn't welcome them.

Lord, what is with her? Brody is trying to keep her safe and alive, is what I'm thinking, but she just doesn't seem to want his help. Cadee simply stood and stared at him as he explained what was going on with Brody.

"Brody? And a lady? Of course, I have some clothes that should work." Cadee spun away from Benen before she was back in his arms. "Thank you, Benen, for not teasing him too much."

"And who said that I did that?" Benen stood, a grin on his face, watching as she quickly sorted through the piles of clothing on the spare room bed.

Cadee shook a finger at him. "I know you, Benen. I know how you fellows are. You tease and torment one another."

Barnabas stood for a moment, watching as Brody and Ker disappeared into the elevator. A frown covered his face. He had spoken with his father and been informed that Ker would need to be kept safe, that threats had been levelled at the private investigations firm her father operated, and that she was a target. He sighed. Another one, Lord? When does it end? And I would say that Brody is involved.

Doc stood in his kitchen doorway, watching as Brody carefully moved towards him, his grip not easing on Ker's hand.

"Brody? What did you go and do, son?" Doc pointed to a chair, a frown on his face at how slowly Brody was walking.

"Got knocked over the head, Doc. It hurts. And the headache is bad." He shoved Ker down in a chair, bending carefully to lift her feet to another chair, shocking her at that. "This is Ker Deeks. We've had to do quite a trek and she had on high-heeled shoes. It was not our choice that this happened. It was through brush and a marshy area. She also lost a heel to her shoe."

"She did, did she? Hello, Ker. I'm Doc and this is my wife, Anna. Let's have a look at you two." Doc nodded as Anna moved around, finding juice for the two, knowing they needed something sweet. "Brody, you have quite a lump there."

"I know." Brody grimaced and then groaned. "I never saw it coming."

"You fellows usually don't. Ker, I'll let you go with Anna. Get yourself cleaned up." Doc looked around as a tap came to the door, and Cadee entered. "Cadee? What are you doing here?"

"Benen was one of the ones who rescued Brody. He asked if I had some new clothes that I was waiting to take in." She held up a pile and smiled at Ker. "Hi. I'm Cadee. I understand that you met my husband, Benen, earlier. Pay him no mind. He loves to tease and torment."

Ker stared at her, not quite sure if she was telling the truth or no. "Hi."

"Here. Benen asked that I bring you these. They are all brand new. Just take your pick." As Ker went to refuse, Cadee shook her head. "No, it's okay. We take in donations for the shelter Mom and Dad run. No one knew these were even coming." She hugged Brody and then was gone, leaving Ker staring after her and then at the three in the room with her.

Early the next morning, Brody tapped at Doc's door, waiting for him to answer. His sleep had been fragmented at best, even with the pain medications that Doc had insisted he take. He was concerned for Ker and just wanted to make sure that she was still there and okay.

Doc stood for a moment, a hand on the door, amusement in his eyes that he quickly hid. Brody was acting just like the others, he thought. The fine young men fall quickly and at first sight for their ladies, or most of them did.

"Brody? So nice of you to drop by and visit us. Come in. I have coffee on."

Brody stared at him for a moment, before he caught the twinkle in Doc's eyes. "Gee, thanks, Doc. I could use a cup of your coffee and your company. We haven't talked in a day or so."

Doc began to shake with his laughter. "Got me there, young man. Here, sit. Anna was up and out early. Something about a breakfast meeting that she had to attend. She did leave her breakfast casserole for us."

"Sounds good." Brody sat, his head in his hands, wishing the drummers would stop their music.

"How are you feeling this morning, Brody?" When Brody just sat, not responding, Doc sighed. "About like that, eh? We'll see what we can do about it." He turned to study the hallway, not hearing Ker moving around yet. "Your young lady isn't up yet. Anna checked on her as she was leaving."

"Was she up in the night?"

"No. Neither of us heard her. She was done in, Brody, as they say. What did you go and do?"

"I have no idea, Doc. At the wrong place at the wrong time, I guess." Brody sipped at his coffee, his mind trying to sort everything out. Lord, I see Your hand in this. I just don't know where it's going.

"No, Brody. At the right place at the right time. Who knows where Ker would have ended up if you hadn't been there."

Ker heard the men talking and hesitated just outside the doorway. She had arisen somewhat earlier, spent her time in her devotions as she always did, glad that a Bible was on the bedside table. She had then stood, her fingers touching the clothing that Cadee had left for her. She had lingered on a pair of beautiful leggings, the jade and cream and peach drawing her in. Her favourite colours, she thought. She had never worn leggings, had always thought that she couldn't. She had known her parents' feelings on them and realized that she had let them sway her from her own decision.

Her decision made, she had quickly dressed, finding a long turtleneck tunic with three-quarter sleeves in a soft cream. She smiled. Yes, she thought. It was time she started making her own decisions. If that meant that she had to set sail on a new career and make a break with her father's company, then she would. She drew on heavy socks, finding her feet cold and still sore. Doc had dressed the cuts and bruises and blisters, not saying much. That had surprised her. If it had been her own family doctor, she would have received a lecture, that she knew.

Brody caught a slight movement in the hall and then was on his feet, moving towards her, his hands outstretched without thinking. Ker studied his face, studied his hands, and then reached for them, finding his grasp warm and welcoming.

"How did you sleep, Kitten?" His voice was low, making sure that only she could hear him.

She heard Doc rattling away in the kitchen and wondered if he was doing that on purpose. She looked up at Brody, finding his attention on her, and not on what was going on behind him.

"Okay, I guess. I was tired. And my feet still hurt."

"They will. Here, let's get you to a seat. Doc said Anna left us breakfast." Brody drew her into the kitchen and to a seat, waiting for her to decide what she wanted in a tea.

"Brody? Your head? Is it any better?" Ker glanced up quickly, disquieted to find him watching her intently.

"Not really." He held up a hand as she went to protest. "It's okay, Ker. I'm just glad I was there. I hate to think of what might have happened to you." He looked around as he heard the door open and close. "We're going to need to speak with the police."

"Yeah, right. About that." Ker studied her hands, not willing to look up. "They will never believe me. I know that."

"And why not?"

"Just because. They have never believed the ladies in town."

Barnabas and Bruce had entered the kitchen quietly, listening to the conversation before they exchanged a glance. Bruce was puzzled. He knew of Ker, but not that this was her opinion of her town's police. Barnabas merely shook his head, took the plate of food held out to him, and sat beside Ker.

Brody nodded at the two men but kept his attention on Ker. He frowned for a moment, seeing the conflicting emotions flitting across her face.

"Ker? Talk to me. What happened yesterday? It's more than just nothing. And we do have to talk to the police and give our statements."

Ker drew a deep breath, a sober look on her face. "I know we do." Her voice was barely a whisper. "But I can't. Not to them."

"Okay. So, I have a detective friend. He could come out and take the statements. He's been through a lot with us over the last couple of years."

She shrugged, finally looking up at him. "Brody? Why? Why did this happen?"

Bruce began to pray, causing Ker to jump and stare at them. She had not heard them come in, so focused was she on Brody. That's not good, she thought. I could have disappeared again.

Looking up at last, Bruce picked up his fork and then pointed it at Ker's plate. "Eat, young lady. Then, we'll talk. And yes, Brody, I have spoken to Will. He's sending Dallas out. He hasn't said but he seems to give the impression that he shares Ker's opinion of some of her police force."

"He does? Who's he?" Ker looked between the four men.

"He's our chief of police, Kitten." Brody chewed his mouthful of food and then swallowed. "He's also a good friend of ours, and a member of our church."

"Oh!" They could see Ker relaxing. "That's good. I don't know that any of our force even goes to church."

An hour later, Dallas tapped the papers of their statements together and set them into his briefcase. He was puzzled. What happened didn't make sense.

"Ker? What else can you tell me? This is puzzling."

"I know. Keefe let slip that there had been threats against our business. He didn't say that they had been directed at me." She paled. "Why?"

"Talk to us, Ker. Tell us exactly what it is your father does. I can guarantee, it goes no further. Not unless we have to do that, and that is only with your permission." Barnabas leaned forward, his pen in his hand.

"It won't? Okay. Dad is a private investigator. He searches for missing and exploited children and teens. It is dangerous, that I know. He has a team that works with the authorities wherever he tracks down the children. He never goes in on his own or sends his team in. He leaves that to the ones who are trained in that."

"Okay. So has anything happened recently that would make someone come after you? And how well known is it what your father does?"

"Dad flies undercover, as he says. He works by word of mouth. There is a network out there that has the names of those willing to help find these children. Even our building and the business name gives nothing away. But someone has to have learned what we do. Keefe did tell me that there had been an incident six months ago, I think it was. Dad has found a child, told the authorities where the child was. They refused to believe him and didn't go in. That child died. The inquest stated that if the child had been found even two days earlier, that child would have survived."

Brody nodded. It was what he had suspected, his mind searching all the scenarios that he could imagine during the night.

"And your father was blamed. Someone has to have told someone."

"That's what we think. Dad did have to testify, but it was a closed court. No one should have known he was there."

"Someone saw him, put two and two together, and then tracked him down." Bruce sat back, frustrated. "We'll need to talk with your parents and Keefe. Make sure they take extra care."

"Good luck with that." Ker's growing bitterness showed.

Brody just reached out and hugged her, finding her struggling at first before she relaxed against him. What is going on, Lord? What has she been through that has caused her to react like this?

Dallas stood, Barnabas walking him out, shutting the apartment door behind him.

"What's your reading on the situation, Dallas?" Barnabas was puzzled as well.

"She's scared, Barnabas. And my reading is that she will become angry. I talked to Benen and Brandon, and they said that she did grow angry with Brody." He rubbed a hand on his face. "I just don't get what they were after. Brody said the men never spoke, never asked for anything, just took them out and dumped them."

———

"I know. That doesn't make a lot of sense. Unless it was a threat directed towards her father. Dad knows him but hasn't said much about him. I don't know that he has seen him much in the last few years. Dad gathers friends and acquaintances."

"Like someone else I know." Dallas grinned and waved, walking away.

Barnabas stood for a moment, watching him, before he shook his head. Footsteps stopped beside him and he turned. Breck, his good friend and the one just under him in the work of the Foundation building, stood there.

"What's this I hear about Brody? I was away yesterday, just got in."

"Brody is off on an adventure, I would say." Barnabas brought him up to where they stood at the present time with the situation.

"Ker Deeks? I know her. I met her just recently at a church event. Brody and Ker? Now that is one couple I wouldn't have seen."

"Would we with any of them?" Barnabas stood for a moment, lost in thought. "I'm off, Breck. I have meetings that I can't miss."

"They're with Doc and Anna? Go on then, my friend. I'll pop in and see what I can find out."

Breck stood where he couldn't be seen, watching Brody and Ker. What is it, Lord, with our fellows? The lady has to be in danger before they find their life mates, the ones who You have chosen for each one.

———

Chapter 6

Brody slumped down in the corner of Doc's sofa, his head cushioned against a pillow that Anna had tucked under it. He was asleep, his body unable to stay awake any longer. Pain lined his face and dark shadows lined under his eyes.

Doc stood and watched him, wondering how long it would be before he could actually talk Brody into going for an X-Ray. He doubted that he could. His eyes dropped to Ker, and he smiled. She was quiet, he thought, but there was a desperation and anger in her that he seldom saw. Brody, you have your hands full.

Ker's head was on a pillow on Brody's knee, his arm cradled around it, as she too slept. His other arm cradled her body, holding her to him, her hand tight in his. She had not thought twice about lying down as she was, too tired and sore to even worry about it. She had had to admit to herself that her sleep of late had been troubled and worrisome, the nightmares driving her awake. She had not been able to pace as she would have liked to. Her mother would have been at her door, telling her to go back to bed.

She slept, this time without worries or dreams. Her grip on Brody's hand and the way that he cradled her so carefully to him brought reassurance to her that someone cared, that they would take care of her.

Doc turned as he heard a tap at his door, watching as Anna opened it, greeting Bruce and Barnabas and then stepping back as they entered, another couple with them. Ker's parents, Doc surmised. He sighed. Somehow, he just knew, didn't he, Lord, that things would not go well. Ker had not said, but he gathered from what she didn't say that she had not been allowed to make many decisions on her own.

Introduced to Keene and Kelly Deeks, Doc pointed to the kitchen.

"In there, I think. Brody and Ker are asleep in the living room and I won't disturb."

"Just what do you mean?" Kelly Deeks was instantly hostile. "That's not right. Let me find my daughter." She moved past him, standing and staring at her daughter, before an angry sound came from her and she moved to enter the room.

Doc took one look at her, clapped his hand over her mouth, and bodily carried her from the apartment and down the hall where he set her back down on her feet, removing his hand.

"How dare you! How dare you touch me! Let me by!" Kelly found that she could not bluff Doc, or make him move. "Out of my way!"

"No, you're not going back into my apartment. Not with that attitude." Doc had dealt with too many unruly patients to step aside. He could see some of the men from the building heading their way, grim looks on their faces. Word had gotten around that Brody had been hurt and that he was at Doc's, along with the lady everyone was surmising was his.

"I most certainly can. That's my daughter in there." Kelly tried her best to move past him, not seeing Keene and Bruce standing watching them. Barnabas had stayed at the apartment, standing guard at the door.

"Not in my apartment. I get to decide who is welcome there."

Kelly finally looked up, anger sparking from her eyes. "We'll see about that. Bruce, make him move."

"Sorry, Kelly. He is correct. It is his home. I don't make those decisions for him." Bruce watched her closely. "As for Ker, she is an adult. She can make her own decision as to where she wants to be and who she wants to be with. It's time that happened."

Keene drew in a deep breath, knowing that Bruce had just hit at Kelly where she grew the most angriest. She did not tolerate anyone telling her what to do with her children, not even her children themselves.

"Kelly, enough. Let's go." Keene reached for her arm, having her jerk it away from him.

"I'm not done. I'm not leaving until I remove Ker from there."

"It's not happening, Kelly." Bruce nodded at Keene and they both grasped one of her arms, leading her away, directly towards the men of the building who had gathered. Brady, the paramedic, still in his uniform, followed them, Breck on his heels.

"Breck? What's going on? I was just coming in when I heard the shouting."

"You were on duty, I gather yesterday?" At Brady's nod, Breck continued. "Brody had gone out on an assignment, ending up dumped in the woods somewhere with the owner's daughter. He's likely got a concussion. She was trying to walk back in high-heeled shoes. Brandon and Benen went to find them and brought them here." Breck nodded towards the car waiting outside the door of the building, watching as Kelly was shoved inside, Bruce and Doc standing in such a way that she was not able to open her door and return to the building.

"I know of them. He runs an investigations firm. His daughter works for him."

"I would say that she did. I doubt that she'll go back. Brody will have something to say about that." Breck smiled at Brady's quick grin. "Yeah, he's one of you. On his adventure. I'm not sure what brought this on."

"She found Brody asleep in Doc's apartment, Ker's cuddled up to him. She took offense at that." Barnabas spoke from beside the two men. "We'll have to deal with this aftermath. I doubt Ker will want to return home."

"Let's pray that she doesn't. If that's what her life has been like, we need to rescue her." Brendon spoke from Brady's other side. "Sorry. Brody will have to rescue her."

"And he'll drag us all along on his adventure. You other nine have done that." Buckley, the minister in the group, grinned at Brady and Brendon.

"Yeah, there's that. I would not want to face her. What drives people to be that angry?" Bradon spoke up.

"Loss of control for one." Burnie, the author, had used similar ploys in his novels. "I fear for Brody and his Ker."

Moving restlessly, Brody awoke, finding Breck setting down a mug of coffee on the table beside him.

"Thanks, Breck. What time is it?"

"Almost one. Doc said not to wake you. He's off for his shift."

"That late? I didn't think I would sleep." Brody rubbed at his face, his eyes on Ker as she still slept. "Ker hasn't woken up?"

"No, and it's a wonder that the two of you didn't, with the commotion earlier." Breck sat, his own mug of coffee in his hand.

"What are you talking about?"

"Ker's mother. Her parents showed up, she took offense at the two of you in here, and was adamant that she was going to awaken Ker. Doc took care of her." Breck gave a low laugh.

"He did? Moved er out of here, did he?" Brody gave a quick smile.

"He did. Carried her out of here, Barnabas said, and set her down in the hall. Her husband and Bruce finally moved her out and to Keene's car." Breck shook his head, sobering. "We're not done with her. I fear for your lady."

"I know. She hasn't said much, but I sort of got the impression that there was not a good relationship there." Brody sighed. "Not like it was with my sister and our mom and dad. We all got along, had our differences, but worked through them. I miss them."

"I'm sure that you did. You said once that the bodies had never been found."

"No, they were. They were heading home on the snowmobiles, coming across a lake that should have been frozen solid. They seemed to have hit a pressure crack, and then open water. The lake is too deep and murky for anyone to risk their lives. I was only fifteen at the time." Brody blinked rapidly. To have lost his whole family like that still troubled him.

Ker roused in turn, sitting up, and pushing her hair back from her face, frowning. Why was her hair loose, she wondered? She looked around, startled to find that she and Brody were no longer alone in the room. His arm kept her close to him, bringing comfort to her.

"Hi. I'm Breck. And you are Ker." Breck grinned at her.

Ker stared at him before looking back up at Brody. "Brody? What happened?"

"You had a much-needed rest, Kitten. So did I." Brody nodded at Breck. "This is another of my friends, but he is also just under Barnabas in the chain of command here."

Breck continued to grin at her. "That I am. Welcome to the family."

She frowned at him again. "Welcome to the family? Just what are you talking about?"

"Your mother was here." Brody's arm tightened around her as she jumped and then tied to stand up. "It's okay. Doc dealt with her. She's not here now."

"She's not? That can't be right. She would never walk away, not if she saw us."

"She saw you, Doc dealt with her as he would an unruly family member in Emergency, and Bruce and your father moved her out of the building. It was quite the sight to see." Breck just continued to grin at her. "She wasn't hurt, but you would have been. How much hurt has she done over time to you?"

Ker withdrew slightly into herself. "You don't understand. She won't let this alone. Brody, what did we do?"

"We did nothing. Doc and Anna were with us the whole time. After yesterday, we needed to be together, just to heal. And sleep is part of that." Brody's heart broke for his lady, as he began to pray for her.

"But you don't get it. Brody! You don't know her!" Ker was becoming more and more agitated.

The two men exchanged glances, not quite sure what was going on, before Brody simply bowed his head and began to pray, asking for peace for his lady, wisdom in the situation, and a swift resolution to whatever it was that Ker was facing.

Ker felt herself relaxing against Brody, feeling content, at peace, and loved. How that was, she couldn't figure out, but his character was coming through to her, and she didn't want to move from his side. She had never had that in her life, not even with her parents or brother.

Breck pulled out his phone when Brody finished, a frown on his face as he read the text message.

"This is not good, Brody. Bruce says Kelly is still on the warpath as he puts it. She is adamant that Ker is leaving here, today, and that you won't have any contact with her. If either of you refuses, she will have you charged with kidnapping, Brody."

"She will too, Brody. Oh, what will I do?" Ker fought her emotions, but for once, her tears got the better of her.

Brody simply turned her into his shoulder, taking the burden from her, seeking to bring her comfort, all the while his mind racing as to what they could do.

"Brody? There is one way out of this." Breck was hesitant to name it, but Brody nodded, knowing exactly what he was thinking.

"Marry her." Ker raised her head at that, staring at him as he repeated his words. "I marry her, Kelly can't touch her or me. If Ker agrees of her own free will and seeing that she is an adult, there is not a lot that they can do."

"You would do that?" Ker's question was soft, barely audible.

———

"I would, Kitten. I would do that, just for you. You need this." Brody dropped a kiss on her forehead. "We'll pray about it. Breck here will pray for us now, knowing Breck."

"That I will. And if you do decide to do this, be quick. Bruce said that she's trying to find an officer to come in and arrest you."

"She is, is she? She can try." Brody's face and voice were grim.

Chapter 8

Standing in the building chapel doorway late that afternoon, Brody stared down at Ker, her hand tight in his. They had prayed, discussed it, and then agreed. Ker hadn't shared with him, not yet, the relief that she felt, knowing he was taking on her fight for her, a fight that she hadn't known either that she was in. She looked up at him, a puzzled look in her eyes at the look in his.

"You are sure, Kitten?" Brody's voice was low.

"I am. But this is asking so much of you, Brody." Ker was troubled.

"I want to, Kitten. I truly do. For one thing, I can't walk away from you. Not now. Not ever." He nodded towards where Buckley stood waiting, his friends and their ladies in the pews, turned to watch them. Brody knew that the security in the building had been tightened for the next few days.

"Mom will try to get it set aside."

"She can try, but she had the Barnabas Foundation to go against. She won't win."

"I guess. But I don't understand."

"We'll talk later, Ker. But just understand that now that you are becoming a member of the Foundation family, you are part of a group that takes care of one another."

"Oh! I guess that we do need to talk." She walked forward on unsteady feet as he drew her to the front.

Later, Ker stood hesitantly in the conference room, not quite sure where to go. She felt like running, but the only way that she wanted to run was towards Brody. Right now, though, he was speaking with some friends, standing just a few feet away from her, his eyes on her. Cadee watched Ker closely before she approached.

"Ker? Welcome to the family. May I hug you?"

———

Ker spun, startled. "I guess. I've never been one for hugging."

"That's okay. We hug here, a lot. Just tell us if you're not comfortable with that and we won't. I have a friend who can't hug because of health reasons. She gives virtual hugs instead. We could do that." Cadee's face was alight with laughter.

"No, it's okay. I'm needing to make a change." Ker looked around. "I didn't realize there were so many here."

"There are. There are fourteen of the fellows. Nine, sorry, ten of them are now married. Berneen's brother is here. That's Darbie. And Hagen's twin sisters, Hailey and Holly, are around. They have Hagen's twins with them."

"Twins? Oh, my! That's a handful."

Hagen laughed from beside her. "Both sets are. But the girls are good. We had been on our own for a bit before Brandon and I married. I understand that he gave you a bit of a hard time the other day."

"That was your husband? I'm sorry. I don't think that I was too nice to either one of them."

"Hey, they are used to that. We've all given them a hard time. Still do." Fynn spoke up. "I'm married to Brady, by the way. I'll get you a flow chart of who's who. That will help."

"A flow chart? I'm sorry. I don't think that I understand." Ker was bewildered at the laughter that sprang up.

"We're not laughing at you, Ker. Fynn is known for her flow charts. She's an entomologist and before she moved here, was working in the medical examiner's office."

"You were? Fascinating. I would like to talk to you about that." Ker's interest was piqued.

Brody watched her closely, seeing her opening up to the ladies.

"She's making steps to get to know the ladies, Brody." Blair spoke from beside him.

"She is. It is going to be hard for her. She hasn't said much, but I would like to have a long talk with her mother."

"You and the rest of us. We saw what happened this morning with Doc. She's brutal." Blair shook his head.

"I heard it was bad. I didn't realize it was that bad."

"Trust me, it was. If it had been anyone other than Doc, Ker would not be standing here with you."

"Okay. That's good to know." Brody bit his lip as he looked around. "Listen, can you do something for me, you and the others? Can you do some research on her family?"

"Already started, Brody." Bradon spoke from where he stood behind him. "You know us. If something affects one of us, it affects us all." He nodded towards Ker. "Your head is hurting, isn't it? And Ker needs a rescue. She's trying hard but she's at her limit."

"That she is. Thanks, guys." Brody walked towards Ker, an arm coming around her. "How about it, Kitten? Ready to go?"

She looked up at him, a frown on her face. "You need to explain, buster."

Brody grinned down at her. "Explain what?"

"That word that you're always calling me. Kitten. And why you keep taking the tie from my hair."

Brody shouted with laughter, causing all eyes to find them.

"Kitten? You were like a little, itty bitty kitten yesterday. All fluffed up, hissing and spitting at us. Claws out. Sorry, but you were just so cute." He smiled down at her look of outrage. "You're adorable when you are like that. I love your spirit. And the hair? You look beautiful with it down around your face."

Chapter 9

Two days later, Ker wandered the gardens on the grounds, amazed at the variety and extent of the plantings. She stopped to watch Jaxcy, she thought it was, working in the vegetable garden. She had always wanted to get her hands dirty doing just that, but she had not been allowed. Almost without thinking, she walked towards Jaxcy, who stood, a smile on her face.

"Ker? Welcome to our building garden."

"What did you call it?"

"Our building garden. I'm supposed to be in charge, but everyone works it at some point or another. We are enjoying the fresh produce." Jaxcy looked with satisfaction at the long rows.

"Oh, that's wonderful. I've wanted to do that."

"And now you can." Jaxcy was wise enough not to question Ker's wording. "I didn't get a chance to speak with you but I do welcome you to our family."

"It's a huge family."

"It is. The fellows are all orphans." Jaxcy laughed freely at Ker's expression. "That's right. All orphans. All from different provinces. Brennen and I are both from Newfoundland and Labrador. And no, we didn't know each other before we married. It's a long story."

"And one I would love to hear. Brody said the men all share initials as well."

"That they do. All the same as Barnabas. He set it up that way. He was directed by God, he states, to do just that. All of the fellows are employed by the Foundation even though they work out in the community."

"That's an odd way of doing things." Ker was puzzled.

———

565

"It is. But part of the premise of the Barnabas Foundation is to be encouragers, just like Barnabas in the Bible. This is how it's been set up. And each of the wives has their own income from the Foundation, as part of their plan to encourage the couples." She paused. "I guess you and Brody haven't talked about that."

"We have, but we didn't get very far. He still fighting headaches and sometimes he's found it hard to articulate what he wants to say." Ker was silent, her mind racing though. "Does that mean that I don't have to go back to Dad's?"

"That it does, if that's what you and Brody want. I know that you two are still young in your friendship. Marrying as you did though as something into it that changes it." Jaxcy bit at her lip. "Brennen ended up in my town. At the time, there was a law that said if a newcomer didn't marry someone from the town, they were jailed. I stepped in to marry him, but he had been beaten soundly, all because of me. We were married a week before he really roused. We moved back here." She reached to rub at her Shetland Sheepdog's side. "This is Kerry. He'll be around if you need protection, as will Bradon's Kade. Never once worry about asking for help."

"I have never felt free to do that. I just didn't realize how controlling my mother has been. Dad too, but not as much. Keefe? I'm not sure about him anymore."

Jaxcy reached to pick up a basket of produce and handed it to her. "Here. I was picking these for you and Brody. A welcome to our garden gift for you."

"Thank you." Ker blinked back tears. "You have no idea what this means. I mean, I had friends." She stopped, anger colouring her face. "And every one was handpicked by Mom. Now, what do I do?"

"Make your own. There are nine of us here. Fynn's sister-in-law is around, as is her cousin Eric's wife. We meet once a week just as the ladies of the building for Bible study and prayer. Tonight is the night. You are welcome to join us. Now that we are even numbers again, we can split up in twos. The men do that."

"They do? Oh, how wonderful. There are so many things I am seeking to know. I just didn't know that." Ker's voice died away as she eyed the woman standing in front of her, a hulking man standing beside her. "Mom, what are you and Robert doing here? My understanding is that you were banned from here."

"I have come to take you home. Robert, bring her with us."

Robert moved towards Ker, as she backed away. She could hear Kerry growling from near Jaxcy but didn't see Jaxcy frantically sending a group text to the men, asking for help. She stumbled as she moved, almost falling.

Reaching for her, Robert's hand was cruel in its grasp. She began to fight him, yelling at her mother in anger that she was married, that she no longer had to do what Kelly said.

Kelly stared at her and then waved her hand. "Married? Not really, my dear. It can be annulled very easily. If not, you could always become a widow."

Ker stared at her mother in horror. "Mom? What did you just say?" A cruel blow across her face stopped her words, as her head whipped around from the force of her mother's hand.

"Enough of that. Robert. Head for the car with her."

Ker fought harder to escape, her free hand clawing at the man's face, her feet kicking at him as best she could. He stumbled when he tripped over her foot, taking them both to the ground. A cry of pain was wrenched from Ker even as she fell, his weight trapping her underneath him.

The men who were in the building had looked up at the text message that they received, threw down whatever it was they were doing, and ran, calling for the security guard to call for the authorities.

Breck, Brendon, and Blair raced for Robert, pulling him up and off Ker, fighting to hold him, twisting his arms behind him, and taking him to his knees. Brennen raced for his wife, pushing her behind him, a quiet word of command to Kerry.

Burnie and Brendon restrained Kelly, loud questions in the air, even as Brady dropped to his knees beside Ker. Buckley was beside him, his phone out to call for help. He could tell that Brady was worried, even from a cursory look.

"Baird?"

"Her hand, for one." He winced as Ker whimpered as he touched it. "She's broken some bones." His hand touched her face lightly. "She's taken a blow to the face as well. He's a brute." Baird turned slightly to watch the struggle going on with Kelly. "Her mother?"

Jaxcy had moved closer to him. "We were talking and then they appeared. She was taking her away. She threatened to have Brody killed."

"I did no such thing." Kelly sneered at her.

Jaxcy held up her phone. "Sorry, lady. I have it on a voice recorder. You told Ker that she could end up widowed."

Dark looks covered the men's faces even as they heard the sirens shut off in the parking lot and slamming doors and then the sound of running feet as the officers approached.

Throwing open his truck door and letting it slam behind him, Brody ran for the door to the Emergency Department. Breck had tracked him down, let him know that Ker had been hurt and that Brady was on the way in with her. His heart thundered with sudden fear. *How bad, Lord? How badly hurt is she? I don't think that I could stand it if she's hurt bad.*

Breck's hand stopped his forward motion and drew him to one side.

"Brody, wait. Doc's been looking for you. He took the liberty of putting you down as her next of kin."

"That's good. What happened? She was fine when I left two hours ago. She said she was going to explore the gardens." Brody was bewildered, fear driving cohesive thought from his mind.

"She was. She found Jaxcy and they were heading back from the garden. Her mother and a bodyguard appeared. Kelly tried to take her. Jaxcy said Ker fought the man, somehow tripped him, and ended up on the ground." Breck looked around, seeing the men and ladies circling them.

"How bad?" Brody was scared to even think.

"She was backhanded, Jaxcy said. Bruising there. But it's her hand. Brady said he felt broken bones. Doc has called in the surgeons that he needs to but he'll need to talk to you."

"Surgeons?" Brody paled, Breck's hand on his arm steadying him. "That bad?"

"It is, Brody." Doc's hand rested on his young friend's shoulder. *How many times have I done this, Lord? I pray each time it's the last.* "Come. I'll take you to her."

Brody didn't hesitate at all, heading directly for Ker, his eyes on her face. He grew angry when he saw the bruising and the cut on her lip. His hand reached to gently touch her face, finding her turning into his hand.

Ker's eyes flickered open. "Brody? You're here. I was so afraid."

"I am. I hear that you decided to have an adventure without me."

She snorted. "That's not true. I would not call this an adventure. Mom showed up with Robert and tried to make me leave." Anger sparked in her eyes. "She threatened you. She said we would annul the marriage. Or she could have me end up a widow. I have no idea what she will do."

"We'll take all the precautions that we can. I am sure that your mother and Robert have been arrested."

"I am sure that they have been. This will destroy Dad."

"Somehow, I don't think so. We need to talk, Kitten, but right now, they need to take you to have your hand fixed."

"Why? What did I do? Slug Robert?"

Brody began to laugh, picturing her doing just that. "No, but I wish I could have. You two fell and you have broken some bones in your hand."

"Oh? Does that mean the claws will be gone?" She smirked at him as he laughed before growing quiet. "Brody? Are we sure?"

"Sure? About what? Getting married? I am. You are the one that I have been waiting for. Bringing to justice those that need to be? It seems that has become our lot?" He bent to kiss her forehead and then moved back, watching as she was removed from the room.

He stood, sorrow on his face mingled with anger. Breck and Buckley exchanged glances even as they reached to lay their hands on his shoulders and pray with him.

Two hours later, Brody once more stood beside Ker, his hand resting on her cheek, his eyes on her bandaged hand, resting as it was on a pillow just to elevate it. Anger burned inside him, anger that he knew he had to release, only he didn't know how. He would need to talk to someone, he thought, before his thoughts returned to Ker and her questions.

Bradon approached him. "How is she?"

"Still sleeping. The surgeon said that she likely would for a while. They were able to repair the breaks, thank God."

"That's great. Now for her to heal. How long, did he say?"

Brody shook his head. "I didn't ask. I was just happy that they could do the repair. He'll be by in the morning before I take her home."

They spoke for a few more moments before Bradon turned to leave. "Some of us will be in the waiting room all night, Brody. Come find us if you need to talk."

"Thank you. I might. For now, this chair will do."

Ker stirred in the night, frightened for a moment at not knowing where she was. She moved her hand and bit her lip to control her groan of pain. Staring at her hand, she could feel her anger growing, praying that God would remove it. She turned slightly, pausing, watching Brody as he slept, slumped down in an uncomfortable chair, his arms tucked across his chest, his chin down. Wonder grew in her that he would stay with her. That was not what she had been trained to expect. Her eyes closed and she slept, a prayer for protection on her lips for her husband.

Sighing with frustration, Ker stared down at the clean clothes that she had chosen, her shower done. She hadn't been able to wash her hair and that bothered her. She struggled as best she could before she heard Brody's voice behind her.

"Ker? Just put on your pajamas. It's okay to do that." His hand rested on her head and she heard his softly whispered prayer for her. "Even if someone drops in, they won't care."

"It's the middle of the day. I can't do that." She fought back tears of anger.

"Yes, you can. Your mother doesn't control what you do or what you wear. Is that what she did?" He waited until she gave the barest of nods. "Okay. So, I see that we have to have a discussion about things. But for now, put on your nightwear and then come out to the kitchen."

She turned slightly as she heard him leave and quickly did what he said, reaching for her dressing gown once more before she grabbed up a pair of socks. Those she would need help with, she thought. Brody turned as she entered the kitchen, reaching for the socks, kneeling in front of her to put them on her feet, her good hand resting on his shoulder. He looked up at her as he finished, finding her studying him, confusion on her face.

"Here. I know that you can't do your hair. Let me help you. I used to help my sister every once in a while. She had a habit of spraining her wrist or fingers."

"That's so sweet, Brody. My brother wouldn't help me. At least, I don't think he would." She waited until Brody had finished, seated her at the table, and then began to brush her hair. "Brody, what if he's in the same situation as I am? What if he wants to escape and can't?"

"We thought of that, Kitten. Barnabas has tracked him down and spoken with him. For now, he has Keefe stashed away somewhere that he won't say where."

"He does? But Dad is friends with his father."

"Doesn't make a difference, Kitten. Barnabas and Bruce pray about something and then do what they are led to do."

"That's a strange way to live."

"It's the only way. We are told to seek for treasures. Right now, I have the treasure I was seeking for right here in my home."

She spun to stare at him, finding her watching her, a light in his eyes that she had caught a glimpse of before. She blushed.

"Brody, what happened to Mom and Robert?"

"Your mom was released and sent home, with a court order that she cannot contact you or come with a certain distance from you. The fellows and security here know that. Our police department has a copy of that. Seeing as you are now part of the Foundation family, you will be watched carefully."

"I don't like that feeling."

He grinned, even as he prepared their lunch. "It's in a good way, Kitten. They don't track you down and monitor your every move. They just watch for our vehicles, us, and make sure that we stay safe. It's how our town works." He turned, the knife that he was using to butter the bread for their sandwiches held up in the air.

"Okay. It's just strange." She looked up at him. "I'm angry about all this. Mom took so much, and I let her."

"You didn't know any different. Now that you do, you'll never let her again. I'll help to make sure of it." He sat, reaching for her hand before asking the blessing on their meal. "We'll talk, Kitten. I'm angry too, but there is something about what your Dad did that bothered me."

Ker didn't respond, not quite sure how to. She finally pushed back her plate and stood, wandering through the apartment, seeing the office that Brody had set up for himself, and then inspecting the bedrooms, before she returned to the living room and then headed for the balcony, finding a wicker rocker to sit in.

Brody stood and watched her, before he too sat in the matching wicker chair, his hand out for hers. "I love this balcony. I come out here to pray, to think, to meditate."

"It's a quiet place to do that. Brody, what did you mean about Dad's work?"

"I mean that we've been looking into it. It's not what it seems. I'm sorry, Kitten. I don't mean to put your parents down."

"I know, Brody. In the last six months or so, something changed with them. Mom became more angry and controlling. Dad didn't say anything, just let her. He was away more. What does that mean?"

"It means that the fellows will do more digging, trying to determine what has happened. To try and find out where the problems started." He tightened his grip on her hand. "And for you, it means that you heal. Not just physically. You have a lot of healing to do. And I am thankful God chose me to help you do just that."

A week later, Ker stood beside Cadee and Berneen in the lobby, watching as the men searched outside the area. Ker had received a text from her mother, threatening her. When it was traced, the signal came from the Foundation property. She was afraid but also angry. She couldn't see Brody and knew that he would be a target of her mother, her mother not liking being thwarted in her plans.

"Ker? Come. Let's sit." Berneen's arm around her drew her to a chair in the lobby. "Let's pray."

"I can't, Berneen. I am just so angry."

"We get that, Ker. We really do. We can still pray for you, and for the anger to leave." Cadee looked up as some of the other ladies approached.

"I know. I guess that I'm just not sure that I want to let it go. And I have to." Ker sighed, not sure how to word what she wanted to say.

"We get that, Ker." Hagen smiled at her. "We all went through anger when we had what we term as our adventures.

Brody turned as he heard a sound from behind him, ducking the fist heading for him. His own fist drove upwards and into the man's jaw, dropping him to the ground. Brody pulled the man's belt from him and tied his hands behind him, waving at Bradon as he approached.

"Is he the only one?"

"I don't think so. Security picked up on at least two on the cameras near the building." Bradon touched Kade's neck. "Okay, boy. Let's search." Kade gave a low woof and moved off, his hackles rising.

"He's found a trail."

"That he has." Bradon sent off a quick text. "Dallas is on his way out. He was anyway. He needs to talk to you two."

"Doesn't he always?" Brody paused, his eyes on Kade. "What's he doing?"

"He's found someone. That's his signal." Both men had kept their voices low. "Wait here, Brody. I'm going forward. I'll be back."

Brody waited, not liking the feeling that he was getting. He crept forward, suddenly not wanting to be on his own.

"Brody?"

"Bradon? What did you find?" Brody stared at the man lying in front of them.

"He was out when I got here. That's what was throwing Kade off."

"Who?"

"That I would like to find out. He's on our side, I would think." Bradon stood, his hand on Kade's head. "Okay, boy. Release." Kade relaxed, leaning into Bradon.

Ker's head was still down as the men returned to the lobby, the security guard unlocking the doors. She didn't hear the murmurs from the ladies or see Brody walking towards her. She jumped as she felt arms around her, her head whipping around to stare at Brody.

"Brody? I was so worried."

"It's okay, Kitten. We have the two men that were here. Dallas is outside. He'll be in shortly to talk to us."

"I don't understand, Brody. What happened?"

"What happened is that Brody took out one man. Kade alerted to the second one but someone beat us to him." Bradon sank down, Ennis perched on the arm of his chair. "It's so strange."

"It is. Someone was out there watching us. I don't like that feeling."

576

"Nor do I." Barnabas had approached, the rest of the men gathering around them. "Fellows, we'll be putting in more security once more. Make sure you know who's around you at all times. Ladies, I'll leave it to your fellows to figure out what you are going to do. I know we can't lock any of you up. It wouldn't work anyway." He turned and walked towards Dallas.

"Barnabas, we need to talk, but first I need to talk to Brody and Ker." Dallas was watching the couple.

"I know you do. Just so you know, I talked to her brother. He's safe and way from here. No one knows where he is."

"Okay. Just keep him there. Word on the street is that someone is after him as well as Ker."

"That's what I had heard." Barnabas nodded towards them. "Finish up with them, and then find me. I'll throw something on the grill and we can eat. We haven't done that in a while."

"Sounds good. I'm going off the clock once I finished with them."

Ker paced the apartment that night, worrying the bandages on her hand. Bradon had stepped out into the hall with Dallas, their conversation coming to her through the open door. What had Mom gone and done? She had been receiving messages from her and was just ignoring them. The anger in the content was growing. Her father had not been in touch, and that puzzled her. He always kept in touch with her, checking in three to four times a day.

"Ker? You okay?" Brody's arms came around her.

"I really don't know. I know that I am angry and I need to get rid of that. Brody? I haven't heard from Dad. Not in a couple of days." She looked up at him. "I haven't answered them. Mom keeps trying. But Dad always checks in during the day."

"I see. Dallas asked if we had seen him. They haven't been able to find him."

"Oh, no. What did she do?"

"Your mother? That's what we're looking into. The fellows are hard at work. I'll take you down to the conference room tomorrow and you can talk to them yourself."

Ker nodded. "Do you know if Keefe is okay?"

"He is. Barnabas talked to him today. No one has been around him."

"That's good." Her head went down on his shoulder and she just let him hold her, finding herself relaxing, and her anger abating. "Why do you calm me, Brody?"

"It's not me. It's God. I'm just a channel for Him to use." He dropped a kiss on her forehead. "How be you head off to bed? It's late and you're tired."

"I will. Thank you, Brody, for being who you are." She walked away, leaving him staring after her, a bemused look on his face.

Brody reached for his phone as it gave a muted ring. Dallas? He wasn't on duty and had just left.

"Dallas?"

"Brody. I'm heading back your way. Where's Ker?"

"I just sent her to bed."

"Keep her up. I need to talk to her."

Ker had returned, intent on asking Brody something, as he turned and reached out a hand for her.

"She's still up. Dallas, what is going on?"

"I'll explain when I get there. Keep your doors locked. And I mean them all, including your balcony door. Don't answer except for myself or one of the building people." Dallas' phone clicked off, leaving Brody heading to check the balcony doors.

Ker followed him, a puzzled look on her face. "Brody?"

"Dallas is on his way back. He wants us to lock ourselves in."

"But the balconies? They can't get up to them."

"Oh, but they can. Jaxcy and Brennen were kidnapped by men using the balcony."

Ker paled and then dropped to the couch. "I don't like this, Brody. You're scaring me."

He was beside her, a hand reaching for hers. "I don't mean to, Kitten. Let's pray until Dallas gets here."

Dallas tapped at their door, Barnabas and Brady with them, Buckley hurrying up to be with them. Brody stared at the four of them, concern on his face.

"Dallas? What's going on?"

"Let us in, Brody. We need to talk." Dallas' face was grim.

"We're in the living room." Brody watched as his friends seated themselves, Buckley raising a hand to indicate he wanted to pray. When they looked up, Brody's attention was on Dallas. "Dallas?"

"Brody. Ker. Have you heard from your father in the last few days?"

She shared a look with Brody. "No, I haven't and that's unusual. Not that I was answering his texts or voice mails. Why?"

"Because we found his car. It had been dumped near where you two were. It was burnt." Dallas' hand went up at her exclamation of shock. "No, he wasn't in it. We searching but with night coming on, it is tricky. We'll be taking in dogs in the morning. And that area is in our jurisdiction, just in case you wondered."

"It is? Then, you can investigate what happened to us?" Ker was puzzled. "I still don't get it."

"None of us do. We're working through what we know. We'll get it sorted out."

"But at what cost? I know enough to know someone will be seriously hurt or even killed. Mom threatened Brody with that."

"We know, Ker." Buckley's voice broke in. "What Dallas needs, I think, from you is a list of anyone that your father had problems with, no matter how small or minor it seems."

"Why do you ask?" Ker felt Brody's hand tightening on hers.

"We need to know if you have any idea of someone who would want to harm him. We need to track his last movements." Dallas frowned down at his notes. "Did you hear from him yesterday?"

"No, not since the day we married." Ker sank back against the couch. "What did she do?"

"What did who do?" Barnabas had a good idea of who she meant.

"Mom? What did she do?"

Dallas stared at her, puzzled for a moment, before he caught the look on Brody's face and then nodded. *He suspects something, doesn't he? Lord, I am getting tired of this. Fighting for my friends. Having them hurt, almost killed. Their ladies worried and hurt as well. How many more months and years can I do this?*

"Explain, please, Ker, if you will." Barnabas spoke up, Brady watching him intently.

"I'm not sure that I can. I'm sorry. Right now, I am so angry with her. She's damaged me without me being aware of that." Brody's hand tightened on hers again. "I am not aware of anyone who would want Dad hurt, or that he had run-ins with. I wasn't privy to that information. If there were any issues, they were never discussed in front of me. Keefe might know more than I did. Mom kept a tight control over what I did at the office, who I saw and when." She turned to look at Brody. "That's why I was surprised with Dad asked me to meet with you. He had never in the past."

"Do you think, then, it was planned for you to be on your own when the men came in?" Dallas shared a look with Brody.

Ker shrugged. "I have no idea. Dad had set up the appointment. Then, that morning, he just told me I was to meet with the new paralegal that was coming in. I was to go over the forms with him and find out what he would do to change them." She looked back up at Dallas. "The only one I knew that Dad had concerns about was the new lawyer in the law firm that he had dealt with for over twenty years. He wouldn't say why he all of a sudden pulled all the legal work from them."

"He did? That's something that he would not do under normal circumstances?"

Shaking her head, Ker watched Dallas closely, not seeing Buckley and Brady watching her. "No, he wouldn't. They were both adamant that they had to use that firm. I never felt comfortable around the men. I refused to go near them. In fact, I would leave the office if I knew they were coming. That was what was so unusual." She paused, thinking back over the week or so before that. "But then, Dad had not been himself for a week or so. I thought that he was worried about one of his contacts or someone that he was trying to find."

"That is possible." Dallas studied his notes. "Now, that day. I know that you have given me your statements. Have either one of you thought of anything?"

Brody spoke up. "I didn't see much, but it just seemed strange how we were just taken out there and dumped. Brandon and Benen said that they didn't see any vehicles in the area."

"And didn't you say it was in your jurisdiction? Why there?" Ker was puzzled but she was also angry. "Dallas, find these people. Find out why they did this. There has to be a reason."

"I am sure there is. We are hearing rumours on the street regarding you, Ker. I can't emphasize enough that you stay close to the building or if you are out, be aware of what is around you. Stay close to whoever it is you are with." Dallas rose, his thoughts dark. He had felt his phone vibrate and needed to take the message that he knew was waiting for him.

Brady and Barnabas walked out with him, their conversation quiet, as Dallas pulled out his phone. He sighed. He was to be off at midnight. That was not happening, not now.

"Brady, Barnabas. Make sure they stay close to someone. I need to run."

"We will." Brady watched him walk away. "I don't like that he left like that."

"No, but we have no idea why. All we can do is pray for him. And for Brody and Ker. She's seeking for freedom and peace, Brady."

"She is. I pray that she finds them. Catch you later." Brady walked away.

Barnabas hesitated and then headed for his office. He needed to talk to his father, but he knew his father was out west and not readily available for that very conversation.

Buckley had remained, talking with the couple, reading from the Testament that he pulled from his pocket, and then praying with them. He rose, his eyes on the wall in front of him, suddenly hesitant to leave, but not knowing what else to do.

"Thanks, Buckley. Your support of all of us is so appreciated." Brody walked out with him, shutting the door behind him. "I am afraid for her."

"I know that you are. I can feel that fear. She's afraid, too. What was that about her mother?"

"Her mother was or is rather controlling. Ker has been talking more and more as she finds release from that control. She is struggling with life-long emotions."

"I am sure she is. I will continue to pray. Come and find me if you need to talk."

"I will do that." Brody stood, his hand on the outside of his door, praying, before he entered, finding Ker standing waiting for him, coming readily into his open arms and welcoming his hug.

"Kitten? You okay?"

"I don't know, Brody. I just don't know. I hate this." Her voice was muffled against him.

"I know that you do. We'll make it through. I have no doubt about that. Here, head off to bed. The surgeon wants to see you tomorrow, doesn't he?"

"He does. I just don't get all this." She turned and walked away, her shoulders slumping in defeat.

Brody watched her walk away, his heart breaking for her, before he moved to clean up the mugs and whatnot from the coffee that they had shared with their friends. He walked through the apartment, checking doors and windows, turning off lights. He hesitated at Ker's bedroom before he entered, the light from the bedside lamp low. He stood, his head tilted, a sad smile on his face as he watched the tears creep down her face as she slept. He simply laid down beside her, pulling a blanket over himself, and cuddling her to him. Tonight, this was what she needed, to be held.

A week later, Ker turned from studying the roses in the rose garden. She had clipped a few to take up to the apartment, needing that today. She stopped as she saw the man waiting for her.

"Who are you?" Fear drove her anger.

"I'm here for you. You need to come with me."

"I don't think so. I'm not going anywhere with you."

"Oh, but I say you are. Your mother wants to speak with you."

Ker backed away, knowing that she was near the edge of the garden, and just might be able to escape and make her way back around to the building.

"Sorry. She can't contact me."

"That paper?" The man flicked his fingers. "That's nothing. She stated that you are to come with me and now."

"Sorry. She has no control over my movements. I'm married now."

"That's what you say. She says that you aren't." The man moved towards her.

Ker dropped her roses and dove behind a bush, her breath held as she crept away from the garden and then around to the edge of the walk, not seeing the man, but hearing his curses from behind her. She ran, her feet flying over the path, heading for the building, not sure if she would make it in time.

Blair had turned as he heard running footsteps and then held out his hand.

"Here, Ker. Let's get you inside. I don't like that you're running."

"Mom sent someone. He's behind me, I think."

"Okay. In you go. Head for your place."

"I will. Thank you, Blair." She ran, not waiting to see if the man had appeared.

Blair stepped back outside, his eyes searching but not seeing anyone. He frowned. Ker would not have been running like that if she hadn't been afraid. Benen appeared beside him.

"Blair?"

"Ker just ran back from the rose garden. She said her mother had sent someone to bring her to her."

"That's what we've been waiting for. Come on." Benen held up a hand. "There. Just behind the tall shrub. That's not one of us. I'll head this way. You go that way."

The strategy worked as they approached the man from either side, their hands on his arms preventing him from leaving. They directed him back to the building and to the security office. The patrol officer who responded just shook his head.

"Twister, what did you get involved in this time?"

The man, Twister his street name, simply refused to answer, knowing that if he did, he would be locked away for a long time. Maybe, he thought, if he didn't say anything, he would be out soon.

"He tried to kidnap Brody's wife. Her mother sent him. And there is a restraining order to keep her mother from contacting her." Benen spoke from behind the man.

"Is that right? Twister, it doesn't matter if you talk or not. With that, we can put you away. You're wanted for too many crimes."

Twister finally looked up, a whine in his voice as he spoke. "If I talk, what's in it for me?"

The officer just shook his head. "This time, Twister, that doesn't work. Out you go."

Benen finally tapped at Brody's door, Blair beside him. He could hear muttering as Ker approached the door.

"Ker? It's me, Blair. Benen is here as well."

She cracked open the door, only one eye visible. "I can see that. Are you sure?"

"Sure about what?" Benen grinned, having seen her sense of humour before.

"That's is just you. That no one is hiding behind you somewhere."

"Nope. It's just us. Oh! And Brody." Benen grinned at Brody as he approached. "Brody, will you ask your wife if we can come in? We've asked politely but she has refused to open the door."

"I'd refuse to open the door to you as well if I was Ker. But since I'm not and we're friends, I'll let you in." Brody grinned as he moved past them, his arms out for Ker. He had received her panicked text and headed home as soon as he explained to his employer. Ker didn't understand, he didn't think, that their employers didn't pay their wages.

"Ker, what did you do to these two?"

"Me?" Ker's voice rose in frustration. "I did nothing. It was that man."

"Man? What man?" Brody sobered instantly.

"The man who tried to take me to Mom. Does she not get it? That I want nothing to do with her." She glared at the other two men as they tried to cover their snickers. "I'm so glad that you find this funny."

Benen's grin grew. "Ker, you are so good for us all. We need that refreshing voice that you bring to the family." Then, he sobered. "Twister, as he is called, was brought in by her mother, Brody, to bring her back to her. Between Blair and I, we managed to stop him from leaving."

"Thank you. I'm glad no one was harmed."

Blair shook his head. "She doesn't give up very easily. Ker, what is it that you know?"

"I'm sorry?"

"Do you know something or someone that you're not supposed to? It seems to me that it is going well beyond just control for her." Blair tried to be polite, not saying what he really felt.

"I wish I knew. I didn't meet anyone. They kept me in the office. Any meetings were after hours." She twisted to stare up at Brody. "So, why did Dad arrange for you to come in the daytime?"

"Trying to protect you? Give you a way out of the business and the building?" Benen had been brainstorming with the others. "We've been doing some research, Ker. That research? We need to talk to you about, but some of your father's work has not been real legal."

"It hasn't? Then, that's why." Her anger flared and then died away. "Getting angry doesn't help, does it? So, what do I seek for then?"

"Peace. Understanding. A closer walk with God." Benen raised a hand as she went to protest. "I know, Ker. You're trying all that, but sometimes we try too hard. We need to just be still and let God work. Sometimes, we go through things that we won't expect. Know that we are praying for both you and Brody."

——

Twister refused to cooperate with the investigators, frustrating Dallas, who finally just shut the door to the interrogation room and walked away. He has to know more, Dallas thought, but how do we reach him. He had been working away, bringing his notes up to date on all his cases, when a sudden commotion roused him from his computer. He was on his feet, out of his door, and heading for the cells.

"What is going on?" He stopped one of the officers running towards him.

"Someone got to Twister. He's dead."

"What? I talked to him, what an hour ago? How did that happen?"

"That's what we don't know. We pulling surveillance tapes now."

Dallas nodded. "Let me know what you find out. Right now, I have to tell a friend and his wife that the man who tried to abduct her is dead." He turned as Will Peters, the police chief, stopped beside him.

"Dallas?"

"It's Twister."

"Twister? When did we arrest him?"

"Earlier today. He tried to abduct Brody's Ker."

"What are you talking about?" Will pointed to the break room. "In here. I need my coffee and you look like you could use one too. Fill me in. And who is Ker?"

"That's right. You've been away on vacation. Brody's married. And her name is Ker." Dallas explained in a few succinct sentences what was going on. "Today, Twister appeared on the Foundation property and tried to get Ker to go with him. She outwitted him and ran for the building. Blair and Benen managed to trap him."

"And now he's dead? Is that what you're saying?"

"It is. Her mother is the one who hired him."

"Her mother? What was her last name?"

"Deeks. Her father ran a private investigations business. Ostensibly, it was run to go in and find missing and exploited children and teens. But we're finding out that there was a lot more to it than that. And now, her father is missing. We found his vehicle, burned, near where Brody and Ker were dumped."

"I see." Will rubbed at his head. "It doesn't pay to take a vacation. Too much happens when you're away."

Dallas laughed before he sobered. "That's true. I need to call Brody. I fear for them."

"I know what you mean, Dallas. Keep me up to speed, please."

"That I will. Oh, her father? He was friends with Bruce Carey."

"He was? Well, that certainly puts a wrinkle in it, doesn't it?"

Setting his phone done carefully, Brody rose from his desk chair, looking for Ker, finding her curled up on the couch, wrapped in a blanket, staring at the bandage on her hand.

"When does the bandage come off?" Brody dropped down beside her, an arm around her.

"In a couple of weeks. The surgeon thinks that it is healing well. Brody, who was that you were speaking with? Or shouldn't I ask?" She tucked her head up under his chin, finding comfort in that.

"Dallas. He had some bad news. Twister was killed tonight in the jail."

"He was? That's so sad. He never had a chance, did he?"

"No, I don't think he did. I mean, he made his choices in life, but it still doesn't mean that he had to die this way." Brody grew silent, content just to sit and hold his lady. "What are your thoughts about all this?"

"I'm just so confused, Brody. Everything that I have known all my life has been upturned. What if Dad is dead? Would Mom do that?"

"I don't know, Kitten. We don't know that your father is dead."

"I think that he is. Where they found his vehicle and where we were dumped? There are a lot of abandoned wells from old cottages. I'm surprised that they didn't drop us down into one."

"They could have, but I think that you'll find God intervened in that. I am still puzzled by that."

"I know. Did they take us as a threat towards Mom and Dad? Or did Mom arrange that as a threat against Dad?" Ker drew a deep breath. "Then, maybe something I overheard about a month ago and shrugged off makes sense."

"And that would be?"

"Dad and Mom were fighting, real angry words. He had accused her of stepping in on a case, making it impossible for him to reach the children that he needed to. They were gone when he got there. Mom had prevented him from leaving the day that he should have. What if Mom was playing both sides all along, and Dad found out?"

"That's a possibility. I can say that the fellows have thought of that, and are busily researching it."

"They are? No one said anything."

"No, they didn't, but from now on, we will. We just needed to make sure of our facts. After all, it is your family."

"A family that has held me back all my life." She sighed. "Brody, isn't tomorrow your potluck dinner?"

"It is. Why?"

"What do we take?"

"This time? It's our turn to bring a dessert. I have some squares in the freezer that I'll pull out unless you want to make something."

"No, it's okay. It's dressy, isn't it?"

"What do you mean?"

"I mean, dress clothes, and all that."

"Kitten, it's not. We are casual. Jeans, T-shirts. Some of the ladies wear those leggings that you seem so thrilled to find out that you like. Buckley quite often will appear in shorts and a polo shirt."

"Oh, I see." She shifted. "I would have dressed up in nice slacks, blouse, and heels. And been totally out of place."

"If you had dressed that way, then I would have been in dress slacks, dress shirt, tie, suit, whatever would make you comfortable."

"You would do that?"

"I would, Kitten. You are that important to me." He didn't say and wouldn't, not yet, that he was head over heels in love with her. He just prayed that she would respond when the time was right for him to tell her of his love.

<hr>

Three days later, Brody opened the door to the conference room, not surprised to find eleven other men there. Barnabas was involved in meetings, and Breck was out of town that day. He set down the mug of coffee that he was carrying, walking over to study the map.

"Do we have the location right?" Brendon approached him.

"You do. I don't get it. Why out there?"

"That's what we are working on."

"Ker said that there are a lot of abandoned wells out there." Brody paled. "How many? And is her father in one of them?" His voice was barely audible.

"Brody? Do you know what you just said?" Brendon looked around, finding the other men watching them.

"I do. I fear that is exactly where he is. How do we prove or disprove it?"

"I take Kade out. Do we have something that we can use to search from?" Bradon stood beside him, a hand on his shoulder.

"I'm not sure. Not likely. But we do need to search. With the search team?"

"Of course. I'll set it up."

"I won't say anything to Ker, not yet." Brody's body sagged for a moment, the sorrow he was anticipating dragging it down. "She is going through so much with her mother. She thinks that her mother had her father killed."

"That's what our feelings are." Bradon's hand tightened on his friend's shoulder. "We'll search, Brody. I'll talk to Dallas."

"Ker is scared. She's not saying much." Brody sighed. "This is wearing on her. To find out her mother has tried to have her abducted twice, charged in that, the man who tried to abduct her killed."

"We know, Brody." Buckley spoke from beside him, his eye on his friend. "Does she need to talk to someone?"

Brody shrugged. "She might. Right now, she's just trying to make sense of what happened." He shot a glance towards the door. "What I am about to say is more on the lines of a prayer request. She said her mother held her back all her life, told her what to wear, where to work. Chose her friends. She didn't realize how bad it was until now."

"And she's not sure what to do with all her freedom?" Blair shook his head. "And how does she feel about our ladies?"

Brody shared a look with him. "She is so glad to have them here. She feels overwhelmed at times, not sure how to approach them. Can I suggest that they just continue what they have been doing? Include her if that's what she wants."

"That they will do." Blair paused. "Devaney is quite concerned."

"I saw that." Brody paused, not wanting to break a confidence. "She's really not sure about her dress and what to wear when. If one of the ladies would help her out?"

"They will do that, and in a way that she would never know." Benen spoke from where he was standing beside Blair. "Cadee is quite taken with her."

"Ker has spoken about Cadee, wishing that she had had a friend like that years ago." Brody turned to face the room. "Now, where do we stand on the research?"

"About there." Burnie grinned at him. "We're finding all sorts of wonderful things about your in-laws. Her brother is still up north, I think?"

"I have no idea. Dallas has him stuck away somewhere, and isn't telling." Brody slid into the chair he usually used, reaching to boot up his computer. "What do we know about this Twister?"

"Nasty person, he was. Into a lot of stuff that would curl your hair." Baird sat beside Brody. "Here. This is for you and Ker. Read through it, talk it over, and then talk to one of us. It details a lot of what he was doing, and a lot of it was for her mother. Her father seems to have been on the edge of it all."

"So, if he found out and tried to stop her?" Brandon left his sentence unfinished.

"Would she remove him?" Brendon picked up the thought. "Somehow, I think that she would. I was out to her hometown yesterday, Brody, and spoke with some of the merchants in town. Her mother is not liked. Her father was to some degree. Everyone knew what her mother was up to."

"How involved was the police force?"

"Some of them very much involved." Brendon slid another file folder towards him. "Ask her about these officers. See what her reaction is."

"You're throwing a lot at us." Brody glanced through the files, a grim look crossing his face.

"We are, Brody, just like we did for the others." Buckley looked up from where he was seated. "We need to dig deep on this one. I called Emma but she's away. Jace is working on something that has priority over everything else. He said they'd look at it as soon as they could."

Brody sighed. "That's all we can ask." He dropped his head onto his hand. "How do I keep her safe? She's finding her freedom and I can't fence her in, no matter the risk. And I can't be with her all the time."

"No, you can't. We'll pick up where we can. Our ladies will help. If she's out and about on the grounds, the security team has volunteered to trail her. There have also been calls from Dallas with names of officers if we need them."

———

595

"That's good." Brody answered absentmindedly, his thoughts already on the file he was reading.

Throwing his truck into park a day later, Brody flung open his door and ran for the building. He hit the stairs still on a run, not waiting for the elevator. He fumbled with his keys, dropping them repeatedly before he was able to unlock the door and throw it open. Searching frantically for Ker, Brody stood in the hallway, not seeing her anywhere. Where is she, Lord? Where is she? I got her text message and now she's not here.

He paced back to the door, stepping into the hallway, finding Ker running down it, heading for him. He simply stood, his arms open, his stance widened as she hit him full force, tears streaming down her face. His face on her hair, Brody watched as Cadee and Ennis approached, worry on their faces.

"What happened, Ker?"

"Mom was here. I could hear her at the door. How did she get in?" Ker leaned back, staring up at him. "Cadee and Ennis were here. Cadee checked to make sure the way was clear and took me to their apartment, to wait for you. What did she want?"

"I don't know, my love, but she's not to be here. Ladies, did you see her?"

"We did. We peeked out after Ker did. She was smart, Brody. She didn't answer the door and kept really quiet as she looked out." Ennis rubbed at Ker's back. "Now, what do we do? How do we keep you safe?"

"That's what I would like to know." Ker hugged Brody tighter. "I can't do much more of this, Brody. This is how she is. She keeps hitting at you until you give in."

"But you see, you have secret weapons. You have all of us here, the police force, friends who will step in." He looked up at the ladies waiting. "Ladies, how be you find all the rest of you and come back? We need to make some plans. The fellows have been working on something, but you ladies need to be in on this."

———

"How be we meet in the conference room? An unscheduled potluck dinner sounds good to me." Ennis grinned. "And no, Ker, you don't have to bring anything, except yourself. And Brody, if you want to." She waved as she walked away, Cadee beside her, Brody's laughter following them.

"Did she really do that? Plan a meal without asking anyone else?" Ker was dumbfounded, staring after her friends.

"She did. It's what we do. It's not the first time that we have met like this, researching and planning, with the ladies planning a meal for us. Come on. I need to change and you need to find that cup of tea that I know you didn't finish."

Ker sighed. "No, I didn't finish it." She made no move from his arms, and he made no move to release her.

He finally turned them to the apartment. "As much as I enjoy having you in my arms, we do need to meet with the others."

Ker just looked at him, not quite sure what he meant before she headed for her neglected cup of tea, not caring that it was cold, her thoughts on Brody, and just what he had meant. She knew in her heart that he was the knight that she had dreamed about, that she was falling in love with him. Her hand paused as it set her cup down. Did he really call me his love? Lord, did I hear right? If I did, then we need to talk, don't we? Protect him, dear Lord. Let no harm come to him.

Watching the men closely as she helped to clear up from the meal, Ker frowned. They were joking and teasing one another, even as they bent over files or stared at computer screens. She could see Barnabas and Brady at the map, pointing at different areas.

Imly had been watching her. "Not used to this?"

Ker shook her head. "It seems like chaos, to tell you the truth."

"Organized chaos. They do this, teasing one another, just to relieve the stress. Soon, they'll be bouncing ideas and thoughts off one another. They work well together. God brought them together, years ago, and it has been a blessing to all of us."

"That He did, Ker." Devaney took the tray out of Ker's hands. "Each of the men, with the exception of Breck and Barnabas, are from each of the other provinces and territories. Those two are from Ontario, this area, and have been friends for life. Barnabas searched for these fellows, watching them, finding out about them, before he offered them employment and a home. God had to be the one making the decision, he said. It was God who has led them here."

"They all have unique talents. Not just in their work. They also volunteer." Berneen snapped the lid back on a casserole dish. "Your Brody? Did he tell you that he tutors preteens in English? No? He does. He doesn't like a lot of praise, but we hear talk from them. The parents are blessed with his compassion for the young ones."

"He did hint at that." Ker leaned back against the table. "But what do I do? I can't go back to where I was. Not that I want to."

"Take your time to make a decision. Talk to Brody. Talk to anyone of us. Talk to Breck or Barnabas. As for now, enjoy the time that you are not working." Fynn pointed to her hand. "That still needs to heal, doesn't it?"

"It does." Ker sighed. "I just wish things were different."

"We all have had that wish, Ker." Hagen spoke up. "All of us."

———

Brody stared at the man blocking his path before he moved backward. He didn't know him, but he didn't think the man was there for the good of Brody's health. Coming to an abrupt halt as he felt something poke him in his back, his hands raised.

"I think you have the wrong person. I don't have anything that you would want."

"On the contrary, Mr. Corcoran, you do. We need you to have Ker come here. And now." The man facing him approached to stand with two feet of him.

"No, not happening. I won't bring her here." Driven to his knees by the vicious blow to his back, Brody drew in as deep a breath as he could. "Was that really necessary?"

"Absolutely. You need to cooperate with us, Mr. Corcoran. Bring Ker here." The man repeated his request, studying his fingernails on his right hand as he did so.

"I told you. That's not happening."

Five minutes later, the second man stepped away from Brody, staring down at the bloodied body in front of him, tucking away the brass knuckles that he had used on Brody.

"That didn't work. He just wouldn't cooperate with us."

"No, he wouldn't." The first man looked around before he turned away. "I told her that it wouldn't."

"Ker is too well protected." The second man stared back at Brody. "You know, is the pay really worth it?"

"I know what you mean." The first man turned, before he searched for a payphone, making an anonymous call about a man down. "Let's hit the road. I hear the weather out west is better for our health."

"She'll track us down." The man slipped into the seat of the car.

"Not if we're careful. I have a stash of aliases that we can use. Let's pack what we need and blow this town."

Brady drew in a deep breath as he approached Brody, his eyes finding those of his partner, Patrick.

"Brody? What on earth? Brady?" Patrick was on his knees beside Brody, Brady on the other side.

"Whoever did this worked him over well." Brady studied him. "And not with his fists."

Dallas had heard the call and headed their way. He studied his friend. "Brass knuckles."

"Brass knuckles? They still use them?" Patrick's comment was low, even as he and Brady worked to stabilize Brody. "Where all is he hurt?"

"A better question would be where isn't he." Brady rolled Brody to one side, a deep groan coming from his friend. "His back is really bruised." He slipped the shirt back down. "Okay, when you're ready, let's move him and get him in. Dallas? Ker?"

"I'll call Breck. Have him bring her in." Dallas paused. "They'll need an escort."

"Have the patrol vehicle meet them on the way in. I won't want to answer to Ker if she's delayed waiting for that."

Dallas stared at him. "Just what does that mean?"

"You didn't hear? Apparently, she was ticked off at Brody when Brandon and Benen found them. She threw her shoes at him. So, I wouldn't want to be the one not telling her right away." The men moved away, their equipment boxes gathered up, Brady's eye on Brody, watching him closely.

Answering her door, Ker stared at Breck and then Ennis.

"Come in, you two. What can I do for you?"

Breck stepped inside, his frown deepening. "We need you to come with us, Ker. Brody has been hurt. Dallas is sending a patrol car to meet us."

"Brody? I just spoke with him, about twenty minutes ago. How could that be?" Ker refused to move.

"Ker, we need you to move and move now. Brody is on his way to the hospital. Brady is with him. Dallas would not be sending out a car unless he felt it was urgent and necessary."

Ker's face paled. "She got to him! I hate her!" She turned and ran for a jacket, and her purse, struggling to pull on sneakers as she returned. "Well? What are we standing here for? Are you driving?" She pulled the door closed, locking it, and then running for the stairs.

Breck stared after her, shooting a look at Ennis. "Is she for real?"

"Oh, yeah! Hurry, Breck. She just might jimmy open the doors on your truck, hotwire it, and take off." Ennis ran after Ker, finding her waiting just inside the lobby door.

"Well? Is he coming or are you driving?"

Ennis broke out into laughter. "Ker, even in your fright, you are just too funny for words. Here he is. Quick. I told him that you'd jimmy the lock and hotwire his truck."

"You did what?" Ker stared at her before shooting a look at Breck. "You know, I just might do that."

Ker was out of the truck and running for the door to the hospital before Breck could even come to a full stop, Ennis behind her. He shook his head, found a parking spot, and ran after them. Dallas met him just inside the door, pointing to the examination rooms.

"She's back there already. Doc was watching for her."

"He was? Good. Any word?"

"Not a lot. He's been beaten badly, Breck. And not with just fists."

"No?" Breck's eyes slid closed. "Don't tell me."

"I won't, then. We both know what was used. Doc's not saying much, nor did Brady. I'll keep an officer with him for now."

"Ker won't leave him. I can guarantee you that. If we try, she'll hide somewhere and sneak back to be with him."

"That's our assessment. We'll clear it." Dallas watched as Ennis returned, walking towards them. "Ennis?"

"She's with him. She made me leave." Ennis brushed a tear away. "He looks awful, Breck."

"I'm sure he does. Here, have a seat. I'll send out a text and let them know what's going on. Dallas?"

"I've been called to another case. I'll touch base when I can. Have Ker call me with any news." Dallas walked away, his heart sore for his friend and his wife. Why, Lord? I just don't get it. Not anymore. I just don't understand the evil that's out there today, and touching so many of my friends.

———

Her hand resting on Brody's cheek, feeling the stubble on it, the cuts and scrapes from his beating, Ker blinked back tears. I don't get it, Lord. Why? She bent to drop a kiss on his cheek, before she raised back up, to stand watching him.

Doc stood watching her in turn before he nodded. Anna was right, once more. She had insisted that the young couple were in love, just not ready to let each other know. This may do it, Anna. And Lord, he's going to need a real touch of the hem of the Master's garment. I haven't seen someone beaten like this in a while.

Doc's arm around her shoulders startled Ker for a moment before she relaxed against him. Doc had become like a father to her, and she needed that father right now.

"Doc?" Her voice was a mere whisper.

"He's hurt bad, Ker. Has anyone talked to you? No? Then, I guess I must. Dallas has confirmed from what he's seen that brass knuckles were used. We can see the marks that they left. That being said, we need to talk about his injuries."

"Is he going to die, Doc? I can't handle it if he does. I won't want to live if he does." Ker didn't take her gaze from Brody.

"No, but he will need time to heal. For starters, he has massive bruising all over. His kidneys are bruised, and we need to watch them. His liver has a laceration. But it's his spleen. He's bleeding from it."

"And you need to go in and remove it?"

"That's what the surgeon is deciding now. We will make no decision without talking with you first. Is someone with you?"

Ker nodded. "Ennis was with Breck. She's in the waiting room." Her voice died away. Doc could barely hear her next comment. "And this is when I could really use my Mom. Only Mom is the one who did this."

Doc hugged her to him. "Let me call Anna for you."

Ker nodded. "Thank you."

Anna approached her, much as Doc had, not saying anything, just gathering her close, holding her as she would her own daughter. She felt the shudders and then the sobs as Ker broke down. Breck's hand on Anna's back directed the ladies to a chair. He watched, compassion on his face before he looked up. Anger took over for a moment, before he turned, finding the men of the building standing around him.

"Who?" Brendon spoke for the group.

"Her mother, we think. The man or men who did this were long gone." Breck frowned. "It was strange. There was an anonymous call that came in from a payphone."

"Guilty conscience?" Buckley held up hope.

"Possibly. Right now, Brody is headed for surgery. Ker needs us. Where do we stand with the investigation?"

"Not where we need to be. That's a given." Brandon paced, a prayer raising for his friend.

"What do we do now, then? Seek until we find the answers?" Burnie spoke up. "It's like trying to solve one of those puzzles that have only one solution and we don't know how to find it."

Brennen stared at him. "Burnie, how do you do it? You just said the magic words."

"I did? And what would that be?"

"A puzzle. Like in a logic problem. What we need to do is draw up one of those diagrams and work it like you would one of those problems." Brennen's eyes had lit up.

"I see what you mean. Of course, it's a puzzle. They all are." Burnie paced before he drew out a pad of paper and clicked his pen to open it. "Okay, so we brainstorm. We'll have some time. We split up in teams like we usually do."

The men worked away, quiet conversation among them, glancing up every once in a while to check on Ker. Buckley sat for the longest time, his eyes closed, his heart hurting for his friends. Why, Lord? I don't get it. Not at all. How do we trust? How do we seek to find the answers? I know You care, that You will heal. It's just so hard to see this young lady hurting and hurting because of her family.

Ker sat, her eyes on the door to the operating room that she could barely see around the corner, her cheeks wet with her tears. Anna's arm was around her, her hand in Ennis' as they sat with her, whispered prayers murmured every once in a while. The other ladies had been in and out, checking on her, whispering a prayer or a Bible verse. She had simply nodded, her eyes not moving.

How long, Lord, just how long do I have to wait? It's not fair and it's not right. I hate my mother for this, and that I know I shouldn't do. How do I forgive when she has caused so much hate and destruction? The men don't have to say. I can read it on their faces. She sank back, her hand reaching for the bottle of water Fynn was handing her, to simply twist it in her hands.

Doc watched for a while before he returned to his duties. He never understood how families could hurt one another like this. He saw it all too frequently in the Emergency Department. He had had a quick word with the surgeon, whose grim look had not boded well for Brody.

Hours later, Ker was on her feet, moving rapidly towards the surgeon as he appeared, pulling the surgical cap from his head, his mask tucked down under his chin.

"Doctor? How is he?"

"He's in recovery, Ker. May I call you that?" At her nod, he continued. "We had to resect the spleen. That is, we had to remove it. He can live without it, just needs to take precautions, that's all. The liver laceration was not as bad as we feared. It will heal on its own. The kidneys are bruised. Those we need to watch. Overall, considering the beating that he took, I was surprised not to find more internal bleeding."

"I'm not. God had His hand on him."

"If you say so. Now, he's in recovery right now. Once we can stabilize him more, we'll move him to a room. Likely ICU for the night. And yes, you can see him once we get him moved." He looked around the room, surprised to find himself the centre of attention from so many eyes. "These people are with you?"

"They are. For all intents and purposes, they are my family and Brody's. Just don't take too long to get me to him." Ker moved away, back towards Anna who had stood, ready to hug Ker to her again.

"Ker?"

"He's in recovery. Lost his spleen. Needs to be careful. He's going to ICU soon." She looked around at the room, not surprised at the silence. "Thank you. Thank you for being here. Thank you for the support. Thank you for praying." Her legs gave way, Brennen there to catch her and help her to a chair. "I don't know why I did that."

"Release of stress. It happens, Ker." Brennen crouched in front of her, taking the bottle of juice handed him to give to her. "Here. Drink this. And drink all of it. You need it."

"Yes, boss." Ker drank deeply, her eyes closed, not seeing the grins on the faces of the men. They were beginning to understand how she thought.

Searching for Ker the next afternoon, Dallas finally found her in the waiting room of the surgical floor, standing in front of a window. Her stature was hunched, and he could see the hurt in it. He sighed. Why, Lord, again he questioned. What do they want from her?

"Ker?" Dallas gently touched her shoulder. "Is Brody worse?"

Ker shook her head, her hair moving with the motion. She pulled at a lock. "I used to wear my hair in a braid or a ponytail all the time. Mom made me. It became just too hard to fight her on it. I don't know. Brody likes it down." She looked up at him, a lost little girl look in her eyes. "Why is she like this, Dallas? Have you found out yet?"

"Not yet. Here, Ker. Sit. First, tell me about Brody."

Folding her arms around herself, Ker shuddered. "He's back in surgery, Dallas. They did some sort of imaging this morning and found something or other bleeding. The surgeon didn't think that they could wait."

"Oh, Ker! And you've been here on your own?" At her nod, he shook his head. "Let me call one of the ladies for you." He looked up. "Wait. Here are Ennis and Devaney. They will sit with you."

"Thank you. I didn't want to bother anyone." Her voice was almost too low to hear.

"It is never a bother, Ker. We are family." Ennis hugged her and sat beside her. "Now, Dallas is here. Did he say why?"

Ker stared at her and then at Dallas. "No, he hasn't. I don't think he's here for his own health."

Dallas stared at her before he shook a finger at her, a grin briefly appearing on his face. "Behave, Mrs. Corcoran."

Ker blushed and then spoke, a wistful tone to her voice. "I think you are one of the first to address me as that. It's like it never happened." Her voice faltered. "Do you know where Keefe is?"

"I do. And you want to talk to him? I can see what I can arrange about that. He's one I needed to talk to you about today."

"How deep is he into all this?"

"Not at all. Just like you. He didn't know anything. He knew about the threats and packages but not what your mother was up to. He told me that your father insisted that he take the two weeks off that he did."

"Dad did? And he called in Brody on a pretence. I understand that now. He was protecting us. How much does he know?"

"That we will ask him when we find him."

"And just how sure are you that he is alive?"

Dallas pulled out his phone and sorted through his photos, pausing at one. "I am going to show you a photo, Ker. I need you to tell me if you recognize it."

Ker took his phone, her eyes searching his for a moment before she looked down. Her fingers covered her trembling lips even as she blinked back tears. "Dad! What did she do?"

"You confirm that this is your father?" Ker nodded at his question. "He was found about one hundred miles from here, unconscious and with no identification on him. I have been in touch with a detective there. Your father is still unconscious, but we have now placed him under police guard."

Ker's face hardened. "She just doesn't stop. Do we even know why?"

"We are working on that, Ker. Trying our best to solve it. The fellows are working on a thought that one of them had. It may take some time, but we will get there."

"I know. I just don't know how much time we'll have. That's the thing." Ker was on her feet, moving towards the surgeon as he approached.

"Ker? These are friends of yours?" He nodded towards the group.

"They are. That's the police detective." Ker looked back at them. "You can talk in front of them if you like."

"I would. I also need to sit for a few moments. I have been here doing surgeries since midnight."

"You have? That's not good." Ker sat, waiting for him to speak, Ennis and Devaney reaching for her hands.

"How are you holding up, Ker, first of all?"

She shrugged. "I have no idea. I'm here where I need to be. And I am scared. Scared for Brody. Scared that my mother or one of her henchmen will appear."

"And that is an issue?"

"It is. She's the one responsible for this. For putting Brody in there. For making my father and brother disappear from my life. What else would you like to know?"

The surgeon, Dr. Wight, just shook his head. "We'll take precautions for you and Brody, Ker. Now about Brody. We went in, as we told you we had to, to find the bleeding. It was from the liver laceration. We've done what we need to for now. We'll wait for a day or so, and redo the imaging for him."

"And if he's still bleeding?"

"That we will address as we need to. For now, he is stable. We'll monitor him. Give us about an hour, and then the nurse will come for you. He's in recovery right now."

"Thank you, Dr. Wight. You are a blessing from God." Ker's words startled the surgeon as he stood, and he studied her for a moment before he turned and walked away with a thoughtful look on his face.

Finally back beside Brody, Ker watched as he moved restlessly before she reached to lay a hand on his shoulder. His movements stopped for a moment before his head began to toss and turn.

She bent closer to try and understand what he was muttering, her face paling as she did so. He had been beaten because he refused to bring her to the men? Anger once more surged through her and then faded. Lord? I am trying to forgive, but it's hard. I need to seek for Your peace but it's just not so easy. I need to hear Brody's prayers for me, for us. And I can't. Lord, please? Heal my husband.

She bent close again, to lay her cheek against his, finding that gesture stilled him. She stayed like that even as she continued to pray before she dropped a kiss on his cheek and whispered that she needed him. He had all of her love, and she wanted to grow old with him.

An hour later, Brody's eyes flickered as he fought his way out of the darkness towards the light flickering between his eyelids. He finally managed to open them, his gaze wandering across the ceiling and then around the room. Disoriented, he tried to raise himself but his pain kept him flat on the bed. A groan came from him, and he looked around to see who had groaned.

Ker was on her feet, her hand reaching for his, her eyes watchful, even as Brody's gaze found hers.

"Hi! Do I know you?" Brody's voice was hoarse.

Ker just shook her head. "You should. We married."

"Married? No, I don't think so. I'm tired. And why am I in a hospital room?" Brody's head moved restlessly until Ker placed her hand back against his cheek.

"Because you were beaten severely. You've had surgery, Brody. And you can't be moving around."

"I will if I want to." Brody pulled himself upright despite her protests, an arm clamped around his abdomen before he fell back. "I hurt."

"Yes, you do. You have had major surgery, twice in the last day. So, stay still." Ker was getting angry with him and then relaxed. It wasn't his fault, now was it?

Brody's eyes closed as he drifted off, his hand reaching for hers, his grip tight. She just shook her head and then looked behind her. There was no way that she could reach her chair, and he was just not letting go of her.

Breck studied the couple for a moment from where he stood in the doorway, shaking his head finally as he walked towards them. He reached to pull Ker's chair closer, earning himself a soft thank you.

"He's been awake?"

"He has." Breck grinned at the disgruntled tone. "He says that we're not married. And then he wanted to get up."

Breck's head tilted as he studied their linked hands. "He may have said that. I know that he doesn't handle coming around from anesthesia too well. But that grip on your hand? That tells me that he doesn't want you to move away from him. He may not say it in words, Ker, but he is deeply in love with you."

"He is? I need to hear it. Actions don't prove anything, not lately." Ker was disheartened but also cheered by Breck's words.

Brody had awakened once more, listening to the voices, Ker's voice calming him even with the frustration he could hear in it. Breck was right, he thought. I don't do anesthesia well.

Breck caught a slight movement on Brody's part and his attention shifted to him.

"Brody? You awake?"

"I am. What do you want?"

"Nothing much. Just wanted to see how you were faring. I hear tell you are giving the love of your life a hard time." Breck just grinned at the frown Ker sent his way.

"I am? I wouldn't do that." Brody's eyes opened again, and he squinted in the light. "Where am I again?"

"In the hospital, my friend. Someone beat you up pretty badly."

"Is that why I hurt? I don't remember much." Brody suddenly jerked upright. "They wanted me to bring Ker to them. I couldn't do that. I need to find her."

"She's right here, my friend. You're holding pretty tight to her hand." Breck laughed at the expression on Brody's face. "It's okay, Brody. Lay back down. We don't want you to undo all the stitches that the surgeon decided you needed."

"Stitches? I don't do stitches. I thought I told you that."

"You might have but they didn't have much choice. Ker, make him lie still, will you? I have a meeting to get to but I'll be back. I'll let the others know that Brody is awake and running true to form." Breck's laughter sounded behind as he left.

Ker stared after him, knowing he wasn't laughing at them or making fun of them before she felt a tug on her hand. She turned back, to find Brody watching her intently.

"Ker? Are you okay?"

"I am now. An hour ago, you told me that you weren't married."

"I did? I certainly didn't mean that. You are the one I love, Ker. No other. I'm sorry if I made you sad." Brody watched as she frowned at him.

"Not sad, Brody. Mad. Mad at my mother for all this."

"I know, Kitten. I know." He tugged at her hand even as he reached to raise the head of the bed. "No, don't stop me. I need to sit up." He wrapped her in his arm, his head on hers. "What all have you been told?"

———

613

"About you? That you no longer have a spleen, that the liver laceration had to be dealt with again this morning, that your kidneys are bruised. Not to say anything about all the other bruises and cuts."

"I'll get better. But have you heard anything else?"

"Dallas was around. He has talked to Keefe, who knows nothing of what was going on. Keefe told Dallas that Dad made him take those two weeks of vacation. And then he called you in. He was trying to protect us, wasn't he?"

"I think he was. He must have found out something and knew you two were in danger."

"And Dallas has found Dad. He was found unconscious somewhere with no identification on him. Dallas had me identify him from a picture." Her head went against Brody even as she struggled with her tears. "Why, Brody? I just don't get it."

"I don't either. The fellows are working on something, that much I know. How long am I in here for?"

"Dr. Wight didn't say. I wish this was over, Brody."

"I do too. I have a beautiful lady right here beside me that I want to live life with and right now we can't."

"We can, Brody. We can." Ker turned to him. "I refuse to let her win, to dictate how I live my life anymore. Breck questioned me this morning about my hair, for some reason. I realized then that what I was doing was following Mom's rules for me. It's not how I want to live. I don't like dressing up and being on stage all the time. That's how she made me feel."

Brody hugged her tighter to him, not letting her see his grimace of pain. "Then, we take back your life and make it our life. We start today, my love."

Her arms wrapped around herself, Ker stood in their kitchen doorway two days later, her eyes on Brody. She could hear the quiet conversation behind her from Cadee and Guenivere, as they moved about, preparing a meal, putting away what they didn't need that had been delivered by the building family. She sighed. Brody was being typical, she thought, not wanting help but needing it.

"I don't want to lie down." Brody was protesting, his finger pointing to the living room. Brandon and Buckley exchanged glances and shook their heads.

"You need to rest, Brody. That's what the surgeon said. As in bed. Lying down." Brandon tried to steer his friend that way as both he and Buckley held him upright by their grasps on his arms.

"Absolutely not." Brody finally shrugged off their hands, wrapping an arm around himself, and shuffling to the living room, to drop down on the couch, his eyes closing from pain and fatigue. "I'm sorry, fellows. I know that you're trying to help. But I don't want to go in there. Not yet."

"Brody? You do realize that you just had major surgery, don't you?" Brandon sat down near him.

"How can I forget? Everyone keeps reminding me." Brody squinted through one open eye at his friend. "Now, tell me. Where do we stand with what we are looking at?"

"Not today, Brody. Tomorrow." Ker finally moved in, simply picking up his feet and making him lie back on the pillows that she had already positioned on the couch. "Today, it is enough that you are at home. Tomorrow, someone will come up here, bring what they can for you to look at and we'll talk. Today, you'll do what I say."

"And if I don't?" Brody knew he was petulant but felt he deserved to be. He hurt all over, more than he had in the hospital.

"Remember, I have a good pitching arm. And I have shoes handy." Ker perched beside him. "Please, Brody? I don't want to have to wake anyone up in the middle of the night to take you back in. And if you keep up this way, I will." She rose and walked away from him, heading for the kitchen.

Brandon looked after her before he exchanged a glance with Buckley, who simply nodded at Brody. Brody had sank back onto the pillows, his eyes closed in his white face, pain drawn on it.

"She's right. I just want this over yesterday." Brody's voice was gruff.

"We know you do, Brody. But you do have to take care. Ker wants you around for a long time. So do the rest of us." Brandon was on his feet. "I need to run. I have my volunteer work later. Call if you need anything."

"Thanks again, Brandon."

"No problem. You were there for us when we went through what we did. It's our turn to return the favour."

Buckley studied his friend. "How can I pray for you best, Brody?"

"Pray this over and quickly. For her father and brother. For resolution of whatever it is that needs to be resolved. For Ker. This is hitting her hard. She won't show it unless it comes out in anger. Right now, she's dealing with that and trying to find out how to forgive her mother."

"We have been doing just that, Brody. But for you two, how do I pray on a personal level?"

Brody shrugged, his eyes closing. "I don't know, Buckley. I really don't know." He lost the battle to stay awake and slept.

Ker stood watching. "He's asleep."

"He is, Ker. And will do this off and on for a few days, I suspect. Now, what I asked him? How do I pray for you?"

Ker shrugged. "What he said. I really have never had anyone ask me that before, do you know?"

"I gathered that. I'm off. I see the ladies are gone. Call one of us, no matter the time of day or night, do you understand?"

Ker reached to hug him, surprising herself. "Thank you, Buckley. You are what I imagined a minister should be like." She stood, listening as Buckley walked away, the door closing quietly behind him before she sank to a sitting position beside the couch, her arm across Brody, her hand on his cheek. Tears sparkled on her cheeks as she prayed, asking for forgiveness and strength. She knew they were not done yet, not by a long mile, as her father would have put it.

Brody stirred, his hand reaching for his phone, hearing it ringing. He couldn't find it, but his hand stopped as he saw Ker sitting just as she had sat a few hours previously. Worn out, she too slept. He smiled, before he reached for his phone, frowning at the text message. This is not good, he thought. Her mother's in the area. She's been spotted but how do we stop her? She'll harm Ker unless we do.

Carefully sitting up, he reached down, not listening to his body, to scoop Ker close to him and up onto the couch. She turned into him, and he dropped a kiss on her hair. Lord, it's coming up to that point where it gets so dangerous. With her mother here, looking for her, we both have to be so careful. Who knows what she will do to either one of us. I fear for her.

He rose, walking slowly through the apartment, before he stood, staring at his face in the bathroom mirror. He winced, seeing the varied colours of the bruising and the cuts and lacerations. I am thankful, Lord, that I survived. They wanted Ker, but something seemed off. Why there, Lord? He shrugged, turning on the water in the shower, knowing it would hurt but he needed to clean up and shave. He hated the smell of the hospital that always lingered.

Ker stood and waited for Brody to return, not sure what he would want. She had received a text message from her mother, and the viciousness of it frightened her as no other message ever had. Lord, she whispered, I thought that she was a believer. She worked in the church. She has hidden this from us all. I need a mother, and I don't have one. She wiped at the tears, jumping as she felt arms around her.

"Kitten?"

She would never have thought of that word as a term of endearment but Brody had made it theirs.

"Mom sent a text message. She is getting more brutal. What did I do to make her like that?"

"It was that bad?" He took the phone she thrust at him. "Ker? You really are in danger. We can't let you out anywhere." He forwarded the message to his own phone and then on to Dallas. "She's here in the area, isn't she?"

"She has to be. I just don't understand what she wants. I'm not in her life. Keefe is in hiding. She's made Dad disappear. I don't think that she planned for him to be found."

"Not likely. But she has lost control of all three of you." Brody moved away, reaching for the mug of coffee that she had poured for him, sitting at the table. "Let's have something to eat, and then make some plans."

"I don't know what plans that we can make. We have no idea what she's planning." Ker slid bowls of soup onto the table for them. "I'm sorry. I didn't cook this. In fact, I'm not that great a cook. I was never allowed to cook."

Brody reached for her hand, blessing their food, and then speaking softly. "We'll learn together. I had to, Ker, just to survive. Anna was a great teacher. She'll work with you."

"But she'll judge me. I just know that." Ker's voice held defeat.

"Not at all. Anna loves to teach cooking and baking. She's always finding something new to do just that. She misses having her daughter around all the time. The ladies in the building are precious to her."

Ker shrugged. "What did we need to talk about?"

"First, before I was hurt, the fellows were making progress in what they think your mother was involved in. It's not pretty."

"Did you think it would be? Given what Dad did, finding missing and exploited children and teens, was Mom involved on the other side?"

"That's what we've heard. We are still working to confirm that. Dallas has been given what we have and he has someone working on it as well." Brody paused, his spoon halfway to his mouth before he lowered it. "Is there a particular point in time where your mother seemed to change?"

Ker stared at him. "You know, I think there was. Let me think for a moment." She ate absentmindedly. "About the time I turned fifteen and Keefe sixteen. She had always been hard, but she became harder on us, harsher. We could do nothing right. I think that over time, beaten down as she had us, we just gave up and let her control us."

"What was your Dad working on at the time? Was he always involved in this type of rescue?"

Ker stared at him, surprise on her face. "No, he wasn't. He used to do other stuff, I'm not sure what now. But about that time, I can remember him being approached by a friend's father. Their young son had gone missing, and he wanted Dad to find him. The boy was around seven, I think. Dad found him, and that decided him to change his investigations to that."

"So, if your Mom was involved in these disappearances, she wouldn't want your father involved in tracking the children and teens." Brody rose, paused to catch his balance, and then moved to clear the table with Ker's help. "Now, Ker, we have something to work with. Let's head for the office."

"Not tonight, Brody. Tonight, you rest. You need that." She stood in the hallway, refusing to let him pass. "The only way past me is if you head for the bedroom. Other than that, it's the living room and the couch. Please?"

Brody just swept her into a hug, and turned them to the living room, sinking down gratefully.

"Thank you, Kitten. I really didn't want to go there, but I want this over for you."

"And we'll get there. I just hate that she has done this to you."

"I hate how she's treated you, beaten you down. I know you're angry. I would be too if I were you. But don't let the anger consume you."

"I'm trying, Brody. I'm trying, but it's hard. Buckley asked me how he could pray for me. That's all I could think of."

"And he will have already been praying that way. He's good at reading people." Brody grew silent, content, he thought, just to sit there, holding the love of his life. "We still need to talk, Kitten."

She twisted to look up at him, reading him correctly. "And we will. Right now, hush. You're talking too much." She smirked as he grinned at her and then kissed her forehead.

———

The next morning, Brody sat at the table in the conference room, eyeing the boards on the wall, amazed at how much work that his friends had done. He shook his head at Ker as she hovered near him.

"Sit, Kitten. We'll find out what's going on." He groaned as his phone chimed. He stared at the text before he handed her the phone.

"Brody? What is it?" Ker stared down at the text. "This can't be right. Mom wouldn't do that. At least, I don't think that she would."

"Brody? You look troubled." Barnabas sat beside him.

"Here. Ker's mother has gone to the media, stating that Ker is being held against her will by us."

"I heard that this morning. Our lawyers are already dealing with it. They want a statement from you two, to pass on." Barnabas paused. "I don't know where your relationship is right now. That's none of my business. But in the video, we need you to look happy and together."

"That's not a problem." Ker looked up at him, anger making her eyes spark. "I know how she thinks. We'll make her eat her words, in more ways than one. What can we do in the meantime to help move this along?"

Barnabas stared at her for a moment. "Tell us whatever you can about your mother, what she was involved with. What you can without breaking confidentiality on your father's cases. What was your brother involved with? That will help."

"How long a day do you have? I could talk for hours. I'm finally ready to." She looked at Brody, finding him watching her, his trust in her evident. "Brody and I figured out last night about when she changed. I was fifteen, Keefe sixteen." She detailed the account for him, not realizing that there was silence in the room, and that her voice carried to everyone.

"Do you think she was involved in that?" Brendon had moved closer, taking notes.

"I do. Her reaction was off if I remember. She wasn't that concerned, not like she should have been. Dad was. It drove him night and day to find them." She looked up at Brandon. "They found the boy, hurt but alive. They never found who kidnapped him. And he never said. Whether it was because he didn't know or because he was too scared, that didn't become clear at all."

"Can you let us have the names? I'll pass them on to Dallas." Brandon took the paper that she handed him. "Prepared, were you?"

Ker shrugged. "It's just habit, I guess. I used to make notes of everything and anything." Her face grew sad. "With my house gone, all of that is gone."

"I'm sorry, Ker. That should not have happened. Brennen, did we get the report on that?" Barnabas looked around.

"We did. Emma found it for us. She's back, Brody, and working on this." Brennen handed over the file folder. "It was arson. I'm sorry, Ker, that it happened."

Ker nodded. "It is what it is, isn't it? We can't go back. Things can be replaced." She looked up at Brody. "And to tell you the truth, now that I no longer have the house, I'm glad. Mom picked it out, decorated it, and all. I had no say in anything. If I did say something, she just ignored me and went her own way."

Barnabas made a sound, his eyes meeting Brody. "This is Brody's place to say it, Ker, but understand. If there is something in the apartment that you want changed in any way, at any time, talk to us. It will happen. It is your home as well as Brody's. The ladies have made changes to their own places, just to make it theirs. Yours is no different." Barnabas was on his feet, walking out of the room before Ker could respond.

She stared after him, then reached for the folder, opening it and reading through the report. She frowned when she finished, going back to something that had puzzled her.

"I don't understand this. It says the fire started in the gas stove, that it had been tampered with. I didn't have a gas stove. That was one thing that I refused. Mom could not change my mind on that."

"You didn't? That's interesting. We never thought to ask you. What about the dryer?"

"Electric. So was the water heater. If it says different, then someone has changed them. And it had to be that day. What did she do?"

"We'll find out. Now that we know, we can start canvassing the companies."

"Wait. She has a friend who is a gas fitter. She would have had him do it. He would have gotten the appliances as well." Ker reached for another piece of paper. "This is who he is. He's not that well liked in the community."

"Thank you, Ker. We'll handle this." Bradon reached for it. "Now, Brody looks as if he's going to faint or something."

"I know. Would someone help us, please?" She stood, a hand on Brody's shoulder. "But before we leave, may I thank each one of you? I know you're not doing it for thanks, but you have no idea what this means to me."

Brody rose with Brady's assistance, and then headed out, his arm around his bride, Brady's hand under his other arm.

"Brody? What are your thoughts?"

"My thoughts? Someone is setting it up to make Ker look like she is unstable. I don't like that. This is just an opening wedge, I suspect. Let Barnabas know we want to do that video for him. And today. I want the world to see what her mother has done."

"But you know that people will say it was Ker who arranged it."

"I know. Ker, your phone please." He took it when she offered it to him, a puzzled look on her face. "Hand this off to Dallas, please. Have the techs go over it. Ker has had no access to any phone other than mine, and I know that it hasn't been used for that. She hasn't been in town to use any payphones, either."

"I'll need yours too, Brody. I'll grab a phone from the security team for now for you two."

Ker's mother stared at the television, anger growing within in, disfiguring her face. She threw the glass she was holding, just missing the screen, having it shatter against the wall, liquid running down to the floor. How dare she, she thought? How dare she go on television and into the papers with that story? Who would believe her, anyway?

She paced the room, Ker's voice detailing her life and what had transpired in the last few weeks. Brody was beside her, an arm around her, her hand tight in his. His face looked garish in the lighting, the varied colours showing clearly what had happened.

One of the Foundation lawyers drew them out, asking the questions that would tell the story. Her mother sneered. A likely story, she thought. Of course, Ker had gas appliances. She had seen to that. It just didn't matter that Ker hadn't known that they had been replaced. Her car had been in the driveway. She was supposed to have been home that day and died in the fire. Why hadn't she? Who had mixed that up?

Ker looked directly at the camera as she finished, Brody's arm tightening around her. They had talked about what they needed to say. Ker had been adamant that she would address her mother.

"Mom, I know that you are out there and listening. You always listen to the news. Well, this time, you're the news. I want it out there that you tried to kill me. You tried to kill my beloved Brody. I have no idea what you tried with Keefe. Or what you did to Dad. But this ends now. If you come after me again, you will not win. I refuse to let you control me anymore. I don't know what made you change, or if you were always this way, but you have lost a daughter. You could have gained another son, but you blew it. Don't come after me. I want nothing to do with you. Anything or anyone that I can think of that might solve this, that information has been handed over to the police department here." Ker grew silent, unable to speak any further.

Brody spoke, his eyes on Ker. "Mrs. Deeks. I know that you sent the men who assaulted me. They wanted Ker to be brought to them. That will never happen. If you come after her again, I will stop you. She is my bride, the love of my life, and I will not tolerate any harm done to her. I am not threatening you. Merely stating that I will cooperate with the authorities in any way that is necessary to prevent that from ever happening."

The screen on her television went black as Ker's mother stared at it. How dare they, she thought once more? She spun, looking for her phone. They had warned her. Warnings never worked. She had too many people that she could call to end this with her daughter.

Only this time, she had been branded by the news story. Everyone that she had used in the past for her dirty deeds refused to answer her call or said they didn't have time to help her. She was growing desperate. The man and woman that she worked for were demanding she provide more children and teenagers. She had never thought of what happened to them. She was just glad for the money that she was accumulating in the bank. Soon, she would have enough to leave Canada and find some island or tropical paradise where she could live. She didn't care that she was leaving death and destruction in her wake.

She paced through the downtown area of Brody's town, looking for an accomplice and finding none. She didn't realize the esteem that the Foundation was held in. No one would go against the Foundation or the men and ladies who lived in the Foundation building.

Dropping down onto a park bench, Ker's mother slumped down, not holding herself in the usual haughty manner that she normally she did. The patrol officer drove past her and then circled the block, leaving his vehicle to stand in front of her.

"Mrs. Deeks? You need to come with me, please." He reached for her hand just as she slammed forward into him. They fell together, the officer rolling her over, and seeing the spreading red stain on the front of her blouse. He frantically tried to stem the flow of blood, calling for help. But she would never face justice on earth. Someone had taken care of that.

Dallas stood, listening to the report, a somber look on his face. He had been part of Brody and Ker's story, standing in the background as they spoke, listening to the reports that were coming in. He shook his head. Now, he had to face Ker and let her know that her mother was dead, murdered, but they were no further ahead in finding the ones responsible for that or who it was her mother worked for.

Brody stood for a moment watching Dallas walk towards him across the lobby. He had been restless and Ker had sent him out for a walk, telling him that he was bothering her and she needed a break. He had looked at her, hurt for a moment, before she reached to hug him.

"I didn't mean it that way, Brody. I'm sorry. I just need a few minutes on my own."

"I understand. I am just oversensitive, I guess. I'll walk in the lobby. That way, you can come to find me if you want me." He walked away, puzzled at her mood. Please, Lord, don't let her do anything that would harm her. She needs to talk to me and I am not sure that she will.

"Brody? You're out and about. Where's Ker?" Dallas stood watching him move not as carefully as he had been. "You're healing."

"I am. Ker needed some space. This is why I am down here. But you have some bad news."

"I do, Brody. I need to learn to school my expressions better. Can we find Ker?"

"You can. I'm right here." Ker's grin lit up her face as Dallas jumped at her voice.

"So you are. Can we sit? It's been a long day already, and my feet are tired." Dallas pointed to one of the sitting areas in the lobby.

"You have bad news. I can tell. What did Mom do now?" Ker barely let him get seated before she spoke.

"I'm sorry, Ker. Your mother was shot earlier today. She didn't make it. One of our officers had found her and had approached her to bring her in for questioning. He didn't see where the assailant was."

"She's dead?" Ker paled, her hands clasped together. "No, it can't be true."

Brody swept her close to him, his eyes on Dallas. "You're sure it was her?"

"We are. I'm so sorry, Ker. I know that this will not bring any closure for you."

"No, it won't. She had to be working for someone, but who? That's who did this." Ker looked up. "I was listed at one point as her next of kin and executrix if Dad couldn't serve. I need to contact her lawyer." She groaned. "And it's the law firm that Dad wanted nothing to do with."

"I can obtain a court order for records, Ker. And if you need to go to that office, I will personally escort you. How be we talk in the morning?"

"That will work, Dallas. Right now, Ker needs some time." Brody reached to shake his friend's hand. "I know this is not easy for you. Call me later."

Breck looked up as Brendon stopped beside him. He had found a quiet moment or two and had gone to sit in one of the gardens, just to commune with God.

"Brendon? I don't like that face of yours." Breck moved over so that Brendon could sit beside him.

"You'll like what I have to say even less. Ker's mother was killed earlier today."

"She was what?" Breck groaned. "That's not good. Ker knows?"

"She does. Dallas came out himself and talked to them. Brody said that Ker's really quiet right now, not saying much, but she is hurting."

"That she would be. What can we do?" Breck rose, heading back for the building. "The fellows are in the conference room?"

"Those who can be. Ker seems to think that her mother was working for someone else."

"That's been our feeling. How do we prove it?" Breck stood for a moment outside the conference room.

"I have no idea. It only gets worse. Ker is one of the executors, and the lawyer her mother used is the one her father was trying to get away from. Dallas will go with her, he said, whenever she needs to go there. Both he and Brody are adamant that she's not going anywhere on her own."

"No, she can't. Whoever it is will be waiting for her." Breck began to pace. "How far are we in the search?"

"Far enough along that we've been able to start feeding information to Dallas for him to verify. Emma's been sending us information, but she and Jace are still tied up on that priority case."

"That's good. We need to talk to her brother. How is her father?"

"Still unconscious. Dallas hasn't said much other than that." Brendon held the door open. "I can work for a while before I need to leave." He looked around at the men gathered, somber looks on their faces. He knew that Brody had been in.

"I think that it's time we pulled you all back in for now. Talk to your employers. We may need some of you to head to Ker's hometown."

"We thought of that. Bradon, Benen, and Burnie are heading that way tomorrow. They haven't said anything to Brody, not until they're back."

"My advice is not to hide it from Ker. She will not accept that it was done for her own good."

Brendon nodded. "I'll head up and talk to them. It's hard in this situation to know what to say."

"It is difficult. Let them know that they are in all our prayers."

Brody stepped back from the door, letting Brendon in, early that evening. He had tried to comfort Ker, but she had shut down to some extent. He could relate, he thought, knowing that was how he had reacted all those years ago.

"Brendon? What can I do for you?" Brody pointed towards the kitchen. "I just made a fresh pot of coffee. I won't be going to bed very early, I don't think. I need to try and do some work, but Ker comes first."

Brendon took the mug with a word of thanks before he looked around.

"Where is Ker?"

"In the office. She finally settled down on the couch in there. She's not talking much." Brody studied his friend. "You need to talk to her?"

"With her. And you. If she's up to it."

"Let me see." Brody looked past Brendon. "Ker? Brendon would like to speak with us. You up to it?"

Ker shrugged, her eyes on Brendon. "I don't see why not. Brendon?"

"Three of the fellows are heading to your hometown tomorrow, Ker. They have some information that they need to verify."

"And they can't do it from here. That's what you're saying." Ker sighed. "I'm not sure that they will find any assistance there. They might." Ker studied him. "You're not one of them."

"No, I'm not. Bradon, Benen, and Burnie are." Brendon heard a sound of agreement from Brody but did not take his eyes from Ker.

"Those three?" Ker's shrugged again. "I guess that's what will work. I'm sorry, I can't give any names for them to talk to. I'm just not sure about anyone there now." She rubbed at her temple. "Brody, do you have any pain medications that aren't prescription?"

"I do. Have a seat on the couch, Kitten. I'll find that and some juice for you. Brendon, go on in."

Brendon sank into the chair that he favoured when he visited Brody, his eyes on Ker.

"Ker? What can we do to help you?"

"I really don't know, Brendon. Not anymore. Losing Mom, even though she was responsible for so much damage to people, it's hard. I'll never hear her explanation of what went wrong. Keefe isn't around. And Dad doesn't know what's been happening." She looked up as Brody sat beside her, taking the medication and juice that he handed her. "I'll need to go back there, I think."

"Not necessarily at the moment. We could give authorization to one of the fellows to do whatever it is that you need."

"We could. But I still have to face that lawyer."

"And we will. How deep do you think he's involved?" Brody looked up at a sound from Brendon. "Brendon? What have you not told us?"

"That the lawyer is deeply involved, but we don't think that he's the top man. Dallas is obtaining search warrants for your parents' documents from them. That would save you a trip there, even though as executrix you would have access to your mother's."

"They would do that? They could?" Ker shifted to look up at Brody. "Brody?"

"We'll let Dallas work on it first. Then, if that doesn't work, we'll see, Kitten. Brendon, where are we in the process?"

"Getting there. We need your legal mind down there."

"And he's not going down there. Not for hours at a time." Ker was adamant that he wouldn't. "Bring what you need up here. Maybe, we could work together on it."

"And that would be a great idea." Brendon grinned at Brody as he stared down at his wife.

Benen stared out the back window of Burnie's car, glad to be leaving the town behind. The three of them had spent the day there. Ker was right, he thought. Not a lot of information was readily available to them. Someone was preventing that. And he wanted to know who.

"What are your thoughts, Bradon?" Burnie finally spoke.

"Ker was right, wasn't she? She certainly knows her town." Bradon paused. "I would have thought someone would have spoken to us."

"Me, too. It's like they have all been threatened. In a town that size, even small as it is, there should have been someone who was willing to break ranks." Benen stuffed his hand into his pocket, and then withdrew it, a frown on his face. "What's this?"

Bradon looked back at him. "What's what?"

"This? It's a note. From someone in town. Asking that we stop in the town mid-way home. Whoever it is, wants to meet us. They have even given instructions as to where. So, do we?"

Bradon shared a look with Burnie. "Who do we know on the police force there?"

"Eric. That's where he is, isn't it?"

"It is." Benen's phone was out, calling Eric. "Eric? Benen. We're fine. And you? Say, are you working today? You're not? Terrific. You know that Brody and Ker are going through some stuff? She did. Okay, here's what's happening. Bradon, Burnie, and I were to Ker's hometown today. Somehow I was passed a note, asking that we meet in your town. At a local business. The EyePatch company." Benen pulled his phone back to stare at it. "It's what? Oh. That's what I thought you said. So, we don't go? You'll go? Okay. Then, we'll keep on driving. Call when you know something."

———

"Well?" Bradon stared back at Benen as he just sat, turning his phone over and over in his hand.

"Eric said not to go. It's a shady area of town. The business? It's known to be a local drug dealer's but they have never had the evidence to charge anyone. This might be it, he says."

"Home, then. I had to disappoint Ker." Burnie frowned. "Or will we?"

"I don't think so." Benen sighed as he pulled out his phone. "It's Breck. He's called an emergency meeting for tonight with all of us. Something must have come up."

"I would say likely." Bradon grew quiet, his thoughts on their reception in Ker's town. "She knew, didn't she?"

"What's that?" Benen looked up from the research he had been doing.

"Ker knew exactly what would happen."

"She did. She knows her town. But there has to be someone who would be willing to talk to us." Benen was frustrated.

"It depends on how desperate they are or how much they want her town to change." Bradon pulled out his phone. "It's Brody. He wants to know how it went so that he can prepare Ker." He looked at the other two. "What do we tell him?"

Burnie shrugged. "What can we tell him other than it went as Ker told us it would."

Bradon sent off his text, frowning at the response. "Ker asked if we talked to someone named Mary Beth. Did we?"

"I don't remember that name. Where would we have found her?"

"In the library. We were there. I don't remember seeing anyone who had a name tag on with that name."

"Brody said Ker suspects that Mary Beth wasn't there. That it would have been arranged that she wasn't. She's a wealth of information for the town. Ker added that whoever it is that's in charge would keep her from talking with us, somehow, some way."

———

“I don’t like the sounds of that.”

“Nor does Brody. He’s ready to have this solved. Just like you and I were, Benen.”

Burnie frowned at a thought. “She was in the library, right?”

“That’s what Ker said.”

“Only we didn’t find her. Now, if she was there and had hidden herself from us, would she take the card that we left on the desk and contact us?”

Benen stared at him. “I forgot we did that. She just might.”

Breck stood at the head of a table in the conference room, his gaze stopping on each of the men gathered there, before he exchanged a look with Barnabas. Bruce and Dallas were there as well. Crucial information had been handed to Dallas, and he had asked if he could meet with the men. He felt it was too important and too life-threatening for both Ker and Brody to let it go another day.

"Thanks for giving me time this evening, fellows. Before we begin, let's pair off and spend some time in prayer. From what I have been told, we are going to need the Lord's guidance and wisdom in this."

Thirty minutes later, the men shifted around to stare back at Breck, who looked up from where he had been talking with Barnabas, Bruce, and Dallas. He sighed. What Dallas would say would rock Brody's world, to put it one way. He was just glad that Bruce was there. They would need his wisdom, he thought, before the night was over.

"Fellows, Dallas approached Bruce and Barnabas late this afternoon. He has come into contact with someone who he has interviewed. That person has provided information that Dallas' team is busy verifying. But the content of it was concerning enough that he felt he had to talk to us. Brody, this directly affects you and Ker. Dallas?" Breck turned to Dallas, who had approached him.

"Fellows, Brody, in particular. I have no words for how I feel right now. It's disheartening and discouraging when you happen upon an informant who provides what they have. Burnie, Benen, and Bradon tell me that they hit a dead end today in Ker's town. Other than a message slipped to Benen. That message he relayed to Eric, who asked that they not stop in his town. The area that they were to meet this person was one of great risk to them. Eric was setting up to watch for this person. He has been asked to contact me if and when that person shows.

"Now, the informant that came forward is from our town. I will not give any more details than that. This person was known to Ker's mother and the ones over her. We have been provided with information that directly ties her to the abduction and disappearance of a number of children and teens. Given the names and details, our team is frantically working with the child welfare unit of the social services and the child and teen exploitation section of our department. We have no idea how long this has been going on, but we feel it has been for at least twenty years. Ker would have been a young child when it started. Keefe, just older.

"Now, as to Keefe? We are keeping him apart from Ker. Some of what he has been stating is contradictory to what Ker has said, and more in line with what their mother said. We need to verify if he is telling us the truth and if he is involved in the crimes or not. I pray that he is not. Ker needs her brother." Dallas paused to sip from his water bottle, his eyes on Brody, who was staring at the pad of paper in front of him, his pen moving rapidly.

"Dallas? Are you confident in what you say about Keefe?" Brendon spoke up.

"We are, unfortunately. We are going back over all his trips and vacations, trying to determine if they coincided with any of the disappearances. So far, they haven't. Pray that he is not involved."

"Her father?" Bradon asked. "Has he awakened and been able to talk?"

"He has. He fatigues easily, as you can imagine, but he is willing to talk as much as he can. He didn't see who it was who struck him. He is concerned about Ker. That was his first statement when he was coherent enough to be understood."

"So, calling Brody was deliberate on his part?" Brady studied his friend, Brody, watching him intently.

"It was. He told the investigators who spoke with him that he had been warned that she would disappear the next day or else die. He arranged for Brody to appear, hoping that Ker would go with him. If she hadn't, he had plans to move her from their town. Only, we know what happened." Dallas turned for a moment as Bruce spoke quietly with him.

Dallas' face grew grim as he nodded, his eyes finding Brody.

"Brody, Bruce would like to speak with you in private and then speak with Ker. We'll catch you up on what else we discuss. Buckley?"

Buckley nodded as he rose, following Bruce and Brody from the room, the eyes of their friends following them.

"Bruce? What is that important that you pull me from the meeting?"

"Brody, I have no words to tell you. Ker's father passed away just a short while ago. He had undiagnosed heart disease and had a heart attack."

Brody paled, staggering from the shock, Buckley's hand there to hold him upright. "How do I tell her?" His voice was a mere whisper. "How do I tell her that her father is gone before she could see him again?"

Brody found Ker on the balcony outside his home office, wrapped in a blanket as she sat, staring at the night sky, counting the stars as much as she could. She loved clear nights like this one was. She felt closer to God when she could see the stars. She leaned into his hug, surprised to see him home so soon.

"Brody? Is your meeting over already?"

"Not really. Bruce was there and needed to speak with us. He and Buckley are waiting in the living room for us."

Ker searched his face, seeing the sadness in it. "Which one?" Her voice was barely a whisper.

"Which one?" Brody echoed her words, trying to find his own words to tell her.

"Which one? Dad? Keefe? And how?" She felt herself hugged tightly before Brody drew her to her feet.

"Bruce wants to tell you." He shut the door quietly behind them and reached for her hand, a prayer audible to only the two of them, before he led her towards the living room.

Ker hesitated as she saw Bruce and Buckley stand. "Bruce? Buckley? Brody said that you needed to speak with me."

"I do, Ker. You may want to sit first." Bruce watched with compassion as she sat on the edge of a chair, Brody perching on the arm, holding her to him.

"Bruce? Which one? Dad or Keefe?" Her eyes searched his, seeing the truth in his. "Dad?"

"It was your father, Ker. Did you know he had heart disease?"

"No, not really. He had seen the doctor about six weeks ago. He wouldn't say why, but I suspected something like that. Is that what happened?"

"I'm sorry, Ker, but he had a heart attack. He was alert enough before that to speak with the investigators. His first thought was for you."

Ker drew in a trembling breath, her fingers pushing about her lips to try and stem the tears. "It was?"

"It was. Dallas has spoken with them. Your father confirmed that he brought Brody in to meet with you, in the hopes that he would convince you to leave. If he hadn't, your father had made alternate plans. If you had not left, then you would have disappeared the next day."

"Mom?"

"That's what he implied. He didn't come right out and say it."

"No, he wouldn't. He never laid blame, not unless he had absolute proof. And he wouldn't have had with Mom." She sighed. "Now, what?"

"Now, we work with you on your duties for the estate. Our lawyers have met and one of them will work with you. We are familiar with the firm you indicated has your parents' paperwork. There will be no issues retrieving it."

"There won't? I thought there would be." Ker shared a look with Brody.

"Bruce means that the lawyers will know better than to try anything. The Foundation lawyers will not allow it. If I know them, they will have what they need to convince them to cooperate or they will face a hearing with the law society."

"Brody is correct, Ker. They are already on the radar of the law society. A new complaint that is substantiated would mean they would lose their licenses. And they won't want to do that."

They spoke for a while longer before Bruce looked at Buckley, who nodded.

"Ker, in situations like this, our church works with the families. You are family to the Foundation and to the church, even if you are a new member. We want to do what we can to help you get through this. Brody, when you need to make any arrangements, talk to me. Right now, Ker needs to absorb what she has been told and to begin to grieve. Let me pray with you, and then we're on our way. Ker, I meant it. Call at any time. That's what our church family does."

Brody walked slowly back from the door after the two men had left, not quite sure how to approach Ker. He found her in the kitchen, the kettle plugged in as she watched it boil, his coffee perking in the pot beside it. His arm around her, he just stood, unable to find the words that he needed.

"Brody?"

"Yes, my love?"

"I didn't get to say goodbye to either one of my parents. It's so not right."

"No, it's not. We have some decisions to make. Dallas will be in touch with Keefe. Do you need to talk to him?"

Ker shrugged. "Right at the moment? No. I've been remembering things that I shoved to the back of my mind. Was he involved?"

"That's what we are surmising, but it may be false information that we have been given."

"That's true." Ker sighed as she turned into his hug. "I will need to speak with him, but I don't want him around me. Not if it's unproven. But he has to be, doesn't he?"

"He does. But I can guarantee you that you will have your own bodyguards. Each one of the fellows will be close enough to that he can't try anything."

"And if I'm wrong about him? How do I ask him to forgive me?" She turned as she heard her phone chime. Her face paled as she read the text.

"Ker?" Brody reached for her phone, his own face growing stern. "This is Keefe's number?"

"It is. And only he could be on his phone unless he unlocked it for someone. He is involved, isn't he?"

A day later, Ker looked up from where she was sitting in the lobby, finding Devaney, Ennis, and Fynn approaching her. Fynn handed over a mug of tea before she sat, her feet curled under her.

"Ker? We've been looking for you. We haven't had a chance to gossip in a few days." Fynn grinned at her.

"Gossip? Fynn! You know that we don't gossip." Ennis shook a finger at her friend.

"You know what I mean! We talk, we discuss, we get to know one another. We learn secrets that some people don't want to share."

Devaney laughed. "And that would be my secret that you're trying to find out, is it, Fynn? Not telling."

Ker stared at them all. "You gossip? I didn't think you ladies did."

"We gossip, but in a nice way. We never tear anyone down. When we gossip with one another, it is to try and build up each other. It's our form of gossip." Ennis laughed at the expression on Ker's face. "We have confused you."

"No, I get what you are saying. I just have never heard it expressed that way. And you three are so happy. Even with what you went through."

"We are, Ker. God has been good. We are blessed with husbands who love and adore us. We have a huge family here that loves us. They tolerate our nonsense, the fellows do, but we do the same for them." Ennis watched her closely. "Tell us, Ker. What can we do for you? We have been praying for you."

"Thank you. I needed that." Ker blinked away the tears of thankfulness. "I have never had such prayers as you ladies send forth. It's just so normal and natural for you to talk like that. That is how I've always thought we should be. But I was never allowed to do that. That's what I think I have been searching and seeking for. That freedom."

"You've come to the right place then, Ker." Devaney reached to hug her. "We have all had to learn over time to do just that. It has not been easy at times." She searched Ker's face. "Now, talk to us. You need to tell us what is going on. We can give you a female perspective on what you're enduring."

"Enduring?" Fynn began to laugh. "Devaney! You and your expressions. You have gotten worse over time."

Devaney smirked. "I know I have. It's called growth."

Ker began to laugh. "I needed that, Devaney. You don't know how much. Now, as to what is going on? Where do I start?"

"At the beginning, but I think we've already done that." Ennis laughed at the expression on her face. "What can you tell us?"

Fynn pulled out her ever-present notepad and pen. "And I will take notes. They may be too scientific for you though." She frowned at her pen.

"It's not the pen's fault, Fynn. It's how your brain works. Ker, this lady was in college at age 16, graduated with her degrees and doctorate at age 20, and went right to work in a medical examiner's office. She was one of those who went in and studied the creepy crawlies at a crime scene."

"You were? Oh, that sounds fascinating." Ker looked with new interest at Fynn. "I still haven't made it to your building."

"You will. Brody will make sure. Now, where do you stand?"

"I'm not, I'm sitting." Ker smirked at the laughter. "Seriously? With Mom and Dad gone, it's put a lot of pressure on me. The lawyers here are handling a lot of it. Brody drew up papers and had me sign them. For some reason, Keefe had never been named to an executor position."

"That is strange. But go on." Ennis pushed her to continue.

Ker explained where they stood in the investigation, as much as she could reveal, and then listened to the ladies discuss it. She shifted over as Hagen sat, reaching to take Hagen's daughter from her even as Ennis reached for Hagen's son. Ker cuddled the little girl close, her hand rubbing her back, not even realizing how she was acting like a mother.

"So, with your brother, Ker, what's going on?" Hagen had listened to the update from Fynn.

"I'm not sure. Dallas isn't saying." She sighed. "I thought I had a brother I could depend on, but now I'm not so sure."

"What if he's being set up? Would your mother have put something like that into play?" Fynn looked up, a distracted look on her face. "I have seen that on some of the cases I worked on."

"You did?" Ker hesitated, a finger rubbing at her temple. "I wondered that. I don't know who the investigators are but I wonder if they had been gotten to? That they're feeding Dallas information that's not from Keefe? The brother I know and love would not be acting like this." She paused, her lips compressing even as anger sparked for a moment in her eyes. "Dad sent Keefe away. Would he have done that if Keefe had been involved? Mom would say Keefe had done and said things, things that didn't seem to be him. I never fully believed them."

"Where is he?" Fynn looked up again.

"I don't know exactly. He has been texting me, and Brody and I have been responding."

"Then, we look at the cell records. Emma will help." Ennis had her phone out, sending a text message off to Emma, and smiling at the quick response. "Emma had thought of that and has obtained the records. Her husband and his team are bringing Keefe back today."

"They are? And just who are they?" Ker was confused.

"Emma and Abe are friends. They have helped out some of us. Emma finds people and information that no one else seems to be able to. Abe has a security team. They do training mainly now, but they do go in and bring out people that need rescuing."

"They do? Abe? That name sounds familiar." Ker looked around, surprised to see all the ladies had crowded around. "Oh my, when did you all get here?"

"Over the length of time that you have been here." Cadee grinned. "And we brought lunch. Brody has been told to stay away, that this is our time with you. You need some time with the ladies."

Ker began to laugh, waving at Brody as he watched from near the stairs. "And he's standing guard, you know."

"We know." Berneen smirked. "He's in love, Ker. And he wants this over for you." She tilted her head and watched as Ker blushed. "And Ker's in love." Her voice had softened. "We are so happy for you two. Brody is a wonderful man, and you two are just right for each other."

Brody watched as Brennen paced the conference room, not quite sure what was up. He looked around as the door behind him opened, and then he was on his feet, his hand outstretched to shake that of the man who appeared.

"Abe Finlay? What are you doing here?"

"Looking for you. And I understand that you are married. Congratulations. I would like to meet your wife." Abe studied Brody carefully, seeing the bruises that were fading, but the stress that was showing on his face.

"Sure. We can head up now if you like."

"I would like." Abe waved at the few men who were gathered in the room and looked up as he left.

"You're here for a reason, Abe. I know you that well."

"I am, Brody. That reason is why I need to speak with your wife." Abe waited in the hallway of the apartment as Brody searched for Ker.

Ker studied the man waiting, a frown on her face before it cleared.

"Tell me? You're Abe?"

"That I am. You have guessed well." Abe grinned at her.

"The ladies and I were talking. Someone said that you had become involved. Tell me. Did you find Keefe?"

"We did. We have him at our place, for now, Ker, just until we clear him to come this way. Can we sit? This will take a while."

"Sure. Have you eaten? I have sandwiches and soup ready." Ker looked worried for a moment.

"Sandwiches and soup are just fine, Ker. What can I do to help?"

"Just have a seat. Brody?"

"On it, Kitten. Here, you sit for a change. I'll dish it up." Brody worked quickly, setting their meal in place and then sitting himself beside Ker, reaching for her hand. "Abe, will you?"

"I would be glad to." Abe's prayer covered more than just their meal and left the younger couple refreshed and confident that they could handle what he would tell them.

"Abe?" Ker finally pushed her meal away. "How is Keefe?"

"Not in great shape. Whoever said the police had him in protective custody lied. There is no other word for it. He was not in police custody. Whoever it was that Dallas was speaking with has to be involved in this. We have passed the names on to our own police detectives. We have a friend who will assess him and treat him. For now, we'll keep you two apart. I understand that you are planning the funerals for your parents. We will make sure he's here for those if this is not resolved by that time."

"And you think it might be?" Brody was hopeful.

"It may well be, Brody. Emma has been finding a wealth of information, between her and Jace. Dallas is pleading with her to slow down, but you know Emma. She can't. It's not in her to do that."

"No, it's not. What can you tell us or can you?"

"Emma is the best one to do that. She wants to head this way in two days. She states that she needs that time to confirm some information she's finding. We'll head back here then if it's convenient for you two."

"Any time is convenient." Ker was indignant. "And not soon enough."

"Wow, Ker. Tell me off or what!" Abe was laughing. "You sound like some of the ladies my men are married to. They all had adventures, just like you two, and so did Emma and I. Don't worry. We will keep you updated as much as we can between now and then. Now, if I may take the time to pray for you two once more, I need to get on the road. I have a training session scheduled for early tomorrow."

"And yet you came here tonight." Ker grew silent, her eyes on Brody. "Will you give Keefe a message for me? Will you tell him that I love him? That I miss my big brother?"

"I can do that. If tomorrow he's coherent enough, I will have a call set up for you. May I have your phone number?" Abe took the slip of paper from her and tucked it into his pocket before he rose.

Brody walked him to the door. "Thank you, Abe. That's a relief for us, knowing Keefe is not involved."

"I am sure it is. We'll find out who it is. Emma already has an idea and has been in touch with Dallas tonight, she said.

Ker stared down at her phone. She had just spoken with Abe's wife, Emma, who had called just to say hello and ask how she was. That surprised Ker. She had never had that before. She looked up as Brody's hand rested on her head for a moment before he stooped to kiss her.

"You okay?" His voice was quiet.

"I am. I just spoke with Emma. Did you know that she just called to see how I was?"

"That would be Emma. With Keefe at their place or with one of their friends, she would want to make sure that you are okay with it all." Brody sat beside her, reaching for her phone that she had clutched in her hands and dropping it onto the coffee table.

"It's nice, you know? What have I missed all my life, Brody?" Ker turned to him, finding him watching her intently.

"I don't know that you have missed a lot, Ker. You have missed out on friendships, but you likely missed out on heartaches too."

Ker reached for her phone as it chimed, her face paling at the number. "This is Mom's phone number. Who has her phone?"

Brody reached for his phone, trying to reach Dallas and having to leave a voice mail for him. "Dallas will call us back. I'll let him deal with that."

"Do you think Keefe was involved?" Ker's voice showed that she was hopeful he hadn't been.

"From what we can find out, I don't think so. Emma's fed us a lot of information that we're collating with what we have. Dallas is also copied on everything. I don't think Keefe was. It just doesn't seem to be his character, not from what we have learned."

"That's a relief." Ker snuggled down against him. "Where do we go from here, Brody?"

"With this? I am not sure. The fellows are working it as a huge logic problem."

Ker laughed. "A logic problem? Do they have a diagram and all?"

"They do. It's posted on the wall in the conference room."

"I need to see it. Will they let me?"

"They would never dream of stopping you. How be we head on down there?" Brody waited for Ker to move but she didn't. He tilted his head to look at her and then smiled. She was asleep, just like that. He had heard her pacing the apartment during the night for the last few days. He simply held her and prayed for his lady.

An hour later, Ker stirred, rubbing at her nose and face, before she looked up at him, finding that he was asleep as well. She gave a small smile and then reached for her phone, scrolling through her messages. Some she erased. Some she saved. Some she forwarded to Dallas, those ones scaring her. And then there was one from Keefe. It was not a phone number that she recognized, but Abe had said that would be the case. She smiled sadly as she read it, knowing there were just the two of them left in their family.

Brody had roused, his eyes on Ker as she worked away.

"Ker?"

"I'm okay, sweetheart. It's just a message from Keefe." She blinked away the tears. "He misses me, he says. And he says Abe will be calling us."

"And he will. That I know from experience. If he says he is calling, Abe will." He looked over her shoulder. "And there's a message from him, isn't it?"

"There is. He's heading this way tomorrow with Emma. I wonder if Keefe will come as well."

"It depends on how he is. Abe will bring him if he feels it's safe enough. Whoever was holding him will be watching you, just to see if Keefe is in touch."

"I know they will. Can we go downstairs now, Brody? I want to be part of this now. The lawyers are working on the estate for me. Bruce arranged that."

"I know he did. Here, let's go then, Kitten."

Her hand tucked tight in his, Ker stood just inside the conference room doorway, watching the men at work. She was surprised to see all of them there.

"They're all here!"

"They are. Breck called us all in to work on this." His finger touched her lips as she opened her mouth to protest. "It's what we do, Kitten. We work like this. We have for everyone else."

"I see." Ker moved away from him, wandering the room, stopping to speak with each of the men, before she walked to study the papers on the wall, a finger out on occasion to trace something. Burnie followed her, taking notes as she commented on something before she looked up at the huge puzzle they had placed there.

"A logic puzzle, Burnie? What made you think of that?"

He shrugged. "I have no idea. I used it in a book at one point. This just seemed to fit one of them."

"I can see that." Ker studied what they had written and discarded. "What's this? This name?"

"That name? That's a name and occupation that crossed our desks. We're not sure who it is."

"It's the man who is in charge of the homeless shelter in my town. It has always been rumoured that he was on the take, as they say, but no one could prove it." Ker paled. "He would be perfect for helping people disappear, now wouldn't he?"

"He would, Ker. He's just one that Dallas is looking at." He stepped away for a moment, a thought crossing his mind that he needed to look at.

Baird approached her. "Ker? What can we do for you?"

"For me? You're doing so much." She looked surprised. "Why would you ask that?"

"Because it's what we do, Ker. We look after one another." He shared a look with Brody who was standing behind Ker. "Brody?"

"Thanks, Baird. Knowing that you are praying for us as we seek to find the answers not only on this but on what Ker has been missing all her life helps."

Ker suddenly swayed, her face paling as she did so. Brody reached to swing her into his arms, finding the chair suddenly shoved behind him.

"Ker?"

"I remember!" Ker looked up at Brody, her face growing even paler. "I remember him. He and Mom used to talk at church. I wasn't supposed to hear, but I did. Once when I was young. He was talking about someone who had disappeared. He and Mom knew where they were. She mentioned it. I don't know if Dad ever found that boy."

"Do you remember the name?" Brendon crouched down beside her.

"No, I don't. Brody, this is getting worse and worse." Ker looked up at the men who had surrounded her. "We need to stop this, and now. But how?"

"We're working on it, Ker. I know that we keep saying it, but it's the truth." Brendon looked around. "I don't know about anyone else, but this is frustrating to no end for Ker and Brody. What are we missing?"

Ker was on her feet, moving quickly to a blank sheet of paper on the wall, a pen in her hand. She wrote swiftly, listing names, occupations, relationships between them. She moved to a new piece of paper and began to list names of missing children and teens that she knew of. Where they had disappeared. If they had been found and where.

Finally stepping back into the circle of Brody's arms, she studied the wall, fatigue weighing her down.

"Does this help?"

———

"It does, Ker. We were remiss not to have you in here before. I guess that we were trying to spare you any more distress." Bradon looked worried.

"It's okay, Bradon. I know why you fellows did what you did. Now, if this is what helps, I will do it again and again until we find the ones at the top."

Standing in front of Ker the next day, Bruce and one of the Foundation lawyers, John Timms, watched as she sagged for a moment and then straightened back up, a determined look on her face. John had been instrumental in obtaining all the paperwork from the other law firm and had been dismayed at what he had found.

"Can we go somewhere and talk this over, Ker?" Bruce looked past her to see Brody heading their way. "Here's Brody."

"Bruce? John?" Brody's voice held the question that he wouldn't ask.

"We just asked that we speak with Ker. I'm glad you're here, Brody." Bruce pointed towards the office that he had in the building.

Ker sat, her hands clasped together, her eyes on the men. "Bruce? What did you find?"

"John will explain. First, we need to pray, Ker. That's how we start our meetings."

Bruce watched with interest as Ker took each document that she was handed, reading it through thoroughly, making notes, asking the questions that he would have expected Brody to ask. Then he realized that he was selling her short, that perhaps they all had been. In front of him was an intelligent, knowledgeable young lady.

"Brody? What is this?" Ker finally held the last paper.

Brody peered at it. "It's a power of attorney for financial affairs."

"But it's not Mom or Dad. Who is this person?"

"It's not?" John reached for it. "You're right. We found that with the paperwork. I needed to speak with you about that one. Do you recognize the name?"

Ker shook her head. "No, I don't. Who is this Ted Lowe?"

"That's what we will look into then, Ker. I think that we have covered everything we need to at present." John shared a look with Brody.

Ker walked away from the meeting with a handful of documents, Brody by her side. He watched her intently, not seeing the distress that he had expected.

"You okay, Kitten?"

"I am, sweetheart. I am. I think that overnight I came to the realization that I cannot change what happened in the past. I cannot change who she was or what she did. I am responsible only for myself. That is something I think I was seeking, to be responsible for others. And I can't be."

"That's good. Prayers are being answered then." He unlocked their apartment door and headed for his office. "Bring your paperwork back here when you're ready. I need to check on my emails. Then, if you want, we can do some research." Brody reappeared when Ker didn't respond. "Ker?"

Ker looked up, a puzzled look on her face. "That name. That Ted Lowe? I don't know it. I'm just not sure why Mom would have had that document."

Brody walked back to her, taking the documents and dropping them on the hallway table, and simply enveloping her into a hug.

"We'll figure it out. Right now? Come with me. You can sit and watch me work." He smirked at the playful swat she aimed his way.

"I need to find something to do, Brody. But with this hanging over me, I don't want to put anyone in danger."

"We get that, Kitten. We'll find something for you. What about going back to school?"

Ker shook her head. "I don't think so." She reached for the documents that he was holding. "Go. Do what you need to. I plan on reading back through these."

An hour later, Brody looked up, a smile creasing his face as he watched Ker. She had stretched out on the couch, dropping the documents to the floor, and was fast asleep. He rose, covering her with a blanket and dropping a kiss on her cheek before he reached for the documents and returned to the desk.

Brody was puzzled as he read through them again, knowing that Ker would not mind him doing just that. He made his own notes, reading hers and her questions. She's got a logical mind, he thought. He stopped at the last document, the one naming her mother as power of attorney for Ted Lowe. He reached instead for his mouse, waking up his computer, and then was deep into research. He didn't like that he could find no evidence of anyone by that name. Sitting back, Brody finally reached for his phone, sending off a request to Emma. She was back to him promptly, promising to have something as soon as she could.

He looked up as he felt a hand on his shoulder. Ker stood there, watching him. He simply reached around and drew her down on his knee, startling her for a moment, before she leaned against him.

"Ker?"

"Brody? What did Mom do? Who is that person?"

"Emma's looking into for us. Did you hear from her or Abe how Keefe is?"

Ker shook her head, a sad look covering her face. "No, and I wish I did. This is so distressing, Brody. I want to move on with our lives, but how can we?"

"We will. We will not let this stop us. Now, how be we head into town for dinner? I would like to take my sweetheart out for a meal?"

"Casual, I hope. I have no dress-up clothes."

"No, you don't, but we'll take care of that. Casual works for me." He watched her face for a moment. "Something is puzzling you."

"There is, Brody, and I don't know how to ask. Am I really your sweetheart?" Ker watched him.

"You are, my love. That you are. You were the one I was waiting for." He kissed her and kissed her again.

Ker sat for a moment, her eyes on him before she spoke. "I am glad, Brody. We need to talk about so much, but with this hanging over us, it just doesn't seem right."

"No, and you are grieving as well." He set her on her feet and rose, his hands reaching for hers. "Come. Let's go do something fun."

The next morning, Brendon stood at Brody's door, knocking and waiting for an answer. He frowned. He had talked to Brody last the afternoon before and had made plans to meet him that morning. It was not like Brody to not be there.

A thought had him running for the stairs and then to the parking lot, sliding to a stop. No, Brody's truck was not there. Now, where was he? His phone out, Brendon searched for messages and found not.

"Brendon? You look lost." Brady approached him, on his way home from his shift.

"I am. I was to meet with Brody and Ker this morning. There is no answer at their apartment. And his truck is missing." Brendon spun in a circle. "He hasn't parked anywhere else."

Brady shifted his duffel bag and motioned to the building. "Let's head in there. See what we can find. When did you last speak with him?"

"Late yesterday afternoon. He said something about going out for dinner with Ker. I would have thought that they would be back."

Both men turned as they heard their names called and found Abe running towards them.

"Brendon. Brady. Where's Brody? We've been trying to reach him."

"We can't find him. The last I spoke with him was yesterday afternoon." Brendon pulled open the door, waiting for the other two men to enter. "You're here for a reason."

"My whole team is. Emma got word last night that someone would try and kidnap them. Don't tell me that we're too late." Abe was worried. It was not often that Emma received such messages but when she did, they were always correct.

Brady dropped his bag by the elevators and ran towards the office hallway, searching for Breck.

"Breck? Do you have your key for Brody's?"

"I do." Breck looked up from his desk and was on his feet. "Why?"

"We can't find them. Abe's here. There is word that they were to be kidnapped last night."

"What?" Breck moved rapidly, grabbing the keys to the building suites from his desk drawer. "You're sure they're not around?"

"No answer Brendon says at their apartment. And his truck is missing."

"I don't like that, Brady. I was just about to head up there anyway." Breck peered at Abe. "And Abe is here."

"He has his whole team, Breck. Emma sent them."

"She did? That's not good." Breck took the stairs two at a time and landed in front of Brody's apartment in no time. Hearing no answer, he unlocked the door and cautiously opened it, walking through to search. "Not here. Wait. Here's a note. It's from Brody. Now, how did he know to leave one?"

"What does it say?" Abe stood near the open door.

"Just that they were going out for dinner last night. And that they expected to be back by 7. But he had a meeting early this morning. Brendon? Do you know anything about that?"

"No. He had planned to be here." Brendon reached for his phone as it chimed. "This is strange. A message from Brody's phone, but it's not phrased as he would phrase it. Just that he's running late and would be here shortly."

"No, that's not quite how he would phrase it." Breck left the apartment, locking the closed door behind him. "Now where would they have gone?"

"I would suspect somewhere casual." Brady looked around. "Fynn said that Ker has not yet replaced her dress clothes. Was reluctant to in fact. She felt it too much like what her mother had demanded of her."

"Okay, so casual. But that leaves a lot of restaurants." Abe stood for a moment, studying the sky from where he now stood in the parking lot. "We didn't get a lot of information last night. Emma was still trying to confirm it or track down the source and was having difficulty doing that." He looked around as he heard footsteps. "Micah?"

"Emma called. She didn't want to call you. She found them."

"She has? Where?" Breck pointed towards his vehicle. "Where do we go?"

"You don't. You three stay here. Let us go in." Abe ran for the SUV, Micah on his heels.

The three watched them drive away, not quite sure what had happened.

"Now what, Breck?" Brady walked back towards the building and inside, retrieving his duffel bag, a yawn catching him unawares.

"We work hard to try and find out who is behind it. Brendon? You had needed to talk to Brody and Ker?"

"I had. I came across another name that I needed to run by them. A Tom Light."

"Tom Light? That's a strange name."

"I know. We have documents on him. Dallas has that information as well." Brendon sighed. "This just does not get any easier."

"It never does. What else?" Breck pulled up a chair at the table that Brendon had claimed.

"Not a lot from what we had last night. I feel like we are missing one small piece and that piece is what we need to crack this wide open."

"I know. Has Ker talked to her brother?"

"Not that I am aware of." Brendon frowned. "I thought that was why Abe was here."

"Obviously not." Breck rubbed at his forehead. "I just wish we could figure it out, fellows. This is wearing on Ker. She's grieving in so many ways, but can't fully and opening grieve or attend the funerals without resolution of it."

Standing sheltered partway by Brody, Ker stared at the man standing in front of them. She didn't know him, but he looked familiar. Brody refused to let her move past him, his eyes searching for anyone else that was around.

"I just need to talk with you two. That's all." The man was pleading, desperation on his face.

"And why?" Brody was stern, not willing to show how scared he was for Ker.

"Her mother did me wrong. I just want to tell her what happened. There were others as well. I want them brought to justice." The man rubbed at his face, the sound of his hand scraping across his face loud in the stillness of the early night.

"Okay. Brody, where can we meet him that has people around? An all-night coffee shop or cafe?"

"There's one. Just down the road. Lee's. We'll meet you there in thirty minutes. Be on your own."

"I will be. I want to give her some stuff." The man whirled and was gone before either one of the young couples could respond.

"Brody?" Ker was frightened.

"I know, Kitten. I know. That's why I suggested Lee's. He's a friend and works overnight. There are usually patrol officers stopping in for coffee or a meal. It's the safest place that I can think of." He led her to his truck, tucking her inside, watching for anyone who might approach.

Parking behind the restaurant, Brody took Ker's hand as he walked towards the back door, keying in a code, and then pulling the door open. They stood, just inside the door, watching the activity before Brody pointed to a young man around their age.

"Lee?" Brody's voice was quiet, but the man still spun.

"Brody! Where have you been? You haven't been in for a few days. And just who is this that you're holding onto so tightly?"

"Lee, this is Ker, my bride."

"You're married?" Lee looked surprised before his brows lowered and his eyes narrowed. "Don't tell me. You're having one of those things you call an adventure." He waited for Brody to speak. "You're not saying anything, Brody."

"You told me not to tell you." Brody laughed, Ker's gaze flickering between the two men. "Listen, someone approached us about what we're going through. He's to meet us here. Watch for us, will you?"

"That I can do. Stay here as long as you want. Paul and Peter will be in and out all night. They're on duty."

"That's good." Brody hesitated. "I just want you to watch and see if anyone is around that shouldn't be."

"On it, Brody. You've done a lot for my family, you and the Foundation people." Lee pointed to a corner booth. "Take the one I usually use. I can see you from here. Coffee for you. Ker? May I call you that? I can? Oh, terrific. Tea?"

"Thank you, Lee. I would appreciate that." Ker was quiet as she seated herself on the bench seat and slid over for Brody to sit on the outside. "What are we expecting, Brody?"

"I have no idea. He seemed almost too eager to talk to us."

"I know. That scares me." Ker watched as the man entered the diner, looked around, and then headed their way. "Here we go, Brody. Do we need to let anyone else know?"

The man hesitated before he sat, looking up as Lee approached with coffees for the men and tea for Ker.

"Anything else?"

"Have you eaten today?" Brody watched with compassion as the man finally shook his head. "Lee, bring us a meal for him. For me, a piece of whatever pie you have. Ker?"

"Nothing for me, thank you, unless you have some fresh fruit?"

"I do. I'll be back with some for you." Lee walked away, to stand where he could not be seen and could watch the man. "Peter? Have you seen him before?"

Peter, Lee's brother and a patrol officer, stood behind him. "I have. He's been wandering around the downtown area for the last couple of days. He seems harmless but we're watching him." Peter looked around. "I'm off duty soon. I'll change to street clothes and come back."

"Thanks. Brody and Ker are going through something.'

"Ker? That's her with him? She's a beauty."

"She is. She and Brody are married."

"Where do they find all these beautiful women?" Peter was happily married but liked to tease Lee, who was still single.

"I have no idea, but ten of them have." He turned. "Let me know when you're back."

"I will. Watch yourself."

Lee set the meal down in front of the man, seeing his trembling hand as he reached for the fork, pausing as Brody prayed for the food.

"No one has done that for me for years. Thank you."

"Okay, eat. Then, we talk." Brody sipped at his coffee, even as Ker ate her fruit, both of them watchful.

"Now, tell me. What did you want to talk to us about?" Ker finally spoke, her eyes on the man.

"I know you. I saw you with her."

"With who?"

"Your mother, I think. She wanted me to do something and I wouldn't. Then she stole from me. I just want to know why."

Brody was surprised at what he heard, but then he realized that he shouldn't have been. What they had discovered over the last few days was that Kelly Deeks in fact did steal from people. Not just in money but in identification and documents. It was disconcerting, to say the least. Ker had just looked at them as they had detailed it all and shrugged. To her, it was just who her mother had been and become.

"Why would you say that?" Ker pushed.

"Because it's what she did best. She stole from people. She took my identity and used it for someone else. That ruined me. She stole who I was." The man reached carefully into his pocket and pushed across an envelope. "My name is Lowe. Your pa was kind to me when I met him. I was looking for work, hadn't worked in months. He set me up with a friend of his to do landscaping. I was happy there until your mother came around. She kept after me to do dirty deeds for her. I owed her, she would say. I said no, I didn't owe her or anyone. What I had, I had worked for.

"She kept after me. I finally had to leave town, but when I did, I found that my identification was gone. I had to replace it. She forged a power of attorney using my name and gave it to someone, some lawyer I think it was. I tried to get it, but I couldn't prove that it was fake. I went to the police but they just laughed at me and threatened to put me in jail." The man paused, his jaw working as he tried to control his emotions.

"So then, what happened?" Brody shared a look with Ker, even as he tried to watch the people in the cafe. He nodded at Lee and Peter as they moved around the main portion of the building.

"So, I had to start all over, in another town. I went to a lawyer there, and we managed to stop her. But it didn't help my reputation. I had to rebuild it all. I watched her from afar, just waiting for an opportunity to bring her to justice. I didn't want revenge, but I didn't want her to do to someone else what she had done to me." Lowe paused. "She ran with some pretty bad people. I would see them with kids and teens and then hear that they had disappeared. I tried to follow her one day. Someone must have seen me. I ended up in the hospital with a broken leg from being run down in a parking lot."

Ker looked down at the envelope. "What's in here?"

"As much evidence as I could find. It also has my statements from the police about what happened and when. I kept it, hoping to find you or your brother. Your father? I was never sure about him."

"Dad wasn't involved." Ker looked up at Brody. "Keefe? We don't think he was."

"He wasn't. Your mother made sure that you kids weren't. At least, not directly. I overheard her threaten you two about four months ago. She was speaking with your pa."

"That's about the time Dad became more distracted. Brody, did he know?"

"I would suspect so. Lowe, what else?" Brody nodded as Lee held up the coffee carafe. "Here, Lee. Refill this for Lowe. Would you like anything?"

Lowe hesitated and Brody shared another look with Lee.

"It's okay. Have want you want. It's on the house." Lee nodded as Lowe looked up in surprise. "So, what kind of pie would you like?" He just grinned at Lowe.

Two hours later, Ker had finally given in to her fatigue and cradled her head on her folded arms and slept. Lee had arrived with the plaid blanket that he kept in his office and handed it to Brody to cover her. The men's conversation had drifted to many things, coming back time and again to God. Brody rubbed at his sore eyes, but he refused to give in. There was something about Lowe, that made him want to trust him, even though he still wasn't sure of him.

———

"What do you plan to do now?" Brody turned his spoon over and over, not looking at the other man.

"Move on, I guess. Try and find somewhere that I can live until I can retire. If I can even do that." Lowe sighed. "I regret this. I trusted her pa."

"And your trust was broken not by him. Do you like this area?"

"I do. I moved around the province after my wife died. She was young and had cancer. I just couldn't stay in one place, grieving too hard, I guess. This has felt like home."

"Then, don't move on. Have you heard of the Barnabas Foundation?"

Lowe stared at him. "Who in this area hasn't? They're good people. Take care of people." He was puzzled. "Why?"

"Because I work for them. I am also a paralegal. Let us help you. I want to solve whatever it is that needs solved for my wife. And her brother. I can talk to them. See where we can find you work and a home. In the meantime, try the shelter here. Another one of the Foundation men's in-laws run it. Just tell them Brody sent you. They'll take you in." He nodded at the lightening sky. "It's almost dawn. Why don't we spend some time in prayer, my friend?"

Lowe blinked rapidly as his emotions caught the best of him. "You would do that for a stranger? For someone who might have harmed you or your woman?"

"I would. You're a brother in Christ. I can do no less than give you a helping hand."

It was early morning, the breakfast rush just starting, when Ker roused, blinking to clear her vision. She frowned for a moment.

"We're still in the diner?"

"We are, Kitten. Have a good sleep?" Brody just grinned at her.

"I guess. Where's Lowe?"

"He's gone. I sent him to the shelter. They'll take him in until I can talk to Barnabas." Brody hesitated. "What are your feelings about him?"

"I think he was telling the truth. We'll need to look into that envelope. Or have you already?"

Brody shook his head. "Not yet. Not without you. We'll look at it at home." He glanced at his watch. "I have to meet Brendon in an hour or so. We need to get moving."

"Sure. Whatever." Ker was still thinking about the man who had approached them, a frown across her face again. "How did he find us?"

"That I asked him. He said he had been wandering around the area, recognized you, and took a chance on approaching us. Don't worry. I won't let him near you until we get this resolved."

"Thank you, sweetheart." Her hand in his as they walked towards his truck, Ker's steps slowed. "Brody? What's on your truck?"

"I have no idea. I don't like it. Back to the diner, Kitten. Paul was just coming in off duty. I'll catch him to take a look."

They stood just inside the diner, watching closely as Paul approached the building. He had a grim look on his face. As he entered, he pointed towards the hallway that led to Lee's office.

"Paul? I don't like that look." Brody spoke as soon as Paul closed the door behind him.

"I've called in the bomb squad, Brody. I'm not taking any chances. We've heard what's been going on." Paul peeked around the door as a tap came and he spoke quietly to whoever it was. "I'll be back. I want you two to stay in here. If you're expected anywhere, call or text them that you're delayed. Just not why. Not until we can sort it out." He was gone, the door shut behind him before either of the couple could speak.

Brody sent off a quick text to Brendon, not really aware of what he was saying, and not knowing the consternation and fear that text would cause. He paced the office, Ker watching him from where she had perched on the corner of the desk.

Dallas peeked around the door before he entered, his eyes on the two in front of him. He shook his head. Lord, when can this be over? This is getting worse and worse for these two. I hate to be the ones to tell them this.

"Dallas? You're here?" Ker tilted her head to watch him.

"I am. Ker. Brody. Walk me through the last twenty-four hours." Dallas notepad and pen were out as he sat behind the desk.

Brody did just that, leaving out the part about the envelope. He wasn't ready to share that with Dallas, not yet. Ker watched him, shaking her head at him. Dallas watched the silent communication between the two.

"What did he leave you? And don't tell me that he didn't."

Brody sighed, holding up the envelope. "This. We haven't had a chance to look at it yet."

"May I?" Dallas' voice was stern as he asked.

"Only if you do it in front of us and let us see what is in it. Otherwise, it was given to us and is private material." Ker was digging in her heels, wanting it to be all over, but not willing to give up control of something this small.

"Okay, Ker. We can do that." Dallas reached into his pocket for latex gloves, snapped them on, and then opened the envelope, pulling out the documents.

Brody and Ker crowded close, watching and reaching each one.

"This doesn't make sense, Dallas." Ker was puzzled. "I don't know these people. Who are they?"

"That's what we need to find out. Are you sure he was legit?"

Brody shrugged. "He seemed that way. We spent hours talking and praying. The thing of it is? When Ker went over the paperwork with our lawyers, there was a power of attorney in his name. He says it was forged."

"Okay. I'll talk to John, was it?" At Brody's nod, Dallas tucked away his notepad and pen. "I'll leave this with you. If you can make copies for me, I would appreciate it."

"We will, at some point." Brody looked towards the door, fatigue weighing him down. "What about my truck?"

"Your truck? Oh, that. It was a bomb, Dallas. Set as a threat more than likely. Who did you anger?"

"Me? I have no idea. Unless it's whoever Kelly was working with."

"That's what we think. It will be a while yet before you can have your truck. If you're wanting to leave, I'll make sure that you have a ride home." Dallas looked around as he heard footsteps stop behind him. "Abe?"

"Dallas. Brody. Ker. We've been looking for you two. Brendon was worried." Abe's voice gave nothing away, nor did his face.

"I know. I was to meet with him." Brody looked down at Ker. "Any chance of a ride?"

"Sure. We'll take you home."

"We?" Brody peered at him. "Just how many are we?"

<hr>

“All of us. Emma sent us.”

“Emma? That’s bad.” Brody reached for Ker’s hand. “Back door?”

“Of course. We’re parked right outside. We have two vehicles, Brody. One of you in each.”

“No way. I’m not leaving Brody.” Ker’s anger flared briefly.

“Ker, let them do it their way. This is how they work. This is how they keep people alive.” Brody watched her until she gave a reluctant nod. “Who’s Ker with?”

“You’re with Joseph, Ian, Micah, and Luke. Ker is with Nathaniel, Murphy, Matt, and me.” Abe quickly moved them to the vehicles and watched behind him as they drove away, heading for the Foundation building before the SUV in front of him pulled to the side, Murphy who was driving theirs following suit.

Abe was out of his vehicle, Micah coming towards him.

“Micah?”

“Emma called. She was trying to reach you but couldn’t. There’s news.” Micah looked up, trying to find words. “It’s Keefe.”

“No. Not Keefe.” Abe grew stern. “What happened?”

“He’s admitted that he knew what his mother had been up to the last few months. He was trying to get away, to find someone who could help. That’s when his father sent him away.”

“This is not going to help Ker. Not a bit. She’s sure, I know.” Abe turned to stare at the vehicle behind him. “We need to take them home. It’s almost to the point where we would normally hide our friends.”

“I know. That won’t work with this couple. Brody is ready to break free and go after them himself.”

“I know, and we can’t let them.” Abe rubbed at his chin. “We take them home and make sure that they stay put.”

“It won’t work, Abe. Not there. What was going on at the restaurant?”

"A bomb on his truck. I sent Barnabas a text that we had them and were heading their way." Abe finally turned. "Head on out, Micah."

Abe slid back into his seat, nodding at Murphy. He turned slightly to watch Ker, finding her eyes on him.

"What happened, Abe?"

"We need to talk, Ker, but I want Brody there."

She paled. "Keefe?"

"He's okay, Ker. We'll connect you two today."

"Do more than connect. I need my brother and I need him now. Please?" Ker knew she was begging but she just needed her older brother.

"We'll see what we can do. Right now, we need to get you two back home." Abe shifted around to watch the area around them. "Someone's out there, fellows."

"I know." Matt had been watching the area. "And there's a truck behind it. It pulled over when we did."

"Can you get the plate number?" Abe ducked his head to stare out the back window.

"No. He's staying back far enough that we can't." Matt was frustrated.

Barnabas approached Abe, watching as Brody and Ker were hustled quickly into the building, Abe's men surrounding them, his own men watching from the sidelines.

"Abe? Where did you find them?"

"At a diner called Lee's. They had been there all night, from what I was told. They met someone named Lowe."

"Lowe? That name came up in our research. But all night?" Barnabas was puzzled.

"Lowe. Ker said that they made sure he had something to eat, Brody sent him to the shelter, and then when they went to leave, a bomb was found on Brody's truck."

"A bomb?" Breck let out a whistle. "Someone means business."

"They do. We need to talk, Barnabas. This is getting out of hand. We can't lock them up, but we need to work with you and your security and the local police to determine just what we do."

"Brody won't do that." Breck was adamant in his statement. "And Ker is getting angry. It has been building for years, I would say. She's just as apt to go after whoever it is."

"Don't let her. If you have to, stage the confrontation where you can control it. And there will be a confrontation, that much I can guarantee." Abe watched as his team returned, mingling among the building men for a while before heading for the vehicles. "We need to get on the road. We're leaving tonight for a week. Call Emma if you need to reach me."

"We will." Barnabas shook Abe's hand and then stood back.

The two men watched the vehicles leave before they turned to find all twelve of the Foundation men behind them. They could see the ladies in the lobby, watching as well.

"Brody? What didn't you tell Abe?" Breck walked towards him.

"This." Brody held up the envelope. "Dallas has looked through it. Lowe gave it to us. We need to talk about what he said." Fatigue was making it difficult for him to talk.

"You need to catch some sleep first, Brody." Brendon reached for the envelope. "Head off and get some. We'll meet later this afternoon. You know where to find us."

They watched as Brody hesitated, nodded, and walked away, his arm coming out to gather Ker to him.

"He's about at the end of what he can take. He hasn't let himself heal." Brady spoke as he followed their progress.

"No, he hasn't. And he won't, not until it's all over."

"And that will keep Ker from relaxing as well." Buckley shook his head. "This is the part, isn't it, fellows, where we need to pray and pray hard."

"It is, Buckley. Prayer chain at work?" Bradon grinned at his friend even as he headed for the conference room.

"Absolutely. I didn't have to start it this time. Your wife took care of that. I'm putting her in charge."

"Really? She'll enjoy that." Bradon stood in front of the map. "So, where do we go from here? It's centred back around our town once more."

"It always comes back to that, doesn't it?" Burnie stood beside him, a frown on his face. "I always have felt that there was a common theme running through all the adventures. That there's someone else involved that we have not figured out yet."

"That's what we all think. But going back to Lowe, what's in the envelope?" Brendon walked over to where Breck had opened it and laid out the paperwork.

<hr>

"We need to find out what their discussion was. But this is interesting. Proof of a stolen identity. Police statements. Copies of his identity. And a letter was written to Ker and Keefe from him." Breck sorted through it. "I think it will help move us forward. He names people. Anyone recognize them?" He passed around that piece of paper.

Brandon took it, heading to make copies of it. "We'll each need a copy. A copy of everything and then the originals get sealed into an envelope. He said Dallas has seen it?"

"He did. That helps." Blair took the papers as they were copied, sorting them out and then handing them around.

Four hours later, Brody stood in the doorway, Ker beside him, watching as the men worked away. He had spoken with Dallas, who had confirmed that the bomb had been meant for him. There had been a note inside it. Whoever it was had seemed to think that Brody would not open the box himself.

"Brody? Where do we go from here? They want to lock us up somewhere. I couldn't stand that." Ker drew closer to Brody, leaning against him.

"Nor could I. But if it becomes necessary, we'll have to." Brody nodded towards the men. "They've been at work while I've been sleeping. So have you."

Ker looked down at the sheaf of papers she held. "I was. But I don't know that I did any good. What I found from newspaper articles doesn't make a lot of sense."

"It might when we put it all together." Brody walked them over to the table he favoured and seated her.

Baird approached. "Brody? You two are okay?"

"We are, so far. Thanks for asking. Where do we stand?"

"Further ahead but still not there." Baird blew out a breath of frustration. "We're missing something, Brody, Ker. Just what it is, we're not sure of."

"Can we somehow visualize what you have found out? Sometimes, that makes it easier." Ker looked at the wall. "And I can see that you've started that."

"We have. It's a continuation of the logic puzzle. That we've been able to sort out more for."

Chapter. 40

A week later, Ker approached Brody as he stood on the balcony in the early morning sunlight, his hands clasping the railing. He simply reached to pull her close to him, loving her more each day. He reached to kiss her, finding her face upturned for that.

"Ker? Have I told you today that I love you?"

She smiled, content to be held. "You have. I love you, too." She seemed unsettled for a moment. "Brody? Someone has found my new phone number. There were a lot of awful brutal texts sent overnight."

Brody stared down at the phone that she was thrusting at him. "They have? You read them?"

"I started to and then stopped. I don't want a phone. Not if this is what is happening."

"We'll get you another one." Brody turned them back into the apartment. "Let me call Dallas."

"I did already. He's not in today. I turned the phone off. I don't want them sending anymore." She paced the office, not looking at him, her arms wrapped around herself.

Brody watched her closely, seeing how fragile that she had become in the last couple of weeks. "I wish that I could just take you away somewhere and come back when this is all over."

"I wish you could. I pray every night that I will wake up and find this over or at least that it's a bad dream. That never happens. What am I supposed to be learning through all this, Brody?"

"That I don't know. To trust more, I guess. To seek God in a deeper way." He stared down at her phone. "Let's tuck this away. Dallas is in tomorrow?"

"They said that he would be. They promised to give him my message." Ker was hesitant in how she spoke. "This is so different from what I am used to."

"I am sure it is. We have a good force here." Brody glanced at the clock. "It's too early to go downstairs."

"And why? Does the door not open until a certain time?" Ker was challenging him, she knew.

He shot her a look and then began to laugh. "You have me there. No, it doesn't. We have spent all-nighters in there at times." He reached for her hand. "Let's head down there, then."

His phone ringing as they walked towards the room had him reaching for it, a frown on his face.

"It's Abe. I thought they were to be away."

"I thought so, too. Answer it."

Brody listened as Abe spoke quickly, asking only the question "When" before he pocketed his phone and reached to wrap Ker into a hug.

"Brody?" When he didn't respond, she pushed at him. "Brody? What did Abe want?"

"He and Emma are heading this way. This morning. And Keefe is coming." He watched as her eyes sank closed before they popped open again.

"Keefe? Is it safe?"

"They seem to think so. Emma has more information for us. He said it would be a flying visit, but Keefe would be staying if we can arrange that."

"And of course, we can. Can't we?"

"That we can." Brody studied her again. "Are you ready for this?"

"I think so. I mean, we need to talk. Doing that over the phone doesn't work so well." Ker pulled the door open and looked in. "I thought that you said it was too early. It doesn't look that way."

Brody laughed. "No, it doesn't." A hand to her back, he directed her in, heading for Breck. "Here. Ker's been getting a lot of messages on her phone."

———

"She has? We wondered. And it's a number that shouldn't be out there."

"No, it's not. Dallas is out of the office today, so we'll turn it in tomorrow. If you need to take a look at it, here's the password." Brody scrawled it down for him.

"Thanks, Brody." Breck peered at Ker, watching as she wandered around, reading the papers on the wall. "How is she?"

"Hurting in many ways, Breck. Abe and Emma are heading this way today. Keefe is with them. Abe said that he'd talk to you about what to do for security for him."

"It may make it easier having them together, but it may make it harder." Breck rose, setting the phone on the desk. "Let me go talk with security. See what we need to do."

"Thanks, Breck." Brody stood, lost in thought before a hand on his shoulder roused him from his thoughts, some of which were dark.

"Brody?" Blair stood there, his eyes shifting between Brody and Ker. "How are you both?"

"That is a question that I really don't know how to answer. Ker is hurting in ways that I can't make better for her. Keefe is heading this way today."

"He is? That's good, isn't it?" Blair was unsure of how to read Brody about this.

"It is, and then again, it might not be." Brody blew out a breath. "I'm really not sure how to take it. Ker wants to see him, but she is afraid."

"Afraid of what she might find out from him? Or afraid that he'll be hurt if he's around her?"

"Both, I think. I know that I have real hesitations about him coming. What if he has been involved all along?"

"I talked to Abe earlier. A friend met with him. She's a retired forensics psychologist. She didn't pick up that he was the culprit or that Ker needs to fear him. And Abe said she is one of the best he has ever seen at reading people without meeting them in person. She's even better when she can sit down with the person."

"That's good to know." Brody looked around. "You fellows have been busy in here all night, haven't you? Where do we stand?"

"That's what we need to discuss." Benen had moved closer. "We have some research that we need to clarify with Ker. Brody, in your job, did you ever come across someone who tried to bribe you?"

Brody's eyes shot to him, shock on his face. "I did. About a year ago. I had forgotten. I never got the woman's name or any more details from her. Once she tried to offer me a bribe, I cut the conversation off. I don't even know if I have the number for her now."

"Then, that's part of how you got involved." Benen held out a file folder. "Read this. You'll need to talk to Ker as well."

Looking up from where she had been reading, Ker frowned. The men were quiet, which she found unusual. They were usually joking with one another. Right now, they were all deep in concentration, the occasional question or comment from one to the other breaking the silence. She rose, wandering around the room, needing to move but not wanting to leave where Brody was.

Brody watched her closely, noting the distress on her face before he looked back down at his notes. He sighed, threw down his pen, and rose, heading for his bride.

"Kitten? How be we take a walk around the lobby? We both need a break from here."

"Sure." She shrugged as she took the hand that he held out for her. "Did Abe say when they would arrive?"

"No, he didn't. Just sometime this morning." Brody paced with her, his hand holding hers tight. "When this is over, do you want to run away with me for a few days?"

"You would do that?" She looked up at him. "Where?"

He shrugged. "We could find a nice hotel. Or a cabin in the woods. Or go camping."

"I've never been to a cabin in the woods or camping. Can I think about it?"

"I guess. I was hoping to know today." He laughed at her look of outrage. "It's okay, Kitten. You can think about it, and we'll make the decision together." He smiled widely. "I like the sounds of that. Making decisions together."

"You do, huh? And if we don't agree?" She smirked at his own pretended look of outrage.

"Then, we compromise. We go where you want and then next time where I want."

"Sounds like a plan." Ker's footsteps slowed as she stared through the window, her attention on the vehicle stopped just outside the door. "Keefe?"

"It's Abe and Emma. And that is your brother?"

"It is. It's Keefe. What happened to him? He looks sick."

"He has been, Kitten. Abe hasn't told us where they found him or what happened to him. That, I think, was likely for your own protection."

Keefe Deeks stared up at the building, amazement on his face. "This is the Foundation building?"

"It is, Keefe. The main offices are here. Each of the men who live here has an apartment and also an office. There are a physician and his wife on site as well." Abe watched him closely, knowing how close it had been to losing him as well. "Brody and Ker are here. Just inside the building doors."

"They are." Keefe's attention went to the door. "Can I go in?"

"You can. In fact, it's likely best that we get you inside and under cover." Abe's hand gripped Keefe's elbow to steady him, Emma on his other side with his bag in her hand.

Keefe stopped just inside the door, looking around, his attention drawn to the comfortable feeling of the lobby before he caught movement in front of him. He frowned for a moment and then his face cleared.

"Ker? You're here?"

"Keefe!" Ker broke from Brody and ran for her brother, finding his arms open to receive her hug, Abe's hand on his back to steady him.

Ker's sobs shook Brody as he heard them from where he had moved closer. He finally just reached to encircle the siblings with his arms, his quiet prayer reaching them and calming Ker. She looked up at him, mouthing a thank you to him before she studied her brother.

"Brody, we need to get Keefe somewhere he can sit down."

"That we do. Abe, Emma? Are you with us or with the fellows in the conference room?"

"I'm with them. Abe's with you." Emma moved away rapidly, her worn sneak scuffing softly across the floor.

"Abe?" Brody turned to him.

"Let's get him up to your place for now. I think your Doc will need to see him."

"We can do that. He's at work today." Brody reached for Ker's hand, watching her closely before he led the way to the elevator and then to their apartment.

Keefe sank gratefully down onto the couch, his hand held tight in Ker's. He was exhausted but glad to be with his remaining family. They needed to talk, he knew, but it would come.

"Ker? You're okay? You're happy?" Keefe's eyes opened to watch her.

"I am, Keefe. This is not how I expected to be married. In fact, I didn't think I ever would. Brody is the one God meant for me. That much I know." Ker watched him. "And now you're here. Keefe, are you really okay?"

"I'm getting there, sis. It will be a while. Whatever they gave me drained me and kept me in a stupor of some kind. I just don't know what it was. Abe here said I was on my own when they found me. I don't remember much, other than Dad insisting that I take my vacation at that time."

"I wondered about that. He also arranged for Brody to come in to go over legal documents. That I found it strange that he didn't meet with him. He was afraid for us."

"I think so. I would find him up late at night, working away in his home office. When I would ask him what I could to help, he just waved me away. I did find information that he was planning on shutting down the agency."

"He was? I wondered. Just something that I felt. Did they tell you how he went?"

Keefe nodded. "His heart. He denied that he had any problems, but I could see his health was failing." He sighed, his eyes closing. "I'm sorry about Mom, Ker."

"Why?" Ker shared a look with Brody, who had sat on the arm of the couch, his arm around her, and with Abe, who had seated himself across from them.

"Because you deserved to have a different mother. One who you could have pleased, been friends with. And that you didn't have. You don't know the number of times that I stepped in to shield you."

Ker reached to hug her brother, tears sparkling on her eyelashes. "I know, Keefe. I know of some of them. Mom made sure that I did."

———

Breck paused in the hallway of Brody's apartment, his eyes on Keefe as he slept, before he moved to the kitchen, thanking Brody for the mug of coffee handed to him. He sat, his eyes on Ker, as she too slept, her head pillowed on her arms, a blanket wrapped around her.

"She okay?"

"She will be. She's taken it well, but it bothers her how Keefe was treated. She wants the culprits for that."

"We're tracking them. I spoke with Dallas earlier. He was around, just to take Ker's phone. He's talked to Will, and both feel that they need to work on that. Dallas did say that they were closing in on some of the lower echelons, as he put it."

"That's good, as long as it doesn't cause the head ones to run." Brody sat beside her, his arm around her. "She can't take much more. She's struggling in her faith, the longer this goes on."

"I know that she is. So are you. Do you need to talk, Brody?"

"Not at present, but at some point, I likely will." Brody paused. "What have you discovered about the documents that Lowe gave us?"

"They are legit. That much we know. Dallas didn't say much about them, just took the copies we gave him. He's wearing out, Brody."

"That he is. We've done that to him."

"No, I don't think so. I mean, maybe to some degree, but there's more. His interests are changing, I think. He's not sure what he wants, is what I'm picking up."

"I get that feeling too." Brody sighed again, his eyes on Ker's face. "I want this over, Breck. How do we do that?"

"We'll talk to Keefe. Put together what he can remember with what Ker has. Match it to what we have found out. Our concern is that we won't find out who it is in time, and Ker or you disappear."

"I know. That worries me. It is keeping me up at night, trying to think about how to keep her safe. I have to be back in the office next week. I have no choice. There are some cases and documents that I need to deal with."

"We get that, Brody. The security head has been working on that. They'll take you in and bring you home. If Ker has to go with you, your employer has said that's okay. We've tried to think of everything that we could to try and keep you two safe."

"We appreciate it." Brody was silent for a moment. "Breck, can I run something by you? Something that has puzzled me all along."

"Sure." Breck reached for the pad of paper and pen laying beside him. "I see that you were prepared."

Brody grinned. "Always." He sobered. "Okay, say Keefe was not taken to keep him quiet. That's what we assumed. What if he was taken as a threat against Keene? Or against Ker?" He paused. "But, what if there is another party involved? Keefe was taken as a threat to Kelly? To make her cooperate with them? Only she refused to? That's why Keefe was kept as he was?"

"That's an interesting supposition, Brody. Bradon mentioned that this morning. He seems to think that might be the case. He's working on that, trying to find whatever information that he can."

"And what about you? What are your feelings?" Brody watched Breck closely.

"I think that there is merit in that." Breck looked around to find Keefe standing beside him. "Hi. I'm Breck."

"What you said? How serious were you?" Keefe pulled out a chair, slumping down in it.

"Serious enough that two of our men are heading up that way today. Our Foundation pilot is flying them up." Breck watched Keefe closely.

"Good. My mind has been so foggy but it's starting to clear. I can remember Dad asking me to take my holidays at that time, even though I didn't really want to. He was insistent that I did. For some reason. He never said, but he had been distracted lately."

"What can you remember about that?"

"Not a lot. He wouldn't say much. Not unless he had proof. And if he had proof, then he would confront that person." He groaned. "I can remember him and Mom arguing that last day before I left. He was calm but stern. She was excited, angry, loud. She wasn't like that." Keefe studied his still-sleeping sister. "I can remember Ker being mentioned. I couldn't hear what Mom said, but I heard Dad tell her that there was no way Ker was going somewhere. I left the next day."

"And where did you end up?"

"I headed towards Toronto but never made it. Someone ran me off the road, shoved me into another vehicle, and tied me up. I could see my car following us. Then, we traveled for hours, ending up near the Quebec border. I was shoved into a room with no windows, the door locked. They must have drugged me at that point. I don't remember much until Abe had me at his place. And I can't describe the men. They seemed to be disguised."

Late that night, Brody stared at his computer screen, reading an email that had reached him through his work account. He paled, re-reading it, before he was on his feet, moving rapidly through the apartment, searching it. He pulled out microphones from the office and the living room. His face grew stern. Someone had been in his apartment. The only ones, beside Breck and themselves, were the cleaners.

He stood for the longest time, watching Ker sleep, before he turned away, looking for his phone, sending off a text message to all the fellows. Responses were quick, and he heard a tapping at his door.

Breck and Brandon stood there, Brendon and Blair coming up behind them. Brody stood back and pointed to the kitchen.

"I have coffee on. We're going to need it." He handed out the mugs of coffee and then the email that he had printed. "This is what came through my work email. They have been in our apartment."

"So they have. What did you find?" Brandon looked up.

"Microphones in the office and living room. Nowhere else. No cameras." Brody pointed to the counter. "There they are. I'll contact Dallas in the morning. This has gone too far, fellows. I want to go on the offensive. Put out a statement or two."

"We can do that." Breck nodded. "We'll work with the lawyers and the police public relations."

"No, not the police. On our own. We'll let them know what we plan, but this is for us, Breck. For Ker and myself. For Keefe. They won't stop coming after them until we do. They're cowards and bullies."

"They are. Before we do anything though, we pray. We don't go out there until and unless God says that we do." Breck watched with compassion as Brody finally nodded. "I know that it's tough, Brody, but we can't move without God being there."

"I know, Breck. I get that. I just want this over. Can we do that?"

"We can." Brandon looked up at him. "I found some new information just a bit ago. I have verified it but haven't had a chance to talk to anyone else."

"And that would be?" Brody wanted answers.

"That Kelly had a brother who ran with a shady group. She kept in touch with him behind Keene's back. He is the one who was behind what happened to Keefe. The police in that area arrested the men and they talked. Emma was able to get that information for us. They have a warrant out for his arrest. The thing of it is, he's in this area."

"Lowe?"

"That's who we suspect. You wouldn't have known when you met with him. Dallas was in touch late this afternoon. The documents are all forgeries."

"And he seemed so earnest and honest. Ker had sensed a hesitation about him. We talked through the night. He gives a good line."

"That's what the men who were arrested have said. They said that he was out for revenge, but would play it like he was the one hard done by."

"And that's exactly how he played it." Brody watched Ker as she moved slightly before he rose, scooped her into his arms, and headed for the bedroom, to tuck her into bed. He stood for a moment, praying for her, knowing that they were heading into the roughest part of what they faced.

"Breck, now what?" Brody reached for his mug, refreshing his coffee before he sat again.

———

"We keep you two as safe as we can. We work on your publicity request. If the lawyers say no, Brody, we don't go ahead with it. We have to weigh your safety against what we could find out by doing that. How prepared are you for further violence against you or Ker?"

"I'm not, but I know that we could face it anywhere or at any time. As I said, I want this over with and soon."

The men bent their heads and discussed the options, finally coming up with a plan.

"You'll talk to Ker, I take it, Brody?" Brendon looked up finally.

"I will. We need to do this, fellows. They're hiding. And when they're hiding, they'll strike at us when we least expect it. I don't want that."

"We understand, Brody." Breck paused before he spoke again. "Let's pray, okay? We need that."

Ker shifted uneasily late the next morning. She had not seen Keefe, for some reason, and she was glad that she had not. Something was off about him, and she just could not place what it was. He wasn't the brother that she remembered. She ran quickly down the stairs and headed for the conference room, needing the company that she was sure that she would find there. And she was right. Most of the fellows and all of the ladies were gathered there, looking up as she shut the door carefully behind her.

Fynn approached her, a frown on her face. "Ker? What is going on? You are white!"

"I am? Oh, no. That's not good. I just thought of something and needed to talk to someone."

"Well, I'm here. So are the other ladies. What can we do for you? Here, come over to this corner. We staked our claim on it."

"Staked a claim?" Ennis began to laugh as she heard Fynn. "Fynn, your language and description at times leaves a lot to be desired."

"Well, it's exactly what we did. Isn't it? Ker, sit. And no, I don't think that you're a dog."

The ladies broke out into merry laughter, Ker staring at Fynn for a moment.

"Fynn, stop while you're ahead. You're just making it worse." Cadee grinned at Ker. "Now, that you're here, we're all set. First, let's get you your tea." She was up and away, back quickly with the tea that she knew Ker preferred.

"You're spoiling me, ladies." Ker smiled at them.

"And you deserve to be. We've been where you are right now." Berneen looked up again from her paperwork. "Now, Ker, what can we do for you? You're troubled."

"I am. You know that Keefe has arrived."

"We do. How is he?" Devaney looked Ker over carefully.

"I really don't know. He sounds like my brother and looks like him, but there is something off. Something he has said that just doesn't ring true to what I know." Ker was troubled by what she had remembered Keefe saying.

"And what would that be?" Guenivere had her pen ready to write. "Or can you share it?"

"I can. I need to go back a bit. Keefe has always tied to defend me and protect me, sometimes to my distress and against my wishes. He said that he heard Mom and Dad fighting but couldn't understand what they were fighting about. He also said he approached Dad late one night. He couldn't have. He had his own place and spent little time at home. He was never there late at night."

"That is concerning, Ker. What else?" Hagen looked around at the ladies even as Imly made notes.

"There is just something off about how he is talking. He doesn't sound or talk like Keefe would."

"Was he drugged?" Fynn watched as Ker nodded. "Sometimes drugs do that, but not to the extent of what you're saying. There's more?"

"There is. Someone was sending me texts and voice mail to the new phone that Brody got me. Keefe was the only one other than Abe, Emma, and all of you who had that number. Was it him or did someone get it from him?"

"I would suggest that we need to talk to whoever it was that he was staying with at Abe's." Devaney sent off a quick message. "Emma will get back to us as soon as she can."

"But who would do this?" Ker was troubled and it showed.

"Whoever it is that is behind all this. This Lowe fellow? Do you trust him?" Imly looked up once more.

"Not really. I slept unfortunately most of the time we were together. Brody talked to him at length, but I don't know that he trusted him fully. Cadee, he sent him to the shelter."

———

"He did. Dad has talked to him. He's not sure that he's on the level, as he put it." Cadee smiled sadly. "Dad has a good read on people."

"He does." Ennis looked around, seeing Brady watching them closely. "Brady's watching us."

"He is?" Ker turned slightly. "Brody's not here. I thought that he was."

"Breck and Barnabas have him in the Foundation office. Something about legal paperwork that they wanted him to go over with the lawyers." Imly looked around. "It's lunchtime, ladies. Let's put out the sandwiches and whatever it is that we brought, eat, spend some time in prayer and then reconvene."

Looking behind him, Breck sighed. So much for having security with him. They had been separated from Brody and himself. The three men behind him were not them. Barnabas had sent Breck and Brody into the courthouse with documents that needed to be filed. They all thought that they had taken the precautions that they needed. Obviously not.

"Breck? What happened to the security?" Brody looked around. "I don't see them."

"They're not with us. Somehow, they were separated from us in this crowd. We have a tail of three men that we need to lose." Breck made a sudden move, pulling a door open and tugging Brody with him. "Down this way. This leads to the basement and then out to the parking lot. There's a path that we can take to get to the street. Not many people know of it."

"I certainly didn't. How did you?"

"Growing up here as a kid, you explored. This is one that we explored often. We used to be able to wander the courthouse, but it's too locked down now." Breck shoved open a door, squinting against the sudden light. "Wait for a moment."

Brody waited, barely daring to breathe, shooting quick glances over his shoulder.

"Breck?" He kept his voice low.

"It looks okay, but I'm not sure." He let the door close, glancing around. "There, that hallway. It will take us back upstairs, to the outside door." He ran quickly, Brody on his heels.

The men popped outside, searching for the men who had been following them, not seeing them. They ran for the parking lot, finding the security team frantically searching for them.

"Breck! Brody! What happened to you two?" The older of the three men hustled them into the truck.

"We were separated from you and followed. I found the old tunnels under the courthouse."

"Good thinking. We saw the men. Dallas was here for a court case. He stopped them and they took them in. We were trying to find you." The man stared at them. "What else?"

Brody shook his head. "Nothing. Just that someone seems to be keeping a fairly close eye on us."

"Someone has been. They've been around the perimeter again, Breck. We'll up the security there for now."

"I know you will. It's what they always do, try and catch our people out in the open. Only Brody and Ker haven't been playing that game."

"Not yet. But it's coming. We need to go on the offensive, Breck. Ker is ready to snap." Brody was growing angry. "I know God is in all this, but it seems as if He's gone quiet."

"It always seems that way, Brody. You know that from the others. Let's meet again with the fellows and see what we can come up with."

Breck and Brody stood in the conference room thirty minutes later, staring around, not seeing anyone.

"They should be here." Breck paced the room. "They were planning on working all day."

"I know. No word from anyone?" Brody walked closer to the tables. "Wait. Their phones. They are all on the tables. What is going on?" He spun as the door opened.

"We've been waiting for you two." Lowe stood there, sneering at them. "Fooled you, didn't I?"

"No, not really." Brody stood, arms crossed. "Not really. You put on a good show. You should be in the movies. I thought back over what we had talked about. You just didn't ring true with some of your words."

———

697

"Is that right? Well, let's see how these words ring true. We have your friends and the ladies. They are separated into two different rooms. No one gets hurt if you come with us."

Brody snorted, causing Breck to stare at him. "No? I would suspect that you've already roughed up some of them. It's what you do. I spoke with Dallas this morning. He warned me that you were not who you said. So, who is Lowe?"

"Lowe? What makes you think I'm not him?"

"Fingerprints, for one. DNA. You shouldn't have eaten in the diner. Not when the two brothers of the owner are patrol officers. You threw out garbage that they confiscated and took in for testing. It proves that you're not Lowe. In fact, you're Kelly Deeks' cousin. You're the one who kidnapped Keefe. Threatened my wife. Who is behind you?"

"No one. I'm the boss."

Brody shook his head. "No, you're not. You're not that smart. You left a few clues in the bomb that you deposited on my truck. That note? It wasn't written by you. It's too sophisticated to have been."

"You think you're that smart?" Lowe raised his arm, bringing his weapon down on Brody's head before either he or Breck could react. Brody dropped to the floor, his eyes closed. "Pick him up. I said, pick him up."

Breck did that, carefully dropping Brody over his shoulder, his eyes on Lowe.

"Now what?"

"Now what, is that you follow me. We'll find the ladies. The men will cooperate if the ladies are threatened. It always works."

Breck gave a grim smile. "And you think the ladies will just do what you want?"

"Of course they will. They're too chicken to do anything else."

Breck simply shook his head, walking towards the outside door and then towards the gym near the other side of the parking lot. "You put the woman in the gym?"

"Sure. Why not?" Lowe stared at him before he shook his head. "They won't try anything."

Breck snorted and then corrected himself with only a gleam of satisfaction in his eyes. He knew the ladies. They would find weapons of some kind in there. They would not let these men win.

Lowe pulled open the door, waiting until Breck had entered and deposited Brody gently to the floor before he too entered and looked around.

"What on..?" Lowe spun, staring around the room, seeing the men that he had left with the women unconscious on the floor. "Where are they?"

"I have no idea, but I can guarantee you that they'll find the men, release them, and then come back for you." Breck leaned against the wall, his arms folded across his chest. "Did you really think that the women who had gone through life and death struggles would sit still for you to destroy them and the fellows?"

"And why wouldn't they?"

"Because they are survivors. They are fighters. They don't take what you dish out sitting down." Breck paused, his gaze on the ceiling before he smiled and looked back at Lowe. "Because God is in control." He moved quickly to one side, ducking as a body flew through the air, a wild cry sounding, and feet slammed into Lowe, sending him unconscious to the floor.

Fynn stood up, dusting off her hands, as the other ladies ran from the locker areas.

"Fynn? You could have been hurt! But thank you!" Ker reached to hug her friend. She poked at Lowe with her toe before she dropped beside Brody. "What did he do?"

"Knocked him out. He'll be around soon." Breck stood back up from where he had been bent over tying up Lowe. "You've tied up the others?"

“We have. Now, we need to find our fellows.” Ennis was angry and ready to fight.

“This is how we do it. We move Brody back into the security office. Some of you ladies will stay with him. Some of you will come with me. Figure it out among yourselves. Now, move.” Breck had Brody over his shoulder again and moving quickly for the main building.

Raising a finger, Breck pointed to the office, heading that way and gently laying Brody down. Ker was beside him, his head on her lap, her hands feeling his head.

"He's got a bad lump here." She looked up to find Cadee beside her, an ice pack in her hand. "Thank you. Breck? Who stays and who goes?"

"You and Cadee stay here. Cadee has medical training. Now, ladies?" Breck looked around with a grin at the angry looks on their faces. "Who goes and who stays?"

"Imly stays. Hagen?"

"We'll stay. The rest of you go find our fellows. We want this over today. It's gone on long enough. Now that they have threatened all of us, we will work together to end it." Hagen followed them to the door, shutting it and locking it. Imly reached for a chair, to brace it under the knob.

"That should hold out anyone. Our guys will batter at the door, I know." Hagen looked around, reaching for the phone. "It's dead. They've cut our communications."

"Here. Brody still has his. I can call for help." Ker dialed Dallas, finding him in the office. "Dallas? We need help."

"Ker?" Dallas sounded distracted. "Where are you?"

"At the moment? Imly, Hagen, Cadee, and I are locked into the security office with an unconscious Brody. Breck and the other ladies are searching for the fellows who are locked up somewhere. Lowe and some of his cronies are tied up in the gym. The phone system is down."

"Ker? What are you talking about? I just called and spoke with Barnabas." Dallas' voice died away. "But come to think of it, he didn't sound like he normally does. How many?"

"How many what? Minutes? Hours? Men?"

"Ker! How many men?"

"About eight and Lowe. There are three plus Lowe tied up. He didn't think that he needed to leave more than that with us."

"Obviously he was wrong." Dallas strode rapidly through the department, looking for Will. "Ker, I'm going to hang up. We're on our way."

Ker stared at the phone. "He hung up on me!"

"Of course he did. It's what they always do, isn't it?" Hagen looked around. "Now, we need to find something that we can defend ourselves with if we need to." She looked around as Brody's phone rang. "You need to mute that."

"I know." Ker stared at the number. "Abe? Why are you calling?"

"Ker? Where are you?" Abe's voice echoed over the phone.

"Locked in the security room. Why?"

"Because we got word that Lowe was going to try something today."

Ker laughed. "Well, guess what! You're too late with the warning. He already did. Fynn took him out. Oh, what a sight that was!"

"Ker? What are you talking about?"

"They separated us, ladies and fellows. We managed to take out the men watching us as they say. Then, we hid. Lowe showed up with Brody and Breck. Fynn flew down from the rafters on a rope, knocking Lowe out. And Brody is hurt."

"Where are the fellows?" Ker could hear Abe speaking with someone.

"That we don't know. Breck and the ladies are searching for them. It's just Cadee, Hagen, Imly, and myself with Brody."

"Do you have help on the way?"

"We do. Dallas is coming. Why? Where are you?"

"Not where we can help, unfortunately. Emma just reached out to me. She couldn't raise any of you."

"Of course, she couldn't. They made us leave our phones in the conference room. Breck and Brody were off site when the men arrived. That's how I have Brody's phone. Brody! You need to lie still. Please! Abe? I need to go." Ker hung up on Abe as he protested.

"Ker? You're okay? The others?" Brody tried to sit up and then slumped back down. "My head hurts."

"Of course it does. Lowe hit you over the head." Hagen knelt beside them. "We managed to take out his men in the gym and Lowe too."

Brody looked askance as the ladies laughed.

"We'll explain, sweetheart. Right now, let Cadee check your head."

"No cut but a bruise." Cadee slapped the ice pack back into his hand. "Keep this on it. It will help."

"I know it will but where are the others?"

"Breck and the other ladies are searching for the fellows. Dallas is on his way. And Abe called to warn us."

"Abe did? He's overseas." Brody studied Ker's face.

"I know. Emma couldn't reach us, so reached out to him. Yours is the only phone we have. They cut the lines or whatever it is that they do in the movies. There is no phone system."

Brody slumped back against Ker who simply wrapped her arms around her fellow, her chin on his shoulder. Hagen positioned herself near the door, listening for any sound from the hallway. Imly took up a position near the window, having closed the blinds, just keeping them open enough that she could watch the parking lot.

"Dallas is here." Her whisper sounded loud in the sudden silence. "Wow! He's got a lot of men and women with him."

"He thinks he needs them. This is a big place to search." Brody reached for his phone as it vibrated. "It's Dallas. He wants to know if we're still in the office."

Ker reached for the phone. "You're supposed to be unconscious. Let me answer him." Brody stared at her in disbelief, Imly and Hagen snickering.

Sudden hammering at the door and jiggling of the doorknob startled them, causing squeaks to come from both Hagen and Imly. Hagen refused to move the chair or unlock the door, afraid that it was Lowe's men.

Brody looked up from his phone with a grin on his face.

"It's okay, Hagen. Breck and your fellows are outside. Dallas is with them." He kept grinning. "Go on. Open the door. They'll keep trying to break it down."

"I don't believe them. Have them send me a picture."

"A picture? Are you for real?" Brody was stunned at her response.

Ker simply took his phone, sent the text to Breck, and waited. A grin lit up her own face as she was on her feet, first showing the phone to Hagen and then to Imly.

"We can open the door. Hurry, Hagen." Imly was there beside her to help remove the chair.

The door was barely unlocked when it flew open and Brendon, Blair, and Brennen were through it, gathering their wives close to them. Breck moved towards Brody, a hand out to help him to his feet and then to steady him. Dallas stared among them all.

"You ladies are okay?"

Their chorus of "of course, we are" startled him before he too grinned.

"Good. Now, we need to have Brody here assessed and then we need to meet to talk."

"I'm fine, Dallas. Just get this over with. Tell me one thing. Do you have the ringleader?"

"No, but we know who they are. Officers and detectives are heading that way now, with arrest warrants in hand." Dallas turned and walked away, his voice trailing after him. "Conference room in ten."

"Did he really say that?" Ker ran after him. "Dallas? Ten? Really?"

"Really, Ker. We need to get your statements while we can before you start talking with one another. You know that."

"I do, but a little time would be nice. We'll be there in thirty." She spun and walked away, nose in the air, as he stared after her.

"I think that you were just told." Buckley grinned at him. "I'll make sure that she's there when you want her to be."

"Do that." Dallas' words were clipped as he walked away. He hadn't told them who the ringleaders were. They were people that not one of them had suspected.

Brody seated Ker in her favourite chair, moving to find tea for her. The other ladies had been in as had Anna and Doc, making sure the building inhabitants were all taken care of and unharmed. Doc had stopped him, checked his head, and then told him to come to see him the next morning. Ker took her tea, her hand reaching for Brody's as he sat beside her. She studied the room and then her friends, glad that it was over, she prayed, and that no one was harmed.

"Brody? Why?"

"That's what Dallas will tell us. He's still working through some of it. We've given our statements. Now, they have to take those, work through what we've said for charges against Lowe and his men. They also have to ensure that the cases are airtight for when they go to court. It takes time. He'll give us what he can tonight."

Dallas finally walked through the door, his mind and thoughts not on the men and ladies gathered there. He had had disturbing news from the arresting officers and sighed to himself. It was not what he had wanted to hear. He took the mug of coffee handed him with a quiet thanks before he found Barnabas.

"Barnabas? Can we spend some time in prayer? Your people need it and so do I."

"It's that bad?" Barnabas searched his friend's face.

"It is. I have no idea how Ker will take what I have to say." He searched the room. "Where's Keefe?"

"Doc has him. He collapsed during our adventure. He's in the infirmary. Two of your people are with him."

"Good. I'll talk to him later. How serious?"

"Doc didn't say. Let's get started on the prayers and then you can have the floor." Barnabas moved to the front of the room, drawing all eyes to himself as the room quieted. "Okay. Dallas is here and will speak in a bit. First, let's spend time in prayer. We all need it. Keep Keefe in your prayers are well."

Dallas stood near the front of the room, his head bowed as he gathered his thoughts, a sigh drawn from deep within. Then, he prayed for wisdom and the words that he needed. He looked around at the men and ladies gathered there. They have all been hurt with this one, Lord, just like all the other times. I pray each one is the last, but in Your wisdom and plan, it has not been. I always feel like there is something leftover, something not explained. That has been expressed to me as well.

His eyes found Ker, who searched his face and then nodded, a smile on her face. She knows somehow, doesn't she, Lord? Just how she does, I don't know, but You do. Protect this lady and her fellow.

"Now that you have all given your statements, have had a chance to relax, I need to speak. It's not easy what I have to say. Ker, my apologies in advance. I would not want to hurt you, but I think I will."

"It's okay, Dallas. I understand. I think that I have an idea of where you are heading. Just from what I discovered this morning. Go on, please. We need to hear your words."

"Thank you, Ker, for being so gracious. Brody, when you were asked to meet with Keene, you didn't know that he was actually meaning for you to meet with Ker. We have discussed this before. He had hoped and prayed that you would take her to safety. It was not in his plans for you two to be abducted and then dumped out where you were. That was the working of the couple who were behind it all. Ker was taken as a threat against Kelly. You were incidental to it all. The bomb threat that came was from them.

"Ker, your house burnt that day as well. We have determined that your mother had your appliances replaced with gas ones, which you refused. You were to be home that day, but not be aware of what was happening. She had planned to drug you, tamper with the stove, and then let the gas heater pilot light ignite the gas. Thank the Lord that you were not there.

"Your brother was sent away by your father, for the reasons we discussed. It was for his own safety. However, we have determined that he knew more than what he has said. He had been investigating on his own, and your mother found out. She talked out of turn, and again the couple stepped in, kidnapped him, and kept him away from you. Abe and his team found him and brought him home. His collapse today is related to the drugs that he was on. I am sorry to tell you that they damaged his heart. With care, he will make it." He watched as Ker turned into Brody, her shoulders shaking with her sobs.

"I'm so sorry, Ker. Now, just to continue. We have investigated your father's agency. It was what you said. He had turned to finding missing children and teens when you were young and that young boy disappeared. He was successful in finding many of them and returning them to their families, with the authorities' help. This caused friction between your parents. It was kept low key until the last few months. Then for some reason, and we have not been able to determine why your mother changed and began to try and sabotage his work. Part of it was done through the law firm that he pulled out of.

"Your parents' papers will be returned to you. There was nothing in them that indicated anything but what they were. We are sorry that your father disappeared and we were not able to find him in time. That is a regret we will live with.

"Your mother's killer has been apprehended. He worked for Lowe. Someone saw something and finally came forward. Again, Ker, we are sorry for that loss.

"Now, on to the couple that was behind this. I will give some background and then go on with what we have found. This couple lost a child to an abduction and resulting death when she was only five. She was searched for, your father being part of the search. They blamed him for not finding her when he could find others. However, at that time, technology was not what it is today. The availability of the resources that we have today precluded finding her. It didn't matter to them. They approached your mother with something that she had done illegally as a teen and began to blackmail her. But then, she began to see the advantage of working with them and the lure of financial gain caught her up in it all.

"She made no effort to escape it. In fact, we have documentation that she planned a number of the abductions, using your father as a sounding board. She left this documentation in a safe that you likely didn't know about. Keefe was able to tell us about that a day or so ago. We obtained the warrants and went in and retrieved it.

"Now, Lowe. He is an interesting man. He was never part of the abductions but worked strictly in what you would term as enforcement for the couple. He ensured that the people that they employed did exactly what they were to. He has been tracking you, Ker, over the last few months, finally approaching you and Brody. He has admitted that he planted the bomb on your truck, Brody, more as a scare tactic. He thought it would drive you from investigating."

"He didn't know us very well, now did he?" Brody's face held the sorrow that he was feeling. "He talked the talk well, but there was always something that didn't sit right. I talked to Cadee's father and he never made it to the shelter, even though someone pretended to be him and did."

"That's what we have determined. There are still avenues that we need to investigate, charges to determine, children and teens to find, if we can." Dallas stopped his speech, choking up for a moment, knowing that he had to name the couple.

"The couple, Dallas? Who were they?" Ker's voice was soft but sounded loud in the silence of the room.

"The couple?" Dallas exchanged a look with Barnabas and then Bruce, who had entered with the fellows. "It is a couple that you all know well. They are part of our church. Stan and Lou Clare."

"Stan and Lou?" Buckley's voice could be heard through the muttering before he nodded. "Yes, I can see that. They tried but tried too hard."

A month later, Ker sat contentedly on the balcony outside Brody's office, wrapped up in her favourite afghan, one he had bought her. It had a verse on it that she loved, simply stating that God would be found when He was searched for with all one's heart. I did that, didn't I, Lord? I searched for You for years. It took this adventure, as we call it, with Brody for me to find you in a new and richer way. She turned her head as she heard the door open and then felt herself scooped up into beloved arms and cuddled down on Brody's knee, a favourite activity of theirs.

"All done?" Her head went down on his shoulder and she felt his kiss on the top of it.

"I am. I talked to my employer. We can leave on Monday for our time in the cabin that he offered us."

"That was so nice of him."

"It's rough, he says. Running water and electricity, but they didn't do fancy when they built it."

"That's okay. If you're with me, that's all I need."

Their voices died away for a while, as they watched the sunset spread out over the lake. They had spent many a night wandering the shoreline, watching the freighters as they moved through it, studying the opposite shoreline.

"Ker? Have you decided what you want to do?" Brody wasn't pushing her but he was curious.

"We've talked about that so many times. I'm still not sure, sweetheart. Cadee's parents have asked me to help them at the shelter. And then there's the youth shelter as well. I might give a day or so to each." Ker raised her head to watch his face. "What do you think?"

"I think that you pray about it, take the time that you need to make your decision, we discuss it, and then you decide. There's no rush. I kind of like having you around here when I'm working at home."

"You do, do you? I like that too. When I think of my parents, Mom really didn't want Dad around. Keefe has mentioned it as well."

"Probably because of what she was involved with. I talked to Keefe a while ago. He asked about the memorial service if you still wanted one."

Ker shrugged. "I am not sure. There would only be the ones from here, and they didn't know Dad and Mom. Keefe and I have talked. Given what Mom did, we don't think it's appropriate. We want to for Dad but it's hard."

"We know. How be we just do something simple here in the chapel? With our friends. Buckley would speak, he has already told me that."

"He talked to me. He has a wild sense of humour, did you know that?"

Brody began to laugh. "He always has. Part of his western heritage, I suspect." Brody reached to kiss her, his hand lingering on her face. "I love you, Mrs. Corcoran."

"And I love you, too, Mr. Corcoran. I never dreamt that day you walked into the office that we would have such an adventure, and end up married to the one that God had planned all those years for us."

"Nor did I. I am thankful that I was there. And I am thankful that you are here, Kitten." He reached into a pocket and pulled out a little calico kitten. "With your nickname, I thought maybe you would like a real kitten."

Ker's face lit up and then softened as she reached to kiss him and then took the kitten, holding her against her face, hearing the contented purr from the little bundle of fur. "Thank you, sweetheart. This is what we needed for our family."

Thank you for picking up the story of Brody and his Ker. Once more the characters had led the story, throwing in twists and turns along the way. Ker's mother was not meant to be one of the "bad guys" but that is how it happens at times. It is always interesting to see who they decide is the culprit.

Seeking for God is a daily task that we need to do. We seek Him first for salvation. Then, we seek Him to grow in our faith, to understand His word, to know what He wants us to do. Seeking takes many different aspects, depending on the person, and just where they are in their life's walk.

Abe and Emma and his full team just had to show up again. I love it when the characters walk back and forth between books. Their stories are in the *His Guardians* series. The psychologist mentioned is Darcie. Her story and that of her husband Doug's is *The Heart of a Lion*.

God bless each one of you as you seek Him and search for Him with all your heart, finding a treasure that cannot be replaced.

Ronna

Buckley: Encouraged to Pray

The Barnabas Chronicles
Book 11

By

Ronna M. Bacon

Jeremiah 29:12
Then you will call on me and come and pray to me, and I will listen
to you.

Hebrews 4:16
Let us then approach God's throne of grace with confidence, so that
we may receive mercy and find grace to help us in our time of need.

Table of Contents

Chapter 1

Feeling as if he was standing at the crossroads of his life, Buckley Cullen stared through the windshield of his car, not seeing the scenery in front of him. He had drawn to the side of the road and into a little store parking lot, not really wanting anything, but feeling he was lost and needing some help. Just what kind of help that was, he wasn't sure. He was worn out, he thought. He had needed a break and the church board had agreed. The pastor was important to them, they told him. The two weeks that he had asked for had been freely granted.

Buckley shoved open the door of his car and then stood beside it, looking around. He had not gone too far from home, taking trips by the day, or just staying home. Today, a Sunday, he had driven away early in the morning, not wanting to see the sympathy on his friends' faces. They were a tight-knit group, the fourteen men of the Barnabas Foundation. Even with ten of them now married, they still stood with one another in difficulties. And there had been great difficulties, Buckley thought, some almost losing their lives.

Hearing a commotion from behind him, Buckley spun around and then moved to the other side of his car, watching closely as the young lady, around his age he thought, ran around the corner of the building. He frowned as he saw the fear on her face and then raised his eyes to watch the man chasing her. Buckley moved quickly forward, reaching for her arm and tucking her behind him, standing with his feet spread apart in a protective manner, his fists curled at his sides.

"Hey! What's the problem here?" Buckley's question and his sudden appearance stopped the man in his tracks.

"Get out of my way! That's my woman!" The man glared at Buckley, who simply stood, not moving, not speaking.

Buckley could feel the lady's head moving against his back in a negative manner. He spoke quietly to her.

"Is that the truth?"

"No." Her voice was low. "It's not. It never has been. Can you help me?"

"Certainly. My car's unlocked. Head for it and lock yourself in. I'll stall him somehow."

"Good luck with that!"

He heard her mutter even as he felt her moving away from him and then the click of the car door. His eyes never moved from the man in front of him, so he saw the instant that the man's fist came his way. He ducked, his foot going out to trip the man, who tumbled to the ground and lay still. Buckley was on the move, into his car and backing it out on the road and disappearing with a trail of dust. He caught a glimpse of the man in his rearview mirror through the dust, a fist raised in anger at him.

Driving away rapidly, Buckley chose roads that he knew would lead him home before he pulled over into a picnic area at the side of the road. He turned to the young woman and stopped, mesmerized by her beauty. Her hair, he thought, is the red-gold of a fiery sunset. Her eyes when she looked up at him were the curiously-coloured jade of a canal near his home. He could see the fear in her eyes and the uncertainty that flickered there as well.

Buckley pulled out his wallet and found one of his cards, handing it to her.

"You're safe with me. I'm a pastor in a nearby town." He looked back towards the road. "What was that all about?"

The lady took the card, her finger gently tracing his name. "Buckley Cullen. A strange name for a minister."

Buckley grinned, his teeth showing white against the redness of his neatly trimmed beard and moustache before he ran a hand through his reddish-blond hair. His dark brown eyes studied her more closely.

"You're scared."

"Well, yeah! He's not going to ever give up." She slumped back against the door. "I'm Locklin Dinneen. Thank you for rescuing me, but I have to go back. At least, I think that I do."

———

721

"And why would that be?"

"Because it's my home. I have nowhere else to go. And so far, no one has lifted a hand to help me."

"Explain, please?" Buckley was concerned, knowing that if he returned the lady, she would face difficulties that he suddenly wanted to spare her from.

"That monster? He's Len Forester. He's been trying to make me his girl or whatever he wants to call it since I was a teenager. I avoid him, stay in crowds, lock myself in my home. It has not stopped him."

"And the police? What have they said?"

"I haven't been able to go to them. It would be my word against his. In this area? His family is the one who counts. Mine didn't." Her voice was barely audible as she finished.

"That's not right. I can help you. I have a number of friends who will as well." Buckley started the car again and moved back to the road, heading for home. "I work for the Barnabas Foundation, even though I have a church near there. They will take you in and protect you."

"No one can, Mr. Cullen. I'll sorry, but no one has ever been able to." Locklin blinked rapidly before she screamed.

Buckley shot a look towards her, seeing the truck heading his way. He spun the wheel, heading for the other side of the road, hitting the gravel and losing control. His car hit the ditch and rolled, ending up against a tree, dust, and debris flying through the air before it became to float gently to the ground.

The man paused his truck's forward advance and then drove rapidly away. He would return, pretending to be a Good Samaritan, he thought. Give them about thirty minutes and he would be back. This was a little travelled road, that he knew. It had been perfect for what he had done.

Buckley roused from where he had slumped against the wheel, batting at the deflated airbag to clear his way. He groaned, a hand to his shoulder before he squinted. This is not good, he thought. What did I go and do, that I don't remember going and doing? Hearing a soft moan, he spun, his seatbelt releasing under his fingers. He stared at the young woman, finally remembering their conversation.

"Locklin? Can you hear me? Locklin?" He reached for her, releasing her from her seatbelt. His fingers touched the large lump on the side of her head, blood oozing from it. When she didn't respond, he shifted once more, shoving at his door until he could finally open it. He reached to gently pull her from the vehicle, cradling her against him as he stood. He was scared, Buckley admitted to himself. He was out in the wilds, or so it seemed, his car was wrecked, and he had an injured lady in his arms.

Buckley stared up at the road and then around him, before moving towards a more sheltered area. Scanning the sky, he shook his head. It was spring, granted, but the clouds were moving in. Laying Locklin down, he staggered back to his car, working to open the trunk and find the blanket he kept there. He would need it. He returned to wrap her in it, sitting and cradling her to him, her head on his shoulder. Finding his phone in his pocket, Buckley stared at it, praying that he would have service before he dialled a friend's number.

Buckley began to pray, an ingrained habit of his. He begged God to protect the lady that he held, his interest already piqued. He prayed for their safety, that the man would be kept away. He begged God that Burnie would arrive quickly. His eyes studied Locklin's white face, and he was afraid, afraid that he had hurt her when he moved her. Please, God? Heal this lady. Don't let me have hurt her.

Buckley tucked his phone away once more, his arms tightening around Locklin. She had not stirred, the dark lashes laying on her ivory cheeks. His head down on hers, he thought through the conversation that he had just had with his friend, Burnie.

Burnie had been shocked, to say the least, at the call from Buckley but had readily agreed to come and find him. He would also arrange for a tow truck, he said. Just where was he anyway?

Buckley had given a short bark of laughter. "I was on my way home and someone ran me off the road. I need transportation, Burnie. Can you help? Right at the moment, my own car is up against a tree and isn't about to be driven."

Burnie had been silent for a moment before his cautious voice sounded through the phone. "Buckley, are you having one of those adventures?"

"What do you mean?" Buckley had a good idea what Burnie was asking.

"You know. Those adventures. The ones that our friends have had. The ones we told Brody ended with him? Are you? Because if you are, I'm telling the others. I don't care if it's Sunday or not, and you're not behind the pulpit. I'm telling."

Buckley gave a brief bark of laughter. "Go ahead and tell. It appears that I am. I rescued a lady in distress and got run off the road for my troubles."

"Are you okay? What about your car? Obviously, it's not working if you're calling me for help." Buckley could hear the door slam as Burnie ran out of his apartment.

"The car is likely totalled. I'll need a tow. Dan would come. This is about where I was. As to the lady?" Buckley stared down at her. "Right now, she's unconscious. I just pray that I didn't hurt her when I pulled her out of the car."

"Whose side?"

"What do you mean? Whose side?"

"Whose side got the brunt of it?"

"Hers. The car rolled when I hit gravel. I ended up against a tree. Is Brady around?"

"He is. He's with me as is Bradon. We're on our way. Stay safe, Buckley." Burnie dropped his phone, staring at his friends even as he drove away from the building that they all called home, each with their own apartments.

"What was that all about? You dragged us with you, Burnie. I know that you don't do that without cause." Brady shared a look with Bradon.

"Buckley's been in an accident. He has a lady with him who he says is unconscious. He asked for you, Brady."

"Buckley? And a lady? He's having an adventure?" Bradon shook his head. "I didn't expect him to be the next one."

"Who did you expect then?" Burnie turned towards the road that Buckley had indicated. He knew that had a ways to go, but he was proceeding just as quickly as he could. He could see a tow truck behind him. "Is that Dan?"

"It is. And we expected it to be you." Brady grinned at the look of horror that Burnie pretended. "Your lady is out there, Burnie. Not in one of those books you write."

"Yeah, those books. No readers would ever believe your stories if I ever wrote them."

"Maybe someday, you should. God protected us, led us, brought our ladies and us together, and through it all, showed just what a great God we have." Bradon paused, his thoughts on his own bride. Ennis was truly a blessing sent by God, he thought, the perfect one for him.

"Yeah. Maybe." Burnie finally slowed. "This looks as if there's been some trouble." He pulled to a stop on the shoulder of the road.

"There." Brady was out of the car, running towards Buckley's vehicle. "Not here. Where are they?"

The three men stared around before Bradon pointed. "There. Under those trees. He's hidden them."

Brady dropped to his knees beside Buckley, a hand on his friend's shoulder, even as they heard Dan beginning to work around Buckley's car.

"We'll have to report this." Bradon walked back towards Dan, who nodded at his shouted request. He turned back. "Dan's already done it. Wherever Buckley was, he's in provincial territory."

"Buckley?" Burnie had dropped down by his friend. "Can you hear us?"

"I can. You can stop shouting." Buckley squinted up at them, his headache raging. "You're here. Good. Locklin needs help."

Locklin had roused not long before his friends had arrived. Buckley had questioned her, searched her eyes, but had little response from her other than her statement that her head hurt. And just who was he? He shouldn't be holding her, she stated.

He had simply held her tighter, worry on his face. His prayers were raising but for once, he wasn't sure that they were being heard. He was scared for the lady in his arms. Buckley had kept constant vigil, worried that the man after her would find them and take her, with him not able to protect or shield her.

"We need to call an ambulance, Buckley. She needs to be in a hospital." Brady was busy examining her. "She'll need X-Rays of that lump at the very least." Brady was a paramedic, and very concerned.

"No. No hospital. Not here." Locklin struggled to stand, subsiding back down at Buckley's arms tightened on her.

"No, not here. We'll take you to my town. Doc, a friend, is working today. He'll look after you." Buckley looked past the three men to watch the red and blue lights of the patrol vehicle that had stopped. "Fellows, can we get to your car? I don't want her out in the open any more than we have to."

<hr>

"She's in danger." Bradon reached to help Buckley stand, not questioning his statement. "Let's get you situated in Burnie's car. You'll need to talk to the police."

"I know." Buckley gently set Locklin down, shifting her to the middle of the seat, and fastening her seatbelt. "I'll be right back, Locklin. I'm just going to talk with the officer." He watched as fear whitened her face. "My friends will be here. No one will get to you. I promise you that. God is watching out for you."

Locklin closed her eyes against the pain even as she gave a brief nod. "Please, Buckley. Be careful."

Buckley finally walked back towards his friends, his body hurting in so many places. He could barely keep himself upright. Brady's hand was there to steady him as he approached them.

"All set?"

Buckley nodded, even as he slipped to the seat beside Locklin. "We are. He'll track us down, he said, just to finalize our statements. Locklin?" Buckley bent his head to study her and then wrapped an arm around her. "Let's move, fellows. I feel someone watching us."

Doc peered over his reading glasses as he heard the footsteps approaching him in the Emergency Department of the local hospital and then was on his feet, moving towards his young friends.

"Brady? You're not working today."

"No, I'm not. Buckley has had an accident. He needs to be assessed. He has a young lady with him as well. She's taken a hard blow to the head. She's somewhat disoriented." Brady pointed to Locklin.

"In here, Buckley. Set your lady on the bed." Doc pointed to the door. "And you head for the next room."

"Sorry, Doc. I can't leave her. Someone threatened her and I can't let her be by herself." Buckley planted his feet near the stretcher, finding Locklin's hand reaching for his. "This is Locklin Dinneen, Doc. We were in an accident, rolling my car, and her side ended up against the tree. She was unconscious for a while."

His three friends headed for the waiting room, Brady's phone out to call their employer, Barnabas Carey, of the Barnabas Foundation. He squinted at the clock and groaned. He would be in church.

"Brady? What's wrong? You never call me during church." Barnabas had stepped from the sanctuary, to pace outside.

"It's Buckley. He's here in the hospital, after an accident. And he has a young lady with him, a Locklin Dinneen."

"He was? He does? How is he?" Barnabas headed for his truck, knowing that he might well be needed.

"He says that he hurts. Likely bumps and bruises." Brady shared a look with Bradon. "It's the lady, Barnabas. Apparently, he rescued her and they were run off the road. I don't have many details."

"Okay. On my way. Doc's there?"

"He is. He tried to make Buckley leave but he's refusing to leave her side." Brady suppressed a grin. "He sounds the rest of us."

"Like that?" Barnabas shook his head. "He's fallen already, just like all of you. Love at first sight and all. Okay. See you in ten."

Doc turned to Buckley, making him sit, pulling the curtain around the stretcher where Locklin lay.

"Buckley, I need to assess you. Locklin will need some X-Rays at the very minimum. Do you know who her next of kin is?"

Buckley sighed. "No. We just met. I saved her from a brute. He ran us off the road, is my guess. He was determined that she not escape from him. I couldn't let him have her. Not if I could prevent it, Doc." Buckley kept his eyes on the curtain, not seeing the compassion and concern in his friend's eyes.

"That is all well and good, Buckley, but let me look you over. Were you unconscious?"

"Briefly. I have a headache."

"I'm sure you do." Doc finally moved away, watching as the stretcher bearing Locklin returned. "Stay put, young man. I'll let you know when you can see your lady again."

Buckley nodded, not catching Doc's words, looking up as Barnabas appeared at his side.

"Buckley? You okay?"

"I am. It's Locklin. I'm not sure if she is." Buckley resisted for a moment as Barnabas reached to draw him to his feet. "I need to stay, Barnabas."

"No, you want to stay. Come with me. We need to talk." Barnabas kept his hand on Buckley's shoulder, directing him to the waiting room. "The fellows have left. So, it's you and me and Breck. Talk to us."

Buckley explained just what had transpired, his eyes not leaving the doors to the exam rooms. He didn't see the looks of concern shared between the two men with him.

———

"Buckley?" Breck waited until Buckley looked at him. "Just what were your plans?"

Buckley shrugged, his finger rubbing at his forehead. "I wasn't thinking, I guess. I just wanted to help her, get her away from him. She said he's been after her since she was a teenager. He called her "his woman". No one addresses a lady like that."

"No, they don't. Not gentleman. Does she have any family?"

"From how she spoke, I would say no. And she did tell me that she couldn't go to the police. That his family were prominent in the area and would be believed over her."

Breck nodded. "Then, we set her up in the apartment near you for now. Just until we can sort through all this." He looked up as an officer approached. "Bill? You're here?"

"I am. I just need to talk to Buckley. Buckley? What happened today?" Bill sat near him, taking notes. "Do you know that you were accused of interfering in a domestic situation?"

"There was no domestic situation. She was terrified, Bill. She was running from him. Locklin told me that she wanted nothing to do with him, and he wouldn't leave her alone." Buckley looked at him. "You believe me, don't you?"

"I do. We know of that family and in particular that man. This is not the first accusation of that sort against him. We just haven't been able to prove anything. The ladies retract their statements or disappear." He looked towards the exam rooms. "I need to talk to her. Buckley, just where are you going?"

"With you. She needs me." Buckley walked away from him, looking for Locklin.

"This is Buckley?" Bill shook his head. "Don't tell me. Adventure number eleven."

Breck and Barnabas shared a look. "It would appear so. He's very protective of her. More so than any of the others, and they have been protective of their ladies."

"I know. Let me go see what I can find out. I take it she'll be at the Foundation building?"

"That's correct. Until we can sort out what's happened and where she wants to be." Breck turned away, heading for the door, intent of talking to Anna, Doc's wife, and setting up the apartment for Locklin. "Barnabas, I'll have some of the ladies find some clothes for her. I doubt that she had time to pack."

"Not likely." Barnabas pulled out his phone. "Breck, wait. I just got a message from the police. It appears that the apartment that she had? The building just exploded. There's nothing left."

Breck spun, shock on his face. "What? Just how close was Buckley to not surviving?"

"That's what we need to find out. The authorities will want to talk with her." Barnabas began to pace. "What was Buckley doing there?"

"I have no idea. He's just been lost the last week or so, staying home or going out on his own for the day." Breck sighed. "He'll need to prove that he wasn't involved."

"That is true. And his heart is already involved." Barnabas nodded to the door. "Head off. Do what you need to. I'll touch base with Will Peters, the chief, and see what we need to do. He'll need legal representation."

Locklin stared at Buckley, a frown on her face before her eyes slid closed. He waited for her to rouse, finally reaching for the chair near him to sit. She hadn't reacted when the officer had asked her what had happened that day, simply shaking her head. That had concerned Buckley. It had concerned him, even more, when Barnabas had appeared, to let him know that her apartment had been destroyed in an explosion, and just what was he doing in that village, anyway?

Locklin finally roused, reaching to raise the head of her bed, waiting for her eyes to clear from the vertigo that attacked her. Her hand rested on her abdomen, willing the nausea to stop. Her eyes found Buckley, and wonder grew within her. Just who is he, she wondered? Do I know him?

Buckley looked up, a smile lighting his face. "You're awake. How are you feeling?"

"I really don't know. My head hurts and I don't know why. And just who are you?"

"You were in an accident. I stepped in to stop a man from taking you away and he ran us off the road. I'm Buckley Cullen, a minister. You don't remember?"

"No, I'm sorry." Her voice was low, melodious, sounding like a song to his ears. "I'm... I'm.... I can't remember my name. Just who am I?" Panic began to run through her until Buckley's hand found hers.

"You're Locklin Dinneen. We met earlier today." He looked around. "You don't remember what happened?"

"No, I'm sorry. I should leave, though." She sat up, her legs swinging to the side of the bed. She stared at the blood on her T-shirt. "I need to change."

"We can manage that. I have transportation waiting for us. We'll take you to the Foundation building and get you set up there." Buckley helped her to stand, an arm tight around her as he walked them to the back entrance of the department, knowing his friends would be waiting there.

Barnabas watched as the couple approached him, exchanging a look with Brady, who had returned, Ennis waiting with them.

"She's not in good shape. She shouldn't be leaving here." Ennis was concerned, to say the least.

"No, but Doc can watch her. He wants her with them. Anna's preparing a room for them." Barnabas walked towards Buckley, causing Locklin to stop in fear.

"It's okay, Locklin. It's my friend, Barnabas. He won't hurt you." Buckley's voice held a soothing quality to it that had her looking up at him, searching his face.

"He won't? I don't know him." Locklin looked up at Barnabas. "You're tall."

Barnabas grinned at her. "I am. So are all my friends. I'm glad to meet you. Now, how be we find my vehicle and I can take you two home."

"Home? I don't know where I live. Where do I live?" Locklin crawled into the back of Barnabas' truck and shut the door after herself.

"Buckley? What does she mean?" Barnabas' hand on his arm stopped him.

"She can't remember who she is. It must have been the head injury." Buckley stared at the truck door. "What do I do now, Barnabas? We haven't had this before."

"No, I don't think we have. In you go, Buckley. Let's get you home and out of sight." Barnabas nodded at Brady and Ennis as he rounded the front of his truck and jumped up behind the wheel. He turned slightly in his seat to watch Locklin. *She's like a lost little lamb, isn't she, Lord? Not knowing who she is or who's after her will be difficult to defend against. And my friend, Buckley, here, Lord, is involved all the way. I know his heart, Lord. He will not walk away from her. And that makes me afraid for him.*

Locklin kept her eyes on Buckley, not watching outside the truck. He knew that she was watching him and kept glancing back at her, a smile to reassure her on his face. She finally looked away as Barnabas parked in his designated spot on the Foundation grounds. Her mouth opened at the sight of the three-story building they called home and had their offices in it.

"This is your home, Buckley? It's huge!"

Buckley grinned. "It is. It has apartments on the three floors, offices on the main floor for all of us. There are fifteen of us who live here, including Doc and his Anna. We have security on site as well. This is where the Barnabas Foundation has its offices. Right now, Doc and Anna want you to stay with them."

Locklin took the hand that he extended to her to help her down from the truck, a look of pain on her face as she landed on the ground. He swept an arm around her, leading her into the building, stopping as she did. She stared around the lobby, wonder on her face.

"This is like heaven, Buckley. Are you sure that I'm still alive?" She looked up at him, complete trust in her eyes.

"Not heaven, Locklin. Home. For now. We do need to talk, though. We need to find out what all you remember."

Her brows lowered as she glared at him. "I don't want to remember. That much I know. Whatever it was in my past has terrified me. Can't we leave it there?"

"No, we will deal with it." Barnabas' voice was firm. "Let's get you to Anna."

Anna watched as Buckley walked towards her, unknowing that his heart was on his face as he watched Locklin. She exchanged a glance with Cadee, Benen's wife, who had dropped by, a pile of clothes in her hands. They had been destined for the shelter Cadee's parents ran but Cadee had pulled them from that pile and brought them up at Anna's request.

"I won't stay, Anna. It will be enough for her just to meet you. I'll come back later." Cadee's voice was soft as she moved away. "Call me if you need anything more."

"I will, love. And thank you." Anna's attention went back to Locklin, who stood in front of her, a puzzled look on her face.

"Do I know you?" Locklin's voice was quiet, too quiet Anna thought.

"No, you don't, love. But you will. I understand you met my husband, Doc, earlier."

"I did?" Locklin looked up at Buckley for confirmation.

"You did, Locklin. He's the physician who treated you." He gently nudged her through the door. "In you go. Anna, I suspect that she'll want to clean up. Cadee been around?"

"She has, Buckley. And I have a pile of brand new clothes for Locklin to choose from." Anna's arm was around Locklin, leading her away, not seeing the panicked look the younger woman shot back at Buckley.

"She's got trust issues there, my friend." Barnabas moved into the kitchen, helping himself to the coffee and then pouring a mug for Buckley. "Sit. You're not too steady on your feet yourself."

"No, I'm not. Tomorrow will be worse." Buckley sipped at his coffee, reaching into the cookie tin that sat on the table for one of Anna's cookies. "Where do we go from here, Barnabas?"

"I spoke with Will and then John, one of the lawyers. He'll drop around tomorrow. Both suggested that neither one of you say too much today, now that you've given your statements. There will be an investigation into the explosion. Bill said he'd go by the tow yard and pull the GPS and what he needed from your car. That should prove you weren't around her apartment."

"That's good, considering that I have no idea where she lives. Am I a suspect?"

"No. They just need to verify your whereabouts and hers."

"She's a suspect?" Buckley had to tamp down the anger that rose. "He's still trying to control her."

Staring at the pile of clothes left on the bed for her, Locklin blinked back tears. They are too beautiful for me, she thought, and then wondered why she thought that. She reached out a tentative finger, finally choosing something quickly and rushing through a shower and dressed quickly. She paused to study the bathroom and then the bedroom. One thing that she was sure of, was that she had never had a room like this. Not that she could remember, and right now, she didn't remember a whole lot.

Opening the door quietly, she paused, a prayer rising from her, surprising her. Did she believe in God, she wondered? She must, she felt confident. She stepped into the hallway and saw socked feet in front of her downcast eyes and then felt welcoming arms just sweeping her into a tight hug. Buckley, she thought. He knew when to come and find me.

"You okay?" Buckley's baritone voice, as quiet as he had spoken, swept through her with peace.

"I guess so. I have never had such clothes so. They must have been meant for someone else." Locklin was almost in tears.

"No, they were meant for you. Cadee, a friend's wife and one of the ladies here, collects clothes for the shelter her parents run. She donates them there or to ones who could use them, without any thought of repayment. She has done that for you as a welcome to the family." Buckley turned her to the kitchen, an arm still around her.

"The family? That sounds like a mafia family." Locklin couldn't figure out why Buckley broke out into laughter. "Buckley? What did I say that's so funny?"

"We're a close, God-loving family, Locklin, that just opens up and welcomes the ladies into our midst." He seated her and then paused. "I have no idea what you would like to drink. Or even eat."

"Juice, I think, Buckley. And soup." Anna gave him a hug on the way by, surprising Locklin. "We do that, Locklin. We're huggers in this family. And welcome." Anna was puzzled as Buckley started to laugh once more.

"It's okay, Anna. I said the same thing, and she informed me that it sounded like a mafia family."

Anna laughed even as she bent to hug Locklin. "Far from that, Locklin. And you are indeed a welcome addition to the family."

"But, I'm not. I'm only here for now. I just wish I could remember my past." That distressed her.

"It will come. When you least expect it, you will remember." Doc stood in the doorway, home for the day. "You need to rest and recover, Locklin. That's why you're with us."

Locklin spun, startled, before her eyes closed and she slid for the floor. Buckley was there to catch her, worry on his face as he gathered her to him, and headed after Doc towards her bedroom. Doc shooed him away once he had laid her down.

Buckley paced the kitchen, not sure where he needed to be, pulling out his phone as it vibrated. Brady. Of course, it would be. He stepped out of the apartment to take the call.

"Buckley? Where are you?" Brady's voice was rushed.

"With Doc and Anna. Why?"

"Because I'm on duty and some man was just here looking for you or Locklin. No one helped him out, but it's only a matter of time until someone says something."

"Is that right? Thanks for the heads up, Brady. Stay safe."

"And you. Call if you need any of us. You've been there for us. We'll be there for you. Gotta run." Brady's phone cut off as he answered a call from his partner, Patrick.

Buckley stood in the hallway, back to the wall, head leaning on it, his eyes closed, praying as he didn't think he had ever prayed before. He had never had a lady that had interested him. Not until Locklin. And he had no idea what all that she was involved with. That he would discover over time.

Brandon waited, his eyes searching his friend's face, Burnie at his side. When Buckley finally stirred, they walked towards him.

"Buckley?" Brandon's voice had Buckley opening his eyes and peering at him. "You're in pain. You need to be in bed, recovering."

"I can't, Brandon. Not until I find out if Locklin is okay."

"Locklin? Why? Did something else happen?" Burnie stared between Buckley and the closed apartment door.

"She passed out. Doc startled her and she just dropped." Buckley moved towards the apartment door, pausing as Burnie spoke.

"We're praying for you two, Buckley. But you need to heal as well. Staying up, waiting for her to awaken, won't do that."

"I know that, Burnie. I know that. It's just... I just don't know." Buckley's voice died away as he disappeared into the apartment.

Burnie and Brandon shared a look.

"He's got it bad." Brandon grinned. "Now, we get to tease him."

"Not yet." Burnie grinned as well. "That will come. Let his lady heal a bit. I'm going in. Are you?"

Standing in the lobby the next morning, Locklin looked around, a frown in place. This could not be a business building, she thought. Not with those wonderful seating areas on each side. She moved towards one, a hand out to touch the gas fireplace. This is so nice, she thought. And to think people live in a building like this. Lord, I can't remember what I lived in or how nice or horrible it was. Thank you for letting me see a little bit of heaven on earth before I leave.

She turned as she heard footsteps heading her way and smiled, the smile lighting up her face. Buckley stopped in front of her, his hands reaching for hers.

"You're here. I was just about to head upstairs when I saw you."

"I am. I don't think that I should be." Locklin chewed at her lip.

"Why not? You're part of our family now." Buckley didn't continue, couldn't until he knew more about her. But all he knew was that he was afraid she would just up and disappear and take his heart with her.

"I am?" Locklin looked up at him, a pleased look in her eyes. "I didn't know that. But, you were heading somewhere."

"I was. I was looking for you. I would like to show you around the building. A security guard will go with us when we step outside."

"A security guard? Why?" She stared down at the hand he had extended to her before she took it, liking the feel of his strong grip, and afraid that she would come to like it just a little too much.

"Because someone showed up at the hospital looking for you. No one said where you were. We're just being cautious."

"Oh. I see. But tell me. What is it you do?"

"I'm a minister, pastor, preacher. Whatever it is you want to call me."

"You are? You don't look like one." Locklin studied his face as he grinned down at her. "You're tall."

"I know. Don't hold it against me, okay?"

She shrugged. "Why would I?"

"You're tiny, like Imly. I'll find her at some point and introduce you. I think you two would make good friends."

Locklin finally stood in the rose garden, a hand reaching for an early yellow rosebud. "This is beautiful, Buckley. Someone put a lot of thought into this."

"The Foundation board did. Barnabas' mother, Elizabeth, helped plan the original gardens. The ladies of the family have all had a say in how they have been expanded. Jacxy runs our vegetable garden, although we all pitch in and help."

"Where is that? I think I remember having a garden like that at some point." She took his hand once more as he led her towards the garden. "I can hear waves."

"You have good hearing. That's Lake Erie over here. The waves are running high today with the winds on the lake. I'll take you there once you're better."

"You will? I'll be here that long?" Locklin studied him again, still not sure of what he was saying.

"You will be, Locklin, if I have anything to say about it." Buckley stared down at her. "The fellows are meeting in a while. Do you have any identification on you?"

"Identification? I don't know. I have this." She pulled a small plastic folder from her pocket. "It was in my other jeans. I don't recognize this person."

Buckley took it and opened it. "It's you, Locklin. Somewhat younger and with a different hairstyle. You're wearing glasses." Buckley frowned at her. "You really don't recognize yourself?"

"No. Is that really me?" She leaned against him as she peered down at the driver's license. "I guess it is. But how do I find out about me? I don't remember anything at all." She looked down at her hands. "I'm not wearing rings. So does that mean I am single?"

"I would suspect so." Buckley swung an arm around her and turned her to the building. "Let's go in and head for the conference room. It has been used a lot for research in the last couple of years."

"It has? Why?"

"Because ten of my friends here all had what they term as adventures when they met their ladies. Some of the adventures were pretty severe." He held the door to the conference room open for her. "There's only Brandon, Burnie, and Baird here right now. Fellows, this is Locklin."

The men stood, coming to shake her hands, surprising her at how polite they were.

"Do you do that with everyone you meet?" She stared at each one and then down at her hand.

Baird sent Buckley a puzzled look. "We do, Locklin, if I may call you that. It's polite to shake someone's hand when you meet them."

"I know that. It just surprised me. Now, Buckley, how did I know that?"

"Likely because that was how you were raised. Have a seat. We'll start the research. Burnie, here's Locklin's identification, although she says the picture isn't her." He grinned down at her as she frowned.

"You'd say the same if you had lost your memory." She looked around. "There are a lot of computers in here. Why?"

"Because there are fourteen of us who sometimes are in this room. As well as ten other ladies." Baird frowned for a moment. "Do you know how to use a computer?"

Locklin shrugged. "I have no idea. It's like being a newborn and suddenly growing too fast. I have no idea what I do or don't know." She grinned at them. "Is this the adventure that I'm to have?"

Buckley groaned to himself. "I have no idea, Locklin, but it looks as if it's part of it. Here, let me boot up that computer, and then you can see what you do know." He walked away a few moments later, to stand watching her as she studied the keyboard and then the monitor.

"Buckley? What's going on?" Burnie was concerned.

"She's forgotten everything, Burnie. Everything. I don't know how we can keep her safe if we don't know who is after her."

Buckley finally sat back from his computer and stretched, before rising and heading for the ever-ready coffee pot, refilling his mug and then turning to study the room. Over the course of the morning, Benen and Breck had appeared. Cadee, Berneen, and Imly had been in and introduced themselves to Locklin, finally drawing her away with them. Locklin had looked at Buckley, panic briefly in her gaze before he gave her a smile and nod. She had sighed, he knew, and left with the ladies. He figured that he would need to go find her soon and rescue her.

Breck approached him, a folder in his hand.

"Buckley? What did you get involved in?" His voice was stern.

"I have no idea. All I did was step in to save her from who knows what." Buckley nodded at the folder. "What did you find out?"

"That her father was gunned down in Toronto, coming out of court for testifying against a drug dealer. Her mother had died in childbirth having Locklin. Locklin stayed in her home village, scraping by. The apartment that she had was in a very rundown building that should have been condemned." Breck handed him the folder. "Read this. Come talk to me. And then we'll go talk to Locklin."

Buckley nodded. Then, as Breck turned away, he spoke. "That man? The one that was after her? Did you find any information on him?"

"I did." Breck turned back, concern colouring his face. "He's what we would call the worst guy in the neighbourhood. There have been reports placed with the police about him, but nothing ever has gone to court. The victims, male and female, have either disappeared or retracted their statements."

"That's what she said. That worries me, Breck. How do we help her?"

"For now? We keep her here and safe. I spoke with Will earlier. Dallas will be out. Will wants to start an investigation, but he understands that Locklin's memory is not there."

"I know." Buckley stared at the floor, not quite sure how to phrase his next question.

"She's single, Buckley." Breck smiled in sympathy as he saw Buckley's body sag in relief. "She's single. And very active in her church. That much we have determined. I know the minister through the Foundation. I'll call him and see what else I can find out."

"Please. Let him know that Locklin is safe, and I won't let her come to harm. Not if I can help it." Please, Lord, let her be safe. She's important to me, and I don't want to see her hurt. Not any more. Please, Lord? I've never asked for this before. Never had an interest in a lady. But Locklin is special.

Breck watched him walk away, before he turned, shaking his head. He looked up as Brendon approached him, his eyes on Buckley as he walked away.

"Buckley?"

"He's okay. He's in love, but I'm not sure how far he'll take it if Locklin can't remember."

"That's what is worrying us, Breck. We found some more information on her father. It's not looking good for what happened to him." Burnie held up another file. "Here. You take it. I think you'll need to head to see John about this."

"It's that bad?"

"Concerning, shall we say?" Burnie walked away, the door closing behind him.

"It must be concerning for Burnie to react like that." Benen studied the papers in the folder with Breck. "That's her father? I heard of him. Oh, man, what did Buckley get involved in?"

"It wouldn't have mattered to him. He still would have stepped in. It's not in any of you fellows to step away from a lady in trouble." Breck headed out of the conference room, intent of finding Barnabas.

"Barnabas?" Breck tapped at the office door, having cleared his way through past Amy, Barnabas' secretary.

Barnabas looked up, distracted for a moment. "Breck? Just the person I needed to see. Have a seat. Now, about that land we were looking at in town? What is your feeling on that?"

"I like it. It's in a good location and would make a good place for that apartment building. How does the board feel?"

"They feel the same. John's been given the go-ahead to proceed." Barnabas sat back, his eyes on his life-long friend. "But that's not why you're here. You are worried. Buckley?"

"Buckley. I have no idea what he walked into, but Locklin's father was murdered after testifying in a court case. They have never found the assailant yet."

"They haven't?" Barnabas paused. "Logan Dinneen?"

"Logan Dinneen." Breck handed over his folders. "Read these. I have. It's not pretty. This makes it even worse that Locklin can't remember her past. We have no idea who to look for."

Chapter 8

Locklin looked up as Cadee dropped down on the couch in Anna's apartment, holding out a plate of cookies.

"Have one. Anna makes the best cookies and she always has tins full for us. We drop in whenever we want, provided that she hasn't told us not to. She's taken us all in and under her wings." Cadee tilted her head. "You're tired. We've worn you out." She was on her feet, finding a pillow for Locklin's head, making her lie down, covering her with the afghan Anna kept on the couch. "You lie still and sleep if you need to. Do you need your pain medications?"

"Not right now. The headache isn't bad. It's the bruise that hurts." Locklin opened her mouth to protest at Cadee's exclamation before Cadee was away and back with an ice pack wrapped in a soft towel. "You didn't have to do that."

"But I did. You need this. It will help." Cadee tucked her new friend in. "Now, rest. I'll just sit here and watch you sleep." She grinned at Locklin. "And if you feel like it, I'll pray with you."

"Oh, would you? I think that would be nice. I can't remember if I had any friends who did that. You three ladies have been wonderful." Locklin blinked back tears.

"There are seven others who want to meet you as well. They've met this morning already for prayer. If and when you're up to it, we would welcome you to join us."

"I would like that, but I don't think I'll be here that long." She slept, not catching the softened look on Cadee's face.

"You will if Buckley has anything to say. And I think that he will, Locklin. You have his heart. I can see that by how he looks at you and looks after you." She looked up as she felt an arm around her. Benen perched on the side of her chair. "You're here?"

"I am. I just wanted to make sure you didn't need me for anything. I have to run to town. Now, give me a list. What do you want for Locklin?" He bent to kiss his wife.

"You know me too well." Cadee reached into her pocket. "Here. This is the list. If Haley and Holly are around, take them with you. It's been a while since they've been shopping for one of us. They enjoy it so much."

"They already tracked me down and insisted that I needed to take them to town. They have their own list. We'll see how well you've trained them. Love you, sweetheart." With another kiss, he was gone, leaving Cadee smiling at how much she loved her husband.

Locklin had awakened and had watched with interest the interchange between the couple. Cadee caught her movement and looked over at her.

"That's my fellow. Benen. He married me when I was out on a mission field, just to make sure I could get out of the country safely. Dad asked him to. We had been friends for years. We had an adventure I'll tell you about sometime, but I will tell you that I almost died from a poisoning. We went through a lot, but we are deeply in love. God has blessed us." She looked around, not seeing anyone else. "Can I tell you a secret that we haven't shared with anyone else?"

Locklin nodded, smiling. "Sure. I think I can keep secrets. You're taking a chance, though."

"You can keep secrets. I know that. I have a good read on people, and I trust you." Cadee paused for a moment. "We're having a baby in about seven months. I think you needed to hear some good news."

"Cadee! That's wonderful. How blessed the little one will be!" Locklin grew sober. "I don't think I'll have married. I'm not the type to."

"Don't sell yourself short, Locklin. I think you will." Cadee looked around as she heard the door and then footsteps heading for the kitchen. "Your fellow is here and I think Breck and Barnabas as well. They always head for the kitchen for coffee and sweets."

"My fellow? Oh, I don't think that I have one of those. I never will." Sadness lingered on Locklin's face as she sat up, wrapping the afghan around herself. Buckley paused before he dropped down beside her, an arm around her to hug her.

Cadee exchanged a look with Breck, who had been watching Locklin intently, and frowned. Something was up. She made to rise, but Breck shook his head. She settled back. Okay, he wants me here. This can't be good.

Locklin looked up at the two other men and then at Cadee.

"You're here. I don't like that. At least, I don't think that I do. You look like you have bad news."

Barnabas and Breck sat, setting down their mugs of coffee and Breck dropping the file folders that he held.

"We do need to talk to you, Locklin. First, may we pray with you? That's how we always start off anything that we are concerned about."

She shrugged, Buckley's arm still around her. "I guess. I have no idea what I do or don't do. And that's frustrating. When will I remember?"

"Likely it will come back over time. Or it may come back all at once. There are some things that you might never remember." Breck nodded at Buckley, who led them off in prayer. When they were finished, Breck studied his hands, not quite sure how to begin. He finally looked up at Locklin, to find her watching him.

"You need to talk to me?" Locklin looked between the three men. "I don't like those looks. At least, I don't think I do."

"We have news, Locklin. We have been researching you, as I am sure Buckley has explained." Breck paused, his eyes on Buckley.

"I did, Breck. Go on. What do you need to say to Locklin?"

"Locklin, we have determined something about your family. I'm sorry, but your mother died in childbirth with you. Your father raised you, up until about a year ago. At that point, he had been testifying in a drug trial. He was not one of the parties that were arrested. He just happened to have information that helped to arrest them." Breck paused, not quite sure how to continue.

"And he was killed? Is that what you don't know how to tell me?" Locklin blinked, not quite sure how to react. "I'm guessing that I grieved. I would if he had been my father. But I don't remember him. And that sucks. Big time."

Chapter 9

Breck nodded before looking over at Barnabas, finding his gaze intent on Locklin. He sighed to himself. This was not going the way that they had prayed. They had prayed that this would trigger a memory for Locklin, and it hadn't.

"Breck, do you have a photo of her father? That might help." Cadee spoke from where she had moved to sit beside Locklin, reaching for one of the other lady's hands.

"I do. Locklin, we are so sorry for you. We cannot imagine how difficult this is for you, to be here with strangers, not remembering who you are or your past. Or even why you were on the run." Barnabas handed Buckley the photo. "This is the one that we found. Your father was a hard worker, not making a lot, but enough to keep you two from want. He made sure that you were taken care of. Breck has spoken with the minister in your town. He was very concerned about you. He warned Breck that you should not ever come back there."

Locklin blinked. "But it's my home. I need to go there." Her voice wobbled. "I have nowhere else."

"But you do, Locklin. You have us. We can become your family if you let us." Buckley hugged her tighter, his chin resting on her head. "None of us want you to walk away and into danger."

Locklin had turned to study Buckley, not sure what he was saying. She frowned for a moment.

"I'm not sure that I should. If I am a danger to you, I should leave." She started to rise but found Buckley had tightened his arm around her.

"Locklin, I am about to say something that we should really discuss in private. But I know these friends of mine. I know that they will support me in what I say." He paused, biting at his lip. "I would like to offer you my name in marriage, to have you become my bride."

"You can't do that!" Locklin was shocked. "You can't!" She whispered it again, her eyes on him. "You don't know me. I could be a criminal, setting you up for something."

Buckley laid a finger over her lips, stilling her words. "I see the real you, Locklin. You are not a criminal. You don't have it in you. Just think about what I asked, and pray about it." He shared a look with Cadee, who nodded. "Talk to some of the ladies here. Berneen, Cadee, Imly, for some. They married quickly in order to protect themselves. Berneen married Baird to save his life. I would offer you my home and my name." He dropped his gaze, not wanting to see the rejection in her eyes that he was sure he would see.

Breck and Barnabas shared a look. They had felt this was the step that Buckley would likely take. John had been around, taking the identification that he offered and heading into the court, to obtain the necessary licenses. None of them knew when Buckley would make the offer, but they knew him. They knew that he would not let a lady like Locklin walk out of his life, not if he could possibly help it.

Locklin studied the photo of her father, a finger tracing the face. He should be familiar to me, Lord, but he isn't. I just don't know why. I am so scared and again I don't know why. Buckley is offering to put his life on the line for me. Do I accept or do I walk away, running for my life, not knowing when it will end? Please, dear Lord, I need an answer and a peace withthat very answer. I need to learn to pray as I have never prayed before.

Buckley sighed to himself. He had blown it, he thought. In his eagerness to protect her, he had blown what chance he had with her. He rubbed at his forehead, his headache worsening. He refused to look at Breck or Barnabas, not wanting to see pity on their faces, yet knowing they would never show that to him. All they would show would be their support of him.

"Buckley?" Locklin's voice was low. "Did you mean that?"

"Mean what? That I would marry you? Absolutely." He watched as she glanced at the other three in the room, reading their thoughts and then lifting her eyes to where Anna and Doc stood, their acceptance of her on their faces.

———

"Then, I guess, I accept." She buried her face in her hands. "That's not how I should say that. Thank you, Buckley. I will marry you."

Buckley simply reached to hug her, his cheek on her hair. He blinked rapidly, not sure what had just happened, but realized that he had taken the step so many of his friends had taken. He was sure that it was right. God had given him peace about it.

Breck sighed to himself. He had done it, hadn't he, Lord? Put himself out there as a target, just to protect a lady. Barnabas shook his head at Cadee who rose and walked softly from the room, linking her arm with Anna. Doc sat beside Locklin, waiting for her to look around.

"Locklin? Let me take the place of your father for just a moment? You are sure?" At her nod, Doc continued. "Then, let us arrange it for you. Breck told me that one of the Foundation lawyers had taken both of your identification and headed in to get the license. I spoke with the minister, Jack, who is taking Buckley's place while he is on vacation. He will marry you."

Barnabas spoke in turn. "I have talked to Will, Buckley. He suspected that you would take this step. He knows you fellows too well. He suggested that you not wait for too long. That if you married, she would have your protection but also the protection of the Foundation and its lawyers as well as the protection and support of the police in town."

"That's true." Buckley looked down at Locklin. "I won't rush her. Not at all."

Locklin looked up. "Buckley, do we need to marry right away? I mean, like today. I'm not ready. I don't have a dress to wear." Tears sparkled on her lashes.

"I don't care about that, Locklin. All I care about is keeping you safe." Buckley looked up as Anna cleared her throat. "Here, go with Anna. She'll find something for you to wear. If you are willing, would you marry me today?"

Locklin looked at Anna and then back at Buckley, nodded, unable to speak. Buckley hugged her once more, stood, and drew her with him to Anna, who simply wrapped them both in a hug and prayed for them.

———

Late that night, Buckley wandered his apartment, coffee mug in hand, not sure if he had made the right decision. He felt that he had. He had prayed hard and long and had not felt God stopping him. His friends had prayed with him as they gathered in the chapel, each one knowing that Buckley would not have taken the step if he had not felt it was the right one. They also knew that he would walk away from his beloved church and congregation if he had to, to protect everyone.

He paused at the bedroom that Locklin had chosen, resting his hand flat on the door, his heart raised in prayer for his Locklin, his bride. Mom and Dad, you would love her. I know that you would. I just wish that you were here to meet her. I never knew that day, when I was only a young teen, you left for that mission trip, and that cyclone hit the village you were in, wiping it out and taking everyone with it. I miss you both. Buckley wiped at the tears on his face. His parents had supported him in all his decisions, talking through them with him, and then praying with him. He needed their prayers right now and then felt peace. He remembered the passage in John, where Christ had prayed for those who were His, all those years ago.

Locklin raised her head, hearing Buckley's footsteps pause for a moment and then walk on by. She snuggled down under the covers, for the first time that she felt she could remember being warm with enough blankets. She felt the sheet, the soft flannel comforting. She slept, her heart raised in prayer and thankfulness, her earnest plea that God would teach her how to pray, to support her husband. She knew that she would need it, being a minister's wife, and not having her memory. She slept, not knowing that the next weeks would test both her faith and Buckley's and test the marriage that they had entered into with God's blessing.

Early the next morning, Locklin crept from her bed, dressed, and then wandered the apartment on her own. Buckley had given her a tour the night before, but her head had been aching too much to take in her new home. She stood in his office, a hand on his chair, praying for him, not quite sure what her duties would be. She ran her hands along the volumes of books on the floor to ceiling bookshelves, finding to her delight the classic novels that she had always wanted to read but had no time to do that.

Locklin searched the kitchen, finding it well stocked with food. She stood staring at some of the small appliances, not quite sure what some of them were before she reached for the eggs and bread in the fridge, and then the ham and fresh peppers and onions. She searched and found the cheese. She would make an omelet for breakfast, she thought, finding the skillet that she needed. Humming, Locklin worked away, content to be in such a beautiful kitchen, she thought.

Buckley stood and watched her, a sigh rising from him. He had had a call from Breck, warning him that the man who had been searching for Locklin had tracked her to the Foundation building. Security had stopped him from entering the main gate late the night before. He had become violent with them and they had called in reinforcements. Breck suspected that he would be back as soon as he could. They needed to talk to Locklin again.

Locklin looked around, a smile brightening her face, before she frowned as she looked down at the breakfast that she had prepared. She had searched for the dishes in the cupboard, delighting in matched dishes, not quite sure why.

"I'm sorry. I should have waited to find out what you wanted to eat." She rubbed her hands together nervously.

"Whatever you have prepared is what I want." Buckley grasped her hands, stilling their movement before he raised them to kiss them. "Now, let's get you sitting, and we can eat." He sat beside her, a hand reaching for hers as he asked the blessing on the food.

He finally sat back, his eyes on her, even as he prayed for her. He knew Breck would be around and he suspected Brody would be as well, in his paralegal work mode.

———

Locklin tilted her head, watching him as well. "Buckley? You're troubled. I'm sorry. I didn't mean to make you marry me. I can leave."

"No, it's not that, Locklin love. I will follow you wherever you go if you do ever leave me. It's not that. Breck called earlier. The man from the hospital has tracked you to here. He was prevented from entering the premises last night and arrested, but we suspect that he will return."

"Do you have a picture of him? Maybe I would remember why he's after me." Locklin twisted the china cup that Buckley had found for her tea, simply telling her that it had been his mother's and she would want her to use it.

"Breck likely will. Another friend, Bradon, will be with him. He's a paralegal and wants to draw up some legal paperwork for us."

"Such as?" Locklin was puzzled. She didn't think that she needed any legal paperwork.

"For starters, power of attorneys for us, medical and finance. He also wants to do a preliminary will for us. We can always change it as we need to."

"Oh, I see. To protect us? Is that why?"

"Exactly. He went through some hard stuff with his wife, Ker, regarding her parents' estates. Their story is quite the tale. I'll walk you through them all later today. That way, you'll have an understanding of what happened with each one."

"How many of you are there?"

———

"With Barnabas, there are fourteen of us. Eleven of us are now married. We also need to talk about finances. I am paid through the Foundation, which they do with all of us fellows. That allows our employers to hire on someone else without worrying about money. It's part of being encouragers, as Barnabas was to Paul." Locklin's gaze never left his face. "Even as a minister of the local church, my wages are paid. That has allowed the church to reach out to the community and help where needed." Buckley paused. "As part of their practice of being encouragers, and to help the couples, the Foundation board agreed that the wives would receive a wage through the Foundation as well. That allows them to either work in the community, volunteer, return to school, or just be at home."

"They do that?" Locklin's voice was quiet. "I never knew that people did that nowadays. I think that it's wonderful. But I don't qualify."

"But you see, you do. You're my wife. Breck or Barnabas will talk to you about it later on. But for now, you're here, with me. I am so glad that you are. I think that I've been waiting forever for you." His last words were barely audible.

Locklin studied him, not sure if she had heard him right, or that she had heard him right when he had called her love. It made her happy but she had to remember her history. She might not be the right one for him. And that saddened her.

Locklin turned from where she had been standing at the door of the office, looking out over the grounds. She smiled tentatively at Breck and then at the man with him.

"Locklin. This is Brody. He's here for what we discussed." Buckley's arm around her drew her to a seat on the couch. "I know Breck. He wants to pray first."

"He does? Okay." Locklin smiled at Breck and then bowed her head.

Breck handed over a folder to Buckley. "In this is a photo of the man who tried to break through our defenses last night. He didn't make it. Take a look at it. Tell me if you think you know him."

Buckley opened the folder, peering closely at the photo. "This is not the man who I stopped from harming Locklin. I've never seen him before."

Locklin leaned against him. "I don't know him. I wouldn't, now would I?"

"We were hoping that it might trigger a memory." Breck nodded. "It was a long shot. He's a known associate of the drug dealers whom your father was testifying against. We're not sure why they are looking for you."

"I don't know that either." Locklin paused and then shook her head. "I'm sorry. I can't remember. I keep saying that. It's not right. I should be able to." She rubbed at the receding lump on her head.

"That's okay, Locklin. He's still in jail. He couldn't make his bail. He's also wanted in other areas. He'll be transferred there today." Breck hesitated and then spoke quietly. "We need both of you to be ever so careful. Buckley, you understand, having been part of what the others went through. Locklin, trust what Buckley tells you. I know it will be difficult for you at times. Talk to the other ladies. Hear their stories. That will help."

"You're scaring me, Breck." Locklin's eyes were huge with fright.

"I don't mean to, Locklin. I just want to warn you to be very careful. Even here on the Foundation grounds. Now, I'm off to a meeting that I can't miss. We'll talk again." Breck was gone before either one of the couple could say anything.

"Did he really just do that?" Locklin frowned as she strained to see through the doorway.

Buckley and Brody laughed.

"He did, love. He did." Buckley grinned at the frown she directed his way. "He'll be back. Trust me on that."

"That's what I'm afraid of. He'll be back with more photos of men that I don't know." She glared at the two men as they continued to laugh. "Now, he's here for a reason. What is it?" She pointed at Brody.

Brody laughed. "You got me there, Locklin. Buckley asked me to stop by. I was going to anyway. We need to do some legal stuff for you."

"Legal stuff? How definitive and descriptive. Is that what you call it to your clients?" Locklin was tired and although she didn't know it, when she grew tired, she could become combative to an extent.

"Legal paperwork, then. First, we need to look at the powers of attorney. Financial. Medical. Particularly medical. We'll make sure that the hospital is aware of this, Buckley. We'll also need to let your family physician know. I assume that Locklin will become one of his patients?"

"I would assume so. I'll talk to him on Monday. Now, about the wills?"

"Wills as well. Locklin, I know you can't remember, but have you ever thought about a will?"

———

"You just told me that I couldn't remember that." Locklin was puzzled, not sure if she ever had. "I'm not sure that I ever did. From what I have been told, I didn't have anything of value." She blinked rapidly to dispel the tears that had gathered.

"I'm sorry, Locklin. I didn't mean to upset you." Brody was concerned about her. "How are you feeling?"

"Feeling? Me? How would you expect me to feel? Apparently, I was chased, jumped in a car, run off the road, and ended up slammed against a tree. Then I'm dragged here, dropped into a huge family that's not a family, and then married. How am I to feel?" She looked sheepish, her eyes on Buckley as she finished. "I'm sorry. That wasn't nice of me."

"But it's true, Locklin. It's all true. I'm sorry that it had to happen to you. But I'm not sorry I was the one who rescued you. Now, Brody, what do we have to do?"

"Let me have a few moments. I can do the documents up right away, have you proof them, and then print them. You can sign them. I'll need some witnesses but I know Baird and Berneen are around as are some of the others."

"It doesn't matter, other than for Ker. She shouldn't be the one as a witness."

"No, she shouldn't. Let's get this done and then I'll be gone." He looked up, hesitating for a moment. "Ker asked if you two would like to come for dinner. It's up to you. She just wanted to extend the invitation."

Buckley kept his eyes on Locklin, even as her body sagged against his, fatigue and pain drawing her strength from her.

"Let's see what this afternoon brings."

"That's fair. Now, here. Sign here and here. Berneen and Baird, you two need to sign. Thanks for coming on short notice."

"Not a problem." Baird spoke for both Berneen and himself. "Buckley has gone above and beyond for us all. We have felt his prayers in whatever it was that we have faced, and in the solutions we have found. It's our turn to be there for him."

A week later, Locklin wandered once more in the lobby, the security guard on duty keeping an eye on her. She had become accustomed to that, and to having someone shadow her if she stepped outside. She had wandered the gardens, checked out the gym, looked over Hagen's shop, and been to the lake with Buckley, just as he promised. She was starting to feel better physically, but emotionally she was on a roller coaster ride, she thought.

Hearing her name called, she turned, finding Imly running towards her. It never failed to amaze her how much energy Imly had tucked into her petite frame.

"Locklin! I was hoping to find you here. I'm having a tea party and I want you to come." Imly linked her arm with Locklin's.

"You are? And why me?"

"And why not you? Come on. We have all the ladies together for a change. Hailey and Holly are there. So are Anna and her sister, Amy, who is secretary to Barnabas."

"That sounds like quite a crowd. You don't need me." Locklin hesitated just inside Imly's apartment door.

"Oh, but we do." Fynn appeared, reaching to hug Locklin and then draw her into the living room. "We have a special seat of honour just for you."

"You do? You shouldn't." Locklin looked around. "Wait a moment. This is more than just a tea party. I see all sorts of goodies."

"It is a tea party." Ennis spoke up. "It's also a shower for you. We wanted to do something to welcome you to the family. This is our way of doing it. In fact, you're the first one that we've done this for. So it is very special."

"Buckley is special to all of us. He'll tease and torment us, but he loves us all. He is such an example to us, even when he is struggling. God chose you as his helpmeet. That makes you special." Guenivere spoke for the group. "Please, Locklin?"

Locklin searched each of the ladies' faces, finding acceptance and not condemnation in them.

"What can I say but thank you?" She blinked back tears even as Cadee hugged her.

"Then, let's party!" The women laughed at Holly's comment.

Later that afternoon, Imly and Cadee helped Locklin gather her goodies, as the twins called them, and head for her own apartment. She had been shocked and then surprised at the thoughtful gifts that she had been given. Locklin hugged the two ladies as they left before she headed for her own bedroom, staring down at the gifts. A nice sweater or two, a gold cross from one of the couples, bath stuff that she had no idea even existed. Some nice enlarged photos. A leather diary. A Bible that she reached for, realizing that her own was likely gone in the fire. She blinked back tears as she then reached for the china teapot and cups and saucers that the twins and Berneen's brother, Darbie, had given her, and turned for the kitchen, standing for a moment just staring around.

Buckley found her still standing there when he came in. He hesitated for a moment to watch her, finding his heart opening up more and more to her. A fervent prayer was raised for her, that she would remember who she was. He had met with the church board that afternoon and had been given their blessings on his marriage, and just when did they get to meet his wife, anyway? That had been arranged for that evening, a light supper at the church with the members and their spouses.

Locklin jumped as she felt arms come around her and then she leaned back against Buckley. I could grow to like this a lot, she thought.

"Have a good day, love?" Buckley's voice was low in her ears.

"I did. The ladies gave me a shower. They said it was the first one for anyone here."

"And it is. They're a wonderful group. I'm glad you're part of them."

Locklin twisted in his arms. "They shouldn't have, but it was nice. I got to meet everyone, I think, other than Ennis' cousin's wife and Fynn's sister-in-law."

"Alice would have been on duty. She's a police officer. And Eric and his wife are away on vacation." His finger touched the teapot. "This is nice."

"The twins and Darbie picked it out. I think I like tea, but I'm just not sure about anything." She looked up at him. "You're quiet."

"I am. I had a meeting with the church board this afternoon."

"Oh no! They fired you!" Locklin was horrified at the thought. "It's all my fault." She struggled to free herself from him.

Buckley simply hugged her tighter. "On the contrary, I was given congratulations and asked when we could meet them. They would like to do a light supper this evening. If you're up to it."

She frowned at him, earning herself another grin. "I guess. I'm not sure, Buckley. I know nothing about being a minister's wife. And there's that danger hanging over me. What if it hits the church?"

Looking around, the man snuck into the garden area of the Foundation grounds, watching for Locklin. He knew that she was here. He had seen her. His boss wanted her. The man had no idea why, but there had been enough rumours and gossips among the employees for him to fear for her life.

He looked around and grimaced. She wasn't here. She was always out here at this time of day. He couldn't hang around or else he would be caught. A sound behind him had him stopping in his backward trek.

"All right, my friend. We're heading into the building." Bradon stood there, Kade, his dog beside him. "You're not part of the family. In you go."

The man sighed. He had blown it. Now, his life would be forfeit, that much he knew. Unless he could swing a deal and leave.

Bradon studied the man closely. He was neat and well kept. Just why he was on the grounds, he would leave that for the authorities to determine. He looked around as Baird and Blair approached him.

"Where'd you find him?" Baird nodded towards the man.

"In the rose garden. I suspect that he was looking for Locklin. She's usually out there at this time of day." Bradon looked the man over again.

"Not today. I met Buckley earlier. They were heading out somewhere for a while." Baird kept quiet where they were heading.

"I see." Bradon looked around as he heard a car door shut. "Here's your ride, my friend. My advice to you is to own up to why you're here. It will go easier with you if you do."

Buckley watched from where he stood near his car, Locklin peering out his open door.

"Who's that?"

"I have no idea, love, but I suspect that he was after you." Buckley slipped behind the wheel. "Right now, we're heading for the church. You need to become familiar with where I work."

She studied him. "Are you sure that you're a minister? You don't act like one."

Buckley laughed at her comment. "I am. I have the diplomas to prove that. But I know what you're saying."

"You do?" Locklin rubbed at her temple. "Buckley, will I ever remember?"

"I am sure that you will. Sometimes it takes great fear or sudden shock to do that."

"That's what I am afraid of. They'll try to do something to you, I'll remember, and then you'll walk out of my life."

"Never, love. I would never do that." Buckley pulled to a stop in the church lot and came around to help her from the car, holding tight to her quivering hand. "I will never leave you."

Late that afternoon, Dallas stood in the sanctuary, his eyes closed, feeling peace flowing through him. He always did when he was there. He felt closer to God when he was in church, and knew that was true but he needed it today, more than any other day. His eyes opened to find Locklin standing in front of him, a hymn book in her hands, a puzzled look on her face.

"Dallas?"

"I'm okay, Locklin." Dallas grinned at her. "I'm okay. I just needed to take a moment and commune with God. And how are you this fine day?"

She frowned at him. "I have no idea how I am to be. What news do you have?"

"I like you. Direct and to the point." He pointed to the front pew. "Can we sit? I was hoping to talk with you."

"Sure. Whatever." Locklin shrugged. "Buckley is on a conference call, I think. He should be done soon."

"We can wait for him if you wish." Dallas sighed as he stretched out his legs. "It's been a long day."

"Has it? And you're here, trying to talk to me." She looked around. "Go ahead. We can always catch Buckley up on what we talked about." Locklin jumped as she felt Buckley sit beside her. "You're here?"

"I am. The call was just finishing when I heard Dallas. Dallas?" Buckley looked over Locklin's head at him.

"Buckley. Locklin. I have news. And I am not sure how to express it." Dallas looked puzzled and then sad.

"And why is that?" Locklin studied him. "Is it that bad?"

"Not necessarily. But it does relate to what happened to you." He pulled a photo from a folder and handed it to her. "I know you may not recognize this woman. But can you please just take a look at it?"

Locklin took it, staring down at it, Buckley's arm around her as he stared at it as well.

"It looks like you, love. Dallas?"

Dallas simply shook his head, his eyes on Locklin.

"Locklin?"

Locklin looked up, a frown on her face. "I'm sorry, Dallas. I don't know this person. I mean, she looks like me, but I'm sorry."

"That's okay, Locklin." Dallas shared a look with Buckley. "I can tell you who she is. That might trigger a memory. She is your mother's sister. She died about six months ago. She had tried to find you but couldn't. She even went to your home area and was sent away."

"She did?" Locklin looked shocked. "Oh, I wish I had known. I would have loved to have met family."

Locklin searched for Buckley that evening, not finding him in the apartment. She paused, frowning, before she grabbed her keys and headed for the chapel. Not here, she thought, before she turned in a circle, not sure where to go.

Burnie was watching her and then approached, finding her staring at him.

"Locklin? Can I help you?"

"You can. Do you know where Buckley is?"

"Sure. He's in the chapel. Have you searched there?"

"I did. He wasn't there. Where is the conference room that you all talk about?"

Burnie motioned with his hand. "This way. I'm heading there. How are you feeling now?"

She shrugged. "Physically I am better. It's just this memory loss that I am having trouble dealing with." She stood in the conference room, staring around. "This is a conference room? It looks more like you would see in a police story, where they all try and solve their crimes."

Burnie grinned. "That's what we do here." He looked around. "No, Buckley isn't here. How be I show you around and you can get a taste of what we do?"

"Sure, why not? Maybe it will trigger something with me. But I'm not holding my breath waiting for that. I'd be too blue in the face if I did." She walked away, not hearing Burnie's soft laughter at her expression.

Buckley paused as he entered, surprised to see Locklin there and deep in conversation with Brady. He turned as Burnie approached.

"She was looking for you, Buckley. I found her outside the chapel, looking lost and forlorn."

"She was? I thought I had told her where I was going. I guess I forgot." Buckley rubbed at his cheek. "I need to do better."

"It will come, Buckley. At least she didn't go outside looking for you."

"No, that's something to be thankful for. How'd she end up in here?"

"I brought her. She asked where the room was. She's been going around, watching everything, talking to the fellows. She asks some tough and discerning questions."

"I would think that she does. She's a thinker." Buckley excused himself and moved towards Locklin, finding her looking up as she heard his steps.

"Buckley? You're here. Brady has been explaining this program to me. It's fascinating. I never knew you could find out ancestors and all that so easily." She beamed at him, drawing him into her beauty.

"We can. Has he been searching for you?"

"He has. Brady, did you say that you could print this?"

"I can. I can also send a link to Buckley and he can pull it up on his personal computer for you."

"Oh! He can?" She sat back, frowning at him, causing him to grin at her. "Stop smirking. I didn't know that. Or at least, I don't think that I did. Maybe?"

"You sound definite there, love. How be we print it, take it home, and then go over it? Brady will continue to add and we can find what he's adding as we work through it."

Locklin was on her feet, already moving towards the printer. Not seeing the papers coming out, she spun and stomped back to stand by Brady. "Okay, buster. Where is it?"

Brady was laughing as he pointed to the printer. "Right there. You hadn't given me time to print it."

Buckley bit back his own laughter, not wanting Locklin to think he was laughing at her. She frowned at him as well before spinning and heading for the printer. Her exclamation that there were too many pages had the fellows laughing quietly.

Brady watched as the couple left before he began to laugh harder. "When she recovers her memory, she'll give Buckley a hard time."

"Yeah. She's just right for him." Burnie turned back, a smirk on his face. "He deserves that. Now, where do we stand? And how far have we researched Locklin?"

"About as far as we can. I put in a call to Emma. She's to get back to me." Brendon looked up. "Any word on that fellow who was here today?"

"Not that I have heard. Dallas hasn't been in contact today." Brennen sent off a text. "He'll get to us when he can with what he can."

Buckley set the papers on the kitchen table and then just swept Locklin into a hug. She surprised him by hugging him back before she leaned to one side and looked up at him.

"Where do we start, Buckley? How do we find out who I am?"

"With what we've been doing. Dallas called. The fellow that they found here? He's an undercover officer, apparently. He can't say more than that."

"Oh. Well, okay. I guess that's all right." Locklin moved away, reaching for her new teapot. "Do you want some tea, Buckley?"

"Yes, that would be nice." He grinned at her. "You just want to use your new teapot."

"Well, there's that." She turned, watching him intently. "Buckley, aren't we supposed to be getting packages with photos crossed off in them, death threats, horrible text messages, and emails, being stalked? Is that happening?"

"Not that I am aware of. We would have been told. I hope it never happens."

"But it will. I just know it." She paced to the end of the counter and back. "I don't want a phone, Buckley, but I know I need one."

"You do. I have one here for you. The only ones with the number other than myself are the family here, and Dallas and Will. We're trying to keep it as private as we can." He handed it to her. "We've programmed in all the numbers for you."

"You have? You're so thoughtful, Buckley." Locklin peered up at him, finding that look in his eyes again. "How did you ever not marry before?"

"I was waiting for you." He watched as she blushed before he ran the back of his hand down her cheek. "I was simply waiting for you."

——

Locklin let out a scream as she opened the package, dropping it to the floor and falling herself, to scramble backward. She drew up her knees, wrapping her arms around them, and hiding her face. Buckley slid to a halt, running towards her as he heard the scream. He stared at the package before he was on his knees, fighting her to wrap her in his arms and then draw her up and away from the hallway.

"Locklin? Talk to me. Locklin?" His frantic words finally reached to her and she threw her arms around him. "Locklin?"

"That package. Get it out of here, Buckley. Please?" Her sobs shook her frame, distressing him.

Buckley reached for his phone, called Dallas, and demanding that he send someone. That there was a package that Locklin had opened and that it had frightened her soundly.

An hour later, Buckley still sat in his chair, Locklin tight in his arms, her head buried against him. She had finally stopped shaking but her face was still white, the shock of what she had seen running deep within her.

Dallas watched her before he looked at Buckley, finding his attention on his wife. He sat, waiting until Buckley looked up.

"Dallas?" Buckley's voice was shaken.

"It's gone, Buckley. Did you see what it was?"

"No. All I heard was Locklin scream. She had gone down for the mail, something she will do if I'm on the phone or deep in my studies. That's what she had done today. The mail is on the table, I think. She had opened the box, I guess, and that's when I heard her scream. What was in it?"

"A blood-covered teddy bear. It shook the crime scene techs as well. There may be a note in it, but we'll have to wait to see what they find." Dallas looked at Locklin. "Locklin? Can you talk with me?"

She shook her head, her eyes turning to watch him. "I can't. I don't even want to think about that thing, whatever it was." She burrowed closer to Buckley. "Buckley, make them stop, please? Make them stop? They keep doing this to me. Sending me boxes with stuff in it. I don't want them anymore. Please make them stop?" Her sobs shook her once more.

Buckley could feel anger growing in him and knew that he needed to address it.

"Dallas, who?"

"That's what we'll work on. There was no return address on the box. In fact, it really doesn't look as if it came through the mail. I'm waiting to speak with the security people who were on duty today and to pull the security feed from today."

"Find them. That's all I ask. I won't have her troubled like this." Buckley bit down his words. "I know. You can't help it. And that you can't stop it." Buckley tightened his arms around Locklin. "Maybe we need to go away somewhere."

"That won't work, Buckley. They'd just follow you. You'd be out there on your own. Here, you have your friends. You have us. You need that."

Buckley finally nodded, his eyes moving past Dallas to find Breck and Doc there. Dallas had sent for them. Doc moved towards them, setting his bag down on the table.

"Buckley?"

"She's terrified, Doc. She had only stopped shaking and then she remembered getting packages like this one. That started it all over again." Buckley looked devastated. "I think she is starting to remember things. This is not what I wanted. Not these things."

"We can't pick and chose what she remembers. Locklin?" Doc waited patiently until she looked at him, drawing in a breath at the haunted, hollow look in her eyes. "Can I listen to your heart, Locklin? Buckley can still hold you."

Locklin finally nodded, submitting to Doc's examination, but not moving a fraction of an inch from Buckley's firm hug. She settled back against him, her eyes shifting between the four men, listening to their quiet conversation.

Dallas finally spoke. "Locklin? I think that you remembered something. You told Buckley that you had had packages like these before. Is that correct?"

Shrugging, Locklin refused to answer before Buckley spoke.

"Locklin? We're trying to help you. Do you remember anything?"

She nodded at last and then spoke, her voice so low that the men had to strain to hear it.

"I think so. I can remember seeing something like that bear and the blood before. More than once. I just don't remember when or where." She looked up at him, her face pale and wan, her eyes dark with her fear. "I don't remember when. But I have seen them."

"Okay. That's okay, Locklin." Dallas had been watching her. "Did you tell anyone?"

She shrugged. "I don't know. I'm sorry. I don't know." Her eyes closed and she slept, unaware of the concern on the faces of all the men.

"Doc? What happens now?" Buckley finally asked the question that he had been hesitant to.

"We wait, Buckley. This may trigger her memory, or again, it might not. Time is all we have right now."

"And time may not be enough. They have followed her to here, Buckley. Somehow, they made you and followed you." Dallas stared at his friend before he spoke again. "And that makes you a target as well. You know that from the others. They'll go after you to get to her."

"As long as they leave the church and the people alone, they can come after me." Buckley shook his head. "But that's what they'll do. They'll go after them to get to me."

"The board is aware of that, Buckley. I spoke with the chairman earlier. They want no changes. The board will go to the people on Sunday, explain what is going on, and give the people the option of coming or not. We already live stream the service." Breck stopped, his mind working. "They need you there, Buckley, no matter how hard it is. They need to see you and to see Locklin."

Buckley paced the apartment that night, stifling a yawn. He had finally gotten Locklin settled for the night, not without a great deal of difficulty. She had simply refused to let him out of her sight, and that troubled him. How was he to do his visits to the sick and shut-ins, to the ones hospitalized, keep up with his meetings and studies at the church, if he couldn't leave her? He prayed as he had never prayed before, finding the experience that they were going through driving him deeper and deeper into prayer and into a study about it. His favourite passage in John came to mind. He loved that he had been prayed for in the garden all those hundreds of years ago.

He turned finally, not sure where to go or what to do. Buckley reached for his phone as it chimed, studying the number and sighed. Charles Turner, the board chair, was calling.

"Buckley? You've been on my mind tonight. How are you and your beautiful wife?"

"To tell the truth, Charles? I'm not sure. We had a disturbing incident today, and it frightened Locklin badly."

"Is that right? This morning, you say? I had an urge to pray for you. Listen? Can we meet? Your place, tomorrow, if I can? No, nothing serious. I just need to pray in person with you both."

"Charles, thank you. I am needing that. In fact, I am not sure with what is happening with us how safe the church and people with be with me around."

"We have talked it over as a congregation. We are standing behind you all the way. We'll talk tomorrow. No rash decisions, young man. You came in when we needed an interim, Barnabas finding you in your home province and bringing you here, without any thought that you would be needed so quickly. You are dear to our hearts, son. We'll talk."

Buckley set his phone down, and then cradled his head on his folded arms, his shoulders shaking as he wept. It was something that he did infrequently, but having spent the last year or more fighting to save his friends and their ladies and now facing the unknown with Locklin, he had reached his limit. He didn't hear Locklin as she rose and searched for him, standing for a moment in the office doorway, watching him before she was across the room, her arms around him, her tears wetting his shirt before he simply reached and swept her into his arms, their cheeks touching, their tears mingling.

Locklin finally drew back, her hand on his cheek, her eyes watchful.

"Buckley?" Her voice held the question that she refused to ask.

"Locklin, I love you. I never dreamt that I would have such a beautiful lady in my life. I am so afraid that I will lose you."

She nodded. "I'm scared too, Buckley, that whoever this is will get to you." She tilted her head to watch him. "We've never talked about your family."

"I lost them to a cyclone overseas. They were on a short-term mission trip. I had just about finished seminary when Barnabas tracked me down and offered me a position, paid for by the Foundation. We were working out the details when they needed an interim pastor here. And I took it on and then the church took me on. Mom and Dad would love this church. I miss them so much at times."

Locklin hugged him, her head on his shoulder. "Sometimes that can overwhelm a person. I wish I could remember mine, but it's only bits and pieces that I remember. Not enough to get a picture. It's frustrating." She was silent for a while, content just to be with him. "Something has me puzzled."

"And that would be?"

"You fellows all have the same initials. Is there a reason for that?"

Buckley gave a quick grin. "There is. God was specific with Barnabas. Everyone he hired had to be an orphan and share his initials. He was true to that command. We have been blessed with him as our employer, Breck as his second in command. The fellows are all great friends, and they are blessed with their ladies."

"I see. That's interesting. And I see that each of the ladies' names start with a different letter of the alphabet in order, except it started with the letter B."

"It does. We've talked about that. We figure Barnabas' lady's name will start with the letter A."

"Does he have a lady?"

"That we don't know. He's never said." Buckley paused. "He can be a very private person. I suspect there was someone in his past."

Locklin nodded. "Yes, he is like that." She looked around. "Did I hear your phone?"

"You did. It was Charles. He wants to meet with us tomorrow." His finger laid across her lips to still her protest. "He wants to pray with us. We have the support of the church family."

"But what if I bring harm to them? What then?" Locklin had to admit to herself that she was terrified of doing just that.

"We'll deal with what we have to." Buckley studied her, finding her not looking at him. "When you said you had received packages like that before, do you remember anything else?"

"I said that?" At his nod, she frowned, a puzzled look on her face. "I don't remember that at all, Buckley. I really don't. I was terrified this morning."

"We know you were. I was scared for you, love." He set her on her feet and rose. "How be you head back to bed? You need to rest."

"That's what everyone keeps telling me. I'm fine." She spun and walked away before she was back in front of him. "I'm sorry, Buckley. That wasn't nice of me."

"It's okay, love. I understand totally." He bent to kiss her, and then sent her off to bed, knowing that he would not be sleeping. Instead, he would be spending the night on his knees by his office chair, petitioning heaven to bring his love's memory back and then protect her while they worked to find whoever it was.

Charles' keen eyes watched Locklin closely the next morning as she set his mug of coffee in front of him and then a plate of oatmeal cookies that she had just made. Buckley seated her before he reached for her teapot and one of the cups and saucers, setting them down by her before his own mug of coffee was on the table and he was seated beside her.

Buckley looked between Locklin and Charles and sighed. *She's out of her element, isn't she, Lord? She wasn't ready to be a minister's wife, and I forced her into that.*

Charles' voice caught at his attention and he looked that way, to find Charles grinning at Locklin.

"Locklin, these are delicious. I must have the recipe. Lois has been looking for an oatmeal recipe just like these."

"Thank you, Charles. It's one I can write out for you." Her brow wrinkled. "I don't remember how I knew it. It was just there when I started."

"It's probably one that you made many times. Our hands will take over sometimes in situations like this. Buckley, do you know what a treasure you have here?" Charles nodded at Locklin's look of shock. "He does, Locklin. I can see just how well suited you two are. You are going to be a wonderful addition to our church family."

"But, I'm dangerous. I could bring someone in to harm the church."

"We know that, Locklin, and are prepared for that. As Buckley could tell you, we have sat through many meetings discussing the situations in other churches, where security was needed. We have worked with the local police and a security firm, just to be prepared. We have officers in our congregation that are there every single Sunday. Besides, God protects us, doesn't He?"

She finally nodded. "He does, but it would still be my fault."

"No, not your fault. The fault of whoever it is that is behind this. What can you tell me about what you have remembered?"

"Just bits and pieces. After our scare yesterday, I'm not sure that I want to remember."

Charles studied her. "And just what was your scare?"

"A blood-covered Teddy bear. She opened the package and screamed. Then, she remembered that she had had others of them, but today she's not remembering that she said that."

"Is that right, Locklin? How do you know that you received others?"

Locklin shook her head. "I'm not sure. I could just remember staring down at something similar to what I was holding. Only it wasn't a Teddy bear. It was a doll once. A piece of clothing, a child's sweater, I think, another time. Photos. A Bible." She looked up, surprise on her face. "How did you do that?"

"Do what?" Charles simply smiled at her.

"Get me to remember that?" She frowned at him.

Charles grinned once more. "It's only a matter of asking the questions that will help you to remember. Sometimes, it takes the questions coming from someone not close to us. Dallas would have been around, I gather. You are aware that he is a friend of the fellows here. That would make it more difficult for you to open up to him, in a way. I'm a relative stranger to you. Therefore, I can ask a question that might help you to remember."

"I see." Locklin was lost in thought at that point, not hearing Buckley and Charles talking. Her hands began to shake and then she was sinking to the floor, an exclamation from Buckley as he sprang to catch her.

"Locklin?" He called for her, not having her respond.

Charles had a cold cloth in his hand almost before Buckley had gathered her close. "Here. Use this on her face and then her wrists. We need her to come around and now." He knelt beside the younger couple, feeling for a wrist and a pulse. Charles was a retired family physician, who still kept up his skills by volunteering at the shelter.

"Locklin?" Buckley breathed a sigh of relief as her eyes opened and she stared around. "Locklin?"

His voice brought her attention to him, and she frowned. "I don't know you, do I? Where am I?" She looked around, panic in her eyes, before she looked back at him. "You're the one who stepped in and helped me. I went with you. You married me, didn't you?"

"I did, love. That I did. You remember?"

"Not a lot. I just remember running towards you but not why. I was terrified."

"You were. Do you remember the accident?"

Locklin shook her heard. "No, I don't. Is that what happened?"

"It was. Your side of the car hit the tree after the car had rolled. You lost your memory." Buckley just hugged her tight, not giving in to his fear that when she remembered everything, she would just walk away from him.

Charles stood, waiting for Buckley to stand and set Locklin on her feet. "Locklin? May I examine you? I'm a retired physician and work at the shelter. I won't hurt you. I promise. Head injuries have always been of a particular interest to me."

Locklin shrugged. "I guess. We have to go to the shelter?"

"Not at all, young lady." He simply grinned at her. "We can do it right here, or pop down to the well-stocked infirmary downstairs."

"Here, please." Her voice was barely audible and both men could see the fright in her eyes.

"Here it is." Charles finally stepped back, rubbing at his chin, his eyes on Locklin.

"Charles?" Buckley's voice finally caught his attention.

"Buckley. Locklin. What testing was done when you brought her in?"

"I can't remember. Doc would. Why?"

"Because there is something going on. Locklin, were you ever given any medications to take that you can remember?"

"I don't know. Other than the medications I was given for the headaches." Buckley was on the move, returning with it. "Thank you. This is it. I haven't been taking it much in the last three days or so."

"I see." Charles scanned the label. "I don't recognize this doctor. Who is he?"

Buckley at him. "Doc is the one who prescribed it."

Charles popped the top from the vial and looked inside. "Whatever you have been taken, it's not what is on the label. I have no idea what these tablets are." He looked at the label again. "And it's your regular pharmacy?"

"Actually, no. It's the one that was closest to here."

"I see. Buckley, this must go to Dallas. Locklin, if you have headaches, try an over-the-counter medication. If not, talk to Doc again. I'll see him today. If I have your permission, I'll talk to him."

Chapter 19

Sunday morning, Buckley turned as he heard Locklin's heels tapping on the floor as she approached him where he stood in the home office. He paused, his eyes on her face, thinking how beautiful she was, before he reached for her hands, raising them to kiss them. He stood, their hands linked, his eyes on her face, seeing her uncertainty.

"I wasn't sure what to wear, Buckley. I seem to remember just wearing jeans and a top to my old church. But I can't here." She had chosen a flowered dress that came to her mid-calf and shoes with a low heel on them.

"It wouldn't have mattered what you wore, love. We dress in all sorts of manners. Some jeans, some suits, some in-between for the men. The ladies are the same. Some wear jeans and a top, skirts, and blouses, suits. It's your choice. But you look absolutely beautiful."

She blushed. "I'm still not sure about this."

"I know, love. I know. Here's let pray first." Buckley's prayer was powerful, soothing the nerves that had wracked Locklin's body. He looked up before he dropped one hand to reach for a small box on his desk. "Here. I want you to have this. We rushed into our marriage with only the wedding bands. That didn't do justice to you." He opened the box to pull out a ruby ring. "I can remember my father telling my mother that she was his Proverbs 31 lady, that her worth was far about rubies. It is how I feel about you." The ring landed on her finger, to guard the engraved wedding band that he had chosen.

Two hours later, Locklin looked around the basement of the church, feeling somewhat overcome. She frowned as she caught sight of an older man staring at her and shivered. She spun, intent on finding Buckley, only to have her way blocked by another man. Frightened, she turned and made her way through the crowd, finding Branigan and Breck heading for her, their attention on the second man who was following her.

"Locklin? Just who we needed to see. We need to ask you something." Breck had captured her arm and led her through the crowd, towards Buckley who had been stopped by one of the other board members. "I don't think that you have met Jacob Baker."

Buckley swept her close to him, his eyes on Breck's face, and sighed. Even here, she wasn't safe. They couldn't lock the doors and keep out the strangers. And who to say one of the church members wasn't involved? That very thought frightened him.

Buckley tracked Breck down later that afternoon. Locklin was sleeping, and he felt he had to get to the bottom of what had happened in church.

"Breck? What was that about?"

Breck spun from where he stood staring out the lobby window. "Earlier? There was a man coming after Locklin. Branigan and I moved in to separate her from them. There was one after her, and one on the other side of the room, watching her. Brandon was able to snap photos of them and sent them on to Dallas and to Emma. They're trying to identify them."

Buckley paled. "In the church? With all those people? Where is she safe?"

"I don't know. I'm sorry, Buckley. It shouldn't be happening."

"It's no different for us than the others." Buckley suddenly grinned. "So, now, we know where they will try to capture her. How do we go on the offensive?"

Breck shook his head, a small smile tickling at his mouth. "Buckley, only you. You have your humour to get you through. You've done that with all of us over this. By the way, I see the garden didn't start producing fruit when you told it to."

———

Buckley began to laugh. "No, it didn't listen very well, did it?" He sobered. "Doc spoke with me a while ago. The medication that Locklin had been taking? One of the side effects can be memory loss. It's not a prescription drug."

"So, her prescription was tampered with? Have you talked to Dallas?"

"Not yet. I will. I thought he was away for a few days on vacation."

"That's right. He is." Breck walked back towards the stairs with Buckley. "Then, let's hope Emma can come up with something."

"She and Abe and their little one are away as well. She sent a text a while ago, stating that Jace would work on what we needed." Buckley paused, one foot on the step, his hand on the smooth oak railing. "How do I protect her? If they come into the church like that and try and take her in front of all those people, how do I do it?"

"We try and stay with you, some of us. Our ladies are invested in this as well. They want to keep her safe, knowing what they went through. They don't want that for either one of you. I spoke with Charles earlier. He has asked the officers who attend to stay by the doors for now, to monitor those coming in and out. They will be near both you and Locklin during the time you are at church." Breck held up his hand as Buckley went to protest. "I don't think you fully realize how the church feels about you. And that feeling now extends to your bride. The officers have all come forward to Charles and Barnabas stating that when you are in the church building, one will be there. If you are out and about on church business, you will have someone driving you."

Buckley swallowed hard. "Thank you. I hadn't expected this."

"It's what they want to do, Buckley. And if Locklin has to be out on her own, someone will be with her. Even on the grounds."

Locklin spoke from the step above them. "That's not fair to the men, Breck."

Breck looked up, seeing the dark shadows under her eyes. "It is fair to you and to Buckley. It's what we do, Locklin. Now, I must run. I'm off for a birthday party for a young man and I can't be late."

They watched him walk rapidly away before Locklin spoke.

"This is so unfair, Buckley. They're putting their lives at risk for us."

"I know, love. I know. But we must accept. Sometimes the givers must be receivers. I have been the one always giving. It's tough to be on the other side."

Locklin paused just inside their doorway, her face puzzled. "Buckley? Why do you call me 'love' all the time?"

"Because you are just that. My love. I haven't wanted to burden you with that. And I won't, not until you are ready. But I will still call you 'love'." He touched her cheek gently and walked away.

Staring after him, Locklin blinked back tears. "Oh, Buckley, do you know how I needed to hear that? You are my love as well. Only, I don't know how to tell you that."

Hitting the outside wall of the gym hard, Buckley struggled to escape the hands holding him against it. He could feel the rough wood scraping at his face. There was no release from the hands. Then, he yelped with pain, unable to escape the board driven at the side of his knee, buckling it and dropping him to the ground. His hands clutched at it, even as another blow from the same board landed even harder on his arm. Buckley heard a snap before intense pain darkened his vision. He didn't hear the men leaving.

Sometime later, Bradon and Brennen approached the gym, joking comments tossed between the two before Brennen's hand was on Bradon's arm to stop him.

"What's that by the shrubs?" Brennen was on the run. "It's Buckley. He's been hurt."

Bradon's phone was out as he called for help, even as he dropped down beside Buckley. "They want to know if he's conscious."

"No, he's not. Let them know that." Brennen looked up. "Find someone to bring Locklin."

"Already on it. She was with the ladies today." Bradon was on his feet, running towards the building, finding Breck heading his way. "Buckley's hurt. Brennen's with him. I'm going for Locklin."

Breck stared after him, and then down at his phone. He had just heard from Dallas, who sent a warning that someone was after Buckley. A patrol officer had found a car near the Foundation grounds and stopped it from leaving. The men had not put up a fight, merely stating that they had been hired to scare the minister.

Locklin looked up as Bradon approached her, and then paled. She rose and went with him, listening to his explanation even as he tucked her into his truck, Ennis with them. She didn't wait for him to fully stop, shoving open the door and running into the hospital, desperately seeking Buckley. Brennen stopped her, pulling her to one side.

"Brennen?" She was frantic to hear that he was alive.

"He's been hurt, Locklin. He was ambushed near the gym. I'm not sure yet what his injuries are, but we'll find out. Doc's on duty today. Here, sit." Brennen made Locklin sit, even though he could tell that she was about to refuse to do that.

"How?" Her voice died away and then she tried again. "How bad?"

"The paramedics said his arm and his leg. We'll know more in a bit." He looked up as Jaxcy sat beside Locklin, an arm around her. "We're not leaving you alone, Locklin. One of us goes with you when you go back. Dallas is on his way here. Apparently, he was to meet with you today. He had just talked to Buckley as he was walking to the gym."

"And then this happened. When does it stop, Jaxcy? Ennis? When does it stop? When one of us is dead? Oh! I wish I could remember!" Her voice died away as she paled. "It's him. There. By the door. He's the one who was chasing me. Make him go away."

Brennen shifted in his chair, searching for the man, his eye catching Dallas, who nodded and moved towards the man, preventing him from leaving. A short struggle ensued and then Dallas had the man handcuffed and handed over to a patrol officer.

Locklin had paled even more. The ones with her could her low whisper and looked at one another.

Dallas crouched down in front of her. "Locklin? What was it that you just said?"

"He told Buckley that I was his. That I had to go with him. He tried to hit Buckley but Buckley moved and the man ended up on the ground. I don't know why he said that. I have such fear when I see him. And I don't know why." Locklin looked up. "I am starting to remember things, Dallas, but not enough to put together anything."

"It's coming, Locklin. Maybe if you took a notebook and wrote down the bits and pieces, we can put them together for you."

"I can try, but a lot of times it's in my dreams. And then I can't remember if it was a dream or real life."

"I don't think that matters right now, Locklin." Ennis' arm was around her. "Just write down everything. We'll sort it out for you."

Locklin finally rose to pace, unable to stay in one position for long. Brennen paced on one side of her, Blair on the other, no one wanting her to be on her own and vulnerable. She had looked up at them with a slight smile. Blair had drawn in a quick breath at the whiteness of her face and the dark smudges under her eyes.

Ennis studied her as well. "She's not sleeping."

"No, I don't think she is. She said Doc wanted to give her something but she refused." Fynn looked around. "I think everyone is here."

"They would be. They would do no less for Buckley and his Locklin." Cadee watched the men milling around. "They're working on it. Why don't we work on it as well? We would have a different perspective than them."

"You mean, from a female point of view?" Guenivere nodded. "I agree. I talked to Emma's friend, Kataleen. She asked if we had any more information on Locklin, other than what we had given Emma."

"I don't think that we have. This has to be so frustrating for them." Berneen rose, heading for the gift shop, and returned with note pads and pens. "Here. One for each of us. Now, let's start sleuthing."

Locklin had dropped back in her chair, taking what was handed to her, a frown on her face. "And just how do we do that?"

"You start by jotting down everything you remember, no matter how minor it seems. It is sometimes something so minor that breaks a case." Hagen studied her and then frowned as she saw Charles and his wife entering. She drew in her breath as she stared between Locklin and Lois. She was on her feet, heading for Brandon. "Brandon, did we ever figure out if Locklin had any aunts or uncles?"

"I'm not the one working on it. Brody was. Brody? Did you ever determine if there are relatives for Locklin?"

"I did. Her mother had a sister who lives around here. Why?" Brody stood beside them, a puzzled look on his face.

Hagen turned towards Lois. "Take a look at Lois and then Locklin. What do you see?"

The men frowned at her before they did just that. Brody drew in a breath before he shared a look with Brandon.

"Emma. She could tell us." Brody's phone was out, sending off a quick message to Emma, who responded quickly. "Emma has tracked down the sister. She lives here." Brody froze, unable to continue.

"Brody? Is it that bad?" Hagen couldn't understand his stillness.

"She's Lois."

"Lois?" Brandon spun around once more to stare at Lois and Charles. "As is Charles' wife?"

"Exactly. Now how do we do this?" Brody watched as Locklin rose, heading for the exam rooms as Doc approached her, Dallas and Breck on either side of her.

Locklin stared down at Buckley, watching his beloved face contorting with pain as he moved before he laid still. Her hand was against his cheek in an effort to still his movements.

"Doc?" She looked up at him. "What is wrong with him?"

"A broken arm. And a heavy bruise on his knee. That will take time to heal."

"So, what happens now?"

"Right now, the orthopedic surgeon will set his arm. He can do that without Buckley heading for surgery. The knee will be in a brace for a few days. He can't weight bear for about a week." Doc watched as Locklin's eyes slid closed and a single tear tracked down her cheek. "He'll use a wheelchair for that and then he can start weight bearing using a cane."

Locklin nodded, watching the activity around Buckley. "I want to stay with him. Please?"

"For now. But when they go to set the arm, you'll have to leave." Doc nodded at Breck as he walked away.

Dallas stood beside Brody, shock on his face. "Who did you say?"

"Lois. Take a look at her."

Dallas turned. "You're right. She does look like her. Where's the proof?"

"Check your emails. Emma was sending it on to you." Brody watched as Dallas did just that. "Now, we need to talk to both of them."

"We do. Right now, Locklin's not up to it. I want to talk to both Buckley and her together."

The men looked up as Charles and Lois approached.

"Brody, keep us updated, please? We'll be praying for both of them."

Lois nodded before she spoke. "This young lady? She looks familiar. Do I know her?"

"Locklin? I don't think so." Brody was careful about how he phrased his words.

"Locklin?" Lois paled. "My sister's baby was named Locklin. It's such an unusual name. Where is she?"

"Right here." Locklin stood beside Brody, finding his arm around her and Hagen on her other side. "Why?"

Lois paled even more. "You are the image of my sister. Your mother? Is she still alive?"

"No, I'm told that she isn't. Again, why?"

"Because you are the image of my sister. Oh, please, dear Lord. Let this be our Locklin, our Laycee's girl."

"Laycee?" Locklin began to shake before she whispered. "I remember. Laycee was my mother's name. Are you her sister?"

"I am. Oh, thank you, dear Lord." Lois simply swept Locklin into a tight hug, tears flowing down her cheeks.

Charles stood watching before he turned to Dallas. "How sure are we?"

"Fairly sure. I was hoping to talk with Buckley and Locklin together before we approached you. It looks as if the Lord had other plans."

"He did. Lois has prayed for years to find Locklin. She lost contact with Locklin's father just after her sister died. She would write, try to call, but received no answer. We even went to their home area a few times but couldn't track them down."

"You did? That's interesting. Charles, we will need to talk with you then. I'll call and set up a time." Dallas had pulled out his phone as it chimed. "I'm sorry. I need to run. Brody, have someone keep me updated on Buckley."

———

Locklin abruptly moved away from Lois, heading back towards where Buckley was. She just needed to talk to him, and not likely could. Standing in the hallway, she watched through the open door as the surgeon set his arm, the staff moving around her. She never noticed Breck and Blair standing beside her, their attention on the people around them.

The surgeon studied her as he left Buckley's bedside and then beckoned her forward.

"You're Buckley's wife. I thought I recognized you from Sunday. Here, in you go. He's been awake for a bit. I've ordered some pain medications for him. He can go home tonight. I know the building and that Doc and Brady will be around to make sure that you don't need anything."

"Doctor? How bad?" Locklin could barely get the words out.

"The arm? It will take about six weeks or so to heal. It was a clean break. The knee? I want to do an MRI on it next week. We need to let some of the swellings go down first. The nurse will make sure that you have everything that you need." He paused, his eyes on her pale face. "Locklin, he will heal."

"I know, but it's my fault. I did this to him." Her words were barely audible as she moved away from the men and towards Buckley.

"What did she say?" The surgeon stared after her.

"She's convinced that it's her fault. She can't remember a lot right now, but Buckley stepped in to help her when she was in danger."

"Just like all of you fellows from the building. Make sure that he follows my instructions. I know him. He'll be chafing at the bit to get back to work."

"That we will. We will do our best." Breck stepped into the room, Blair on his heels. "We need to set up for him in the apartment. Thank goodness the doors are built for handicap accessibility."

"There's that. I'm off then, Breck. Call if you need something."

"We will. Thanks, Blair. Send the others home, will you?"

"I can do that. Brennen said he was staying to help with moving Buckley home."

"Thank him for me. I have no idea when that will be."

Frowning in frustration, Buckley pushed at the wheel of the chair he was in, not happy that he couldn't move himself forward. Locklin had stood back, not ready to move, but finally did just that, pushing him into the living room and positioning the chair so that he could slide to the couch. This takes a lot of effort, Buckley thought, and laid his head back for a moment, feeling a blanket tucked over him before he heard Locklin moving away.

Locklin returned, a tray in her hands that she set on the coffee table, before she dropped to the floor, an arm resting on the couch seat beside him.

"What can I get for you, Buckley?"

"I'm not sure, Locklin. You're okay? They didn't get to you?" Buckley had been worried when he had awakened at last late the afternoon before in the hospital, looking around for her.

"No, the fellows and Dallas kept me safe." She bit at her lip, a habit that Buckley noticed she had when she was uncertain.

"What happened, love?" He reached for her hand. "Tell me."

"The man that you saved me from? I recognized him. He was in the waiting room, watching me. Dallas arrested him."

"He was? That's not good. I'm glad he didn't get to you." Buckley waited for her to continue. "What else happened, love? Something did."

Locklin nodded. "I was so worried when they came to get me. I couldn't get you to talk to me at all. And then I remembered my mother's name. Did you know that Lois, Charles' wife, was her sister?"

Buckley started and then nodded. "I wondered who she reminded me of. It is you. You've met her?"

"They were there. She asked who my mother was." Locklin blinked back tears. "That Emma had confirmed it already. Lois said that they tried to find me or Dad, and couldn't."

"So, whatever this is goes back that far?" Buckley whistled. "Wow! Who would have thought that?"

"I don't like it, Buckley. I mean, she says that she's my aunt, and we do look somewhat alike, but I just can't do this. Not right now. You need me. I can't remember a lot."

"I know, love. Charles and Lois will stay back, now that they've made contact. I suspect that Lois will send you photos and a long letter. It's how she is, but they will wait for you to approach them."

"They will? That's strange."

"It's how they are. What else happened?"

Locklin handed him his mug of coffee, trying to think about how to frame what she needed to say.

"The ladies told me to journal what I remember, whether I think it's a dream or not."

"That's a good idea. Have you a journal?"

"I do. Berneen bought one for each of us and a pen as well. She shouldn't have."

"That's Berneen. She gives and gives, without expecting anything in return. I think you should. If you want, we can go over it together."

Locklin's head went down against his good leg, her eyes on him, the trust she felt in him showing as well as the growing love she had for him. "I would like that. Buckley, where do we go from here?"

"With the investigation?" At her nod, he shook his head. "I'm not sure. Dallas is working on it. Emma and Jace are. So are the fellows. And I suspect that the ladies are, if Berneen had bought you all notebooks."

"That's what they want to do. I just don't want anyone hurt. Not one person. It's bad enough that we have been."

"I know, love. It's hard, but they won't think anything of it. We've all been there for each other."

"I get that." Locklin grew quiet and her face pensive as she studied Buckley. "Buckley, what is God trying to teach us?"

"Teach us? As in what can we learn by going through this?"

Locklin nodded. "I have this vision of a conversation with my father. I think that I had been questioning something. Dad told me that God was there with us all the time. That sometimes He allowed things or events to happen, just to draw us closer to Him. To teach us that we need to trust and rely on Him and not ourselves."

"Your father sounds like a very wise man. That's what I believe."

"Is it? Is that how we look at things? It's hard."

"It is very hard when we try to do it in our humanness. We need to set that aside and realize that it is in God's strength that we do that."

She nodded, her eyes closing as she slept. Buckley pulled himself up as best he could to reach for the blanket to drape over her before he laid back himself, his eyes closing as he prayed for his love.

Locklin rose an hour later, her eyes on Buckley as he slept, the blanket that he had used to cover her now over him. Tray in her hands, she headed for the kitchen, as a knock came on the door. She stood on tiptoes to peer out, before opening it, to find Breck, Blair, and Devaney there.

"Come in. Buckley's sleeping." Locklin waited for one of them to speak. "What? No one talking? If you're not talking, I'm going to go clean my kitchen."

Devaney gave a low laugh, linking her arm with Locklin's. "And I will help. These two guys can see to Buckley."

Locklin looked back at them before she shook her head. "If they want. I still have to make us lunch."

A week later, Buckley sighed as he sat at his desk in the church office. Locklin had driven him there, against the protests of some of the fellows. She had simply stared them down, slipped behind the wheel of his car, and driven away.

"Did you really just do that?" Buckley grinned at her.

"Do what?" Locklin was distracted, staring at all the books he had on the shelves.

"Drive away from them? They were supposed to come with us."

She shrugged. "You needed to be here. It would have taken forever for them to decide who was coming with us."

"I know, love, but we really should have waited." Buckley turned his attention to his desk, sorting through the mail. He was lost in his work in short order, a quiet thank you as Locklin set a mug of coffee beside him. He finally looked up, finding her curled up in a chair, a book open on her knee that she wasn't reading.

"Locklin?" He had to say her name twice before she looked over at him. "You're deep in thought."

"I know. I'm thinking about Lois. She says that she's my aunt. Emma sent me documents that prove it. But I just don't see it. How could she lose contact with my Dad?"

"That's what the fellows are working on. You have doubts?"

"I do. I know that they're part of the church family, and I don't want to cause any trouble in it, but I just don't know."

"What is it that is troubling you?" Buckley was willing to take the time to draw her out.

"I'm not sure. I think I need to talk to someone, but I'm not sure who. Someone who would understand about families and family relationships and family trees."

Buckley reached for his phone. "I know just the person. One of Abe's men and his wife. She is into family trees and has a wonderful program that she developed." He paused, looking up at Locklin in surprise. "I have an email from Micah. His wife is Kataleen, who I just described. They are on their way here, this afternoon." Buckley looked down at his work.

Locklin was on her feet, her hands reaching to help him. "Tell me what I can do for you that's not breaching any confidences. There must be something."

"There is." Buckley quickly sorted through what he had on his desk and together they worked away.

"It looks as if we've made good progress." Locklin stood, a hand on his shoulder.

"We have, love. It's at a point where I can leave it for tonight and come back tomorrow to work more." Buckley stood, sweeping her into a hug and then kissing her. "Thank you, love."

Locklin blushed, not sure still if he really meant it when he called her love. "Now, let's get you home. This friend of yours? They're going to the building?"

"I would expect so. Here, let me lock up the office."

They walked out slowly, Buckley giving more of an overview of the congregation to her, just to help her understand.

Micah watched as Buckley made his way towards him as he stood in the building lobby, Kataleen beside him.

"That's Locklin?" Kataleen studied her. "She's just what he needs."

"That she is, sweetheart. The men have all said that." Micah reached to shake Buckley's hand, waiting for the introduction to Locklin.

Kataleen reached to hug Locklin. "I've been waiting to meet you. We all wondered who Buckley's lady would be. You're perfect for him." She grinned as Locklin finally remembered to shut her mouth. "Now, where can we go to talk?"

"Our apartment, unless you want to head for the conference room?" Buckley shared a look with Micah.

"Your apartment is good." Micah grinned as he held up a plastic sack. "We stopped and bought some submarine sandwiches, some salads, and some fresh fruit. How does that sound for a meal?"

"It sounds wonderful. Slavedriver here didn't let me have a break all afternoon." Locklin smirked as she headed into the kitchen, reaching to start the coffee and then put on the kettle. Kataleen searched for plates and cutlery, laughing at Locklin's nonsense and at Buckley's laughing protest that she hadn't told him that she wanted a break.

Buckley finally pushed his plate away, reaching for Locklin's hand. "Let's spend some time in prayer. I have a feeling we'll need it."

"I think that you're correct. Kataleen has found a lot of information, some of which she has confirmed."

"But I'm not sure if I can help. I still can't remember a lot."

"That's okay, Locklin. We'll work with what we can."

———

Buckley fingered the papers that Micah had left with him, not able to sleep. As she had stated, Locklin had not been able to confirm much of what Kataleen had found. It had frustrated her, that much he knew. He sat at his office desk, reading back through every piece of paper, tracing the family tree that Kataleen had drawn up. He shook his head, not knowing how she could do that. It had to be God, he thought.

Locklin rose early in the morning, frowning as she saw the light on in the office. Searching for Buckley, she found him deep into his study on prayer, the papers set aside. Her hand on his shoulder roused him and he swept her down on his knee, despite her protest that he would be hurt.

"You didn't sleep?"

"No, I didn't. I was going over what Kataleen left and then turned to read on prayer. I'm thinking that it would make a good series."

"It would. I feel like such a baby when it comes to prayer. I pray for this to be over, but it's not."

"I know, love. I do the same. God is working on this, but sometimes His timing is not our timing."

"I wish He would hurry up and get it over." Locklin sounded disgruntled. "I'm sorry. I shouldn't have said that."

"And why not? He listens to us and wants to hear our joys and our hurts. This is one of your hurts."

"And yours?" Locklin poked at the papers. "Did you find anything in there?"

"I did. I was waiting to talk to you. We need to turn it over to the fellows as well."

"And?"

"I found your mother didn't have a sister. She had a cousin, who was raised as a sister to her. That was Lois. I'm not sure why Lois wouldn't have known that." Buckley frowned. "We need to talk to them."

"Let's do some more research before you do. I don't want to hurt her. Kataleen mentioned that last night. You and Micah had stepped outside when she did. I thought that you would have heard."

"No, I didn't. That's okay. We'll get there. Anything else that stands out?"

"My father. He had siblings and they must have had children. How do I confirm that? Kataleen said that she couldn't give me that information, as it wasn't ethical."

"I see. Then, we turn this over to Dallas and see what he can find out for you."

"Poor Dallas. He's had so much thrown at him. He told me that he's working a lot of cases now."

"I know. I feel bad that he's involved in this." Buckley finally stood, his hand reaching for hers. "Let's eat and then head downstairs."

Brendon looked at Buckley and then at the paperwork that Buckley was handing him.

"Kataleen? They were around yesterday?"

"They were. They were here long enough to eat and go over this with us."

"I see. Anything we need to watch for?"

Buckley explained what he had discovered and what they were trying to discover. "Locklin still hasn't remembered that much."

"That worries me, Buckley. It's like she's blocking it."

"I know. I had a long discussion with Doc. He said it's likely that she is blocking some of it, knowing it will hurt her deeply. I don't want that, but I want her to remember."

"I know, Buckley. She's off with the ladies?"

"She is. Berneen handed them all notebooks and a pen. They're racing us to try and solve this."

Brendon grinned. "And it wouldn't surprise me if they did just that. I'll make copies. You get off your feet. Do you have to head to the church office?"

"Not right at the moment. I'm working from home for today." Buckley walked away, his limp very evident that day.

"He's hurting." Blair stood and watched him.

"He is. He's not joking with us like he usually does." Brendon looked down at the paperwork in his hand. "Kataleen did some of her magic and dropped it off last night. I guess this just adds to our work."

Brady reached for it. "Let me make copies. Burnie should be here. This is what he enjoys."

"He's back tomorrow. He had no choice. His publisher wanted him to do that book signing." Benen headed for his favourite chair.

"I know. He hates that." Brandon sat. "Let's see how far we can get. I'm told that the ladies will solve it before us. I think that they just challenged us."

Staring down at the envelope in her hand, Locklin shuddered. She knew the handwriting. It was his. How had he found her married name? And her address? She spun and ran for the conference room, seeking Buckley.

The men who were there spun as the door flew open and then were on their feet, moving towards her.

"Locklin?" Blair reached for her arm to steady her.

"Buckley? Where is he?"

"He's in the apartment. He's working there." Blair reached for the envelope in her hand. "What's this?"

"It was in the mail." Locklin's words tripped over each other, she was that frantic and terrified. "It's him. He has found me."

"Who, Locklin? Who has found you?"

"I don't know his name. He kept watching me. He'd follow me all over. Please? Make him stop! Please? Don't let him near me!" Her eyes rolled back as she collapsed, Brady reaching for her before he headed for the stairs and the apartment, Locklin in his arms.

Buckley stared at Brady and then at Locklin. "What happened?"

"She fainted, Buckley. She received a letter, came looking for you, and then collapsed. She recognized the handwriting."

"She did?" Buckley sat on the couch, Locklin's head on his knee, even as Brady crouched down beside her to assess her.

"She did. She was terrified, Buckley. Kept asking us to stop him and to keep him away from her."

"She did? Had she opened it?"

"No, she just was holding it away from her. It needs to go to Dallas. Blair was calling him but he couldn't reach him."

Blair extended the letter. "This is it, Buckley. I'd leave it for Dallas."

"I intend to." Buckley nodded at the table. "Drop it there. Thanks, fellows."

"No problem. Let us know what Dallas says."

"I will." Buckley heard the door close behind them, but his attention was on Locklin. His heart broke for his lady, wanting to make it all better for her, but not able to. Lord? How long? How long until this is over for her? How much more hurt and danger will she face? Teach us, Lord, to pray, to pray as we should, that Your will be done. Protect us, dear Lord.

Locklin roused in the late afternoon, disoriented. She rose, wandering the apartment, frightened. She couldn't find someone to help her. Why not? She wasn't in her own apartment. Where was she? Hearing a sound behind her, Locklin spun, a hand covering her mouth to stifle her scream.

"Locklin, love? You're up?" Buckley moved towards her, stopping as she backed away from him. "Locklin?"

"I'm sorry. I'm sorry. I shouldn't have run to you that day. Forgive me?" She turned and ran, for where she wasn't sure, Buckley moving after her as quickly as he could, his arms reaching to sweep her to him.

She fought him until she heard his whispered prayer and then his words of love whispered in her ear. Locklin looked up, her heart calming.

"Buckley?"

"Locklin? You worried me. Are you okay?" Buckley's head tilted as he studied her

"I think so. I just didn't know where I was. I wasn't in my own apartment. I forgot for a bit. Forgive me?"

"There's nothing to forgive. Here, let's sit. You're shaking." Buckley directed her back to the couch, wrapping her in a blanket and just sitting close to her, holding her tight.

"I'm sorry, Buckley. I'm sorry I brought danger to you. I shouldn't have."

"I could have walked away, Locklin, but it's not in me to do that to anyone, let alone a lady I love."

Locklin stared up at him, her eyes wide. "You love me?"

"I do, Locklin. You are the other half of my heart. God sent me there that day. I had no plans to head that way. I was on vacation and just took off."

"Then, God was in control." She leaned against him. "He really does care."

"And you didn't think that He did?"

Her head shook. "No, I didn't. I mean, I knew in my head that He does. Sometimes, the heart has trouble understanding that."

"It does, but never doubt that God loves you and wants to protect you. He may let us go through rough stuff, like we are now, but unless He wills otherwise, we won't die."

"That's a comfort." Locklin looked around. "The letter?"

"Dallas was here while you were sleeping. He said not to awaken you. He didn't open it, not yet. He was turning it over to the techs and letting them do that. He'll call us with what they found, but it might be tomorrow."

"I felt such evil when I was holding it. I couldn't pray, I really couldn't even think."

"The fellows said you were upset. I can see why." Buckley grew silent, content to sit and hold her.

"Buckley, that family tree? It's accurate?"

"It is. Kataleen is very careful not to include something or someone that she can't confirm. If it's there, then she had made sure it is accurate. You're questioning something?"

"No. I've just never seen a family tree before. Not for my own family. And Lois? Have you talked to her?"

"Not yet. I was waiting for Emma and Kataleen to provide more information, just as they promised. Then, I'll meet with Charles and Lois. Talk to them. See where we go. You're not going to be there, not now. Not until you can remember much more than you have."

"Thank you. I just don't think I can handle that right now. When she hugged me and cried, I didn't feel anything. Is that wrong of me?"

"She is a stranger to you. It's normal not to feel a lot in that situation."

"Okay. I just don't want to hurt her. If she really is Mom's sister or cousin, she's been hurt enough."

"I know, love. I know. We'll get through it. Blair was around as well. He has more information that he wants to go over with us, but I said not until tomorrow. And then tomorrow night, we have our prayer meeting at the church."

"We do? I think I need that." She was quiet.

"You can wear jeans, love. You don't have to be dressed up. In fact, most of the time that's what I'm in. Our church doesn't stress that you have to dress a certain way. The person is more important than the clothes that they wear. They feel it is more in line with how Jesus would approach people, given that he could be found with the outcasts of society in the Bible."

"That's so true and so comforting." She settled back, her head on his shoulder, content to be held.

Two weeks later, Buckley watched as the cast was removed from his arm, Locklin tight to his side, her own eyes on the surgeon. He had healed extremely fast, the surgeon had declared. Buckley had grinned, shaken his head, and said that he always healed quickly.

Hand in hand, they walked away from the hospital, towards Buckley's car, not seeing the man following them. Would it have changed anything, if they had, Buckley wondered afterward? He was never sure. Dallas had asked to meet with them that morning, as he had news.

Dallas seated them at a table in a small conference room in the police department and then sat himself, a thick file folder in front of him. Buckley sent a questioning look his way but Dallas' attention was on Locklin.

"Locklin? Have you remembered anything else?"

Locklin stared at him, a frown on her face. "Not really. Just bits and pieces and even those don't make a lot of sense. I can't tell if it's real or a dream."

Dallas nodded. "That's what we thought." He tapped the folder. "Your friend, Emma, has been sending massive amounts of information, Buckley. I don't know how she does it, but she does. Will has finally managed to have her come on as a consultant with us."

"And that helps?"

"It does. She has provided more information about your father, Locklin, that we can't divulge to you as yet as it is still part of an ongoing investigation."

Locklin frowned. "I don't remember Dad. When did he die again?"

"About a year or less ago. He was murdered. Do you remember us talking about that?"

She nodded. "I do. And you said Mom died in childbirth. I have no siblings. What else?"

"You are twenty-eight years old. You worked odd jobs to survive. Your church was an important part of your life, but you didn't involve yourself in a lot of activities outside of the normal services. I have had conversations with your pastor there. The fire that destroyed your apartment building was deemed accidental. Plumbers were there, to do work on some of the pipes." He paused as she shook her head.

"No, I can remember the landlord. A slumlord, is that what you call them? I can remember that he refused to do any work for us, even when the furnace failed in the middle of winter. We had to go to a lawyer and threaten him with a lawsuit. Even then, it took a while for him to have it repaired."

"Is that right?" Dallas looked down at his notes. "Someone didn't explain that very well to us, then. We talked to the other tenants. They could not say enough good about him."

"He would threaten us." Locklin looked at Buckley, a bleak look on her face. "He would threaten us. I can remember that. We would come home and our doors would be unlocked, our belongings thrown all over the place. There were would be things missing. We found threats written in paint on our walls that we had to paint over. Furniture would be damaged." She dropped her head, her hair hiding her face. "I tried to move, to find somewhere else to live. I couldn't. If he found out, he would go to the new landlord and I wouldn't get the place. I had no transportation to leave town. They had taken Dad's car, saying it wasn't safe to be driven. But it was. Dad kept it up." Locklin didn't realize how much she was remembering.

Buckley's hand grasped hers tightly. "Okay, so the landlord burned the place down, or had it burned down? He can be charged?"

"We'll certainly work that way. Locklin, you have remembered things. Do you realize that?" Dallas watched her reaction closely.

Locklin shook her head. "It's as I said. It's bits and pieces. It's like I'm talking and saying things but I don't remember them if I stop and think about it. Does that make sense?"

"It does. Now, that letter that you received?" As she looked at him, he shared a look with Buckley. "You recognized the handwriting?"

"I'm told I did. I was just so scared. I don't remember even what I said that day." She looked at Buckley. "Brady told me that I fainted, and I don't faint. That's the fear I can remember. It just took over my whole body."

"She was shuddering, Dallas, in a way that I have never seen before. I want this over."

"I know you do. You fellows always do. We still have work to do. And I know you are working on it." He glanced down at the letter, reluctant to tell Locklin what it said, but knowing that he had to.

"What does it say, Dallas?" Buckley kept his eyes on Locklin.

"I won't go into all the details, but it is a direct threat to her life. It states that they know where she is and that when she least expects it, they will take her and kill her. We have an idea who it came from, and they're part of a vicious group of men. Multiple detachments are working together to bring them down. I can't begin to tell you that you must stay safe, Locklin. Stay around the building as much as you can. Stay with someone. We're working hard to bring these men down, have been for months now. It should be soon, but you're now part of it, because of your father."

"I see." Locklin shoved back from the table and stood, feeling vulnerable and overwhelmed. "Can I leave, Dallas?" Her voice was barely above a whisper.

Dallas stood. "You can, Locklin. Buckley, you too must be very cautious. They have proven that they will go after you to get to her."

"That's what they always do. Go after the one to get to the other. God is in control, Dallas. I have His protection, no matter what happens."

Her hand tight in Buckley's, Locklin walked the downtown area, stopping every once in a while to study the merchandise in the windows. Buckley was content to let her, but his focus was also on those around him. He could feel someone watching them and that frightened him. He knew that they shouldn't be doing their walk, but they both needed some normalcy in their lives.

Locklin paused in front of a bakeshop, her hand resting lightly on the window, as she studied the wares.

"We can get some if you like." Buckley's voice above her startled her.

"No, it's okay. I think that I like to bake. I was just curious to see what they offered."

"Now, you know. I have a fairly well-stocked cupboard for baking. I like doing that." He grinned at her. "But for now, how be we head home?"

"We can. You need to finish preparing for your prayer meeting, don't you?"

"Not really. I mean, I'm there and lead it, but we usually just share what's on our hearts. Sometimes, I give a short talk on a subject or a verse. Other times we don't. It's working out well doing that. We are growing closer together."

"I see. I didn't realize that you didn't bring a sermon or whatever it is you call those." She frowned as he laughed.

"It's called a sermon or a message." He slid into the car, having shut her door behind her. "Some people refer to them as talks. I like to think of them as God's speaking to us. I'm just the instrument that He uses. And I'm not the only one."

"No, he uses so many. The ladies have been talking, you know." Locklin smirked as she stared out the side window. "I hear that you suggested dates for a couple of them to marry."

Buckley shouted with laughter, bringing a smile to her face. "They did, did they? I did, and they came right back at me with my own words."

"Serves you right." Locklin sobered. "Buckley, what if we never find out who it is?"

"We will, love. I am confident in that. Dallas seems to think that it would not be long." Buckley parked in his allotted spot on the Foundation grounds and shifted to watch her.

"I know, Buckley. I'm just so scared that someone will get hurt because of me. Or disappear and not be seen." She looked up at him, her eyes dark with her emotions. "I worry about Hagen's little ones."

"They'll watch them closely." He reached for her hands, his head bowing as he prayed for her and for himself.

Late that night, Locklin shot up in bed, drenched in sweat, her hands covering her mouth as she stifled a scream. He was here, wasn't he? He was here in her apartment. She knew he was. He had done that before to her. She would awaken to find him standing in her doorway, or see him disappearing out of the door.

She was out of her bed, running to check the locks on the doors and the windows, spinning in a wild circle as she searched for him, not finding him. But she knew that he had been there. She felt him.

Buckley watched for a moment from his office doorway before he carefully approached Locklin, not sure what had happened. Locklin turned to him as she heard his footsteps, backing away until she recognized his voice and form and then throwing herself at him.

"He was here, Buckley. Here in the apartment." Her sobs shook him.

"Hush, Locklin. It's just us here. No one else." He lifted her into his arms and carried her back into the office, dropping to the couch he had there and wrapping her into a blanket. His own tears wet her hair as his fear for her grew. Her sobs gradually lessened and her body grew heavy as she slept. Buckley watched her, his arms tight around her, his heart praying.

———

Early the next morning, Locklin slipped from his arms and headed for a shower and to dress, stopping on her way by to the kitchen to watch him, reaching to cover him with the blanket he had used for her. A quick kiss was dropped on his cheek, and she touched the roughness of the overnight growth of whiskers with a gentle hand.

Buckley shot up, suddenly awake, sure that he had heard Locklin call for him. He was on his feet, searching, finding her in the kitchen, engrossed in baking. He smiled as he watched her before she looked up.

"I'm sorry! I keep saying that." Locklin was frustrated. She had had enough of her life as she had been living it the last while. She had made some determinations that she needed to talk to Buckley about, but she was too shy with him to do just that.

"Don't be." Buckley grinned at her. "Just tell what you're making?"

"A mess, I think." Locklin looked down at the countertop. "I wanted to make some pancakes but I can't remember the recipe. I couldn't find a cookbook."

"That's because I don't have any." Buckley simply wrapped her into his arms. "I have prepared pancake mix if that will do."

"There's such a thing? I thought you could only make them from scratch." Locklin stood, shutting down.

"Locklin? Love, please talk to me." Buckley shook her slightly, finding her coming back around. "What just happened?"

"I don't know, Buckley. I don't know. All of a sudden, I just couldn't hear or understand. Some days, I feel like I am on a precipice ready to jump off."

"I know, love. I know. Here, you sit. I'll make us something." Buckley swiftly cleaned the counter, keeping an eye on her, before he simply made them toast and set it in front of her.

"I can't, Buckley. I need to be doing something or have to be somewhere. Only, I don't know where that is. Please, help me!"

"I will, love. Here, have some toast." Buckley felt out of his depth right then, watching Locklin. This is too much for her, Lord. I think I am losing her.

———

Slowly closing the door to the church, Buckley turned to walk down the stairs, his keys in his hand, lost in thought. It had troubled him that morning by what Locklin had said. I don't know how to reach her, Lord. How do I? I pray and pray but can't reach her. She's blocking something and I don't know what.

His mind on Locklin, he didn't hear the running footsteps approaching him until he was on the ground, his keys flying from his hand. Stunned, he didn't hear the questions thundering at him, just felt himself yanked to his feet and propelled forward. His vision blurry, he didn't realize that he was being forced into the back of a truck until he hit the seat. He turned, trying to fight his way back out, but his movements still as he saw the knife held up towards him, the sunlight winking of the long, silver, sharpened blade. Buckley sank back, his hands in the air, waiting for the knife to come towards him. He kept his eyes on it even as the truck moved away from the church, his car following.

Locklin paced the apartment living room, her arms wrapped around herself, watching the clock. Buckley had promised to be home an hour ago, and he still wasn't. She began to fear for him, and ran for her phone, dialling his number and only getting his voice mail. She tried the church number and again, only got through to the voice mail.

Running for the stairs, Locklin headed downstairs, intent of searching the parking lot. He had to be here somewhere, she thought. But where? She shoved the door open, her hand up to shelter her eyes as she searched. Not finding him, she moved in a circle, fear coursing through her. They had to have taken him. But just who were they? Did she know who they were?

She walked slowly back towards the building, not seeing the car approaching her, a sound at the last minute raising her head as she screamed. The car moved slightly towards her, the fender driving into her body and sending her flying through the air, to lay, a crumpled broken heap on the pavement as it turned and sped away, almost colliding with Breck's truck as he approached.

Breck slammed on his brakes, his arm along the back of his seat, as he stared after the car. Shaking his head, he turned back to drive forward, once more slamming on his brakes and then slamming the truck into park and throwing open his door. He ran towards Locklin even as Brody and Baird ran from the building.

"What happened?" Breck's words were sharp.

"We have no idea. We heard Locklin scream and ran for the door, just in time to see the car take off. Did it hit you?"

"No, but it came close." Breck was on his knees. "Did someone call it in?"

"Berneen was." Baird was down on the ground as well. "Locklin? Can you hear us?"

"She's not responding." Breck ran his hands over her arms and legs. "I don't feel anything broken here."

"She bleeding from her head." Baird bent over until his own head almost touched the ground. "Oh, no, Dear Lord. Please!"

"Baird?" When he didn't answer, Brody's hand hit his back. "What you do see?"

"Blood. From her ear." Baird straightened back up. "You know what that means."

"We do." Breck stood up and moved back as the paramedics ran towards them. "She was run down about ten to fifteen minutes ago. We didn't see it. Baird here says that she's bleeding from her ear."

The paramedics nodded, working quickly to assess her, reaching for the neck collar and the backboard, shifting her gently to that, before one of them reached to start an IV drip. The three men helped to lift her to the stretcher and then stood back. Breck moved forward suddenly.

"Wait! I'm riding with you! She needs one of us with her."

"Is she married?"

"She is. Buckley Cullen."

"Buckley? Where is he?" The paramedic ducked to look out the window on the back door.

"That's what we don't know. He wasn't around." Breck's phone was out as he called Buckley. "No answer." He sent a swift text to Baird and then to Barnabas. "I'll have Barnabas meet us at the hospital. He's power of attorney after Buckley."

Barnabas hit the Emergency Room doors on the run, heading for the exam rooms, finding Breck moving towards him on swift feet.

"Breck? What happened?"

"As far as we can tell, Locklin was run down in our parking lot. They almost nailed me on the way out. I wish I had known. I would have gone after them." Breck hit the wall with his fist, anger at the men flaring.

"You didn't know. Were you able to get any description?"

"Not much of one. They were moving too fast. I passed it on to the patrol officer." Breck pointed behind him. "She's in rough shape, Barnabas."

"I see. Have they said anything yet?"

"No. They wanted to talk to Buckley. We can't find him."

"What?" Barnabas paused in his pacing. "He was at the church earlier. I saw his car as I drove by."

"It's not there now. He's not anywhere around. And he's not answering his phone or text messages."

"The fellows are searching?"

"They are, as best they can. So are the patrol officers. Dallas was in touch. He's tied up on a case and can't make it here yet." Breck looked behind him as he heard the door swish open. "There's the nurse. She was looking for you about ten minutes ago."

"Heidi?" Barnabas walked towards her, a hand on Breck's arm pulling him along.

"Barnabas? I understand that you have power of attorney for Locklin Cullen?"

"I do. We're not certain where her husband is at the moment. Do you need me to sign or authorize something?"

"We do. Dr. James will be along in just a moment." Heidi stopped at a door. "In there. I must warn you, she's in rough shape, Barnabas."

Breck caught the look that Heidi had on her face that Barnabas didn't see and his heart sank. They don't expect her to make it, do they, Lord? Please, Lord? Heal her. Give the medical personnel the wisdom to treat her.

Barnabas stood at Locklin's bedside, his eyes on her white face, seeing where the blood had not yet been washed away. He saw the blueness of her lips. His heart sank as he prayed, petitioning the heavens for Locklin to survive. He did not want to be the one to tell Buckley that his bride had died and that they had no idea where to find him.

Dr. James paused beside Barnabas, his own eyes assessing the young lady in front of him. He had seen the X-rays, the CT scan, and feared for her very life.

"Dr. James? What can you tell me?" Barnabas spoke without looking away from Locklin.

"She is in critical, life-threatening condition, Barnabas. I know you well enough, to be frank with you. I have seen the imaging studies. It's not good. She has what we call a brain bleed. You understand that?"

Barnabas nodded. "I do. So, what are we looking at? We can't find Buckley, to have him talk to you. I'll have to make whatever decision is necessary for him." Barnabas reached to touch Locklin's hand, finding it cold. "So, what are we looking at? Surgery?"

"That is a distinct possibility. This time, her head hit on the other side from her other injury. I understand that she couldn't remember much."

"Not a lot. Buckley told me that she was starting to remember bits and pieces, but not enough to put together much of her life. How long do we wait?"

"I want to wait until morning, repeat the imaging, and then see where we stand. I don't want to transfer her to a larger hospital if I can avoid it. The travel just might be too much for her at present."

Barnabas paled. "It's that bad?"

"It is, Barnabas. It is. Here. This is what I am proposing for treatment." Dr. James walked Barnabas through the treatment options, answered his questions, and then stood watching as Barnabas prayed and then signed the paperwork. "Thank you, son. I know it's a huge responsibility to put on you."

"Other than Buckley, she has no one. Buckley asked if I would consent to stand behind him like this. I can't say no to the fellows."

"We know you can't." Dr. James grew quiet as he assessed Locklin again. "She's about the same. We may need to intubate her at some point if her breathing worsens. I'll talk to you if that's necessary. For now, you can stay with her, if you wish. We'll be moving her upstairs to an ICU bed shortly. And I have the neurologist on call coming in to assess her as well."

"Can you send Breck in, please? I'll need him to talk to everyone for us."

"I can do that." Dr. James stood and watched Barnabas before he walked away, looking for Breck, who was on his feet heading for the exam rooms as soon as he was told to.

"Barnabas?" Breck's voice was quiet as he stopped beside his friend, drawing in a deep breath as he saw Locklin.

"It's bad, Breck. He said life-threatening. She has a brain bleed as he put it. They may need to do surgery." Barnabas turned to face Breck. "If she dies, how do I tell Buckley?"

Breck drew in another deep breath. "Are they planning for the surgery tonight?"

"No. I just wanted you to update everyone for me. I'll be staying here with her for now. They're moving her to ICU shortly." Barnabas' face hardened for a moment. "We need to find these people, Breck. Where do we stand on that?"

"Not where we want to be. Just like her memory, we're getting bits and pieces. It's trying to piece them together that has us frustrated."

"Find whoever it is that you need to help. Bring in whoever it is. I want this solved and solved soon. Buckley doesn't deserve to have his bride lying here on her death bed."

"No. I've already started that process. The fellows are all drawing back from their work and focusing on this. Emma has been in touch. She and Abe were planning on heading this way in the next day or so." Breck was frustrated and angry and knew he had to pray it through to get his perspective back. "I'll go talk to the ladies. They're out there. They sent the fellows back to the building."

"Did they? And are they working away out there?"

"I suspect so. I talked to Dallas earlier. They found the car, but it was wiped clean, plates were pulled, and the VIN was damaged enough that they can't make it out. Whoever it was also pulled any computer chips that might help."

Barnabas stared at him. "An organized group that knows what they need to take. Organized crime?"

"That's what he's saying. It's what we've been feeling all along, given how Locklin's father died."

Barnabas nodded. "Okay, so that's that. Head off, Breck. I'll be in touch."

Two days later, Breck stood watching as Barnabas paced his office. Locklin was still unconscious but so far, had not had to have the surgery that she had been threatened with. Breck knew that the fellows and the ladies were waiting for Barnabas to show up and give an update.

"Barnabas? You need to get some sleep."

"I know, Breck. I've had some. Dad had an interesting observation that I need to speak with you about. Only I'm not sure how to express what he said."

"Just say it like he did." Breck perched on the corner of the desk. "What did he say?"

Barnabas returned to his desk, sitting in his chair, leaning forward with his elbows planted on the desk blotter. His cheek rested against his clasped hands.

"We were talking this morning, he had dropped in. He was asking how the investigation was going and if Buckley had appeared. When I say no, he then asked how Locklin was. He is very concerned, I must say as he is for all of us here."

"I know he is. What else?"

"He said that Mom had had a thought. If they wanted to get to Locklin, they would take Buckley and hide him somewhere. But running her down as they did, that was deliberate. I agree with Mom. Dad said she then commented that if they were trying to get to her by taking Buckley, they did it all wrong. They would have stopped, threatened her, and then made her life miserable with taunts about him. She doesn't think it's the same group."

"Doesn't think they're the same group?" Breck stared at him. "You know, that's what Bradon and Blair said. Benen agreed. We've been arguing back and forth that it is."

"Two groups. Two different methods. Two different threats. Two different motives." Barnabas sat back in his chair. "I have to agree. It has never made sense to be one."

"No, it hasn't. Buckley made the same sort of comment, late last week. He also wondered if Locklin had been given something when she was hurt that caused the amnesia. I have to talk to Doc yet about that. He's been working so many hours and then they're away right now."

"That they are. I wondered the same thing. The medication she had wasn't what it was supposed to be." Barnabas stood. "Let's go find the fellows. This may move what they're doing along faster."

"Or complicate it further. I would say that the fellow Buckley put down is one group. He was after Locklin, nothing more. The other group would be related to her father. But what if Locklin knows something and has forgotten it?"

"That's what Brendon asked me last night. I think that's probably the case. But we have no way of knowing. And with her belongings all destroyed, whatever she had in proof would be gone." Barnabas pulled the door to the conference room open and stopped. "Abe's here."

"So he is. And all of his fellows and their ladies. It looks as if we have more help than we planned on."

"I'm glad. Abe? What brings you and Emma and everyone else here?"

"Buckley. We want to help find him. And we want to help solve this." Abe stood for a moment, surveying the room. When he spoke again, only Barnabas could hear him. "I don't think you understand that Buckley has been in touch with each one of my fellows and their ladies every single week since he met them. He talks with them, prays with them. Teases and torments them as Emma would say. They want to help."

"No, I didn't know that, but he does the same here. He thinks differently than the rest of us do."

—

825

"He does. He has a servant's heart. He models Christianity in a way that I have seen few do. Maybe, just maybe, he was kidnapped to do that to the group after Locklin." Abe shot Barnabas a look. "How is she?"

"Still unconscious. The physicians are not ruling out surgery yet to relieve the pressure. But if the imaging continues the same or improves, they won't have to. That is how we are all praying."

"As are we. Listen, can we go somewhere and talk? I have some information that I want to run by you before I talk to your men and mine."

"Sure. My office works. Amy is there but if the door is closed, she doesn't interrupt." Barnabas settled Abe down in a chair in front of his desk, mug of coffee handed to him. "It seems that all we do is drink coffee."

Abe grinned. "I know that feeling. Now, about Locklin? Had she remembered anything?"

"Not a lot. Buckley said that she was starting to. She would come out with something about her life or what had happened without thinking. If she was stopped or questioned, she would just look at us and wilt, unable to remember any more details."

"That's what I thought you would say. Now, how do the physicians think this will affect her memory?"

"They have no idea." Barnabas studied his friend. "But that's not what you want."

"No, it's not. Joseph and Luke were doing some research on her home area. I know that the provincial force has authority there. But they have discovered a secret group that runs the area, does their own policing, and keeps people in line. They have ties to a drug lord in South America."

"South America? Drugs? Her father was testifying in court against a drug dealer."

"And he was killed to keep him quiet. We've discovered that. What we have also discovered is who the leader in the area is. It's someone you would least expect."

———

"That's what Mom said. Who?" Barnabas paled as Abe said the name and occupation. "Him? That really changes it, doesn't it? She would have trusted him completely. Buckley did say that she didn't have many friends or trust too many people. That much she could remember."

"And he would have played that with both her father and herself. We've been tracking him. He's moving back and forth between her area and here."

"That doesn't help, Abe. Now, what? With your experience in security, how do we keep her safe, and then find Buckley?" Barnabas stared at his friend, not sure on where this was taking them.

Her head moving restlessly, Locklin's hand found the sore spot. Her eyes flickered open and then shut against the brightness of the lights. She sighed. Now, what did he do to me? Lord, I am so tired of him. I want to move on but he won't let me.

Dr. James watched her movements before he reached to assess her eye movements, earning himself a frown before Locklin drifted off again. He reached to flick on the computer monitor near the bed and signed in to view the images that had been taken that morning. He frowned himself. This can't be right, he thought. He verified that they were the images taken that very morning and that they did indeed belong to Locklin. He shook his head.

"I don't understand. It is like she had no injury at all. But I know she did. I saw the evidence." He stepped back, after exiting the program, and watched her. "She's dropping into a natural sleep, isn't she now?"

Barnabas had hesitated as he approached. He would rather it be Buckley that was here, but to date, four days after he seemed to have vanished into thin air, they had not yet found him. He was worried that he would make the wrong decision for Locklin and then have to explain to Buckley why she died.

"Dr. James?" Barnabas spoke quietly.

"Barnabas. Just how much have the people been praying for this young lady?" Dr. James watched him intently.

"Every hour of every day. For both Locklin and Buckley. Why? Is she worse?" Barnabas was almost afraid to hear the answer.

"No, it's the opposite. There is now no evidence of any brain injury. And she had roused." Dr. James peered at him intently. "That's your God at work?"

"It is." Barnabas drew a breath of relief. "Sometimes, this is how He works. Complete healing. Are you saying that she is going to be all right?"

"I would suspect so. We'll have to wait until she fully rouses and then assess her completely. But right now? I would say that it's as if she has never been injured. Even the other injury on the other side of her head that we saw some residual from is gone." He turned to walk away. "Now, just find Buckley and bring him home. I'll be in your church Sunday morning. I want to hear him preach."

Barnabas stared after the physician as he left. Dr. James was known for doubting any divine intervention. As he put it, that was a bunch of garbage. He turned to stare back at Locklin, his mind racing as to why God had allowed this. Finally walking away from the room, he sat in the waiting area, not sure where to go or even who to talk to. The fellows and ladies of the building were deep in either the investigation or their employment.

Berneen found him, Cadee in tow, and paused, not sure if she should approach him. The two ladies shared a look. Barnabas, hearing their footsteps, looked up and then stood, surprising them by hugging both of them.

"Barnabas? Don't tell us!" Berneen blinked back tears.

"It's okay." He smiled, the first genuine smile in a few days, he thought. "She's better."

"Better? How can that be?" Cadee was puzzled. "I thought that she was still critical."

"Last night, she was. I just spoke with Dr. James. God has been good. She's healed. Dr. James just told me that." Barnabas blinked rapidly. "And he is starting to believe. He said he'd be in church on Sunday."

"He will? Wonderful." Berneen looked around. "Is it okay if we go in?"

"I would assume so." Barnabas stepped to where he could see Locklin's room. "Go on. I need to call the fellows and let them know."

Breck paused as he walked through the conference room, stunned at the words he heard. Silence greeted him as all the men stared at him as his eyes slid closed and he couldn't speak. The men exchanges glances, sorrow in them, as they waited for Breck to speak.

Breck had trouble speaking, blinking rapidly to clear his vision. Burnie approached him, a hand resting on his shoulder.

"Breck? When?"

"What?"

"When did she go?"

"She didn't." Breck waited for the murmurs to cease. "Dr. James told Barnabas that she is completely healed. That he would be in church on Sunday and that we needed to find Buckley. He wants to hear him."

The men sat in stunned silence before they broke into cheers and praises.

"He said that? He's known to shun anything like that." Brady stared down at his notes. "That is amazing."

"God is at work. Maybe that's why Locklin was hurt." Blair stood, heading for the door. "I'm finding the ladies. They need to hear this."

Breck nodded, missing Buckley greatly at this time. He should be here, Lord. He would be the one leading us off in a prayer of thanks. I don't know where he is, but You do.

A day later, Locklin moved slowly through the apartment, not really recognizing anything. She stared at her wedding band and her engagement ring, knowing that she was married, but not really believing it. Where is my husband, she thought. They said he's missing. That he had been missing since I was hurt. And hurt the second time. That doesn't make a lot of sense. I don't remember him.

Locklin reached for a photo that sat on the mantle of the gas fireplace, a finger tracing the face of the man in it. This is Buckley. And me. I wish I could remember him, Lord, but I just don't. And they tell me that I couldn't remember my life from before. I am just so confused. I need healing, Lord, but I can hear a man praying for me, praying that we will both learn to pray. Was that Buckley?

A knock at the door disturbed her thoughts and she moved that way, holding the door partly closed as she stared at the three young ladies, around her age, she thought, who stood there.

"Locklin? I am told that you don't remember us. I'm Cadee. This is Hagen. And this is Fynn. May we come in? If you don't feel like company, that's okay. We'll just leave what we have for you and go on our way."

Locklin finally nodded, standing back to let them in. "I guess, the kitchen? I'm not sure."

Fynn grinned at her. "That's okay, Locklin. We understand how strange this is for you. We've all had our troubles, not quite like you, though. Here, can I put this food in your fridge?" She waited for a nod and then did just that.

"Now, what can we do for you?" Cadee watched Locklin closely. "What can we tell you about what has happened?"

"Everything." Locklin dropped into a chair, pointing to the others. "Oh, I'm sorry. I should have offered you coffee or tea." Her brow wrinkled. "I'm not used to company."

"You will be. We drop in and out on one another. There are eleven of us ladies, plus Anna, Doc's wife, and Hagen's twin sisters. You'll be tired of us all." Hagen moved to make the coffee and tea. "I hope you don't mind, but Buckley would say just to go ahead."

"No, that's fine." Locklin looked around. "I just feel so disoriented. I can remember my own apartment. It was so tiny, just a bachelor one. And rough at that. I had hardly anything."

"That's sad, Locklin." Cadee reached for her hand. "May I pray with you?"

"Of course."

After the ladies had left, Locklin still sat at the kitchen table, her finger rubbing along the edge of it. She was disoriented, she thought, and needed to talk to someone who knew her. But she was afraid to do that. Dallas had spoken with her that morning, finding time in his busy day to do that. He had not been able to tell her much about who had run her down, but he had cautioned her to be extremely careful. In his words, he didn't think whoever it had been was done with her yet.

That scared her. She rose, almost running through the apartment, hearing a phone ringing and not finding it. She paused, frowning. There, it was ringing again. She searching, finally pulling it from under a cushion on the living room couch. Locklin stared down at it, before she touched the screen, to waken it.

Her hand covered her mouth as she stared down at the photo. Buckley? But where was he? What had happened to him? She crumpled to the floor, sobs shaking her body as she mourned for him. In her mind, he was dead. Reaching again for the phone, she studied the photo and then say the text that went with it.

She was not ready to meet with anyone, that much she knew. But if she didn't, would Buckley remain alive? Who could she talk to?

Grabbing her keys and locking the door after her, she slowly walked down the stairs, to stand in the lobby, searching for someone, anyone, who could help her. Seeing no one, she dropped into a chair, drawing up her legs and burying her face against them.

———

Blair and Brennen paused as they moved by her, sharing a look, before they walked towards her. Blair crouched down beside her, a hand on her arm, causing her to jump.

"Locklin? What happened?" He stared down at the phone that she kept thrusting at him. "Your phone? What about it?"

"Buckley. There's a photo. I think he's dead. They sent a picture and a text message."

"Who did?"

"I don't know. They're sending me messages. I can't read them." She looked up at them. "Make them stop."

Brennen studied her before he reached for the phone. "May I?" At her nod, he scrolled through her messages. "I don't see any voice mail. Some of these have come from Buckley's phone. Some from a blocked number. Locklin, I'm taking your phone and giving it to Dallas. Don't worry, we'll find you another one."

"Buckley said no one should have that number. How?"

"From his phone, more than likely." Brennen stood watching her. "Locklin? Are you going to be okay on your own? You've just come home and it must be hard to be on your own."

Locklin shrugged. "I guess. It's what I've been used to for the last while. I miss my dad." She blinked rapidly before she was on her feet. "Fynn said that you were all working on this. How can I help?"

"Right now, we need you to finish healing." Blair watched her closely, seeing the fatigue in her face.

"I can't. Not when this is going on. Where do we start?"

"For tonight, you rest. We'll come to find you in the morning. After 9. Not a moment before." Brennen had returned with a phone for her. "Our numbers are in there. Call us if you need anything, even just to talk. Buckley is always there for us. We can do no different for the one he loves."

"He loves me? How can that be?" Locklin was shocked at the thought.

"He told me that when he saw you running towards him and he stepped in, that he knew he had found his lady. His love for you had just grown day by day. Those are his words." Blair escorted her back to her apartment and waited for her to enter before he walked through it. "It's good, Locklin. And we mean that you call us if you need us."

Locklin closed and locked the door, heading for the living room. She curled up on the couch, a blanket over her, not willing to settle into any of the bedrooms. She didn't think that she would sleep, but her fatigue and injury had other ideas. She slept, her sleep full of dreams of Buckley.

Breck ran for his truck, his phone to his ear. He could only faintly hear sounds, but he recognized one of the voices. Buckley! Now, to find out where he was! Driving away rapidly, he headed for town, looking for Dallas.

His phone in his hand, he approached Dallas as he stood in the line at the coffee shop.

"Dallas? It's Buckley!"

"What?" Dallas grabbed his coffee and sandwich with a quick thank you. "What are you talking about?"

"Here. On my phone. It's his phone that I'm hearing. I can hear him but I can also hear others. I just don't know where they are."

Dallas took the phone and then sent the link on to the techs. "I'm hoping that they can trace this. Here, follow me. We'll head back in and see what they can say." He paused, his cup of coffee on the roof of his car, as his phone rang. "What's that? You have a location already? Oh, it was reported to you? Okay. Let me have it. Patrol on the way?" He pointed at Breck as he caught up his cup of coffee. "In. You're coming with me." He tossed Breck back his phone.

"Dallas? What is going on?" Breck barely was seated before Dallas had taken off, driving as rapidly as the traffic would allow, finally moving at a higher rate of speed as he hit the highway.

"We have the address that call came from. Patrol had been out there earlier, following up complaints of noise and gunfire. They had pulled up as close as they could and are watching the building." Dallas shot a look towards Breck. "It's near the old Smothers' place."

"The Smothers' place? As in Brody and Ker and that Smothers?"

"Exactly." Dallas slowed his vehicle as he made a sharp right turn, Breck grabbing for something to hold on to. "We'll get you back to your truck. Right now, check your phone."

Breck did just that. "Nothing more. That was so bizarre." He stared down at a text message. "Locklin is looking for me. She's worried. And now Fynn. She's with Locklin. Says Locklin is frantic with worry about Buckley."

"I thought that she really didn't remember me." Dallas' eyes narrowed against the sun as he slowed and then parked behind the patrol vehicle, his window lowering as the officer approached. "What do we have?"

"A lot of traffic has been going in and out from the other side. I took a walk around, keeping in the shadows. A number of known drug dealers for starters." The office peered at Breck. "Breck?"

"We traced Buckley's phone to here." Dallas watched the building.

"That makes sick sense, you know. Buckley is so anti-drug. Put him in here. Not necessarily get him stoned, but let the smell of the drugs permeate his clothing. Where would that put him with the church?"

"Exactly. Keep an eye on the traffic. I need to call Will and make some plans."

Two hours later, Breck stood back, watching as the various squads moved in towards the house. He jerked as he heard gunfire and then the shouts of the authorities. He paced away, his phone out, knowing that he needed to check in with the fellows but not sure what to say.

"Barnabas?"

"Breck? Where are you? Brady found your truck, but not you. You've worried us." Barnabas paused as he heard the faint noise. "Breck? What is going on?"

"I got a call from Buckley's phone, took off to find Dallas. Right now, I standing watching as they move into a drug house. We tracked Buckley to here."

"You did? I guess you can't say much. Call me when you can." Barnabas cut off the call, rising from his desk and heading for the chapel. He knew that was where the fellows had gathered along with the ladies. He paused in the doorway, hearing the prayers, and just waiting until they were finished.

They all looked up at him as he walked to the front of the chapel and then turned, rubbing at his cheek.

"People? Breck received a call this morning from Buckley's phone. He tracked down Dallas. Right now, the police are moving in on a location where they think he is."

"And they can't tell us where." Brandon was frustrated. "All we can do is pray. I, for one, am heading back to my research." He was on his feet and out of the room, the door swinging closed behind him.

Quiet conversation filtered around the room before the men all rose and walked back to the conference room. They were determined to find Buckley and in finding him, bring to justice those responsible.

Barnabas watched as the ladies gathered around Locklin before he approached her.

"Locklin?"

His quiet voice startled her and she stared at him, fear on her face.

"I'm sorry. I didn't mean to startle you. What can we do for you?"

She shrugged. "I don't know. Everyone is always asking me that. I have no idea."

"Then, we do what we can for you. For now, the ladies are with you. If you need anything, find one of us." Barnabas walked away, knowing that he had a number of calls to make, but they would wait while he spent time in prayer. One of those calls would be to his parents.

Locklin watched him leave, before she too rose, walking away from the ladies, not even aware that she had not excused herself. She settled into a chair in the lobby, her focus on the door. She was expecting God to answer her prayer and that Buckley would walk through that very door that day.

Searching through the rooms in the dilapidated building, his weapon at the ready, Dallas followed after the Emergency Response Team members. He heard the shouts and scattered gunfire from the men around him, but his focus was on finding Buckley. He heard a sharp cry and spun, heading for the small room next to him. He searched the room before his eyes fell on the huddled, tumbled mass of blankets, an officer on his knees beside it.

"Joe?"

"It's Buckley. He's unconscious."

Dallas was on his knees as well, pulling back the blankets and the broken down cardboard cartons that partially covered him. "Is he alive?"

"He is. He's not drugged. At least, I don't think so but he's hurt."

"Here. Let's get him up." Dallas' weapon was back in its holster. "Over my shoulders. Which is the quickest, clearest way out?"

"This way." Joe led him out, watching carefully.

Dallas moved as quickly as he could towards the waiting ambulance, handing Buckley off to the paramedics before he stood back, a dark look on his face. "Joe? You were paired with someone?"

"I was. I'll ride with him."

Breck watched anxiously as the ambulance moved past him. He had heard the sounds of activity around it but had not been able to see much. He looked up to see Dallas walking towards him.

"Breck? In the car." Dallas merely pointed at his vehicle. "We're heading into the hospital."

"Buckley?" Breck fastened his seatbelt, ready for another wild ride.

"We have him, Breck. He's unconscious. We'll find out more when we get there." Dallas shifted on his seat, fatigue setting in as it always did after a raid like that one. "There's a lot of work to do, but right now, Buckley is my focus."

Breck held up his phone. "Can I call?"

Dallas nodded. "Just have Barnabas bring Locklin in. I don't know what to tell her."

"Simply that Buckley is alive and receiving help." Breck's attention shifted as he heard Barnabas answer. "Barnabas?"

"Breck? Where are you now?" Barnabas had tracked down Locklin and was sitting watching her, the fellows and the ladies gathered around. None of them wanted to or were willing to leave her.

"Barnabas? Where's Locklin?"

Barnabas' heart fell. "Right here. Breck?"

"Bring her to the hospital, Barnabas."

Barnabas was on his feet, his hand on Locklin's arm as she looked up, fear briefly showing on her face.

"Breck?"

"We have him, Barnabas. We have Buckley."

Barnabas' eyes slid closed in relief. "He's alive?"

"He is. Dallas said he's out of it. We need Locklin."

"On our way." Barnabas' phone was away as he crouched down beside Locklin, knowing the others were moving closer. "Locklin? We have him."

Locklin stared at him, not quite sure of what he had said. "What?"

"We have Buckley. We'll need to go to the hospital, but he's alive. I'll take you to him."

———

Locklin sat still, unable to move, before she was on her feet, moving towards the door, belying the fatigue and pain that she was feeling. Even though the surgeon had released her, he had warned her about overdoing it. That was exactly what she had done.

The fellows and ladies scattered, moving towards the parking area, sorting themselves out into vehicles. Barnabas tucked Locklin into his truck, and then drove away, a slight smile on his face as he saw the caravan following him. He knew that he would need to call Charles, but for now, Locklin was his priority, and that priority was to get her back with Buckley.

Locklin shifted from foot to foot, unsure of herself where Buckley was concerned, but anxious to meet him in person. She had remembered most of what had happened, but she felt that he was a stranger once more. That bothered her, and she had to pray for forgiveness, she thought, and then for strength and wisdom.

Blair moved with her as she entered the exam room. He had volunteered and she had accepted that. She knew the others were waiting. Doc looked around as she came towards him, his keen eyes on her white face.

"Locklin? He's right here. There, you stand right beside him." Doc moved her to the position he wanted her in. Buckley had been rousing and Doc wanted Locklin to be the first one that he saw.

"Doc?" Blair's voice held the question that he knew Locklin couldn't or wouldn't ask.

"No drugs. Not that we can tell. That's an answer to prayer. He's been ill-used, to say the least. He's starting to rouse, Locklin. I want you where he can see you. The nurses have been around, cleaned him up some. We're running bloodwork to see what is happening."

"Any X-Rays or anything, Doc?" Blair's voice startled Locklin, who had forgotten that he was there.

"Not unless we feel there is a need. So far, we don't see that." Doc stepped back. "I'll find Barnabas, if you like, Locklin."

She shrugged. "I don't care." She missed the looks that the men shared.

Doc watched as the building folks, as he called them, milled around, inside and outside. He shook his head. The family just keeps growing, doesn't it, Lord? Gives me more to pray for, but more to share with. He walked towards Barnabas, who headed his way.

"Doc?"

"I'll take you back to Locklin. Now that she's here, I have to speak with her." Doc looked apologetic.

"I understand. Just one thing, so I can tell the others. He's okay?"

"Seems to be." Doc could hear the breath of relief that wafted from person to person. "Come. Blair's with her, but he needs to be with Devaney."

"I know. They will all want to see him."

"And they can't. I'll put restrictions on him for now. I have to until Dallas or someone can take his statement. It is enough that you and Locklin are here with him." Doc pointed at Blair. "You can leave, but don't say anything."

"I won't, Doc." Blair grinned at Doc's pretended gruffness. "I'll leave it for Locklin."

Barnabas studied Locklin and then turned his attention to Buckley, shock momentarily stopping him in his tracks.

"Doc?"

"I know. He looks rough. That unkempt beard and hair don't help. Stay here for now. We'll move him to a room, if we can, when one becomes available. And those are in extremely short supply today. Everyone in town seems to think that they need to be in the hospital overnight." Doc grumbled away, knowing that Barnabas took it in the spirit he meant it.

"Locklin?"

Locklin looked around at Doc. "Doc? What's wrong with him?"

"Likely malnourishment. Dehydration. Hypothermia. It's been chilly overnight lately, and I doubt he had the heat and covers that he needed." Doc reached to draw her to him, just as he would his own daughter. "He'll make it, Locklin. You both will. God had provided for you. He's brought Buckley back. Why you two have had to go through this, we may never know. If you hadn't, Dr. James, for one, would not be willing to learn about God."

"That's true. I had some talks with him before I left the hospital. He is seeking."

"He is." Doc paused as he saw Buckley moving. "Now, young lady, your fellow is waking up. He doesn't want to see my old face. He wants to see you." Doc moved her closer to the head of the bed and then stepped away. "I'll be back."

Dallas hesitated at the doorway, knowing that he had to talk to Buckley, but not wanting to interrupt. His duties finally won and he walked forward, just as Buckley discovered Locklin standing beside him.

"Locklin? You're here? Thank you! They told me that they had done the same to you as they had your father."

Buckley's hand reached for Locklin and then he withdrew it, seeing the marks and dirt streaking it. Locklin simply reached to take it, her eyes on him, a puzzled frown on her face.

"Locklin, I was so worried. I thought you were dead."

"No, I'm not. But you were gone for what seemed forever. Doc said that they might keep you in." She really wasn't sure what to say to him, now that he was in front of her. All the sentences and words that she had planned to say just flew from her mind.

Buckley looked past her at Dallas. "Dallas? You'll want to talk to me. I'm not letting Locklin leave. And Barnabas? You're here? Where is everyone else?"

"Hanging around the building somewhere. We missed you." Barnabas stepped back, not wanting to intrude on Dallas' questions.

Dallas nodded. "We need to talk, Buckley, but I'll wait for a bit. Just give the basics."

"I didn't see who it was. And I can't remember much of it. Does that help?"

"Not a whole lot. I'll talk to you in a bit. I need to speak with Doc first. Barnabas?"

"With you." The men walked away, Locklin turning to watch them.

"Locklin, love. Are you okay?"

"No, I'm not. I'm not sure of anything anymore."

"Something has changed with you." Buckley reached to raise the head of the bed. "What happened?"

"I was run down, had a brain bleed, spent I don't know how long in a coma, woke up, remembered who I was, and forgot who you were. Isn't that enough?" She struggled to contain her tears and couldn't.

Buckley made an inaudible sound and then swung off the bed, gathering her close to him, his heart breaking as she sobbed. Why, Lord? Why us? Why Locklin? She didn't deserve any of this. I know, Lord, I'm questioning and I shouldn't. But I'm human and I'm a husband with a hurting wife.

"Love? Can you talk to me?"

Locklin shook her head. "I don't know where to start. I'm scared, Buckley. Scared of so much." She sniffed and then swiped at her face. "I am scared to be on my own. And I just know I will be."

"I'm not letting you go. That's what they wanted. They wanted me to give up on you. To let you walk away from me. They planned to take you. They were plotting revenge against you and your father."

"That's what the fellows have said. I don't know why. I didn't know what Dad was up to." She leaned against him. "You shouldn't be on your feet."

"I will be if I need to be, and right now, that's what you need. Can you spring me? I want to go home."

"Not until Doc says so. And Dallas is wanting to talk to you." She stepped back as Buckley reached for her hand. "Buckley, we can't leave."

"We can. I know, it's against medical advice, but I can't be in a small room. Not tonight. I need space." He looked both ways in the corridor and then headed away from the waiting room, towards the bays where the ambulances offloaded their stretchers. "Out this way. One of the fellows will be watching for me."

"And just how would they know that?" She was shocked that he would leave like that.

"Because it's what I do. I come in and out this way all the time." He pointed. "There. Benen and Cadee are watching for us. Quick. Into their truck." Buckley shoved her in, jumped in after her, and slammed the door, a grin on his face. "Home, James."

"James? Memory failing you, Buckley? No offense, Locklin." Benen just grinned at him. "Didn't get your discharge, I take it?"

"Nope. I'll talk to Doc later. Right now, I just want to go home, get cleaned up, and have a decent meal. As well as spending time with my love." His arm went around Locklin. "Benen. Cadee. Thank you. And which one of you won the bet?"

"Cadee. She said you'd be coming out in ten minutes from when Barnabas appeared back in the waiting room. I thought twenty."

Cadee grinned. "I know our minister. He doesn't hang around when he needs to be somewhere else. I sent out a group text. They'll head for home. They will all want to see you."

"I know. Can it wait until tomorrow? Dallas will have tracked me down by then." Fatigue was setting in. Buckley yawned, his arm around Locklin, content for the moment.

Late that night, Buckley paced his office. He had had a chance to clean up, trim his beard, and let Locklin trim his hair as best she could. She had frowned at him as he had grinned when making his request. He was puzzled. Something had changed with her, and he wasn't just quite sure what. He still had to talk to her, to find out what all happened in the days that he had been gone.

Dallas had appeared a few hours prior, staring at Buckley before shaking his head.

"You just had to, didn't you?" He dropped his laptop onto the kitchen table and then headed to dish up a plate of food offered to him. He hadn't had a chance to have his dinner and this was welcome.

Buckley had grinned. "Of course. Doc called Locklin. He wasn't surprised."

"No, that what he said. Now, I need to talk to you, to find out what exactly happened." Dallas looked up as Locklin left. "Did she just leave?"

"She did. I'll talk to her. Now, what is it that you want to hear?" Buckley knew that Locklin had stopped just outside the kitchen doorway. Her footsteps had not gone much past there.

"Tell me what happened. I know that you wouldn't in front of Doc or Barnabas." Dallas wiped his hands on the napkin that he had been given and brought up his word processing program on his laptop. "You've been through this before, only not as the victim."

Buckley's hand paused as he rubbed it on the tabletop. "That's what I am, isn't it? A victim? A victim of crime. I have often counselled those very victims. I never expected to be one myself."

"But you have been in the past. With Baird and Berneen." Dallas watched him closely, seeing the fatigue in his friend's face. "Let's get started, Buckley. Doc gave me strict instructions to tell you that you were to rest. And that he would be around later tonight or early tomorrow morning."

"I am sure that he will be." Buckley hesitated, a prayer rising from within him, knowing that he could give few details. "I'm not sure what is going on. Something involving Locklin. But there seems to be more than one involved."

Buckley began by giving his full name and the date before he began to speak.

He had just walked down the steps at the church and towards his car when he was tackled and then shoved into a vehicle. A blindfold had been slapped around his eyes and his wrists bound behind him. Shoved to the floor in the backseat of the car, he had felt a foot resting on his back. Drawing in his breath, he wasn't sure what was going on. He just prayed for safety and for protection for his beloved Locklin.

Buckley had felt the car driving around for what appeared to be hours, and he was sure that they were just driving in circles, although he could feel the different speeds and sounds of country and town hitting at his ears.

He had finally been pulled from the vehicle and shoved towards a building, stumbling as he struggled to keep his feet. A hand was bunched in the back of his shirt, the brutal manner of that scaring him. And Buckley knew that few things scared him. This did. This unknown of what he was facing scared him. And all he could do was pray. And even that was difficult.

The door slammed behind him as he rested on his hands and knees. A violent push had sent him through the doorway and to that position. He could feel the nicks on his wrists where the knife had slashed at his bonds. Buckley finally rose, pulling off the blindfold, and staring around. A ramshackle room, he thought, trying to wrap his mind around the fact that he had been kidnapped. The fading sunlight barely made a dent in the dimness of the room, the window was that streaked with dust and mud and dirt.

Buckley sank back down to the floor in the middle of the room, staring around at the debris that littered it. Broken cardboard cartons, broken bottles, wine and beer, he thought, crushed plastic bottles, other garbage. Then, his gaze centred on the debris in the corner, and his eyes slid shut. A drug house, he thought. They've brought me into a drug house. Even against my will and as a prisoner, how do I explain that to my church?

Days passed. Buckley saw no one, received no food or water. He began to grow weak, his prayers the only thing that kept him sane, that and his quoting of the Bible verses that he had memorized over the years and the hymns and choruses that he could sing. He wasn't aware that when he slept, one of his captors would stand over him, just watching.

His captors had been given strict instructions. Buckley was to be left alone, no contact with them. They were only to approach him when he was sleeping. The men had looked at one another and then shrugged. They didn't know who was giving the orders but they were being paid good money to follow those very instructions.

On the last night, Buckley had roused as he heard the door open and the man approached him. He was on his feet, his hands in fists at his sides, as he demanded answers, answers that he didn't receive. He had charged at the man, desperate to escape, only to fall to the dirt and debris-covered floor, blood trickling from the cut on his head, a cruel blow from the wooden bat that the man held.

Buckley had been unaware the next morning as he had been roused, that he had dialled Breck's number and then tucked his phone under some of the debris. He had protested that he didn't know what they wanted and why him, anyway? He was a minister, a pastor, a servant. He didn't have contacts on the wrong side of the track. He had dropped once more from the blows across his face, his head hitting in a sodden manner on the floor, before he lay still.

Unaware that Breck had received his call and gone for help, Buckley had not moved from where he had fallen. He didn't hear the shouts and gunfire in the dilapidated house or hear the running footsteps. He didn't hear the door broken down and the cries for help when he was discovered, covered as he was with tangled blankets and garbage hastily kicked over him.

Dallas had approached and then dropped beside him, joining the officer who had found him, before they had him on his feet and draped over Dallas' shoulder, moved rapidly from the house and then to the waiting ambulance. Buckley had not felt the hands that assessed him. He was unaware of the race to the hospital or Doc standing staring down at him. He had been unaware of anything until he finally roused and found Locklin standing beside him.

Buckley looked up at last. "I'm sorry, Dallas. I can't tell you much. I was too out of it and it was too dark to be able to see what the man looked like."

"We get that, Buckley." Dallas read back through what little Buckley had been able to tell him. "You really don't have much of a statement. Here. I'll print it off, have you sign it, and then take it in. I'll have another detective go over it and then talk to you again, just so they can't say anything, seeing as I was the one to find you."

"I never thought of that, you know. That's a possibility." Buckley sat back. "Is that all?"

"It is. I know you won't say much, but that house was a drug house, just as you thought. We've made arrests, including the men who have admitted kidnapping you. But they don't know who they are working for."

"I see." Buckley's attention was on the far wall, not seeing how Dallas was watching him. "Now what, Dallas? How do we find them?"

"We work on it. We need you fellows to pull back. These are dangerous people that are involved in this." Dallas watched him and then sighed. "And I know that you won't pull back. Not one of you will. Just stay safe."

"We will. Doc muttered something about Dr. James hearing me preach. What was with that?" He turned as Locklin appeared beside him, and simply wrapped an arm around her to draw her down on his knee. "Locklin?"

"He treated me, Buckley. When I was healed without any medical intervention, he asked Barnabas if it was God, in words something like that, and then said that we had to find you. That he would be in church on Sunday and that he wanted to hear you preach."

"Dr. James? Wow! God is at work in all this."

"He is, Buckley. No matter how dark or how dangerous, He is at work." Dallas stood, gathering his belongings and then walking away, the door closing softly behind him.

Locklin stood at long last, her eyes on Buckley, before she reached to clear the dishes and set the food away. He watched her, a frown on his face. Something has changed, he thought, and I don't know what.

"Locklin? What happened?"

Locklin hesitated before she turned. "What do you mean?"

"I mean. What happened to you? You seem different."

"I guess that I am. I was run down in the parking lot here. I was in a coma for a bit, with a brain bleed. They thought I would have to have surgery, but God intervened and healed me. I have remembered my past, Buckley, and the last year or so is not pretty. I'll pack and be gone in the morning."

Buckley sat in stunned silence, staring at the spot where Locklin had just stood before he was on his feet and following her. A hand on her bedroom door braced him on his feet.

"Locklin? Just like that? You walk away without talking it over with me? Without giving me a chance to say yes or no?"

Locklin refused to look at him. "It's for the best. I brought this trouble to you. I don't want you to be hurt anymore. Or have anyone else hurt."

Buckley moved towards her, his hands raised to touch her, opening and closing before he reached to turn her towards him and then sweep her to him, his hug tight. He felt her stiffen and then her arms wrapped around him, her tears soaking into his shirt, his soaking in the red hair that he had dreamed about when he was away from her.

"I can't let you go, love. You would take my heart with you if you did. Please? Don't walk away from me."

"I don't want you to be hurt." Locklin repeated herself. "I couldn't live with myself if they killed you."

"God is in control, love. He is in control. We need to trust Him."

"And that's so hard. I am learning all over again how hard. And to pray, Buckley." She leaned back, her eyes clouded with her tears. "We'll talk. I promise that I would leave without letting you know. But for now, you need to seek your rest. Doc made me promise that when he called a bit ago."

"Checking up on me?" Buckley grinned before his head lowered and he kissed her. "That's a promise, love. I love you so much. You're my Proverbs 31 lady."

She frowned at him for a moment. "Buckley? It's Friday. You have to preach on Sunday, don't you?"

He grinned again as he shrugged. "I suppose I must. But it's okay, love. We'll figure it out." He kissed her again, reluctant to let her go, before he walked away, closing her door softly behind him, to stand with his head back against it, fear in his heart that she would do exactly what she had said, walk away from him.

———

Locklin stared at the closed door, her fingers on her lips, a softened look on her face. No, she thought, I just can't, Lord. Please help me. I just can't walk away from him, and I should. She felt peace in her heart, knowing that to stay with Buckley was exactly where God wanted her. She frowned for a moment. She didn't know anything about being a minister's wife, now did she? She felt ill-fitted to do that. She only had a high school education, not having the money to go on to college or university. And even if she had, she wouldn't have known what to study.

Walking around the conference room the next morning, Locklin's hand tight in his, Buckley studied what his friends had discovered. He was not surprised at how many details had been added to the boards that now lined the walls, taking the place of the paper that had been there. Whose idea is that, he wondered?

Locklin paused as a board, her finger tracing her father's name, before she read what was there. There were details that she had not known about her father. He had been reluctant to talk about his family, and now she knew why. They were involved, his cousins, ones that she never had heard about. She then turned to the board that held the information for Buckley's family.

"I didn't realize that you were here for such a short time. I thought this was your home area."

Buckley's arm around her, he shook his head. "No, Just about eight or nine years. For all intents and purposes, it is my home. I won't leave it, not unless God wills."

"I pray that He doesn't, but I know that's not right."

"No, it's not. We have to trust Him, no matter how hard." He turned as he heard the door.

The fellows had gathered for prayer in the chapel before heading to the conference room, stopping in surprise at seeing Buckley already there.

"Buckley! You're here!" Burnie walked towards him, reaching to hug him before he stood back. "You look rough."

"Only you, Burnie, would greet someone that way." Bradon laughed as he reached to shake Buckley's hand and then hug Locklin, to her surprise. "Welcome home. Now, what can you tell us?"

“Bradon! Give him a moment or two to get used to us again.” Baird simply shook his head. “Buckley, I agree. What can you tell us?”

Buckley shook his head, seated Locklin at a table, and then proceeded to tell them what he could.

“I don’t know a lot more than that. I don’t recall seeing enough of any of the men to give any descriptions.” He looked around. “Thank you, all of you, for praying for me and for taking care of Locklin. She won’t say, but I know that you all did just that.”

“Okay, so where do we go?” Benen rose and walked to the empty board. “Buckley? What was your sense of where you were? Dallas isn’t saying.”

“In a drug house. I would say around the edge of town somewhere. I know they drove me around for hours, in and out of town, but it seemed aimless. I didn’t get much of a sense other than that.”

“Okay, so they drove you around. Why?”

“Waiting for dark. Waiting for orders. To terrorize him. To get to Locklin.” Brady spoke from where he stood near the door. “They would want him to be frightened for her. Did they say anything about her?”

Buckley had to think about that one. “No, they didn’t. I’m surprised. When I asked them why, they simply said that they were told to hold me and that I had to cooperate with them.” He was puzzled. “I’m not sure why. They didn’t give any names or any reason.”

“That doesn’t surprise me.” Breck had appeared in the room. “You weren’t that far away from here, Buckley. Security has had numerous hits on the system, picking up men wandering around the building and gardens at night. We suspect they are trying to find a way into so that they can get to Locklin.”

“Her father?” Buckley shared a look with Locklin.

"That's the supposition, but we have to prove that or have Dallas and his fellow officers do that. And the ladies are on a race to beat us in solving this."

"That they are." Brendon spoke distractedly, his eyes on what he was reading. He looked up at Locklin. "Locklin, do you know a Tommy Hall?"

"No, should I?"

"He's from your area, but younger than you. He's been a suspect in a lot of drug dealing in that area and then moving outwards, towards here."

"He is? And just who is he?"

"Brother to the man who was chasing you. They had different names." Brendon watched her closely, see her frown, but not reacting any differently. "Locklin?"

"I'm sorry. I don't know him. That monster didn't live with his family, that much I know. He lived on the streets or whatever abandoned building he could find. He was well known for that. That made him difficult to avoid."

"We understand that. About this man who was chasing you? Have we talked much about him?"

"No, because I couldn't remember. His name is Len Forester. He's older than me but not by much. He had no visible income, not that we could find out. Dad tried to find out for me. I talked to Dad and he helped me to avoid Forester." Locklin felt Buckley's hand tighten on hers. "He was horrible. I think that he was involved in a lot of the crime that went on in the area. I just couldn't prove it."

"He was." Brennen's voice was gentle. "We have proven it, Locklin. Dallas and his team have proved it."

"You have?" Locklin sat back, stunned, before she leaned forward. "Does that mean this is over for me?"

"No, unfortunately, it doesn't. They still have to arrest him. They are working on the charges and hope to do that soon." Brandon approached the board, paper in hand, as he added notes. "We are finding out more and more about his habits and who he hangs around with."

"The lowlife in town and area. That's who." Locklin was on her feet, moving towards the door before she stopped. She didn't look around as her head went back and her face was raised to the ceiling. They watched as her head dropped back down and then she just quietly left, the door closing softly behind her.

Buckley finally tracked Locklin down that morning, finding her curled up in a chair in the lobby, a mug in her hand. Cadee had been around, just sitting with her, not saying anything. The other ladies had come and gone, their quiet chatter and laughter helping to heal her. She felt out of place, not because they made her feel that way, but just for what she had gone through and what she felt that she had put Buckley through.

Dropping down on the floor beside her, Buckley stretched out his legs, his eyes on the sitting area on the other side of the lobby. He waited, not sure how to approach his bride, knowing that she had remembered her past.

"Buckley? Where do we go from here?" Locklin's question was not unexpected.

"We wait, love. We wait for God to direct our paths. We pray. I have learned more about praying than I ever thought I could. It's a work in progress."

"It is. Dad used to refer to it as a conversation with his best friend. He would talk to God anywhere and everywhere."

"That's how it should be. We complicate it."

"I know. But where do we go? I have a lot of garbage in my past."

"We all do. Garbage of all kinds." He tilted his head to look up at her. "I love you, Locklin."

She stared down at him. "You keep saying that, Buckley." Her voice was very soft. "I know you do. But I'm not lovable."

"But you are, love. You are. He's done this to you, made you feel cheap and unlovable, just by how he's treated you." Buckley was on his feet, his hands drawing her up, and then he was leading her from the lobby, towards the rose garden. "Mom explained something to me one day. She loved her roses. She picked a rosebud and forced it to flower. She said it wouldn't smell the same as a rose that had been allowed to bloom naturally, facing all the forces that nature could throw at it. She was right. The bloom had very little scent. But the ones in the garden? They smelled wonderful. When I smell a rose, I think of her illustration." He looked down at her, finding her gaze intent on him. "You are like the bud that has been allowed to grow naturally, facing all the elements, fighting to survive, and finally bloom. You have something about you that draws people to you."

"But I'm not a minister's wife."

"Don't judge what a minister's wife must be based on what you were raised with. Each lady is unique, just as the minister is unique. Where God has placed you, is right where He wants you. He planned that for you."

"He did? I never thought of it that way." Locklin looked thoughtful before a smile brightened her face. "So, what I have been through, the elements and forces of human nature that I have faced? They have made me who I am and ready to face this?"

"Exactly." Buckley stooped to kiss her. "And made you my help-meet." He hugged her, content to just stand and hold her. "Together, love, we'll get through this. We'll come out victorious. Battered and bruised, with scars more than likely, but together and with God, we'll win."

"I know, Buckley. I know, sweetheart. But it feels like there is no end to the battle." She looked around him as she heard footsteps. "Barnabas?"

"I was looking for you two. Buckley? How are you feeling?" Barnabas pointed to the benches and sat, watching the young couple closely.

"Not quite myself. It will take a bit." He studied his friend. "What is it?"

Barnabas grinned. "You know me too well. Charles has called. The board is concerned that you won't be up to giving a message tomorrow. They would like you to just talk, about whatever, no notes or formatted message. They also plan on a prayer and praise portion."

"They do? I guess he must have tried to call me. I have to get another phone."

"That you do. Breck has one for you. Locklin, your phone is okay? No more messages?"

"No. That stopped. They must have gotten the number from Buckley's phone."

"That's strange, you know. They never took my phone."

"No? They were waiting for you to use it to call for help. I would suspect that if you had, you would not have been found in the condition that you were."

"No, I suspect not. Now, about this investigation? Abe has been involved?" He looked between the two with him as they laughed.

"He has been, Buckley. Abe and Emma and his men and their ladies all showed up here one day to work with our fellows and ladies. They moved it forward a lot. Kataleen had her family tree worked out for both of you."

"That doesn't surprise me. Not one bit." Buckley's attention was drawn back to something Barnabas had said. "You were receiving messages, love?"

"I was. Nasty, horrible ones." Locklin looked up at him. "I hate that they were doing this to us. Trying to drive us apart."

Barnabas made a sound, drawing their attention to him. "What did you just say, Locklin?"

"What part? That they are trying to drive us apart. That's exactly what they are doing." She looked disgruntled. "Why?"

"If it is Forester or his friends, it is because he lost you. If it is Hall and the ones that he works for, he is trying to discredit you and through you to discredit Buckley. Buckley?"

Buckley raised his face, a thoughtful look on it. "That could be it, Barnabas. I don't remember making any enemies, but who is related in the church to the drug dealers that her father was testifying against?"

Barnabas pointed at his friend. "I think that you just broke through the barrier that we were stuck against." His phone was out and he sent off a quick message to Brendon. "Brendon was going that route if I remember correctly. He just wasn't sure if it was correct."

———

A week later, Buckley stood in his office, his hand resting on the door frame as he stared out across the Foundation property towards the road. He usually enjoyed the view, but today, he was troubled. Just by what, he couldn't say. He had been back in the church office, out visiting his people, but never on his own. Barnabas had insisted that he have one of the security teams with him from the building. He had been reluctant but one look at Locklin had him acquiescing to the request.

His mind drifted to the past weeks and what his friends had been through. God, I have no idea what is going on. You do. You allow this. Teach us to trust. Teach us to pray, Lord. We need to pray, to have that communication with you.

Locklin's arm slid around him. She was opening back up to him, her love for him declared in words as she became more confident. They just stood, not speaking, not needing to.

"It's Sunday again tomorrow, Buckley."

"It is. I am ready, I think. I'm not sure that the people are."

"And why is that?" Locklin looked up at him, finding him still watching the outside.

"I am planning on starting the series on prayer. With Christ's prayer in the garden. There is so much in that."

"There is. It's one of your favourite passages, isn't it?"

"It is." Buckley turned them away from the door, reaching to close the drapes. "And what have you been up to?"

"I have been with the ladies." She grinned. "We are working on our adventure, as they call it, We have made progress, I think."

"You have? Care to share?"

"After dinner. I have that ready when you are. Just a green salad and grilled chicken. I love all these appliances that you have that I can't put a name to."

"You do, do you? I make up placards and place them around for you." He ducked the elbow that she playfully shot at him.

Later that evening, Locklin snuggled down against Buckley, content, even though she knew that the dangerous part of what they faced was approaching. Everyone had warned her of that fact.

"What did you ladies discover?" Buckley finally broke the stillness.

"That Lois is in fact not related to me. She thought she was but Mom never had a sister or a female cousin. So, why did she say that? I asked Cadee. She says Lois has always maintained that she had a sister who died in childbirth and that her sister's husband refused contact with her."

"That's strange." Buckley sighed. "So, you ladies researched Lois?"

"We did with some help from Emma. She found that out about Mom. She said it was hard to find, that Mom's history was buried. And she found out who by." Locklin was hesitant to continue.

"Lois?" Buckley groaned as she nodded. "This really complicates everything. Not your fault, love."

"I know. We can't figure out why though. Emma has promised to keep looking into Lois. She says that Lois' family had quite a few numbered companies that don't seem to exist."

"Numbered companies?" Buckley grew silent, the possibilities racing through his mind. "As in crime?"

"That's what we are trying to determine. They may be legitimate, or enough to be legitimate that it could be overlooked. We talked to Dallas, who wasn't happy."

"No, I didn't think that he would be. He has enough on his plate."

"Something is going on with him. I sense that he is searching for something, and not finding it. He needs to find another line of work."

"Why would you say that?" Buckley waited, knowing that Locklin would speak when she was able to.

"I don't know. It's just that he has a look that he's haunted by something or someone. Does he have a girlfriend?"

"Not that I know of." Buckley suddenly groaned. "You realize that we have to face Charles and Lois tomorrow? That we can't avoid them?"

"I know. I've been praying about that. You have taught me to remember what my Dad did. That was to pray without ceasing."

"And you've reminded me. It's easy to forget, to slip into the mode that the world lives in. I have tended to do that lately."

"Maybe that's why we're going through what we are. To remind us that we need to trust God more and part of that trust is praying."

"It is, love." Buckley grew pensive. "You are happy here in the apartment?"

"I am." She shifted to look up at him. "I like that my friends are here but that we have our separate spaces. We're not in one another's faces. Your friends are here. This family here? It's closer than a normal family can be. Part of it is because you are all orphans and so are some of us ladies. There are enough others around to bring balance to our lives." She frowned. "Are you?"

"I am. I just wondered." Buckley dropped a kiss on her forehead. "Barnabas has asked what we want to change in decor. Paint. Flooring. Appliances. Furniture."

"He would do that? Of course, he would. I'm content for now. Other than all those little appliances that I don't know the name for." She grinned as he shook a finger at her before he reached to kiss her.

———

Standing behind the pulpit the next morning, Buckley sought for Locklin, finding her sitting with Burnie and Breck on either side of her, near the back of the church. Breck had approached him, asking where he wanted Locklin to sit.

Buckley had stared at him and then stuttered out that he hoped she would be near the front, frowning as Breck shook his head.

"Not yet, Buckley. Not until we find the ones responsible. We want her near the back. That way, we can get her out of here as quickly as possible. The fellows want this for you."

He had finally nodded, agreeing with their logic. "Have you talked to her?"

"Not yet. We'll come to find her when you're done with your prayer before the service. She needs to be there with you."

"She does. She has expressed that plan." Buckley looked past Breck. "Locklin, love? Breck will come and find you when it's time for the service."

Locklin had stared at him before she turned questioning eyes towards Breck. "Protecting me? Who's on duty this morning?"

Breck had grinned. "This morning, Burnie and myself. We will be sitting with you in church until this is over. And it will be at the back of the church."

"Of course, it will. I was going to suggest that. Buckley, the worship team leader is looking for you for prayer." Locklin simply reached for Buckley's hand, leaving Breck grinning at her.

There was the usual bustle and stir as the people settled themselves for the message. Buckley looked down at his notes, and then found Locklin's gaze once more. He frowned and then nodded. *Lord, I'm going to be talking without notes this morning. You need to lead my words, given me what You want me to say.*

Locklin stood beside him after the service, greeting his people. No, her people as well, she thought. How did this happen? She stiffened as she saw Charles and Lois approaching, stepping back just a bit so that she was slightly behind Buckley. He glanced down at her and then up as Charles spoke. He needed to be polite, he knew, but he also needed to protect his wife. He quickly moved them on, and then drew Locklin away, heading for his office and towards his friends who were waiting.

"Everything okay, Buckley?" Brennen stared past him, to find Lois watching them. "What's with Lois?"

"We are trying to get away from her, if you must know. Did Jaxcy talk to you?"

"She did. Come on, we can lock up for you. Out the back door, Buckley. I have the codes for the system. Head on out." Brennen and Brady walked through the building, locking things up and then standing outside as Brody approached them.

"Lois and Charles?"

"You've got it. We sent Buckley and Locklin on." Brennen was frustrated. "This isn't right. They shouldn't have to be running like this. Not from the church."

"No, they shouldn't." Brody pulled out his phone. "It's Emma. She just sent an email." He paled as he read it. "Did you know that Lois is Charles' second wife? That his first wife drowned?"

"No, I didn't. Wait!" Brady groaned. "And let me guess. Lois was on the scene when it happened."

"Emma implied that. She said she'd confirm that and let us know. We need to go talk to Buckley and Locklin."

"After lunch, Brody." Brady moved away. "I'm taking my lady out for lunch. We'll meet about three?"

"Sounds good."

Buckley stared down at the photo and then read the attached email before he looked up at Brody. "I know Emma. She's sure of this?"

"She is. She's sent it on to Dallas. This complicates things, Buckley. It also places you in a difficult position."

"It does. It means that the board has to confront the chairman and question him." Buckley rubbed at his forehead with his thumb and forefinger. "I don't see in here where she gives the name of Charles' first wife."

"She hasn't. She's working on confirming information on her, but she hinted that somehow it connected to Locklin."

"I wish this was over. She's had enough. And frankly, so have I." He sighed again. "I know, Brody, I know. You know what I mean. She's fretting and trying hard to hide it from me. I also worry about the church family, what could happen to them, if for some reason whoever it is decided to go after me when we're meeting."

"Don't resign, Buckley. You're where God has put you. Everyone is confident in that fact. We'll work through this."

"I know we will, but it's so hard. I feel like I am walking through this deep ravine with only the faintest of light reaching down, and that the path is strewn with so many rocks and stones and thistles."

"He knows, Buckley. You and Locklin are in our prayers." Brody's hand rested on his friend's shoulder as he did just that, prayed for his friend.

Buckley stood for a moment, his eyes on the picture, before he spoke.

"Who is she, Brody? Are we sure that she is dead?"

"What?" Brody spun from where he had taken a few steps away. "What are you saying, Brody?"

"What if she is still alive? Somewhere in the world? Look what happened to Jaxcy's parents. They were held for so many years overseas, both them and Jaxcy thinking the other was dead. What if she was removed, her death faked, and this Lois moved in? How long have they been married?"

"I don't know. I'll find that out." Brody was away to the computer that he favoured, booting it up, and beginning his search.

———

Buckley sighed. He needed to go speak with Locklin, but he knew that she was meeting with some of the ladies for prayer and Bible study. He would not disturb that, not unless it was an absolute emergency, and he didn't feel that it was. Not yet. It might come to that, but he wasn't ready to scare her. She needed the time with the ladies, for their support. They could relate to what she was going through, better than most.

His friends watched as he walked away before they exchanged glances, knowing it was at the point in the adventure that things could and would break loose. And they feared for their friend. They felt that he would face worse than they did, and from within the church he loved. And if that was the case, how would he continue as the minister that was just who they needed there?

Looking around the kitchen doorway, a huge smile on her face, Locklin watched as Buckley entered, setting his shoes in the closet, and then pausing before he looked up. She frowned as she saw that his smile didn't reach his eyes.

"Buckley? Sweetheart?" She walked towards him and into his hug.

"Locklin, love. Have a good time with the ladies?"

"I did." She accepted his kiss before she hugged him, standing with her arms still around his neck. "You're troubled."

"I am. Brody received some information from Emma that we need to talk about."

"He did." She stepped back, her hand reaching to draw him to the kitchen. "Sit. I have your coffee and some Irish baking. Blair and Devaney were to Riverville yesterday and stopped in the Irish bakeshop. They brought back goodies for all of us."

"They did? It's the wife of one of Abe's lifelong friends who has it." He sat, a sigh rising from him. "Sit, Locklin, with your tea. We'll talk of other things, then spend time in prayer. We are going to need it."

Locklin finally reached for Buckley's hands, finding his chilled. "Buckley, how bad is it?" They had spent time in prayer, seeking protection and wisdom.

"It's bad, love. Lois is Charles' second wife, and we don't know that his first wife is even dead. Emma's looking into that."

Locklin nodded. "That's what we discovered. We were talking about it this morning. Fynn digs deep, and she will, given that she likes that kind of thing. I still want to see her building with all her creepy-crawlies."

"And you will. What did she find out?"

"That Lois is indeed Charles' second wife. She talked to some of the older people in the church, who could remember things. No, we weren't gossiping. They want this over for you. Some of them have never really trusted her."

"They haven't? That's interesting. Nothing has ever been said to me."

"And they won't. They have no proof. Without proof, it's just gossip. Anyway, Fynn is able to draw them out. Guenivere was with her. The consensus is that his first wife just disappeared. She is reported to have drowned in the lake, caught in the undertow, but no one found her body."

"It would be easy to have placed her on a freighter, the freighter work its way through the canal, and then down the St. Lawrence River and to the ocean. From there, they could go anywhere. It sounds so much like Jaxcy's parents."

"It does. Jaxcy was intending to speak with her parents. To see if they had heard of any female on a neighbouring island that might be her." She paused, to sip at her tea, her finger running along the edge of the cup when she replaced it on the saucer. "Where does that leave Charles?"

"In a lot of trouble, unless he is cleared. What else, Locklin? I know there is more."

Locklin sighed. "There is, sweetheart. Dallas was around just before you came in. He wanted to clarify some things from my past. The forces are planning on moving in shortly, to clear up the drug houses and dealers both here and at home. He warned me that we will need to be extra cautious."

"And we will be. I just want this over." Buckley sighed, running a hand through his hair. "I keep saying that. I know that's what the others said as well."

"And it will be, Buckley. It will be. It is God's timing, not ours. He has plans for this, that we don't know about."

"He does, love. He brought me you." He reached to kiss her, not wanting to let her go, suddenly afraid for her. He looked around as he heard a tap at the door. "Were we expecting anyone?"

<hr>

"Not that I am aware of." Locklin moved to the door, standing to stare out of the peephole before she opened it. "Barnabas. Bruce. Come in."

"Locklin. You look beautiful." Bruce grinned at her, Barnabas' father a favourite among the ladies for the father figure that he had become.

"Thank you, Bruce. Please? We're in the kitchen, although we could move to the living room or office."

"The kitchen is fine. Buckley, son. How are you?" Bruce greeted Buckley before moving to find his own mug of coffee.

Barnabas hesitated, his eyes on Locklin. "Locklin?"

"Barnabas? I know this is more than just a casual call. Find your coffee and we'll talk."

Bruce paused as he studied the younger couple, Buckley in deep conversation with Barnabas, Locklin with her eyes on him, a frown on her face. He shook his head at her and she nodded.

"Buckley? I think Bruce wants to talk to you." Locklin had no problem interrupting the men.

"Oh? Sorry, Bruce. I can get carried away."

"I know you can. It's okay, Locklin. I expect that from these young fellows." Bruce shoved a file folder across the table towards them. "Here. Read this. And then we talk."

"Bruce?" Buckley nodded when Bruce refused to answer. "Just tell me. Is it good news or bad?"

"We think it's good news. It's up to you two how you look at it."

Buckley opened the folder, Locklin leaning against his arm, to find photos of both of them. Buckley looked up, finding Bruce watching him intently.

"Go on, Buckley. Read through it."

Buckley exchanged a look with Locklin and then began to read through the paperwork, hearing some exclamations from Locklin. He turned back and read through it before he looked at his bride, finding a look of wonder on her face.

"Bruce? What is this?" Buckley didn't look at the older man.

"This paperwork? It is from the Foundation board. We want to set up a new ministry, dedicated to those who are seeking to heal from violence or crime, or domestic abuse. We have been praying over this for many weeks. We decided that we would each pray for a specific couple to head it. Every single one of us came to our meeting three days ago with a single name. Yours and Locklin."

"What?" Locklin stared at him, then at Barnabas, and finally at Buckley. "I don't understand."

"What Dad is saying, Locklin, is there was complete consensus that they want you two to prayerfully consider moving on to this. We go no further until you two have had time to pray about it and consider all aspects of it. If you say no, that God wants you to stay with the church, then we move on to pray for another couple. If you say yes, you will take on this new challenge, then we move forward with it, and with the church to find someone to fill the vacancy. We are in no rush. We are moving forward with the plans and paperwork, and setting it up with the legal team. But until you accept or decline, it remains as it is. In the planning stages."

Buckley had to swallow hard. "I'm not sure what to say. I didn't expect this."

"No, son. You wouldn't. You're too humble to expect something like this. We have seen the growth that has occurred particularly over the last months that you have worked with and counseled your friends. We have seen the change in you as you and Locklin go through this, a maturity that we don't often see in someone your age. Both of you are blessed by God with gifts that will be used by Him wherever you decide to serve. Buckley, if you need counsel, I have spoken with a couple of pastors who are willing to meet with you as an individual or as a couple. That choice is yours." Bruce watched the couple closely, seeing how close to tears Locklin was. "How be we pray and then we'll leave, letting you start the process of praying and discussing this."

Buckley stood in his office thirty minutes later, staring down at the closed folder. He could hear Locklin singing softly to herself as she cleaned up the kitchen for the night. They had not felt like eating, neither one of them. Buckley finally went looking for her, finding her curled up on the couch in the living room, staring at the fireplace that she had lit. He had laughed at her one day when she said she would use it whenever she wanted, that she found it relaxing.

"Locklin, love?" She leaned against him, welcoming his arms around her.

"I was not expecting this, sweetheart. Were you?"

"Not in my wildest dreams. You know, Dad and I had discussed something like this years ago, that someone needed to start this. I think that if he had not died, he would have. But Bruce is right. We have the experience of sorts that we need."

"We do. Unfortunately, we do." Her head on his shoulder, her finger rubbed at the black button of his flannel shirt. "They didn't give a time to let them know."

"No, they wouldn't. They are like that. They put forth something like this and then let God lead. It's how they are all. I think that's why they are so successful."

"I see." She looked up at him, watching his face closely. "What are your thoughts?"

"Right now? I'm stunned, I think. I certainly will pray about it. But unless we are agreed, we don't do anything. We have to agree on this."

"Thank you, sweetheart. I'm scared, I think, to move on. But I shouldn't be. I guess there has just been so much lately. In the last year, in fact."

"They know that, love. They know that and considered that when they discussed offering it to us." Buckley grew pensive, wishing his own father was there so that he could discuss it with him.

"Tomorrow's Sunday again. How do we face Charles and Lois?" Locklin finally spoke.

"The same we do every week. With a smile on our face and in God's strength. I don't know how people who have no faith get through times like this."

"I don't either. It's been hard, Buckley, so very hard. When I saw you that day, I ran towards you, praying that you would help me. If you hadn't, I don't know what would have happened to me."

"I am thankful that God sent me there. I just fear for what we might face. It's not over, but I sense that it will be soon. We need to pray for that hedge of protection, love."

———

"And I have been." Locklin grew quiet, finally dozing off, Buckley's head on hers.

Locklin's steps slowed the next morning as she approached the church office. She could hear angry words and hesitated about approaching Buckley. She stepped to one side as Charles stalked past her, anger on his face. She frowned as she stared after him before she turned to find Buckley beside her.

"Buckley?"

He swept her into a hug. "I need you to stay close to me or one of the fellows today. Breck is bringing in some of our security guys. Charles seems to think that he is under suspicion. That's what that was all about. It's coming to a head, love."

"I know it is. He was angry and hurt." She looked back towards the door to the sanctuary. "What can he do to threaten your position?"

Buckley shrugged. "He can go to the board and then the congregation, try and make it seem that I am incompetent or evil or something. We won't worry about that now. Here, let's go meet the team for prayer. I really need it this morning."

Buckley paced through the gardens that afternoon, deep in thought. It had disturbed him that Charles had approached him like that. It was not him, he knew. What had happened that morning that set him off? He turned as he heard a throat clearing near him.

"Burnie?"

"Buckley, can we talk? I heard what happened this morning. I had come to find Locklin and overhead. I'm sorry. I didn't mean to." Burnie looked contrite and unsure of himself.

"It will soon go through the church. Charles threatened that." Buckley pointed to a bench and dropped down to it. "I can't stop it. I didn't ask for him to be investigated."

"No, his wife did, approaching Locklin the way she did and spreading around that she is Locklin's aunt." Burnie nodded at Buckley's look of surprise. "You didn't know that?"

"No, I hadn't heard that. And we know that's not true." Buckley sighed. "Now, where do we go? Charles will carry through with his threat. We can't stop him. If we did, it would look like we are trying to hide or cover up something."

"I know. You may need to leave the church that you love and that loves you. I pray that isn't the case. We have all grown under you so much, particularly with your messages on prayer."

"That was what God had laid on my heart. We need to be more like Christ when He prayed in the garden." Buckley grew silent. "I don't know what to do, Burnie. Locklin and I are praying through something right now. I feel as if I am on the edge of a cliff, ready to jump and it's too high for me to survive."

"That's an interesting way to phrase it. But it makes a good picture." Burnie looked around as he heard a sound. "Locklin, come on and join us. We're not talking about anything that you can't hear."

Locklin nodded, sitting beside Buckley, but the men could tell that she was upset.

"Love, what is it?"

"It's Lois. She showed up at our door. I didn't answer, but it was horrible what she was saying. She just kept banging on the door. I called security and they came and escorted her away." She looked at the two men. "She's accusing me of not being who I am. That I am an imposter and trying to corrupt you and the church." She blinked back her tears. "I'm not. She is."

"And we're proving it. I suspect that she knows, given what happened this morning." Buckley hesitated in what he needed to say. "It's going to get worse, love. We'll be in more danger, particularly you. You're the one that she seems to be going after. I don't understand why."

"This might explain it. Kataleen emailed me. I had just read it when Lois came to the door. Maybe if I hadn't I would have opened the door to her." She handed over her phone, the email ready to read.

Buckley read through it, drew in his breath, and then handed the phone to Burnie. Burnie read it and then read it again.

"We were right. His wife is still alive. How did Emma do that?"

"I don't know, but Abe is heading out to bring her home. Abe and his team. Where does that leave us now, Buckley? She'll be after us for sure. Her carefully crafted life is crumbling around her."

"It is. God will protect us, love. I don't know how or from what, but He will. Burnie, we need to get this to the others." Buckley reached for her phone. "I'll send it out as a group email and then we can meet. We are meeting, aren't we?"

"We are. The ladies are meeting with us as well." Burnie was on his feet, moving towards the building.

"Buckley? I'm so scared." Locklin crowded closer to him.

"You and me both, love. You and me both. This is getting out of hand." Buckley was on his feet, her hand in tight, rushing them back to the building. "We need to stay in here as much as we can. Barnabas will make sure that we have security with us if we need to be out."

"I sent the email on to Dallas. I wasn't sure if I should have."

"He needs to know. I would not be surprised if he knew already." Buckley paused outside the conference room door. "No matter what happens, Locklin, I love you more and more each day, more than I ever thought I could love someone. I don't want to see you hurt, but I am afraid."

"I love you too, sweetheart. We go forward, hand in hand, with God's protection. What He allows will happen."

His heart in his mouth, Buckley ran from his car, heading for the building and racing up the stairs. He had been speaking with Locklin when he heard her scream and then silence. He hit the apartment door, flinging it open, not finding Locklin even though he searched. He stood, hand on his head, frantically looking.

The note of the back of the entry door caught his attention and he ran towards it, sliding to a halt and then pulling it loose. He opened it, his heart sinking as he realized that whoever was after them now had Locklin in their control. He would obey their directions but he had to let someone know. He snapped a quick picture of the photo, sending it on to Burnie, knowing that of all of them, he would be the one to receive the text the quickest.

Running for his car, Buckley sped away, not seeing Burnie waving frantically at him before Burnie ran for his car and followed him. Burnie frowned before he reached for the button on his steering wheel, calling Breck and telling him that he was following Buckley.

"Burnie, what are you talking about? Buckley's at the church."

"No, he's not. He was in their apartment. He sent me a copy of a note that was on their door. I'm following him." Burnie slowed as Buckley's vehicle slowed and then shot down a side road. "He's heading towards the old Wallace place."

"He is? That's one that Dallas has been looking at. Dear Lord, protect them." Breck was gone, hitting his own apartment door on the run, heading for the conference room. "Fellows, Locklin's missing. Buckley had a note on their door. Burnie's chasing him and will keep us up to where they are."

The fellows were on their feet, the ones who were there, rapidly following Breck as he ran for his truck, separating themselves into a few vehicles as possible.

"Brady's on duty?" Breck shot a glance at Bradon.

"He is. Pray that he's the one they call if paramedics are needed."

Breck slowed his truck and came to a stop behind Burnie. The men congregated around Burnie, questions flying at him.

"Whoa! Wait, guys!" Burnie's hands went up. "We need to move some of our vehicles. I don't think they can see us, but we can't take a chance."

"Have you called for Dallas?" Breck peered through the trees, towards the house. "Wait a moment! That's Charles and Lois' home."

"It is. Buckley has gone in. He was met by someone holding a rifle or something on him." Burnie was scared, he had to admit to himself. He had had to leave a voice mail for Dallas and then had opted to call Will, speaking with him. Will was on his way, he said, with patrol vehicles. He sternly ordered Burnie and whoever it was with him to stay put.

"Have you seen Charles or Lois?" Bradon stood beside Burnie, watching the house.

"I saw Lois. She appeared in the doorway after Buckley had gone in." Burnie turned, his phone in his hand. "I just got a text from Emma. Abe's home with Charles' first wife. She was correct in her supposition. The lady was kidnapped, taken to a freighter, and shipped overseas. Close to the island where Jaxcy's parents were. Emma can't find any evidence that the islands are connected. She did say the lady had been forced to be a cleaner in a drug lord's home."

"That's is what we thought." Breck looked around. "How long do we wait?"

"As long as it takes." Bradon turned and faced them. "We can't go in. We have to let the police go in. If we did, it would be seen as trespassing and they could shoot us. I'm sure that Will has all the help he needs."

Will approached the building fellows, shaking his head. Of course, they would all be there. It was what they did.

"Any sign of them?"

"Not since they took Buckley in." Burnie pointed to the front door. "They walked him in through the front door. Lois came out just after and was looking around. I have not seen any sign of Charles."

"No? Okay. I want you all to stay right here. We're moving in. The judge has signed off on warrants for us. So it will be all legal." Will was away, heading for Dallas and the waiting officers.

The fellows watched as the police moved in. Lois appeared briefly at the door before she tried to slam it back shut in their faces. The police moved in. The fellows prayed as they had not for a while, not knowing what condition that their friends would be in, or even if they would be alive.

Dallas and Will moved quickly through the two-story house, searching. Lois screamed at them that they had no right to be there, that they were intruding on her, until she was handcuffed and removed, a stern warning given her and the search warrants shown to her.

"Where are they, Will?" Dallas was puzzled. They had searched the house. "They have to be here."

Will looked around. "You know, this house was rumoured to have belonged to a bootlegger. It's that old. There were tunnels running to the lake and secret rooms, or so it's told. Let's start searching for that. Find out who would know."

Will was away, down to the basement, officers with him to spread out, searching. Dallas was frustrated. He hadn't been able to find anyone who could verify the rumours. At a shout from one of the officers, he ran for the stairs, almost falling down them in his haste to descend. He met Will running his way.

"Where?"

"In the root cellar." Will slid to a halt on the dirty concrete in the room. "Of course, it would be in the root cellar. Here, let's get that door open. Break it down if you have to."

A few solid kicks from many feet had the door splintered enough that it could be pulled away from the frame. The officers in protective gear went first, shouts rising in the air for the men they found to halt and raise their hands. Will and Dallas followed, their hearts dropping as they saw Buckley bound hand and foot on the floor, trying to move but unable to do. They followed his line of sight and then were across the room, dropping to their knees beside Locklin, cries for help sounding from them.

Turning to call for paramedics, Will moved swiftly towards Buckley even as an officer's knife sliced through his bonds. Will restrained him from moving towards Locklin.

"I have help coming, Buckley. What happened?"

Buckley shook his head. "I don't know. She was like that when I found her. I didn't have a chance. They had me down and bound before I could get to her." He was almost sobbing as he watched Brady and his partner, Patrick, appear and then begin to work on Locklin. "They said they had given her something. An overdose."

Patrick spun at his words. "An overdose? With what?"

"I don't know." Buckley didn't feel the tears that were running down his face. "They didn't say, just said an overdose."

Patrick was on his feet, running for the rig, grabbing the kit that he needed, with the medication that he prayed would save Locklin's life.

"How long, Buckley?" Brady's sharp voice cut through the silence. "I don't know. I was here for fifteen or twenty minutes before they forced me down here. They said it was just before that. Please, Brady?"

"I know, Buckley. We're working on it." Brady and Patrick exchanged glances even as Brady spoke.

"We need to move, Brady." Patrick was reaching for Locklin, to help transfer her to a stretcher. "Will, we're off. An escort?"

Will pointed to two officers. "In front and back. Now move. Buckley, no, we'll get you there. Just let them move." Will's hand on Buckley's arm stopped him from moving forward. "Dallas, you've got this. I'm with Buckley."

Will's hand on his arm propelled Buckley up the stairs, through the house to the outside and then to Will's car. He was shoved roughly inside before Will was behind the wheel, lights flashing and sirens blaring as he raced after the ambulance. He could see the building fellows scattering and gave a grim smile as he saw them pulling in behind him. He lost them on the race to follow Locklin, but he knew that they would be there, for Buckley, just as he had been there for them.

Doc looked around as the charge nurse hurried his way.

"Doc, we have an overdose coming in. Brady and Patrick are on their way in. Brady asked that we tell you that it's Locklin."

"Locklin? There is no way that she would do this on purpose. She doesn't do drugs. Clear room 1." Doc was on the move, heading for the ambulance bay.

"Already done. Our people are ready, Doc. Brady also asked that you be told Will Peters was heading this way with Buckley."

Doc helped pull the doors to the rig open, even as Brady and Patrick reached for the stretcher.

"She's starting to code, Doc. I don't know if we got to her in time." Patrick was standing on the bars of the stretcher, his hands working to perform CPR even as the stretcher was rushed in a rapid manner to the room.

"Keep it up, Patrick. Sue, heart monitor. Brady, do we know what it was?"

"No, we don't. They told Buckley what they had done, but not with what." Brady's hands were busy, starting the IV line and then reaching for the defibrillator. "We need this. Patrick, here."

They watched as Locklin's body jerked with the electric shock sent through her. And it was repeated.

"We have rhythm, people." Doc's rapid orders were followed, the debris from needles and other equipment flying through the air.

An hour later, Doc finally stepped back. Locklin had been intubated and was still on the heart monitor. He watched closely, finally nodding.

"We did it, people. We did it. She's still alive and steady. Brady, Patrick, thank you. Now off with you two. I know it's after your shift."

"We would have stayed, no matter who it was. You know that, Doc."

Doc nodded and then turned, fatigue weighing him down. He had called in an extra physician to cover the busy Emergency Department even as he fought for Locklin's life. She was stable, he knew, but for how long? She could regress, that he knew. But for now, he'd send her to the ICU, find Buckley and then go home and hug his Anna. He needed that. It had been a brutal day, too many accidents. Losing the young mother and her small son had been hard, harder even to talk with the young husband.

Breck was watching for Doc, seeing the fatigue in his steps as he approached. He walked towards him, trying to assess his mood.

"Doc?"

Doc looked up, a hand rising to tap Breck's shoulder. "Where is he?"

"We found an empty room and have him in there. He was looked over. Rope burns on his wrists. He was bound and couldn't get to Locklin."

"Was he? All right. Let's go find him."

Pausing just inside the doorway, Breck's hand resting this time on his shoulder, Doc watched as all the faces turned his way. He could see that Will was still there, in a chair beside Buckley. Buckley sat, not looking around, his form crumpled and grieving, Doc could tell. Brody moved from the seat beside him, to let Doc sit.

Doc waited for Buckley to look up, a prayer on his lips for his young friend.

"Buckley?" He drew in a breath as Buckley raised his head.

"She's gone, isn't she? They don't survive overdoses. Not after that long."

"She's alive, Buckley." Doc waited for Buckley to hear him and then he repeated his words. "She's alive, Buckley."

Buckley's eyes shot to Doc. "She is? She's still alive?" He could barely get the words out.

"She is, Buckley. She crashed on the way in from the ambulance, but with Patrick and Brady's help and the staff here, we were able to revive her. She's intubated right now and on a heart monitor. But she is alive."

Buckley's eyes slid closed. "I was afraid, Doc, afraid that I had lost my heart. Can I see her?"

"Give us a few moments to get her situated in her room. Then we'll come to get you." Doc stood, his eyes on Buckley before he spoke to everyone in the room. "Locklin is still with us. God worked His healing touch there. She is still not out of danger, but she is alive." Doc paused for a moment before he walked away, a heaviness to his steps. No, there was no guarantee that Locklin would even make it, despite what they had done.

Chapter 48

Buckley haunted the ICU for three days, not willing to leave to sleep, to shower, or to even eat. His friends made sure that he was taken care of but he just shook his head and walked away if they even suggested that he leave. Barnabas had been around on the third day, worried about Buckley, finding him standing in the middle of the waiting room, staring into space.

Barnabas touched his arm lightly and then grasped it to lead him to a seat.

"Sit, Buckley. You're going to fall over if you don't." Barnabas watched with compassion as Buckley sank down, dejection, worry, and sorrow in his bearing. "How is she?"

"They've been able to take the ventilator off. She's on room oxygen but she'll go back on it if she can't keep her oxygen levels up. Why, Barnabas? Do we even know why?"

"I'm not sure that all the pieces are together yet. I haven't talked to Dallas today. He said that he was around last night."

"He was. He didn't say much." Buckley sat back, scrubbing his hands down his face. "Where do I stand with the church?"

"What do you mean?"

"What I said. Where do I stand? I'm sure the board will want me out with Locklin overdosing even though it was done to her."

"No, that's not what they've said. Charles resigned from the board and left the church. Edward Styles took over. They are meeting nightly to pray for you two. He wanted me to tell you to take the time that you needed. This was not your fault or doing."

"He said that? I still don't know if I can go back and preach again." Buckley sighed. "Maybe this is God's way of telling me to move on."

"It might be but don't make any decisions without prayer, talking to us, and talking to Locklin. I have every confidence that she will heal. We're praying for a touch of the Master's garment for her."

"Thank you." He looked up to see Dallas standing in front of him. "Dallas? You're back. That can't be good."

"Actually, Buckley, it is. I just wanted to update you. Locklin?"

"She's improving, they tell me. I don't see it." Buckley rubbed at his sore, red eyes. He had wept too much, he thought, ready to weep some more. "You're here." He repeated himself without meaning to.

Dallas nodded. "I am, Buckley. I have a photo to show you." He opened the portfolio that he had set on the chair beside him. "Take a look at this photo."

Buckley finally reached for it, blinking rapidly. He frowned. "That's Locklin's father, isn't it?"

"It is. We have received word and have confirmed it that it was not her father who was shot and killed at the courthouse. The police are working on identifying that man. He was close enough in looks and had her father's identification on him." Dallas tapped the photo. "This is her father. We have traced him to a property in Quebec. The authorities are moving in on it as we speak."

"He's alive?" Buckley was stunned. "He's been alive all this time."

"Yes. We'll have to get his statement and that will take time. Once we can get him cleared and back here, I'll talk to Locklin."

Buckley slumped back against the wall. "So, what has been the point of all this?"

"Locklin? We suspect that she was being used against her father. If he shut up and didn't say anything, then she would be safe. But the rumblings that we have heard from someone undercover is that he is starting to rebel and make noise, threatening to run. He's been put under harder lockdown from what we can determine."

"What about Lois? Where does she fit in?" Barnabas watched Buckley closely, seeing how near to collapse that he was.

"She's related to the drug lord in South America. She has refused to talk but others who worked for her have. They are getting ready to arrest him in that country. That should happen today."

"Charles?"

"He was innocent or so he claims. We're still talking with him. We have him under house arrest at the moment. His first wife has returned but wants nothing to do with him. The Foundation lawyers are working with her."

"That's good. Find her someone to talk with." Buckley was on his feet, moving towards the ICU units, without saying another word.

"He's shutting down, Barnabas." Dallas watched him walk away.

"He is. But there is nothing that we can do. Not until he collapses. He'll hold himself up as long as he can."

"Locklin?"

"She's recovering. He won't say much. He's losing his hope, Dallas."

"I see that. I need to run. Keep me updated. I'll be back around as soon as I have more word on her father."

Buckley stood beside Locklin, his hand on her cheek, his heart still even though he knew he should pray. He just didn't have the words he needed. But God knew, Buckley thought. This is when the Holy Spirit prays for us.

———

A week later, Locklin curled up once more on their couch, glad to be home, but still struggling to recover. She had been given a list of symptoms to watch for. She had read it over and then tossed it on the kitchen counter. Refusing to acknowledge it, Locklin had simply shut her mind to the possibilities. God was healing her, she thought. That is all that mattered.

Fynn watched her carefully from where she sat near her.

"Locklin?"

"Fynn?"

Fynn grinned at her. "We need to plan a date when you can come play with my creepy crawlies."

"We do. I just wish that this had never happened." Locklin didn't look up as Buckley sat beside her. "It's taken too much from me, too much from Buckley."

"It takes from all of us, but you two in particular, it has taken a lot." Fynn was not sure how to continue. "God kept you alive, Locklin. I don't know why. But He loves you both. Let me pray with you and then I'm leaving. You two need to talk."

Buckley rose to follow her to the door, locking it behind her, a hand resting against it, in what seemed to have become a favourite position of his. He looked over his shoulder. He had asked that he be the one to tell Locklin that her father was still alive, had been returned to this area, but was still being debriefed, as they put it.

"Buckley?" Locklin studied him as he sat beside her, sweeping her into a hug and then just holding her.

"Locklin? Are you sure that you should be up?"

"For now. What is going on?"

"Locklin, Dallas approached me a week ago. He handed me a photo." Buckley reached for the envelope he had set down on the end table. "This is it. Before you look at it, we need to pray."

Locklin finally reached for it, puzzlement on her face. Pulling open the envelope, she then extracted the photo. A hand went to her mouth as she blinked rapidly. "It's Dad. Oh! It's Dad." Then she frowned. "But, Buckley, the date. It has to be wrong."

"No, love, it's not. The man who was killed testifying in Toronto? They have finally determined that it was not your father. I don't know all the details and I am not sure that we will as it was an undercover officer who contacted the force there. Your father was held in Quebec."

"He's been alive all this time? So close and yet so far. How is he? Where is he?" Locklin's words tumbled over each other.

"He's as well as can be expected. He's receiving treatment. And he is in the area. They're still talking with him. The police do not want you two together for a few more days. Not until they can make all their arrests."

"He's here? Oh, Buckley! Dad is alive and here? Now, I can heal! But I want to see him!"

Buckley hugged her tighter. "You will, love. You will. Barnabas has the Foundation lawyers and some others working with him."

Locklin snuggled down against her husband, wiping at her face. "I am suddenly so tired. That's not right."

Buckley gave a soft laugh. "Yeah, it is. You're recovering from dying. You did die, you know."

"I know. Brady talked to me about it. He was so scared, he said. He didn't want to have to face you if I didn't make it back."

"I would not have blamed him. I blame the ones who did this to you."

"What happened with Charles and Lois?"

———

"Charles has been removed from here. They moved him somewhere to protect him until he can testify. Lois? Let's just say that God has avenged so many people. Somehow she managed to get some drugs and overdosed. They didn't find her in time."

"That's so sad. What about his first wife?"

"She's given her statement and then moved on. She divorced Charles. She has a lot of healing to do. And no, neither lady was related to you. Lois apparently made that up, to try and get close to you. She's been playing everyone for years."

"That's sad. What drives people to that?"

"Greed. Money. Lust." Buckley's voice had softened as he felt Locklin's body relaxing. He was content, for the moment, to sit and hold her, and spend time in prayer. He eventually reached for her Bible, opening it to read the passages that he loved on prayer.

Three weeks later, feeling mostly recovered, Locklin moved restlessly around the rose garden. Something was up, she could tell, something that no one seemed to want to share with her. She shrugged, not willing to push it. Life was too precious, she decided. She jumped as arms surrounded her and she felt the familiar beard brush her face as a kiss landed on her cheek.

"Buckley, that had better be you."

Buckley's deep laugh caused her to smile. "It is, love. It is. I was looking for you."

"You were? Well, you found me. What did you want?"

"I want you to turn around but keep your eyes closed." She could hear the joy and laughter still in his voice.

"Really? My eyes closed? And why?" She was laughing as she questioned him.

He laughed with her. "Just humour me? Please? Okay, I have your hand. Your eyes are closed. Trust me, love. I won't let anything harm you. Okay. We're stopping right here. Now, when I ask you to, I want you to open your eyes. Yes, love, I need you to drop my hand."

Buckley watched her closely before his quiet voice whispered in her ear. "You can open your eyes."

Locklin blinked as she did so, the few moments that she had her eyes closed causing the light to be too bright. She looked around, her gaze coming back to the man who stood five feet in front of her, a bouquet of yellow roses in his hand. Locklin's hands covered her mouth, even as she blinked rapidly to clear the tears.

"Dad! Dad! It's you? It's really you? Oh, Daddy, how I missed you." Locklin was across the few feet, her arms around her father's neck even as his arms surrounded her, the roses dropping to the ground. She sobbed even as her father wept.

Buckley blinked back his own tears. It had been God who had spared them, he thought, and brought them back together. Logan had a lot of healing to do, that he had admitted, but to be near his daughter? That was all he had asked. Buckley had met with him and Dallas the day before, making the arrangements for him to move into one of the spare apartments in the building, just until he was healed enough to know where he wanted to live. He nodded at Barnabas who had walked with the two men to find Locklin. Barnabas gave a small wave, heading off to find the building family.

Locklin finally stepped back, leaning against Buckley, taking the roses that her father handed her. He had always given his wife yellow roses and for him, there was no other colour to give his beloved daughter. They spoke for a while before the three of them moved towards the building, finding all the fellows and the ladies waiting for them. Barnabas had arranged for that.

Locklin wandered the lobby, her arm linked with her father, introducing him, telling him bits and pieces of the fellows and ladies. She prayed that he would not be overwhelmed, but was so glad to have him nearby. Doc had approached her, letting her know that he would be checking in on her father, just to be sure that he was okay. Doc had hugged her and then walked away, wiping at his eyes, complaining that he had dust or something in them. No one believed him, knowing the soft heart that Doc had.

Late that night, Locklin found Buckley on the balcony, just watching the stars. She cuddled close, her emotions still raw.

"Thank you, Buckley. I think you prayed Dad home."

"We all did, love. We all did. Burnie admitted to me today that he never felt it was your father. I think he was putting out feelers all along."

"Bless Burnie. He needs to find a lady."

"It will take a special lady for him. You have to be careful around him. You just might end up in a book."

"Is that right? I feel like we have lived a mystery story or a police drama or something. But God was there, just as you said."

"He was, love." Buckley stooped to kiss her. "Have I told you today how much I love you?"

"You have, and I never tire of hearing that. I love you, too. I just never expected to be a minister's wife."

———

A month later, Locklin was on the hunt for Buckley. She had searched for him at the church, and then through the building, finally tracking him down in the rose garden. He reached out a hand to draw her to the bench with him.

"Missed me?" He laughed as she swatted at him.

"Always. I just needed to ask you something but I can't remember what." Locklin snuggled down against him. She never grew tired of being held, finding his love just what she needed to help her heal, that and his prayers.

"It can't be important if you don't remember."

They sat, watching the sun set, throwing out the rose and purple streamers over the lake. They had made a decision about what they wanted to do but were still praying it through.

"I guess that we need to talk to Barnabas and Bruce." Locklin finally broke the silence.

"I guess that we do. You're sure?"

"I am. God led us through things to give us the knowledge to help others. He had brought others into contact with us who will help." Locklin looked up at him. "I'm scared, Buckley."

"Me, too. This is jumping off into the unknown, isn't it? But God will guide us. I will miss the church and it's people."

"So will I. Even though I'm not a minister's wife." Locklin laughed at the face he made. "I'm not."

"Yes, you were. And you are so suited to this new venture." He stood, a hand reaching for hers, helping her to stand, then bowing his head to pray for them.

Barnabas looked at them as he opened his door.

"Come in. I wasn't expecting you. Mom and Dad are here. They'll be glad to see you. Mom was asking about you, Locklin. And you're in time for a meal."

Laughter and conversation helped to ease the nervousness that Locklin was feeling. She looked up at Buckley as she helped to clear away the meal, finding him watching her and then nodding.

Bruce had been watching the young couple closely and then nodded himself. They have reached a decision. I guess, then, Lord, we'll be putting our plans for the new ministry on hold.

"Dad, how be we head for the living room with our coffee for the men and tea for the ladies? Mom, you had that tray of sweets?"

"I do. Now, find those little glass plates that were your grandmother's. We need them. I feel like we're going to be celebrating. She always used them for that."

Barnabas merely grinned, digging out the plates that his mother wanted. He watched as the ladies were seated and served and then sat himself, his eyes on Buckley and Locklin.

"Dad? Will you lead us in a time of prayer? I think we need it."

"I agree, son. Now, any special requests?" Bruce's eyes twinkled as he asked that.

"Not really, Bruce." Locklin reached for Buckley's hand. "But I do appreciate your prayers."

Thirty minutes later, their heads raised and conversation and laughter flowed among the five before Bruce took a chance and broke into the conversation.

"I think you have something to tell us, Buckley. I don't think you ended up here for just a visit."

Buckley shook his head, his hand reaching for Locklin's.

———

"We do. Just bear with me for a moment. Locklin, when I saw you running towards me that day, I could do nothing else but step in. I didn't realize what an adventure we would end up on. I certainly never expected to find the love of my love that way. God was good. He protected you from Hall and brought him to justice. He also protected you and myself over the weeks that we struggled to make sense of everything.

"With you not having your memories when we married, I always felt that you were short changed. But you never let it or seldom let it come between us. I love the lady that you are becoming. You are my Proverbs 31 lady. Mom and Dad would have loved you.

"To find out that your father was alive and to have reunited you two? That is an answer to a prayer I don't think we asked. God moved there. Your father has healing to do, as do you. But we're working on that." He stopped for a moment, overcome with his emotions.

Bruce nodded. "You two are a testimony to your faith. Buckley, I hear that your messages are reaching and changing people. But what is it that you wanted to say?"

Buckley looked down at Locklin and swallowed hard. They were confident in their decision but now that the time had come to give it, he wasn't so confident.

"A while ago, you approached us, asking us to consider a new ministry that the Foundation was planning. You asked us to take the time to pray it over and when we had made a decision to come and find you. We have made that decision." Buckley raised his eyes, searching the faces of the three in front of him. "We have tendered our resignation to the church board. We are accepting the new ministry that the Foundation offered us. Going through what we did? We both feel that God led us through that, to give us some understanding of what is needed. I can no longer just serve in a church. And Locklin keeps reminding me that she is not a minister's wife."

Bruce nodded. "No, she's not but she is fitted for her new role. Thank you, Buckley, Locklin, for accepting this. It's a position that will grow and grow, we suspect. We will need to meet but first, let's spend some time in prayer."

Locklin walked back through their apartment late that night, not really heading anywhere in particular, and ran into Buckley as he stood watching her.

"You're sure, Buckley?"

"I am. And you?"

"I am. I mean, I'm scared, nervous, excited, not sure about what emotion to have."

"Bruce was right. You are suited to this new duty. And I feel the same as you. Let's spend some time in prayer. Tomorrow is Sunday, and Edward said that he would read our resignation after the service. This will be hard."

"It will be, but God is leading us on to different ministries. I have a vision when Bruce was praying for us. That this ministry started here and then kept expanding, town by town."

"God will lead in that, love." He bent and kissed her, wrapping her tight in his arms.

Dear Readers

Thank you for choosing the story of Buckley and his love, Locklin. They had an adventure that I had not planned on. Once more, they just took over the story and kept on going. It was not planned that Locklin have amnesia. They threw that in to move the story along. I love it when characters just take over. Mine always do. We call them unruly characters, who did not share the story and just take over the steering wheel.

Prayer? How do we pray? When do we pray? Only when we need something? Only when something prompts us to? When we think of someone that we promised to pray for?"

We are exhorted in Scripture to pray without ceasing. For me, that means a day-long conversation with God. He wants to hear from us, hear our joys and sorrows. He knows them already but we need to vocalize them to Him. I often turn to the passage in John, where Christ prayed in the garden. Just to think that He prayed for each one of us all those years ago. That is something to meditate on.

Drugs are becoming more and more dangerous. It has become common for emergency personnel to carry the antidote, but even then, it is sometimes too late. My heart goes out to those who have lost loved ones to drugs and to overdoses.

And of course, Abe and his men and their ladies had to return. I am always happy to see them, even though they drop in unexpectedly. Their stories are in the *His Guardians* series. And the Irish bakery? That is Dave and Rylee, whose story is *A Touch of His Garment*.

Buckley is well loved by his friends. He needed a special lady to love. And Locklin needed that special fellow. I think that they found one another. Love at first sight? Sure, I believe in that. But this is a book, which gives me the opportunity to have that happen. Nothing was planned, really, for them. For Buckley to move from the church that he loved to a new ministry, something totally new and untried? Not in the planning, but it added to the story, giving another dimension to his character.

God bless each one of you.

Ronna

Burnie: Encouraged to Teach

The Barnabas Chronicles
Book 12

By

Ronna M. Bacon

Psalm 32:8

I will instruct you and teach you in the way you should go; I will counsel you with my loving eye on you.

Psalm 25:5

Guide me in your truth and tech me, for you are God my Savior, and my hope is in you all day long.

Psalm 143:10

Teach me to do your will, for you are my God; may your good Sprit lead me on level ground.

NKJV

Table of Contents

Staring glumly at his wrist as he tugged against the handcuffs that shackled him to the side rail of the hospital bed, Burnie Cummings wasn't quite sure what had brought him to that or even to the hospital bed in some little town. He stared around the room, his head dropping back on the pillow as his eyes closed. He hurt. All over. And he couldn't remember why. He raised his free hand to stare at the bandages that covered that hand and arm. He had been told, forcefully, that he had burns on them. But no one would tell him how or why. Burnie tugged again at his wrist, desperate to escape yet held in place by two pieces of metal attached by a small chain.

He tried to pray, but he felt that his prayers didn't hit the ceiling. Burnie knew God was there. He just needed some reassurance of that.

Burnie's eyes turned towards the door as it opened and a head appeared, followed by a body and then another man. He frowned.

"Breck? Andy? What are you two doing here?" His voice was low and rough.

"We're here for you." Breck held up a small key. "Dallas gave me this. He's outside, trying to find out why you're chained up." Breck quickly undid the handcuffs and then helped his friend to sit up. "Watch yourself. We were told that you had been unconscious when you were found."

"I was? I don't remember. All I remember is waking up here, with those things on my wrist." Burnie pointed to the handcuffs now laying on the bed. "Can I leave?"

"That's what we're here for." Andy dumped out the plastic bag he had been carrying. "Here. Breck raided your apartment for some clothes."

With Breck's aid, Burnie dressed quickly, his head spinning as he finished. "I don't feel so good, fellows."

———

"No, we didn't think you would." Breck looked around as the door opened and Dallas, a police detective friend, appeared. "Here's your key. Can we leave?"

"We can. They tried to say that Burnie was a material witness and was on the run from them." Dallas shook his head as he studied his friend, whose dark brown hair was tousled badly and deep green eyes were filled with pain and uncertainty. "Burnie, what did you go and get involved in?"

"If I knew, I wouldn't have." Burnie shoved his feet into his sneakers, staring down at the laces. "I'm not doing those up. They may come and arrest if I take time for that."

Breck grinned for a moment. "Not likely. But let's get you out of here."

The four men moved cautiously away from the hospital, heading for the vehicle that Andy, the Barnabas Foundation pilot, had borrowed from the maintenance man at the small airport. Burnie was tucked into the back seat beside Dallas.

"Burnie, what did you go and do?" Dallas stared at him, unable to see him clearly in the dark.

"I don't know, Dallas. Breck asked me that. I remember leaving on my vacation, needing some time. But I don't remember what happened." Burnie stared out of the window. "I think someone else was there, but I don't know. What happened, anyway?"

"We'll talk, Burnie, once we are into the air. I don't have a good feeling about this small town force." Dallas shifted in his seat to look behind him. "Andy?"

"Five minutes to the airport, Dallas. And then we can take off. I'll just need to do my preflight."

"Okay."

Dallas and Breck hustled Burnie up into the cabin of the Barnabas Foundation plane while Andy did his preflight, buckling him in and then seating themselves. Andy soon was in the cockpit and the plane lifting off.

———

Once in the air, Breck moved towards Burnie, watching his friend closely, noting the bruises and cuts on his face.

"Burnie, you can't remember anything?"

"About what happened to me?" Burnie shook his head and regretted it, the headache now pounding behind his eyes. "Why'd you make me do that?"

Breck gave a quick grin. "I didn't. You decided to do that." His voice died away as his head tilted. He shared a look with Dallas. Both of them had heard something, a soft rustling when there shouldn't have been any.

Breck stood, a finger on his lips to hush Burnie's question. He turned, eyes narrowing, as he moved through the cabin, stopping in front of a cupboard door. It had been closed tightly, he thought, but now was ajar. He yanked at the door, pulling it open quickly, and then reached it, grasping the arm of the youth, as he thought, who was hiding in there, a blanket pulled over themselves.

A startled sob shook the three men as Breck pulled the blanket off the youth.

"What! Wait! You're a lady!" Breck was shocked.

They stared at the young woman who stood in front of them, her hands covering her face as her body shook in fear. Her short auburn curls were tangled and her flannel shirt and jeans were torn, dirty, and covered with burn marks.

"Here! Sit! I'm sorry!" Breck gently shoved her down into a seat, a frown on his face before he reached for her hands, pulling them away from her face.

Startled violet eyes stared at them before she focused on Burnie. She was up from her seat to kneel beside him, a hand reaching to touch his face.

"You're alive. I thought that you were dead!"

"I'm not, but I don't know you. And why are you on this plane?" Burnie's voice sounded harsh and he winced. "I'm sorry. I didn't mean to sound like that. Here. Sit beside me." He reached for the bottle of water that Dallas held out to him. "Drink this. And then talk."

She swallowed a mouthful too quickly, choking on it, sputtering out water as she coughed.

"I'm sorry. I didn't mean to do that."

"Can you tell us your name?" Burnie's voice had gentled.

"I can. It's Muir Donachie. I'm sorry. I shouldn't have snuck on here. But I heard you talking and that you were looking for someone named Burnie." She turned to Burnie. "Is that you?"

"It is. I'm Burnie. The one who pulled you out of the cupboard is Breck. And this is Dallas." He watched her closely. "Can you tell us why?"

"I guess." She rubbed her hands along her jeans, studying the dirt and debris that covered both her hands and her jeans. "I think I'm responsible for what happened to you."

"You are? And how would that be?"

"You came into the shop that I was working in. Just a little shop where you can buy snacks, soft drinks and some groceries. You heard someone talking to me, took offence at his words and language and removed him. He threatened to come back. You had come back in to talk to me. Then, a fire started in the back of the store and the propane tank exploded. You had made me leave when the fire started. We were running away when the explosion happened. I tried to get back to you, but I couldn't. He was there. He was watching you and then me and threatened you. I couldn't help. I couldn't call for anyone. I had no cell phone, if that's what you call them."

"And then?" Dallas' voice was gentle as he prompted her to continue.

"The police came. I heard them talking to him. He said that you had caused the fire and that they should arrest you. He couldn't prove it. And you weren't awake. I saw them handcuff you and then take you away. They dragged you to one of the cars and just drove away." Her eyes were sorrowful as they watched Burnie.

"Wait a minute! Didn't they call for the paramedics?" Breck shared a look with Dallas, puzzled.

"No, they didn't. We don't have them here, anyway. When they left, he searched for me. I hid. Then I heard the plane and came to the airport, thinking that somehow I could escape. I have never been able to leave this town."

"And then you heard us talking about Burnie?" At her nod, Dallas sat back. "Okay. We'll talk more."

"I don't understand." Muir's eyes searched Dallas' face.

"I'm a police officer, Muir. I can look into this."

Muir looked horrified. "Oh, now! You can't! They'll find my Granny and hurt her. They threatened me with that." The stress that she had been under for an unknown time finally took over her body. Her eyes closed and she was lost to them.

Burnie stared at her. "Is that for real?"

"It's not one of your mystery stories. At least, I don't think it is." Breck commented on Burnie's occupation as a mystery writer. "Dallas, we'll need to look into this."

"And we will. Once we have both Burnie and Muir looked after." Dallas nodded towards Burnie. "We've lost him too."

"So we have." Breck was on his feet. "I need to talk to Andy and then see if I can get through to Barnabas."

Breck carefully gathered Muir into his arms, heading for the airplane stairs and then his truck, tucking her inside. He turned as he heard Burnie's stumbling steps as he approached, an arm across both Andy's and Dallas' shoulders. They had landed safely on the airstrip on the Barnabas Foundation lands.

"He's alert?" Breck gave a brief grin before concern for his friend coloured his face.

"If you can call it that." Dallas helped Burnie into the truck and then stood back. "What did he get involved in?"

"I have no idea, but I don't like it. I'm glad that you went along."

Dallas nodded. "Will called me. Barnabas had been in touch with him. Did he ever say how he found out about Burnie?"

Breck shook his head. "No. He called as he was heading to a board meeting. Just said that Burnie was in trouble and asked me to fly up with Andy and bring him home. He had asked Will if you would go."

Andy nodded towards the truck. "This is not over for him. At least, I don't think so."

"No, I don't think it is." Breck sighed as he ducked his head to watch Burnie, finding the other man with his arm around Muir, tucking her close to him. "We're off on another one, fellows. Pray that this time neither one of them is so critically injured."

Doc stood in his apartment doorway twenty minutes later, watching as Breck walked towards him, Muir in his arms, Burnie's stumbling steps leading him that way as well.

"Breck? Who do you have? And what happened to Burnie?"

"This is a stowaway on our plane, Doc. A lady by the name of Muir Donachie. And Burnie was involved in an explosion. We couldn't get a lot of details from his physician. They were very reluctant to talk to us."

———

"In with you then." Doc peered at the clock. It was getting close to midnight, and he had been up since early morning for his shift at the local Emergency Department. "She can go into that room. Burnie across the hall."

Doc's wife, Anna, gently touched Muir's hair. "What happened to them, Doc? It's not just the explosion for her, is it?"

Doc shook his head. "I don't think so, love. She's too thin." He paused as he lifted the back of her shirt to listen to her chest. "She's been beaten, Anna."

"Oh, Doc! Who would do that?" Anna blinked rapidly. "The poor thing. You finish up and then I'll get her settled. Who was with her?"

"Burnie." Doc was distracted, listening to Muir's heart. "An explosion, the boys said."

"Who?"

"Breck and Dallas." Doc stepped back. "She'll do for the night, love. Get her settled and I'll be back. If she rouses at all, we can talk."

Burnie had dropped back off to sleep, not feeling the sneakers pulled from feet, or the gentle hands as Breck pulled the covers over him. Doc stood for a moment, his eyes on his young friend, even as a prayer was raised for him. *Lord, what has he gotten involved in? And is he off on another adventure, just like his friends? If so, please protect him.*

Breck stood back beside Doc, uncertainty on his face.

"Doc? He was injured in an explosion a day or so ago. We tried to get information on him but the hospital refused. He was also handcuffed to his bed."

"Handcuffed? That's not our Burnie. Has he said much?" Doc peered at Breck and then down at Burnie.

"Not really. Muir did mention that he was unconscious, or dead as she thought." Breck looked behind him. "She's worried about her grandmother. She doesn't want us talking to anyone."

"And that won't happen, you not talking to anyone, not if I know you fellows. You'll be deep into an investigation on the morrow." Doc walked towards Burnie, bending over him. "Did he say why the bandage?"

"He said burns, but I really question that, Doc." Breck was hesitant to say what he really thought. Lord, please heal our friend.

Doc reached to unwrap the bandage, a puzzled look on his face. "What are they talking about? There are no burns."

Breck shared a look with Doc and then reached for the bandage, feeling it. "There's something in here, Doc. Something small and metal?"

"Then I suggest that you remove it from here." Doc peered at the clock. "It's not too late. Take it into town and give it to the police. Dallas can get it from them."

"I agree. I'll check in on him in the morning, Doc." Breck walked away, leaving Doc to assess Burnie.

Rousing in the early morning hours, Burnie lifted his head and frowned. This wasn't his apartment. Where was he? He slipped from his bed, stumbling over his feet and the blankets, before he felt his way to the door. Cracking it open, he watched as a lady walked the halls, her arms wrapped around herself, muttering quietly. He opened his door fully, startling her.

"I'm sorry!" Burnie's words were barely audible. "I didn't mean to scare you." He looked around her, seeing Anna in their own bedroom doorway. "Can't sleep?"

Muir stared at him, her violet eye huge. "No. I don't know where I am. Is he here?"

Burnie cautiously reached out a hand, finding hers reaching for his. "No, I don't think so. I'm not sure who you mean." He led her to the kitchen, seating her and then switching on the light over the sink. Anna had followed, standing back from the door where she could watch Muir. "What would you like to drink?"

"Water, I guess." Muir rubbed her hands on her legs. "I don't want to make any work."

"You're not. I'm making coffee. Anna had all sorts of different teas or hot chocolate." Muir's mouth dropped open when Burnie opened that cupboard door.

"I didn't think they made that many." She was on her feet, leaning against him as she counted them. "There are so many."

"Pick one. It won't matter to Anna."

Muir reached for one that said peppermint. "I have always wanted to know what peppermint tea tasted like. We could only get tea once in a while. Granny and I didn't have a lot of money."

"Then, peppermint tea it is." Burnie didn't move, his eyes on her as she continued to lean against him, staring at the selection of teas and coffee. "Muir, are you hungry?"

Her eyes turned to him again, even as she frowned before she saw the time. "Burnie? It four in the morning. It's not breakfast time."

"Doesn't matter. Anna and Doc won't care. Doc is sometimes up at this time of the morning. He's a doctor and works in an Emergency room."

"He is? He does? Oh, that's what I always wanted to do. But I couldn't afford to go to school." Muir turned, stopping abruptly as she saw Anna standing inside the kitchen door. "I'm sorry. I am disturbing you. I shouldn't have." She looked down at her nightwear and the dressing gown that she have found to wear. "If you tell me where my clothes are, I'll get dressed and leave. Only I don't know where I am." Distress coloured her voice.

Anna simply reached to hug the younger woman, finding her stiffen at first and then reach to hug her back, even as sobs shook Muir's body. Burnie stood, his eyes on Muir, not knowing that it was his heart that she had already staked a claim on and that was visible in his eyes.

Burnie paced his office later that morning. He needed to work, he could feel the plot and characters in his latest novel burning inside him, but his thoughts were on Muir. After he had fed her toast and tea, she had barely been able to keep her eyes open and had shuffled off back to her rest. Anna had watched her before she simply hugged Burnie, a prayer for the young couple whispered in his ear.

He finally dropped to his chair, booting up his computer and then staring at the screen. He sighed, reaching instead for his Bible, needing that time with his Father. An hour later, he set it aside and rose, heading back for Doc's. He paused as he entered the lobby, watching Muir as she just stood and then turned in a circle.

Burnie smiled as he approached her, standing just short of where she was, waiting for her to turn back towards him as she spun. Muir stopped abruptly as she saw him.

"This place is so big!" Her eyes were huge as she spoke.

"It is." He grinned at her, reaching out a hand and then leading her to one of the two seating areas in the lobby. "It's our home, Muir. You met Breck last night. He has an apartment here as do I. On the main floor are the offices that each of us fellows have. And then we each have an apartment here on the three floors."

"You do? They must be small."

"Muir, you saw Doc and Anna's place?" He waited patiently until she nodded. "All of our apartments are that big. And there are some that are used for visitors or for short-time occupancy. And before you ask, there are fourteen of us fellows. Eleven are married. One couple has a set of twins and I know two more who will adding to their family in the next few months."

"There are? How tall is this place, anyway?" Muir craned her neck, trying to guess the height. She stared at the skylights. "Those are pretty. I would not have thought of having stained glass up there."

"Barnabas' mother wanted that. The stained glass is sandwiched between panes of glass that are almost unbreakable."

"They are? Someone went to a lot of work." She was on her feet, moving away from him and towards the door. "Are the doors locked?"

"Not during the day." He ran after her, reaching for her hand, waiting for her to pull away, surprised when she didn't. "We can go outside and walk around the gardens if you like."

"We can? We're allowed?" Muir stared at him. "No one will say anything? I'm not used to that."

"We can and we are allowed. No, no one will say anything, unless you are in danger. The grounds are our home as well. Come on. The roses are still in bloom."

Burnie watched as Muir slowly walked the rose garden, his steps matching hers. She reached to touch a petal on one.

"These are so beautiful. Granny had one, but it really didn't grow much. She was always so disappointed in it." Muir breathed in the scent from the roses. "There are just so many colours. I am not sure which one I like best."

Burnie smiled before he reached for his pocket knife, finding the blooms that were just opening, and picking a selection for her. His knife made short work of the thorns before he turned, finding shock on her face.

"Burnie! You shouldn't have done that! We're not allowed!"

Burnie simply wrapped her into a hug, the roses resting against her back. "Muir, I don't understand why you're stating these things, but here? We're allowed to come outside or stay inside. We can roam wherever we want on the lands. We can pick whatever flowers we want. There is also a vegetable garden that we all work in and can pick what we want from there. The fruit trees? We can pick the fruit."

She finally nodded against him. "Okay. I wasn't allowed to do that. Do you have any animals?"

Burnie grinned. "Other than a couple of kittens, cats, and two dogs? No."

"I had to look after the chickens for the store owner. I won't miss them." Muir moved back, her eyes on him. "Burnie?"

"Here." He held up the bouquet of roses. "There's are for you. Roses for a beautiful lady."

"Oh, you don't mean me. I'm not beautiful. I'm ugly and a runt." Muir was just above average height for a lady and had the classical looks of a beautiful lady who would age well.

Standing where he could watch Muir, Barnabas caught the look on Burnie's face and sighed. Here we go again, don't we, Lord? Another adventure? I don't know how much more our fellows can take, that's the thing. It just keeps adding on to our stress. But You are in control. That much I know.

Burnie looked up and around as he felt eyes on them, a frown on his face. He nodded towards Barnabas before he looked behind him. Someone else was there. He just wasn't sure who.

Burnie reached for Muir's hand, turning her towards the main walkway, pausing as he felt her steps slowing. He searched her face, seeing the momentary fear and the puzzlement on her face.

"Muir, this is Barnabas. He's my boss, and he is also represents the Barnabas Foundation." Burnie waited, not finding her responding. "It's okay, Muir. You're welcome here. In fact, Barnabas is the one who sent Breck, Dallas, and Andy to find me yesterday."

"He did? Why?" Muir didn't take her eyes from Barnabas.

"Because he's a friend. He does that." Burnie nudged her closer. "He won't bite, Muir. Nor will he harm you."

"He won't? I don't know him."

Barnabas grinned, lighting up his face. "No, you don't, and you are correct to be careful. But I am a friend of Burnie's, and I hope to be your friend. I found out yesterday that Burnie needed me. I just did what I do best, sent in help."

"Oh! I'm not used to that." Muir's hand tightened on Burnie's. "Burnie? What happened?"

"I don't know, Muir. The store exploded and burnt. So did my car." Burnie watched in horror as her face crumpled.

"It's my fault. I did that."

Burnie gave a growl of disbelief and simply swept an arm around her. "No, you didn't. Whoever set the fire did that. It's not your fault." He exchanged a glance with Barnabas. "Is that what you have been living with?"

Muir finally nodded. "It's always my fault. That's what he told me. He would beat me if I didn't say that."

Burnie froze, his words dying on his lips, as he stared down at the head resting against his shoulder. He shared another look of concern with Barnabas.

"He told you that? He beat you?" At her nod, Burnie grew angry. "Who told you that?"

"The owner of the store. It was the only work I could find in our village. He threatened Granny if I didn't do what he said. I was finally able to get Granny away from him. That's when he beat me the worst. He would beat me to try and find out where she was. I couldn't tell him." Muir's head went back as she looked up at Burnie. "I miss her. And you're tall!"

"I am, Muir." Burnie gave a grin that didn't reach his eyes. "Would you like your Granny to come here?"

She nodded and then sighed. "But I can't. I don't have anywhere to live."

Barnabas's hand rested on her back, startling her. "Muir, you have a home. You have a home here for as long as you want it. Anna will welcome you to stay with them. There is also an apartment available right beside Burnie. It's furnished and everything. You can use it."

"I can? Oh, that would be wonderful. But I don't have any work. I can't pay you."

"Muir, we don't expect you to pay. No one who has a need is ever turned away." Barnabas was patient as he watched the conflicting emotions cross her face. "We don't charge people who are in need. It's part of how we encourage one another."

Muir finally nodded, her eyes on her roses. The effect of being free from the cruel store owner and his physical and verbal abuse was hard for her to understand. To have a male reach out to her in this way? She just didn't understand it.

<hr>

"I'm sorry. Burnie picked these for me." She tried to shove the roses at Barnabas, who simply grinned and shook his head.

"No, keep them. Beautiful roses for a beautiful lady. That's what they're for, Muir. All the ladies pick the flowers." Barnabas pointed towards the building. "How be we go back in? I can walk you through the apartment next to Burnie. And then we can talk about your grandmother coming to live with you."

"Thank you." Muir blinked back the tears that clouded her eyes. "No one has ever been so kind."

"This is just the start, Muir. Once you have met the fellows and their ladies, I assure you that you will find everyone kind here."

"I will?" Muir turned to Burnie, finding him nodding in agreement.

———

Walking through the apartment next to Burnie that night, Muir wrapped her arms around herself. She didn't think that she had seen such a beautiful home. And to know that it was hers? And her Granny's? She felt like she was in heaven. It would take a while for the fear that gripped her in such a tight grasp to fade, but Burnie had sensed that she was fighting to free herself. He had simply hugged her, kissed her cheek and stepped back as Anna had approached her.

Muir spun and almost ran for the master bedroom, sliding to a stop to stare around at the soft yellow and cream walls and trim, feeling for the first time, she thought, a sense of peace and hope. Burnie had done that, she thought. If he had not been there, she would not have been able to escape. She was afraid to talk to him, to tell him what she had overheard. She had prayed for someone to walk in and rescue her and Burnie had.

Approaching the bed, Muir stared down at the piles of clothing, all brand new, that Anna and she thought the lady's name was Cadee had brought in for her. She couldn't remember the last time that she had had new clothes. Certainly not is such an abundance. She had tried to protest but Cadee had simply shrugged, hugged her, and told her to enjoy them.

Muir stopped finally in the kitchen, her hair wrapped in a towel that she kept fingering, her eyes searching the kitchen. She touched the different appliances and then investigated the cupboards, finding more small appliances and an abundance of food stuffs. She didn't realize that Cadee had gone to the other ladies and together they had shopped for her.

Sinking to the floor, Muir wept. God, I think that You heard my complaints and just dropped me down into heaven. She finally crept to her bed and slept, wishing that her Granny was there with her, but knowing that she couldn't be. She didn't know that Burnie had gone to Breck, handing him her grandmother's name and where she was. Burnie had managed to find that out without Muir understanding what he was asking or why.

Breck had frowned for a moment before his face cleared.

"We'll bring her here, Burnie. Muir needs her. She hasn't said anything about her parents?"

"Not a word. She's so overwhelmed right now." Burnie paused, blinking back tears as he thought of Muir that day. "She was beaten, Breck. She has so little self-esteem right now."

"I know she does. Barnabas spoke with me." Breck sat back in his armchair, reaching for the ever-present pad of paper and pen. "What do we do for her?"

"Cadee took care of clothes for her. The ladies stocked her kitchen, although I'm not sure how well she'll cope with the modern appliances." Burnie bit at his lip. "We need to find something for her to do, something that will build her up. I hate that she's so downtrodden."

"We'll get there, Burnie. Right now, the best thing is for her to rest. She's been through a harrowing experience from what I understand. I know you have deadlines for your book."

"I do, but I can work at anytime, most days. Do you know she asked if we could go outside? If we were allowed?"

Breck sat forward. "She said that? It sounds as if she was kept a prisoner."

"That's what I think. I have remembered the words directed at her." Burnie paused, a sick feeling in his stomach. "There was a reason for how she was treated."

"Human trafficking?" Breck was quick to pick up on Burnie's thought.

"I think so. I think he was threatening her grandmother to shape her into doing what he wanted. It almost succeeded."

"It has. Did Doc talk to you?"

"He did. He's puzzled as to why they told me I had a burn, other than to put the GPS tracker on me. Thanks for looking after that." Burnie paused. "He won't say, but I know that Muir was beaten."

"More than once, I would suspect." Breck sat back, a prayer in his heart. "Burnie, you don't have to answer, but I know your heart. How invested are you in Muir already?"

Burnie didn't answer right away, knowing that was something he had to pray through. He finally looked up at Breck, finding his friend watching him closely.

"At the moment, I know I am attracted to her. She is a beautiful lady who I want to get to know. But I have to be careful of her. I can't rush her into anything."

"No, you can't. It's different for her. She watches to see who is going to hurt her. Only prayer can help to change that. If I might suggest, talk to Buckley. See if Locklin will speak with her. That might help."

"I will. Buckley and Locklin are away for a couple of days. I'll call when he's back." Burnie finally stood, stopping his walk towards the door as Breck's hand came down on his shoulder.

"Let me pray with you, Burnie, before you leave. You're carrying a burden tonight, my friend."

———

Two days later, Muir wandered the lobby of the building, not seeing how intently that she was being watched by Breck. He stood just out of her line of sight, praying for her, not quite sure how to do that. She had not told Burnie much more than she already had. The fellows were concerned, working away as they could with the little information that Burnie had been able or willing to give them.

Muir paused in front of the lobby door before she pushed it open and stepped outside in a hesitant manner. She wasn't used to that kind of freedom, not any more. The store owner who had employed her had made sure that she knew she was not allowed outside unless he told her that she could. She had been like that for months, she thought. Lord, I'm trying. But it's hard to let go.

Moving around the building, Muir found her way to the rose garden, a garden that she just knew she would spend a lot of time in. She hesitated as a dog approached her, sitting in front of her, a paw raised for her to shake. Jumping as she heard a male laugh from in front of her, her eyes shot towards him in a frightened manner.

"It's okay. This is Kade. He's friendly. I'm Bradon. I live here as well." Bradon waited, having heard of Muir from his wife, Ennis. "You must be Muir, Burnie's friend."

"I'm Muir, but I'm not sure if I'm Burnie's friend or not. I caused him a lot of problems."

"Not from what he says." Bradon pointed to a bench nearby. "Would you like to sit? Kade, move out of the way."

Muir studied him for a moment before she nodded, sitting on the edge of the bench. "This is nice here."

"It is. Except for Barnabas and Breck, we're all from different provinces. This is home now and has been for a number of years. Those of us who are married? Most of our wives are from the area." Bradon watched Muir closely, seeing her begin to relax a little. "Where's Burnie?"

Muir frowned at him. "I have no idea. I have not seen him at all today. He brings me here and then abandons me." Sighing to herself, she apologized. "I'm sorry. I didn't mean that. I know he's writing and has to. I am just thankful that he came and that I could get away. I don't think I would have lasted there much longer."

"What do you mean?"

Shrugging, Muir didn't respond, her eyes on the ants scurrying around her toes. "I heard him talking." Her voice was barely a whisper. "He was planning on sending me somewhere. I didn't like what I was hearing him say about me." She looked up, bewilderment and pain in her eyes. "I am glad that I am not there, but I think I brought danger to here."

Bradon gave a soft laugh, even as he noted Burnie heading their way. "Muir, you have no idea what we have been through here. Some of us almost died. I was drowned and revived. My wife, Ennis, was stabbed. Just a bit ago, Locklin, Buckley's wife, was given an overdose and her heart stopped. So no, you're not bringing anything that we haven't dealt with."

Muir stared at him, her mouth slightly open before she shook her head. "That's hard to believe. Anna talked to me, told me about all of you but she never told me that." She jumped as Burnie's arm came around her.

"It's true, Muir. And we all want to help you stop this man from hurting you or anyone else." Burnie kept his eyes on her profile.

"You do?" Muir kept her eyes on Bradon. "All of you?"

"All of us, Muir. We would like to consider you a friend, if we may." Bradon smiled even as Kade stood up at Muir's knee, sniffing at her face.

Muir's arms went around the dog as she hugged him, a swipe of Kade's tongue against her face.

"He's beautiful. I always wanted a dog, but we just couldn't do it. Granny only had a small pension that we had to live on. I tried to find work but it was hard." She sniffed, not willing to give into her tears.

———

"You don't have to worry about that here, Muir. If you want a dog, or a cat, or even a bird, you can have that." Burnie watched as she mulled over his words and then turned to him.

"I can? Oh, I have so wanted a cat. We had a kitten when I was just so tiny but it disappeared."

"Then, that's what we can do today. I know of someone who has some kittens that they want to re-home." Burnie waited for her to speak, his eyes meeting Bradon's and finding only concern in them.

"I don't think so, Burnie. I need to find work first." Muir was on her feet, running for the building, not hearing Burnie's call for her to wait.

"Burnie? What just happened?" Bradon was on his feet, standing beside Burnie.

"I'm not sure, Bradon. I am really not sure." Burnie sighed. "This is so hard. I don't know how to approach her or what to say. She's terrified, I know that."

"Her grandmother?"

Burnie nodded. "I suspect so. Branigan and Brady are heading out with Dallas to bring her here. They leave early in the morning. It's really not that far from here."

"Will it help her?" Bradon paced beside Burnie as he walked slowly back towards the building.

"I pray it does. She is so scared for her grandmother. If we can get the two of them together, maybe Muir will open up more."

Chapter 7

Seeking refuge and solace in the rose garden late the next afternoon, Muir reached to touch a red and white rose. She sighed. Granny, I want to see you, but I am afraid to see you. He'll find me and then you. I just wish, God, that I had never been born. She turned as she heard a soft sound, blinking rapidly, before she was running towards the tall, slender, older lady who stood watching her, arms open to receive her.

Barnabas stood and watched from the distance, Burnie beside him.

"Was there any trouble, Barnabas?"

"No, Brady said there wasn't. Her grandmother stood for a moment assessing them, asked what took them so long, and just reached for a bag sitting on the table in the apartment hallway. She told them that God had spoken to her, that she was to expect three men that very day, and that they would take her to her granddaughter. She also stated that she had been given their names."

Burnie shot a glance at Barnabas before he nodded. "Yes, in this situation, God would do just that, wouldn't he?"

"He would. Come find me later, Burnie. We need to talk." Barnabas walked away, his heart raised in prayer for his friend and his lady and her Granny as she called her.

Moira Donachie finally stood back, her hands on her granddaughter's upper arms and studied her. She's thin, Lord, thinner than I ever remember seeing her. What did that monster do to her? Please, Lord, we need healing, the pair of us.

Muir wiped at her eyes, a smile finally reaching them. "Granny? How? I didn't think that we should be in touch."

"God willed otherwise, love. He brought three young men to my door earlier today and had already told me their names and that I was to go with them. That they would bring me to you. That you were safe." Moira turned Muir back towards the building, their arms around one another. "You have a beautiful place to live, Muir."

"For us, Granny. For us. Barnabas told me that the home here is for us."

"He did, did he? Then I guess it is." Moira watched Burnie as he stood, roses in his hands for them, and just waited. "This young man in front of us?"

"Burnie? He was hurt, Granny, when the store exploded. He and his friends brought me here." Moira gave a wavering smile at Burnie. "He's been wonderful and kind, Granny."

"Like the knights of old that I wove into your bedtime stories?" At Muir's nod, Granny smiled. "Then, Muir, why the hesitation that I hear in your voice?"

"I'm afraid, Granny, that the monster from home will find me. He threatened horrible things. I don't even want to tell you about them. He told me that if I showed any interest in anyone, he would kill that man."

"Somehow, love, I don't think that this Burnie will let him. I hear there are a number of men who live here who have had adventures. His friends talked today, I think in part, to reassure me that we would be safe." Moira stopped them in front of Burnie. "We will talk, love, alone and then with this man of yours."

Burnie's smile lit up his face. "Flowers for two beautiful ladies." He then stepped around them, moving between them, and holding out his arms. "May I escort you to the meal that I know Anna has prepared for us? Tomorrow, it is our usual potluck meal in the building. Tonight, we'll go easy on you."

"You will, will you, young man?" Moira gave a soft laugh. "I like you. You'll be good for my Muir."

Muir stared at her grandmother, aghast that she had said that. Moira just shook her head at her granddaughter. She and her Lord had had plenty of time to talk, she thought. Muir needs someone just like Burnie. He'll draw her out, teach her how to live. She needs that. That monster beat her down. Now, to settle with him.

———

Late that night, Moira stood watching her granddaughter sleep, sorrow on her face, a prayer in her heart. Lord, protect my girl. I know that she's not safe. Not yet. I know what that man was. I hated for her to go and work for him, but there was not a lot of work in our community. And we were prevented from leaving. How Muir managed to get me out, I don't know. But she did, and because she did, You were able to get her out. Thank you, Dear Lord. Moira then turned and sought her own rest, a peace in her heart for her beloved granddaughter.

Burnie stood on the balcony outside his living room doorway, his head tilted back to watch the clouds scudding across the night sky. It was a favourite time of day for him, one where he could commune with his Lord. Tonight, his heart was full of thankfulness that Muir and Moira were together again. He had spoken briefly with Moira, heard her story in part, and then had just hugged her. He had never known his grandparents. Or his parents for that matter. He had been placed in foster care as an infant, and no one had ever offered to adopt him. That had always puzzled him and driven him to stay apart from people. The men and ladies in the building had changed that. He had become part of a large family, he thought, when Barnabas had tracked him down and offered him a position with the Barnabas Foundation. Barnabas had simply waved away Burnie's protests that he couldn't, that Burnie wanted to be a writer, stating that part of the mandate of the Foundation was to encourage others, and this was what Burnie needed.

Chapter 8

The next evening, chatter and laughter filled the conference room that was used for the monthly potluck dinners the Foundation family had. Moira, welcomed by all of them, stood beside Anna, watching them all but in particular her Muir as she stood as close to Burnie as she could get, her hand tight in his.

"Anna? This is a wonderful family that my Muir has dropped into."

"And you as well, Moira. They are a good bunch. Brady said that they explained what had happened to them all."

"That he did. God protected them, didn't he? He protected my Muir and brought that young Burnie into her life just as she needed him."

"He did that." Anna exchanged a look with Blair and Breck who stood beside Anna.

"I fear for her, though. The man she worked for will not let her go. A number of young ladies disappeared from our village and those who came through were at risk."

Breck rubbed his hand along the back of his neck. "Moira? Are you suggesting that he removed them?"

"I can do more than that, young man. I have proof that I have worked on over the last few years that I can turn over to you. I feared that Muir would disappear into that world and I would never see her again."

"She's here, now. We will do our best to protect her." Breck hesitated as Moira shook her head. "There's a problem?"

———

"There is. He is a very vindictive man. With Muir escaping him? He will come after her. You fellows that were with her? He'll come after you. But he'll go after Burnie in particular. This man seeks revenge and violence against those who thwart him." Moira studied her granddaughter as she moved away hesitantly with Cadee and Ennis. "She's scared, Breck. More scared that she will admit to anyone."

"She is. We've seen that." Breck sighed. "Did you know that he had beaten her?"

"I suspected as much. I felt her flinch when I hugged her yesterday. That is not my Muir. She was always free with her hugs."

Burnie had moved to stand near them. "Moira? I think you and I need to have a talk, in private, but I will state this here and now. I will do my utmost to protect our Muir."

"Our Muir, is it, young Burnie? Then, we will work together, you and I, and your friends as well. Now, I see that Barnabas is trying to get our attention. What do we do now?"

Muir turned as she felt someone beside her, watching Burnie as he stood there, his head bowed as Buckley blessed their meal. She was distracted, she thought, as he reached for her hand, his grasp tight and warm and comforting. She looked up as the prayer finished, to find his eyes on her, a light in them that she didn't or wouldn't allow herself to understand.

Fynn watched the pair closely before she turned to Brady.

"He's serious about her, isn't he?"

Brady studied his friend. "I would think so. He's like us. One look and he knows." He gave her a quick kiss. "We have to pray for them."

"We are. The ladies are meeting on Monday, seeing as tomorrow is Sunday. I would like to ask Muir and her grandmother to join us."

"Ask, but don't worry if they say no. Muir needs healing, Fynn, in so many ways."

"She does. She's like a lost little kitten. Burnie will bring her out."

"That he will." Brady turned away at a question from Branigan, leaving Fynn to watch Muir closely.

Muir stood at the end of the evening, feeling overwhelmed and lost, not quite sure how she would fit in, if she ever would. Berneen and Devaney had approached her, quick smiles on their faces.

"Muir? The ladies in the building are meeting on Monday for a Bible study. We're all off during the day for a change. We would like you and your Grandmother to join us, if you wish." Berneen didn't push, knowing that she couldn't.

"A Bible study? Oh, I don't know. Can I let you know?"

"You can do just that." Devaney spoke up. "We're in the apartment next to you. We're meeting at 9, so come if you wish. If you don't, that's okay. We understand. We've all been the new kids here at one time or another."

Muir nodded, her eyes searching the room for all the ladies. "I understand that. It's just that you wouldn't know that."

"We were. And we would really like you to come, but if you're not able to, maybe next time."

The ladies spoke for a bit longer before the two walked away.

"She's so scared, Berneen."

"I know. I haven't heard what all happened to her. But we can still pray for her."

Cadee had approached them, overhearing their conversation. "Muir reminds me of some of the young girls that come through the shelter, who had been abused and threatened. Some have escaped from human traffickers."

"You don't think?" Berneen drew in her breath. "Until she tells us, we don't speculate. We pray."

"That we do." Cadee looked contrite. "I didn't mean to insinuate that was what had happened to Muir."

"No, you weren't. But something did." Devaney shot a look behind her. "Good, Burnie's with her. He'll take care of her."

———

934

“He will. He’s needed that special lady. Muir is it.”

Staring at the gates that led to the Barnabas Foundation property, the man hammered at the steering wheel in the battered truck that he drove. He glared at the woods surrounding the gates, knowing that he wouldn't make his way through there. She was there, he thought, and I need to get to her but I can't. Not yet. I need to find someone familiar with the property who can help.

Shoving the truck transmission into gear, he gunned the motor, speeding off, gravel flying behind him as he did so. Brandon and Brendon exchanged a glance as they stopped at the gate before following him.

"What's his problem?" Brandon shot a look behind him before he turned back around, his hands steady on the wheel.

Brendon shrugged, his eyes on the photo that he had snapped. "Good. I was able to get the plate number. Now, to send it on to Dallas." He looked up and through the windshield. "You don't suppose that it's the man from up north?"

"More than likely. He'll have had some way of tracking us." Brandon pulled off into a coffee shop. "This is where you were to meet?"

"It is. Thanks, Brandon. Four work for you?"

"It does. I'll see you then. Listen, if you hear from Dallas, let me know. But we need to let Burnie know."

"On it. I sent him a text with the picture as well. He's deep into something, he said, and would get back to me."

"His books! See you tonight."

Brendon watched Brandon drive away before he pulled out his phone again. Dallas had been in touch.

"Dallas?"

"Brendon? Where was this taken?" Dallas sounded distracted.

"Just outside the gates. He had been parked on the side of the road and pulled out in front of us. Why?"

"Where's Burnie?"

"Still at the building. He said he had to concentrate on some stuff for his publisher today, proofreading or something like that."

"He'll have to talk to me. I'm heading that way. Is Muir there?"

"I would suspect so. The ladies are getting together for a Bible study today and asked Muir and Moira to join them. They hadn't said that they would, though."

"Okay. Stay safe, my friend. If this man knows you snapped a picture of his vehicle, you're not safe."

Brendon grew still. "He's that bad?"

"He is. He's all and more than what both Muir and Moira think. We need to watch them closely. He'll go after Burnie just for getting Muir away from him." Dallas was gone before Brendon could say another word.

A quick text to both Brandon and Barnabas and then Brendon was running to meet his friend. They were off on a quick road trip that day but Brendon's heart was raised in prayer for his friends.

Burnie gave a groan as he heard a knock at his office door, glancing down at the paperwork he was almost through, before he rose and headed for the door, opening to find Dallas standing there.

"Dallas? You're here? Come on in. I've about ten minutes left on paperwork that I have to get done and in this morning. I think the coffee is still okay." Burnie was back at his desk, immersed in his documents, not noticing that Dallas had made a fresh pot of coffee and set a new mug down beside him.

Finally sitting back, his documents done and sent on to his publisher, Burnie reached for the mug of coffee and sipped.

"You made fresh?"

"I did. That sludge that was there had to have been from first thing this morning." Dallas simply grinned at his friend. "How are you faring, Burnie?"

Burnie shrugged. "To tell you the truth? I feel like I just jumped off a cliff into an undertow,"

"Good analogy. I think that's exactly what you've done." Dallas pulled out his phone. "Did you get a text from Brendon?"

"I think so." Burnie reached for his phone, paling as he read it. "I hadn't read it before. He was outside the gates?"

"He was. He took off when Brandon drove through them. What we need to determine is if this is the man from up north. Where's Muir?"

"With her grandmother." Burnie squinted at the clock. "They might be with the ladies. I'm not sure. Their Bible study is likely over by now." He was on his feet, heading for the door when Dallas' voice stopped him.

"Burnie?" When Burnie turned back, Dallas stared hard at him. "Think hard about what you are going to say and do. She's not used to the world. She's been sheltered up there. To have had to work for this storekeeper and be abused like she has been? She needs tenderness."

"I know, Dallas, but she's also got a tough streak in her. I've seen it." Burnie waited for Dallas to exit before he locked his office door and headed for the stairs.

Chapter 10

Standing in the lobby, Burnie watched as Muir and Moira walked towards the elevators, not seeing the two men waiting for them. He shook his head. He needed to talk with her, he supposed, and warn her that she needed to be aware of her surroundings.

Muir looked up, sensing eyes on her, frowning first at Dallas and then smiling at Burnie. Moira reached to hug Burnie and then hugged Dallas, surprising him.

"Ladies? Having a good morning?" Burnie just grinned at the frown Muir directed his way.

"We were. We spent the morning in the garden. I'm sorry. I just couldn't face all the ladies this morning." Muir looked upset at that.

"They understand, Muir." Burnie reached to hug her. "God was there with you, wasn't He?"

"He was." Muir's face lit up, showing the beauty that was there. "But you're here? I thought you had to work."

"I'm finished what I needed to do for my publisher. The plot of my next book is still mulling around in my mind. My characters aren't sharing what they want to do, so I have to wait. Listen, Muir, Moira? Can we talk?"

"We can, boys, but it's lunchtime. We'll eat first, spend some time in prayer and then talk. Dallas? You have time?"

"I do, Moira. I do. I have some interviews to do but that's later this afternoon. And I'm not on call, so I can take some time." Dallas walked off with her, climbing the steps beside her.

Muir watched her grandmother closely before she spoke.

"Burnie? What happened?"

"Your storekeeper? What kind of vehicle did he drive?"

———

939

"A brand new truck. I don't know the make. He used to have a beaten up one but that one he burnt."

"He did?" Burnie paused, then pulled out his phone. "This truck was outside of the gates this morning. Brendon snapped a photo of it."

Muir leaned against him, her hand tilting his in order to see the photo. "That's his brother's truck. They have tracked me down?"

"I would assume so. Dallas would have had to say what force he worked for." Burnie's arm came around her as they walked up the stairs. "That's what he needs to talk to you about."

"All I can say is that his brother is as brutal as he is. There have always been rumours about what they are involved in. Any female in the area avoided them as much as they could." Her frown deepened. "Is he that desperate to get me back in his control?"

"I would think so, Muir."

Late that afternoon, Moira found her granddaughter stretched out on the couch in their apartment, sound asleep. She reached for a blanket to cover her, a hand resting on her head as she prayed for Muir. She turned as she heard a tap at the door and opened it to find Burnie, Breck, and Barnabas there.

"Gentlemen? Come in. The kitchen, I think. Muir is asleep."

"She is?" Barnabas frowned for a moment. "We needed to speak with her."

"First, we pray. Then, we talk. And then I'll awaken her. She's rundown physically, boys, as well as emotionally and mentally. She needs time to heal."

"Unfortunately, Moira, it doesn't look as if that will happen." Breck slid a photo across the table to her. "This man was around this morning. Muir told Burnie that he's the storekeeper's brother."

"He is." Moira paused, before she shook her head. "He's been after Muir for years. I have been so afraid that he would harm her."

"But he hasn't, yet. We plan to see that doesn't happen." Breck's voice was stern and his eyes raised to where Muir stood in the doorway. "Muir? I thought your grandmother said that you were asleep."

———

"I was, but I'm not. What is this about Walter?"

Burnie reached to pull her down beside him, keeping his arm across the back of her chair, just touching her. "We talked, Muir. He's in the area."

"I know he is. But why?"

"He's looking for you, Muir." Barnabas caught the look that the two ladies shared. "Why?"

"Why? It's obvious. Stewart didn't like that I left." Muir rubbed at her forehead, a headache starting. "I can't do this." She was on her feet, running from them, the apartment door slamming behind her.

Burnie gave a sound and then was on his feet, following her, catching her in the lobby and just holding her, not seeing Baird and Berneen and Blair and Devaney as they were heading out. His audible prayer finally reached through her panic and she relaxed against him.

"Muir? How do we do this? How do we keep you safe?"

Muir shrugged, her hair brushing against his chin. "I don't know, Burnie. I don't know. How do we? And why would you care?"

"Why would I care?" Burnie's arms tightened around her. "I care about you, Muir, not just as a friend, but as a beautiful lady who I would like to get to know better. God brought us together, Muir."

"He did?" She leaned back enough to look up at him, seeing the look in his eye. "Just what are you saying, Burnie?"

"That I would like to date you, be your beau, look to the future." He watched with compassion as her eyes closed and a single tear traced down her cheek.

"Do you mean that? Burnie, do you really mean that?" Muir looked back up at him. "Do you know how I prayed for someone to walk in and save me? And then you did?"

Burnie directed them to a seat in one of the lobby sitting areas, his eyes on Brennen as he and Buckley were seated on the other side, a nod towards them. He seated Muir, his arm still around her.

"I mean that, Muir. At first, it was because you were a lady in distress. That's when I stepped in, to protect you at the store. Now? I'm starting to understand who you are and who you can be. That's my prayer, sweetheart, that God will work in your life and bring out the beauty that's there."

Muir listened to him pray, before she looked up at him. "But it's dangerous. He's an evil man with a huge streak of meanness and anger in him."

"He's a coward and bully. We'll take him on, you and I, and Granny, and all my friends here. He will not win. He will not overcome. We may have to go through things, but we'll emerge victorious."

"You sound so sure." Muir was hesitant, knowing the character of the man who Burnie was willing to take on for her.

"I am. I have no doubt that he and his henchmen will try their best to overcome us and take you back. We won't let them." Burnie hugged her tighter. "I promise that I will do my best to protect you and Granny."

"That's my fear, Burnie. Granny."

"We'll look after her. She's a smart lady, your Granny is. I imagine right now that she, Breck, and Barnabas are coming up with a plan. I'm not sure that we'll like it."

Muir found that hilarious. Her charming bell-like laughter echoed through the lobby. "You can count on that, Burnie. Granny can come up with some wild plans. She used to do that with my bed-time stories. Now, about Walter?"

"Dallas called before we came up to find you. Walter was arrested on a break-and-enter charge in town. When they looked into his record, he's wanted for so many charges and violations of his parole that he will be going back to prison and that will be today. So for now, he's out of the picture."

"And Stewart will be angrier at me. I know that. He'll come after you." Muir chewed at her lower lip.

"He can come and try. He will not succeed. Not in the long run." Burnie sat, Muir cuddled against him, trying to come up with words that would calm and reassure her both.

"Burnie? What was in the store that he didn't want anyone to find?" Muir's question got Burnie off guard.

"You think that there was something there?"

Muir nodded. "I do. I think that he had someone hidden there. I would hear sounds in the night, like someone walking around."

Burnie paled. "Are you saying what I think you are? That he killed someone?"

"I am. It was always rumoured that he had killed before. How do we prove it?"

"I'll talk to Dallas, see what he or Will Peters, the police chief, can do. It may mean that the provincial force can move in and do an investigation. We'll have to see. Did you have a mayor?"

"Yeah, Walter."

"Oh, I see. But if Walter's not able to act, then who does?"

Muir thought about it and then her face lit up. "Granny. They put Granny in as deputy mayor but told her that she'd never be able to act. They never took that away. Part of it, I think, was a threat against me."

"Do you know what you just said?" Burnie hugged her. "That means that she can request outside investigation." He was on his feet, pulling Muir with him, running for the stairs and then Muir's apartment.

They appeared in the midst of the four, no, five, as Dallas has appeared, breathless, startling them.

"Muir?   What is going on?"   Moira stared at her granddaughter.

"Granny?   Did they ever remove you as deputy mayor?" Muir's words tumbled over one another.

"No, they didn't. I asked them to and they refused. Why?"

"Because Walter is in jail and unable to act. That makes you the mayor. I told Burnie that I think there was someone in the store when it burned down. You can call in outside investigators?"

"She can, Muir." Dallas had been listening closely. "We can look after that for her. Moira, we'll need a formal request from you."

"Then, how do I do that? And I want an investigation in Stewart Holman as well."

"We can look after that."

Burnie looked up from his laptop the next morning, working on the balcony outside his home office. He closed his eyes, listening to the sounds of the early morning. This was when he wrote the best. He had been awake, he thought around two, finally rising and coming out to write. His characters were cooperating and he had put many words into the latest mystery he was authoring.

He frowned, hearing a faint tap, and then rose, heading back into his apartment, his laptop on his desk before he paced through to the front door. Hearing another soft tap, he opened it, to find Muir there, her face covered with tears. Burnie simply swept her into his arms and stood, Muir cradled tight to him as his prayer reached her ears.

"Muir? What happened, sweetheart?"

"Granny. I can't find her. Where is she?"

"What? You've looked through the apartment?"

"I have, Burnie. I haven't gone anywhere else. I was afraid to."

Burnie reached for his shoes and then her hand, closing his door behind him. "We'll go back through your apartment and then head downstairs. You didn't find a note?"

She shook her head. "I was too scared to look."

Burnie walked through the apartment, appearing back in the kitchen. "No sign of her. Let's head down to the lobby and then the chapel."

"You have a chapel?"

"We do. It's never locked." Burnie paused outside the chapel door, praying that Moira would be there. He gently shoved open the door. "There's Granny, Muir. She's found a place to pray."

Moira turned as the door open and then was on her feet, moving swiftly to gather Muir into her arms.

"Muir?"

"I was scared, Granny. I couldn't find you."

"I'm sorry, Muir. I thought I left a note for you on the kitchen counter."

Muir looked sheepish. "You might have. I didn't see it. I just panicked. I thought somehow Stewart had taken you."

"He hasn't. Now, sit, child. You too, Burnie. Let's pray this through as I taught you, Muir."

Muir nodded. "I know, Granny. I know. It's just that lately I didn't think God was hearing me."

"He has, child. He always has. Sometimes, it takes time for Him to work, but His timing is perfect. You wouldn't have been put here if you had left earlier. This is where we stand and fight."

"That's true, Granny. You've remembered something."

"I have, Muir. That's what had me out walking the building. The security guard was kind enough to show me this wonderful chapel. I didn't mean to scare you."

"I know, Granny. I know." Muir leaned back in Burnie's arms, not realizing that she had.

Moira shared a look with Burnie who simply shrugged.

Dallas turned from his phone, a troubled look on his face. Burnie had called, letting him know what had transpired that morning. He sighed. Another friend head over heels in love. How do we protect them this time, Lord? He rose and went looking for Will.

"Will? Got a moment?" Dallas tapped at Will's open door.

Will looked up, a smile on his face. "Sure, Dallas. Come on in. You look troubled." Will sat back in his chair.

"I am. It's this thing with Muir and her home village. I spoke with the provincial force. They'll be talking with Moira. They have been watching that village for a while now."

"Any particular reason why?"

"What we thought. Human trafficking. White slavery. The rumours that they are getting is that the teens and young women who are disappearing are shipped overseas."

"And that's what the plan was for Muir?" Will blew out a breath. "How do we keep that from happening?"

"That's what I am trying to think through. Burnie is fully involved. He doesn't have to say anything but he's in love."

"That just increases his danger. He'll put himself between Muir and anyone coming after her."

"He will. And we won't be able to talk him out of it. And she'll try her best to protect her grandmother." Dallas paused, thinking through the possibilities. "Walter was moved off today to eastern Ontario."

"That's good and also bad, I suspect. Muir will be blamed for that."

"She will." Dallas stood, his eyes on Will. "If you have any advice that you can give, please?"

Standing outside of the library in town, Burnie watched as the unkempt man walked towards him and sighed. Stewart is in town and he's found me. Looking around, Burnie ducked back into the library and then through it, to exit from the employees' only door, and then around to his car, quickly disappearing into it and driving away. He pulled over and placed a call to Dallas, frustrated to get only his voice mail. He sighed, heading for home. He had done the research that he had needed to and now had to put that into his plot.

His mind on Muir, Burnie didn't see the vehicles that boxed him in until he was forced to slow down. He frowned. That's his game, is it? Burnie volunteered at a local driving school, teaching evasive maneuvers to the students. He watched closely, seeing that he had enough room to get around the car in front. He hit the accelerator as he pulled out and then flew past the car, slowing just enough to turn into a side road and then sped along it, heading for the back entrance to the Foundation grounds. Watching closely, he didn't see the cars, but figured that they would head for the front entrance.

The men in the two cars stared in disbelief as Burnie disappeared. This was not going well, the leader thought. Stewart will not be pleased, not at all. He wanted Burnie, to use as leverage against Muir and now that wasn't happening.

"How do we tell him?" The leader's companion finally spoke.

"I have no idea. I didn't think he would get away."

"Well, if you had done your research, you would have found out that he volunteers as a driving instructor. Stewart should have known that."

The leader snorted. "As if he'd bother looking into anything." He pulled to a stop and pointed to the door. "Out!"

"What do you mean?" His companion stared at him in disbelief.

"What I said. Out!" He barely waited for the door to close when he spun the wheel and headed back the way that he had just come and kept on going, heading for another province down east. He had had enough.

Burnie ran for the building after he had parked, fear in his heart for his lady. Muir was in the lobby, sitting with Ennis and Imly, and looked up as he slid to a halt near them.

"Burnie? What on earth?" Ennis stared at him.

"Muir? You're okay?"

"Of course, I am. It's you that doesn't seem to be."

"Just had an incident. I saw Stewart."

Muir paused, her eyes on him. "You did? Of course, you did. That's what he'd do. Come to town. Send his men after you to get to me. Okay, so what do we do?"

"We do nothing, sweetheart. We wait. I don't know that we can do much right now."

Ennis and Imly shared a look before Imly spoke.

"Okay, Burnie. What would one of your characters do about now?"

Burnie began to laugh. "Imly, only you would ask that. Let me think." He was on his feet pacing.

"He does that, Muir, when he's thinking." Imly grinned at her. "He'll come up with a plan that will be so outrageous it will work."

"He came up with a logic problem for one of us." Ennis laughed at the remembrance. "It really did help."

"He did?" Muir was on her feet, standing in Burnie's way.

Burnie stopped abruptly, his hands out on Muir's arms to balance himself.

"Muir?"

"Burnie? What are you thinking?"

"What am I thinking? I'm not really sure. I am angry that he did what he did to you, that he showed up here today. I am angry that they tried to take me to use against you. That was their plan, more than likely."

"Anger doesn't help."

"No, it doesn't, and I'm praying my way through that." He turned her, an arm around her and led her to the conference room. "In here, sweetheart. This is where we plot and plan against the bad guys."

Muir stared at him. "Burnie? Really?"

He grinned. "Really. You're getting freer with how you talk to me."

Muir flushed. "I'm sorry. I didn't mean to." Her face shut down.

"Oh, sweetheart. Don't shut down on me. I like that."

She stared at him again. "You do? I was being obnoxious and impolite."

"Whoever told you that?"

"He did, when I would object to something."

"I'm not him. I want you to talk back to me. It's part of learning how to be human again. He had tried to drive that out of you."

Muir looked up at him, a surprised look on her face that turned to determination. "He did, didn't he? Burnie, will you teach me? Will you teach me how to live again?"

"That, sweetheart, would be an honour. And if it's something that the ladies or Granny or Anna can help you with, talk to them."

"I will." She surprised them both by suddenly hugging him before she turned and disappeared into the room.

An hour later, Burnie looked up, surprised to see most of the men were in there, working away. He searched for Muir, a smile softening his face as he watched her sleep, her head down on her folded arms, as she sat in the chair next to him.

"She drifted off about forty-five minutes ago, Burnie." Brody looked up at him. "Her body's giving in."

"It is. She has been under so much stress. And the beatings that she took didn't help."

Brody stared at him, his mug slowly go back on the table. "Burnie? What are you talking about? What beatings?" His voice, though low, had grabbed the attention of the other men.

Burnie sighed, his eyes on Muir. "She was beaten, Brody, likely to break her spirit. She wasn't allowed outside of the store building unless she was told that she could be. I heard him talking to her. It was brutal, the language and the words." Burnie blinked rapidly as he looked up at Brody. "I know what the plan was. He didn't have to say it in words. The implication was there."

"Overseas?" Blair looked at him before looking at Muir, compassion on his face.

"That would be my guess. She wouldn't have survived."

"No, she wouldn't. And he'll be after her for revenge because she thwarted him. You too, Burnie." Brennen had moved to a chair beside Burnie. "So, how do we stop him?"

"For starters, Granny is now the mayor of that village. She is working with Dallas to bring in an outside force to investigate. His brother was the mayor but he's in custody for murder." Burnie's hand rested gently on Muir's back. "I fear for Granny. He'll try and stop the investigation."

"I'm sure he will." Baird spoke from where he was standing near the printer, his hands full of papers. "What else?"

———

Burnie drew a deep breath. "Muir thought that there was someone else in the building, someone who didn't make it out when the fire happened and then the propane tank exploded. Dallas is working on that."

"Murder?" Brendon nodded. "Of course, he would do that."

Buckley stood in the doorway, watching and listening before he spoke. "Burnie, how do you wish us to pray for you and for Muir?"

"For safety. For peace. For resolution of this. She asked me today to teach her how to live once more. I need prayer for that."

"And you have it, for all that. Let Locklin talk to her at some point. She may be able to help, given what our ministry is. This is when I miss being pastor of the church."

"But you are where God wants you. Maybe just for Muir." Burnie stood, gathering Muir into his arms. "I'll be back, fellows. I need to take my lady to Granny." He walked away, leaving them all staring after him.

"His lady? Granny?" Blair smiled. "He's found his family."

"That he has, just like some of us have with our wives' families. But we are still his family and as such, let's get to work. I don't want to see him go through what any of us did." Bradon dove back into his research, missing the looks that were exchanged.

Moira nodded as Burnie entered the apartment and pointed to the living room.

"In there, Burnie. That's where she's been sleeping." Moira reached to cover her granddaughter before she pointed back to the kitchen. "What happened?"

"We were working in the conference room and she dozed off. I gather she's not been sleeping?"

"No, I don't think so. I've been listening for her but she's quiet when she moves around at night. More so now than she used to be."

"That's from being held like she was."

———

"More than likely. Burnie? What did you go and do?" Granny searched his face.

"The fellows are working on solving this, Granny. It's what we've done for the others. They are successful." Burnie bit at his lip. "If we can talk to you, find out everything that you can tell us, that will help."

"I can do that. How be you go get your laptop and work from here? And then I'll slip down and talk with them." Moira reached to hug Burnie. "Thank you, Burnie. You are bringing out my Muir again."

Burnie raised his head hours later, realizing that Moira had not returned, or if she had, he had not heard her. He watched as Muir sat up, brushing at the hair on her forehead and then rubbing at her eyes.

Muir jumped, realizing that she wasn't alone, her eyes huge as she stared at Burnie.

"Burnie? What are you doing here?"

He grinned. "Writing. Watching you sleep. Did you have a good nap?"

She shook a finger at him. "Behave or I'll sic Granny on you. Where is she?"

"She was heading down to the conference room to talk to the fellows. She hasn't come back, not that I know." He sighed as he reached for his phone, having ignored it. He scrolled through his text messages. "She's still there. Brennen said that she has provided a wealth of information for them."

"That's good. She knows that village and the people." Muir stood, her feet tangling in her blanket for a moment before she shook it off. "I need to eat. I didn't get enough when I was working."

Burnie froze as he stood as well. "Muir? How often?"

"How often what? Burnie, you're not making sense." Muir looked over the fridge door at him.

"How often did you eat?"

She shrugged as she turned back to the fridge. "Once a day, twice if I behaved."

"Muir!"

"Burnie!" She echoed the sound of his voice. "There wasn't a lot I could do. I tried at first to get more, but that just had me deprived of meals for days on end."

Burnie simply shut the fridge door and gathered her into a hug, startling her.

"Burnie, you need to warn me."

"What? Warn you when I want to hug you? Then I give you fair warning now. It will happen and happen a lot." He grinned down at the outrage on her face. "You need this, Muir."

"I do?" She sounded disgruntled. "I also need to eat."

Moira looked up at last, her eyes on Barnabas as he stood speaking with Breck. He's the one I need to speak with, she thought. And I will, at some point. He needs to know Muir's history and I guess I need to talk to both Muir and Burnie. She has never known her full history or why I had such trouble leaving the village.

Barnabas turned at that moment, finding Moira watching him. He spoke with Breck for a few more moments and then walked towards her, detouring to fix her a cup of tea and himself his inevitable mug of coffee.

"Moira? How are you?" He sat beside her, his attention focused on her.

"Barnabas? To tell you the truth, I'm not sure. But I do need to talk with you. There are some things that even Muir does not know about her history."

"There is? Shouldn't you be speaking with her?"

"I will. With both Muir and Burnie. They're a couple, whether they acknowledge it or not. He's good for her and she's good for him." Moira stared down at her clasped hands. "I don't want what I have to say to tarnish Muir."

"It won't, Moira. It won't. You've met our ladies here. You know that we treat them just as that, as ladies."

"I know." Moira sighed. "Muir never knew her parents. We have emigrated from Ireland just before Muir was born. When she was about nine months old, her parents had to return to Ireland for business reasons. There was a plane crash into the Atlantic Ocean and they were killed. There were in fact no survivors. The authorities assumed that they had crashed. But there was always a question about that."

"We can look into that. I have a friend who can do that. Just let me have all the details and I will send it on for you."

"You would do that?"

"I would, Moira. I would. You need this closure as well. You have always questioned it, have you not?"

"I have." Moira blinked for a moment to clear the moisture from her eyes. "Bless you, Barnabas. Now, as to the village. Stewart Holman was not the original owner of the store. My son had been. During my grief, he moved in, forged documents and took it over. I tried to fight him but he threatened to have me declared incompetent and take Muir away from me. I couldn't allow that.

"As she grew, I would find him watching her. Not in an appropriate way, I would add. When his brother became mayor, they decided that I would be deputy mayor. They laughed at me when I refused, stating that I had no choice. They once more threatened Muir. They were never specific with their threats."

Barnabas looked past her for a moment, watching at Burnie and Muir stood behind her, Muir tight in Burnie's arms.

"What else, Moira?"

"I tried to leave but was prevented on so many occasions. The village is mostly his friends and relatives. I wanted to get Muir away. There was no work, other than for the store. It was fine at first, but then Muir become more distant and troubled. She was finally able to arrange for a stranger to take me with him, hidden in his car. I am sure that she suffered for that."

"I am sure that she did. Where did you go? To where we found you?"

"I did. I didn't want to go somewhere that Muir could not find me. The man had willingly helped us, made her memorize the address and not write it down. He was only there for about thirty minutes, and we took advantage of that. We had nothing that we wanted to bring with us."

"That's sad, Moira." Barnabas reached to hug her. "Now, I will take this information that you have given me and speak with my friend." He looked behind her once more. "Muir and Burnie are right behind you. They have heard what you had to say."

"They have?" Moira's eyes slid closed. "There is so much to tell Muir that I don't know where to start."

———

"Start by telling her that you love her. That you loved her father and mother. That you tried your best to get her free of the village and the control there. Talk it over with her and with Burnie. I don't think that Burnie is walking out of her life." Barnabas reached to hug her before he rose, his hand resting on Burnie's shoulder before he walked away.

"Granny?" Muir's voice was barely audible.

"Muir, my love. I'm sorry. I should have spoke with you earlier." Moira was on her feet, her beloved granddaughter in her arms.

"No, you couldn't, Granny. Now, you can. We're free of that village. These men are working to ensure that. Granny?" Muir touched the tears on her grandmother's face. "Can we go and talk?"

"We can."

Burnie stood back, not sure where to be. Muir saw his hesitation and reached for his hand, including him in her family and the discussion that would follow.

Burnie walked the paths around the building that evening, twilight coming down on him as he did so. He was troubled, that much he knew, by what Moira had told him and Muir. She had added to what she had told Barnabas. He turned as he heard a sound behind him, an arm up to deflect the blow aimed for his head and then staggered as a knife slashed at his abdomen. He went down, his foot kicking out in a desperate move to stop his assailant before a blow to the head rendered him senseless.

The man stood over him, before a sound caught at his ear. He turned and then ran for the woods, anger building in him that he had not been able to take Burnie with him. He would need to return. Stewart would not be happy with him, that much he knew.

Kade gave a low growl, staring off into the woods. Bradon stopped, puzzled, before he shrugged, calling Kade to follow him. Kade's attention went then to the huddled form in front of them. With a bark, he had forged ahead, his nose nudging at Burnie's face.

"Burnie?" Bradon was on his knees, his hands feeling for a pulse. Relief coursed through him before he had Burnie up and over his shoulder, heading for the well-stocked infirmary in the building.

Brady stared at Bradon for a moment as he watched him heading for the infirmary before he was running after him, his work duffel bag dropped at the door. Brady had been one that Bradon intended to call, a paramedic who willingly stepped in to help his friends.

"Bradon?"

"It's Burnie. Kade and I found him. I think that it just happened. He's taken a blow to the head, but it's the abdomen I'm worried about. He's been slashed across it."

Brady had reached for the scissors, slicing through Burnie's shirt and T-shirt. He grimaced as he saw the wound.

"I'll need your help, Bradon. Is Doc around?"

"He should be. I saw him about an hour ago. He said that he was planning on being home, he had some Bible study that he wanted to do."

"Okay. Find him."

Bradon was off on a run, his quiet command to Kade keeping the dog in the room, his eyes on Burnie.

"What happened, Kade? Did you see it?" Brady spoke quietly to the dog, even as he worked to clean around the wound. He drew a breath of relief. It wasn't quite as bad as he had initially thought.

"What do you have, Brady?" Doc's voice startled him for a moment, and he heard Bradon call Kade back.

"Burnie has a slash across his abdomen. Not as bad as I thought. And I haven't had a chance to check his head. Bradon said he had been hit."

"Okay, let's take a look." Doc looked around. "Bradon? Muir?"

"I'll go find her and Moira."

"I think they were heading for the chapel, if I heard Anna correctly. The ladies were meeting tonight."

"Oh, okay. I'll head there."

Bradon hesitated just inside the door that he had opened quietly, watching as the ladies had their heads bowed in prayer. Ennis had looked up and then moved towards him, following him as he exited the room.

"Bradon?" Her voice held a question.

"I didn't see Muir. Is she here?"

"She is. She's on the other side of Fynn. Moira's beside her. Do you need her?"

"I do. Burnie's been hurt and Doc wants her with him."

"Oh, no! Let me go get her." Ennis was back in short order, Muir almost running from the room, Moira hurrying after her.

"Bradon? Ennis said Burnie was hurt." Muir was frightened that he had been badly hurt, but was afraid to ask.

"I didn't mean to frighten you, Muir. He's here in our infirmary. Doc and Brady are with him. Let's get you to him." He paused, a thought crossing his mind. "Are you afraid of blood?"

"Blood? No, not that I am aware of." Muir ran ahead of him, shoving open the door, and then coming to a halt beside Doc. "Doc?"

"Muir? You can handle blood?"

"I can. What can I do?"

"Just step around me to the head of the bed. He's starting to rouse and keeps asking for you. I need you to calm him down while I finish with this."

Muir moved to stand by Burnie, a hand reaching out to touch his face. Burnie turned into her hand, his eyes flickering open and closed.

"I need to get up. I need to find Muir." He struggled to rise, despite the admonitions of Doc. Bradon moved into help hold him down.

"Talk to him, Muir." Brady glanced up at her before his attention went back to Doc. "Stitches?"

Doc shook his head. "Just a couple where it's the deepest. Has anyone called it in?"

"I did, Doc." Bradon shot him a look. "Dallas is on his way out. He said he was heading this way anyway."

"Muir? I need to find Muir?"

"I'm right here, Burnie. Now, please lie still." Muir bent over him, coming into his line of sight.

"Muir? You're okay? They didn't hurt you?" Burnie's eyes slid closed even as pain crossed his face.

Burnie's arm over his shoulder, Brady moved slowly into the bedroom that Moira pointed him to. She had just refused to let Burnie go back to his own apartment, insisting instead that she would look after him. Burnie sat for a moment on the side of the bed, an arm wrapped around his middle, his head down before he nodded at Brady's quiet question asking if he was okay.

"I think so, Brady. Thanks."

"Then, let's get you horizontal." Brady helped him before reaching to pull off his sneakers.

Moira was there, pulling up the covers, a gentle hand touching his head before she turned and pointed to the door.

"I'll call you or Doc, Brady. Thank you." She reached to hug the young man. "Go on, now. You're just off shift, aren't you?"

"I am." He grinned at her use of words. "You're a quick learner."

Moira smiled at him. "I always have been. Stop by in the morning."

"I will." Brady stopped to hug Muir, much to her surprise. "He'll be okay, Muir. Doc said that."

"I know. I'm just worried."

"We know you are. You are in our prayers."

"Thank you." Muir disappeared down the hall, to stand in the bedroom doorway watching Burnie before she moved to sit beside the bed, her hand on his shoulder. Exhaustion got the best of her at last, and her head went down on the pillow, her hair just touching his cheek.

Thirty minutes later, Breck stood and watched, listening to Moira's quiet comments. He had been out when the event had happened and had just returned, coming quickly to see what he could do for the two ladies.

"Here, let me move Muir." He reached to gently lift her, turning towards the door.

"The living room, Breck. She's been sleeping on the sofa there."

"She has? That's unusual?" Breck tucked a pillow under Muir's head even as Moira covered her granddaughter with a soft yellow blanket.

Moira pointed to the kitchen. "There's coffee on. I expected some of you fellows would be through."

"They would have been, but Brady sent out a group text to us all."

"He did? How does that work?"

"It's a text message that goes to all of us. And we respond when we get it. I just got mine as I was coming in. I had had my phone turned off."

"Oh, I see." Moira hesitated. "Did you have your dinner, then?"

"I didn't." He went to protest as Moira reached for a bowl and then the soup, making him a sandwich to go with it. "Thank you, Moira. I didn't expect this."

"No, you didn't. And you would never ask." Moira sat near him, her tea cup on the table, her hands wrapped around it. "Brady never said what happened."

Breck wiped his mouth on the cloth napkin, fingering it as he studied the older lady. "I didn't get a lot of the details, other than Bradon and Kade found Burnie outside with knife wound and a head wound."

"He was walking by himself?"

"He was. He does that. He says it helps to clear his head. His characters also talk to him when he's doing that."

"They do? That's an interesting thought." Moira turned her head to listen before she looked back at Breck. "Breck, you were there when I spoke to Barnabas. Do you know if there is any news?"

"I don't think so. Emma, our friend that he was speaking of, did get back to us. She's working on it, but she had a priority investigation that she was working on."

"I understand. I don't expect her to find out much, not after twenty-seven years."

"It's a long time to wonder, Moira. We'll do what we can to find out for you and Muir."

"Thank you, Breck." Moira rose to clear away his dishes, stopping as his hands reached to them.

"I'll do them, Moira. And then I'm taking my mug of coffee, heading in for that nice comfortable easy chair and spending the night here. You may need help with Burnie."

Moira reached to hug him again. "I just might. There are towels and whatnot in the bathroom of that bedroom. I'll find a blanket for you. God bless you, Breck. And why have you not found your lady yet?"

Her question shocked Breck into silence before he smiled. She's out there somewhere, isn't she, Lord? I just have not found her yet. I pray for my friend and his lady. Please, dear Lord, protect them. Help us to find what we need to bring these men to justice and please prevent Burnie and his lady from going through what some of the others have.

Early the next morning, Burnie roused, his head coming up from the pillow as he stared around the dimly-lit room, before he sat on the side of the bed, one arm wrapping around his middle, the other hand on his head. He searched for his shoes, finding them, and grimacing with pain as he bent over to shove his feet into them. That he wasn't in his own apartment, he knew. He just wasn't sure where he was.

Stumbling somewhat as he walked through the hallway, he kept his focus on the door, opening it and peeking out before he closed it behind him.

"There's my apartment. But whose was I in and why?" He shut the door to his own place behind him, kicking off his shoes and then heading for his bed. He could barely keep his eyes open. Pulling the covers over him, Burnie was soon asleep again, knowing that he had to be up soon to work on his manuscript. He was now on a deadline with it and needed to finish it.

Muir had raised her head when she heard Burnie closing the door and then had risen herself, standing in the bedroom doorway and not seeing him. She sighed. Where did he go, Lord? She reached for a blanket to wrap around herself and headed for Burnie's door, thinking that was where he was. Fatigue soon had her sitting on the floor, wrapped in the blanket, her head against his door.

Doc paused the next morning as he approached Burnie's, a frown on his face before he shook his head. Burnie must have gone home, Doc thought, before he bent to draw Muir to her feet.

"Muir? How long have you been out here?"

Muir rubbed at her eyes and then squinted at Doc. "I'm not sure. Burnie came home and I wanted to make sure that I didn't miss him leaving again."

"Here, young lady. Let's get you back to your home." Doc persisted in leading her there, despite her reluctance to do that. "I'll come find you. In you go. Breck? You're here?"

"I am, Doc. I can't find Burnie, though."

"He's at home. I found Muir sleeping against his door. Make sure she had her tea and something to eat. I'll be back."

Doc tapped at Burnie's door, then twisted the knob, shaking his head at finding the door opening. He quietly called for Burnie as he entered before he walked through, searching for him. He stood at the bedroom doorway, watching as Burnie slept, before he approached him and then shook him gently awake.

"Burnie? Can you wake up for me?"

Burnie frowned at Doc's voice. "Doc? What are you doing here?"

"Looking for you. I left you in Moira's care last night but I find you at home. Did you let her know that you were leaving?"

Burnie stared at him. "Why would you do that?" He groaned as he sat up. "My abdomen hurts. So does my head."

"You don't remember? You were hit over the head and slashed across your upper abdomen. Brady and I put in a couple of stitches to the wound. How are you feeling?"

"I have no idea how I am supposed to feel." Burnie groaned. "I'm sorry, Doc. I didn't mean to sound like that."

"I know you didn't. Let me have a listen to your heart and lungs and then check out your wound. I found a young lady wrapped up in a blanket, sleeping against your door just a few moments ago."

Burnie watched him, and then sighed. "Muir? She did that?"

"She did, Burnie. She was that concerned, I suspect, when she couldn't find you. She wouldn't have tried to enter your place."

"She was? I need to find her." Doc's hand on his shoulder kept Burnie in place. "Doc?"

"She's at home. Breck was there as is her grandmother. I would suggest that we get you cleaned up. You're still in the clothes Bradon found you in."

"I am?" Burnie stared down at himself. "I don't remember what happened."

"Kade and Bradon found you outside, down on the ground. Kade alerted to something but Bradon called him off, not seeing anything himself. Come on, son. On your feet."

Showered, shaved, in clean clothes, and feeling refreshed, Burnie moved slowly towards the entrance door, Doc's hand on his back.

"Muir is okay?"

"She is, other than being worried about you." Doc closed the door behind him and then moved the few feet to Muir's door, finding Breck waiting outside for them. "Breck?"

"Doc. Burnie. How is he, Doc?"

"I'm fine, Breck. Any reason that you're standing out here?"

Breck just grinned and shook his head, standing to one side at Burnie glared at him before moving past him and soundly shutting the door behind him.

"You shouldn't have done that, Breck." Doc shook a finger at him, all the while grinning himself.

"I know. I just couldn't help myself. Muir is wandering the apartment, still wrapped in a blanket." Breck shook his head. "She's that worried."

"I know that she is. We'll need to see what we can do to help her out." Doc paused before he too entered the apartment, Breck staring after him before he walked away.

"Barnabas?" Breck tapped at his friend's office door, not surprised to find him there already.

"Breck? You're up early." Barnabas pointed to a chair.

"I am. I stayed at Muir's last night as Burnie was there. Only Burnie left in the middle of the night. Muir followed him. Doc found her sleeping against Burnie's door this morning."

"He did? Is she that worried?"

"She is worried, but I think there's more. Burnie is her lifeline right now to reality and to getting back to who she is."

"He is. So, what do we do? The fellows are working on his adventure as they can?"

"They are." Breck was quiet, his eyes on his hands that he was rubbing together, an uncharacteristic move for him. "Who do we question about this, Barnabas? Dallas is trying his best, but he's tied up with his other cases. Moira has talked to the police force who will be investigating but she says that will take months. Muir doesn't have months."

"No, she doesn't. Emma is working on finding out what happened to Muir's parents but since it's so long ago, she's needing to do some deep research."

"That's what worries me, Barnabas. I don't think either Muir or Burnie have months."

The next day, Burnie raised his head from his work, a frown on his face. He had just completed the rough draft of his manuscript and needed a break. He rose, stretching, a hand to his abdomen as he grimaced with pain. His headache had returned in full force, and he had been fighting himself against taking anything. Burnie turned as he heard soft sounds from the kitchen and then a smile lit up his face.

"Muir." His whisper didn't go far.

Burnie smiled as he remembered her that morning, frowning at him adorably as she had shoved him from her apartment back to his and then down the hallway to his office, forcing him down into his chair.

"You need to work, Burnie. You have a deadline, don't you?"

"I do, Muir, but it's not for a week yet for the rough draft." He grinned up at her.

"But, you need to finish it now. Who knows what tomorrow or the next day will bring that will prevent you from finishing." Muir had paced his office, her hands on her cheeks.

Burnie had been content to watch her, wishing that he dared speak from his heart. He could envision her in his apartment all the time. But she's not ready yet, is she, Lord? I won't rush her. I know my friends married quickly but I just can't do that to her. She needs to have this time, to relearn how to live and to learn to enjoy life. If it means she moves on, dear Lord, then I must let her.

He stood in the kitchen doorway, watching as Muir worked away, not quite sure what she was doing. He finally approached and stood behind her, watching over her shoulder as she prepared sandwiches, muttering away to herself as she did so.

"Those look delicious, Muir." He reached around her to snag a piece of cucumber, earning himself a smack on his fingers as he did so.

"No snacking. You'll ruin your lunch." Muir paused, horrified at what she had done before she spun, a hand to her mouth as she opened it to apologize.

Burnie simply shook his head. "You are quite right, Muir. I shouldn't have helped myself." He grinned. "But it was just so tempting, sitting there. And the sandwiches do look good. You are joining me, are you not?"

Muir hesitated, not sure if she should or not. "I was hoping that I could, Burnie." Her eyes sought his and she once more found that look in his eyes, that said she was special and wonderful and that he cared for her.

Burnie simply reached to hug her, a kiss on her forehead, before he stood, just waiting for what, he wasn't sure. He felt Muir move and then her arms come around him even as her head laid against his chest, over his heart.

"Burnie?" He could hear the question in her voice.

"Muir? I know it's too soon. You need to enjoy life, to find what you haven't had. I don't want to take that from you. But I care for you, deeply. At some point, if you are willing, I would like to date you, to see where our friendship goes."

Muir had raised her head to look at him. "Just how long will you give me?"

"As long as it takes, sweetheart. As long as it takes."

Muir nodded before she spoke. "We need to eat, Burnie. I need to think over what you have said and pray about it."

"I know that you do. Talk to Granny. Or any of the ladies, if you feel you can."

"I might. Locklin seems to be willing to do that." Muir moved from him, to set their meal on the table, sitting herself beside Burnie, not surprised when he reached for her hand as he asked the blessing.

———

Moira watched her granddaughter later that afternoon, finding her quieter than normal. She sighed. Burnie? What did you go and do? Lord, this child needs You so much right now. We need to work with her, to teach her that she is free and help her to find the peace and joy that she has lost.

"Muir, child?" Moira wrapped an arm around her and drew her down to the sofa, as she called it. "What happened?"

Muir blinked, coming back from her thoughts and the dreams that she had buried.

"Burnie kissed me, Granny, on my forehead. He wants to date me." She sounded surprised, yet hopeful.

"He did, did he? And?"

"And?" Muir turned to her grandmother.

"And is he?"

"Not yet. I asked for time to pray about it."

"You did? Thank you, Muir, for not rushing into anything." Moira hugged her granddaughter.

"He told me to talk to you, to any of the other ladies."

"That sounds like a wonderful idea, child. I have been talking with them, learning their stories. They all have such different ones, even though they do sound similar. When the ones married quickly, it was to protect them, they said. The men have all stated to me that they knew when they saw their ladies that they were the ones God meant for them."

"I didn't think there was such a thing as love at first sight." Muir's voice was quiet.

"There is, child. And I would say Burnie is one of those men too."

The ladies sat in silence for a while, each busy with their own thoughts.

"Granny? How do I know?"

"How? Pray and ask God to show you His plans for you. We are working with you, to teach you once more how to live and love and have that joy and peace that disappeared from you."

"I know, Granny. I know that you are. I just don't know how I will ever know."

Two days later, Brennen looked up from his computer in the conference room, searching the room, before he rose.

"Brandon? Did you see this?" He held out a sheet of paper that he had detoured by the printer to retrieve.

"What's that?" Brandon looked up, distracted, before he reached for it to read it. "Is this for real?"

"It is. It says that Holman was in Ireland when Muir's parents were to be there. That sounds strange."

"It does. Moira never said anything about that." Brandon was on his feet, heading for the door. "We need to talk with her."

"We will but she's not home. She headed into town with Anna and Locklin."

"Oh. Then I guess we can't." Brandon turned back, a frown on his face. "Do you think that he had something to do with the plane?"

"That's my thought. I know it was a small executive-class plane. With only the pilots and Muir's parents. Whoever it was that arranged for them to return to Ireland set it up."

"Set it up?" Brendon spoke from behind Brennen. "That's an interesting choice of words."

"Because I think that's exactly what happened." Brennen stared down at his feet. "I found news articles about Holman and his link to the company in Ireland."

"You did? I don't like that." Brady spoke up from where he sat. "How do we prove what we think?"

"More research and investigation. It may mean someone will have to head over there." Branigan looked up. "I think that I found a link to that as well."

"We need to bring Burnie in on this." Blair was on his feet. "I talked to him earlier. He was heading into his office down here to work on his last manuscript."

Burnie stood just inside the door, his eyes on his friends, thinking back over the years. Barnabas had approached each one of the men, offering them employment with the Barnabas Foundation, an organization set up to serve as a source of encouragement for others. Each of the men were orphans, each from a different province, and they all shared the same initials as Barnabas. The Foundation paid the men their wages, letting their employers free up that money to hire others without worrying about finding the finances necessary to do so. The Foundation itself was named for Barnabas, but also for the Barnabas in the Bible, who served as an encourager to the apostle Paul.

"Blair? You were looking for me?" Burnie's question broke through the quiet chatter.

"I was. We have some information that we need to go over with you." Blair beckoned him over.

"And I have some information for you. I've been receiving some nasty messages in the last couple of days, since I was hurt. I spoke with Dallas. He's heading out this way later. Will is sending him." Burnie sank into a chair, fatigue gnawing at him. He had been unable to sleep the night before, his headache keeping him awake, as well as his worry about Muir.

"Where's Muir?" Benen looked around, a question on his face.

"With Berneen and Cadee. They've decided that they needed to pray with her on a daily basis. I'm glad."

"That's good. Now, where do we go?" Benen looked down at his work. "I think I'm just making a mess, is what I'm doing."

"We need to start using the whiteboards, fellows. And combine what we're finding. I'm sure there is overlapping." Brody moved to start with what he had found. "Burnie, want to set up a logic problem again?"

Burnie nodded, wishing that he had not done just that. "We can, once we start finding out more."

———

"I think we can start now." Brady's hand on his shoulder kept him in his chair. "You sit there and direct me. I'll get started."

Two hours later, Muir peeked around the door that she had opened, Berneen and Cadee behind her, before they entered, trays of sandwiches and fruit in their hands. Berneen and Cadee worked away to set it up, Muir standing watching in amazement the concentration going on around the room.

"It's how they work, Muir." Cadee grinned at her. "It's a wonder to see them still like this. All of them are athletes and spend time in the gym or out on the track running."

"They do? I haven't seen the gym yet. I would be interested in doing that. I've never seen one."

Berneen stared at her. "We have been remiss. Tomorrow, Muir, we'll do a field trip. Fynn also has a building full of creepy-crawlies that she would love to show you. Hagen has a woodworking shop attached to the gym."

"Wow! All that? And where's your library?"

Berneen and Cadee stared at one another.

"That is one thing that we have never thought about. We should set up one." Cadee reached to hug Muir. "I nominate you to run it."

"Oh, I couldn't do that. I'm not educated." Muir kept her eyes down, not wanting to see the pity in them.

"That wouldn't matter, Muir. If it's what you want to do, and you want to go to school for it, Barnabas will have the Foundation sponsor you."

"Oh, they can't do that!" Muir was horrified.

"They can and they will, Muir. Pray about it." Berneen hugged her before moving off to find Baird.

"They would?"

"They would, Muir. Each one of us ladies have a wage through them. They are encouragers that way. We can work, volunteer, be a student, or not, depending on where we want to go with our lives. I'm working through a nursing program."

———

"You are?" Muir became quiet. "I'm not that good. I mean, I had good marks through school but I'm not good enough to do anything like that." She jumped as she felt arms come around her.

"You are, Muir. You are right up there with the other ladies. God is working in you. I can see the change. You don't have to rush into anything. And I think you would do wonders with a library." Burnie dropped a kiss on her cheek, causing her to blush.

"You think so?" She turned to find herself almost nose to nose with him.

"I do, sweetheart. I do." He dropped a kiss on her nose. "Come, let's eat and then I'll walk you through everything that we've been working on today and yesterday." He nodded through the boards. "That's only part of it."

Muir's eyes grew round. "That? That's us?"

"It is, Muir. It is. And our friend has sent on a whole raft of material that we need to sort through."

"She has? I can't afford to pay her." Muir grew distraught at the very thought of how much it would cost.

Burnie sighed, realizing that they had overlooked something with Muir. He resolved to not let it happen again.

"She won't charge us, Muir. She never charges a friend, and she considers us and the ladies all friends. In fact, she has asked to meet you."

"She has? Why?"

"Because you're special to me, and because you're part of the Foundation family."

Moira watched as Muir curled up in the corner of the sofa that night, a frown on her face before she began to pray for her granddaughter. Something had happened that day, she decided, and Muir was unsure of how to deal with it.

"Muir? Can we pray?" Moira sat beside her, reaching for Muir's hand.

"We can, Granny. I'm so conflicted, I think you would say. We need to talk, but we need to pray more."

Muir finally raised her head, her hand still tight in her grandmother's, feeling a peace once more in her heart, a peace that she had not felt in years. She reached to hug her Granny, hanging on tighter than she had been.

"Thank you, Granny. I needed that prayer. I always like to think of how Christ prayed for us but I had forgotten."

"You may have forgotten, but you are not forgotten. You have many here praying for you. I talked to young Buckley this morning. He stated that the church they attend have you and Burnie on what they call their prayer chain. Just asking for protection and a solution. He said the people don't need a lot of details in order to pray."

"I think that I have felt those prayers. I have felt someone watching me when I'm outside, and that scares me. I have talked to the security guard. He is willing to go outside with me."

"That's a smart move you made, child. I wouldn't have thought of it."

Muir's head went down on her Granny's shoulder. "I hadn't, not really. I was going outside today and he was at the door. I think he saw that I was hesitating and offered to go with me. That gave me peace, Granny. Is that the Lord teaching me to think and live again?"

"I am sure it is. God will teach you to live again. I can see the change already. Young Burnie is good for you."

"He is, Granny. I am still praying through what he asked."

"He doesn't want you to rush into anything and then regret it. I've seen how he watches you, child. He is in love with you, and not quite sure how to tell you."

"He is? He said he wanted me to learn to live again, to enjoy this time. I wouldn't be able to if he's not in it."

"You're falling in love, Muir. I wish your parents were here to share this with you." Moira stopped to wipe at a tear that trickled down her cheek.

"Do you really think that they are dead, Granny?"

"I always thought that but there has always been a question. I thought it was because they couldn't find the plane."

"Burnie said his friend is working on that. She wants to come and meet me." Muir sat up. "Granny, I just remembered. Stewart was talking with someone one day. I wasn't supposed to be near him but I had to clean the shelves. He said something about Mom and Dad. That he was sure that they wouldn't give in."

"He said that? Did you tell Burnie?"

"No, I just remembered it. Can it be that they might still be alive?"

"It might. We'll get Burnie to sort it out for you." Moira grew quiet, a prayer in her heart for Muir. "Muir, I regret that I let you work for Stewart, but I can see that God was at work. We would never have been able to leave the village if you hadn't been there and approached that man."

"What happened to him?"

"I don't know. He dropped me off at that apartment and then just disappeared. I never saw him afterwards at all."

"An angel." Muir's voice was low.

"It could be, Muir. It could be. Now, we need to do some planning. We need to look after that wardrobe of yours and mine. Barnabas has assured me that the Foundation will fund it for us."

"They will? They are so wonderful." Muir looked up as a tap came to the door and then Burnie appeared. "Burnie?"

———

977

"Muir?" He grinned at her before he sat in Moira's favourite chair.

"How are you feeling, Burnie?" Moira shook her head at him.

"Better than I was. I think working in the conference room has helped. The headache, or rather that one, has disappeared."

"Which one hasn't?" Muir frowned at him.

Burnie grinned again, a sparkle of mischief on his face. "The one where Muir has not agreed to go out to dinner with me."

Chapter 22

Turning from the whiteboards the next morning, Burnie frowned, a thought crossing his mind. He pulled out his phone and scrolled through his messages. It was as he had thought. He was beginning to get the text messages threatening him. Only the threats were vague. He looked up as he heard footsteps stop in front of him.

"Dallas? How'd you do that?"

"Do what?" Dallas was puzzled.

"Appear just as I needed to speak with you." Burnie held out his phone. "You need to see these."

"Messages?" Dallas took his phone, scrolling through them, sending the ones he needed to on to the crime lab.

"Those ones. Muir refuses a phone. I've tried to talk her into one."

"No talking into it, Burnie. Just give her one. Tell her the police have asked that she have one. Or I can do it."

"It might be better coming from you. It would have more weight." Burnie stared at his friend. "You're here for a reason."

"I am." Dallas frowned as he stared around. "Where is everyone?"

"At work. I have to head that way soon." Burnie nodded at the boards. "This is what we have so far."

Dallas wandered along the walls, reading the boards, taking notes as he needed to.

"It never fails to amaze me how you all find this information. You don't have access to the sites and programs that I do."

"I know we don't. I would say it's God that is leading. What can you tell me?"

———

979

"Right at the moment?" Dallas grinned for a moment, the look of worry and care dropping from his face. "We're working on Holman and his brother. Emma has found a wealth of information that she is couriering over today, she said. She specifically mentioned Muir's parents."

"She did? Muir and Moira are wondering if they are still alive, if the plane wreck was staged."

"That we are looking at. I talked to Barnabas. He said something about sending a couple of the fellows over there like he did before."

"He did mention it in passing but we haven't heard yet who he wants to send."

"He didn't say." Dallas turned to lean against a table, his eyes on the whiteboards. "Burnie? What is your feeling on all this?"

"My feeling? That Muir was being beaten down so that she would not make any trouble when she was sent overseas. That she would just do what she was told and not fight them. I hate to think of how she had lived in the last six months or so since Granny moved away. She hasn't said a whole lot but I heard him, Dallas. He was brutal and didn't really care how he talked to her. She just stood there, her head down and took it. Her spirit was almost broken. That's what he did to her." Dallas frowned. "He was no amateur, Dallas. He was too smooth and good at what he was doing."

"I see. And the beatings? Has she said much?"

Burnie shook his head. "It's as if she's ashamed that it happened, that she wants to forget them. But she never will. I am praying that she will learn to let God handle that for her. Granny says that she's sleeping on the couch, not in her own bed."

"She is? Because of?" Dallas didn't finish his question, not quite sure how to.

"I think that she is afraid. She told me once that she didn't really have a bed at the store, just a small pallet. He refused to let her go home, told her that she couldn't when he employed her. She managed to get away when Granny was there but once Granny was gone, he locked her in the store and refused to let her leave. She doesn't know what happened to the home that they had. Granny owned it."

"I'll look into it. Sounds as if we have him for kidnapping, physical and mental abuse, unlawful confinement."

"At the very least." Burnie grew silent, his eyes on the floor as he thought through what he knew. "I am sure that he is the one who started the fire in the store. He didn't like that I stood up to him for Muir."

"You did? You have not mentioned that."

"I didn't? I thought I had. I guess with the explosion and all, I just sort of forgot it. I know that I stepped between them, refusing to let him hit her. The look of hatred was horrible. He disappeared and it was shortly afterwards that we smelled smoke and saw the flames. He must have done something to the tank to cause it to explode. The fire wasn't near it, not from what I can remember." He slanted a look at Dallas. "How much investigation didn't happen?"

"All of it. There was no investigation and when the other force went in, the store site had been completely cleared away."

"Hiding the evidence? That makes sense. Muir was worried about someone else being there."

"I know. But unfortunately we can't prove or disprove that. Not unless someone talks and then tells us where the debris would be." Dallas turned as he heard a sound beside him. "Muir?"

Burnie took one look at her distressed face and wrapped her into his arms. "Muir?"

"Dallas, there's a ravine outside of town. Look there. He's claimed that he has dumped people there. We just thought it was talk."

"We'll do that, Muir. But first, I need to give you this." Dallas held out a phone, finding her shaking her head at him.

———

"No, I don't want one."

"But you see, Muir, it has now become a necessity. I have been told that you will take this and keep it on you." He gave her no choice but to take it. "That order comes from the chief, Will Peters. He has insisted that you take it. He programmed in every number that he could think of that you might need." Dallas showed her how to operate the phone.

Muir stared down at it. "I don't like it. But I will keep it with me. How do you turn off the sound?"

Burnie gave a quick grin that he hid. "You don't want to do that, Muir. You need to be able to hear it ring."

"I know. I just don't want to." She walked away, leaving the two men staring after her.

———

Muir stared at the phone that she had set on the table in their kitchen, a finger lightly poking at it. She sighed. This was not what she wanted. She had heard the other ladies talking about how they had received messages that were brutal and nasty, and she wanted no part of that. She felt her grandmother's hand on her head and then heard the chair beside as it slid back to let Moira sit.

"Muir?" Moira watched her closely. "Is that phone going to bite you or something?"

"It's the something that I am afraid of, Granny." Muir looked up at the ceiling, a bleak look around her eyes. "What if Stewart finds out the number? Can he track me?"

"I am sure that Will Peters would have ensured that the number was private and not available to just anyone. I met him the other day, Muir, when I was at the church with Locklin. He was troubled about you."

"He was? I haven't met him, so why would he be?"

"Because you're a young lady in trouble. Because you're friends with Burnie, and possibly something more to him. Because, as he put it, we're part of the Foundation family now and he looks after them, just as he does anyone else in the area."

"He said that?" Muir's eyes turned to Moira. "We never had that, Granny. We always felt threatened by the officers in our home village."

"I know, Muir. And that should not have been. Stewart was not working on his own, of that I am sure. He didn't have the smarts to set up the network of disappearances that happened."

"There were others, weren't there?" Muir's voice was barely above a whisper. "I remember two of the girls, just mid-teens, who disappeared. Their parents never said a word, but they looked so sad and beaten down. Where did he send them?"

"I don't know, Muir. We need to give the names to that young Dallas or to Breck. Maybe they can discover something."

"He almost succeeded, Granny."

"Who?"

"Stewart. He almost succeeded in breaking me. If Burnie hadn't stepped in and helped me, I would not have been able to resist whatever it was that Stewart had planned. I was ready to just give up."

"I know, child. I know. I am thankful that God provided a way for you to escape." Moira reached to hug Muir, holding on for longer than she normally did. When she sat back, she studied Muir. "Muir? You are healing. There is no rush to decide what you need to do for the rest of your life."

"I know, Granny, but I feel so useless. I need to be doing something, but I'm not sure what."

"Talk to Burnie. Or talk to one of the ladies."

"I have talked to Devaney and Ennis. They told me to talk to Locklin, but I don't know her well enough to do that."

"That will not matter to her, Muir. If you wish, we could have them for a meal and you could talk to both of them."

"Maybe, Granny. But I know Burnie wants to help so badly. I don't know if I should let him."

"He loves you, child. I can see that. Let him help as much as you are comfortable with. I am sure that if we ask Breck or Barnabas, they could find someone we could speak with."

"I know, Granny. I just feel awkward. I feel ashamed of how he beat me down so much." Muir was on her feet, running for her bedroom, the door closing quietly behind her.

Moira sighed, rising to walk where she could stand and watch Muir's door. Lord, I have no idea how to help her. How do I? She is hurting in so many ways. I guess it's good that she is. She losing the numbness and sense of loss that she had. I hate that she has lost her innocence though, Lord. I am sure that Stewart told her exactly what he had planned.

———

Burnie tapped at the door, and then peeked in, coming to stand beside Moira, an arm around her.

"Muir?"

"She's hurting, Burnie. She is starting to feel again, and is so ashamed of herself."

"I know, Granny. I know. I just wish I knew how to help her." Burnie frowned as he too stared at Muir's door. "Moira, will you please bring her out here? If she will come? I need to talk to her."

"I will do what I can but I can't promise that she will."

They both looked up as Muir's door opened and she appeared in front of them, tears on her face as she reached to hug her grandmother.

"I'm sorry, Granny. I shouldn't have left you like that. It's not how you taught me."

"No, it isn't, Muir, but you are an adult. And you have been through so much." Moira held on her a lot longer, feeling Muir not wanting to let her go. "Your young man is here, Muir. He says that he needs to speak with you."

Muir looked over at Burnie. "He does?"

Burnie nodded, before he dropped to a knee, his hands coming out for Muir's. "Muir, you are a beautiful, sweet, compassionate lady who has been through so much. I love you, more than I thought I would ever love someone. Muir, I know that you are hurting and that you are healing. I would like to be the one who walks alongside you for the rest of your life." He paused, swallowing hard, his eyes on his lady love. "I do not want to put any pressure on you, sweetheart. I just wanted you to know how I feel and how I see you."

Muir blinked rapidly, trying to clear the tears from her eyes, and unable to. She finally struggled to free her hands, causing Burnie's heart to fall, as he thought that she had rejected him. He swallowed hard, his mouth opening to speak, watching as her hands covered her mouth. Muir was overcome for a moment, before she dropped to her own knees and threw herself into his arms, her own tight around his neck as sobs shook her body. Unable to speak, she simply nodded. Moira watched the young couple, saddened at how they had met but delighted that they were speaking of a future together. Bless them, Lord. They have a long ways to go, I understand that, but You are leading. I can see that.

Breck watched Burnie the next morning as he ran for his car, not sure what was going on. He had been late coming home the night before and saw the lights still on in Burnie's office. He's going to wear himself out, he thought, before he shook his head, turning to find Muir standing near him.

"Muir? Looking for Burnie?" Breck grinned at her.

"No, actually, I'm not. I know he was heading into town. I wanted to talk with you for a moment, without Burnie around or without Granny hearing me." Muir looked troubled.

"Sure, let's head for the gardens." Breck didn't speak, instead watching Muir, trying to assess what she was thinking and unable to. "Here, this looks like a nice spot." Breck pointed to a wrought iron bench in the perennial gardens.

"Thank you, it does." Muir sat, her hands rubbing along her jeans, not sure how to begin to ask what she needed to.

"Muir? You were looking for me. For a reason, I know. Before we begin to talk, I want to pray with you. That's what I always do." Breck didn't wait for her to respond, instead bowing his head, his prayer full of verses about peace, about learning, about letting go, and then he prayed specifically for that for Muir. When he finished, he looked up to find her face wet with tears. "Muir?" He reached for his handkerchief, holding it out for her.

Muir took it, wiping at her eyes and face, and then twisting it in her hands. "I never had an older brother, someone who could teach me, or listen to me, or torment me, or just be my friend. Breck, you are that to me. You helped me when I needed help." She looked up at him. "Burnie talked to me last night. He told me that he loved me, that he wanted to walk alongside me for the rest of my life. I'm broken, Breck. How do I let him do that?"

Breck had suspected something like that. "I see. Burnie will have prayed and prayed hard about this. He may also have talked to Buckley, to get a pastor's perspective on what he would be facing, and what he should be doing. He has not rushed into this, not Burnie." He paused. "I know you are afraid for him. All the ladies were. Some suffered more than others, but God had provided for them. The couples each love each other more than anyone other than God."

Muir nodded. "I know. They've told me that. It's just that I feel like a failure. He's educated. I'm not. There is just so much uncertainty hanging over me right now, though."

"And Burnie will have considered that. Tell me, Muir. If you walked away from Burnie, how would you feel? Could you do that very thing?"

Muir shrugged. "It's just so new, Breck. I would walk away if it meant he survived. I know Stewart. He's evil and vindictive. He will go after Burnie for revenge. It won't matter if I'm around or not." She sighed, a hand rubbing at her forehead. "I just am so conflicted, I guess is what Granny would say. I don't want to ruin his life, but he sees something in me that no one other than Granny has seen in a long time. He makes me feels special and wanted and beautiful."

Breck smiled. "I think you have answered your question, Muir. If a man makes a lady feel like that, there is something there. I can't find the words to describe it, but it is how I would like my lady to feel, if I ever find her."

Sitting quietly, Muir mulled over Breck's words, knowing that just talking to him had helped her to sort through her thoughts. "Thank you, Breck. You have helped me. If Burnie and I do ever marry, can I ask a favour?"

"Sure, and it will happen, Muir. I see how he watches you. He won't let you escape him."

"I don't have someone to walk me to him. Would you?" When Breck didn't respond, Muir sighed, thinking that he would refuse. She looked up at him, finding him smiling at her.

"I would be honoured to, Muir. I would be honoured to." He gave her a quick hug and then prayed for her once more.

———

Muir finally rose, unable to speak, and almost ran for the building, leaving Breck standing and staring after her before he shook his head and moved on to where he had parked. He was needed at a meeting but for now, he didn't care that he was cutting it close to getting there. Muir had needed to talk with him and she came first today.

Tucking the small box into his jacket pocket, Burnie left the jewelry store, pleased with his find. He walked back towards his car, his steps slowing as he neared it, watching the man leaning against it, before he shook his head.

"Murphy O'Brien! What brings you to town? And Ian Galbraith as well?" Burnie reached to shake their hands.

"You do. You and your lady." Murphy grinned. "Doing some shopping?"

Burnie laughed, his face lighting up as he thought of Muir. "I was. And no, I'm not showing you. Muir gets to see it first."

Ian grinned. "That's not fair, you know. When do we get to meet this lady?"

"Now, if you like. I'm heading home. Did you bring your ladies?"

"We didn't, not this time. Emma sent us and told us to talk to you and to Dallas." Murphy sobered as he spoke.

"I see. Unfortunately, Dallas is out of town today, up where Muir and Granny came from."

"Granny?" Ian and Murphy exchanged looks.

"Moira, Muir's grandmother. I call her Granny, just as Muir does." Burnie moved to the driver's side of his car. "I'll meet you there?"

"Burnie? Perhaps we should talk away from there first. I know you'll want to speak with Muir."

Burnie shook his head. "No. If it involves her, I want her in our discussion. I can't do it any other way. I'm sorry."

"Don't apologize. Micah told us that would be what you said. He was right." Ian shrugged. "So, let's go find your lady."

Burnie watched the two men walk away before he pulled out his phone, finding no messages, but sending off a text to Muir, telling her that he loved her and would see her in a few moments.

Muir stared at the phone. "Did he really say that, Lord? Did he really tell me once more that he loves me?" She looked up as Imly and Locklin sat beside her.

"Muir? I know that look. Message from Burnie?" Imly just grinned at her.

"It was. He's special." Muir's face held a bemused look.

"He is, Muir. Very special." Locklin reached to hug her. "He has always made sure that we ladies are okay. The fellows all do."

"Thank you, Locklin. I never had that, you know. I am finding out how hard it was living in our village."

"It was difficult. Jaxcy had it hard for a few years, when she was on her own. Her town was really restrictive." Imly hesitated. "Muir, please don't take this wrong. But I do want to ask you something."

Muir shrugged. "Go ahead. Right now, everything just seems so mixed up."

"I understand." Imly reached to touch Muir's hair. "I would love to see you do something with your hair. I don't think it's you to have it so uneven."

"It's not." Muir blinked, not sure how to respond. "I loved my long hair and the curls and waves and ringlets. Stewart wanted it kept long. He kept touching it, telling me that I could never cut it. It was a hold he tried to have on me. One day, I just grabbed the scissors in the store and chopped it off. I kept doing that. He was so angry that he beat me. That was the first time that he did. I could hardly move for a few weeks, it was that bad. It didn't stop him from beating me again and again."

"To wear you down, I suspect, Muir." Locklin reached to touch her hair as well. "We would love to help you with it. If you like."

"I would like. I hate that it's like it is." Muir blinked as she stared down at the shoes in front of her. "Burnie? What are you doing here?"

"Looking for my sweetheart." He crouched down in front of her, his head tilted to watch her.

"Why?" Muir sighed. "I'm sorry. It hasn't been a good day."

"No, I suspect not. But these ladies here are waiting for you. I have a couple of friends as well who would like to meet you and speak with you."

Muir's eyes raised to where Murphy and Ian stood, their eyes on her.

"Who are they?"

"That's Murphy and Ian. They work for a friend's security team. They were sent here with some information for us."

Muir shrugged. "I guess. Which do I do first?"

"Whichever you want, Muir. I won't tell you that. You get to decide and we back you on your decision."

Muir stared at him before she spoke quietly. "I would like to go with Imly and Locklin, but I don't want to put the men out. Not if they have travelled to come here."

"It's okay, Muir. They understand. We can work away on what we need to. You just come and find us when you're ready to." He reached to kiss her forehead and then stood, watching for a moment before he walked away.

"Did he really just do that?"

"Do what?" Imly grinned at her.

"Walk away from me?"

"He did, Muir. He did. You made your decision, he's fine with it, and he'll find you later." Locklin stood. "Now, let's see how we can fix you up to make you even more beautiful. Cadee had some more clothes for you, she said."

"She can't. Others need them."

<hr>

"According to Cadee, these were given to her specifically for you."

Two hours later, Muir approached the conference room, hesitation in her manner. She didn't see Imly following her, watching to see what she would do. Muir stopped, staring down at the new coloured jeans and the nice sweater that she was wearing, a multicoloured scarf tied around her neck, new leather loafers on her feet. Her hand touched her hair that Locklin had trimmed and shaped, telling Muir that it would grow long once more.

Muir finally stepped through the door, her eyes searching for Burnie, finding all the men but Breck and Barnabas there. She didn't see Burnie at first, and she frowned.

Benen looked up as the door closed, pausing for a moment before he turned to Burnie, who sat beside him.

"Burnie? Muir's here."

Burnie paused for a moment, his finger on the place he was reading.

"What was that?"

"Muir's here." Benen nodded towards the door. "I think she's looking for you and can't find you. She's ready to run."

Burnie shifted in his chair and then was on his feet, heading for Muir, finding her turning to him. He paused, a smile of delight lighting up his face.

"You are even more beautiful. What did they do?"

Muir gave a tentative smile. "Locklin trimmed my hair for me. Cadee gave me more clothes."

"They did? Just outward dressing on a very beautiful lady. Will I muss the outfit if I hug you?" He reached to do that as she gave a shy nod and then kissed her cheek. "I meant what I said. I love you." He reached for her hand. "Now, are you able to stay and talk to us? Or do the ladies have more plans for you?"

"I have time. Where do I need to sit?" Muir frowned at him for a moment. "Burnie?"

"It's okay, Muir. You have just taken my breath away. Here. Ian and Murphy are over at this table. Let me grab what I was working on and then we can speak with them."

Two hours later, Muir sat back, exhausted at the amount of material that she had just gone through. She was hurting, she thought, about what they had discovered and who had disappeared from her village. She had not realized that there had been so many over the years.

"Does Granny know?" Her voice was quiet. "She may but I don't know if she'll have put it all together." Muir was saddened. "Did he do that?"

"We suspect so." Murphy paused, watching her closely. "It's not your fault, Muir. You didn't cause him to do this or to hurt you or keep you locked up. It's the evil in him that did this. Emma is working on tracking down who he is working for and she has a good lead on that person. She'll forward what she finds to Dallas or Will."

Muir nodded. "I see. Burnie, I need to leave." She was on her feet, running from the room, leaving Burnie standing, staring after her before he too was gone.

Murphy and Ian exchanged looks, knowing well enough the emotions going through the couple, both of them having faced things with their ladies.

Barnabas dropped down into the chair Burnie had used and shifted through the papers.

"Finding who it is?"

"We are. Muir was gone before we could continue. Is she okay?" Ian was worried.

"No, I don't think that she is. She was held captive, as I am sure Burnie has told you, beaten and almost broken by this man." Barnabas' finger tapped Stewart's picture. "If Burnie hadn't been there, stepping in, and then the fellows bringing her here, she would not even still be in Canada."

<hr>

"It was that close?" Murphy's face hardened.

"It was. We think that she was the only one to get away from him. That's driving him to plot revenge and try to extract it against both Burnie and Muir. Dallas, Breck and Andy are also on the radar as they're the ones who went up and brought them back."

——

Chapter 27

Catching up with Muir as she stopped in the lobby, Burnie just wrapped her into his arms, standing with his chin on the top of her head. He could feel the shudders running through her and grieved, knowing that part of what Muir was facing was grief as well.

"Sweetheart?" He finally spoke, before he directed her to a seat on the sofa in one of the sitting areas.

"Burnie? Why?"

"Greed. Money. Evil." Burnie sighed, not quite sure how to explain the darkness of a man's soul to a beautiful hurting lady.

"I get that. I just don't know how it happened in that village. We are less than one hundred in numbers."

"I know, sweetheart. I know. Evil doesn't look at numbers. Satan looks for someone he can use, and he found that in Stewart. From what Murphy and Ian said, Stewart was always like that. The people are starting to talk, now that his brother is no longer there. They were too afraid of retribution before."

"The ones who disappeared? Can we track them?"

"I'm not sure if we can. Emma and her team will give it a try, as will Dallas and his team and the provincial force will as well."

Muir sighed, her head going down on Burnie's shoulder, seeking comfort from him. "I hate this, Burnie, but if I hadn't been in that situation, God wouldn't have brought you to our village."

"Perhaps not, but you are the one that He meant for me. Of that I am confident." He grew silent, before he reached into his pocket. "I have something for you."

"You do? Everyone is always giving me something. I don't know what to give to the ladies in return."

"We'll come up with something, but I know for a fact that they don't want you to repay them. It's who they are. They model encouragement to others in their actions."

———

"That they do." Muir stared at the box in Burnie's hand. "What is that?"

Burnie grinned, before he lifted the lid from it with one hand, and then dropped the little velvet case from it. He paused, his eyes on Muir, a prayer raising in his heart. He had no idea what her answer would be.

"Muir, you are the one who completes my heart. I love you, more each hour and each day. I would like to be the one who walks alongside for as long as God allows us on this earth. Will you be my sweetheart for life? Will you marry me?" He opened the case to reveal a beautiful emerald ring.

Muir's hand covered her mouth and then tears sparkled in her eyes. "Burnie, even if I were to say no, your words have made be feel beautiful and loved and wanted." She looked up at him, to see the uncertainty that he was feeling on his face. "I will. I love you."

Burnie reached to kiss her and then slipped the ring on her finger, raising her hand to kiss it. "Thank you, sweetheart. I won't rush you into setting a date. You're healing and we need to let you do that."

Muir frowned at him, an adorable pucker between her brows. "What? Making me wait?" She snuggled down. "Thank you, Burnie. You have no idea how you make me feel."

"I think I do, to a certain extent." The couple grew quiet, content just to be together, not seeing the looks that were sent there way by the other members of the building family as they moved around the lobby.

Moira stood for a moment, her eyes on the two, before she turned to Murphy, who had tracked her down.

"Murphy? You said your team is heading for Ireland tonight?"

"We are, Moira. Emma is sending us. It's okay. We do that kind of stuff." He grinned at her. "She has found someone over there that we need to speak with. We'll be gone for a few days, but when we return, I'm brining my lady over to meet your granddaughter."

"Thank you, Murphy. I just wish I could find someone for her to speak with, even on a causal basis. She needs that."

——

"I have a friend whose wife is a retired forensics psychologist. She used to do a lot of profiling. She has been working with Emma on this. Darcie said that she would love to meet your Muir and talk with her."

"She did? Even without meeting her?"

"She did." Murphy looked around as Ian approached. "Listen, we have to run. You have our numbers. Call us for anything, even if you just need to talk. We'll be available."

Moira watched the men walk away before she turned back to her granddaughter and then approached the couple, sitting down beside Muir. Muir looked around at her grandmother, contentment on her face, before she reached out a hand.

"See, Granny? Burnie asked, I answered, and he's going to be part of our family. He's not leaving me."

"Did you really think that he would?" Moira touched her granddaughter's ring and then reached to hug the two, a prayer of blessing ringing in their ears. "Not rushing into it?"

"No, Granny, we're not. Muir needs this time to heal and to be absolutely sure of what she wants. That was taken from her. When we set a date, that will be her decision, or our decision as a couple." Burnie's eyes were on Muir as he spoke. "Muir?"

"I don't want to wait, Burnie, but I know that if we marry, it will make things a lot worse with Stewart." She closed her eyes as she drew a deep sigh. "Will I ever be free of him and his evilness?"

"Soon, child. Soon. Dallas called me earlier. He had tried to reach either you or Burnie but couldn't. He's on his way back. Tomorrow is Sunday but he wants to meet with all of us, if he can."

"I'll speak with Breck. I'm sure that there will be no problem with most of us being there." Burnie sat back, content with the two ladies he now had in his life. Thank you, Lord, for Muir and Moira. I have a family now, all of my own, something that I never had.

Chapter 28

Dallas spoke with Burnie quietly before he moved to the front of the conference room, a heavy sigh coming from him as he dropped the folders that he had been carrying onto the table. This is not how I wanted to come today, Lord. I just don't know how much more Muir can take.

Barnabas studied his friend before he turned to Buckley who stood beside him, Locklin's hand tight in his.

"Buckley, we need your prayers right now. Lead us, please?"

Buckley did just that before he found his seat, his eyes on Burnie and Muir as they sat across from him, a prayer in his heart for his friends.

"Dallas? You have word?" Barnabas spoke from where he had taken a position leaning against a wall.

"I do. Thank you, Buckley. We needed your prayers." Dallas' eyes moved to Burnie and Muir. "Muir. Burnie. Moira. As you know, I was to your home village, Muir. I was working with the investigators who were brought in." He paused, once more, swallowing hard. "It was as you had suggested and suspected. We found the debris from the store in the ravine. We found human remains in that debris. But the cadaver dogs also made other hits."

Burnie's face grew stern. "More than one?"

Dallas nodded. "More than one. I am not at liberty to say how many but there were a number. The investigators now begin the gruesome task of identifying the remains and then following through to find their killers."

"Stewart." Muir's one word sounded as if it had been pulled from deep within her. "There will be others who aren't there. Where are they?"

———

"The investigation continues at his home, with the proper search warrants. Thanks to you, Muir, we have found the link that we were looking for in disappearances in the area of young men and women. I am sorry, though, that it had to be you."

"Where's Stewart?" Burnie had his eyes on Muir.

"We are actively looking for him, but have not found him. That's why we need you two to be as careful as you can for the next while. He will be coming after you both, that's a given."

"We know that, Dallas. We know that. But what else can you tell us?"

"At present, not a lot. Muir? Have you had any unwanted messages on your phone?" Dallas grinned at the look that she threw him.

"No. I thought you made sure I couldn't."

"We did that very thing, Muir." Dallas shook his head at her. "We just have to ensure that it doesn't happen."

"I've been getting them, Dallas, more and more brutal as each one comes. I've saved them to a file and sent them on to the lab."

"Thanks, Burnie. Now, I don't have much more information for you. I know you fellows are working away. Emma and her team are as well."

"What do they need to watch for?" Breck spoke from where he sat at the back of the room.

"The usual. Burnie, you've been through this with the others. Muir, stay close to someone at all times. Stay close to the building, although the building has been invaded at times. Keep your cells charged and on you at all times. Be aware of your surroundings where you are out and about." Dallas finally walked away, not satisfied with what he could share with the couple and Moira.

Quiet conversation broke out among the men and the ladies, Muir just sitting quietly, her eyes on the hands that she had folded on the tabletop. Moira watched her closely before she rose, turning to find Breck nearby.

"Breck? How do I keep Muir safe?"

"By doing what Dallas asked. That's what we do. It also helps to pray."

"I know that." Moira was frustrated, wanting this over for her granddaughter. "But how do we find this man and the ones over him?"

"That's what we're working on. I know that it's frustrating, Moira. It is for all of us. I can't tell you how to live, but please be as careful as you can. You are at risk as well. Stewart and whoever it is that employs him will not think twice to take you to get Muir to come out of hiding."

"I am aware of that. I have dealt with this man for years, Breck." Moira paused. "Let me think through the years and see what else I can discover for you."

Breck watched Moira walk away before he turned to find Branigan and Baird standing beside him.

"Fellows?"

"We've been talking, Breck, us and our ladies. I have a feeling the others have as well. What can we do to help Muir? The ladies are helping with her clothes and hair, but there is still more that we can do."

"Right at the moment? Pray. Be there for them both." Breck's eyes following Muir as she walked around the room, Berneen beside her. "Has she found someone to talk to?"

"Not that we know, but Burnie mentioned that Darcie was willing to speak with her." Baird watched his wife, Berneen.

"That's good. If it helps, we can arrange that." Breck pulled out his phone as it vibrated, frowning. "It's Abe. Sorry, fellows, I need to take this."

Breck walked away, answering Abe's call as he did so.

"Abe? You sound far away." Breck unlocked his office door and then sat behind his desk, reaching for a pen and paper out of habit.

"Breck? Are you somewhere you can speak freely?" Abe's voice held a tone that Breck could not place.

"I am. We just had a meeting with Dallas, but I'm in my office. Alone. What's going on?"

"Muir's parents? We found them."

Breck sat stunned, unsure that he had heard correctly. "What did you say, Abe? I thought you said you found Muir's parents."

"We have. That's why we came to Ireland. Emma found a clue, traced it, and we found them. We have them with us. We'll working with the authorities now, both here and at home. It will take a few days before we can head home, what with needing passports and whatnot, but we're be there."

Breck blinked rapidly, tears flooding his eyes. He swallowed hard. "I'll talk to Barnabas. How much do you want us to say?"

"At present, until we're on Canadian soil? Nothing to either Muir or Burnie. We're trying to keep it as quiet as we can. Pray for us."

"Done, my friend. And thank you." Breck set his phone down, wonder in his heart, a prayer of praise on his lips. Just like Jaxcy, Lord, just like Jaxcy. Her parents were alive. So are Muir's. Bless our ladies, dear Lord.

———

Muir made her way the next morning towards Hagen's shop, Hagen's little girl in her arms, Hagen carrying her son. She looked around, interested for the first time, she thought, in the land that would become her home for real. She had stared hard at her emerald ring that morning, a prayer rising for Burnie, and then for herself. She felt unworthy to be the one that he had chosen but he had chosen her and that filled her with happiness, despite what she had faced and was still facing.

"We're near Lake Erie, Muir. Have Burnie take you down there sometime. It can be wild when the winds come up." Hagen nodded towards the distance, where Muir could see water.

"Is that what it is? I've stood and watched it, not knowing it was one of the lakes." She turned her face to the little girl, finding her staring at her before she grinned at Muir, a tooth peeking through her bottom gum.

"This is your shop, Hagen?" Muir stared around, amazed at the work. "These are wonderful."

"Thank you." Hagen placed her children into the playpen that she had set up near the desk. "We put in the wall here after I was attacked by the madmen who was after me. Come on through."

Muir finally stood back, her finger touching a small wooden puzzle. "These are amazing. I often would make things for myself, just to amuse myself, as the children weren't friendly or weren't allowed to play with me."

"That's so sad." Hagen studied her before she reached for a paper and pen. "Talk to me, Muir. Tell me what you want to do. I could use some help in here if you are interested."

Muir's face lit up. "You can? But can you afford to pay me?"

Hagen began to laugh, causing Muir to frown. "I gather Burnie has not yet spoken to you? He should do, but each of us ladies receives wages through the Foundation, just as our husbands do. It's part of their mandate on encouraging couples."

"They do? It is? Oh, that's so wonderful. I thought I would be a burden on Burnie." Muir sank down onto a stool.

"Never a burden, Muir. Not with Burnie. He would never think that." Hagen was off then, describing her work, what she had done, what her goals were, and how she just knew that Muir would be an asset to her. "Have you had any training in art?"

"No, but my father was an artist on the side. He wanted to establish himself but never got a chance to do that. Granny says that I follow in his footsteps, with my drawings and little crafts that I did." She frowned. "Stewart took that away from me."

"Not any longer. Here. Draw me something. A new toy that you don't see here, that would work for children ages three to five." Hagen walked away, talking to her children, and then reaching for the computer, drawing up her website and then printing off the orders. The business was growing, she thought, thank you, Lord. It is reaching out to be the blessing that I want it to be. She turned as she heard Muir approaching her.

"What's that?" Muir pointed to the computer monitor.

"My website." Hagen was off the chair, pushing Muir down. "Here. Use the mouse and work your way around it." She reached for the paper that Muir still held and drew in her breath. "Muir? You are a true artist. I like this. It's whimsical but so like a little fox. What made you do that?"

Muir shrugged, not really listening to her. "I guess I used to watch them at home. They fascinate me." She pointed to a section on the website. "What's this?"

"That? A friend is providing photos with verses to go along with the toys. It's another avenue to reach out and witness."

"I like that. Do you do cards and stationery as well?"

"No, but we could expand. Muir, I think you just found what you want to do. You can take her photos and design the cards. A printer in town already works with me. He would do the cards and stationery as well."

"He would? Oh, then, okay. Let me think it through and pray about it."

"And talk to Burnie."

"Oh, no! He won't want me doing this." Distressed, Muir sat back, not having heard the door open and Burnie and Brandon approach, the children squealing with glee as they saw their father.

"I wouldn't want you to do what?" Muir jumped as Burnie crouched down beside her, an arm around her.

"This. These photos. Hagen has suggested that I design cards and stationery using photos." Muir bit at her lip with uncertainty.

"I think it's a wonderful idea. Working like this, with Hagen? You two suit each other as friends. I know Hagen has wanted to expand, but is busy enough or almost too busy already with her tools." Burnie grinned at Hagen.

"You do? You wouldn't mind?" Muir turned to him, wonder in her heart that he would even consider letting her do that.

"I do. I am not going to step in and tell you no, not if it's what you really want to do. You're free here, Muir. You can make your own decisions. I just ask that you talk to me when you do. When we marry, then we discuss whatever it is as a couple, pray about it and make a decision together."

"I see. Granny told me that was how it should be. I didn't have a married couple that I could watch or follow, not with Mom and Dad gone."

"We understand that, sweetheart. Any of the ladies here will talk with you. Buckley will advise you as a pastor. I know that he's no longer the pastor of our church, but he is still our pastor as well as a friend. Anything you discuss with him, stays with him, unless you give permission for him to talk to someone. And that someone is usually just Locklin."

Stewart Holman stood in the shadows of the trees, his gaze fixed on the door to Hagen's shop. He had watched as the two women had entered and then the two men. His anger burned inside him. He would deal with that man, get him out of the way, and then deal with Muir. It was too late now for him to receive the money that had been promised, the buyer moving on to someone else. She had cost him millions, he thought, and she would pay with her life. Stewart really didn't care how she died, just that she did.

He turned and made his way from the forest to the road where he had left his vehicle, a high-end vehicle at that, one that stood out on the gravel road. He didn't know that he had been spotted by a neighbour to the Foundation family, and that his license plate and vehicle description had already made its way to the police department. He drove off, the patrol vehicle just missing him.

Muir shuddered with sudden fear as she and Burnie walked back towards the building they called home, her hand tight in his. She eyed the woods with anxiety and sudden knowledge that Stewart had been around, but she could not prove it. She just knew how she felt when he was.

Burnie watched her closely before his eyes too sought the woods. It had been used before to harm the ladies and men who he called friends. He picked up his pace, walking more rapidly towards the building and inside, stopping for a moment to glance out the windows.

"Is Granny around today?" His question brought Muir's attention back to him.

"She should be. We can go find her." Muir started to move away but stood still as Burnie tugged at her hand.

"Are you sure about the design work?"

"I am. I would like to try it. I told Hagen that my father was hoping to establish himself as an artist." She turned to look out the window. "Stewart was out there."

"He was?" Burnie reached to hug her. "I'm sure that he was. Dallas said he was in the area. I have no doubt that he knows exactly where you are."

"But I don't want him to hurt anyone." Muir was growing agitated.

Burnie hugged her tighter and then bent his head and began to pray for her. He felt her relax against him. When he was finished, he raised his head, searching her face and then bent and kissed her.

Muir stared up at him, wonder on her face, her fingers touching her lips. She finally moved away from him before turning and coming back into his arms, welcoming his second kiss.

"Muir?"

"Burnie?" She leaned back to stare up at him. "You told me that it was my decision. I fear for you, that Stewart will harm or kill you, but I have peace about us. God has been working in my life. That much I know. My decision? That we wed and now. I don't know how long we will have. Only God knows that."

Burnie just smiled and kissed her again, then turned her towards the stairs, her hand tight in his. "We need to find Granny. Do you know how long I have waited to have a grandmother? All my life."

Moira took one look at the young couple and then swept them into a hug, her prayer of blessing on them. She stood back, a hand on each of their arms.

"You have made a decision." Her statement was just that, a statement of fact and not a question.

"We have, Granny." Burnie's eyes were on Muir. "I told Muir that the timing of our wedding would be her decision. She has made that. We want to marry now, not wait until this is all resolved."

"Somehow, that's what I thought you would say." Moira turned to her granddaughter, seeing the flush of first love on her face. "Muir, I wish that your parents were here today, to walk with you through this exciting time in your life. But they aren't. I have something that I did manage to bring with me when the man helped me to escape. Michael gladly brought the box for me." She pointed towards Muir's bedroom. "Your mother's wedding dress is on your bed. I kept it for you."

Muir's tears blinded her for a moment, as she realized that she would have part of her family with her that day. She reached for her grandmother, holding on tight, before she spun back to Burnie's arm.

"Now what, Burnie?"

He grinned down at her. "Now what? I need your identification to get the application for the wedding license and then I can do that. We need to speak with Buckley, if you want him to marry us."

Muir nodded. "And here in the chapel? Can we do that?"

"We can and shall." Burnie swooped in for another kiss, dropped a kiss on Moira's cheek and then was off, running for his car and then heading for town.

"Granny? Did I just do something I might regret?" Muir was troubled.

"No, you didn't. It has been prayed over by all of us, and if you have peace, then you know you have made the right decision. Burnie has been teaching you to trust and pray, has he not?"

"He has, Granny. He has taken the lead in our relationship in that, just like you taught me."

"Then, let's move on to what we need to do. When are you thinking?"

"Tomorrow night? If everyone is around that is." Muir was troubled again for a moment before she pulled out her phone. "I can check without going door to door, can't I? Oh, this phone is so wonderful. Now to figure out how to do a group text. There. Did it." She spun as she heard a tap at the door, stepping back as the ladies of the building, including Anna and Amy and Hagen's twin sisters, bustled in, ready to help plan her wedding.

Stewart stared at the newspaper two days later, frustration in his demeanour. She had to do that, now didn't she? She had to marry and move on. I won't let her. He crumpled the paper and tossed it into a trash can, stopping as he saw a man standing in his way.

"Out of my way! I want by." Stewart went to move around him, but felt instead his wrists caught behind him and the feel of steel on them even as he heard the snap of the handcuffs.

"I don't think so." Dallas stared him down. "We've been watching you, Holman. For starters, you are under arrest for kidnapping, forcible confinement, assault. We'll be adding murder to that. Read him his rights." Dallas turned away, his stomach roiling at the memory of what he had seen when he had been in Muir's village.

Pulling out his phone, he stared down at it, listening to the protests that Stewart was making. Dallas shook his head and moved away, dialling Burnie's number.

"Burnie? It's Dallas. Call me when you get this." Frustrated at only receiving Burnie's voice mail, Dallas reached for his keys, knowing that he needed to be across town at another crime scene. This is wearing me out, he thought. I need a break and just can't catch one.

Burnie frowned as he listened to Dallas' message, and then shrugged, setting his phone to one side and reaching instead for his Bible. He could hear Muir as she moved around the apartment, just getting to know it, she said. He smiled. She was just who he needed, he thought. Thirty minutes later, he reached for his phone again, this time leaving a message for Dallas. This is what is going to happen, he thought. Phone tag.

Muir hesitated in the doorway, her eyes on him. Burnie rose, a smile on his face, and went towards her, sweeping her into a hug and then kissing her. He stood back to watch her face, keeping his arms around her.

"Muir?"

"Dallas called. He said that he had been trying to reach you."

"He had. He left a voice mail that I finally had a chance to return. What did he want?"

Muir chewed at her lip for a moment. "He arrested Stewart this morning."

"He did? In town?"

Nodding her head, Muir snuggled closer to him. "In town. But he's sure that Stewart is not here on his own."

"No, he wouldn't be. He'll need to go through the courts now for the charges and then make bail if he can."

"I think he will. Whoever is behind him will not want him talking."

They turned to walk back towards the kitchen, and then to the entry door. Moira stood there, her hand raised to knock.

"I didn't get a chance to knock." She smiled at the couple. "Apparently, I am to bring you two down to the conference room. The other conference room."

"You are?" Burnie grinned as he kissed her cheek. "Then, if you must, you must. Muir, I can almost guarantee that there's a meal set out in there."

"There is? Why?"

"Because we refused one on Thursday night, when we married. They'd have made plans for today. Everyone is around."

Dallas stood for a moment, watching the couple, before he turned to Barnabas, motioning towards the hallway.

"What's up, Dallas? You're not happy." Barnabas paced beside him.

"I'm not. Holman has confessed to being out here. We know that's not on his own. I just wanted to give you a heads' up and let you work your wonders, if you can, with your security people."

"Thanks. We found evidence of someone or more than someone around. Near the gym in fact. It doesn't surprise me." He turned back towards the conference room, heading for the door. "You're staying."

"I wish I could. I have too many investigations on the go. I'll be back." Dallas walked away, fatigue in his body weighing him down.

Barnabas shook his head, opening the door to find Breck heading his way, pointing behind him.

"Abe called. He's heading for here."

"He is? Did he say why?"

"He did. He has news for Moira and Muir."

Barnabas froze and then nodded. "He was over in Ireland, now wasn't he?"

"He was. I'm heading up to make sure the suite beside Moira is ready. He asked that we not say anything, not until he lands here and is in front of them."

Her eyes on Burnie as they finally stood, alone again, in the rose garden, she just reached to hug him. Thank you, Lord. You are healing me, teaching me how to live again. She frowned as Burnie's hand reached to touch her face and then he kissed her. His arms around her, he hugged her to him.

"Have I told you today that I love you?"

"You have. I love you too. Did you see Dallas?"

Burnie shook his head. "Was he here?"

"He was, but he left quickly. He's burning out, as you would say, Burnie. He's doing too much." She looked up again at him, finding him staring past her. "Burnie?"

"Muir? Can you turn around for a moment?"

"I can, if I have to."

"I think that you need to. Abe, Ian and Murphy are here. They're looking for us."

Muir turned, her eyes on the men before she saw movement behind them. Her head tilting, she broke free from Burnie's hug and walked towards Abe, looking past him. She looked up at him, seeing the smile on his face and then his nod. Muir moved past him, Burnie reaching for her hand and walking with her.

Burnie stopped short of the couple who stood there, his eyes flickering between Muir and the lady. He waited for Muir, finding her struggling to free her hand from his, her hands then covering her mouth.

"It's you! I dreamed about you last night. That you were here." She moved to stand directly in front of the lady who looked so much like her. "Are you my mother? And my father?"

"We are, Muir." The man hesitated before he reached out a shaking hand, to lay it against her curls. "You are alive. We were never sure."

"And I was told you were dead. So was Granny." She drew back, wonder on her face. "Does Granny know?"

"Not yet." Abe spoke from behind her, even as his team of seven tall men surrounded them. "How be we head inside?"

"We can do that." Burnie reached for Muir's hand, finding her reluctant to move. "Muir? Sweetheart? We need to move inside."

"Oh, we do? I'm sorry." She turned and walked with him, glancing frequently over her shoulder. "Did you know?"

"No, I didn't. I'm so happy for you, Muir, and for Granny." He stopped just inside the lobby door, watching as Moria walked their way.

Moira came to a sudden halt, her eyes on Muir and Burnie and then drifting past them, to stop on the other couple.

"Morgan? Oh, Morgan, is that you?" She was across the room, in her son's arms as they both wept before she freed herself to turn to Muir's mother. "McRae? You as well? Oh, the Lord has answered my prayers." Both ladies wept as they stood, arms tight around one another. "How?"

"That's what we'll explain." Abe spoke from beside them, looking around, uncomfortable at being in the open, even though they were inside. "Can we move to a room?"

"Certainly. How about the chapel?" Breck pointed that way.

The men and ladies from the building filed into the back seats, leaving the front for Muir and Burnie and her family. Abe paced at the front, suddenly at a loss for words. He looked at Murphy, who simply grinned and nodded.

"Abe? How?" Burnie finally spoke.

"It's a long story, and we don't have it all yet. Morgan and McRae have been working with the authorities on both sides of the Atlantic to give their statements. There is still a lot of work to be done." Abe nodded towards where Muir sat, her parents on either side of her. "They have quite the story."

"Holman?"

"Holman. According to what they have said, he has had his eye on Muir since she was a baby. That's immoral and heartbreaking."

"He separated them because of that?"

Abe nodded. "That's what they were told. He was afraid that if they stayed, they would move away. Have you seen her baby pictures?"

"No, but I am sure that she was a very pretty baby."

"She was. When we walked into the house where they were kept captive, all Morgan asked was if Muir was okay. That has driven them all these years. He did say that they were very close to escaping when we walked in. They had been able to reach out to someone in the government."

"I am glad to hear that, but it doesn't change the fact that a baby was without her parents all of her life."

"No, it doesn't." Abe looked around. "Listen, we have to run. Emma and I will be back in a couple of days. She wants to talk with Muir and her family as well as you, Burnie. Do you want Doug and Darcie to come as well?"

"I think so. Maybe Darcie can give us some more light."

Abe grinned. "Check your email. Emma passed your email address on to Darcie, who was sending you information."

"Okay. I haven't seen it but I'll check my spam folder. I've been trying to work through some revisions."

"I'm sure you have." Abe suddenly laughed. "Did a mystery writer ever expect to become involved in his own mystery?" With that, he walked towards Muir and her family and then out of the chapel, his men filing out after him.

Muir wandered their apartment that night, troubled that she had been the reason that her parents had been taken out of her life. She had always thought that it had been business that had done that. Burnie stood and watched from his office doorway before he approached her and wrapped her into his arms, finally sweeping her up and then finding his favourite chair, just holding her as she wept, his own tears dampening her hair.

She was finally still, her emotions spent, but there was still a turmoil inside her. Burnie knew that and prayed for her. He finally felt her relax as she slept. He refused to move, just shifting to a more comfortable position. He heard his phone ringing from the office and ignored it. Right now, Burnie decided that Muir needed him. His head went down and he slept.

Muir roused hours later, surprised to find herself wrapped in Burnie's arm as he slept in his chair. She slipped away, squinting at the clock. Five in the morning, she thought. Burnie is usually up soon. Muir paused in the kitchen, finally deciding to shower and change her clothes. She didn't know what the day would bring, but she felt refreshed in her heart, knowing that her parents were still alive and right here, in the building. She searched for her phone, smiling as she found Abe's phone number programmed into it. She sent off a short text to thank him and then headed for the kitchen, finding Burnie already there, her tea ready for her and on the table, his mug of coffee there as well.

Burnie turned as he heard Muir and simply opened his arms, catching her as she threw herself at him, her arms around his neck as she hugged him tight.

"Did yesterday really happen?"

He nodded. "It did. Your parents are here, in the apartment next to us for now. Barnabas will let them decide where they want to be. But for now, he'll keep them here, until we can find the ones responsible."

"I am still in shock. God knew all along, didn't He?" At Burnie's nod against her head, she hugged him tighter. "This is what you mean, isn't it? What you're trying to teach me about God? That He knows our path and has plotted it out for us?"

"It is, sweetheart. It's been hard for you. I can't begin to imagine how your parents have felt, knowing that you were in his sights, and not knowing if you would escape him. Abe sent me a text last night. He had a chance to speak with them, telling them what had happened to you and how you and Granny escaped."

"Granny! How is she taking this?" Muir leaned back to look up at him.

"She's taking it just fine, she tells me. I talked to her a bit ago. She's planning on coming for breakfast in about twenty minutes." Burnie squinted at the clock. "That will give me a chance to shower, shave and change. That is, if a certain bride will let go of me." He grinned at her look of pretended outrage before he kissed her thoroughly and then headed away to do just that.

Muir stared at the doorway, before she shook her head, a smile on her face, and headed for the fridge and then the pantry, not sure what to make for breakfast, or even if there were would be more than three of them. She looked back at the doorway and then headed for the entry, to tap at the door where her parents were. Morgan stood for a moment, staring at his daughter, all grown up and married now, and felt the sadness and yes, anger in him.

"Dad?" Muir sounded hesitant. "Have you and Mom eaten yet? I know there's a time change."

"We had some toast earlier, child. Come in."

"Oh, I wanted to ask you two for breakfast. We're just getting up." She stepped backwards, ready to head away when Morgan spoke.

"It wouldn't matter, child. We will come with you. Even if it's only tea that we have, we want to be there. We need to get to know you and your young man." McRae had appeared beside him as he spoke.

"Oh, okay. Come over when you're ready."

"We'll come now, if we may." McRae searched her daughter's face, finally reaching to hug her, missing all the years of just being able to do that.

Burnie looked around as he heard their voices and then reached to hug them. I like this, he thought. All the hugs that I missed as a child, I'm getting now. Moira stood beside him, an arm wrapped around him.

"They're hurting, Burnie."

"I know. So are you and Muir. We'll need to find someone for you all to talk with."

"I've been talking with my Lord, but I know what you mean. That Abe said he had a friend he would send our way."

"Darcie. I hope her husband, Doug, comes as well. He's a lieutenant on their Emergency Task Force in his hometown. They may have insight that we don't."

———

Breck was on a hunt. He needed to speak with Burnie, and just couldn't find him. His car was in the parking lot. He sighed, as he stood outside, his hand rubbing at the back of his neck. He could feel eyes watching him, waiting for what, he wasn't quite sure.

"Bradon? Have you seen Burnie?" Breck called to Bradon as he walked by with Kade.

"Burnie? I think he was heading for Hagen's shop. Muir was there with her parents."

"Okay, thanks. The one place where I didn't look." Breck headed that way, his steps slowly as he neared the woods. We need to clear that back, he thought. It's getting too close to the building. A nice playground here for the little ones would be just the thing. I know Hagen would like it.

Popping open the door to the shop, he listened, smiling as he heard Burnie's voice teasing Hagen and then Muir, Hagen responding in kind. He stood for a moment in the doorway to the shop itself, watching as Morgan and McRae wandered the area, stopping examine the toys and puzzles.

Burnie looked around, and then excused himself, heading towards Breck, who backed away into the reception area.

"Breck? You're here for a reason?" Burnie pulled the door closed behind him.

"I am. Abe called. He didn't call you, not knowing if Muir would be around. He's had word that someone is in the area, looking for her."

"Holman?"

"He's still in jail. Hasn't made his bail, Dallas tells me. No, it's someone related to him. Abe didn't have all the specifics. Dallas also called. They're getting word on the street that someone has put a hit out on you."

"That's par for the course." Burnie frowned, his eyes on the floor. "So, what do we do? We can't stop living. I won't ask that of Muir."

"I know. We don't expect you to. We need to up our security around you. I talked to the security head. His people are moving in around you two. You go nowhere without one of them."

Burnie sighed, and then nodded. "We knew this would happen. Muir and I talked about it. The thing of it is, she doesn't want security. She wants whoever it is to come after her."

"She what?" Breck stared at Burnie. "That's exactly what we don't want."

Shaking his head, Burnie held up a hand to stop Breck's words. "Think about it from her perspective. She was confined for how long? Beaten? Threatened? Demeaned? Broken? She doesn't want to live like that again, to feel like she is a prisoner. She knows that's not what this means, but she still has that hesitation or fear, I guess you could say."

"I understand that, Burnie, but how do we do it then? We can't have them coming after you, if we can help it. You might not survive."

"We've talked about that too, Breck. Since we married and she feels safe with me, she's opening up and talking. A lot. Some things we will need to reach out to Dallas with. Other things? That's between her and I. I will not break her confidence in those."

Breck nodded. "Okay. Just talk to her? Please? She's part of our family, and you know that we take care of our own." Breck paced. "How is it going with her parents?"

"That? It's difficult. They're strangers yet related. It's going to take a long time. Muir may never fully accept them. She and Granny are a pair who have faced what life has thrown at them together. There's a bond there that she will not break. To have Morgan and McRae here? She feels threatened by them. I won't tell them that. They need to work that out."

Breck nodded. "Is Darcie heading this way?"

"Doug called and said they were. Hoping to make it today or tomorrow. I promised them a suite for the night if they wanted it. Doug seemed to think that they would."

"Sure. The guest suite on the first floor is available. We'll need to make arrangement for Morgan and McRae for wherever it is that they want to live."

"I know. For now, let it lie. I spoke with them briefly. Morgan knows how hard it is for all of them. He seemed to think that at some point they would need to put some space between them."

"I see. Okay, then. I'll need to speak with him, then. Dallas said he's on his way out later as is Will."

"Good. Dallas needs to talk to them. I worry about them now that they're here. I also worry about my bride. This is the point in my novel when things heat up. I don't want to see that for Muir."

"And it will, Burnie. The fellows all want you to know that they're starting to pull in from their work, heading to the conference room every day. And Phil called. He said not to worry about your volunteer work with the driving school. He'll look after it for now."

"He did? I had a text from him that I haven't had a chance to answer today. I'll call him."

Burnie watched as Breck walked away and then left the building himself, to stand and stare towards the lake before he walked around the building, his eyes on the trees and underbrush near it. Like Breck, he became concerned.

Muir looked around the gardens later that afternoon, feeling scared suddenly and then turning and running for the building. She had just needed to be outside for a bit, on her own. She knew the security guard had followed her but had stayed back to let her have space.

"Muir?" The guard was beside her, a hand on her back as she stopped suddenly, staring back the way that she had just ran from.

"I'm sorry. All of a sudden I felt scared and alone. I shouldn't have come out."

"No, it's okay. I was watching you. I just couldn't figure out what happened. In you go. I'll go back and see what it was." He looked up as Brendon and Brennen approached. "Fellows, can one of you stay with Muir and the other come with me?"

Brendon nodded, heading inside with Muir, as Brennen walked beside the guard.

"What happened, Paul?"

"Muir was frightened. I was watching and didn't see anything. I told her I'd have a look around."

Brennen finally stopped, staring at the ground. "She was right. With the rain last night, this is muddy. Someone has been here and here for a while. The footprints are too trampled on from him moving around."

Paul nodded and then looked through the trees. "The animal path. That's how they're getting in here."

"They are. We can't block it off." Brennen turned back to study the building. "She can't be caged."

"No, she can't. Not after what she went through." Barnabas had had a brief talk with all the security guards, giving a short history of what Muir had faced. Paul remembered the anger that had flooded through the whole group. "We want to help her stay safe."

"We know you do. We'll need to talk to Burnie."

"That we will." Paul hesitated and then pointed. "What's that?"

Brennen turned back, his eyes following the direction that Paul was pointing in. "An envelope. What do you want to bet it's a threat?"

"That would be my guess."

Brennen pulled out his handkerchief and picked up the envelope. "It's thick. They must have put in more than one threat."

Burnie turned from his computer monitor as he heard Brennen's voice.

"Brennen? What are you doing here? I thought you and Brendon were off somewhere."

"We were. We met Paul and Muir coming back in. Muir had been to the gardens and was scared. Paul and I searched around, found this." Brennen handed over the envelope. "We found a spot where someone had been waiting, but the tracks are too muddled now to try and figure them out. It looks as if whoever it was used the animal path."

"The animal path? Of course, that's perfect for them getting in and out." Burnie laid the envelope down and then reached for his phone, pulling up the camera app. "Here, take pictures as I open it."

"Are you sure that you should?"

"I am. I send the photos on to Dallas or the lab. This has gone on far enough. I want it to end."

"I know you do. Okay, I'm set."

Brennen began to take the pictures as Burnie turned the envelope over and over and then reached for his letter opener to slit the envelope. Burnie paused, a prayer raising, before he pulled out the papers inside.

"There are a lot. More than what I would expect if it was just a threat." He looked up at Brennen.

"That's what Paul and I thought. Okay, go for it, Burnie. Let's see what's there."

———

Burnie unfolded the papers, and counted them. "There are twelve of them, Brennen. He pulled back the last one. "This one has a signature and a date. What is this?"

"I have no idea. Sounds like a confession or something."

"Or something, is right." Burnie began to read, finally sitting down, setting each page where Brennen could take a picture of it. He finally looked up, finding Brennen staring at him in shock.

"Is that a confession?"

"It seems that way. He has named a lot of people that I would never have thought of. Wait! Ker's mother is named in here." Burnie sat back abruptly. "She was involved in this?"

"Oh, man! That sucks. Now we have to talk to Brody and Ker as well."

"That we do." Burnie looked past Brennen as the door opened and Dallas peeked in before he entered. "Just the man that we need to see."

"I am? Why?"

Burnie pointed to his desk. "Take a look at this. It's a confession from someone. And he names Kelly."

"Kelly? Ker's mother? Involved with Muir?" Dallas frowned as he reached for the papers and read through them. "I need a copy of these." He rose and headed for the copier, making copies and then returning the original to the envelope. He reached into his pocket for an evidence bag. "I need to take this."

"We know that. Now, how do we proceed? I can't hide this from Muir or from Brody and Ker."

"No, we can't. Burnie, go find Muir. Brody and Ker were around. I saw them as I came in." Dallas rose, following Burnie from the room.

Muir, Ker and Brody stared at the three men before they took the copies of the papers that they were being handed.

"Burnie?" Brody's voice had a stern tone to it.

"Read through them. Then we talk."

Muir looked up as she heard a strangled sob from Ker, not understanding what was wrong. Brody simply wrapped Ker into his arms, their papers falling to the floor. Turning to Burnie, Muir was surprised at the sadness on his face.

"Burnie?"

"Ker's mother was involved in helping people who made teens and young children disappear. She was killed during the investigation. Ker was at risk." Burnie wrapped Muir in his arms. "That's the Kelly who is mentioned."

"Oh, Ker! How sad!" Muir moved to hug Ker. "I'm sorry. I didn't know."

"Nor did I. Keefe and I didn't know until Brody became involved in it all."

"Oh!" Muir turned back to Burnie, finding Brennen and Dallas watching her closely. "This person who signed this? He is a cousin of the Holmans. He wasn't around a lot. In fact, I hadn't seen him for the last six or seven months I was there." She sighed. "About the time Granny disappeared. Did he follow her?"

"We don't know. And somehow I don't think that we'll find him to verify this statement." Dallas looked down at it. "He has had it notarized, which tells me that he wrote in out in the presence of a lawyer, likely. Where he is now is anyone's guess."

"He was the one who was here today. Wasn't he?" Muir looked up at Brennen.

"More than likely, Muir. We found evidence that he had been waiting for a while. Dallas, I'll show you where. There is an animal path that he could follow."

Dallas had left with Brennen, returning shortly, a stern look on his face. He nodded at Burnie and Brody before he looked back down at the evidence bag. For once, he wasn't sure what to do. Normally, he had no trouble with that.

"Dallas?" Muir's voice brought his head back up. "We need to talk to Mom and Dad. You need to, I should say. I can't. I don't know them well enough to say anything."

"I will, Muir. I understand that they are in town with Barnabas and Amy at the moment. I'll track them down." He stayed for a few more moments and then left.

Brody watched the door close before he spoke. "Burnie?"

"I know, Brody. I know. It now involves you and Ker. And Keefe. Ker, where's Keefe?"

"I have no idea. I have not heard from him in a month. He said that he was taking off and would be in touch. I didn't expect it to be this long. He's not answering his phone. I've been sending texts and leaving voice mail."

"Let Dallas deal with that, then." Burnie sank back into his chair. "We need to start looking into this, but right at the moment? I have an email that I have to answer. Muir? Please?" He reached for her hand even as Brody and Ker said their goodbyes and left.

"Burnie?"

"Muir, how good are you at proofreading?"

"I was top of my class in English. I always enjoyed it. Why?"

"Because I could use your help. It will help distract you from what's going on." He pointed to a binder. "In that is my latest work. Would you consider it?"

"Do you have to ask?" She eagerly reached for it. "Of course, I will. Can I work here? And what do I use to mark it up?"

"Mark it up, is it?" Burnie grinned at her as he stood and swooped in to kiss her. "Hmm. I think I could handle having you working with me."

"Listen, fellow. You just hired me. No kissing the staff." She smirked at him as she reached for a highlighter and pen and then settled herself down in an easy chair, soon immersed in the story.

———

Burnie watched her, content for her to be with him. That way, he thought, I can keep an eye on her. Lord, protect my bride. Keep her safe. Lead to a resolution of this and soon. I love to see how she is opening up to You and asking questions that drive me back into the Word, to find the answers that she needs.

Burnie finally stood, his work done for the day, to find Muir still engrossed in the story. He reached to gently shut it, bringing a protest from her.

"I am at the most interesting point, Burnie." She reached for the binder, finding him holding up and away from her, a grin on his face.

"It's supper time, Muir. I'll give it back. I promise. How be we call it a day for now?"

"Only if you bring that with you." Muir stood and stretched, keeping the highlighter and pen in her hand. "These go with me."

Burnie ran for the rose garden the next morning, knowing that Muir had headed that way. Dallas had called, sounding rushed, and warning Burnie that Stewart had escaped from custody as he was being transferred to another city. They had word that he was heading their way.

Sliding to a halt, Burnie watched as Muir stood, her hand on a rose, before he approached her.

"Burnie?" She looked up, her smile lighting her face. "I didn't know you were here."

"I just got here. That's a beautiful rose. You can pick it."

"No, I don't think so. God is such a wonderful creator. I don't know how someone can look at flowers or nature and not see His hand in it."

"I don't either." Burnie's arm was around her, turning her back towards the building. "What are you up to now?"

"I had hoped to find Hagen, but she said that she had to head for town. Something about needing more material. I'm at a loose ends. Mom and Dad are away again, this time with the police. Granny is off with Anna."

"Then, let's find something fun to do. I don't have to work right now, I'm between books. The proofreading that you did has helped." He walked them to the building. "How about running away for the day?"

"We can do that?"

"We can. Let's head into town. I'll take you out for lunch and then window shopping."

"Window shopping? I've never done that. But what do we do with the windows when we buy them?" She smirked as Burnie stared at her before he broke out into gales of laughter.

"Got me there, sweetheart."

Three hours later, Muir pulled Burnie into a little shop, her mouth rounding as she stared at the treasures there. It was a little gift shop, full of unique gifts, mostly of glass. She wandered the store, listening to Burnie as he talked to the owner, a lady from the church. He finally moved to stand beside her as she stood, her finger lightly tracing a hand-blown rainbow.

"This is what I feel like right now, Burnie. That God saw me and promised me His rainbow." She looked up as he didn't speak, finding his eyes on it.

Burnie reached for it. "Then, you'll take it with you. You need these visual reminders as well as the ones that you find in Scripture." He nodded towards the store. "Find anything else?"

She shook her head, her eyes still on his. "No, just that. Are you sure, Burnie?"

"I am sure." He covered the price tag, before she could protest. "The cost doesn't matter, sweetheart. What matters is what it means to you. Evelyn?"

Evelyn shook her head as Burnie tried to pay. "No, it's a gift to Muir. I know that she's been struggling. No, Muir. No one but God has told me that. I can see the peace of His that you are finding. God bless you, dear." Evelyn watched them walk away before she wiped at her eyes and then dug into her purse to pay for the rainbow.

Muir set the rainbow carefully on the mantle when they got home, her finger once more tracing the colours on it. God, You have provided hope and a promise in Your rainbow. I need that. Burnie is part of the hope I have. Thank you, dear Lord.

Burnie had watched Muir before he stepped from the apartment, tapping on Moira's door. When she answered, he simply hugged her and then guided her back to his own apartment.

Moira watched Muir before she reached to hug her granddaughter.

"Found your rainbow?"

"I did, Granny. The lady in the shop wouldn't take anything for it, said it was a gift. That's what God does, isn't it? Gives us gifts when we least expect it."

<hr>

"He does just that, child. He delights in surprising us. You always liked your rainbows, calling them pretty when you were tiny. Burnie, thank you for finding it for her."

Burnie shrugged. "Muir needed to do something fun for a change, something that she had never done. She wanted to buy the windows though when we were window shopping." He grinned at Muir as she sputtered before she began laughing.

"He wanted to take me window shopping, Granny. What was I supposed to think?"

Moira laughed, liking the lightness of spirit she was seeing in Muir, but knowing that the darkness still hung over the couple.

"Have you talked to Dallas today, Burnie?" Moira turned to find him heading for the kitchen.

"No, I haven't. I didn't expect to. He's off for a few days. Will made him take some time."

"Oh! The poor man. He's wearing out. He won't be on the force much longer. He's needing to find what he's searching for."

"He has been through a lot. He's become a good friend to us, but remains the police officer that he needs to be when he's investigating the mysteries and adventures that we get involved in."

Running for the building, Muir looked back over her shoulder, tripping over her feet but managing to keep upright. She could hear the running footsteps behind her and reached for the door, yanking it open and flying through it and towards the security desk. Paul had looked up and then ran for the outside door, pointing towards the security office and ordering Muir inside and to lock the door.

Paul headed around the building, watching in frustration as the man ran away from him. He headed after him, Burnie following as he saw Paul.

"Paul?" Burnie finally caught up with him. "What's going on?"

"That man. He was chasing Muir. She made it into the building. I sent her to lock herself into the office." Paul was frustrated. "He got away. And I didn't get a good enough look at him to be able to describe him."

"No, I didn't either." Burnie spun and ran for the building, hammering at the office door, calling for Muir.

Muir stood, her back against the door, hearing Burnie calling for her, but too afraid to answer. She felt the door shoving against her as Paul opened it enough for Burnie to squeeze through. She flung herself into his arms, sobs breaking Burnie's heart as he listened to them. Paul headed for the desk, calling it in, but knowing that there wasn't much that the police would find.

Breck paced the conference room an hour later, the eyes of the men on him. The only one missing was Burnie and he had been adamant that he was not leaving Muir. Not just then. Barnabas had appeared, sent them off to their home, and then found Breck, calling a meeting with all the men.

Blair spoke up. "Breck, Barnabas? What happened?"

"Someone made an attempt to take Muir a while ago, from here on the property. She was able to get inside and Paul headed out. This is getting dangerous, fellows. We need to concentrate on solving this. I'm pulling you all back in to investigate." Barnabas had done this for each one of the men, knowing that their employers would be in agreement.

"Okay. What do we need to add to the whiteboards?" Brady was on his feet, heading that way, collecting papers on the way by the men.

"Has Emma been in touch?" Benen sorted through the papers that he had amassed.

"No, she's been quiet. I don't like that."

"She and Abe are away this week. They needed a break. Jace is working on everything, but he said he's got a lot on his plate." Bradon spoke up. "He's shooting me what he can later today. I'll get you all copies of it." He paused, a frown on his face. "That cousin of Holman's? Did we ever get any more information on him?"

"No, we didn't. It's like he didn't exist." Brendon looked up. "And somehow that's what I think we'll find. That he didn't really exist. Or else he's dead and someone is pretending to be him."

"Now, that would throw a curveball into it, wouldn't it?" Buckley looked up and then approached the boards. "Burnie was working this again like a logic problem, wasn't he?"

"We all were. He hasn't been doing a lot. He's had timelines that he has had to meet with his latest book." Brandon rose as well, heading to add information to another board. "I have found a link between Holman and Keefe."

"Keefe? How?"

"Holman approached Keefe a year ago and asked him to investigate something. Keefe refused. That is in the paperwork that Emma forwarded. I'm not sure how she found that."

"Likely from when she was investigating Ker's family." Brody looked up. "She does that. Finds connections, sets them aside, and then remembers them. I wish I had her memory."

"Me too. She's scary." Breck looked around as a tap came to the door and then a man looked in. "Can I help you?"

"You can. I'm looking for Burnie."

Breck walked towards him, Barnabas beside him. "He's not here. Can I ask your name?"

The man grinned as he pulled out his identification. "I'm Doug Foster. Cousin to Abe. He sent my wife and me to find Burnie and Muir."

"Doug? He's spoken of you." Breck reached to shake his hand. "Come on. I'll show you where he is."

Doug didn't move, his eyes on the walls. "I see that you have a nice setup."

"We do. We used to have paper, but then Barnabas had these installed." Breck looked over at Barnabas. "Barnabas?"

"Go on and find them, Breck. I'll stay here for now. Call if you need me."

Burnie looked askance at the tall man and the lady with him that Breck had brought into his apartment. He knew Muir was in the office, he had left her there when he had answered the door.

"Burnie. This is Doug Foster and his wife, Darcie. Abe is cousin to Doug."

"Doug? Darcie? You have been mentioned. Glad to meet you." Burnie shot a look behind him. "I was about to make coffee but first, let me introduce you to Muir. We're in the office." Burnie led the way back, Muir rising to her feet, fear rising in her for a moment.

Burnie simply swung an arm around her. "Muir. This is Doug and Darcie. We talked about them."

"We did." Muir studied the couple before she focused on Darcie. "You did profiling."

Darcie grinned. "I did. I run a gift shop now." Her eyes went to the rainbow. "Oh, you have one of Ella's rainbows. She prays over each one she makes, that the new owner will be blessed by God."

"She does? That's why I feel such peace. Sit please." Muir sank back down onto the couch. "Tell me why you're here."

The three men walked away, conversation quiet between them. Doug was assessing Burnie and not liking the stress that he could see. He shared a look with Breck, who simply shook his head.

Muir watched Darcie for a moment. "Talk to me, please. I need help and I just can't seem to find the words to ask for it. Burnie is trying but I just don't want to burden him."

"Trust me, Muir. It is no burden for these fellows. You need to speak with him." Darcie reached for her hand, bowing her head to pray for Muir. When she looked up, she looked past Muir. "This man who held you?"

"Stewart? What about him?"

"He's older than you by about twenty years. He has been ruthless with so many people. Everyone is afraid of him. He resorts to violence and murder to get what he wants. His home life as a child was the same. Brutal. Full of violence. No love. Drugs and alcohol a large part of it. He saw an opportunity by chance when he saw a young woman abducted and taken overseas. He blackmailed the man who did it, making money to start doing it himself. Only he needed contacts and that he had to buy. You thwarted him, Muir. He will not forget that. He will come after you. To get to you, he will go after Burnie."

Muir drew in her breath. "I don't know how you did that, but that describes him. The man that held me? He was brutal and violent. I don't know how I survived, but for God. He told me exactly what he planned for me."

"I wondered." Darcie reached to hug her. "That's what they do. They beat down their victim, both physically and mentally, until there is no resistance. Part of their conditioning is to describe what will happen to them. I'm sorry, Muir, that it happened to you. You lost something through him that you should not have."

"I know. I get angry when I think of it, and have to pray for peace and for God to take vengeance. Is it wrong to ask that?"

"Not at all. He does say that vengeance is His. I saw that with what Doug and I went through. I almost died because of a bullet. Many people died because of the man who was responsible."

"You did? Oh, Darcie. How horrible!" Muir looked up as the men returned. "Burnie?"

"It's okay, sweetheart. Doug has some information from Abe and Emma that he needs to go over with us before we pass it on to Dallas and the fellows. But I know Breck. He wants to spend some time in prayer."

"That I do, Burnie. We need to cover you two with that. Doug? Will you lead us?"

Doug simply bowed his head and began to pray, Breck following and then Burnie, before Darcie took up the petition. When they were finished, there was a stillness in the room. Muir maintained afterwards that she could feel the presence of God in a powerful way, that He had spoken to her, to lead her to learn to trust Him deeper and fuller.

Burnie headed into town the next morning, needing to mail documents to his publisher. He paused as he turned from the counter in the post office, not sure of the feeling of doom that suddenly overcame him. *Lord, what is going on? I feel like I am at a crisis and don't know why or who.*

He drove away, not seeing the car following him. There was enough traffic that the car could not get close enough to him to run him off the road, which had been their intent. The two men exchanged glances as they noted a patrol vehicle pull in front of them and then follow Burnie to the driveway of the Foundation property. The driver pounded at the steering wheel. They had missed a perfect opportunity, he complained loudly.

Burnie paused at the end of the driveway, watching as the car drove by and then returned, trying to catch the license plate number but unable to. He finally shook his head and drove forward, parking in his designated spot. He sat for a moment, puzzling over the car, before he shook his head. Another thought distracted him. Muir didn't drive. He wondered if she wanted to? He would have to ask her.

Brennen looked up as Burnie sat down beside him, his head tilting to watch his friend.

"Burnie?"

"I was followed. I think if the patrol vehicle had not moved in, I wouldn't be sitting here right now."

"That close?" Brennen whistled, catching Branigan's attention. "So, what do we do?"

"We keep a watch out, be as careful as we can be, and live life. Barnabas said that Morgan and McRae are heading back to Abe's for a time. He needs to debrief them as he calls it for the authorities overseas."

"How does Muir feel about that?" Branigan spoke up.

"I think she's relieved. She needs some time to absorb and accept what happened. Moira is quiet, too quiet. She's praying a lot, she said, but she's not talking a lot."

"None of them are. It was a brutal thing that happened. We're praying for them." Branigan's attention dropped to the paper that he had just picked up. "Burnie, when you were in the store, what did you see?"

"What do you mean?" Burnie sat back, his eyes on Branigan.

"Did you see anyone when you were in there? I mean, other than Muir and Holman?"

"No, not that I remember. Although I felt like someone else was there. Again, why?"

"Because in that pile of material that Emma sent? I found this." Branigan handed over a photo. "It's time stamped for around when you were in there."

Burnie took it, his eyes not leaving Branigan, who simply stared back at him. Burnie's eyes dropped to the photo, and he drew in a breath.

"There was someone else in there. I never saw him. He's standing near me. There was no one there. Just the three of us." Burnie looked up as he felt a hand on his shoulder.

Moira stood beside him, her eyes on the photo. "Michael? What is he doing there?"

"Michael?" Burnie shared a look with Branigan.

"Michael. He's the man who helped me to escape. Only he disappeared after he did. I never could find him."

"Moira, sit please." Burnie paused for a moment. "Have you and Muir discussed him?"

"We have. Muir decided that he was an angel. But I don't understand why he was there."

"To save Muir, I have no doubt. If we had been just a moment slower getting out of the store, we would have died. I felt a hand pushing me forward even as Muir and I ran. I shrugged it off as just stress and fear."

Moira shook her head, a slight smile on her face. "He gives us angels to protect us. I think Michael was provided just for Muir." She looked up. "Who to say that he wasn't there just for that reason, to get you out of the store in order for you two to survive?" She rose and walked away, leaving a stunned silence in the room.

The men gradually went back to what they had been working once, soberness in their hearts but wonder as well. Burnie rose and paced along the wall, reading what had been written. He sighed. This didn't seem to be getting him anywhere, he thought. Baird watched him before he too rose and came to walk beside him.

"What are your thoughts?"

"My thoughts? Who did Morgan anger that much? Was it because of Morgan or because of Muir? Would they really have watched her that long? I don't think so. Stewart didn't strike me as the sort of fellow who would. There has to be something that we're missing."

"I think the same. I just haven't been able to put a finger on it." Branigan reached for his phone as it chimed. "It's Emma. She sending you some more paperwork, Burnie. Although why she sent me the text and not you."

Burnie shrugged. "Does it matter if it moves us forward?" His voice died away and then he spun, reaching for a marker, moving to a clean board and frantically drawing and writing.

"Burnie?" Benen stood watching him.

"I'm plotting it out, Benen. Just like I might with a mystery story. That's how my mind thinks. Now, maybe I can make sense of it." He stepped back, his phone out to take a photo. "I need to talk to Muir and Moira but I'll do that later. Right now?" He reached for a different coloured marker and drew a line through the horizontal line he had already drawn. "If this was a story, this is where the crisis would occur. Right here. Right now. It would build to the climax. Fellows, I think this is where it is going to get very dangerous. For all of us. Whoever it is may well go after anyone of us."

"I don't think so, Burnie." Brody spoke from where he stood beside Benen. "You're the one who stepped in, who stopped them. You're the one who walked away with Muir. Did we ever figure out why they had you handcuffed?"

"You know, I don't know that we did. Dallas didn't seem to be able to find out why." Burnie turned, a puzzled look on his face. "They tried to tell him it was because I was a material witness. You don't handcuff a material witness to a bed."

"No, you don't. They did that to keep you there. They thought that Muir would appear, to see how you were. If she had, then they would have nabbed her and had her disappear then." Breck spoke from where he stood just inside of the doorway. "There was always something off about that. I am glad that Muir had the sensibility to go to the airport and stow away. That got her out of there."

"It did." Burnie looked around, a thought niggling at his mind. "Breck? What was your sense of the airport there?"

"The airport? I'm not sure that I noticed much about it. It was small, not well maintained, but the planes were expensive." His words dropped off. "That's what you mean. The planes didn't fit the airport."

Burnie sighed. "I think that is exactly what I mean. I had noticed that when I drove into town and wondered about it. I think that there is more going on that what we have discovered. What if Muir was not to be sent overseas, but was being used to break her and then use her against her parents? Let them know that she was alive and that she would never be reunited with them unless they did something the men wanted?"

Muir paced their living room later that day, her arms wrapped around herself. Burnie had been in, spoken briefly with her and then headed for his office downstairs. He had hated to do that but he had to write. He was driven to work on his manuscript, the words tumbling over one another in his mind. She returned to the kitchen, her finger lightly touching the photo that Emma had sent and that he had printed for her.

"There wasn't anyone else that I could see in the store. Just Stewart, Burnie and myself. But this is Michael, the man who helped Granny escape. Was I right? Was he an angel sent from God." Muir stopped speaking out loud, her eyes raising to the ceiling. "Was that You, God, looking after me?"

She then turned to the photo he had taken of the time line. She frowned. What was he after, Muir wondered? What was he looking for? She picked it up, returning to curl up on the couch, or sofa as Granny called it. Muir was puzzled. There was something missing, and she wasn't sure what.

Finally dropping the photo beside her, she reached for the Bible that Burnie had given her as a wedding gift. Muir's hand rubbed along the cover before she opened it, seeking verses that would calm her and then teach her to trust. That, she decided, was what she was needed. To learn to trust. And that came with difficulty.

Moira tapped at the door and then entered, watching Muir for a moment. She's been through so much, Lord, so much more than I would have ever expected. She needs this break from Morgan and McRae. I am not sure how they will ever become a family. There is too much time between them. Even I feel like I never knew them.

Muir looked up as her Granny sank down beside her, and then handed her the photo.

"Burnie did this. He plotted our adventure, as he calls it, out as a timeline in one of his novels. But there is something or someone missing. I just don't know who."

Moira studied it, before she tapped the photo. "He's really thought it out. But this here, where you ran for the airport? How much time passed by? I thought it was the next day."

Muir shook her head. "No. The explosion happened in the morning. I saw the plane landing that afternoon. Did Burnie ever say how they knew?"

"I'm not sure, child. That's something you'll need to ask him. But the plane? The airport was a ways from the store."

"I know. I had hidden in the trees and watched as they dragged Burnie away. Stewart kept calling for me. I just kept moving away from the store, away from town, and towards the airport. I don't know why I did that. I didn't want to go into town. I was that afraid. But I was worried about Burnie."

"I am sure that you were." Moira looked across the room, before she spoke. "Did you ever notice that the number of planes coming in had increased in the last years?"

"I did, Granny. They would come in, the men would go into town and then come back a few hours later. Why?"

"There had been rumours that there was an illegal gaming site there, for gambling." Moira watched her granddaughter. "Did any of the men ever come into the store?"

"Never. I couldn't understand that. I also couldn't understand why the store was off by itself like that."

"It hadn't been. Morgan had chosen a nice spot in town, but when he disappeared and Stewart took over, he moved it outside of town. There were protests that really didn't do much."

"I never knew that, Granny." Muir paled. "Was there something under the store?"

"What do you mean?"

"Like a tunnel or store room or something?" Muir searched frantically for her phone, finding it on the table beside her, and then sending off a text message to Dallas. "I'll ask Dallas. Maybe there was something there that he couldn't tell us."

"That's good." Moira's hand came out to stroke Muir's hair. "I'm sorry, Muir, that you had to undergo this. You shouldn't have had to."

"I know, Granny, but you always taught me that God was in control, that He allowed things and events."

"I know, child. That's what I believe. But to keep you from your parents for all these years? That's difficult to understand."

Muir shrugged, her eyes on the flowers on the coffee table in front of her. "I don't know that we will understand here on earth, Granny. But how do we do this? How do we stay safe and keep Burnie safe? Stewart is around. I can feel him. He'll go after Burnie for revenge."

"And you as well. We need to keep you safe, Muir." Moira was silent for a moment. "Did I ever tell you why you are called Muir?"

Muir stared at her for a moment before she shook her head. "I don't think so. I never thought about it, to tell you the truth."

"Muir was your mother's maiden name. In her family, it was tradition that the oldest girl took her mother's maiden name for her name. Your maternal grandmother was a McRae, that's how your mother got her name. And then your grandmother's name was McKenzie." Moira paused, a thought crossing her mind. "Have we traced back our trees, Muir? I don't remember doing that. Maybe there's something there."

"I thought of that, Granny. I emailed that Emma friend of Burnie. She got back to me right away. One of Abe's men? His wife has a family tree program. She had asked Emma for any information on us. I sent what I could. Emma said that she'd be back to me as soon as she could. Do you think there was something there?"

"Perhaps. It was always odd that your father and mother had to return to Ireland for business. As far as we knew, we had settled everything before we left."

"So they were enticed back there?" Muir shook her head. "I don't understand why." She looked up as she heard footsteps and Burnie and Blair appeared. "Burnie?"

"Muir. I think I have found a connection. Emma sent me some information. Kataleen, a friend, is working on your background, she said, but she wanted me to have this." Burnie held out a sheet of paper. "Your family is connected years ago with Holman."

"We are?" Muir paled. "We're related? Is that why?"

Burnie paced the conference room later that day, his friends watching him. He was puzzled. How had Kataleen traced that back, he wondered? He wasn't sure how she did what she did, but he was unsettled. Muir and Moira had not said much and that concerned him.

"Burnie?" Branigan waited for Burnie to turn towards him before he held out the sheaf of papers that he was holding. "You need to see these."

"And these are?" Burnie took them, his eyes on Branigan.

"Confirmation that there was a cellar to the store. Muir asked Dallas about it. He just got back to me. He tried to reach you."

Burnie sighed. "I muted my phone when I was writing. I need to stop doing that."

"Yes, you do. It could mean your life or Muir's." Branigan simply shook his head and walked away.

Burnie returned to the chair he favoured, dropping the papers to the desk, and praying first. He read through them, looked at the photos, and then raised his head. "What was the meaning of this room?" He was puzzled. The room, Dallas noted, was empty and had been cleaned recently. The techs had not picked up on anything there, or had the dogs that had been brought in.

"Puzzled, Burnie?" Blair sat beside him.

"I am. Muir questioned if there was a room or something under the store. Dallas has confirmed that there was and provided photos that he said could be released to us. I didn't think that he could."

"If they're not relevant, then he likely cleared it. May I?" Blair reached for the photos. "These are interesting." He frowned. "There were shelves there. You can see the spots on the walls."

"I noticed that. I wonder what they had down there."

"Something illegal for sure." Blair leaned closer to the photo and then paled. "Burnie? Did you see this?"

"See what?" Burnie had already moved on to new research.

"Here? The shackles?"

"What?" Burnie stared at Blair before he reached for the photos. He paled. "Shackles. Who did they have down there?"

"Somehow, I think they would have put you down there, if the fellows hadn't turned up. Who called Barnabas?"

"You know, I'm not sure that I was told." Burnie frowned. "And we can't ask him. He's away for a couple of days, he said."

"He is. Breck might know." Blair was on his feet, heading out of the room, to try and track down Breck. He was back in short order, returning to sit beside Burnie. "It was an anonymous call, just that you were in trouble and someone needed to come rescue you."

"Michael?"

"Michael? It might have been, but it could have been anyone in the town." Blair frowned. "I guess it's not relevant."

"But it could be." Burnie pointed to the timeline that he had created. "I added some stuff. I'm not sure how far or deep to probe."

"As far as we need to. Burnie? Has Muir talked much more about what it was like? Don't tell me if it's confidential."

Burnie shrugged. "She's not saying much. She's burying it and I don't like that. I have tried to get her to talk, but she's not ready to. Not yet." He buried his face into his hands. "This is so hard."

"We know, Burnie. We know. We are praying for both of you. Has Buckley talked with you?"

Burnie nodded, as he looked up, a bleak look around his eyes. "He has. And Locklin has been talking with Muir. And I know that Darcie has been calling Muir every day. Muir says that helps, that Darcie is able to give her advice and a perspective that no one else can." Burnie sat back, his eyes on Blair. "How do I help her?"

"By doing what you're doing. Loving her. Letting her have her space. Let her rage and cry and scream if she needs to."

"You went through that with Devaney?"

"I did. Even now, there are times when it all comes back. With our little one almost here, she's finding her emotions are all over the place."

"I can understand that." Burnie stopped for a moment. "Blair, if it was you, what would you do? What would you look into?"

"Me? I would start with Morgan and McRae. It just seems odd that they didn't make any attempt to escape, not until now. Who did they talk to over there? And if they talked, why didn't it go any further?"

Burnie pointed a finger at Blair. "There. That's what has me puzzled. Why now? Why not before? Emma might have an idea. I'll call her." He was on his feet, almost running from the room, heading for his office, needing the silence that he would find there and the privacy that he needed.

Burnie finally set his phone now, determination on his face. He had just had a long conversation with Emma and Kataleen who had been there. The two ladies had thought of questions that he hadn't known he needed to ask. He stared at the myriad pages of notes that he now had to make sense of. He glanced at the clock and rose, gathering his papers and heading for his home.

Muir turned as he entered, coming towards him eagerly for his hug and kiss, and then just standing, their arms wrapped around one another, feeling the doom that was gathering over them.

"Burnie? You have changed. What happened?" Muir leaned back to look up at him.

"We'll talk, sweetheart. But you have lunch ready for us?"

"I do. Breck was by. He was looking for you." She turned to ladle out the soup that she had heated.

"He was? I'll catch up with him later."

The meal over, Burnie rose to clear the table, his hand on Muir's shoulder keeping her in her chair. Then he sat once more, his hands reaching for hers, his head bowing as he prayed for them, a desperation in his prayer that Muir had not heard before.

"Burnie?" Muir raised her head, to find him staring at the papers in front on him.

"Muir? You said that your family had been tracked back to Holman. It's not the Holmans here that you are related to. They are a totally separate branch. Stewart had tried to take advantage of your lack of knowledge. I had a long conversation with Emma and Kataleen just a while ago. This is what came from it." He tapped the papers. "We need to sort through it all before I talk to the fellows. I think this will help a lot."

"So, where do we start?" Muir reached for the papers, sorting through them, and then beginning reading. "I didn't know that Dad was one of the founders of the village. Granny never said."

"We'll ask her, but I don't think that it was common knowledge. He had been approached by a friend to move here and do that. They had drawn up a village charter, set the details out for a village constabulary as he called it. I don't know where Emma found all this, but she did. She'll forward it to us and to Dallas. It helps to explain Stewart's motivation."

"It does. He wanted to be rich. He would tell me that. It angers me that he did what he did to me. And to Mom and Dad." Muir sat back, a thought passing through her mind. "How do we know for sure that they are Mom and Dad?"

"Emma said Abe thought of that and has asked for DNA samples from them. They have been resisting."

"And that makes them suspects, doesn't it? Are they even my parents or are they imposters?"

"At the moment, they are suspects and that's why Abe pulled them back to where he could watch them. He doesn't trust them. He'll keep them on his Rebel's compound for now. He's working with both the force here, the force in his town, and the authorities overseas. It's a priority for him. Emma said he'd be sending someone over to talk with us at some point over the next few days."

"I'm getting tired of talking. I want this over with. How do we do just that? Put ourselves out as targets?"

Burnie grinned at the disgruntled look on her face. "We could do that, but I think Dallas would want to be involved in the planning. For now, we stick close to here."

"And it's not much safer, is it?" Muir rose, heading for the kettle to make herself another cup of tea, reaching to refill Burnie's mug of coffee, before she reached for the plate of cookies sitting on the counter. "I worry about Granny."

"I know. I do too. Emma talked to me. They would like to have her come and visit them, staying with some friends who don't live on their property."

"They would do that?" Muir finally nodded. "We should get her to do that. But it might be difficult."

"Emma has approached her already. She is agreeable."

"Emma did? What doesn't Emma do?"

"Emma and Abe had their own adventure as did all of his men and many friends of theirs. I trust him to keep her safe."

"When?" Muir's voice was barely above a whisper, knowing that she would be going through the next while without the stability that her Granny had provided.

"Soon, Muir. Soon." Burnie simply reached to draw her to himself. "I'll do my best to step up and keep you safe. So will all the fellows. It's what we do for one another."

Muir nodded against him. "I know, Burnie, but it's hard. The six months that she was out of my life were so long. Not just because of what I went through."

"We know, sweetheart. We know. We'll do our best. Right now, let's pray. I need to learn to trust even more than I do."

"I need to see Granny." Muir began to sob, her heartbreaking weeping breaking Burnie's heart as he held her, finally shoving back his chair enough to simply draw her to his knee and weep with her. Muir's tears finally stopped, but she made no effort to move from him.

"Muir? I love you more each day. I will do my utmost to keep you safe." Burnie bit at his lip. "Right now, it's what we know to be the most dangerous part of this. Stewart will be after both of us. We don't know who else is involved, so we have to be extra cautious. We still live. We go about our normal daily walk. We go out for dinners, on dates. We work."

"I understand, Burnie." Muir's voice was still tear-filled. "But it's dangerous for anyone around us."

"We know that, too, Muir. We take as many precautions as we can." Burnie's head tilted as he watched her. "Right now, I'm happy just to hold you and comfort you. But we do need to work."

"I know." Muir sighed. "What can I do to help you? Am I banned from the conference room?"

"Absolutely not. Here. Let's wash your face and we'll head down there. In fact, I think it's a great idea that you're down there. We sometimes have questions that we need to set aside. If you're there, we can ask right away."

Two days later, Muir walked along the wall in the conference room, studying the material and noting the new information that had been added. She stopped at the logic problem, her finger up to trace the questions and names. She frowned. What had they been trying to discover, she wondered? Brody stood near her.

"Muir? You're puzzled by the puzzle?" He grinned as she frowned at him.

"I am. I don't understand what you were trying to discover. It doesn't make sense."

Brody nodded. "Sometimes things don't." He reached to hand her a marker and pointed to a clean board. "How be you try one?"

"Me? Make up a puzzle? I'm puzzle enough without that. Besides, I wouldn't now what to ask."

"Just write down what is puzzling you. Then work from that." Brody turned to walk away, stopping as Muir asked him to stay.

"I need your help, Brody. I don't understand how this all works, but I'll give it a try." Muir stepped back after a while, the board covered in her neat handwriting. "I did all that?"

"You did, Muir. You did. You think out loud, do you know that?" Brody grinned as he held up a pad of paper. "I made notes."

"You did? Care to share?"

"Certainly. There are some things here that aren't on the board." Brody looked up as Buckley and Benen approached. "Muir's working on her own logic problem. She didn't like ours."

"Yours is okay. It just didn't make sense to me." Muir read through Brody's notes, pausing at one comment. "I said that? Stewart had no sister, not that I know of. Why would I refer to her?"

"A lady?" Benen reached for the notes. "When was this?"

"I think about eight months ago. She was around for about a week. He introduced her as his sister, even though we all knew that he only had a brother." Muir paled. "What happened to her?"

"Did you have a name?"

Muir shook her head. "No, no name. He just called her his sister. Funny thing is that he wouldn't let her out of his sight."

"No, I don't think he would. Can you describe her?"

Muir did that, not catching the glances that the men were exchanging.

Burnie stopped beside her, an arm around her. "Muir, this lady? Do you know how much she resembles you?"

Muir turned her head to watch him. "No, not really. She was only five foot tall, if that. And heavier. Her hair was the wrong colour. I think it had been dyed. And her eyes were strange."

"Contact lenses, then." Brody made notes. "I wonder if she was there as a captive or as someone who was in control. It may have looked as if Holman was keeping her in his control. What if it was the other way around? She was watching him, keeping him in her control?"

"I would hazard a guess that's what it was." Brendon reached for the papers, reading through them. "I want a copy of this. Do you mind, Brody?"

"No, go ahead. Make a copy for Dallas as well."

Muir walked back along the wall, the marker in her hand underlying certain events and statements. Brandon watched her, before he turned to Burnie.

"Burnie? What's she doing?"

"Making sense of it all. I think that we were remiss in trying to protect her from being here. She's driven so much down inside that I think it will all come out at once." Burnie watched her closely once more. "I wonder what she's found."

Muir turned back to Burnie, walking into his arms and hugging him. "I found out who it is, Burnie. It's been there all along. I just needed to follow the steps."

———

1053

"You know who it is?" Burnie looked up at the sudden silence in the room.

"I do. Everything that I have underlined? Write it all down in the order that I numbered it. Then we talk. Right now, I need to see Granny and she's already left."

"I'm sorry, Muir. She has. What can we do?"

"Just find this monster. He's here somewhere, I just know." Muir sank into a chair, her head going down on her folded arms, her body shuddering from the deep sigh that she drew.

———

Her hand tight in Burnie's, Muir wandered along the sand by Lake Erie, her hair tossed by the light wind that had come up. She was amazed at the sight of the lake, watching the waves roll in.

Burnie grinned at her smile, knowing that this was what she had needed, to do something that took her away from her thoughts. He reached to kiss her, and then pointed to a lake freighter.

Muir nodded, her eyes on Burnie instead. Lord, I am afraid. I am afraid for my man, that something is going happen and happen today. How do we stop that? Or do we? Do we really have to go through more danger and trials and troubles? I know that You are here with us and if You chose, nothing would happen. But sometimes we need those trials in order to grow. Teach me to trust You as I should.

Burnie hesitated for a moment and then turned their steps back towards the pathway to the building.

"Having fun, sweetheart?"

"I am." Muir nodded. "I needed this. There is something calming about watching the waves. I want to see this lake in the middle of a storm, to remember that I know Who it is who calms them."

"We can do that. Late fall is a good time for that. We can get gale-force winds at that time."

"Burnie? Have you heard from Granny?"

"No, I haven't. Abe said that would likely be the case. To try and hide her away somewhere that she couldn't be used against you." Burnie sighed, knowing what she was asking. "If something had happened to her, he would have been in touch."

"I know. I just need to speak with her." Muir's eyes raised to the trees that they were asking under. "How many paths are there to the lake?"

"A few. Some go through the fields and clearings around us. This is my favourite one. But somehow, I think I made a mistake." He suddenly began to run, heading for home, Muir's flying feet keeping step with him.

Burnie slid to a halt as a man appeared in their path, a weapon held on them. He tried to back up, feeling a weapon against his back. His free hand raised, his other hand keeping a tight grip on Muir.

"What do you want?"

"You two. You're coming with us." The man motioned with his weapon. "Now, head off that way. And no funny stuff."

Muir's hand tightened on Burnie's as they moved away, away from the safety of the building and their friends, away towards what, they didn't know. They were forced to walk for a couple of miles before they were shoved into a cave and then deeper into another cave. Burnie's arm came around Muir, as they stood, staring at the empty entrance, but knowing that the men were still out there. They could hear their movements.

"Muir? If you get a chance, run. Head back the way we came. I know this area. If you head towards the tallest pine tree that you can see, that's where our building is."

"Not without you." Muir's imploring look almost broke his heart.

"I need you to do that for me. Promise? I'll be right behind you. That I will try to do."

Burnie paced the cave, his eyes on the entrance before flickering to Muir, watching as she huddled on the floor, her arms wrapped around herself. He sighed. That was not a good idea, he thought, going to the lake. How did he get word to the others? He had let Baird know what they were doing and giving him a time that they should return. Baird would check on them and then head for help to come and find them. Please, Lord, let my lady live and get away.

———

Burnie listened closely late that afternoon, hearing nothing from the other cave. He walked that way, Muir's hand on his back. He stopped, listening, and then peered outside. He couldn't see the men.

"Run, Muir. Head for home. I'm right behind you." Burnie shoved at her, watching as she ran, before he ran after her.

A sudden sharp pain in his chest drove him backwards and to the ground, where he lay, sprawled on his back, an arrow protruding from his chest. The world disappeared into a swirling darkness as he lost consciousness. He didn't hear Muir's scream or feel her hands on him, trying to rouse him. Burnie didn't see the men who stood over them before one of them pulled Muir to her feet and away from him. She began to fight him, breaking free and running, the sound of his pounding feet coming after her.

Muir searched for some place to hide, not finding anything, her fear spurring her on. She gave a scream as the land dropped off in front of her before she plunged over a cliff, to lie in a sprawled, motionless heap on a pile of evergreens. The man following her peered over and then nodded, moving away, a smile of satisfaction on his face. There was no way that she'd survive that, he decided. He ran back the way that he had come, finding his companion ready to leave.

"He's not going to be going anywhere." The man's voice was gruff. "Let's get out of here? What about her?"

"Ran over a cliff. She's likely dead. I'm not going down to find out. Let's move." They disappeared, leaving the two forms crumpled and appearing lifeless behind them.

Pounding at Burnie's door, Brody finally just rested his hand against it. There was no answer, just as there had been no answer at Burnie's office door. It was past time that Burnie thought that they would be back. Burnie, where are you? Brody turned and ran for the conference room, the door flying open as he ran in.

"Brody?" Barnabas was on his feet.

"Burnie and Muir. They went for a walk towards the lake. I tried to talk him out of it. They were to be home by now and aren't. I can't get an answer at his office or his apartment."

The men were on their feet, flying from the room, heading to dress for the weather and their search, backpacks in place as they met in the parking lot.

"We'll pray and then split up into teams, each team taking a path." Barnabas led them off in prayer and then watched as they scattered. "Bradon? You're ready with Kade?"

"I am. We're taking the path through the woods?"

"We are. He likes that one, I know."

Kade suddenly alerted, drawing Bradon's attention before he tugged at his leash, wanting to head away from the lake.

"He's hit on something, Barnabas. I say let's follow him."

"I agree. I don't like this, Bradon. Rain is moving in."

"It is. Let's move ourselves."

Kade surged ahead, suddenly stopping before he gave a loud bark and then frantically tried to move away from Bradon. Bradon dropped the leash, watching as Kade ran forward, not waiting for his master to follow.

"He's hit on something." Barnabas ran after him, following Bradon.

"It's Burnie." Bradon was on his knees, shoving Kade away. "An arrow?"

"An arrow. Who did that?" Barnabas looked around. "No sign of Muir. Where is she?"

"I don't know, but I'm calling in." Bradon did that, and then shoved his pack from his back, pulling out a folded emergency blanket and wrapping it around Burnie. "He's not coming to at all, Barnabas."

"I know." Barnabas knelt beside his friend, his hand resting on his arm, even as a prayer wafted heavenward for him.

Thirty minutes later, the two men stood back, watching as the emergency personnel worked on Burnie, and the officers searched the area.

"Burnie would not have left her, not on his own." Brady spoke up. "Where is she? Bradon, can Kade track her?"

"Likely." Bradon moved away from the commotion, then hand on Kade's head, gave the command to find Muir. "Go, boy. Find Muir."

Kade raised his head, gave a woof, and then started his search, heading towards the cliff, intent on following the scent that he associated with Muir.

"Oh, no! The cliff!" Breck ran towards it, followed by most of the men, sliding to a halt as he watched Kade alert at the edge. He gripped a hand and leaned over. "I see her. She's not moving."

"Can I get down there?" Brady was on his knees, looking over. "It's not that far. Six or seven feet." He was over the edge, dropping and rolling as he landed, before he scrambled towards Muir, a hand reaching for a pulse. "She's alive, fellows. But I'll need a backboard and neck collar."

"On it!" Breck ran back towards where the emergency personnel were still working on Burnie, ready to move him. "We found Muir! She's over the cliff. Brady needs a backboard and collar!"

The men spun, one running towards him, one running for the rig parked not far away, even as the other two paramedics lifted Burnie's stretcher and moved away as rapidly as they could.

———

Two hours later, Barnabas paced the waiting room in the Emergency room. The men from the building paced as well, both inside and outside. The ladies had gathered in the chapel, praying for their friends, Anna with them. Doc was on duty in the department, appearing briefly just to let them know that Burnie and Muir were being taken care of.

Dallas appeared and then headed back to speak with Doc, not liking the report that Doc gave him. It was grave enough for Burnie, but with Muir, they were still awaiting imaging studies to be reported, he said. He had simply shaken his head at Dallas and then pointed him away. Emergency was busy that day, and Doc was rushed. They didn't see the men standing in the corner of the waiting room, eyeing the doorway to the examination rooms. Breck finally pulled Barnabas aside.

"What is Doc not saying?" Breck kept his eyes on the waiting room, watching carefully.

"I don't know. You know Doc. He's careful with patient confidentiality. I suspect that until he has permission from Moira to talk about Muir, he won't. Do you know if she's her next of kin?"

"I have a call into Abe. He's faxing something in once he's talked to her, to let them speak with you or I."

"Good. I hate this, Breck. All of the men have ended up here at some point."

"I know. That just leaves you and me, you know."

"I know." Barnabas grew silent, his mind drifting back in time before he shook his head. "I always feel like there has been something left hanging, though."

"I know what you mean. I think that there is." Breck nodded towards Doc as he headed for them. "Here's Doc. I'll just step away."

"Breck, stay. You're named in the document that Moira signed." Doc sighed, getting tired of treating his young friends. "She's given permission for me to talk to you both. Until Burnie is able to make decisions, she has asked that you or Breck do, Barnabas. Abe will bring her here if we need her to be."

"And do we?" Barnabas prayed that was not the case.

———

"Not yet. And I don't know that we will. What did Muir land on?"

"A pile of evergreen branches." Breck shared a look with Barnabas. "But how did they get there? There shouldn't have been."

"God again." Doc pointed to the outside. "Let's walk for a moment. I need a breath of fresh air." He tucked his reading glasses into his pocket.

After a few minutes, Doc began to talk, to detail Burnie's injuries.

"The arrow missed anything vital, even to blood vessels. He's being stitched up by the surgeon in the exam room. He's been awake and refused to leave there, wanting to get up and find Muir."

"Of course, he would. Muir?" Barnabas was almost afraid to ask.

"Now, Muir. I have no explanation, Barnabas, Breck. She's battered and bruised. She knocked herself out somehow, but she has not internal injuries. No broken bones. I can't explain it."

"That's God at work, Doc." Breck blinked rapidly. Muir had become like a sister to him, as had all the ladies. "Thank God. But I can't explain how the branches ended up there."

"Nor can I. They shouldn't have been." Barnabas stared at the pavement in front of his feet. "Someone prepared that, knowing that Muir would run that way. I'm not going to probe it any further."

"No, I don't think we can. Give us some time and I'll get you both in to see them. They can go home today."

Burnie moved carefully through the apartment the next day, his arm in sling to prevent the muscles from pulling. He sighed. This is not what he needed, not at this time. He turned as he heard Muir moving around in the bedroom and headed that way, finding her sitting on the side of the bed. He sat beside her, an arm around her.

"Muir?"

She nodded, sniffing, wiping at the tears on her face before she leaned against him.

"I'm tired of this, Burnie. I'm tired of being chased and hurt and destroyed. For what? We haven't even figured that out. I talked to Dallas a few moments ago, when you were in the shower. He's heading this way. He wants to talk to us. All we seem to do is talk."

Burnie dropped a kiss on her head. "I know, sweetheart. It's hard. It's hard to trust at times like this."

"It is. I keep praying this to be over." She wiped her hands along her jeans. "I heard from Kataleen. She said she's sending more material to us."

"She is? Did she say anything?"

Muir nodded. "She's proven that Stewart is not in our line at all. So what he was saying was all talk. She also said she was sending a document that we needed to look at together. She refused to say what it was, only that she was praying for us."

"She did, did she? That's what getting us through, you know. The prayers of our church and the prayers of our friends." Burnie grew quiet, not sure what to say.

"Burnie, what would have happened if you had not been there? Given what we know now, was I to be sent overseas?"

"I doubt it. I think it was all talk on Stewart's part. He wanted to control you, and keep you down and in the store. He didn't pay you, did he?"

Muir shook her head. "No, he said he provided room and board. That was all I could expect to get." She grew angry for a moment. "I let him do that to me."

"You didn't have an escape."

"Not until you and your friends showed up. Did Dallas ever say anything more about what they found?"

"No, he hasn't. I asked him. He said it was still in the preliminary investigation stage. That there was a lot of work to do. Ker wonders if some of the teens that disappeared from her town ended up there."

"That's sad, you know. I guess that's the evil that we have around us. God protects us, I know that, but there is just so much evil." Muir finally rose, heading for the kitchen, reaching for her tea that Burnie had made for her. She turned as she heard his footsteps. "How's your shoulder?"

"It hurts and will for a while. The surgeon said I was lucky. I told him it was God. He just stared at me."

"We've been able to witness to others through all this, haven't we? Even the others have commented that they have been able to share with the medical staff and others." Muir sipped at her cooling tea. "Burnie, when this is all over, do we stay here?"

"Here? As in the building?" At her nod, he simply hugged her. "If you want. I would like to. It's been my home for many years. But if you feel you want to move, I will do that."

"You would?" Muir tilted her head back to look up at him. "No, I love the building here. The family that we have. I never had that, other than Granny."

"Then we stay." The young couple stood for a while. "I would like to take you away for a vacation, belated honeymoon, whatever you want to call it, when this is over."

"You would? Where?"

He shrugged. "I have no idea. Ireland?"

———

Muir shook her head. "No, I don't think so. This is my country. I have always wanted to go to the Maritimes."

"Then, we'll head there. There are lots of areas that we can explore. And we can take day trips here in Ontario. And when I get to travel for my books, you come with me."

"I do?"

"You do." Burnie stepped back, a frown on his face as he heard a tap at the door. "Were we expecting anyone?"

Muir shrugged. "Not that I know of, but it's become like a train or bus station lately."

Burnie was laughing at her comment as he opened the door, to find Barnabas and Breck standing there, Branigan with them, and Abe coming along the hallway.

"Fellows? Come on it. The coffee's on, but somehow I don't think that you're here for coffee."

"We can be, but we need to speak with both of you. Dallas is about five minutes out, he said." Breck hugged Muir on the way by. "And how are you, Muir?"

"Sore and puzzled."

"You are? About what?"

"About that pile of evergreens. Who put them there?"

"God. That's the only explanation that we can come up with." Branigan gave her a hug as well, before reaching for the mug that Breck was extending to him. "Can we meet in the office or the living room?"

"Office, I think, Branigan. That way, if we need the computer, we'll have it." Burnie reached for Muir's hand, finding hers cold.

Muir sat beside Burnie, her hand tight in his, watching the other men carefully. Breck had taken a seat at Burnie's computer, after Burnie had signed in, ready to search if needed. Abe had simply shaken his head and handed over the folder that he had brought with him.

Burnie had taken it, a frown on his face, then bowed his head as Abe prayed. The other men followed, Branigan bringing it to a close. They sat for a few moments before Burnie opened the folder, staring down at the picture.

"These are the people who said that they were Muir's parents."

"They are. They look enough like them to fool even Moira. Although Moira has said that something seemed off about them. She put that down to being so many years."

"But it's not, is it?" Muir leaned against Burnie and frowned. "I see what you mean, Burnie. They aren't my parents." She was on her feet, running from the room and then returning with a faded photograph. "These are my parents. Who are these people?"

"Actors that were hired. They had to undergo plastic surgery to alter their looks. They were paid well enough that they agreed to it." Abe looked at Muir. "I'm sorry, Muir, for our part in this."

"You didn't know? How could you?" Muir watched him. "But you had hesitation, didn't you? That's why you removed them."

"You're correct, Muir. Something just seemed off to all of my men. We agreed that we needed to pull them away. We have been in constant contact with the Irish authorities. The couple finally confessed last night as to what they had been hired to do." Abe looked down before he looked up at Muir, sorrow in his eyes. "I'm sorry, Muir. We have confirmation that there was a plane crash on a remote island. Your parents' remains have been discovered. If you wish, we can return them here for you to bury."

"Talk to Granny. I'll abide by what she said. Who?" Muir's voice had dropped to a whisper. She didn't remember her parents, so to bury them here was not really a thought that she had had.

"We have. She has said to bury them in the family plot in Ireland."

Muir nodded, before she reached to flip the photo over. "Who is this person?"

"That's what we're finding out. He was a business partner of your father. In fact, he is the one who your father was to meet with when he returned to Ireland. This man? He's skirted close to the edge of the law all his life. We are surmising that is why your father moved away. He was trying to draw your father into illegal activities and was making it difficult for your father to continue to live in your home town."

"I see. You know, he looks like Stewart. Are they related?"

"You have a good eye, Muir." Burnie turned to the next page. "He's a nephew of the man. How did he end up here?"

"He was sent over before your father came over. Holman sent him over. And yes, the man's name is Holman. We talked to Moira. She had never know the man's name, only knew of him. Your father had never given the name." Abe looked up as Dallas appeared, Branigan having gone to the door.

"Dallas?" Muir looked up at him, seeing the fatigue in his face. "You're here."

Dallas grinned for a moment. "I am. I need to talk to you as well."

They talked for a while longer before everyone but Dallas left. He sat back, his eyes closing for a moment.

"Dallas? You needed to talk to us?" Burnie spoke quietly

Dallas nodded before his eyes opened. "I do. Muir, I regret to inform you that Stewart Holman was killed in a hit and run last night. We just got word this morning."

"He's dead?" Muir was shocked. "Now what?'

"Now we continue to piece together the parts that aren't. We're still a long ways away from that. I can't stress how much you two need to still practice safety."

"We know that, Dallas. What else?" Muir watched him closely.

"One of his known associates is in town. He's asking about you and Burnie." Dallas sighed. "The people on the street aren't talking. They respect the Foundation too much to do that, the Foundation having helped out many of them over the years. He knows where the building is. He was followed here one day. We had no reason to stop him."

"I see. So that leaves us vulnerable?" Burnie shut his eyes, picturing a possible scenario. "How do we go on the offensive, Dallas? I want this over."

"We've been discussing that with our PR people. We could do a television interview, but they think just a statement issued by them will help. It means that it will draw out whoever it is and they will come after you even harder."

"We understand, Dallas, but we can't continue to live as we are. It's not fair to Muir."

Dallas finally rose, his eyes on the couple before he walked away. They're planning something, aren't they, Lord? Protect them.

The next morning, Muir paced the walkways in the garden, Burnie keeping step with her. They had spent the night in prayer and made a decision to go on the offensive. They had stopped in the conference room before they came out, the men listening to their plans, discussing it, adding to it. She knew that some of the men were hidden around them, as were some of the security team. That they were taking a risk, she knew. She just prayed that no one was hurt.

"Burnie, are we doing the right thing?" Muir looked up at him.

He nodded. "I think so. I pray so. We had peace about it, Muir, when we left the conference room. I pray that it ends today. I know that there will be investigations to complete, court to face, but if we can trap the men and the ones responsible then it's over."

Muir sighed. "I just wish it was all over. I hate living like this. Stewart has taken so much from me. His uncle took much more. Did they arrest him?"

"They have. They found all sorts of information that the authorities over there will be working through. They also found confirmation that you were a target, just because. Apparently in the town bylaws, you would take over the biggest portion of the town when you turn thirty. They were trying to prevent that. They had a nice little scheme going."

"I was? Does Granny know that?"

"Abe was going to speak with her, but Dallas asked him not to. He wants Moira to return here and then he's planning on talking with both of you."

"I see." Muir's footsteps slowed. "Burnie?"

"Yes, love." When Muir didn't respond, he looked up, a frown on his face before it cleared. "Of course, Dennis Holman. I never connected you."

The man, in his late sixties, stood in front of them, a heavy walking stick in his hand. His face was a true picture of pure evil as he glared at them.

"You should have. That oversight will cost you dearly." He motioned to Muir. "Walk towards me. Now!" His voice rose as she retreated. "I said, walk towards me."

Muir simply shook her head and retreated some more, Burnie moving with her. "I don't think so. I remember seeing you in the store and around the village. I didn't know who you were, though."

"No, we kept that carefully from you and your granny. It wouldn't have made any difference. You see, you've just written a will, deeding your property there to me when you die. Not to your husband or anyone else. It belongs to me. It should have all along." The man's face grew more cruel as he paced carefully towards her, his limp pronounced as he held his walking stick up high.

"I don't think so. I wouldn't do that." Muir screamed as the heavy stick landed on her shoulder, sending her to the ground in horrible pain. She heard Burnie cry out and then there was silence.

Burnie was on his knees beside her before he swept her up and ran for the infirmary, Brady beside him. Brady's hands were gentle as he felt her shoulder.

"Broken?" Burnie was afraid, his own chest hurting from the movement and weight of carrying his sweetheart to safety.

"I don't think so. She was moving down when he struck at her. Kade took him down before he really hit her hard."

"Thanks to Kade, once more. We own him a nice raw steak dinner." Burnie's hand rested on Muir's face. "Do we need X-Rays?"

Brady nodded. "We will. Let me talk to the officers who are out there. One of them will take us in." He was back in short order. "Okay, let's move, Burnie. We have an escort. I'm driving and you're with me."

Muir turned restlessly that night, her shoulder paining her, before she stilled, watching Burnie as he slept, her head pillowed on his shoulder before she too slept. Dallas had called just as they were heading off for the night, weariness in his voice, but jubilance as well. He had stated that Holman was the head of it all, and that they would be arresting everyone else over the next day or so. Could the two of them just stay out of trouble for a bit, he pleaded.

A week later, Burnie sat in the conference room, his sling gone, his arm around his sweetheart, pulling her tight to him. She smiled up at him, peace on her face at long last. It had been a long time coming, he thought. Dallas had asked for the meeting. Now, to find out why and who.

Dallas entered finally, Will Peters with him, a sheaf of folders in his hands that he dropped onto a nearby table. He searched the room, finding Moira and heading towards her.

"Moira? I am sorry about Morgan and McRae."

Moira nodded before she reached to hug him. "I knew it wasn't them, but I couldn't be sure. It had been too long. I am glad that we know where they are now. It will give us closure." She looked towards Muir. "Muir is happy, and that makes me happy. I have not told Muir yet, but I'm moving into an apartment in town. I need to. For my sake and for hers. She has a life now with Burnie."

"They won't want you to." Dallas reached to hug her again. "They will want you nearby."

"I know that, but they need this time to themselves. They're newlyweds. They need to learn about one another without an old woman interfering."

"Not interfering, Moira. You have become Granny to all of us here. All of the men but Breck and Barnabas have no family. Some of the ladies as well. The little ones who are coming will be delighted to have a great-granny to spoil them."

"I know that, Dallas, but I can do that from town. It's time for me to move on." Moira nodded towards the front. "I think that they are waiting for you."

Dallas moved to the front, pausing beside Buckley. "Buckley, will you? I know that it's Barnabas' place to ask you."

"He already has. Thank you, Dallas, for what you've done for all of us. I know it's been a strain on you. I can tell you're wearing out."

"I am, Buckley. I am trying to make a decision and would appreciate your prayers."

"You have had them." Buckley was on his feet, moving to the front, waiting for the room to quiet before he prayed, a powerful prayer that seemed to lift them right up to the throne of God. He waited for a moment when he finished before he raised his head, his eyes on Muir, frowning. No, he was seeing things. There was not someone standing behind her. He blinked, and the person had disappeared.

Barnabas rose, his eyes roaming the room. The men and ladies of the building have been through so much, Lord, some almost dying. You have protected them, strengthened them, and brought them their life partners. His eyes turned to Breck, who stood at the back of the room, leaning against the wall. For my old friend, Breck, Lord, I sense that he is next and that he too will face danger. Protect him, Lord. And for myself? You know what I wish. Grant it if it be Your will.

Barnabas finally cleared his throat and spoke, talking with each couple before he came to Burnie and Muir.

"Burnie. Muir. What can I say? God has provided for and protected you. Muir, you are a welcome part of our family, Burnie's helpmeet. He has waited his whole life for you. Now, it's my turn to be quiet and let Dallas speak. Before I do, I just want to thank each one of you fellows and the ladies for your dedication to helping solve each mystery or adventure. For the support that you have shown. For the prayers that have been raised." Barnabas grew quiet, his hand motioning to Dallas, before he walked to the back of the room, to stand shoulder to shoulder with Breck. Breck's hand rested on his shoulder for a moment before they turned to listen to Dallas.

Barnabas' eyes were on Muir and Burnie, watching them closely. Lord, is this over for them, or is there something else? He drew in a breath and abruptly left the room, running for his office, pulling up an email from Emma that he printed. He ran once more for the conference room, heading to the front for a moment to hand the paper to Dallas, who glanced at it and nodded.

Dallas read the email and then nodded. Thank you, Emma, this is the last link that I needed. I need to prove it, but you have done that. I thank God that we brought you in as a consultant. That helps a lot.

"Muir. Burnie. I am sorry once more that you had to go through what you did. Muir, you had no idea that you were to inherit that village, did you? Moira didn't either. A trust fund had been set up for you with the village as the trust, to come to you when you turned thirty. We have spoken with the lawyers who were involved. Your father didn't wish it to be a burden on you, he said. He would not have imagined what you went through in the last year or so.

"Burnie, when you walked into that store and stepped in, you had no idea what you were getting involved in. We have evidence, confirmed and all, that Holman was running an illegal gaming den or two in the village. The planes that you saw? They were ones that he had to bring in the gamblers. He refused to let them drive in, just knowing that too many cars would raise red flags. Stewart was not to have treated you as he did, Muir. You were to be held until you turned thirty or agreed to turn over the trust fund, which incidentally you cannot do. If you refuse it, it goes back to a trust for the village. No one will have access to it.

"Now as to your parents, Muir." He held up the email that he had just been handed. "Emma has come through once more. She has proof that your parents had been called back to Ireland on false pretences. The plan all along had been to kill them, but it had been planned to happen in Ireland. The authorities there have found a co-conspirator who has talked. The place went down in bad weather, from what we understand. It was a business class jet that had been sent over for your parents to travel on. You were to be with them, but your mother didn't want you to travel. That saved your life.

"Moira, Emma has more information for you that she will send on to you. Your property in Ireland was never sold but had been rented for years. The renters would like to purchase it, if you are willing. She has that contact information for you.

"Now, as to the Holman from here. He had been in Ireland, in contact with the business man that your father refused to deal with, Muir. He wanted revenge and Holman stepped in to help him. When your parents were killed, they went silent, until you were an adult. At that point, Stewart stepped in, wanting to destroy you to obtain control of the village. How he knew about the trust fund, he is not saying. We suspect that he searched your family's home at some point and found the paperwork. His plan all along had been to break you. His threats to send you out of the country were just that. Threats. Stewart had admitted that much in his statement before he was killed. He was involved in a lot of illegal activity.

"The person that you felt was in the store building? You were correct. It was an associate of Stewart's, put there to make sure that you didn't escape. He was asleep when the fire hit and not likely even knew what had happened. We found his remains in the store debris in that ravine. We also found remains from six or seven other people. At this point, it is hard to determine if they were killed or died naturally and were buried. That is still being sorted out.

"You were correct when you stated that there was a room under the store, Muir. We have determined that it was used to hold supplies for the gambling dens. When the fire occurred, it was cleaned out. The shackles that you spotted in the photo? No one had yet explained them or their purpose. Any guess that we would or could make would just be speculation."

Dallas paused, his eyes roaming the room, fighting against a feeling of dread that he had. It was over for Muir, wasn't it? They had found everyone, had they not? He suddenly reached for a folder, opening it and then dropping it, before he was approaching Will.

The two men left quickly, heading for town and an abandoned building in the downtown area. They searched, patrol officers with them, finally pulling out an unkempt man, whose maniacal gleam from his eye scared the officers. When questioned, he admitted that he had been hired to watch Muir and to let someone else know, someone that they had not expected.

———

Dallas had his phone out, calling Barnabas, letting him know that they had to finish up on another day. This left a lot of confusion in the building family, who finally moved away.

The next day, Dallas appeared in Burnie's office.

"Burnie, where's Muir?"

"In our apartment. Do you need to speak with her?"

"With both of you." Dallas followed Burnie through the apartment door, finding Muir standing staring at him.

"Dallas? You're back."

"I am. Sorry about yesterday. We had someone else to arrest, that I just discovered when I was speaking. Burnie, do you know that a post office employee was involved?"

Burnie went to shake his head and nodded instead. "Sean Foster."

"That's him. He was hired by Holman to watch you two, but he hired someone from the street. We have arrested both of them."

"It's over? It's finally over?" Muir turned to Burnie, swept into his arms in a hard hug.

"It is, Muir. It is. Thank goodness."

Two months later, Muir moved around the gardens, contentment rising within her. God had been good, she decided, and *I am finally happy. I have searched all my life for this. God prepared it for me.*

She had had a long talk with her Granny that day, finally. Moira had hugged her and then sat her down. She had told Muir of how difficult it had been those first few weeks and months after Moira had received the call from the authorities in Ireland that her parents' plane had disappeared from radar and they were unable to find it. They felt that the plane had disappeared into the Atlantic Ocean. Moira described how that day, her own face wet with tears, she had turned to pick the little one up from her nap, finding her inconsolable.

"You cried for hours for your Mommy, Muir." Moira's hand had rested on Muir head. "I couldn't calm you, couldn't console you. You would cry yourself to sleep and I would sit and just hold you, your little body shaking with sobs even as you slept. Then you would awaken and sob even harder. It was as if you knew that your mother was gone. This went on for days. I was grieving for Morgan and McRae and grieving for you as well. I had no minister that I could turn to. Only my old Bible and prayer."

"Did I know somehow, Granny?" Muir was thoughtful. She didn't remember her parents, they were only faces in faded photographs.

"I think that you did, Muir. You never asked for them as you grew, instead clinging tighter to me. I tried to explain it to you one day when you were about eight or so. You listened, asked no questions, and then just hugged me. I think that you were trying to comfort ne."

"But God gave you comfort, didn't He? Does it say that?"

"He did, Muir. He did."

"Granny, I've thought about Michael. Was he an angel?"

"I don't know, Muir. He may have been. We'll not likely know until we reach Heaven and can ask."

The two ladies sat in silence, their arms around one another, before Muir began to tell Moira how she was now feeling and then hugged her Granny.

"Granny, I would not have made it had it not been for you. If you had still been in the village that day Burnie showed up, I wouldn't have left. I couldn't have left you there. Stewart would have tortured you."

"I know that he would have tried, Muir. But God provided in that, now didn't He?"

Muir turned as she heard footsteps and then ran for Burnie. He had been away that day, off on a book signing, and she had missed him. She had refused to go with him, saying that she just wanted to stay at home.

"Okay, sweetheart?" Burnie kissed her soundly.

"I am, now that you are home. How was the signing?" She grinned as he shrugged. "That bad?"

"No, it was okay. I just missed you. How was your day?"

"It was good. I spent some time with Granny, and then I finished proofreading that manuscript. I am enjoying that work, Burnie."

"I thought you would. Now, let's head into town. I want to take my sweetheart out for a meal."

"If you want. I would rather stay home." Muir grew pensive as they walked back towards the building. "Breck was around when I was in the gardens. He's heading off for a vacation, or so he says."

"He needs it. It's been a while since he had one." Burnie drew her down onto a bench near the entrance to the garden, listening to the sounds of nature, the late fall sun gleaming down on them. "I am glad that you are in my life, Muir."

"I am too." Muir frowned. "Michael?"

"What was that?" Burnie looked up, following the direction with his eyes that Muir was staring in.

“Michael was here. Oh, he’s gone. Burnie, was he an angel?”

“I am sure that he was. God knew you needed that reminder.” He hugged her tighter and just sat, content himself to be where he was. “I need to learn to trust Him more. This has been a learning experience for me.”

“And for me. Thank you for teaching me, Burnie, in a way that I would understand.” She looked up at him. “What now for the family here?”

Burnie shrugged. “Cadee and Benen and Devaney and Blair have had their babies. Brandon and Hagen’s are growing. Baird and Berneen and Brennen and Jaxcy have announced that they are adding to their family.” He grinned. “The parents that are here are over the moon, as they say. Granny is delighted, she says, to be great-granny to so many.”

“She will be good at that. I don’t know what I would have done without her.” Muir’s head went down against him. “Will we have little ones?”

“God only knows that, sweetheart. I pray that we do, but if we don’t, we can always look at adopting.”

“That’s true. We can do that.”

The couple grew quiet, their eyes on the setting sun, before they finally rose and walked, hand in hand, into the building.

Michael stood and watched before he looked up. “She’s safe now, Lord. My work is finished. I will miss her, but I need to move on. Bless her and Burnie, Lord.” Michael turned and walked away, disappearing into the rays of the setting sun.

———

Thank you for choosing to read Burnie and Muir's story. He certainly threw in some added plot lines that I never saw coming. Must be the mystery writer in him.

Muir had been beaten down in many ways. As an orphan, she missed her parents and their guidance on her life greatly. Moira or Granny led her as best she could, teaching her to trust in God. That trust was sorely tried on many occasions.

I knew Burnie's would be one of those stories. He's a mystery writer and writers like to throw in plots and plans and curveballs. He is what I term as an unruly character, always ready to change the direction of the story. And he did that towards the end.

How do we teach someone to trust in God, to depend on Him? First, by our example. Then, by directing them back to His word. Our Christian walk should be that: teaching others, leading them to a closer walk with Him. We are human, and we stumble and fall and fail. But we pick ourselves up, dust ourselves off and continue on, our hand in Him.

Of course, Abe and Emma and his men and ladies had to show up again. Their stories are in try *His Guardians* series. Beloved characters that just have to keep coming back. Doug and Darcie's story is in *The Heart of a Lion*, written as a challenge for my first Nanowrimo try.

Now, Michael? Was he an angel or wasn't he? I leave that up to you to decide. I firmly believe that there are occasions when angels become visible presences to help us.

God bless.

Ronna